Praise for Dale Brown and His Electrifying Bestsellers

CHAINS OF COMMAND

The riveting story of Air Force involvement in a Russia-Ukraine border skirmish—that may result in all-out nuclear holocaust . . .

"*Chains of Command* is as convincing as nonfiction. Dale Brown is the best military writer in the country today and is a master at creating a sweeping epic and making it seem real."
—Clive Cussler

"Dale Brown takes a hard look at the future of America's Armed Forces. . . . A great story of war in a modern, unstable world. It's an exciting ride." —Larry Bond

FATAL TERRAIN

China is on its way to a nuclear high noon—and the Doomsday clock is ticking. . . .

"Well-handled action and hardware . . . another consistent page-turner from Brown." *—Booklist*

"Nobody, in detailing the lethal excitements of high-tech aerial combat in at least plausible geopolitical contexts, does it better than Brown." *—Kirkus Reviews*

STORMING HEAVEN

The explosive story of America's worst nightmare—terrorism in our own backyard . . .

"Brown has mastered this genre. . . . Riveting."
—Kirkus Reviews

continued . . .

SHADOWS OF STEEL

The new Gulf War is erupting—and this one will be far bloodier than the first. . . .

"*Shadows of Steel* is a pulse-pounding novel of the near future that never ignores the human agony of combat."

—*San Francisco Chronicle*

"Brown is a master . . . bringing life to his characters with a few deft strokes. More than just a military thriller."

—*Publishers Weekly*

"State-of-the-art action in the air, on land, and at sea from a master of the future-shock game." —*Kirkus Reviews*

NIGHT OF THE HAWK

The exciting final flight of the "Old Dog"—a shattering mission into Lithuania, where the Soviets' past could launch a terrifying future . . .

"Dale Brown brings us the gripping conclusion of the saga that began so memorably with *Flight of the Old Dog*. A masterful mix of high technology and *human* courage."

—W.E.B. Griffin

SKY MASTERS

The incredible story of America's newest B-2 bomber, engaged in a blistering battle of oil, honor, and global power . . .

"*Sky Masters* is a knockout!" —Clive Cussler

"A gripping military thriller . . . Brown brings combat and technology together in an explosive tale as timely as this morning's news." —W.E.B. Griffin

HAMMERHEADS

The U.S. government creates an all-new drug-defense agency, armed with the ultimate high-tech weaponry. The war against drugs will never be the same. . . .

"Classic . . . His most exciting techno-thriller."

—*Publishers Weekly*

"Whiz-bang technology and muscular, damn-the-torpedoes strategy."

—*Kirkus Reviews*

DAY OF THE CHEETAH

The shattering story of a Soviet hijacking of America's most advanced fighter plane—and the greatest high-tech chase of all time . . .

"Quite a ride . . . Terrific. Authentic and gripping."

—*The New York Times*

"Breathtaking dogfights . . . Exhilarating high-tech adventure."

—*Library Journal*

continued . . .

SILVER TOWER

A Soviet invasion of the Middle East sparks a grueling counterattack from America's newest laser defense system. . . .

"Riveting, action-packed . . . a fast-paced thriller that is impossible to put down."
—UPI

"Intriguing political projections . . . Tense high-tech dogfights."
—*Publishers Weekly*

"High-tech, high-thrills . . . a slam-bang finale."
—*Kirkus Reviews*

FLIGHT OF THE OLD DOG

Dale Brown's riveting debut novel. A battle-scarred bomber is renovated with modern hardware to fight the Soviets' devastating new technology. . . .

"A superbly crafted adventure . . . Exciting."
—W.E.B. Griffin

"Brown kept me glued to the chair . . . a shattering climax. A terrific flying yarn."
—Stephen Coonts

DALE BROWN

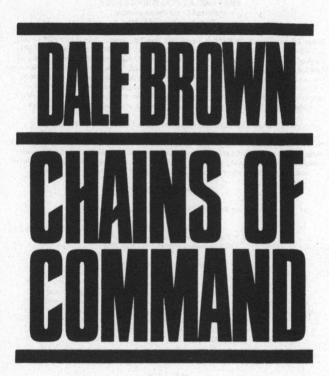

CHAINS OF COMMAND

THE BERKLEY PUBLISHING GROUP
Published by the Penguin Group
Penguin Group (USA) Inc.
375 Hudson Street, New York, New York 10014, USA
Penguin Group (Canada), 90 Eglinton Avenue East, Suite 700, Toronto, Ontario M4P 2Y3, Canada (a division of Pearson Penguin Canada Inc.) • Penguin Books Ltd., 80 Strand, London WC2R 0RL, England • Penguin Group Ireland, 25 St. Stephen's Green, Dublin 2, Ireland (a division of Penguin Books Ltd.) • Penguin Group (Australia), 250 Camberwell Road, Camberwell, Victoria 3124, Australia (a division of Pearson Australia Group Pty. Ltd.) • Penguin Books India Pvt. Ltd., 11 Community Centre, Panchsheel Park, New Delhi—110 017, India • Penguin Group (NZ), 67 Apollo Drive, Rosedale, Auckland 0632, New Zealand (a division of Pearson New Zealand Ltd.) • Penguin Books (South Africa) (Pty.) Ltd., 24 Sturdee Avenue, Rosebank, Johannesburg 2196, South Africa

Penguin Books Ltd., Registered Offices: 80 Strand, London WC2R 0RL, England

CHAINS OF COMMAND

A Berkley Book / published by arrangement with the author

PUBLISHING HISTORY
G. P. Putnam's Sons hardcover edition / July 1993
Berkley mass-market edition / May 1994

For information, address: The Berkley Publishing Group,
a division of Penguin Group (USA) Inc.,
375 Hudson Street, New York, New York 10014.

ISBN: 978-0-425-14207-3

BERKLEY®
Berkley Books are published by The Berkley Publishing Group,
a division of Penguin Group (USA) Inc.,
375 Hudson Street, New York, New York 10014.
BERKLEY® is a registered trademark of Penguin Group (USA) Inc.
The "B" design is a trademark of Penguin Group (USA) Inc.

PRINTED IN THE UNITED STATES OF AMERICA

25 24 23 22 21 20 19 18 17 16 15

Acknowledgments

I've been out of the go-fast kerosene-burning flying game for six years now, so it was time to go back to school. When you want to know about the F-111 weapon system, there is only one place to go, the world's one-stop Aardvark base: The Twenty-Seventh Fighter Wing, Cannon Air Force Base, Clovis, NM, and go talk to its commander, Brigadier General Richard N. Goddard. Thanks to him and his people, I was able to get reacquainted with the swing-wing bomber I loved so much.

Very special thanks go to Lieutenant Colonel John L. Carnduff, Jr., commander of the 428th Fighter Squadron "Buccaneers," probably the "final resting place" for the FB-111A bombers I flew (now called the F-111G), and three of their fine crew dogs, Captains Rich "Hawkeye" Pierce, Tom "LaBrush" Lacombe, and Dirk "Hutch" Hutchison. These gentlemen got me back in the F-111G simulator, gave me an introduction to the new systems, and then got me back to where I belong—hand on the "goat turd," eyes in the "feed bag," checking offsets and shacking targets. It was good to be back in the cockpit again. Many thanks for your time, your help, your ideas, and your inspiration.

Thanks to the following members of the Twenty-Seventh Fighter Wing for their help: Captain Michael M. Pierson, Wing Chief of Public Affairs at Cannon AFB, and SSgt. Fred Espinoza, for setting up a wonderful three-day tour of the Wing's units and personnel; Captain John Ross, TSgt. James Wilkins, and SSgt Tim Jung of Field Training Detachment 528, for their help in understanding the upgrades and changes to the F-111 weapon system's avionics; Major Stephen Hearne and First Lieutenant Gary Gross of Wing Logistics, for teaching me about some of the problems and challenges of unit deployment and mobility; Lieutenant Colonel John Hill, commander, and the men and women of the 522nd Fighter Squadron "Fireballs"; Lieutenant Colonel Dale "Muddy" Waters and the instructors of Detachment 2, USAF Fighter Weapons School, for giving me a taste of flying the F-111F into combat and for answering questions on the F-111 weapon delivery system; and TSgt. Michael Madson and Mr. Kirk Dusenberry of the PAVE TACK laser-pod maintenance shop.

Thanks to the 337th Test and Evaluation Squadron, McClellan Air Force Base, CA, for information and help in formulating the missions and understanding the role of the F-111 and other tactical aircraft in combat, especially Lieut. Colonel Jack Leslie, squadron commander, and Major Steve Webber, Captain Pat Shaw, Captain Russ Smith, Captain Dan Warren, and Mr. Bob Perkins.

Thanks to Ronald J. Kopa for information on the inner working of a Strategic Air Command command post during a crisis situation. I served with Ron at Mather AFB, CA, and he taught me a lot about command-and-control procedures in the Air Force. It was good to get back with him after ten years.

Thanks to Pamela Nault, Chief of Media Relations, Air Force Reserve Headquarters, Public Affairs, Robins AFB, GA, for information on service in the Air Force Reserve; to my good friend Colonel Tom Hornung, USAF (Ret.), former Director of Public Affairs—Western Region, Secretary of the Air Force, USAF, for arranging visits to McClellan AFB, CA, and Cannon AFB, NM, for F-111 research; and to Bill and Harriet Fast Scott, for information on Russia and the city of Moscow.

Special thanks to Jack Hokanson, Media Relations, Sacramento Air Force Logistics Center, McClellan AFB; Colonel Dwight Bass, Chief Flight Surgeon, and Captain Dolly Grise, Flight Surgeon, McClellan Air Force Base, for their help and insight into accident physiology and physiological problems associated with women pilots flying in combat; and to Royal Australian Air Force Commander Philip Campbell for information on the Australian RF-111C aircraft and reconnaissance tactics.

For their help and inspiration, I wish to thank my friends Lieutenant General Robert Beckel, USAF (Ret.), former commander of Fifteenth Air Force, and Lieutenant General Donald O. Aldridge, USAF (Ret.), former vice commander of the Strategic Air Command, for their special insight on potential world conflicts that could affect national security.

Thanks to Lieutenant Colonel Chris Anastassatos, Director of Public Relations, Nevada Air National Guard, for arranging a visit to the 152nd Reconnaissance Group in Reno, NV, that flies the RF-4 Phantom II reconnaissance bird, for their help in understanding reconnaissance systems and tactics; to Lieutenant Colonel Ronald Bath, RF-4 pilot of the 152nd Reconnaissance Group, for detailed information about tactical reconnaissance sensors, cameras, and flight profiles; MSgt William Sjovangen for a tour and explanation of the facilities and photointelligence labs; MSgt Richard Evans for a detailed explanation of the reconnaissance cameras and the film in the Sensor Shop; and CMSgt Mike Patterson of the Image Interpretation department.

Some of the details of the Aurora spy plane are courtesy of aviation expert Bill Sweetman, from his article in *Popular Science* magazine, March 1993.

At the risk of sounding like a broken record, I must extend my sincere thanks to my wife, Jean, for helping me over the rough spots in developing these stories; to George Coleman, Vice President, executive editor at G. P. Putnam's Sons; and Natalee Rosenstein, senior executive editor at Berkley Publishing, for their help in hammering the final story into shape; and to my friend and executive assistant Dennis T. Hall for his support and assistance. The errors are all mine, but a lot of the credit goes to them.

June 20, 1992—March 15, 1993

Author's Notes

As always with works of fiction, this story is purely the invention of my imagination and is not meant to describe any real-world persons, organizations, events, places, or plans. Any resemblance to an actual person, place, or thing is purely coincidental.

Development and production of the AGM-131 attack missile (SRAM II) and the AGM-129 stealth cruise missiles described in this story were canceled in 1991. Supposedly the Russians canceled development of their new nuclear sub- and air-launched cruise missiles at the same time. We shall see.

Real-World News Excerpts

General H. Norman Schwarzkopf, from his autobiography, *It Doesn't Take a Hero;* New York; Bantam Books, 1992 (reprinted with permission)—9 December 1990, C+124, 2100: Phoncon with the chairman [General Colin Powell, Chairman of the Joint Chiefs of Staff]. The two leaders discussed the issue of a declaratory policy with regard to retaliation against biological or chemical attack. The chairman said he was pressing the White House to inform Tariq Aziz [Iraqi foreign minister] that we would use our "unconventional weapons" [quotes added] if the Iraqis use chemicals on us . . .

Adrian Karatnycky, *Foreign Affairs* magazine, June 1992— . . . In their May [1992] meeting [Ukrainian president] Kravchuk and [U.S. President] Bush agreed on Ukrainian participation in the Strategic Arms Reduction Talks agreement . . .

President Kravchuk demonstrated the depth of Ukrainian concern in late April [1992], when he announced the republic's intention to seek Western security guarantees in exchange for scrapping Ukrainian nuclear arms . . .

. . . A free and pro–Western Ukraine would deprive a newly aggressive Russia of its capacity to reassert superpower control over its former satellites. Bolstering a strong pro–Western Ukrainian democracy and assisting a stable Ukrainian state, materially and technically, would not only benefit Ukrainians but the entire democratic West.

PEACE MOVES REMAIN FRUSTRATED AS DNIESTER, SOUTH OSSETIA CLASHES GO ON

06/28/92 Newsgrid News—MOSCOW (JUNE 28) DPA—Fighting continued Sunday in the Dniester and South Ossetia regions of Moldova and Georgia, where peace moves remained frustrated, local media reports said.

In the Dniester region, 16 people were reported killed and 21 wounded in clashes Sunday between Russian and Ukrainian forces on the one hand and Moldovan forces on the other, in defiance of the ceasefire agreed in Istanbul at the weekend by the presidents of Russia, the Ukraine, Moldova and Romania.

LOS ANGELES TIMES, 22 July 1992—About 60 Ukrainian crew members of a Black Sea Fleet patrol boat mutinied Tuesday, raising the blue and yellow Ukrainian flag and sailing to the Ukrainian port of Odessa to protest rough treatment by their Russian superiors.

. . . The mutiny served as a reminder that the Black Sea Fleet is a tinderbox, vulnerable to any spark of nationalism . . .

The incident came close to exploding in the morning when Russian Black Sea Fleet commanders . . . sent several ships and a seaplane to cut it off. Among the interceptors was the missile boat *Impeccable*, carrying an assault team ready to board the boat and seize it.

AVIATION WEEK & SPACE TECHNOLOGY, 5 October 1992—Ukraine is seeking support from Western nations for an ambitious plan to complete the conversion of its defense industry to civilian production in three to four years.

Victor I. Antonov, minister for the military-industrial complex, said Ukraine is pursuing conversion "in a very radical manner." More than 500 commercial programs have been created, mainly involving medical and agricultural equipment . . .

Unlike Russia, Ukraine has decided against a policy of selling arms abroad to keep factories open and generate hard currency, he said. Instead, Ukraine plans to retain only a small military technology base to support its army, converting all other enterprises to civilian production . . .

AIR FORCE MAGAZINE, Mary C. Fitzgerald, September & October 1992 [reprinted with permission]—Russian military leaders are currently focusing not only on creating the Russian armed forces but also on developing a new military doctrine for the 1990s and beyond. A draft of a new Russian doctrine was published recently in *Military Thought,* the main theoretical journal of Russia's armed forces.

This new doctrine identifies two direct military threats to Russia: the introduction of foreign troops in adjacent states and the buildup of air, naval, or ground forces near Russian borders. In addition, a violation of the rights of Russian citizens and of persons "ethnically and culturally" identified with Russia in republics of the former Soviet Union is viewed as "a serious source of conflicts."

. . . The 1990 doctrine held that nuclear war "will" be catastrophic for all mankind, while the 1992 doctrine holds that it "might" be catastrophic for all mankind . . . Russia now views limited nuclear warfighting as a possibility. These changes may stem from the growing proliferation of nuclear weapons on Russian borders, which increases the possibility of a limited nuclear conflict.

. . . [General Rodionov, chief of the General Staff Academy of the Russian Armed Forces] contends that, for centuries, Russia has struggled to acquire an exit to the Baltic and Black seas and that "the deprivation of such free exits would contradict [Russia's] national interests." . . . Attempts by any state in Europe, America, or Asia to capitalize on existing disputes among the CIS states or to strengthen its influence in these states . . . would violate Russia's national interests and security.

. . . General Rodionov's bold views about the new doctrine may well reflect a civil-military rift concerning the extent to which old Soviet imperial interests should be pursued by military means.

AVIATION WEEK & SPACE TECHNOLOGY, 23 November 1992—Military commanders at Supreme Headquarters Allied Powers Europe (SHAPE) and their civilian counterparts at NATO Headquarters, Brussels . . . see dangers looming both inside Russia and among its neighbors as a result of growing military factions in the unstable Russian political situation . . . "There is still an awful lot of hardware in Russia, and an awful lot of nuclear weapons in Russia," [British General Sir Brian Kenny] deputy supreme allied commander Europe said.

This story is dedicated to the memory of my good friend, business associate, and teacher, Jim Harvey. You were always there when I needed you with your knowledge, professional counsel, helpfulness, and most importantly, your friendship.

This story is also dedicated to the memory of my friend, California State Assemblyman B. T. Collins—soldier, statesman, incorrigible Irishman, and determined, inspirational leader.

As the old Irish toast says: May you both be in Heaven a half-hour before the Devil knows you're dead.

If they want peace, nations should avoid the pin-pricks that precede cannonshots.
—Napoleon Bonaparte

LITHUANIA
Vilnius
Moscow
Domodedo
R U S S
Minsk
BELARUS
Br'ansk
POLAND
Brest
VOLYNSKOJE UPLANDS
Kiev
L'vov Air Base
Char'kov
SLOVENIA
Vinnica Air Base
UKRAINE
HUNGARY
Bel'cy
Doneck
Krivoj Rog
MOLDOVA
Iasi
Chisinau
Dnestr R.
Nikolayev
Odessa
ROMANIA
Galati
Braila
Simferopol
Sevastopol
Novoro
SERBIA
Danube River
BLACK SEA
BULGARIA
GREECE
Bosporus Strait
Istanbul
Marmara Sea
Golcuk
Dardanelles
Ankara
TURKEY
MEDITERRANEAN SEA
Kayseri
Adana/Incirlik Air Base
S

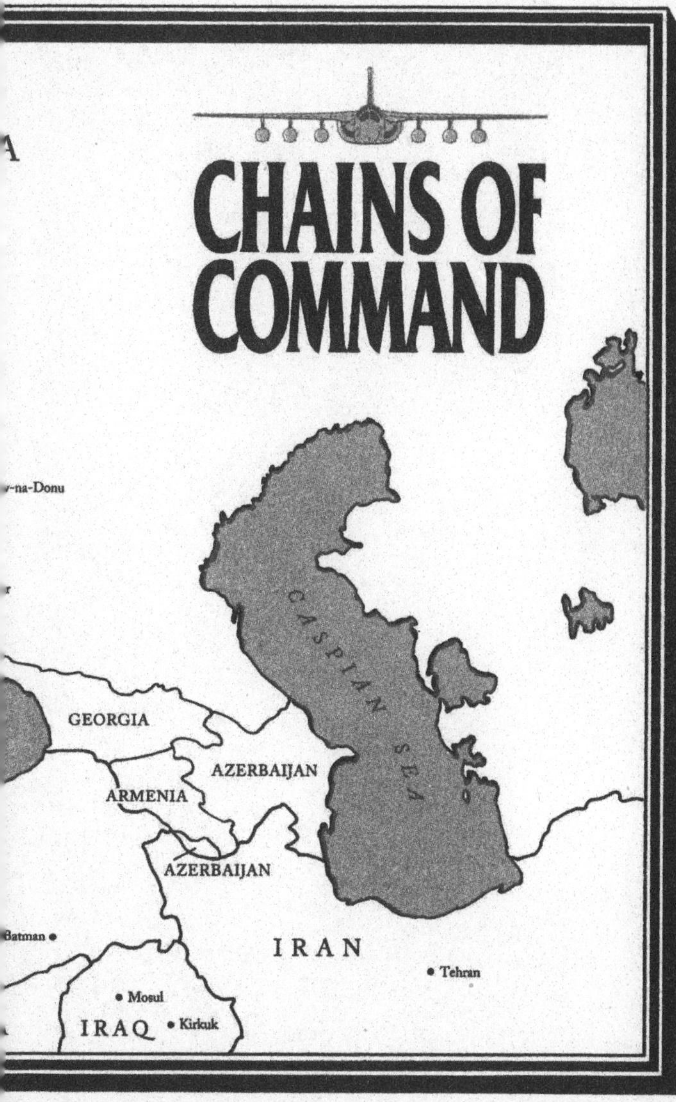

CHAINS OF COMMAND
CASPIAN SEA
GEORGIA
AZERBAIJAN
ARMENIA
AZERBAIJAN
Batman
IRAN
Tehran
Mosul
IRAQ
Kirkuk

CHAINS OF COMMAND

PROLOGUE

**Deliberate with caution,
but act with decision;
and yield with graciousness or
oppose with firmness.
—Charles Hale**

....

L'vov, Republic of the Ukraine, Eastern Europe December 1994

BOUYED BY CRISP, COLD AIR, THE TANDEM TWO-SEAT MIKOYAN-Gurevich-23UB fighter leapt into the air on a tongue of flame like a tiger pursuing its prey through the trees. Pavlo Grigor'evich Tychina, a Captain First Class of Air Defense Aviation of the Fourteenth Air Army, L'vov, Ukrainian Republic, moved the gear handle to the UP position as soon as he saw the altimeter swing upward. It was such a great day for flying, with light winds and near fifty-kilometer visibility, that Tychina didn't even mind when the LOW PNEU PRESSURE warning light came on. He simply started pumping the emergency manual landing gear pressurization handle near his right knee to build up enough pressure in the gear uplock system to fully raise the landing gear. Nothing was going to spoil this flying day, even this cranky twenty-year-old warplane.

Tychina, a twenty-eight-year-old pilot and flight commander in the Ukrainian Air Force, immediately dropped his oxygen mask and took a deep breath, like a platform diver who had just risen to the surface after a deep dive, then swung a small auxiliary microphone to his lips. He never liked flying with his oxygen mask—it was unnecessary anyway, since they rarely flew above four or five thousand meters where oxygen was really necessary. Flying in southeastern Europe was generally pretty good, as long as you stayed above the smog level of about one thousand meters. He raised flaps and slats passing 450 kph (kilometers per hour), then checked out the right side of his cockpit canopy on the progress of his wingman for today's orientation flight.

His wingman was an F-16D Fighting Falcon fighter from the Republic of Turkey. The sleek tandem two-seat fighter and attack plane was on a goodwill visit, representing the North Atlantic Treaty Organization. Since the Ukraine had applied for NATO membership earlier in the year, NATO member countries had been doing more and more of these exchange flights, getting to know their Ukrainian counterparts. While these exchange flights were taking place, Turkish radar controllers and military commanders were inspecting Ukrainian radar facilities and military bases, and Ukrainian military commanders and politicians were doing the same in Turkey, Germany, Belgium, and even the United States. Pavlo Tychina never thought he would ever see his country join a Western military alliance, and he never expected that the West would ever so heartily embrace his country in return.

Someday soon, Tychina thought, the Ukraine will be wealthy enough to build planes like the F-16. Hell, Turkey was an agricultural country, not much more industrialized than the Ukraine, but they were license-building F-16 Falcons there and even exporting them to other countries. He shook his head in disgust. The Ukraine should sell off its MiG-23s, MiG-27s, and Sukhoi-17s. The F-16, as both a fighter and attack plane, could replace them all. That's what they should buy: F-16s. It might take fifty MiGs to get one well-equipped F-16, but so what? Everyone knew the F-16 was at least fifty times better than the MiG-23.

His fantasy of flying an F-16 Fighting Falcon emblazoned with a Ukrainian flag on the tail was just that, a fantasy, so Tychina turned his attention to his backseater: "Are you all right back there?" he called back on interphone in English.

"I'm doing fine, sir," came the reply. Tychina had an American "Combat Camera" military cameraman from March Air Force Base in California in the backseat of the MiG-23UB, filming this entire flight. NATO cameramen and producers had been at L'vov Air Base in western Ukraine and other bases all week, conducting interviews and taking pictures. It was a far cry from the old Soviet multilayered secrecy and isolation. But it made Tychina and his comrades feel good, as if they had finally joined the family of nations, as if they belonged to something other than the stifling, soulless Soviet-Russian domination.

As soon as they passed 650 kilometers per hour airspeed, Tychina swept his MiG-23's wings back to 45 degrees, and the ride smoothed out considerably. They maneuvered east to stay away from the Polish and Slovenian border, then leveled off at three thousand meters. The visibility was well over 160 kilometers. The mountains ringing the Black Sea and the Crimea were beautiful, there were plenty of natural landmarks to help orientate a distracted pilot, and air traffic control restrictions were fairly relaxed, even when flying close to the Russian and Polish borders. The Polish air traffic controllers liked trying their Ukrainian and English out on the MiG pilots.

That was not true of Moldova, unfortunately. For nearly five years a conflict had been raging between ethnic Russians and ethnic Romanians in the former Moldavian Soviet Socialist Republic. Since Moldavia declared its independence from the Soviet Union in 1991, becoming the Republic of Moldova, the Russians living in the Republic, especially the rich landowners and factory owners in the Dniester region, were afraid that they would be persecuted by the ethnic Romanian majority. Moldova used to be part of Romania, back before World War II, and there was a lot of talk about Moldova realigning itself with Romania once again—hell, they even changed the name of the capital city of Moldova, Kishinev, back to its original Romanian name, Chisinau, just like they changed Leningrad back to St. Petersburg in Russia.

Russian fat cats living in Moldova, with their huge farms and modern German-designed factories, were very nervous—even terrified—that Romania might take away the Russians' land and property in Moldova upon reunification, so they rebelled against the Moldovan government, Tychina remembered from his intelligence briefings. That really took a lot of balls—Moldova was still part of the old Soviet Union when the Russians in the Dniester region "claimed" their "independence." But then those guys always had balls bigger than their brains. The new Moldovan government was pissed, of course, but they couldn't do anything because most of their Russian troops sided with the damn Russians in the Dniester region. The former Russian armies, located mostly in two cities in Dniester, Bendery and Tiraspol, were twice as strong as the rest of the Moldovan army.

In comes Romania, offering its military forces to help Moldova retake the Dniester region. Russia steps in, telling Romania to stay out, and backing up their warning with flights of warplanes from Minsk, Brest, Br'ansk, and Moscow. Only problem was, Russia never bothered to ask permission of the Ukraine before sending warplanes into Moldova. A joint Commonwealth of Independent States agreement allows joint military maneuvers and provides for common defense between Russia and the Ukraine, but it says nothing about using a member nation's territory as a staging ground for attacks on another country. The Ukraine insisted on a cease-fire, negotiations, and territorial sovereignty; Russia insisted on free overflight and full support from the Ukraine. Naturally, Moldova distrusted *both* Russia and the Ukraine. It was actually kind of silly: the Ukraine was big, but it was less than one-tenth the size of the Russian Federation in every respect, including the category that mattered here—military strength. Russia could squash Romania, Moldova, and the Ukraine without working up a sweat.

In any case, no one trusted anyone these days, especially not the Russian President Vitaly Velichko, a hard-line nut who had seized power from Yeltsin, who was now living in Siberian exile. So the Moldovan-Ukrainian border area was strictly off-limits, as was the Russian-Ukrainian border. Moldovan air defense units had been taking surface-to-air missile shots at any and all unidentified aircraft straying near. They were usually shoulder-fired SA-7 rounds or small-caliber antiaircraft artillery stuff—not a real threat to fighters above two thousand meters or so—but it was best to give the trigger-happy Moldovans a wide berth.

"So what would you like to see?" Tychina radioed over to the F-16 crew. The F-16D two-seater also carried a Combat Camera photographer, taking films and still shots of the MiG-23. This was really just a technical flight so the photographers could set up their camera mounts; later in the day they would tow some aerial targets over the Black Sea and let the F-16s and MiG-23s shoot them down, then go over to the bombing ranges in the "Bunghole" region of northwestern Ukraine and let some MiG-27s show their stuff alongside the F-16. "The Carpathian mountains farther south perhaps, and the Crimean Mountains along the Black Sea are very nice," Tychina was saying.

"We'd like to try some low-level stuff and tight turns," the chief photographer radioed back, "so we can torque down our camera mounts."

"Okay," Tychina replied in his best English, which he had an opportunity to practice more and more these days. "We must stay above one thousand meters because of the . . . visibility, but low level is better." By "visibility" he meant smog.

"We got a target on radar at two o'clock position, sixty miles—that's one hundred and ten kilometers—low, about two thousand . . . ah, I mean, about six hundred meters altitude," the pilot of the Turkish plane radioed over. He was a big shot in the Turkish Air Force, a colonel or general, and he was always showing off for the cameras. "Let's go get him, shall we?"

Tychina turned his Sapfir-23D search radar to TRANSMIT but did not bother searching for the target—the radar had a maximum range of only one hundred kilometers, and for targets that far below them, they had to be practically right on top of them before the radar would pick them up. "Ukrainian radar coverage is poor in that area," Tychina said. Radar coverage in the Ukraine was poor *everywhere,* but he wasn't going to admit that, either. "We should get permission first." He switched over to his secondary radio and said in Ukrainian, "Vinnica radar, Imperial Blue One flight of two, overhead Vojnilov at three thousand meters eastbound, flight code one-one-seven, request."

It took a moment for the controller to look up his call sign and flight plan, then find his blip on radar; then, in very impatient Ukrainian: "Imperial Blue One flight, say your request."

"My VIPs request permission to descend to five hundred meters and accomplish a practice intercept on the low-flying aircraft currently at our twelve o'clock position, one hundred ten kilometers. Over," said Tychina.

There was another long pause, probably so the controller could look up the flight plan and, more importantly, the passenger status code of the aircraft they wanted to intercept. Most politicians and a few senior officers didn't like fighters, even unarmed ones, flying too close.

"Imperial Blue One flight, you say you have an aircraft near Cortkov at five hundred meters?"

"That is affirmative, Vinnica. Stand by." On the interplane frequency in English, Tychina asked the Turkish general, "Sir, in what direction and what airspeed is that plane headed?"

"He is headed south, heading one-seven-zero, speed three hundred knots," the general responded. "He is not transmitting IFF identification codes."

Tychina forgot that the advanced pulse-Doppler radars on the F-16 Fighting Falcon could not only see low-flying targets at incredible distances, but could even interrogate identification beacons. He keyed the secondary radio mike: "Vinnica, target heading south at five hundred fifty kilometers per hour, not transmitting any identification beacons."

"Imperial Blue flight, acknowledged, stand by." There was another long pause, and that made twenty-eight-year-old Pavlo Tychina very uncomfortable. He could feel his fine flying day going to hell real fast. "Imperial Blue Flight, you are ordered to immediately intercept and identify the target aircraft," the controller finally said in Ukrainian. "The aircraft is unidentified and is below my radar coverage. Report identification immediately on this frequency."

"Imperial Blue One Flight, acknowledged." He sighed. What in the hell . . . had they stumbled onto an unidentified aircraft, a possible intruder? On the primary radio, Tychina radioed: "General, the regional radar command has ordered us to intercept this aircraft. I am not picking this target up on my radar, and he is too low for a vector from ground intercept. Can you assist me?"

"My pleasure, Pavlo," the Turkish pilot replied. "I am in the lead. Stay with me as best you can." And with that, the F-16 Falcon shot out ahead of the MiG, its afterburner rattling Tychina's wings and canopy. Tychina hit the afterburners on the MiG-23—which, unlike the F-16, did not light off in zones but came on full blast with a powerful *bang!*—then swept his wings back to 72 degrees. In the blink of an eye they were at Mach-one and had descended to barely more than three hundred meters above ground.

The visibility was less than twenty kilometers down here because of smog. Tychina's mind raced through a high-detail map of the area, trying to remember if there were any power lines or tall smokestacks in this area, but he was doing all he could just to keep the small F-16 in sight. They did a few sudden climbs when the Turkish general found a few power lines, and Pavlo swore they flew *under* a tall high-tension line strung across the Zbrut River.

There!

"Contact," Tychina called out. It was an Ilyushin-76M cargo plane, a large four-engine military transport. This was the military version of the similar civilian cargo plane—that was apparent as they closed in because . . .

. . . the Il-76 opened fire on them with its two tail-mounted 23-millimeter twin-barrel machine guns.

"*Kemal* damn them!" the Turkish officer screamed angrily on the radio. He immediately banked right and extended to get out of the gun turret's cone of fire. Tychina banked hard left and climbed. Once he was above the Il-76 and forward of the plane's wings, he knew he was safe. The plane had Aeroflot markings and a Russian flag painted on the vertical stabilizer . . .

. . . It was definitely a fucking Russian plane!

The Turkish general was still swearing, half in Turkish, half in English: "That bastard fired on us!"

"Stay out of the cone of fire!" Tychina told him. On the backup radio, Tychina called out, "Vinnica control, Imperial Blue One Flight, we have been fired upon by a Russian Ilyushin-76 transport aircraft. Repeat, we have been fired on by a Russian Il-76. Request instructions!"

There was no response, only the hiss of static—they were far too low to be picked up by Vinnica.

Tychina switched the backup radio to the international VHF emergency frequency, 121.5, and said in Russian, "Unidentified Russian transport plane near the town of Kel'mency, this is Imperial Blue One flight of two, Air Force of the Ukrainian Republic. You are flying illegally in Ukrainian airspace. Climb immediately to five thousand meters and identify yourself." He repeated the instructions in English and Ukrainian, but the big transport kept right on flying. Soon the Russian Il-76 transport had reached the Moldovan border, and Tychina could pursue it no longer. He turned northwest and started a climb so he could regain radio contact with Vinnica, watching it carefully.

"Those bastards," the Turkish general cursed on the primary radio, "if I only had some rounds in my cannon, I would have nailed that son of a bitch for good. I never thought I'd ever let anyone fire at me without returning fire. *Shit.*"

Tychina deselected the radio for the moment so he would not have to listen to the excitable Turk's cursing. On the backup radio, he radioed: "Vinnica, this is Imperial Blue One Flight, how do you read?"

"Loud and clear now," the controller replied. "We could not hear you, but our remote communications outlets picked you up and relayed your calls. Do you have the Ilyushin in sight?"

"Affirmative," Tychina replied. "It is . . . *my God . . . !*"

Just as he visually reacquired the big transport, he saw several white streaks of smoke erupt from the snowy forests below and hit the Ilyushin-76 transport.

Those were surface-to-air missiles, being fired from just across the Moldovan border . . .

"Vinnica, this is Imperial Blue One Flight, the Ilyushin has just been hit by Moldovan surface-to-air missiles. I see two . . . three missiles, small, probably SA-7 portable . . . the Ilyushin is on fire, its left engines are on fire, it is trailing smoke . . . wait! Vinnica, I see parachutes, the crew is . . . no, I see a lot of parachutes, dozens! Vinnica, paratroopers are exiting the cargo area via the rear cargo ramp. Over two dozen, one after another . . . I am turning southeast to maintain visual contact . . . *Vinnica, are you reading me?*"

It was the most incredible sight Tychina had ever seen. Like a giant whale being attacked by tiny sharks, the Ilyushin-76 was being peppered by man-portable SA-7 heat-seeking missiles. As it descended, its entire left wing on fire, it was disgorging dozens of paratroopers. Most of the paratroopers never made it—Tychina saw lots of jumpers but very few parachutes. The plane was so low now that there wasn't time for the jumper's parachutes to fully open before they hit the frozen Moldovan ground. Then, in a spectacular cloud of fire, the Ilyushin rolled onto its left side, crashed, and cartwheeled for at least five kilometers across the earth, leaving bits of metal and bodies under streaming parachutes in its path.

Christ, it had finally started, Tychina thought in a cold sweat. The fucking Russians and Moldovans were at each other's throats. Worse, he knew, just knew the Ukraine would be pulled into it as well. In fact, already had been, when the arrogant Motherland decided it could fly over Ukrainian airspace as well as shoving the Black Sea Fleet through their waters . . . all without permission. Tychina grimaced at the thought of what could happen next. Up until now it had been little more than a bit of sparring and some macho posturing.

But this . . . this, Tychina feared, was just the kind of incident that could be a prelude to something much bigger. And deadlier.

National Military Command Center, the Pentagon, Washington, D.C. The Next Day

"One hundred and forty SPETSNAZ paratroopers, ten crewmen, and a two-hundred-million-dollar transport, all killed by a quarter-million dollars' worth of missiles," Army general Philip T. Freeman, chairman of the Joint Chiefs of Staff, summarized from the report before him. He was in the National Military Command Center, the main military command post and communications center in the Pentagon, previewing the briefing and the edited videotape he was going to give to the National Security Council and the President of the United States in just a few hours. Freeman knew that this briefing was not just important, but vital in determining what the United States' response to this incident was going to be—especially for a President that was busy trying to drastically downsize not just the military's size, but its power and influence in American life as well. After thirty years in uniform, Freeman had learned how to play the game.

Philip Freeman was a tall, distinguished-looking man, with close-cropped dark hair that had gone gracefully, tastefully gray on the sides, and small, quick eyes. He rose through the ranks from a know-nothing Army ROTC second lieutenant from Niagara University in New York, two tours in Vietnam as an artillery and mortar platoon commander, a tour at NATO Headquarters in Belgium, innumerable professional military courses and staff positions, commander of

U.S. European Command, Army chief of staff, and assistant to the President's National Security Advisor, before becoming the highest-ranking military officer in the United States.

Freeman had been privileged to be a witness of the tremendous sea changes that had occurred in the world over the past five years. Unfortunately, now it seemed as if he was seeing a reversal of those changes—just as quickly as change happened, regional and ethnic conflict was threatening to tear it all apart.

The Joint Chiefs of Staff and representatives of the President's National Security Council staff had just viewed the incredible videotape shot by U.S. Air Force cameramen in the backseats of Turkish and Ukrainian fighter planes. They saw the entire intercept, heard the radio calls—the cameramen used "Y" cords to plug their video cameras into the fighter's interphone—and saw the big Russian transport get blown to pieces by Moldovan surface-to-air missiles.

"No one survived?" Air Force general Martin Blaylock, the curmudgeonly chief of staff of the Air Force, asked. "I saw several 'chutes . . ."

"Our information comes from press releases and official memoranda from the Moldovan government," Albert Sparlin, assistant deputy director for Eastern European Affairs of the Central Intelligence Agency, replied. Sparlin was providing a lot of background data on the incident, stuff the Defense Intelligence Agency normally does not gather on its own. "I wouldn't exactly call it *reliable* information. If the Moldovans or Romanians captured any Russians, the first thing they'd do is declare them dead—it's easier to extract information from a prisoner who thinks he's dead than one who knows he's alive. Judging by the tape, several may have survived. But the Moldovan Army pulled off a big one."

"Great. The Russians are ready to blow Moldova off the map over this Dniester stuff—if they find out they're violating their prisoners, they'll kick their asses for sure," Freeman said, feeling a headache coming on.

Everyone assembled in the Command Center knew that when the Russians living in the Dniester region declared themselves independent from Moldavia and formed the Dniester Republic, it had gone up Moldavia's ass sideways. And, of course, Mother Russia couldn't wait to step in and "help" Dneister remain a separate Republic from the despised Moldavians. They knew that it all went way back to when Moldavia was once a province of Romania. Moldova was ceded to Russia in 1940 as part of the Molotov-Ribbentrop Pact with Nazi Germany. They have, and always will, loathe the Russians and the Russians have felt, thanks to the Molotov-Ribbentrop Pact, *very* proprietary of Moldavia (even though the country declared independence from the then-USSR in 1991). The Russians felt especially proprietary now with regards to Dniester. It was a situation that had been brewing to the boiling point.

"All right," Freeman continued, "I've got your staff recommendations, so let's put all this together so I can recommend a military course of action."

"If the President even asks you for one," scoffed Admiral Robert Marise, Chief of Naval Operations.

There was a general nod of agreement around the table at that remark. The President, a young southern Democrat, had to be the most blatantly antimilitary president to come along since Rutherford B. Hayes. In the President's eyes—and, it was noted, in the eyes of his powerful wife, a former attorney who was known around Washington as the Steel Magnolia—the military was nothing but an overblown, unnecessary cash drain that needed to be plugged.

"Russia has publicly threatened Moldova for shooting down the transport," Freeman went on, "and accused Romania of supplying the weapons, and even accused the Ukraine *and Turkey* of assisting in the downing by broadcasting and highlighting the transport's position with the fighters. They think Turkey is assisting the Ukraine, like Romania is assisting Moldova, in driving out all ethnic Russians from their lands and their high positions in these former republics' governments."

"You think Russia has named all of its potential targets for retaliation in that statement, Philip?" Marine Corps commandant Roger Picco asked.

"I'm sure of it, Roger," Freeman grumbled. "The border incursions, the sniper attacks, the firefights, the angry words have all been intensifying over the years. Now, ever since Turkey has come out in favor of Ukraine's admittance into NATO, not to mention its condemnation of Russia for its aggressiveness in the Black Sea region, Russia has been rattling the saber even harder. They say they're being backed into a corner: I say they see their buffer states and regional influence disappearing, and they want to stop the hemorrhaging. The hard-liners have taken charge, gentlemen. We can't afford to just sit back and wait for this thing to blow up in our face."

"But selling any sort of military action to the President will be nearly impossible." Admiral Marise sighed in exasperation, as if his earlier remark hadn't been understood. "He doesn't want to know about the chances of success or failure—he assumes we'll come out of it unscathed—but he'll want to know how much it will cost."

"And then, when Congress comes up with a number," added Army general Patrick Goff, chief of staff of the Army, "the President believes *them* instead of our figures."

"I didn't ask for a commentary, gentlemen," Freeman interrupted. "And we should know better than to air our dirty laundry in front of someone who's not wearing a primary-colored suit." He looked right at the CIA representative.

Sparlin of the CIA laughed along with the Joint Chiefs, then added, "Hey, I'm with you guys—when the President's not hammering away at the Pentagon budget, he's taking a flamethrower to our intelligence budget. But I see big problems in Eastern Europe if we don't do something. Russia lost its access to the Black Sea and the Baltic when the Soviet Union broke up. They got it back when they formed the Commonwealth of Independent States, but now that the CIS has broken up, they've lost it again. Russia's not going to stand for that, especially not that wild-card Velichko. This Moldova thing might be their best opportunity to take action."

"Then we *have* to convince the President to act—diplomatically as well as militarily," General Blaylock of the Air Force decided. "We lost a lot of face when Germany led NATO in the Yugoslavia crisis. We tossed in a few planeloads of MREs and managed to get a few C-130s shot down over Bosnia—then Germany leads NATO into the region, and everyone comes to the bargaining table. We still got egg on our face from that one. Now do we want Turkey to take the lead in doing something about the Russian crisis or just play with ourselves?"

Freeman shrugged. "I don't want a plan of action just for the hell of it—I need a plan that's doable, that'll position our forces in the best possible manner if Russia decides to bust loose. My idea is to support Turkey, to unify and strengthen the

NATO allies. If we tighten up NATO and show the Russians we still got a strong, unified military alliance opposing them, the Russians might think twice before starting any large-scale operation."

"So you're going to tell the President—and our *demure* First Lady—to stop making speeches condemning the joint military operations between the Ukraine and Turkey?" Admiral Marise asked skeptically. When dealing with the chief executive of the United States, everyone knew it was always two-on-one—the President and his wife versus everyone else. But in their few confrontations, General Philip Freeman actually seemed to have a handle on the opinionated, sometimes volatile First Lady—if not cordial or friendly, at least their meetings had been mutually respectful. He just didn't care for women who kept their maiden name *and* their husband's all in one.

"Hey, *I* don't like the Turks flying F-16s close to the Russian borders," Freeman replied, "or having the Turks doing practice bomb runs in a new bombing range that 'just happened' to have been constructed close to a Russian cabinet member's dacha near the Black Sea, or having the Turks *reportedly* accepting surplus weapons and equipment from the Ukraine for safekeeping."

"It's not a rumor," Sparlin interjected. "It's the truth. They averaged ten cargo ships *per day* until the *Washington Post* broke the story last month."

"Turkey says it's not true, so we believe our ally." Freeman sighed. "The point is, I wish Turkey would play straight with us a little more. But yes, I'm going to recommend we support Turkey—all of NATO, but especially the Turks. Turkey has asked for more Patriot missile batteries and defensive aircraft, and they want to buy our surplus F-111 aircraft. I'll recommend we go ahead with the deal."

"Good luck," someone chuckled.

"Thanks a heap. Okay, what else do we need to think about?" Freeman asked. "Let's say the President does nothing about the Russians until well after the shooting starts, but then the country and the allies go into a panic when the Red Army starts rolling across the Ukraine, and the President finally decides he better do something. What are we going to want or need? What can we do to get it into better position once the shit hits the fan?"

There were several ideas tossed around the table, but one comment from Air Force general Martin Blaylock got everyone's attention like nothing else: "Maybe we should consider the absolute worst-case scenario, Philip. What if the Russians try to invade the Ukraine, they drag Turkey into it, Russia nails Turkey, NATO gets dragged into it, and the Cold War heats up overnight? Let's think about putting our Reservists on nuclear alert—putting the B-1s, B-52s, maybe the F-111s and B-2 bombers on alert, with *Reservists*, and the boomers back on patrol. What then?"

It was the question to end all questions. As a major cost-cutting measure, the President had slashed the size of the active-duty military forces by nearly half. But to appease those worried about readiness, he increased the size of the Reserves and Guard to their highest levels yet—there was almost parity between active and Reserve force levels. The cost savings were enormous. But many front-line units were now manned by Reservists, especially in Blaylock's Air Force. If ninety B-1 bombers went on nuclear alert, as many as twenty of them would be manned by Reservists. If the B-52s went on alert, over half of them would have Reservists on board . . .

. . . and in all Air Force flying units, as many as one-fourth of the aircrews would be women as well.

"Good point, Marty," Freeman said. "I think we can see that scenario happening here. I know you're pushing for chairman of this gaggle, Marty, so I'll bet you have a rundown on what we'd have to do and what we'd have if we went ahead and did it, am I right?"

"You've got that right, sir," Blaylock said. "I got together with CINC-Strategic Command, Chris Laird, and put together a dog-and-pony show for you. I'd like to bring him in and lay it on you."

"No," Freeman replied. His response stunned the Joint Chiefs—but he raised a hand to settle them all down, and added, "I want that briefing, but I want the whole National Security Council, including the President and Veep, to hear it. Let's get General Laird in here ASAP and set up a meeting."

"Yes, sir," Blaylock said, then, with an evil smile, added: "But remember to double-check to make sure the First Lady's calendar is clear."

No one laughed.

Over Eastern Turkey, December 1994

"No, no, no," U.S. Air Force lieutenant colonel Daren J. Mace shouted over interphone. "If you go in hot, Lieutenant, you can't dick around—and don't you dare touch those throttles. IP inbound to the target, you're at military power, and you stay there unless you need to plug in the afterburners. Understand?"

"I think I overshoot," Lieutenant Ivan Kondrat'evich of the Ukrainian Air Force replied. He and Mace were flying in a tandem two-seat Ukrainian Sukhoi-17 "Fitter-G" attack plane, over a bombing range in eastern Turkey. They were practicing bombing and aerial gunnery with Turkish F-16 fighters and other NATO aircraft. "I too high, I go around."

"No way, Ivan," Mace said. "You go in hot, you burn your target. Show me your moves, Ivan."

"I not understand, Colonel Daren."

"Like this. I got the aircraft." Mace grabbed the control stick in the backseat of the Su-17, made sure the throttles were up into military power, and rolled the Su-17 inverted. As expected, the big, heavy fighter-bomber sank like a stone. "Wings to forty-five," Mace ordered. Kondrat'evich moved the Sukhoi-17's wing-sweep handle to the intermediate setting—the backseaters did not have wing-sweep control, a serious design flaw—which gave them a much rougher ride at this high airspeed but gave them much more precise control. The big fighter was now aimed at an impossibly steep angle, and the altimeter was unwinding as if it had an electric motor driving it down. Since he had very little forward visibility, the only way Mace could see the target visually was to look out the top of the canopy while they were inverted and try to line up as best he could.

At two thousand feet above the ground, Mace rolled upright. "You got the aircraft," he shouted to Kondrat'evich in the front seat. "Now kill that bad boy." Instead of firing the guns, however, Mace felt the young Ukrainian pilot pop the Su-17's four big speedbrakes. "Don't do that! Retract your speedbrakes, Ivan." He did so. "Now kill the target, Ivan, *now!*"

With Mace's hand on the control stick helping him line up, Kondrat'evich pressed the gun trigger on his control stick. The two 30-millimeter Nudelmann-Richter NR-30 cannons, one in each wingroot, erupted with a tremendous shudder, and a visible tongue of fire at least thirty feet long seared the sides of the Su-17. "Richter" was a good name for that cannon: they had fired only about eighty rounds at the target, an old Soviet tank, but the huge 30-millimeter "soda bottle" shells completely ripped the tank apart and probably slowed the Su-17 down a good fifty knots, even though they were in a screaming descent. "Good shooting, good kill," Mace said. "Recover."

There was no reaction, and Mace was ready for it. Many young attack pilots, especially if they transition from air-to-air fighters, get a bad case of "target fixation," or keeping their noses pointed at the target after completing the attack. Perhaps it was a holdover from firing radar-guided missiles, which usually required the pilot to keep his nose aimed at the enemy to radar-illuminate the target so the missile could home in; or maybe it was just a fascination with seeing a hapless ground target die. In any case, a lot of ground attack crews kill themselves by forgetting to pull up after firing their weapons.

"I got the aircraft!" Mace shouted, hauling back on the stick with both hands. At first he was actually *fighting* Kondrat'evich, who wanted to push the nose down so he could keep the target in sight, until the young pilot realized how low they were. "Wings to thirty!" he shouted, and Kondrat'evich swept the wings full forward to 30 degrees so they could get every ounce of lift and control possible. They finally got their nose up and began a safe climb at only sixty feet above the ground.

"Good dust, Kiev Three, good dust," the range controller called out.

"What does that mean?" Kondrat'evich asked.

"That means they're congratulating us for flying so low but not hitting the ground and killing ourselves, Ivan," Mace replied. "Ivan, you're doing ground attack now, not fighter tactics. There are no ground attack weapons in the inventory that require you to keep your nose pointed at the ground after pulling the trigger." Actually, the Ukrainians had one, the AS-7

"Kerry," but it was an obsolete weapon and they were training for gunnery and Maverick-style TV, imaging infrared, or laser-guided weapons, not old-style radio-controlled missiles. "Shoot, then scoot—don't hang around to admire your handiwork. You understand?"

"'Shoot, then scoot,'" Kondrat'evich mimicked. "Climb or die, eh?"

"You got it," Mace agreed. "Climb or die. Now get on your egress heading and get up to your assigned altitude before your wingmen think you're a bad guy."

"I understand," Kondrat'evich said, making the turn and climbing to five thousand feet to join up on his formation leader. "But it is a very good day to die today. You think so?"

Mace dropped his oxygen mask, looked at the bright sun and clear blue cloudless sky around him, and clicked his mike twice in reply. Yes, he agreed, it was a pretty good day to die.

Back on the ground a few minutes later, Ivan Kondrat'evich was so happy with his performance that he was out of the cockpit and running to join up with his fellow Ukrainian pilots almost before the engines were shut down. Mace had to smile as he watched the exuberant young pilot darting about the tarmac, slapping his buddies on the shoulder, cajoling them for some screw-up they did. When their operations officer came by a few minutes later to tell them their gunnery scores, Ivan practically did cartwheels on the frosty ramp. Mace could tell their scores were good. Despite a few lapses in concentration, Kondrat'evich was a good stick. A few more years and a couple weeks at RED FLAG, the U.S. Air Force air combat exercise in Nevada, and he might just live to see age thirty.

It was a long time since Mace had been that happy after coming back from a mission, and even longer since he'd seen age thirty. Mace was a tall, rugged-looking man, with close-cropped blond hair and dark green eyes. Six foot, 180 pounds of naturally well-defined muscle, Mace would have been Central Casting's dream for a war movie. A younger, less-weathered Robert Redford, they would have said. He was a former enlisted man in the Marine Corps for two years, with an assignment as a weapon systems specialist at Marine Corps Air Station El Toro, California, first in the A-4 Skyhawk and then in the F-4 Phantom. It was the big, powerful Phantom that ignited his desire to fly military jets—in two years on the flight line, he had never flown in the planes he fixed—so he applied for officer candidate school. But the Marine Corps was looking for more infantry soldiers, not more officers, and the only place he could get accepted for officer training was Air Force ROTC at Eastern New Mexico State University.

He graduated in 1974 with a degree and a commission in the United States Air Force. He entered navigator training virtually on the very day the U.S. embassy in Saigon was being overrun by the Viet Cong. His years as a prior enlisted man helped him past the "new guy" syndrome common to second lieutenants, and studying hard in military classes was something the Marine Corps hammered home. Mace graduated top of his nav class in 1975, and got an assignment in the F-4E Phantom II at Moody Air Force Base in Georgia.

But it was during a Tactical Air Command bombing exercise in Nevada that Mace was introduced to the F-111 "Aardvark," and he was hooked forever. He cross-trained to the sleek, sexy-looking FB-111A in the Strategic Air Command in 1980, shortly after pinning on captain's bars, and was assigned to Pease Air Force Base, New Hampshire, in 1982, pulling strategic alert duties with nuclear-loaded Aardvark bombers. He and the FB-111A became one. He became an instructor, simulator panel operator, senior navigator, and wing weapons officer, shuttling between Pease and Plattsburgh Air Force Base in New York, the only two FB-111 bases in the country.

Daren Mace wanted to be involved in every aspect of the F-111 mission. He became instrumental in ushering in the new digital avionics modernization program for the Aardvark's weapon and navigation systems, won Strategic Air Command's Bombing and Navigation Competition once as S-01 senior instructor navigator, and participated in tests of several new weapons for the FB-111, including the AGM-131 SRAM II attack missile, the AGM-84E SLAM (Standoff Land Attack Missile), and the AIM-9 Sidewinder self-defense missile. As the nuclear deterrent role of the FB-111 diminished, Mace saw to it that SAC crews adopted skills in non-nuclear bombing tactics, and he helped design and test new weapons and new missions for the F-111, including "Wild Weasel" enemy air defense suppression and tactical reconnaissance. He was an expert in high-threat bomb delivery tactics, precision-guided munitions employment, and defensive tactics.

He was at Pease as the DONB (Deputy Commander for Operations, Navigation, Bombing) in 1989 when the decision was finalized to transfer the FB-111 to Tactical Air Command and close Pease Air Force Base. Mace began shuttling FB-111s to McClellan Air Force Base in California to begin their conversion to the F-111G, giving them full integration with Tactical Air Command units. While at McClellan, a major aircraft maintenance and repair facility, he learned more about the inner workings of the Aardvark than ever before—his training as a former Marine aircraft mechanic helped him. In just a few months, Daren Mace was recognized as one of the country's leading experts on the F-111 weapon system.

Then, in 1990, the Iraqi invasion of Kuwait. America at war. A secret assignment, no questions asked. In one fateful night, Daren Mace's life was turned upside down. Nothing was the same ever again.

After Desert Storm, Mace wanted to get as far away from the United States, as close to virtual exile, as one could get. He still had his wings, but he rarely flew—completely by choice. He was promoted to lieutenant colonel without fanfare in 1992, was allowed to attend Air War College, and was then sent to Turkey in 1993 for his third overseas assignment.

The Islamic Wars of 1993 and 1994, in which a strengthened Iraq, allied with Syria, Jordan, and other radical Muslim nations, tried to throw the entire Persian Gulf region into chaos once again, signaled the rebirth of Daren Mace. As weapons officer for the 7440th Provisional Wing at Incirlik Air Base in Turkey, Mace supervised the weapons requirements for a hastily formed NATO coalition, successfully arming every strike aircraft that was sent to him in the first few critical weeks of the outbreak of war. He helped keep two hundred Turkish, U.S. Air Force, Saudi Arabian, and a few Israeli aircraft in fighting shape until help could arrive in force. Daren Mace did everything—refuel planes, upload bombs and missiles, change engines, and even flew as a weapons officer in F-15E, F-111F, and F-4E and -G fighter-bombers.

Now, as senior weapons and tactics training officer of the Thirty-Seventh Tactical Group at Incirlik Air Base, it was Mace's job to help train NATO crewmembers on how to fight together as a team. He had many crews rotate in from all over the world, including F-111s, and in the past few months he started to get MiG-27 and Sukhoi-17 planes and crews from the Ukraine and Lithuania training with NATO forces. He got to fly—and fix—them all, but he loved it. It was an exciting time to be in Turkey . . .

. . . that is, Mace thought, if it wasn't for the Russians. The closer the Ukraine got to full integration with NATO and eventual full NATO membership, the testier and more forceful, even unpredictable, Russia was getting. At the same time, it seemed the United States was getting weaker by the day. Mace saw lots of Reservists at Incirlik, including units that he *knew* used to be active-duty ones but were now either full, partial, or Enhanced Reserve Program bases. Now was not the time to downgrade the military, he thought—it was time to gear *up*. All they had to do was check the winds.

As Mace gathered up his gear and stepped out of the cockpit of the Sukhoi-17, he was met by the group commander, Colonel Wes Hardin. "Hey, hotshot, how did it go?"

"Except for almost getting myself killed, great," Mace replied.

"I saw on the range video," Hardin said. "You had about a tenth of a second to live, you know that."

"Sixty feet is as good as sixty miles. I take it by the way young Ivan is jumping around that we did good."

"You did good. Two for two. You're making it look too easy." He motioned to a pod mounted on the right wing fixed section, inboard of the swiveling section of the wing. "The electronics interface pod worked good?"

"Sure did," Mace said. The AN/AQQ-901 electronics interface pod was designed to give older Soviet-made aircraft the look and feel of modern warplanes by giving them all the necessary electronic "black boxes" in one easily installed unit that did not require massive aircraft modifications. The pod provided satellite navigation updates by the U.S. GPS or Russian GLOSNASS constellations; a ring-laser gyro for precise heading and velocity information; a MIL-STD data interface bus for precision weapons such as Western laser-guided bombs and inertially guided missiles; and sophisticated weapon targeting and monitoring capability.

Someday when the Ukraine joined NATO, it would have access to very sophisticated weapons like the British Tornado or the American F-16 and F-111 fighter-bombers, but for now they had to settle for their old Soviet equipment with a handful of high-tech electronics pods to bring them up to Western standards. Even so, it took nothing away from the Ukrainian crew's ability to fly and fight.

"These Ukrainian kids are good," Mace replied. "They need to fly their planes, not just drive them. They need to think in three dimensions. But once you show them how to do it, man, they go out and *do* it. I pity the next guy who has to fly with Kondrat'evich—he's going to spend a lot of time upside down, I think. So who's my next victim?"

"Nobody, Daren," Hardin said. "I got news for you. I don't know if it's good news or bad news, but I got plenty of news."

Mace had been expecting this ever since passing twenty years as an officer—he was not going to be allowed to make full colonel. "Get it over with, Wes. When's my retirement party?"

"Last month," Hardin said. "You were officially RIFed as of last month."

The RIF, or Reduction in Forces, was the current Administration's ongoing program to reduce the size of the U.S. military to below one million members by 1996. The cuts were far-reaching and relentless. Mace wasn't surprised to find himself on the hit list, but now that it really hit him, it hit hard. "So when's my DOS?"

"You don't get a date-of-separation, Daren—you get a Reserve commission, effective last month," Hardin said. "You got thirty days to decide whether you accept it or not. Your thirty days expires in . . . oh, about five minutes."

"Hell, then let's go to the club and celebrate my last few minutes in the service, Wes," Mace said, "because I'm not accepting a Reserve commission. You work just as damn hard as an active-duty type, but for half the money. Tell our wonderful President and his crew, thanks but no thanks. Forget it. Let's get drunk."

"If you accepted the Reserve commission, it comes with a new assignment."

"Who cares? I don't want it," Mace said, shaking his head.

"How about Maintenance Group commander of the 394th Air Battle Wing at Plattsburgh Air Force Base, Daren?"

Mace stopped and stared at Hardin. "I said I don't . . . what did you say, Wes?"

"You heard me, hotshot," Hardin said with a smile. "MG of the hottest base in the force. This is *your* base, my man, *your* plane. You developed the design data for the RF-111G reconnaissance and Wild Weasel variant, you test-flew the -111 with HARM antiradar missiles and photo pods on them. This is the assignment you should have gotten. You accept this, you're sure to make full bird colonel in two to four years."

"Isn't this the unit that's supposed to be prima donna central?" Mace asked. "Full of mama's boys and weak-dicks . . . ?"

"And flybabes too, Daren," Hardin reminded him. "Six or seven women on the -111 side, including Paula Norton, the big-titted blonde who did the hot-pants poster a few months back, the ex-NASA astronaut . . . ?"

"Shit, Wes, flying with women?" Mace said. "It's just . . . ah, hell, weird. Especially in the -111, sitting side-by-side. It's too strange."

"Welcome to the new military, son."

"And Furness, the first female combat pilot—she's there, right?" Mace interjected. "A real winner, huh? Busts guys' balls and eats 'em for lunch."

"The Iron Maiden, Rebecca Furness." Hardin laughed. "Yeah, she's one of the flight commanders now, transitioning crews from training flight to mission-ready. I don't know if 'iron' describes her ass or her chastity belt. Do you want to find out or not? Daren? What about it?"

But Mace wasn't listening. That name . . . Rebecca . . . as well as the thought of returning to the RF-111G he loved so much . . . the RF-111G, the reconnaissance and Wild Weasel variant of the F-111G, which used to be known as the FB-111A.

He flew the F-111G years ago, during Operation Desert Storm—the only time the FB-111A/F-111G model had ever been flown in actual combat. He flew a combat mission on the morning of January 17, 1991, along with thousands of other Coalition forces—except he wasn't part of Desert Storm. His classified mission was called something else. The more he thought about it, the more he wanted to block it out. For so long now he had. And yet, in his heart, he knew he could never escape that terrible incident, even if he tried. It would always be a part of him. The memories seemed as real as yesterday. . . .

PART ONE

How good bad music
and bad reasons sound when
we march against an enemy.
—Nietzsche

1

Over the Murat River valley, eastern Turkey Thursday, 17 January 1991, 0539 hours local

U.S. AIR FORCE MAJOR DAREN J. MACE STRIPPED OFF HIS OXYgen mask and cursed in a voice loud enough to be heard over the scream of the engines and the high-speed windblast just a few inches away. "The damned stealth fighters missed. They fuckin' missed. Our mission's been executed." Mace waved a slip of paper he had just pulled from a satellite communications printer. His aircraft commander, Lieutenant Colonel Robert Parsons, sitting to Mace's left in the close confines of their fighter-bomber cockpit, wore a stunned expression.

It was not the news they had been waiting to hear.

Mace and Parsons were at twenty thousand feet in an F-111G "Aardvark" fighter-bomber, holding in a "parking" orbit over the city of Elazig in eastern Turkey. They had launched two hours ago from a small air base called Batman, in eastern Turkey, two hundred miles east of the main Coalition air base in Incirlik. The radio channels were filled with the excited, jabbering voices of men going to war.

Now, it appeared, Parsons' and Mace's turn had come as well.

It was the opening hours of the largest air invasion since World War II. Operation Desert Storm. The only thing that was definite about the war so far was the intense level of confusion that reigned.

Dozens of aircraft were departing Incirlik Air Base to the west, sweeping across Syria, and hundreds of others were racing northward from Saudi Arabia, the Persian Gulf, and the Red Sea. All were directed to use the radios only in an emergency, but it seemed as if half the fleet had emergencies, because the channels were jammed. Aircraft from earlier raids on Baghdad were returning, and a lot had suffered battle damage—which didn't help the tension levels. Reports of sheer curtains of triple-A—antiaircraft artillery—and hundreds of radar- and infrared-guided surface-to-air missile launches were echoing through the radio channels in a dozen different languages. The full might of the Iraqi military, with some of the world's most sophisticated air defense weapons on-line, was being brought to bear against the coalition of countries aligned against it.

Once airborne, Daren Mace and Robert Parsons were cut off from communications except for two vital radio links: one was a discrete UHF link to their tanker for the precious fuel they would need; the other, a special UHF link to a Strategic Air Command satellite twenty-two thousand miles in space, which would relay messages from U.S. Central Command (CENTCOM) headquarters or from the Pentagon in Washington, D.C.

The last message the crew had received, printed on a tiny thermal printer on the navigator's right-side instrument panel in the cockpit, was not from Schwarzkopf or Horner at CENTCOM—the addressor said "NCA," the National Command Authority. It was from the President of the United States himself, relayed from the White House to the Pentagon directly to Parsons and Mace.

There was only *one* kind of message that would come directly from the President himself.

"Gimme the entire message, Daren," Parsons asked his radar navigator nervously, "then let's go through the authentication together. Show it to me step by step so I can be sure."

"I don't like the smell of this," Mace mumbled. He opened the red-covered decoding booklet, onto which he had clipped the Air Force Satellite Communications printout and recopied the encoded message. Pointing to each section block in the decoded message so Parsons could follow along, he read:

"NCA sends, actual message, reference date-time group, SAC Eighth Air Force units, operation code X-Ray-Bravo."

Mace opened a second folder marked top secret and flipped it open to the proper page, as indicated by the date-time group in the decoded message. "Page sixty-three, XB decodes to Operation Desert Fire."

Parsons nodded.

The code book had listings for dozens of preplanned missions involved in the opening morning of Desert Storm, but only one pertained to Parson and Mace: Desert Fire. If it decoded out to any other mission name, even if the authentication was correct, the message would be invalid.

Mace continued: "Here's the code for the flight plan set, the weapons unlock code, and here's the authentication code and sequence."

Using a third top secret code book, Mace looked up the proper document letter from the authentication code and withdrew a thin, stiff card from his secrets bag. After Parsons confirmed that he had the right one, Mace snapped the card open and laid a series of uncovered alphanumerics next to the last six characters in the decoded message. They matched and were in exact sequence.

"Message authenticated," Mace said. "We're going in. *Shit.*"

Parsons sighed in resignation while Mace began composing a reply message. Parsons was silent, thinking about the challenge that lay ahead. It was a challenge no one ever wanted to *really* face, but it was part of the job. He'd faced them before, though not on this scale, in Vietnam, Libya, Panama. But he was an older breed of flyer. He glanced over at Daren Mace and wondered how this talented hotshot navigator would handle what they were inevitably going to do.

Not much younger than Robert Parsons' own forty-five years, Daren Mace was typical in so many ways of what one would expect an Air Force officer to look like: tall, blond hair, good-looking chiseled features, pearly white teeth, and a hint of a tan. But Daren Mace was atypical in many other ways, his attitude a sharp contrast to his appearance. He hated exercise (and didn't need it, being that rare breed who neither gains nor loses, but maddeningly stays the same year after year), and preferred lifting mugs of Coors and chasing women to anything resembling sports. The Air Force's 391st Bomb Wing kept a close eye on Mace, who vocally scoffed at the monthly fitness tests as a waste of time and delighted in pencil-whipping them simply to aggravate the flight surgeons. When the Air Force began using additional duties to evaluate its officers instead of real yardsticks—like job performance, for example—Mace rolled his eyes, usually muttered that it was a "bunch of shit," and challenged any rule that did not involve flying. For in Daren Mace's mind, flying ruled the day. Period. No ifs, no ands, no buts.

Despite his attitude, which was a constant thorn in his superiors' side, no one could deny that Daren Mace was the best. It was why on this day, the opening hours of Desert Storm, Mace was Robert Parsons' partner. Mace could navigate the hell out of the F-111G bomber, and nobody knew the Aardvark bomber better than he.

Because of his abilities, Mace usually flew the "newbies," the new pilots in the squadron, until they had enough hours under their belt, usually getting assigned to work with the lower-rated "R" (ready) crews, not the "E" (experienced) or "S" (superior) ones. His independent attitude usually lost him consideration for the more high-profile sorties or exercises. The wing commanders knew where their bread was buttered, and as talented as Mace was, one bad impression on the brass could destroy an entire wing's reputation . . . and their careers. So, in effect, Mace was kept in the closet.

"I really can't believe this," Mace muttered as he composed, encoded, and keyed the reply message into the AFSATCOM terminal keyboard. "Those stealth fighters were supposed to be such hot shit, and they can't even hit the target."

"Take it easy, Daren," Parsons said to his radar navigator. "What do you expect when the rag-heads have a triple-A on every rooftop in Baghdad? The Goblins *aren't* supersonic, you know."

"Tell me about it," Mace said. "They couldn't hit anything in Panama, either. What a waste! If Schwarzkopf wanted the job done right, he should have sent the F-111s in right away."

"Hey," Parsons said, "what's done is done. The -117s had their chance. They blew it. Now it's up to us."

Lieutenant Colonel Robert Parsons was the commander of the 710th Bombardment Squadron (Provisional), a Strategic Air Command F-111G medium bombardment squadron secretly deployed to Batman, Turkey. Parsons' thin gray hair and baggy eyes attested to the high degree of thinking and planning he did in preparation for every mission, from the easiest "cake-walk" training sortie to the toughest combat mission. He had been flying various models of the USAF/General Dynamics F-111 medium bomber for nearly twenty years, but he studied, planned—and, yes, worried—like a cherry lieutenant.

Parsons' contingent included four bombers, sixteen crew-members, forty aircraft maintenance and weapons handling personnel, thirty security troops, and five support personnel, but officially his small provisional unit did not exist—in more ways than one. The two F-111G (what had then been known as the FB-111A bomber) bases in the northeast United States had both been closed and the bomb wings disbanded, the result of severe budget cuts enacted long before the Persian Gulf War. The FB-111A supersonic bombers of the Strategic Air Command, in service since 1970, had been transferred to USAF's Tactical Air Command, upgraded, and redesignated the F-111G, so officially the FB-111A bomber itself did not exist. The four bombers deployed during Desert Storm had been kept in mothballs in storage hangars at McClellan Air Force Base, an aircraft maintenance depot in northern California, when Operation Desert Fire had been executed.

This mission was possibly the last flight of the F-111G. It was no longer the unstoppable supersonic avenger: the winner of more bombing trophies than any other bomber in history, the hero of Operation El Dorado Canyon, the bombing mission against Muhammar Quaddafi of Libya in 1986, and of thousands of successful, precision air raids in Vietnam that forced North Vietnam to the negotiation table. Now it was the advanced warplane no one wanted, the twenty-year combat veteran forgotten in the U.S. military's current budget crunch, the orphaned stepchild that had never even been given an official nickname.

Even the bomber's forward operating base in Turkey was a secret. Batman was a Turkish army air base being used by the United States for special operations missions into Baghdad—inserting Special Forces troops deep within Iraq, mounting rescue missions within enemy lines to retrieve downed aircrews, eavesdropping on or jamming Iraqi radio messages, even dropping leaflets with surrender instructions printed on them over Iraqi military bases or over cities. All the American aircraft there, including Parsons' four orphan "swing-wing" supersonic bombers, were concealed in carefully guarded hangars. The F-111s had flown in directly from California after a grueling twenty-two-hour-long nonstop flight, always flying apart from other Coalition aircraft, to make sure their presence was a strict secret.

Although no one would ever officially know they were there, the tiny unit was destined to play one of the most important—and deadly—roles in this war.

"Spin out our LLEP times so we can arrange to get our last refueling," Parsons ordered.

"Right," Mace replied. Using the reference date-time group in the execution message, Mace computed the bombs-away times for their two assigned targets, then backed that time through the flight plan and came up with a time to cross the LLEP, or low-level entry point, then back to the end air-refueling point, then to the air-refueling control point, or ARCP.

The TOT, or time over target, was so close that he would have to hustle to make the air-refueling control time as well as the time over target good within fifteen seconds. No leeway in this flight plan at all.

"Toad One-Five, Toad One-Five, this is Breakdance. CT at 1255. Repeat, ARCT at 1255. How copy?" asked Mace. It took three attempts, fighting through the horrible maze of accents and languages of the Coalition aircraft using the channel—American, British, French, Arab, Australian, even South American—before his tanker's navigator acknowledged the new rendezvous time.

"This is the shits, Bob," Mace said. He punched commands into the flight computer, and a box-shaped bug on the heading indicator, called the "captain's bars," swung to a northwesterly heading. "Captain's bars on the ARCT. We gotta be there in fifteen minutes."

Parsons glanced at the TIME TO DEST readout on the Multi-Function Display on his instrument panel, made a quick mental calculation, and shoved the throttles up nearly to full military power. He then selected HEADING NAV on his autopilot, and the F-111G Aardvark bomber obediently banked left and automatically rolled out on the new heading. "We gotta go balls to the wall to make the LLEP, then push it up to 540 on the low-level. That leaves us very little leeway for . . . stuff."

"Stuff" on a low-level combat mission usually meant countering enemy air defenses. Circumnavigating antiaircraft artillery, dodging surface-to-air missiles, and outrunning enemy fighters at treetop level usually gulped a lot of extra fuel, which was rarely accounted for in fuel calculations on a flight plan.

"If we can't make it, we abort," Parsons said. "You got the flight-plan range estimates?"

"Right here." Mace compared the flight-plan fuel calculations with the new fuel-burn figures in his performance manual for the higher airspeeds necessary in the low-level route. "If we get this air refueling, we have plenty of gas," Mace said. "No abort. We have to abort if we can't get both external tanks to take gas or if they won't feed."

Parsons turned to his partner, gave him a wry smile, and asked, "Praying for a busted boom or bad feed, Daren?"

Answering his squadron commander's question was a Catch-22: he'd be lying if he answered no, and a coward if he answered yes. Instead, he replied, "If the -117s had done their job, we wouldn't be talking about this in the first place, sir."

The hotshot F-117A stealth fighter jocks from supersecret Tonopah Air Force Base in the Nevada desert, the ones who were flown to and from work in plush airliners and who got promoted just by shaking a few hands and showing their unit patches to gaga-eyed generals, had apparently missed their assigned targets. Just like Panama in 1986: the nonsense about the stealth fighters being used just to "disorient" the Panamanian Defense Forces was hogwash. They missed their targets then, and they missed them again now. That did not sit well with the young F-111G crewdog.

The tanker was late to the air-refueling control point. Parsons and Mace had to wait for their companion aircraft: an EF-111 Raven tactical jamming aircraft, which was a modified F-111 fighter-bomber loaded with state-of-the-art electronic jammers, from the 42nd Electronic Combat Squadron, RAF Upper Heyford, England, deployed to Incirlik. Normally the F-111Gs were accustomed to going into a target alone, but the importance of the mission dictated that it be accompanied by the supersophisticated robin's-egg-blue jamming aircraft; the EF-111 could fly as far, as fast, and as low as the F-111G, so it would follow Parsons and Mace all the way to its target and back.

All aircraft completed their air refuelings—all tanks refueled and all tanks were feeding, Mace noted with private disappointment, negating an abort—and they turned toward the Iraqi border and made preparations to attack. The EF-111 Raven had its own flight plan, carefully choreographed with Parsons' and Mace's, that would both deconflict the two aircraft and put it in position to best defeat any enemy radars that might highlight the Aardvark bomber. That was okay with Mace—he didn't like having to worry about watching a wingman during night formation flying anyway.

They had ten minutes to fly to the low-level entry point, and they did so at just below the speed of sound to try to get their time pad back. On this mission, timing was not just important—it was a matter of life or death. Not just for Parsons and Mace, but for the hundreds of other aircraft that would be airborne over southern and central Iraq when Mace completed his bomb release. The ten minutes to the start-descent point was wall-to-wall checklists: TFR (Terrain-Following Radar) Confidence Check, cockpit check, route briefing, and fuel tank jettison checklists.

"Tanks gone," Mace announced. He refigured all switches to normal, then announced, "Weapons coming unlocked."

Using the unlock code from the execution message, Mace used yet another decoding book, broke out the six-digit weapons prearming code, and entered it into a code panel. Two minutes later, a green ENABLE light illuminated on the weapons arming panel. He then accomplished a weapons connectivity and continuity check on the weapons, checking that full electrical and data transfer capabilities were intact, then put the weapon arming panel from OFF to SAFE.

"Gimme consent," Mace said.

Parsons reached around to his left instrument panel, twisted a thin wire seal off from a red switch guard, opened the guard, and flipped the lone switch up. "Consent switch up."

Mace clicked the interphone, reached to his weapons arming panel, twisted a similar safety wire off a sliding silver switch, and moved the switch to CONSENT. In nuclear-capable aircraft, as in all American nuclear launch systems from sixty-pound battlefield shells to hundred-ton intercontinental ballistic missiles to two-thousand-ton nuclear submarines, two physically separate switches had to be activated before the weapons could be prearmed. Mace moved the large knob on the weapon arming panel from SAFE to GND RET. Two white switchlights on the weapon status panel illuminated; both read AGM-131X. He moved the missile select switch on the missile control panel to

ALL and the silver arming switch from its center OFF position up to ARM. The status indication on the panel changed from SAFE to PREARM.

"If this shit wasn't so serious," Mace said to Parsons, "I'd swear I could hear 'When Johnny Comes Marching Home' right now, just like in *Dr. Strangelove.*"

"Right," Parsons said, his voice low and tense. "What have you got?"

"Weapons prearmed, racks locked," Mace replied. "Double-check my switches." He swiveled a small reading lamp down to the weapons arming panel so Parsons could check the indications, then he began composing another coded message to inform the Pentagon and U.S. Central Command headquarters that he had successfully prearmed his weapons . . .

. . . Two thermonuclear AGM-131X Short-Range Attack Missiles.

"Checked," Parsons said uneasily. He sank back into his seat, and realized that he had just witnessed an historical event—this was the first time that a combat aircraft had prepared thermonuclear weapons for use since World War II. Plenty of aircraft had launched with nuclear weapons aboard during the Cold War, and there had been accidental releases and airplane crashes with atomic weapons on board, but this was the first time that a thermonuclear weapon had been prearmed and made ready for attack. It was all because the twelve F-117 stealth fighters, with their load of two-thousand-pound bombs, had failed to destroy one single building near the provincial capital city of Karbala, about fifty miles southwest of Baghdad and thirty miles west-northwest of the ruins of the ancient city of Babylon. Along with a large military base, railroad yard, warehouses, and a large military airfield, Karbala was the site for one of the world's most sophisticated military command posts. It was a deep underground reinforced-concrete bunker that reportedly controlled all of Iraq's fixed and mobile offensive rocket forces—nearly three hundred medium-range SS-1 Scud missiles, over one hundred short-range SS-7 Frog missiles, and an unknown number of SS-12 Scaleboard missiles, a tactical nuclear-tipped surface-to-surface missile purchased from the USSR after the signing of the Intermediate-Range Nuclear Forces Treaty with the United States. Each weapon could carry a high-explosive warhead—or biological, chemical, nerve agent, or even nuclear warheads—that could quickly devastate Coalition forces.

Karbala had to be destroyed early in the conflict, before Iraq could mount a heavy missile assault on Saudi Arabia, or the Coalition airfields near the Iraqi border, or Israel. If Saddam was foolish enough to launch Scud missiles against Israel, she would almost certainly use nuclear weapons to stop the Iraqi war machine. It was so important that Karbala be destroyed, that Iraq not launch any Scuds on Israel, that Israel not enter the war, that the United States planned the ultimate contingency mission—employ a low-yield nuclear device against Iraq.

Except for the standard nuclear strike weapons on board Navy ships, the two AGM-131X missiles aboard Mace and Parsons' bomber were the only thermonuclear weapons deployed as part of Desert Shield and now fielded as part of Desert Storm. The warhead of each missile was a "subatomic device," a very low-power weapon with a yield of less than one kiloton, or one thousand tons of TNT—about one-twentieth the size of the bombs that destroyed Hiroshima and Nagasaki during World War II, but still packing the same explosive power of fifty fully loaded B-52 bombers carrying non-nuclear weapons.

Mace knew the delivery procedures—he had practiced them often enough back home. The missile would be launched from low altitude, climb to fifty or sixty thousand feet with the power of its dual-pulse solid rocket motors, then follow a ballistic path to its target, steered by its inertial navigation system and the superaccurate, satellite-based Global Positioning System. The missile would fly for about forty miles—plenty of room for Mace and Parsons to escape the blast effects.

Only one missile was planned to be launched; the second missile was a backup. Mace had seen charts predicting the fallout path, likely contaminated areas, and a list of things that might happen when the electromagnetic-pulse (EMP) hit, but the bottom line was much simpler—there was going to be widespread, global fear, panic, and a bloody outcry directed against the United States, the Pentagon, the Air Force, and him.

The Pentagon planned, and the White House hoped, that Iraq would sue for peace immediately after that attack.

While speeding toward their low-level entry point, Mace had tuned his HF (high-frequency) radio to the Israel National Radio broadcasts from Tel Aviv—everyone stationed in the Middle East knew the INR's HF single sideband frequency, 6330, by heart, as well as the Voice of America (2770) and the BBC (3890)—and a few minutes later they got the confirmation they had been dreading: "Fuck. Just heard it on the INR, Bob," Mace told Parsons. "'VIPER SNAKE.' Tel Aviv and Haifa were hit by Scud missiles." VIPER SNAKE was the Israeli code word to all its military posts of a mass attack against the country. "Report says that the missiles that hit in Tel Aviv were carrying chemical warheads. Israel is launching attack aircraft."

"You're shitting me," Parsons said. He knew that civilian news broadcasts should never, never be used as sources of official information, but the report only seemed to confirm the orders they had already received from the Pentagon. "Boy, never thought they'd do it."

"One thing about ol' Saddam," Mace pointed out, "is that he's never failed to do something he said he'd do. He told everyone he'd destroy Israel if Iraq was invaded. I hope he's under this SRAM when we cook it off." Mace checked his bomber's chronometer: "The Scud missiles hit shortly after four A.M. We got our execution message about ten minutes after the missiles hit. Christ, the brass didn't waste any time."

"Looks like we were primed to do this mission right from the start," Parsons pointed out. "We haven't heard much from Israel during the military buildup—we must be Israel's secret guarantee that Saddam won't destroy her."

Mace was silent for a moment, then said over interphone, "Well, that's typical of the brass—do a fucking back-door deal and keep us in the dark, then let *us* drop the nuke and bear the guilt of obliterating thousands while they sit back, smoke their cigars, and slap each other on the backs for a job well done. Then it's off to the White House for victory cocktails with the Old Man. The bastards."

Parsons knew the aggravation Mace was going through. He was feeling it himself, as well as a slow, sinking queasiness in his stomach that he hadn't felt for some time—not since 'Nam, when he'd seen little Vietnamese children running through the rains of fiery napalm—ordered by the brass—burning their flesh to the core. It had sickened him then, as this sickened him now. But he was an officer serving his country, with a job to do. The President—their Commander in Chief—had ordered it and they *would* do it.

"Daren, I don't like the thought of it any more than you do. *But* we *are* going to do it. You've trained for this. You knew there was a chance we'd have to when you stepped into the cockpit."

"Christ, but I never . . ."

"Listen to me," Parsons snapped. "You signed on for this just as I did. Nobody put a gun to your head. If you're gonna flake out on me, say it now, before we head into Indian country."

"And what if I don't want to?" fumed Mace. "Killing thousands upon thousands of people . . ."

"Then we turn around. Our careers will be over. We'll spend ten years in prison breaking big rocks into little rocks, and then we'll receive dishonorable discharges. No one in their right mind would launch a nuke, but we'd be treated as cowards and pariahs for the rest of our lives because we refused to follow orders." He turned to his radar navigator and added, "After all these years in the Air Force, are you so afraid to die that you would give up all you have, all you've accomplished . . . ?"

"I'm *not* afraid to die, Colonel," Mace answered firmly, "and I'm *not* afraid of becoming a pariah. What I don't like doing is something completely abhorrent simply because I've received a message to do so."

Parsons said, "You know, Major, you should've sorted out all that before you stepped into the cockpit, before you volunteered for duty overseas, before you joined the bomb squadron. Sixty minutes from our TOT is *not* the time to have second thoughts. But let me tell you something: I'm not going to risk my life flying in combat with someone who's not giving me one hundred percent. I don't want to spend ten years in prison, but I don't want to die needlessly because my nav is having a guilt attack. We either both say 'go,' or we abort and pay the piper back home. Do we go—or do we turn back?"

Mace looked at the time-to-go indicator on his Multi-Function Display—only three minutes to the LLEP. The EF-111 Raven would have already zipped out ahead, scanning for enemy threats and shutting down enemy SAM sites and long-range fighter-intercept radars.

The war is on, Mace thought. The Iraqis invaded Kuwait and threatened Saudi Arabia and Israel. He was committed long before he had received that execution message.

"We go," Mace said.

"You sure, Daren?"

"Yeah. I'm sure." He fastened his oxygen mask in place, slipped on his fingerless Nomex flying gloves, and nodded to his aircraft commander. "'Before TF Descent' checklist when you're ready . . ."

While still one hundred miles from the Iraqi border, the crew of the F-111G fighter-bomber, call sign "Breakdance," began a rapid descent to terrain-following altitude.

They were still thirty miles in Turkish airspace when the AN/APS-109B radar homing and warning receiver (RHAWS) blared, and an "S" symbol appeared at the top edge of the circular RHAWS display. The unit had been displaying several "H" symbols, arrayed along the border—these were American-made Hawk antiaircraft missile sites, operated by the Turkish Army. The line of H symbols clearly outlined the border. But the S symbol was new, and it was not friendly.

"Search radar, twelve o'clock," Mace reported. "Threat detection system is on, trackbreakers off." The bomber's internal AN/ALQ-137 internal electronic countermeasures system, called trackbreakers by the crews, was an automatic noise/deception jammer system that was effective on short-range, low-power radars like airborne missile guidance radars and mobile surface-to-air missile systems, but virtually powerless against big, heavy, ground-based radars like enemy search or fighter-intercept control radars—that was the reason Mace kept it off. The EF-111 Raven electronic-warfare aircraft escorting them was designed to jam these radars anyway. "Ready to step it down?"

"Give me four hundred," Parsons said.

Mace twisted the terrain-following knob two clicks to the left, and the big F-111G bomber nosed gently toward the dark, unseen ground below. They were now flying only four hundred feet above the rugged terrain, screened from view of all but the closest and most powerful enemy radars. Seconds later, they crossed into enemy territory—and the real terror began.

The border region between Turkey and Iraq was one of the most heavily fortified in the world, with over 120,000 troops spread out on both sides along the two-hundred-mile frontier. As the friendly Hawk radar symbols disappeared on the radar warning receiver, they were replaced by "A" and "3" symbols—these were Iraqi antiaircraft artillery units and Soviet-built SA-3 mobile surface-to-air missile batteries, deployed with the Iraqi border army units to guard against hostile aircraft. Neither was a great threat to the fast, low-flying F-111G, but there seemed to be a solid wall of A symbols ahead. "We can't go around them," Mace said. "C'mon, Raven buddy, don't let us down."

"Give me two hundred, hard ride," Parsons shouted over the continuous *deedle deeedle deeedle* of the radar warning system. Every time a new triple-A system appeared on the scope, the warning tone blared. Soon there were five, ten, then more than a dozen A symbols on the RHAWS scope, aligned straight ahead. Occasionally they could see intermittent bursts of heavy-caliber gunfire slicing the darkness outside, but it was random and just sweeping aimlessly across the sky—obviously the EF-111 was doing its job. Mace clicked the TF switch twice to the left, then moved the large center RIDE knob from NORMAL to HARD—this would command steeper climbs and descents over the mountains. At night, in rugged terrain, and while under attack, this was the most difficult flying imaginable for a bomber crew.

"Two hundred hard ride set," Mace reported. "High terrain, six miles, not painting over it . . . five miles . . . four miles . . . give me twenty left to go around this sucker."

In his attack radar, a high mountain peak resembled a yellow ripple across the screen, with black beyond it. The black indicated how high above the bomber's flight path the terrain was: if the black receded as they approached, the bomber was climbing over the peak; if the black grew larger and began to stretch toward the top of the scope, the bomber would eventually hit the hill. At two hundred feet aboveground, there was a lot of black on the scope.

Parsons thumbed a button on the control stick, which briefly disconnected the heading control portion of the autopilot to allow for minor course corrections (without disabling the critical terrain-following and fail-safe flyup features of the autopilot), and edged the control stick left. When they were clear of the hill, Parsons released the NWS/AP HOLD switch, and the bomber automatically swung right toward the next turnpoint.

"We got triple-A at two o'clock, just outside lethal range," Mace announced. "SA-3 search radar, one o'clock, outside lethal range. Sirsenk army air garrison." Sirsenk was the northernmost air base in Iraq, but more importantly Sirsenk protected the northern edge of the Torosular mountain range. "High terrain, eleven miles, not painting over it."

Parsons did not acknowledge all those important calls.

"Sirsenk now at three o'clock. Still got an SA-3 up, but it's not locked on," Mace reported. It was Mace's job to coordinate the terrain outside—which Parsons could not see with the naked eye—with Parsons' only terrain indicator, the "E-scope" on the forward instrument panel. The E-scope painted a distorted one-dimensional picture of the terrain ahead, with a squiggly line depicting the bomber's flight path; if the terrain broke the line, they would hit the ground. Mace would call out terrain ahead until Parsons saw it on the E-scope and could confirm that the bomber's terrain-following autopilot was responding properly. Also, Mace had to coordinate all that with the radar threat scope and with the flight plan route—it wouldn't do any good to successfully avoid a hill only to fly right into lethal range of an SA-3 missile or "ack-ack" artillery battery, or fly so far off course as to get off time or miss the target area completely.

Suddenly, just a few miles ahead, a streak of antiaircraft artillery fire lit up the sky. Streams of tracer bullets seared the darkness. Parsons unconsciously swung farther left to fly away from the tracers, and the bomber's nose zoomed upward.

"Don't turn left!" Mace shouted. "High terrain to the east!"

Parsons' throat turned dry—he thought he could feel the jagged, frozen rocks scraping the bomber's belly as they crested yet another ridgeline. The hard-ride TF autopilot yanked the bomber's nose into the darkness of a crevasse so abruptly that both crewmembers felt light in their seats, as if they were momentarily weightless.

"Those tracers looked like they were firing well to the south of us," Mace pointed out. "It must be the Raven beating the bushes for us. Those guys will never buy another beer in their lives as long as I'm around." As the radar warning receiver scope cleared, Mace deselected the four jammer switchlights, shutting off the ECM system until the next threat.

The first half of the Torosular mountain range was one hundred nautical miles long, and at nine miles per minute it was the hairiest ten-minute ride of Mace's life. The tops of the ridges were sometimes two thousand feet higher than the bomber's flight level, and some mountain passes narrowed to less than twelve thousand feet wide or ended abruptly with a one-thousand-foot sheer wall of rock. Parsons had to go to zone 3 afterburner a few times to safely clear a ridgeline—losing an engine while climbing fifteen thousand feet per minute over a jagged ridge would mean certain death—and they knew that the bright afterburner plume only increased their chances of detection, even in these desolate mountains.

"Better step it up to one thousand feet," Parsons said. "We're safe for now in these mountains, and we can't afford to use blowers to help us get over these ridges."

"Amen to that," Mace said, quickly resetting the TF ride switch to the higher clearance plane. As they inched higher above the rugged mountains, he could breathe a bit easier as the effective range of his radarscope expanded from just a few miles to almost twenty miles. "Got a three-hundred-foot FIXMAG on the last fix," Mace said to Parsons. "System's running pretty well." The FIXMAG was the difference between the radar position fix and the computer's position—a three-hundred-foot difference after thirty minutes of hard maneuvering was very good. With a new, accurate radar update in the system and the bomb-nav system running well, Mace could afford to take his mind off the navigation system for a while and concentrate on getting ready for the missile launch run—the most important one of his life.

Things were quiet in the cockpit at the moment, and they were at the higher clearance plane setting, so Parsons said, "Good. Station check, oxygen and switches."

"Roger." A station check was a quick but thorough and coordinated check of all the cockpit instruments and systems, and all the personal systems in use.

The entire check took about thirty seconds: "Checks over here," Parsons said as he checked the autopilot and flight controls by "stirring the pot" with the control stick and jockeying the throttles.

Mace nodded and gave his partner a thumbs-up. "Everything looks—"

He never finished his short sentence. A loud, fast *deedle-deedledeedledeedledeedle* erupted in the interphone, and a circle with a flashing "9" was centered in the middle of the RHAWS radar warning receiver. At the same time, bright-yellow MISSILE WARNING and MISSILE ALERT lights on the forward instrument panel illuminated.

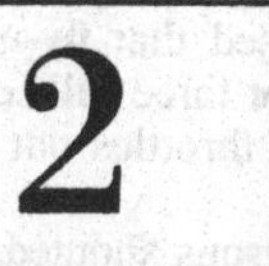

"JESUS!" MACE SHOUTED, "SA-9 MISSILE LAUNCH!"

He reached up to the ECM panel with both hands, depressing the jammer switchlights; at the same time, he used three fingers of his right hand and hit the L CHAFF and R CHAFF and FLARE buttons, which would pop white-hot magnesium flares and bundles of tinsel-like strips of metal from the AN/ALE-28 dispensers to decoy radar- and heat-seeking missiles fired at them.

"Chaff! Flares!" Mace shouted. It was vital to make the SA-9's "Dog Ear" surveillance radar break lock, because once the SA-9 missile launched it almost never missed. "Break! Accelerate! Descend! I'm ready on the TFs!"

"Two hundred hard ride!" Parsons shouted. As Mace twisted the TF clearance plane knob back to two hundred feet, Parsons swept the wings back to 72 degrees and cobbed the throttles to full military power, then into zone 5 afterburner. "Clear my turn!"

"Go right!" Mace shouted. Parsons threw the bomber into a 120-degree bank turn to the right and the bomber knifed downward. As the bank angle exceeded 45 degrees, the automatic safety fly-up feature of the terrain-following radar system commanded a full pitch-up maneuver, but because they were nearly upside down, the fly-up only helped to drag the nose earthward—Parsons used that fly-up to quickly lose altitude. He held that altitude for three full seconds, then abruptly rolled upright and pulled the throttles out of afterburner and back to military power.

"Chaff! Flares!" Parsons shouted, after he was sure the TFs were in control of the bomber's altitude. When he saw Mace punch the ejector buttons, he made another hard bank, this time to the left, pulling on the control stick and letting the fly-up pull the nose left so hard that the bomber began to stall. When the stall-warning horn blared, Parsons relaxed the back pressure on the stick. "Find the missile!" he shouted.

Mace was practically climbing up the back of his ejection seat and onto the canopy, searching behind and to all sides for any sign of an SA-9 missile in flight. But the missile weighed only seventy pounds and was only six feet long, and unless you were very lucky it was impossible to acquire it visually. "Nothing!" Mace shouted. The blinking 9 and the MISSILE WARNING light were still going, so Parsons had to assume that the SA-9 missile was still in flight and still tracking them. He shouted for chaff and flares again, and threw the bomber into a gut-wrenching break to the right so hard that Mace's head slammed against the center cockpit beam.

The flashing 9 was still on the radar warning receiver. "Radar's still up!" Parsons shouted. "Check the track-breakers!"

Mace ran his fingers across the ALQ-135 control switches and found two buttons had not been depressed. As soon as he pressed them in fully, their XMIT (transmit) lights came on, meaning that they had detected the SA-9's tracking radar and were jamming it.

The 9 symbol in the radar warning receiver scope went out a second later—right in the nick of time. Mace saw the rapid flash of light above and to their left as the SA-9 missile careened past them and exploded harmlessly about fifty feet away. "Fuck! It just blew up to the left! One more second and we would've been toast."

"Get ready for another launch!" Parsons said. "Those SA-9s got four rounds per unit." He had just finished that sentence when the 9 symbol and the MISSILE WARNING light illuminated once again. Parsons pushed the throttles to zone 3 afterburner, yelled, "Chaff! Flares!" and made a hard jink to the right as Mace pressed the ejector buttons. He then checked the trackbreaker buttons and noticed the XMIT lights on, indicating that their jammers were working. Seconds later the MISSILE WARNING light and 9 symbol on the threat scope went out. "I think we lost it."

"I see it! I see the missile!" Mace shouted. Far off to the right and behind them, a streak of light from the tiny splash of light that was Bashur army air base raced across the darkness, crossing ahead of them from right to left. It was followed a split-second later by two more shots. Just before the F-111G bomber ducked behind a ridgeline, Mace could see a stream of tiny blobs of light fly off into space. "Flares!" he shouted. "It must be the Raven! He's dropping flares!"

"Clear my turn, Daren," Parsons said. He wanted back into the protective radar clutter of the mountains right now.

Mace checked his radarscope. "Very high terrain to the left," he said. "Get your nose up to clear it. One ridgeline and then we'll be down in the next valley and away from Bashur."

"How much do I have to climb?"

"It'll be about a thousand feet, but we're really close . . . nose up, Bob, and give it some juice . . . high terrain three miles, not painting over it . . . check your fuckin' wing sweep."

The AN/APQ-134 terrain-following radar system was issuing its audible climb/descent cues, a low-pitched *boop boop boop* in a descent and a high-pitched *beep beep beep* when signaling a climb was necessary, and the rate of the sound was commensurate with the rate of climb or descent. Right now the TFR audio was beeping so fast that it sounded like one continuous tone. Parsons had to shove in zone 5 afterburner and move the wings from 72 degrees (full aft) to 54 degrees, then to about 30 degrees, to get the heavyweight bomber over the ridge without stalling.

They ballooned over the ridge traveling less than three hundred knots—only about a hundred knots above their stall speed. The TFR audio switched to a steady *boop boop boop* and the nose eased over. For a moment the SA-9 symbol and the MISSILE WARNING light came on, but it went out almost immediately as they nosed lower. "Steering's good to the next point, Bob. Gimme thirty."

There was a bright flash of light and a fiery streak not more than five or six miles ahead. The winks of flames could be seen clearly, like a big, slow meteor. At the same moment they heard on the tactical command radio channel, "Breakdance, Breakdance, this is Windfall, we are hit, we are hit. Mayday, Mayday, Mayday . . ."

Then there was nothing. Mace could not see the streak of fire impact before the terrain blocked his view.

"God damn . . ."

"They got out," Parsons said quickly. "I thought I heard the pyros going off in the background."

Mace heard no sounds of the EF-111's escape capsule blowing free of the stricken jet, but he wasn't going to argue. "They took a missile meant for us," he said soberly. "I'm sending a Glass Eye report. Better step it to a thousand feet." As Parsons gently climbed the bomber to a safer altitude, Mace recalled a canned Glass Eye aircraft-down report from his AFSATCOM computer, inserted the EF-111's approximate position and time, and transmitted the report. The report would go to Washington first, but the brass in Washington would eventually flash the message to Central Command headquarters in Saudi Arabia so they could arrange a rescue sortie. Normally an E-3 AWACS radar plane would be tracking the planes and would call in a search and rescue mission, but Mace and Parsons and the crew of the EF-111 from Incirlik had no AWACS following them. "Message sent."

Parsons checked his BNS time-to-go readout: "I've got thirty minutes to the IP. Station check."

Mace called up the "SRAM Air Operations Page" on the CDU (Control and Display Unit) on his right-side instrument panel and double-checked that both missiles were prearmed and ready to fly. "Weapons unlocked," he told Parsons.

"Copy," Parsons said. "Daren, make sure those suckers are in manual."

Mace bristled. He paused a bit, then touched the floor-mounted interphone switch with his left foot: "I got it, Bob."

"Just check the damned switch," Parsons snapped.

"I said I got it."

"Check the fucking switch!" Parsons shouted.

Mace had never seen Parsons this rattled. Normally the weapons belonged to the nav, and the aircraft belonged to the pilot, and rarely did either one question the other's responsibilities—but one look from the pilot made Mace hold his tongue. Parsons was obviously still hoping that this deadly mission would be called off, and the last thing he wanted was the nuclear-tipped missile to launch before the White House had a chance to terminate it.

"Hey, you keep the damned plane out of the rocks and I'll worry about the weapons," Mace said. But if the pilot wanted to double- and triple-check switches, that was fine with him. Mace put his hand on the launch mode switch—it was in MANUAL, and the bombing system switch was OFF. "Manual and off, Bob," Mace said. He paused for a moment, then added, "I got this bomb run wired, Bob, so ease up."

"I want full control of those missiles, Daren," Parsons said. "*Full control.* That switch doesn't leave manual under *any* circumstances."

"It's not supposed to," Mace replied. "Chill out."

Parsons nodded, then flexed his right hand on the control stick as if to relieve the tension in his arm and hand. "Sorry, Daren. Station check."

This time the cockpit and instrument check found a malfunction, and a serious one: "Shit. The fuel totalizer is reading zero. I've got the fuel feed selector switch in 'wing,'" Mace reported.

"What?" Still at terrain-following altitudes but one thousand feet above ground, Parsons checked the total fuel gauge—it read zero, with both body tank needles at zero. "Dammit, jettisoning the tanks must've shorted out the fuel gauge electronics."

"Shit, we've been dumping fuel overboard," Mace interjected. The automatic fuel management system worked off the gauge's needles, automatically maintaining a proper center-of-gravity balance between the forward and aft fuel tanks. If the forward-tank needle was too low, pumps would transfer fuel to the forward tank to prevent a dangerous aft center of gravity—but if the needle had malfunctioned and the forward tank was in reality already full, fuel would spill overboard through overflow vents. "It's been a long time since we punched the tanks off."

"Three minutes, at five hundred pounds per minute—that's fifteen hundred pounds of fuel we could've lost," Parsons figured. "How does that work on the fuel curve?"

Mace had been copying down the fuel readings on almost every turnpoint on the flight plan, comparing the flight plan's fuel figures to their actual ones. "We were two thousand short the last time I took a reading," Mace said. "This puts us three point five below the curve. We were flight planned to recover with six thousand."

"And we can recover with no less than two thousand, according to the mission directives," Parsons said. "We're still five hundred pounds on the 'go' side."

"Five hundred pounds ain't spit, Bob," Mace retorted. "The gauges can be off by a thousand pounds at least. We've got a no-shit *emergency* here. If we start losing body tank pumps or lose the generators, we can have an aft CG problem so fast—"

"But we haven't lost any pumps," Parsons insisted. "The system's working fine in manual. We got no choice but to continue."

"Maybe so," Mace said, "but I'll report the malfunction on SATCOM and ask for instructions. They can still abort us."

"No one makes a decision to abort this mission except me," Parsons snapped.

Mace turned to his pilot in absolute surprise.

"The Pentagon can either recall or terminate this mission, but it cannot order us to abort because of a systems malfunction. You got that, Major?"

"Hey, *Colonel,*" Mace said. "This plane didn't come with just *one* seat. It came with *two.* It's a crew decision to abort."

"*I* decide where this warplane goes and when," Parsons declared. "Your job is to maintain the navigation and bombing systems and assist me."

"Hey, don't tell *me* what my job is," Mace retorted. "I don't know when you developed this emperor complex."

"About the same time you chickened out," Parsons shot back. "You've wanted to turn tail and run ever since we got executed. You probably noticed that gauge malfunction a long time ago."

"That's bullshit," Mace said angrily. "I don't dump my computers or roll weapons on purpose, and I'm sure as hell not afraid to do this mission. We have instructions to transmit status messages anytime we have a serious aircraft or weapons malfunction, and that's what I'm going to do." He immediately began composing a status message and transmitted it to the Pentagon via AFSATCOM; Parsons could do nothing but monitor the instruments.

The bomber's flight path took them just east of Dukan Reservoir in eastern Iraq, then directly south between the cities of Kirkuk and As-Sulaymaniyah, but no missile launch indications were received.

They were now out of the Torosular Mountains and into the endless desert plains, only fifteen minutes to the missile launch point. Without the mountains to hide them, it seemed as if the entire Arabian Peninsula was visible to them—and, in turn, every fighter pilot, radar operator, and gunner in Iraq could see *them,* yet no dangerous radar emissions locked on to them.

A yellow light marked SATCOM RCV blinked on the forward instrument panel, and Mace waited impatiently as a thin strip of thermal paper rolled out of the printer. Parsons' attention was riveted on the instruments as they zoomed around low, rocky outcroppings and dove into dry riverbeds, but every now and then he sneaked a peek at his partner as Mace decoded the message: "Acknowledging our rescue and aircraft status messages," Mace said a few moments later. "No other orders."

Parsons said nothing.

The bomber skirted the Iraq-Iran border east of the As Sa' Diyah Reservoir, and it was here, near the city of Tolafarush, that they were "tapped" by their first fighter. A search radar with a height-finder from Subakhu found them and locked on. "Search radar . . . height-finder item of interest. Descend and accelerate."

"Clear me on those power lines and a left turn," Parsons said. "Stand by on chaff."

"Clear left and clear for two hundred feet," Mace said, checking the radar. Power lines and transmission towers showed up fairly well on the AN/APQ-114 attack radar, but the AN/APQ-134 terrain-following radar sometimes had trouble with them. He switched the TFR clearance plane to two hundred feet and punched out chaff as Parsons banked steeply left. "More power lines at twelve o'clock. We gotta climb in about sixty seconds. Twelve minutes to the launch point. We accelerate to six hundred in two."

"I'm already at six hundred," Parsons reported. The exasperated tone in his voice told Mace that he was thinking the same thing—the earlier they went to higher power settings, the farther behind they'd be on the fuel curve. Their five-hundred-pound fuel margin to bingo would be eaten up in no time, and then he'd have no choice but to abort the mission—but by then they'd be in the center of the air defense beehive of Baghdad, risking their necks for nothing. But Parsons had already made his decision, and he wasn't about to give the likes of Daren Mace the opportunity to be right. Parsons took a firmer grip on the control stick, swallowed hard, and added, "We're continuing. Gimme a countdown on those power lines."

Boy, Parsons would rather bust the minimums than do a fuel abort now, Mace decided. Something really serious was going to have to happen before Parsons would call this mission off.

Resigned to keep his mouth shut and press on, Mace turned back to the attack radar: "Roger. Range five miles. Thirty—" Just then an inverted "V" symbol appeared on the RHAWS scope, along with a high-pitched fast warbling tone. "Fighter at our three o'clock," Mace said. The symbol stayed on the scope and moved from the three to four o'clock position. At the same time, a yellow warning light marked MISSILE WARNING illuminated, and an "I" symbol appeared on the RHAWS scope, indicating that the AN/AAR-34 infrared warning receiver, a supercooled heat-seeking eye that scanned behind the bomber looking for enemy aircraft, was tracking the fighter. "He's locked on . . . Jesus! *Climb now!*"

He had almost forgotten about the power lines, and the TFR radar had not commanded on them. Less than two seconds before impact, Parsons hauled back on the control stick. Mace was slammed back in his seat, then slammed into the centerline rail as Parsons executed a steep right bank, then pressed down into his seat as the TFR system pulled them out of the steep descent back to two hundred feet above ground. Parsons was yelling "Chaff! Chaff!" as the radar warning tone continued to sound.

"Unload, dammit!" Mace shouted. The G-forces from the violent turns were preventing Mace from reaching the ejector buttons.

Parsons decreased his bank angle slightly, allowing Mace to reach the chaff/flares ejector panel, but Parsons was reaching for it first: "Dammit, Daren, punch that chaff out *before* I turn!" The fighter "bat-wing" symbol was still present and still locked on to them, so Parsons hit two chaff buttons and then reversed turn and jinked left. The bat-wing symbol disappeared—they had successfully broken the fighter radar's lock. It only made Mace feel even more helpless and edgy to watch his pilot activating the switches he, not Parsons, was responsible for. "I'll kick your ass all the way back to New Hampshire if you don't get with it," yelled Parsons.

"Fuck y—" Another high-pitched warbling tone erupted in the interphone, followed by a red MISSILE LAUNCH light. When the AN/AAR-34 infrared threat sensor was locked on to a target behind them and then detected a second pulse of energy, it interpreted that second flash as a heat-seeking missile launch. As it notified the crew, the system automatically ejected chaff and flare decoys. Parsons shoved the throttles to max afterburner, banked left, and pulled on the control stick, squishing Mace into his seat. The sudden, rapid-fire changes in direction made Mace's head spin, and for the first time he found himself completely disoriented—his inner ear was telling him he was turning, his seat told him he was not turning but descending, and his eyes were believing both of them. For the first time in his flying career, he felt an uncontrollable wave of nausea wash over him, and he ripped his oxygen mask off just before vomiting on the control console between his legs.

"Flares! Flares!" Parsons screamed as he reversed his turn. The stall-warning horn was blaring—even though they were careening through the night sky at well over seven miles per minute, the wings at full-aft position, and the airspeed bleeding off during the tight turns meant a drastic loss of lift. Mace jabbed his thumb at the flare ejector button, then gripped tightly to the glare shield and stared at the standby attitude indicator on the front instrument panel to reorient himself.

Although the engines were roaring, in and out of afterburner power, Mace could feel the aircraft sinking as Parsons held the bomber right on the edge of the stall—the airplane wasn't flying anymore, it was wallowing. *"Stall horn!"* Mace shouted over interphone. Parsons looked as if he was fighting the stall-inhibiting system, which was trying to lower the nose to regain flying speed. *"Get the nose down! Wing sweep!"*

Parsons finally shook himself out of his panic, grasped the wing sweep handle, and shoved the wings forward past the 54-degree lockout and all the way to 24 degrees. He also eased up on the back pressure on the control stick. The Aardvark's nose was still ungainfully high in the air—it was as if they were on final approach to landing, and flying almost that slow. The stall-warning horn was still blaring, but the plane felt solid and stable again. "Find that fighter!" Parsons shouted.

Mace checked the RHAWS scope—it was clear, with no symbols except for intermittent "S" symbols denoting the search radars at Subakhu, now several miles behind them. He switched the RHAWS briefly to IRT mode, looking for a small white dot that would be the system tracking the fighter, but it was clear. Just to be certain, he scanned the dark skies outside the cockpit, although he knew it was impossible to see a fighter out there at night unless he was just a few feet away. "We're clear," he told Parsons.

"When I say 'chaff,' Daren, you better give it to me," Parsons said irritably. "Get your head out of the radarscope and you won't get airsick. If you punch out chaff and flares while we're in the turn instead of before we turn, the missile will fly right up our ass." Mace was too dazed and dizzy to argue, but he continued monitoring the threat scope and scanning the skies as they continued at two hundred feet above the desert floor toward the launch point.

The numbers of ground-based early warning and missile radars decreased rapidly—south of Baghdad there didn't seem to be any at all. But Mace had no time to think about that—once they headed west and crossed the Tigris, they were on the missile launch run.

"Missile select switch to 'all,' status check . . . all missiles powered up, prearmed, and ready. Racks unlocked and ready," Mace reported as he ran the Before Missile Launch checklist. "Missile target data checked. Launch mode switch in manual. Bomb door mode switch auto. Consent switch."

"Consent switch up, guard closed," Parsons reported.

"Copy. Checklist complete. Three minutes to launch point."

It was less than one hour to sunrise, and the brightening sky began to reveal more and more details of the battle-scarred country below, and more details of the raging battle that was Desert Storm. One by one, Mace could see the gleaming office buildings and towers of Baghdad far to the north, the ancient city of Al Hillah, the ruins of Babylon ahead—and, to his complete amazement, aircraft filling the skies overhead. "Bogeys, one o'clock high," Mace reported. "More at ten to eleven o'clock high. All heading north-bound. Nothing on the RHAWS—they must be friendlies." He paused for a moment, then said, "They're heading north, Bob—they're heading right toward the target. Right towards Karbala."

"I'm standing by for the safe-in-range light, Mace. You got the launch point fix?"

Parsons was ignoring the obvious—there were friendlies flying within the lethal zone of a nuclear blast. Obviously someone had screwed up, and it wouldn't be too great to nuke a bunch of Coalition aircraft. "What time do you have, Bob?" Mace asked.

"Jesus, Mace . . ." Parsons scowled.

"Dammit, Bob, there's got to be a reason all these other aircraft are here. Maybe I screwed up the time. When I thought we were late before, maybe I got it backwards and we're really early."

"You didn't screw up anything," Parsons said. He pointed at the SATCOM clock on the forward instrument panel, which had Zulu time set for satellite synchronization. "That time checks with my watch. Now, unless we both got bad time hacks, we're dead on time. But if you got a bad time hack and set a bad time in the SATCOM receiver, we wouldn't have gotten anything on SATCOM. We received a message, you sent a message, and it was received and acknowledged. Everything's on schedule. I don't know why those other planes are up there, but it's not *my* problem—this mission, and getting my butt back on friendly territory in one piece, is my only concern right now. Now, get back on the damn bomb run."

"Whatever you say," Mace muttered. Mace took his eyes off the nearby Coalition aircraft and went back into the radarscope: "Stand by for launch point fix." Mace stepped the bombing computers to the launch point fix and selected the first offset aimpoint. After refining his aiming, he selected a second aimpoint, a tomb fifteen miles south of the dry lakebed. A semicircle of seven forts and tombs surrounded the lone tomb, so identification was positive.

Mace switched the radar to GND VEL to magnify the radar image, carefully laid the crosshairs dead on target, then reduced the range and selected offset three, a transmission tower just west of another lone tomb just twenty miles southeast of Karbala. The transmission line could be seen on radar as a thin, silvery sparkling line across the scope, making a definite jog southwestward where the right transmission tower was. The crosshairs were dead on. "I got the lead-in aimpoints," he told Parsons as he reconfigured the radar to wide field-of-view. "Checking switches. Launch mode switch is in."

Suddenly, on the international emergency GUARD channel, they heard, "Breakdance, Breakdance, this is Nightmare. Stop launch, stop launch. I repeat, Breakdance, this is Nightmare, stop launch. Time one-seven-zero-three-two-five, authentication poppa-juliett. Acknowledge. Over."

It was an incredibly eerie feeling to hear your call sign, which was supposed to be a secret from most of the Coalition, being broadcast in the clear over an international emergency channel. The cloak of invisibility they felt by being part of a secret mission was shattered—it felt as if everyone in the entire world, bad guys as well as good, could see them now. Mace didn't recognize the call sign Nightmare—they had a top secret codebook that would tell them who Nightmare was, but Mace had no time to look—but "stop launch" was a standard range director's order to cease all missile firing activities. "What in hell was that?" Mace cried out. "That can't be for real."

"Ignore it," Parsons said nervously. "It's, uh, a message in the clear, and we don't respond to clear-text messages. Take the fix and let's go." He turned to his radar navigator and found him furiously digging through an AQK-84 tactical decoding card. "Mace, I said ignore it."

Mace ignored him. "It checks, Bob," Mace said. "Jesus Christ, it *checks.* Someone just gave us a stop-launch order."

"We don't accept clear-text messages," Parsons repeated, "and we sure as hell don't accept a 'stop-launch' order, whatever that means."

"It's a standard range order," Mace said. "You hear it on live-fire exercises all the—"

"This is *not* an exercise, Major," Parsons snapped. "We're probably being MIJIed by the Iraqis—they might have captured the Raven, its crew, and their classified documents and devised a phony order to keep us from launching." MIJI, which was an acronym for Meaconing, Intrusion, Jamming, and Interference, was a standard tactic to try to divert aircrews from their mission or issuing false orders by the enemy. Aircrews had specific procedures for dealing with MIJI, and they had to be followed to the letter.

Mace knew that, but this still did not make sense—somebody was trying to tell them something.

"What are you doing now?" Parsons asked.

"If we get a recall or termination message," Mace replied, "it'll be on this page in the decoding book. I want to be ready."

"Forget about that and get back on the bomb run."

Mace silently muttered a "Fuck you." The crosshairs tracked perfectly as well, which meant the heading and velocities in the bombing system were perfect. "Got the final aimpoint . . . taking the fix." He set the right side MFD to the NAV Present Position page, checked that the update mode was in RADAR, then pressed the ENTER FIX Option Select Switch. The reverse video on the ENT FIX legend went out, and the FIXMAG readouts went to zero, indicating a successful position update. Mace switched his right side MFD from the Present Position page to the SRAM Air page and placed the Bomb Data page on the left MFD. "Got the fix. I need—"

"Holy Mother of God!" Parsons suddenly heeled the bomber into a steep right turn, then rolled left again to stabilize. Mace looked up from the radarscope and saw two American F-15E Strike Eagle fighter-bombers streak away to the north. The Strike Eagles were two-man versions of the F-15 Eagle fighter, modified for precision low-level bombing but retaining their air-to-air intercept and dogfighting capability. They had crossed the F-111G's path less than five hundred feet away. "Jesus!" Parsons shouted. "Where did they come from?"

"Those were F-15s!" Mace said incredulously. "They had Sparrows and bombs on board! Why are they heading toward the target area?"

"What difference does it make? We're on the bomb run."

"Bob, this attack should have been deconflicted," Mace said. "Any aircraft within twenty miles of ground zero will probably get blasted out of the sky. Those guys will be practically right over the target when the SRAM detonates."

"Jesus, Mace, we got a valid launch message . . . just punch that fucking missile out," Parsons said. "Put the launch mode switch in 'auto' if you got any problems. When I see the 'safe-in-range' light, I'll start a turn and head outbound. When I roll out of the turn, the missile will launch."

"Parsons, don't you get it? Something's wrong here!" Mace snapped. "Somehow I think we decoded an invalid message. I don't know how, but something's *really* wrong."

Parsons said, "It's impossible to validate an incorrect message. Either the message doesn't make sense or the authentication doesn't check. Both were correct. Stay on the missile run."

"We'll be killing our own guys!"

"You don't know that, Mace!" Parsons shouted. "Those guys can be heading anywhere. All we know is the orders we're given. Now stay on the goddamn bomb run!"

But Mace kept on looking across the gradually brightening sky, and the more he looked the more he was shocked to see dozens of other aircraft passing nearby, going in all directions—but mostly going north into Baghdad.

"Safe-in-range light," Parsons reported. "Countdown to turn started." The SAFE IN RANGE light indicated that the SRAM missile was within its launch envelope, or "footprint," and capable of hitting its target. The SRAM footprint extended not only ahead of the bomber's flight path but *behind* it as well, so Mace and Parsons could accomplish an "over-the-shoulder" launch. They would fly westbound until they were about fifteen miles from the target, then turn 180 degrees away from the target and launch the missile after rolling out of the turn. At detonation, the F-111G would be at least forty miles from ground zero, safe from the blast and EMP effects.

The sixty-second high-speed run toward the turnpoint was the most frightening of Mace's young life. "Thirty seconds to turn . . ."

It was sheer luck that Mace was looking right at the very spot on the ground—he saw a bright flash of light, like a searchlight or beacon light, then a long streak of yellow light. The spot of bright light began spiraling toward them at incredible speed. He had never seen one before, but he knew exactly what it was: "SA-7, three o'clock!" he shouted. He hit the FLARE button, then shouted, "Break right!" It was a Soviet-made, shoulder-fired surface-to-air missile, as common as ants in Iraq, and they were deadly at this close range.

Parsons did not hesitate—he rolled into a 90-degree bank turn and pulled on the control stick. Mace stopped popping decoy flares as soon as he felt the G-forces hit. He lost sight of the missile in the break—he was lucky enough to stay conscious, let alone maintain visual contact on a Mach-two missile—but as soon as Parsons rolled out of the break, Mace saw more flashes of light on the ground. "More SA-7s, two and three o'clock!" He popped more flares as Parsons did another right break.

Parsons had to sweep the wings forward once again to keep from stalling—two hard-break maneuvers in a row bled off a lot of airspeed very quickly. In just a few seconds the wings were forward to 26 degrees, he was in full military power, and the angle of attack was still just 5 degrees below the stall. "I'll roll wings level," he said to Mace. "Punch out the missile! Do it!"

"Keep at it, Bob," Mace shouted. "Level turn back left to the launch point. Still twenty seconds to the turn."

Just then they heard on the GUARD channel, again in the clear, "Breakdance, Breakdance, this is Nightmare, *abort* your missile run, repeat, *abort* your missile run. We show you ninety seconds to launch time. Do *not* fire your missile. Repeat, do *not* launch. Acknowledge." They then gave another date-time group and a new authentication code. Mace flipped open the code book he had already opened to the proper page, and in just a few seconds he discovered it was another valid message—valid, but still not acceptable to the Aardvark crew.

But the voice was definitely American, and the messages were real messages. Either it was a very clever, very well trained Iraqi, or it was for real and meant for them. But they had no choice in the matter—they *had* to ignore clear-text messages . . . they *had* to! But how could anyone else but the Pentagon know their launch time? "Christ, Bob, they know our launch time—down to the fucking second!"

This time Parsons hesitated, and it was obvious that he was scared and worried. Someone, anyone, could fake the first clear-text message they'd received—the second was impossible. They had indeed named their target time down to the second. Parsons shouted, "I'm rolling out for a few seconds to get our smash back. Get on GUARD and talk to someone. We've gotta stay on the missile run, but try to get confirmation. Clear my left turn, then get on the radio."

After making sure there were no missiles nearby being fired at them, Mace cleared Parson's left turn, then used the IFF/COMM page on his CDU and switched his radio to UHF 243.0, the international emergency channel that the voice who called itself Nightmare was using. The SA-7 missile was no match for an F-111G bomber at high speed and low altitude, and they had avoided or decoyed all the missiles fired at them so far. But they were down to about a dozen flares remaining, enough for two or three more attacks.

"Nightmare, Nightmare, this is Breakdance. We copy your message, but we cannot comply. We need a coded message to authenticate. Over." There was no reply. Maybe it *was* a fake radio message. "Nightmare, this is Breakdance, how copy? We need a coded message over our tactical network to authenticate. We will not respond to clear-text messages. Over."

Parsons turned hard left and rolled out, carefully watching his airspeed tapes. "Those damn SAMs are all around us," he said. "I've seen at least six so far! We're right in the middle of a damn Republican Guard division or something!" The airspeed was building rapidly, and he was able to sweep the wings back to 54 degrees to build up even more.

"I've got us at the turnpoint," Parsons shouted. "Coming right. Stand by for missile launch." The SAFE IN RANGE light began blinking—the missile countdown would hold until he rolled wings-level. "Verify launch mode in auto."

"It's in auto," Mace replied.

"Forty degrees to roll-out," Parsons said. "Stand by on missile launch. Stand by on bomb doors. Check cockpit lights up full and PLZT down. Close the curtains."

No one knew for sure what it would be like to fly in the vicinity of a modern-day nuclear explosion. There would be no fallout and less total energy released, but the effects on a "hardened" jet aircraft were just impossible to predict. They had had briefings on EMP and blast-shockwave effects, and they had their game plan laid out—radar fixpoints to re-initialize the navigation computers if they dumped, which circuit breakers to pull if the flight control computers went haywire, even small radiation dosimeters taped next to their skin to check for the amount of radiation they had been exposed to. They had lowered their special PLZT (Polarized Lead-Zirconium-Titanate) goggles in place and checked to make sure they were operating. PLZT goggles were electronic visors that would instantaneously darken to protect their eyes from serious damage from a nuclear flash. The PLZT goggles were like wide, bug-eyed sunglasses, so Mace and Parsons had turned up the cockpit lights not only to see the instruments before the burst, but to help see them after the burst as their eyes readjusted.

They had metal curtains and shields to cover the canopy and windscreen, and just seconds before roll-out they unclipped the curtains and pulled them across the canopies, then raised the windscreen shields and locked them into place. They were flying blind now. Every bit of skin was covered—gloves were on, collars were pulled up, zippers were up and tight; their oxygen supply was turned off to prevent any chance of fire; and their shoulder straps and lap belts were as tight as they could make them. One of the last items on the checklist was to shut the radios off to prevent the EMP from traveling through the energized external antennas and frying the electronic circuits. He reached down to his CDU to set all the radios to OFF—

—and just then the SATCOM RCV light blinked on the forward instrument panel and the thermal printer clattered to life. Mace heard it and gasped aloud. "Jesus fucking Christ, Bob, a SATCOM message."

"Coming up on missile launch."

Mace waited an interminable, spine-tingling thirty seconds for the printer to finish, then tore a long strip of thermal printer paper out of the printer, his hands and lap filled with decoding documents. He ran down the phonetic names one by one against the correct page of the decoding book. "Actual message . . . all Eighth Air Force units . . . I've got a SATCOM message for us, Bob."

The F-111G bomber rolled wings-level, and the SAFE IN RANGE light stayed on steady. "Screw it, Mace. The missile's gone. Turn off the radios, lower your PLZT goggles, and stand by on bomb doors."

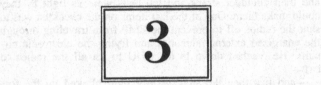

IT WAS A TERMINATION MESSAGE. HE KNEW IT WAS, WITHOUT even decoding it. The clear-text messages were for real, meant to warn them that the termination order was on the way. The Pentagon, the White House, did not want them to launch this missile.

He knew what he was doing was wrong—until he decoded the message and authenticated it, he was obligated to carry out his current orders and launch the SRAM, but Mace didn't feel he had a choice. He reached down to the weapons control panel and moved the bomb-door mode switch from AUTO to CLOSE.

When the SAFE IN RANGE light stopped blinking, the AGM-131X missile computer activated the MSL POWER light, and it began blinking as inertial guidance information was transferred from aircraft to missile. It took only two-tenths of a second for a complete computer dump; then the computer would command the bomb doors to open. The MSL POWER light continued to blink as the computer tried to open the bomb doors, but Mace had seen to those. The computer could not override the position of the bomb-door switch. It would wait about thirty seconds for the doors to respond; then the computer would automatically shut down the first missile, power up the second missile, and attempt to launch it. By then Mace thought he would have the message authenticated with Parsons, and he would either allow the second missile to launch automatically or just manually power it down.

But he had to decode this new message.

The timer in Parsons' brain ran out: "Standing by on bomb doors . . . safe-in-range light steady . . . doors . . . check doors, Mace . . . " He looked over to his radar navigator and saw him, his PLZT goggles off and his shoulder straps loosened, furiously checking data from the SATCOM printer. His lap and glareshield were full of decoding documents. *"What in hell are you doing?"* Parsons screamed.

"We got a SATCOM message. I'm decoding it."

"Why didn't the bomb doors open? Why didn't the missile launch?"

"I got the doors closed until I—"

"You what?" Parsons screamed. He leaned over and saw the bomb-door mode switch. "Are you crazy? Have you lost your mind? Open those damn bomb doors *now!* That's a damned order!"

"I *know* it's a recall order, Bob," Mace said, pleading with his aircraft commander. "I know it is. It'll just take me a second."

"Dammit, I'll have you fucking court-martialed! Open those—"

On the computer control panel, the MSL POWER light stopped blinking and the red MASTER MAL and MSL MAL lights came on. At the same time, the SAFE IN RANGE light on Parsons' panel went out—and he knew why. Since they were doing an "over-the-shoulder" SRAM launch, they had been flying *away* from the target. Now, thirty seconds past the launch point, they were out of range. They would not get a SAFE IN RANGE light unless they turned *back* toward the target—and now all of the Iraqi air defense units on the ground were alerted to their presence and ready for them.

"Jesus, Mace," Parsons cried out, "we lost the safe-in-range light! We have to turn back."

"Just wait," Mace argued. "If this is a recall message, we don't have to turn."

"And if it's not a recall, we have to fly over that infantry formation out there again," Parsons said. He snapped open his PLZT goggles and opened the flashblindness curtains on his left-side canopy with an angry wave of his hand, scanning carefully for any more enemy SAMs coming at them before jabbing an angry finger at his radar navigator. "You son of a bitch, you fucked up big-time. Your flying career is history, Mace. You chickened out and screwed up. I'm coming left. We'll launch the second missile as soon as we get a safe-in-range light—no over-the-shoulder launch this time. Make sure the second missile is powered up and ready to—"

Mace saw it out Parsons' left cockpit canopy, a bright burst of light from the ground, a stream of yellow fire, and a bright ball of light spiraling right toward them, and screamed "Shit! SA-7! Break left!" The large spot of light with a long, bright yellow tail climbed over Parsons' canopy sill, then descended straight at the hot leading edge of the F-111G's left wing.

The warhead of the SA-13 man-portable SAM is only two point two pounds, but the explosive energy is directed forward into a round cylinder designed to punch a hole through titanium- and ceramic-armored attack helicopters—against glass, thin steel, and aluminum, it found little resistance. The left cockpit canopy shattered, the entire left side of the windscreen disintegrated, and the blast blew a three-foot hole in the left side of the bomber just aft of Parsons' seat.

Parsons' steel seat took the entire force of the explosion, but the sheets of shattered Plexiglas windscreen battered his body, and the sudden force of the six-hundred-mile-per-hour windblast drove him unconscious and almost ripped his left arm out of its socket. The only thing holding his shattered body in the plane was a few bits of metal and the remnants of his right shoulder-harness strap.

Mace was knocked to the right by the blast, but Parsons' body, and the hard left bank that shielded his body with the aircraft, protected him from the worst of the explosion. His front windscreen cracked, but it did not disintegrate. His body felt as if it was on fire, then instantly it felt bone-numbing cold as six-hundred-miles-per-hour winds pounded into the cockpit. Mace needed to get on the controls and climb for lifesaving altitude before the engine shelled out.

F-111G navigators are not required to fly the plane and they are not permitted to log second-pilot time, but all navigators must know the emergency procedures just as well as the pilots, and most experienced navigators like Mace were frustrated or hopeful pilots themselves and take the controls and fly the plane whenever possible. The bomber heeled sharply left, threatening to enter a flat spin and hurl itself like a twenty-ton Frisbee into the desert, but Mace immediately applied full right throttle and full right rudder, and was able to thumb in full right rudder trim before the FIRE lights came on in the left engine.

Mace accomplished the engine-fire emergency procedures without thinking and without even consciously remembering he had done them.

The airspeed had dropped from six hundred to two hundred knots in just a few seconds. But for now they were flying and they were upright—that was the important thing.

Parsons was in really bad shape, but Mace thought he was still alive. The left side of Parsons' face and body were black, and his left arm was shredded below mid-bicep; he could not see his legs or much of his torso, but Mace guessed his injuries below the waist were thankfully minor. The windblast was streaking fresh blood from his chest across his helmet and up onto the aft bulkhead. Mace ripped the first-aid kit off the Velcro attachment point behind his seat, fumbled with it with one hand in the dark, and tried to stuff a handful of gauze and a large combat dressing pad into the worst of Parsons' wounds near his chest, but the windblast was too great and the gauze went flying. He was more successful in placing a flight jacket over him and taping it in place. Parsons' helmet was cracked, but the visors and oxygen mask were still in place and intact, and Parsons had suffered no injuries to his face or neck, so Mace decided to leave the mask and visors in place. Mace checked that Parsons' oxygen was on 100-percent oxygen and flowing, tightened Parsons' last remaining shoulder strap, then used the last of the medical tape to secure Parsons to his seat. If they had to eject, Parsons had to be as straight in the seat as possible or the G-forces would snap his spine in two.

Mace then returned his attention to flying the plane. A safe landing was probably impossible. He had a low-fuel situation, wings stuck at 24 degrees or greater, and one engine was out, with all the related hydraulic and electrical malfunctions. He had major structural damage, a blown windscreen, and an injured crewmember. He had no navigation systems, no engine monitoring systems, no computer assist for any function, and no primary flight or performance instruments. He nosed the bomber southward, determined to at least get away from Baghdad and across the Iraqi border before he punched out. The controls felt mushy and unresponsive—soon they would give out altogether. Mace decided to gain a little more altitude, cross the border if possible, then eject. The F-111G bomber was the best plane in the world to punch out from. The entire cockpit section was a winged capsule, complete with its own parachutes, rocket motors, stabilization fins, and landing shock absorbers—it would even float, and the pilot's control stick was a handle for a manual bailing pump. He was at two thousand feet now . . . plenty of altitude for a safe ejection . . . just grab the yellow handle by his left knee and pull . . .

But not with two fucking nuclear missiles on board.

The mission directives said do not bail out until at least thirty miles into Turkish or Saudi airspace, and then jettison the weapons safe over the Arabian Sea or Red Sea, or let the weapons crash with the aircraft. It was possible that the weapons would not be destroyed in a crash, and letting two SRAM-X missiles fall into Saddam Hussein's hands was unthinkable. No, he had to fly the machine a little longer, find a Coalition airfield, maybe get some gas from an aerial-refueling tanker, then try to set the thing down.

Straining against his shoulder harness to see the console between Parsons' legs, he checked the electrical systems panel. The indicator read EMER—that meant that both hydraulically powered electrical generators had kicked off-line and he was running on battery power alone. He flipped over to the emergency checklist for electrical malfunctions, checked the circuit breaker panel near his head between the two seats, made sure the autopilot was off, checked that the battery switch was on, then flipped the generator switch from ON to OFF/RESET, held it there for a few seconds, then switched it to RUN. The indicator read TIE instead of NORM, but with one engine out, TIE was a good indication—it meant that one generator was successfully energizing both electrical systems. Several lights popped on in the cockpit . . . and the radios came alive.

He completed the electrical system malfunction checklists, shutting down unnecessary electrical systems and the autopilot, then switched the IFF, or Identification Friend or Foe, thumbwheels to 7700, the emergency code, and the number one radio knob to the emergency GUARD position. Over the howl of the windblast in the shattered cockpit, he yelled into his oxygen mask microphone: "Mayday, Mayday, Mayday, any radio, any radio, this is Breakdance, 7440 Provisional, squawking emergency. Position south of Karbala, heading southwest at five thousand feet, declaring an emergency, injuries and weapons on board, requesting refueling and vectors to divert airfield. Come in. Over."

He then remembered the earlier radio transmissions and, forgetting proper radio procedures, yelled, "Nightmare, goddammit, this is Breakdance. You must be monitoring my position by now. My pilot is injured and I'm in deep shit. Give me a vector and help me get this thing on the ground *now!*"

4

An American E-3C AWACS Radar Plane, Flying Over Northern Saudi Arabia Same Time

ON BOARD AN E-3C AWACS (AIRBORNE WARNING AND Control System) radar plane, a converted Boeing 707 airliner with a thirty-six-foot-diameter rotating radome atop the fuselage, there were fourteen radar controller consoles, each scanning a specific segment of sky and watching every aircraft in their sector, enemy as well as friendlies, all throughout southern Iraq, Kuwait, the entire Arabian peninsula, western Iran, Syria, and eastern Jordan. Nine consoles were for air controllers, two were set aside to monitor sea vessels, two were tasked to monitor commercial and other noncombatant air traffic along the periphery of the Kuwaiti theater of operations, and one was set aside for the task force commander or other special operations missions. This fourteenth console was manned that morning by a special task force of Army and Air Force general officers who were representatives of the Chairman of the Joint Chiefs of Staff himself. Their call sign was "Nightmare."

The two general officers and their aides had seen Mace's F-111G dodge enemy fighters and missiles, had watched in horror as it began its missile run, then watched it turn away from its launch point without the nuclear explosion they all feared. "Sir, the F-111G crew is calling," the radar controller said to the two-star general in charge of the task force. "He says the pilot is injured and he has aircraft damage."

"Give them a southwest vector clear of known triple-A sites and tell them to climb to ten thousand five hundred feet," Air Force brigadier general Tyler Layton of the U.S. Air Force's Strategic Air Command replied. "He'll get chewed alive by triple-A if he stays at five thousand feet." The short, rather stocky and barrel-chested officer had been listening to the GUARD channel and had heard the call. Layton normally looked very boyish when surrounded by his taller, more powerful-looking colleagues from the Army, especially when a smile came to his lips as it often did, but right now his gentle, friendly features were etched with concern. There was no doubt this Aardvark crewdog had to get down *now.* Layton, the former commander of Eighth Air Force, in charge of all SAC bomber units in the eastern half of the United States, was an old B-52 and F-111G bomber pilot and was familiar with the tactics and procedures used by the supersonic fighter-bombers. He knew navigators didn't have very much stick time, so he was going to need all the help he could get.

"I'll send them over to the frontier, over Seventh Corps," Layton said to his task force commander, Army major general Bruce Eyers of U.S. Central Command. Eyers was the former chief of intelligence for U.S. Central Command, assigned to the Pentagon specifically to mastermind Operation Desert Fire. "We'll have to have Seventh watch out for him and cover their six," said Layton. The U.S. Army VII Corps in northern Saudi Arabia—they called it a "Corps" but in fact it had only about twenty thousand troops, about division size, scattered across a seven-hundred-mile frontier—were responsible for Coalition ground-based air defense. "Thank God the crew didn't launch the SRAM. We got to them in time."

"But they *should* have launched," Eyers said angrily. Eyers was an experienced airborne infantry officer and knew little about the world of aviation, but he did know about success and failure—from Vietnam to Grenada, he was familiar with both. Given a set of tools to work with, he expected nothing less than perfection and performance. Operation Desert Fire was his creation; it was he who pitched the idea to Schwarzkopf, Powell, and then SECDEF Cheney himself, and it was he who was given the honor of overall on-scene command of the operation by Schwarzkopf. Eyers was fifty-one years old, five feet ten, 220 pounds, with short dark hair, dark eyes, broad shoulders, and a "fireplug" build. He was a West Point graduate who was very political, with substantial aspirations for higher promotion. Rumor was he was good at conceptualizing, but not good with details or managerial skills. Still, he was popular with senior NATO commanders as an "idea man" but very poor with field work.

In less than an hour after execution, Eyers had seen his perfectly planned mission unravel. The order terminating Desert Fire was received in the AWACS plane, but not in the F-111G bomber. Only the President, through the Pentagon, could direct the employment of nuclear weapons, and that was true for halts as well as execution orders. That message was not relayed to the crew until very, very late, well after the appointed launch time. Still, for some reason, the crew did not or could not launch the Short-Range Attack Missile. Now he had a crippled plane on his hands with nukes on board—and the mission was not accomplished. One by one, the Air Force was screwing up. "You said the launch time had come and gone—the crew should have launched," Eyers said to Layton.

"I radioed to them to stop launch."

"But even you said they shouldn't respond to that call," Eyers said in exasperation. "The crewman, whoever the hell he is, verified it himself. The recall didn't reach them until after launch time, so what happened? Why didn't they cook it off?"

Layton sat staring at the console in front of him, not believing what he was hearing. Slowly, with deep suspicion burning in his eyes, he turned to Eyers. "You mean you *wanted* that nuke to go?"

Eyers looked at him as if he were a moron. "No, I want a long protracted ground war so we can get our asses kicked all over the place. *Of course* I wanted it to go. Launch it and the war's over in an hour. Done, *finis.* Nice and tidy. God knows if we'd done it in 'Nam, the gooks wouldn't have piled up our body count the way they did. In Libya, we should have done the same thing. We *still* have Qhadaffi to fucking deal with. And now, thanks to your fly-boys, we *still* have Saddam."

Layton swallowed hard, thinking: this is the problem with some of these honchos. They're so self-absorbed in the military, they forget about the real world. Eyers probably modeled himself after the Robert Duvall character in *Apocalypse Now.*

Worse, the guy was in *his* military. It sent a shiver down his spine.

"Have you considered," Eyers was now asking smugly, "that perhaps our President *wanted* to launch the missile? That that's why the termination order came *after* launch time? He really wanted it to go, but had to place a termination on record so he could defend himself later? Think about it."

Layton did. And concluded that Eyers was nuts. Operation Desert Fire was executed only because they believed Israel had been hit by chemical weapons. When that report proved to be false, the termination message was sent. Bruce Eyers, not the President, wanted to launch the nuclear missiles.

"The point remains, the recall message was received *after* the launch time. The damn bomber crew should have launched."

For Layton, the question was moot right now—his problem was to get Mace and Parsons safely on the ground. "Sir, I think we should recover that -111 first, then worry about the whys later," Layton said.

"You've made your point, Layton," Eyers said. "We'll find out how they screwed up later."

Obviously Eyers' mind was made up and the court-martials were already in the mail, Layton thought.

"All right, General, where are you going to set them down?"

"Bandanah would be perfect. Only forty miles from the border, about an hour flying time for the F-111G. We could scramble a tanker and fighter escort from King Khalid Military City and—"

"Bandanah doesn't exist," Eyers snapped. "And I don't want any other aircraft joining on that -111."

"Bandanah *does* exist, only not officially," Layton said. "We know it's a special-ops staging base for gunship crews penetrating into Iraq and setting up forward refueling bases in the desert. It's only a highway, but it's wide enough, lighted, and isolated enough in case there's a . . . crash."

"Can the crew bring that plane back or not?" Eyers asked impatiently. "If not, we'll send it out over the Red Sea and ditch it."

"I'll talk to the crew," Layton said. "I think the navigator is flying the jet."

Eyers' eyes opened wide in shock at that news.

"If that's true," Layton said, "he'll have real problems bringing it in."

"You mean navigators aren't trained in flying those things? They have a stick and throttles, but they can't fly it . . . ?"

"About as well as a tank commander can drive an M1A1," Layton replied. "They can start it up and buzz around in good conditions, but they aren't trained to drive it in combat or emergency conditions. But we've got experienced crews on these planes, so we might just bring it back in one piece." Eyers waved his hand impatiently, telling Layton to just get on with it. "And," said Layton, "I'm ordering an F-111 escort and a KC-135 tanker to refuel the bomber."

"Disapproved," Eyers said. "It'll draw too much attention to the mission. With your flaky nav flying the thing, he's likely to hit someone."

"More fuel gives us more options," Layton explained. "It may be that they can't refuel, but we have to try."

"All right, Layton," Eyers relented. "Just try to keep this quiet, all right? Don't screw it up. I'll call CENTCOM and advise them of what *you* want to do."

"Yes, sir," Layton said, thankful that Eyers finally wanted out of this business. With his precious "final solution" mission in shambles, he was looking for ways to cover his ass, forgetting that he still had men and machines to return safely. He said to his radio operator, "Okay, Lieutenant Cassenelli, let's bring that rascal home:

"I want a KC-135 from refueling orbit HOLLYWOOD to set up a point-parallel rendezvous with Breakdance." A point-parallel rendezvous was the standard join-up procedure for aircraft coming from different directions; the tanker would offset itself a few miles off the receiver's nose, then turn in front of the receiver, putting the receiver a mile or two behind the tanker and ready for hookup.

"A whole lot of receivers coming off targets aren't going to like losing their tanker," Cassenelli pointed out.

"They can get another strip-alert tanker from King Khalid Military City to cover," Layton said. He didn't know that for sure, but the Strategic Air Command had sent half of its entire fleet of aerial refueling tankers to the Kuwaiti theater of operations, and he knew that standby tankers were available. Even so, Layton added, "Try to find one that won't have too many receivers scheduled with it—but get one. If the crew needs confirmation, refer them to General Eyers immediately.

"Then I want an F-111 from Tabuk scrambled immediately to join on Breakdance for emergency recovery . . . nope, cancel that last." There were no F-111s at Tabuk—the closest base was Incirlik to the north, but it would have to fly through heavily defended west Iraq to rendezvous with Breakdance. The other F-111 base was Taif to the south, but it would take several hours for a plane to get that far north.

"We could get an F-15 from Tabuk to join on him," Cassenelli suggested.

"If we need to, we will," Layton said, "but to get Breakdance back safely I'd like a more similar aircraft, and one with a second set of eyes to look our guy over. Pull up the ATO for Tabuk."

The second monitor on console fourteen showed the computerized version of the ATO, or air tasking order, the "game plan" for the entire Coalition air armada in the Kuwaiti Theater of Operations. Broken up into three eight-hour blocks, the ATO showed what each and every aircraft would be doing—what time and from where it would launch, when and where it would refuel, what targets it would hit and when, which poststrike refueling it would make and where, and its approximate recovery time. Only with a computerized ATO, and with well-disciplined crews, could the Coalition ever hope to get two-thousand-plus combat sorties per day—half of which were armed aircraft striking targets in Iraq or Kuwait—off and safely home again.

Tabuk Air Base, in northwestern Saudi Arabia, was home to mostly allied air defense units guarding the northern part of the Red Sea and the southern portion of the Suez Canal, as well as keeping an eye on one of Iraq's few allies in the region, Jordan, should they or the Iraqis try to open a second front into Saudi Arabia or stage an attack on Israel. Tabuk had USAF F-15 fighters, Royal Air Force Tornado Gr.Mk 1 fighter-bombers, Royal Saudi Air Force F-5E fighters, and U.S. Navy HH-60 rescue and assault helicopters—Tabuk was the Navy's main abort base for planes that couldn't land on the carriers in the Red Sea. By checking the ATO, Layton found that the F-15s were scheduled for air patrols all day, escorting the British Tornado bombers on attack missions. The F-15s were scheduled for "hot turns"—land from a sortie, rearm, refuel, and take off again, all within ten to twenty minutes and with the pilots never leaving the cockpit.

"I think we got something, George," Layton told his radar operator. "Several Tornados are coming off targets at Al Asad, Al Taqaddum, H2, H3, and H4 airfields in western Iraq right now." The British Tornado was very similar to the F-111G bomber—both had started out as fighters (the British still had an air interceptor version, the F.Mk 3, in service in the Gulf); both had two engines and two crewmembers; they were of similar size and weight; and both had variable geometry "swing wings" and similar flight control and high-lift surfaces such as all-moving tailplanes, spoilers, flaps, and slats. Could this really work . . . ? "Can you call up these Tornados on the radar and find out where they are?"

Cassenelli punched in the sortie numbers from the ATO and asked the computer to locate the aircraft—there were hundreds of aircraft on the screen right now, all with data blocks showing their sortie number and flight data, and finding one particular aircraft manually would have been impossible. Seconds later he had his answer: "Got 'em, sir. Coming off targets now, at Breakdance's three o'clock position, sixty-one miles, climbing to one-five thousand feet. The ATO shows four flights of four, but I see only three flights. They're scheduled to tank at track Hollywood."

"Shit, this may work," Layton said. "Put in a call to those Tornados and ask them to divert toward Breakdance."

"Might be difficult, sir," Cassenelli said. "Those Tornados will need to refuel first, and there's"—he counted aircraft on the ATO scheduled to refuel in Hollywood aerial refueling track—"at least fifty planes scheduled to tank in the next hour. If they do their refueling, they'll be far behind Breakdance, and they'll have to hustle to catch up. I don't think you can afford to make Breakdance wait."

Cassenelli checked the ATO for the roster of tankers at the refueling orbits in northern Saudi Arabia, clapped his hands excitedly, and said, "Wait, sir, I have the answer. Shamu Two-Two, a KC-10 with buddy pods. They're supposed to exit the refueling track for a crew swap now, then climb to a higher altitude in the block. I can divert them to MARVEL to meet up with Breakdance. I'll just send the Tornados over and have them hook up with Two-Two. If it gets close, they can even hook up together."

"Perfect." Layton grinned. "Give them a call." The KC-10 refueling tanker was a converted DC-10 airliner, configured for aerial refueling and cargo transport. Unlike the KC-135, the KC-10 could do two different types of refueling in one mission, but normally not both kinds at once. But with "buddy pods"—pods attached to the wingtips with refueling hoses and rogues—the KC-10 could do both types of refueling at one time, with a boom-type receiver on the boom and a probe-and-drogue receiver on each wingtip. It could refuel both the F-111G and the Tornado at the same time. "I'll get on the horn to CENTAF and to Vice Marshall Wratten in Riyadh." Wratten was in charge of all British air assets on the Arabian Peninsula; although General Horner of USAF's Central Air Forces (CENTAF) was the Coalition's overall air commander, it was proper and expeditious to give the British counterpart a "heads-up" before committing his forces to a mission.

"Get the CO of Bandanah highway airstrip on the line and let me talk to him," Layton continued. "Let's get a mobile aircraft-recovery team heading out from Taif or Tabuk, preferably with an arrester cable crew. Everything on a secure scrambled channel—if it has to go unsecured, let me know right away." He paused, then added, "And let's get Admiral Mixson of the Red Sea naval task force on the carrier *Kennedy* on the line. We may need his help to recover the -111 and the weapons if we have to ditch Breakdance in the drink."

5

Over Northwestern Saudi Arabia
A Few Minutes Later

AIR FORCE CAPTAIN REBECCA C. FURNESS GRASPED A HAND-hold and tried to pull herself out of the pilot's seat in the cockpit of her KC-10 Extender tanker. "Jeez, my ass thinks my legs have been cut off. They're like Jell-O." She stepped over the wide center console, gave the new first lieutenant copilot a crewdog pat on the shoulder, slid between the pilot and copilot seats, and eased out of the cockpit. She felt wobbly and weak and tried to rub her legs to restore some circulation. She'd been sitting in that one seat, without a break, for eight hours.

Captain Sam Marlowe, the oncoming pilot, passed Furness and said, "Trouble with your legs? Let me help you." He gave her a wink, then reached down and ran a hand along her left leg. Marlowe, thirty-eight, with dark hair and a constant five o'clock shadow and one of two full crews on board, was rested and feeling cocky, which was always trouble.

Rebecca Furness took the word "professional" seriously. But in the time she'd spent in the Air Force, she'd learned very quickly that for all the lip-service the brass gave about nondiscrimination and harassment, the reality was, women in service faced both almost every day. Grimly, she put up with it as part of the job, but that didn't mean she had to put up with assholes like Marlowe who thought she'd be impressed with their fly-boy swaggering. The fact that they were in wartime was all the more appalling, but not surprising, to Furness.

"Sam," she oozed in her best, breathy voice.

"Yeah, babe?" he asked, patting her thigh.

Furness smiled, suddenly flicked her hand upwards, catching the tip of Marlowe's nose. She twisted it hard. He yelped, his head jerked back, bumped into the flight engineer's overhead pane, which startled his copilot, who was hand-flying the big jet, and the 590,000-pound tanker burled and shook as the copilot fought to regain control.

The boom operator, a chief master sergeant in the tail section, who had more years in the Air Force than all of the cockpit crew put together, felt the jolt, but not before his coffee went all over his flight suit. "Hey, pilot, what the hell is going on up there?"

Everyone's attention was on the two pilots now.

"You know, Sam, it's a shame your ego isn't as small as your cock probably is. If it were, it would make everyone's life on this plane a lot easier."

The flight engineer, a senior noncommissioned officer sitting at his console behind the copilot, turned and smiled at Marlowe, who was rubbing his nose, wincing in pain. But the smile disappeared and he turned back to his instruments when he caught a disapproving glare from Furness. She exited the cockpit and shut the door behind her with an exasperated bang.

Rebecca Furness—"the Iron Maiden," as she was known—visited the lavatory (for the first time in eight hours), then poured herself a cup of coffee from the coffeemaker in the galley, curled up on two empty front seats in the airliner-like forward passenger cabin of the KC-10 Extender, used a wadded-up flight jacket as a pillow to rest her head, and opened a four-day-old issue of the *Los Angeles Times.* It was a hell of a way to go to war—comfortable seats, modern airplane, pressurized cabin, relief crews, bunk beds, a bathroom, a kitchen, a newspaper, and, most importantly, staying far from the front lines. The fighter pilots got all the glory, but they had to be shoehorned into a tiny, uncomfortable cockpit, pee into a plastic bag, and suck oxygen through a mask strapped to their face for hours at a time—and there were bad guys shooting at them out there. The "tanker war" was not as glamorous, but it had much better working conditions.

She tried to read the *Times,* tried to forget about the incident in the cockpit, but her mind kept drifting back to it. She was seething. This wasn't the first time something like this had happened—there had been plenty of others—and it wouldn't be the last, but the idea of it happening in the middle of a damned war . . . . What would the men think if enlisted women were suddenly coming up and grabbing crotches in the middle of an operation, when their concentration needed to be totally focused on the task at hand? she wondered. The jerks. She sighed and wanted to forget about it, returning her attention to the *Los Angeles Times.*

She ignored the mission radio headset on the overhead console of her seat and stuck a pair of earplugs in her ears to blot out the gentle roar of aircraft noises. The two seats on which she lay were not wide enough for her to stretch out on, so she had to curl her long legs up to keep her boots from dangling into the aisle. Furness was tall, an athletic one hundred and thirty pounds, and if Marlowe could have gotten a good feel of her thigh, he undoubtedly would have found it nice and firm, a result of her almost-daily exercise regimen. She had below-shoulder-length brown hair, but no one on her crew really knew that because she always wore it pinned up and off her collar when in uniform, which was almost all the time. They did notice her dark-brown almond-shaped eyes, her strong nose and jaw, and her habit of talking rapidly and in a very officious pilot's monotone, which was how she had acquired the boys-only nickname of the Iron Maiden. She knew about the nickname and didn't give a damn.

Well, she conceded, that wasn't *exactly* true. The moniker did bother her, but not because she was tough and professional in the cockpit, which was why most people assumed she had the name. No, she'd earned it for an entirely different reason: her steadfast refusal to date anyone on the base or in her wing. She hadn't really thought much about the rule, until she'd heard the nickname. She wasn't even sure why she'd made that policy for herself other than wanting to maintain distance from the men she might ultimately have to go to war with.

But her policy had generated a lot of gossip, especially after her polite but consistent refusals for dates. She'd hear the word "dyke" whispered more than once in passing. She shook her head in exasperated amusement. That was rich. If they only knew about the men she'd had in her life. Some truly wonderful guys, and none in the military. Men who could have run circles around these fly-boys in bed.

But her private life was her own. If they wanted to think she was gay, that was their problem. Another typical, arrogant male assumption. Like little boys, trying to show the girls who had the larger member. And if you didn't want to play with it, well, you must be . . .

Rebecca sighed. Now that she thought about it, having just one to play with now and then wouldn't be so bad, but her time at home was usually focused on recurrent training and simulator sessions.

Not that she really minded, of course. Flying was in her blood, and she spent most of her free time building her flight experience outside her military duties. The military was cutting back flying hours, eliminating squadrons, and closing bases, and the civilian airlines were still hiring, so she turned her attention to a future outside the Air Force. To make herself more marketable to the major airlines, she had accumulated almost a thousand hours of civilian flying time in the past six years—which was quite impressive, seeing that she was away from home for nearly five months every year—and had earned her civilian commercial and airline transport pilot licenses and instrument, flight instructor, multiengine, and even seaplane ratings.

But if life was tough for women pilots in the military, it was equally tough in the civilian world, and although American Airlines and United had practically set up recruiting offices at March Air Force Base, nobody had called her—not even the smaller regional airlines like America West or Southwest, for whom she was probably overqualified with all her multiengine heavy-jet time. Male KC-10 pilots were being actively and aggressively recruited by the airlines at March because Air Force KC-10 pilots got the world's best heavy-jet training at no cost to the airlines. Some had letters of commitment from a major airline two years before their tour of military duty was up. The airlines were hiring, all right, but not women.

Becky Furness made a few inquiries and got the runaround every time. Women pilots, they said, were paid less to start because they were given more time off and had to be replaced or retrained and requalified more often than men. Bullshit. As a senior squadron flight instructor, she had access to her fellow pilots' flight records, and she knew that a lot of the guys leaving the squadron who ended up flying in the majors had fewer total hours, fewer pilot-in-command hours, and fewer civilian hours than she did.

She also knew her résumé was a lot more impressive than most.

Born in Vergennes, Vermont, in 1955, she was a 1977 graduate of the University of Vermont at Burlington, majoring in biology, and received a commission in the U.S. Air Force through ROTC that same year after going through a two-year scholarship program. She attended pilot training at Williams AFB in 1978, graduating in 1979 in the top 5 percent of her class. In 1979 Rebecca graduated from KC-135 Combat Crew Training at Castle AFB, Atwater, California, and was assigned to the 319th Bombardment Wing, Grand Forks AFB, North Dakota, in 1980, flying the KC-135A tanker on strategic combat alert. After upgrading to aircraft commander and instructor pilot, she transferred to the 22nd Air Refueling Wing, March AFB, California, in 1988, flying the KC-10A Extender tanker. She also upgraded to aircraft commander just before Operation Desert Storm.

Yeah, it was a pretty good résumé, she thought, but what good was it doing her?

Just then, to Furness' surprise, Sam Marlowe emerged from the flight deck, noticed her sitting by herself, and came over to her. She was surprised, not because he dared to approach her after his embarrassing dressing-down earlier, but because she had been so busy since takeoff that she had no time to get up for relief—now, only minutes after taking over, Marlowe was roaming around. "What's going on, Sam?"

By unspoken consent, they both were determined to ignore the previous incident.

"We got a call to do an emergency refueling farther north," Marlowe said. "An F-111 and a Tornado."

"An Aardvark and a Tornado? We gonna do a buddy refueling?"

"Buddy refueling—one-eleven on the boom and Tornado on a pod—then escort all the way to his divert base," Marlowe said. "All we got was a set of coordinates for the base—no name. Probably a desert strip for the special-ops guys. We rendezvous in about ten minutes at ten thousand feet."

"Cool," Furness said. The refueling altitude, ten thousand feet, was an indication of what the emergency was—a decompressed cockpit, probably from battle damage. Aircrews flying with no cabin pressurization would stay at or below ten thousand feet to avoid oxygen starvation. The strange mix of aircraft was a puzzle, which made the situation that much more interesting. "So which one's broken?" she asked.

"I don't know . . . I didn't catch the whole thing," Marlowe replied. "All I know is, we're going into Indian country."

"We're *what?*"

"They're sending us over the border to go get the -111," Marlowe said. "Only about fifty miles or so, but we'll be over enemy territory. That means a Bronze Star at least, maybe even a Silver Star."

So much for a cool, safe, secure little world on board the KC-10 tanker. This plane was a big, slow, inviting target for enemy gunners or missiles even at its best performance—at low altitude with a crippled aircraft on the boom, it was a real sitting duck. Even the world's worst fighter pilot could down a tanker with one arm tied behind his back. Dread went up and down Furness' spine. This could really get hairy.

She heard herself say, "I'll be in the boom pod. I gotta see this."

"Lucky dog," Marlowe said. "Maybe you'll see a really chewed-up fighter jock out there. Take some pictures for me."

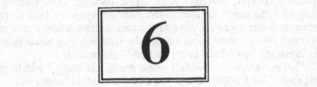

MACE EXAMINED PARSONS CAREFULLY. HIS FACE WAS SHEET white from the cold, but his oxygen indicator was still blinking, which meant he was breathing. Fresh blood was still oozing into his mask. Good, his heart was still beating. Holding the control stick between his knees, Mace wiped the stuff out of his mask to keep it from clogging and suffocating him. Parsons' head rolled to the right, and it appeared that he was trying to tell him something, but in the howl of the windblast thundering through the broken windscreen it was impossible to hear him.

Mace shouted, "Hang tough, Colonel. We're almost home!" then reattached Parsons' oxygen mask and strapped him in tight.

Back on the controls, Mace surveyed the instrument panel. Without an operable fuel gauge and with an electrical emergency, he had to manually control the fuel flow to the right engine, and that required almost constant monitoring. The wing fuel had burned down to zero, so now he had to maintain the longitudinal balance by burning fuel from the forward body tanks. But without boost pumps the forward body would never keep itself filled, so Mace followed an emergency checklist and had to pop a fuel-dump-valve circuit breaker, backflow fuel from the aft body tank to the forward body tank through the fuel-dump system, then push in the circuit breaker and watch the angle-of-attack gauge to make sure they weren't too tail-heavy or nose-heavy. Normally the F-111G fuel management system was automatic and he rarely thought about it, but it was amazing what a no-shit inflight emergency sometimes did for your memory—he was able to remember all the funny spaghetti diagrams, the fuel-pump relay logic, even the specific tank quantities and boost-pump flow rates. When it came to life or death, the human mind kicked into overdrive.

Once the fuel panel was set up, Mace got on the radio. "Nightmare" had sent him over to a discrete UHF channel, unsecure but assigned all to themselves, so he knew the bozos in charge—and probably half the Iraqi military command staff—were listening in: "Nightmare, what's the fuckin' plan? My pilot is still alive, but he looks like Dracula on a bender, and I need some gas or I'm likely to be walking."

"Breakdance, this is Nightmare." The irritated voice of General Eyers (although Mace didn't know that) came on the line. "Unless you have a *specific* request or *emergency* that we need to be notified of, keep *off* the radio. And use proper radio procedures and terminology on this channel. Over."

"Hey, asshole," Mace exploded on the radio, "I haven't heard *squat* from you guys in over fifteen minutes. You want some emergency info? I figure if I don't have any more holes in me, I got about twenty minutes' worth of gas, at most. My pilot's hurt bad, and he needs attention. I figure I can't punch out because of structural damage to the capsule, so I gotta set it down. Now I can see lots of nice, straight paved roads down there, so unless you want to come get me and my *car-go,*" emphasizing the nukes in the bomb bay, "you better fuckin' talk to me. *Over.*"

There was a rather long, silent pause; then a different and far less official-sounding voice came back: "Breakdance, this is Nightmare. We're doing everything we can. You're still in Indian country, there are border air-defense units all around you, and this is an unsecure channel, so we can't tell you too much, but we're going to bring you down soon. Just hang in there. We're watching you and your airspace very carefully. If there are any bandits nearby, we'll tell you immediately.

Do your best to avoid SAMs. Otherwise, if you see any aircraft approaching you, maintain your last assigned heading and don't try to evade. Let us know if your a.c.'s condition looks worse. Stay off the air unless it's an emergency. We're right here with you."

The channel went silent.

The voice sounded like he knew what he was talking about, like a former Aardvark driver. The other guy was a southern Army grunt all the way, probably a general, maybe even Schwarzkopf himself. Well, he was still an asshole for not talking to him. Mace was able to take a deep breath to help some of the tension flow out of his body.

Mace was scanning the skies around him when he saw a small speck of an aircraft. The speck's position on the canopy did not change, which meant it was on a collision course. At six to eight miles it looked like another F-111, but when it got within five miles Mace recognized it as a Panavia Tornado, Western Europe's most advanced fighter-bomber.

At first Mace thought the Tornado was joining too fast, and he was ready to dodge away, but the big aircraft swooped quickly but easily into place, about fifty feet away from Mace's right wing. He could see that it was a British Tornado—the UK, Germany, Italy, and Saudi Arabia all flew Tornados—and that it carried two Sidewinder missiles and two fuel tanks, with all of its underbelly weapon stations empty.

The RAF backseater gave Mace a thumbs-up, then gave him a signal Mace did not recognize. Seconds later, the Tornado dipped under Mace's F-111G, appeared briefly on the left side, then, in a very dramatic display of expert airmanship, rolled inverted and flew atop the stricken Aardvark so the British backseater could look up through his cockpit canopy and get a good look at any damage on the top side. He was giving Mace a visual inspection; now he felt bad because he was too surprised to give the Tornado as thorough an inspection, because Mace knew he must be coming back from an attack against Iraq. The Tornado then moved away from Mace and, as Mace watched in sheer fascination, the British crew jettisoned its external fuel tanks, leaving only the two Sidewinder missiles. He then moved in close again, and the backseater gave Mace another thumbs-up. To his surprise, Mace noticed the very large portrait of a nude woman sitting atop a bomb painted on the left side of the Tornado, along with the name

"Gulf Killer" and the names of its ground crews. The Brits had obviously wasted no time putting nose art on their combat aircraft.

"Pretty slick moves, Gulf Killer," Mace said aloud, being careful not to talk on the radio. As if he had heard him, the Tornado backseater clasped his hands over his head in self-congratulation.

A few minutes later the Tornado backseater pointed above Mace's head, and the sight astounded him: the huge, looming fuselage of a KC-10 Extender tanker appeared as if out of nowhere, accelerating easily ahead of the crippled bomber. It was at least two thousand feet above him, but it still looked as big as a thundercloud. The Extender's air refueling boom was already lowered into the contact position, the nozzle extended all the way into the yellow region, and the buddy pod refueling hose and drogue was extended on the tanker's right wingtip.

The tanker descended and decelerated a few moments later, so now it was only five hundred feet above Mace's altitude. A white flashing light appeared on the tanker's right wingtip and the basketlike drogue was extended, a signal that the Tornado was cleared in for refueling. The RAF Tornado backseater waved as the Tornado hungrily moved up and, a few seconds later, slid his refueling probe effortlessly into the round white drogue. Then Mace saw two white flashing lights on the director lights along the tanker's belly, the signal that he was cleared in to the boom.

He's going to do it, he thought grimly, flipping his checklist to the "Before Air Refueling" and "Before Pre-Contact" pages. *He's going to do a single-engine refueling with a KC-10 tanker at low altitude over enemy territory.* The checklist did not take long because he could not do most of the items: exterior lights were not working, wings wouldn't move, autopilot was already off, fuel system was dead, radar was dead. Mace flipped the air-refueling-door switch and was relieved to get a green AR/NWS light, meaning the air refueling system was ready for nozzle contact.

Slowly, carefully, Mace eased the throttle forward and inched the nose upward. The F-111G responded sluggishly, rumbling in protest as it climbed. The airspeed did not want to increase at all, it seemed, and Mace nudged the throttle forward some more. Before he realized it, he was at the military-power throttle stop, ready to go into afterburner. He knew he couldn't do that—lighting the 'burners with structural damage and an engine out could start a fire. He could do nothing else but remain patient and hope his crippled bird could catch up.

It took several long minutes, but Mace finally climbed up behind the KC-10 and was inching toward the refueling boom. He was still a good fifty feet from contact, but the huge underside of the tanker blocked his view of everything else. He was now even with the nozzle and moving toward it. The open end of the nozzle was dark, like the barrel of a cannon aimed right at him. The tanker's director lights urged him forward and up. God damn, he wished he could talk on the radios! *Someone please talk to me!*

The nozzle was now directly over the shattered windscreen, less than two feet above Parsons' head. It was huge, eight inches in diameter, with colored markings along its length to visually indicate the distance between aircraft. Mace could see every scratch, every mark, every little word stenciled on the boom and nozzle. It seemed as if it was going to come right inside the cockpit with him. . . .

The nozzle was hovering right over Parsons' head, less than a foot away. The wind rumbling around the boom's control vanes and under the big tanker's belly seemed to suck the bomber right up into it. Mace watched it slide aft, getting closer, closer, *closer* . . .

Suddenly all of the lights on the tanker's director-light system flashed rapidly on and off—the breakaway signal. Mace didn't react very fast—he was watching the boom instead of the tanker and didn't notice anything wrong until the boom started to move away—but the tanker reacted immediately: it accelerated ahead like a shot and climbed as if it was on an express elevator. The sudden acceleration and the roar of the KC-10's three huge engines quadrupled the noise in the bomber's cockpit, and the smell of burning jet fuel was overpowering. For a moment Mace thought he had been struck by the boom and his jet had caught fire. Mace automatically pulled the throttle back, but almost immediately the stall-warning horn blared, so he shoved power back in. When he did so, the F-111G swerved violently to the left and Mace almost lost control.

Just when Mace was about to give it up and try to eject, he glanced over his right shoulder and saw the RAF Tornado tucked in close on the right wingtip as if he was cemented there. Normally a wingman stayed with the tanker on an emergency breakaway, but the Tornado crew chose to stay with the crippled bomber. The presence of the Tornado really helped steady his hand, and several minutes later he had his airspeed and wits back. Mace steered toward the tanker, determined to get it right this time—and then the MASTER CAUTION light, a large yellow light right in the front center of the instrument panel, snapped on.

Mace quickly scanned the instruments and found the problem: the FUEL LO PRESS light was on. The boost-pump lights for the aft body and fuel-dump system were on, indicating no flow, and two of the four forward body-pump lights were on. That meant less than one thousand pounds of fuel remaining. About five to ten minutes, less if he had really bad fuel leaks, until the last engine flamed out. And there was only one step in the "Double Engine Failure" checklist, and he knew it by heart: EJECT. But with all the damage they had sustained on the left side, the capsule might not separate from the plane, and even if they made it, Parsons would probably not survive the impact.

Mace had one more chance: plug the tanker this time or die.

It was as simple as that.

REBECCA FURNESS DIDN'T HAVE A CHANCE TO SEE THE F-111G the first time—the other boom operators and the rest of her crew were already in the pod watching—so she waited patiently, watching the Tornado through the starboard porthole, until the breakaway call. She asked her copilot in the pod to switch with her, and he complied immediately—that close call, with the bomber coming only inches away from smacking into the tanker, had rattled him, and he scrambled out of there in a hurry. Furness waited for her tight-lipped, white-faced copilot to climb out, then took a short, steep ladder down into the boom operator's pod in the aft belly of the KC-10.

Before her was a huge window, four feet by three feet, which was the largest one-piece glass panel in any pressurized aircraft. The senior boom operator on board, a chief master sergeant, was in the instructor's seat, while Furness' crew boomer was in the other seat, so she took a position between them and donned a headset.

"Oh . . . my . . . God . . ." she gasped when the F-111G hovered into view. She had seen lots of Aardvarks coming in for refueling, some even with emergencies on board, but in her eight years in the service she had never seen one as bad as this. The pilot looked as if he was hanging out in space, being held in place only by the relentless windblast pounding on his body. The entire left front side was blackened, and huge gashes of torn metal were clearly visible. It looked as if a giant clawed hand had tried to rip the pilot bodily out of the plane and had almost succeeded. The Tornado fighter-bomber was so close now that she could see it, too, close enough so that either one of them could plug into the boom.

"The nav looks scared shitless," the boom operator, Technical Sergeant Glenn Clintock, said on interphone. "He can hardly keep it straight."

"Wouldn't you be?" the senior master sergeant asked. He was the air refueling wing's senior enlisted adviser and still an active boom operator. "If he stays fixated on the nozzle, he'll ram us for sure."

"What's he doing?" Furness asked.

"He's staring at the boom nozzle," Clintock replied. "It's a typical new-guy reaction. You can't help but watch the boom nozzle because it's so close to your head just before it plugs you. When you stare at the boom you unconsciously fly the airplane up into it, and when you realize what you're doing you jerk the plane away too fast and waste time. He's got to concentrate on his visual cues and let us worry about the nozzle—except most navs don't know what the visual cues are. He's really in a world of hurt."

"So tell him."

"Can't. We're still over Iraq. One squeak from us and we'll get hosed by SAM sites or fighter patrols. We're also still within triple-A gun range—one lone Zeus-23 unit that gets a bead on us could eat our lunch."

As Clintock explained the problem, Furness concentrated on the figure of the navigator. She could barely see his hands working the control stick and throttles—rather, the *throttle,* because the left engine was obviously dead—and his visored eyes nervously watching the boom and the tanker. She could somehow feel his fear, sense his anxiety. "What's his fuel state?" she asked.

"Don't know," the chief replied. "We're supposed to be radio-silent until after contact."

"He's clean configuration . . . does he have any stores on board at all?"

"Don't know that either," the chief said.

Furness watched in horrible fascination as the F-111G unsteadily made its way closer.

"This guy's not going to make it in," the chief said. "I recommend we call it off and let him find a flat piece of ground to land on." The chief master sergeant turned to Furness and said, "You're senior officer on board, Captain. What do you think?"

Furness didn't reply right away. Of all the aircraft in the Kuwaiti theater of operations, the aerial refueling tankers, especially the Air Force models, were the most important. No bombing missions could be conducted, unless by long-range bombers like the B-52 or F-111G, without refueling, and even the bigger jets, because they were based so far away, needed at least one refueling en route. Tankers were force multipliers. One tanker not only serviced dozens of other aircraft every hour, but they refueled other Navy and Air Force tankers, which in turn refueled dozens of planes. That meant that losing one tanker was akin to losing several dozen strike aircraft. Losing one tanker like the KC-10, which could gas up USAF, Navy, and allied aircraft as well as carry cargo for long distances, was probably equivalent to losing one hundred strike aircraft. What commander, even at flag or general officer rank, in this day and age, could sustain the loss of a hundred combat aircraft at once? His career would be over instantly.

It was Furness' responsibility to make sure her aircraft was safe and mission-ready—if this was going to be a long war, and there was every indication that it would be so, the KC-10 was probably the most important aircraft in the Coalition fleet. The chief was right: risking the KC-10 like this, with the bomber crew so inexperienced and rattled, was not only unsafe but operationally improper. The chief master sergeant was reminding her of her responsibility: some two- or three-star general could ask them to try to refuel this stricken plane, but it was her job, and hers alone, to protect her aircraft and her crew.

"Captain? He's moving in again. What do you want to do?"

Furness unplugged her headset from the interphone cord and into the boom operator's observer's cord, then flipped the switch to radio one. "Pilot of the F-111, this is the commander of Shamu Two-Two. How do you hear me?"

"Open channel!" someone shouted on interphone. "Check switches!"

"Captain, we're supposed to be *radio-silent,*" Clintock said, his eyes wide. "You're on interplane."

"I know," Furness replied. "But we've got to talk this guy in or he won't make it."

"But you're going to get us all killed!"

Furness wasn't listening: "F-111 pilot, this is Shamu Two-Two. How do you read?"

"This is Breakdance. I read you loud and clear, lady. Have we broken radio silence? Acknowledge."

"Yes . . . and no," Furness said. "I can give you one more shot, and this time we'll do it, or else I have no choice but to send you to an alternate recovery strip."

"Then let's do it," the voice from the F-111G said. "I'm running on fumes. Clear me in to contact position."

Furness nodded with satisfaction. She was expecting a scared, totally out-of-control nav on the radio, but instead found a determined, realistic fighter. She nodded to Clintock and said, "Clear him in and let's get it on, Glenn."

"You got it, Captain," Clintock said. On interplane, he said, "Breakdance, this is Shamu Two-Two, cleared to contact position, Two-Two is ready."

"No, no, not that way, Glenn," Furness said. She motioned for the senior master sergeant to get out of his seat beside Clintock—he had no choice but to comply, but he was obviously perturbed about it—then strapped herself in and got on the radio: "Okay, guy, c'mon in. What's your first name?"

"Say again?"

"I asked you, what's your first name—or do you want to be called Breakdance all morning?"

That got his attention: "Daren," he replied with obvious humor in his voice.

"Okay, Daren, I'm Rebecca. My friends call me BC. We're going to dispense with the normal radio calls and do this my way. It's just you and me, cowboy. I've got the juice, so come get it."

"Okay, BC," Mace replied with a hint of amusement. "Here I come."

Furness watched as the F-111G began moving closer. She could see the long black nose bobbing a bit as the nav made rather large pitch changes—too large for being less than fifty feet away: "Use nice, easy power and stick changes," she said. "Nothing drastic, nothing sudden. Forget about your fuel state, forget about your pilot, forget about everything. Relax. It's like pulling your big Jaguar into your garage and parking it. Concentrate on slipping that big Aardvark nose right under my tail. We'll tell you when to stop."

"You're starting to turn me on, BC," Mace radioed back.

The F-111G eased itself gently into position, the tip of its long black fiberglass nose all the way under the boomer's pod, the refueling receptacle less than ten feet from the nozzle.

"Look at the plane, not the nozzle, Daren," Furness said, ignoring his last remark. "Look at me. Start developing a picture of the underside of the plane in relation to your canopy rails. Don't look at the nozzle—that's our job. Keep coming . . . keep coming . . ."

Suddenly, Mace's radar warning receiver came to life: a loud *deedledeedledeedle* came on the interphone, and a bat-wing symbol appeared on the right side of the indicator. He automatically started to back away in preparation for a breakaway maneuver. "Two-Two, I've got a bandit at three o'clock," Mace shouted on the interplane frequency. "Repeat—bandit at three o'clock. Stand by for evasive action."

"Wait! Hold your position, Daren," Furness said. "You've got a fuel emergency. Get on the boom and get your gas, then we'll do a separation."

This time, before the chief master sergeant could react, Sam Marlowe shouted on interphone: "Furness, that's not the SOP! If we come under attack, we do a breakaway and begin evasive maneuvers. That fighter can be on top of us in no time!"

"I'm not losing this guy."

"But you're willing to get our asses killed!" Marlowe thundered. "I'm calling a breakaway."

"Like hell!" Furness shouted. "This is my aircraft and my sortie!"

A calm but determined British voice said on the refueling frequency, "Shamu, Breakdance, this is Elvis Three-Ought-Seven, we have a bogey at our three o'clock, turning starboard to engage. We'll be back shortly, Elvis Three-Ought-Seven." The Tornado suddenly banked sharply right and climbed steeply, with afterburners glowing brightly and its wings tucked all the way back against its fuselage.

"Daren, continue in to contact position, and do it quick," Furness said. "If my crew gets a visual on the bandit, we'll begin evasive maneuvers."

"I copy," Mace replied. "Coming in."

But it wasn't going to happen. The Tornado had disappeared from sight, the radios were silent, and the bat-wing symbol on the threat scope kept on closing. "Shamu, the threat's approaching lethal range, and I can't see the Tornado. You better—"

Just then, they heard a calm British voice on the refueling frequency: "Lousy bugger . . . don't try it . . . yes, thank you . . . lovely . . . lovely . . . missile away, missile away." There was no sign of excitement, no sign of stress at all in the voice—except for a bit of strain against the G-forces. The bat-wing symbol disappeared from the threat scope. "Splash one MiG, chaps. Elvis Three-Ought-Seven, splash one. Coming in on the rejoin."

Furness found she was holding her hands to her face in absolute, sheer horror. Just like that, as if it was a simple stroke of a pen or a brush of a hand, the Tornado crew had killed an Iraqi pilot and shot down his plane. It was only now that the threat was gone that she realized the threat to herself—had it gone any other way, *she* could have been the one crashing to the desert floor in pieces.

Even now, she could see a small column of smoke rising from the ground, not that far away. Death was that close for all of them, but especially for the crew of the KC-10 Extender tanker. The F-111G could descend to hill-hugging altitude, fly faster than most fighter-interceptors, use jammers, and dispense decoy chaff and flares to protect itself; the Panavia Tornado could do all that *and* launch air-to-air missiles itself. But the KC-10 was powerless, as vulnerable as a newborn baby. The KC-10 could not even *detect* nearby threats, unless the pilots got lucky and *saw* the missile or fighters coming—at night or in bad weather, they would be dead long before they saw the threat. Flying these behemoths over enemy territory was *crazy,* simply insane. Aircraft flying in combat needed to be able to *fight.* More than that, she *wanted* to fight. She wanted to be the one in the F-111G dropping bombs, or the one in the Tornado shooting down bandits. Refueling was fine, and it was a necessary mission, but if she was going to fly, she wanted to *fight.*

"Thank you, Elvis," Furness said shakily to the Tornado crew as they maneuvered their jet up beside the F-111G again.

"My pleasure, mademoiselle," the Tornado pilot replied in the very same voice he used to announce that he was blowing away the Iraqi.

"Okay, Daren," Furness said, "you're cleared back in. Remember, nice and easy. There's a little bump when you get inside, but don't try to anticipate it or try to smooth it out. Ride the bump and keep moving in."

Mace again eased the crippled F-111G into position. He struggled momentarily with the bow wave, overcompensating for the push by pulling back on the stick, then fluttering dangerously close to the tanker's belly when he broke free, but he managed to stay in position through the momentary oscillation and moved slowly but steadily into contact position. "Okay, right there," Furness called out. "That's perfect. You don't have to look up, just get your bearings from the markings on the belly . . . I said don't look up, Daren, just remember the picture you see right now."

She saw the signal from Clintock that he was ready to plug the F-111G. "Here we go, Daren . . . a little push from the boom . . . don't try to help it or back away from it, just hold your picture."

Clintock carefully eased the boom down a bit lower and extended the nozzle. It scraped only a few inches against the slipway, then plugged into the bomber's receptacle with a satisfied *ch-clunk!* The green AR/NWS light went out, indicating that the toggles had made contact and the nozzle was locked in place. "I've got contact," Mace reported.

"Contact, Two-Two," Clintock reported. "Taking fuel."

The director's lights on the tanker's belly automatically illuminated, and Mace found himself right in the middle of the envelope, with the UP-DOWN elevation marker and IN-OUT boom-extension markers both right in the center.

"Okay, Daren, good job. Now just ignore the director lights. Maintain that last picture you see through the canopy. You can glance at the lights every now and then as a crosscheck, but they'll just confirm what you should already see. Relax your hands, take a deep breath. You're taking fuel, and we don't see any leaks. Good job, guy."

Mace was afraid to breathe, afraid to move, but he tried to do as the tanker commander said and relax. He found that, once it was trimmed up and at the proper aimpoint, it was very easy to stay in the contact position—the KC-10 practically dragged the bomber along. One by one, the forward-body low-pressure lights and the LO FUEL PRESS caution light went out.

"Thanks, BC," he said on interplane. "You really saved our bacon. I'm grateful."

"Don't mention it," Furness said. "Give me a ride in your plane someday." If she ever had her choice of planes to fly, without any women-in-combat restrictions, the F-111 would be it.

"You got a deal."

After over three minutes on the boom, the nozzle suddenly popped out and Clintock pulled it quickly away from the bomber. "Pressure disconnect, Breakdance," Clintock reported.

"We can't give you any more fuel because your system says it's full, Daren," Furness added. "What have you got?"

"My fuel system is dead, so I don't know what I got," Mace said. "I can try manually transferring fuel, but I don't think that's a good idea."

"You took on fifteen thousand pounds of fuel," Furness reported, "and I see no leaks up here. We'll follow you all the way to landing."

"This should do me for at least three to four hours," Mace said. "I think I'm done for now. Thanks again, BC."

"Don't mention it," Furness said as she saw him wave at her. "See you when I see you." Furness removed the headset, slumped in the seat, took a deep breath, and let it out in one expansive sigh.

"Good job, Captain," Clintock said, then added with a mischievous smile, "For a lady, you got a lot of balls."

"I just hope the brass sees it that way," the chief master sergeant said as he took his seat beside Clintock again after Furness got out, "when they review those radio transmissions. And thank God we had a fighter out there with missiles on board, or else we'd be a flaming hole right now."

"We got the -111 and the Tornado its gas," Furness said. "That's what we were ordered to do. Any other problems they have with my procedures are moot if the Aardvark makes it back in one piece."

The chief shook his head but said nothing else.

Furness made her way back up to the forward passenger cabin to get back to her newspaper when she met up with the flight engineer and the pilot Marlowe again coming out of the cockpit. The engineer looked as white as a sheet, and specks of white and a large stain spread over the front of his flight suit. "Hey, Pete, what's the matter?" The engineer made no reply, but avoided Furness' eyes and hurried over to the lavatory. "What's with him, Sam?"

Marlowe made sure the engineer made it, then turned angrily toward Furness. "He's sick, that's what, Furness," Marlowe snapped. "He can barely stand up."

"Why? What happened?"

"*You're* what happened," Marlowe said. "That attack by the fighter . . . it really rattled him. He's scared shitless, all because of you. I was coming back here to advise you that I'm making a full report of this incident to the wing," he said.

Furness' smile disappeared in a fraction of a second. "You're . . . what . . . ?"

"You think you're some kind of hero for refueling that bomber with enemy fighters in the area? Bullshit. I say you're an egotistical prima donna that gets her kicks from breaking the rules when it suits her."

"Well, you go right ahead and make your report, Marlowe," Furness seethed. "I was ordered to refuel that bomber, and that's what I did."

"And you broke technical, procedural, and tactical rules to do it—not to mention putting this entire crew and this aircraft in jeopardy."

"I didn't put anyone in jeopardy," Furness said. "In emergency situations we can continue the rendezvous."

"We saw the damned fighter, Furness," Marlowe said grimly.

Furness' jaw dropped open in surprise. "You *what* . . . ? How far? When . . . ?"

"He was *right there,* less than three, maybe four miles away," Marlowe said. "He was rolling in on us . . . Jesus, he fired on us, Furness, we saw him launch a missile at us! We couldn't do anything."

"You didn't try to evade? You didn't say anything?"

"It was too late to do anything," Marlowe said. "By the time we saw him, he was coming at us and the missile was in the air. God, I don't know how it missed us. The Tornado dropped a flare, and I think it went after the flare."

"So the bandit was firing on the Tornado."

"It was firing at us, Furness!" Marlowe shouted. "It shot at *us!* You set us up like a sitting duck for that bandit to shoot us down!"

Furness was completely speechless—she had no idea the fighter was so close: "Greg, the bomber reported the bandit outside lethal range."

"That doesn't mean *shit*, Furness. We don't know from lethal or nonlethal range—we know 'attack.' We were under attack, and you ordered us not to evade."

"You were on the flight deck, Marlowe," Furness said. "You saw the bandit. You should have called a breakaway and begun evasive maneuvers."

"Hey, that's good, lady, that's *real* good," the stunned pilot retorted. "Blame it on me now. Just what I expected. *You* are the senior officer and the mission commander, *you* were talking on the radios over enemy territory when we were told to maintain radio silence, *you* ordered me not to evade, *you* told the receivers to stay in contact position—but now you're blaming *me* for not doing something."

Marlowe turned away, a look of resigned defeat on his face, and said, "Well, I was the pilot-in-command at the time, and I know I'm in charge when I'm in the left seat, so they'll take me down too . . ." But then he snapped a look of pure anger at her and added, "But I'm going to make sure you go down with me, you *bitch*. And if they don't bust you, I'll make sure no one in the Command ever flies with you again."

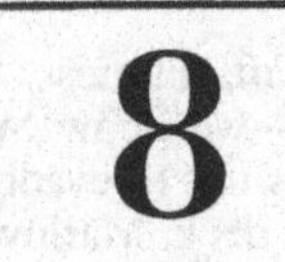

"EMERGENCY-GEAR EXTENSION HANDLE—PULL," MACE SAID half-aloud. He unwrapped the stainless steel safety wire from the yellow handle on the center forward instrument panel and pulled. Immediately the main gear-down lights came on steady green, but the nose-gear light was still out. Mace didn't panic—yet. The emergency gear extension system used very high-pressure air to shove the gear out into the slipstream and throw the downlocks into place, but the book said that it might take much slower airspeeds, higher angles of attack, or as long as five minutes for the nose gear to come down because its shocks were so big.

"Your nose gear looks like it's halfway down, my friend," the British pilot aboard the Tornado chasing Mace radioed. They were just a few miles inside Saudi Arabian airspace, but no Iraqi fighters had dared to fly this far south yet so they were given permission to use the radios. The Tornado crew had configured their fighter-bomber to look exactly like Mace's plane—clean wings (they had used their last two remaining Sidewinder missiles to kill the Iraqi fighter, which turned out to be a MiG-29—a very impressive kill considering that the MiG-29 was a front-line Soviet-made fighter, similar to the

American F-15 Eagle, and the Tornado was a "mud-pounder" that happened to carry air-to-air missiles), gear down, and wings swept back to about 30 to 35 degrees. The Tornado was about thirty feet from Mace's right wingtip, accomplishing some of the steadiest "welded-wing" formation flying Mace had ever seen.

"Yeah, I know," Mace radioed back. "Fuckin' thing is falling apart around my ears. I'll give it a few more minutes."

"Right," the Tornado pilot replied skeptically. Judging by the tone of his voice, he strongly believed in Murphy's Law—"if it can go wrong, it will go wrong"—and Mace's Corollary to Murphy's Law: "Emergency-Gear Extension Handles won't."

"Breakdance, this is Ramrod," a new voice on the radio announced a few minutes later. "How do you hear?"

"Loud and clear," Mace replied. Ramrod was a standard call sign for a maintenance officer at most Air Force bases, a sort of on-site foreman who coordinated all repair, supply, and emergency activities at a base during aircraft launch and recovery.

"Roger. We have an emergency recovery team in place to assist you. The landing zone will be marked by vehicles, and we have a mobile BAK-6 arresting cable set up with a line of trucks marking its location. Land well short of the cable. Check hook extended now."

Mace reached across Parsons and pulled a yellow hook-shaped handle. With all the other warning and caution lights illuminated on the front panel, Mace almost missed the new one: HOOK EXTEND. "Hook is down," he radioed.

"Confirmed," the Tornado crew added.

"Say gross weight, Breakdance."

"Estimating five-five thousand."

"Status of weapon bay stores."

"Unknown," Mace replied. "One store may be hot."

"We copy," Ramrod replied. There was a long, strained pause; then: "Breakdance, do you require assistance to complete your checklists?"

"What I need is to get this beast on the ground," Mace replied. He took a few deep breaths, trying to flush the nervousness out of his eyes and hands, then said, "No, I think I got everything I can. I'm flying upright, the gear is down, and I'm cool for now. Over."

"We're about thirty miles out," the pilot aboard the RAF Tornado radioed. "Let's try a controllability check, shall we? Slow to your computed approach speed and let's have a go."

"Let's," Mace replied curtly.

His computed approach speed of 195 knots—about 60 nautical miles per hour faster than normal—wasn't that much slower than the airspeed he was flying right now, but the effect on his control just by pulling off a little power was dramatic. Immediately the nose came up, the stall-warning buzzer sounded, and the F-111G sank like the anchor on an aircraft carrier. He had to shove in military power to get his airspeed back up above 185. Through it all, the Tornado stayed on his wing, matching his airspeed swings and threatening to send himself crashing in the desert. "Sorry about that," Mace offered as he climbed back up to two thousand feet and accelerated back to a comfortable, stable 220 knots.

"Pulled off a bit too much too fast, I think," the Tornado pilot said. "Not recommended for a normal approach, but keep it in mind if you have a short-field approach. Any serious vibrations or directional control problems?"

"No." Mace replied. "Let's give it another shot—can't do much worse. Ready?" No reply. "Elvis, you ready?" Still no reply. Then he saw the Tornado pilot point to the side of his helmet, tapping his earpieces, and Mace knew what had happened even before he looked back into the cockpit. He punched the MASTER CAUTION light out and found the RGEN and UTIL HOT caution lights illuminated. With one engine running, the primary hydraulic system from the one good engine had to supply power to the entire aircraft. Because of this, it was easy to overload it, as Mace had obviously done with his recovery efforts.

Now the system was in "isolate," which meant that the backup hydraulic system had activated and only a few vital systems were getting hydraulic power—namely, the stabilators, which controlled pitch and roll. Since the electrical generators ran on hydraulic power as well, all electrical systems were out now. Mace tried switching to battery power only, which powered radio one, but when he keyed the mike, nothing happened. The game was just about over. It was all up to the Tornado crew now to get him to the recovery base.

A few minutes later they did reach the recovery base—except it wasn't a base. They had descended to one thousand feet and had first aimed right at a group of trucks parked alongside a highway. But when the Tornado began a right turn and started to parallel the highway, Mace knew what was happening—the highway *was* his recovery base. He was going to land on the highway!

The Tornado pulled ahead of Mace's F-111G for the last two left-hand turns, keeping his airspeed up to two hundred knots for maximum controllability in the turns and making sure the maneuvers were gentle and easy. They lined up perfectly on the highway after the last turn on final. Three trucks on either side of the highway marked the BAK-6 arresting cable location, and off in the distance a few more trucks blocked the highway just before a curve—a little less than two miles available.

Once they turned onto final, all Mace had to do was keep up with the Tornado. The backseater was watching him intently for any other signs of danger.

Mace couldn't keep the damn throttle steady. As hard as he tried, he couldn't find a power setting that maintained the proper glide angle. Every tiny pitch change required a power adjustment, which changed his altitude, which required another pitch and power change to compensate. Several times he found himself well above the Tornado, and once he was so high that he lost sight of it. While the Tornado's approach was a straight line, Mace's approach was a series of roller-coaster hills that—

Suddenly the pilot pointed forward. Mace looked up. He was still twenty, maybe thirty feet above the highway—well above the touchdown point. Mace tried a last-ditch dive for the cable, yanking the nose up just before the nose gear hit, but the hook bounced off the pavement and missed the arresting cable.

"Breakdance, negative cable! Negative cable!" Ramrod shouted on the radio. "Go around! Go around!"

Mace didn't hear the warning, but he knew his landing attempt had gone horribly wrong. He shoved the power back in on the good engine and tried to raise the nose, but the control stick felt as heavy as an iron girder and the nose wasn't moving up. He had no choice—he was going to land.

The line of trucks blocking the highway at the curve seemed to be right in front of him. Although they were still at least a mile and a half away, at his speed he would close that distance in a hurry. Mace tried to ease the big bomber down with small power changes, but thermals coming off the highway were buoying him up, refusing to let him settle gently to earth. He was high and fast, with no highway left. When he reached the trucks ahead, both he and Parsons would die in a spectacular ball of fire. He had only one chance left to save himself . . . Please, God, he prayed silently, don't let the nukes blow. . . .

Mace chopped the throttle to idle and pulled the wing-sweep handle back to the 54-degree lockout. That dumped every last erg of lift remaining in the F-111G, and it sank tailfirst almost straight down. The sudden power loss shut down the backup hydraulic system, and Mace suddenly had no directional control at all—he was at the hands of the gods, the same ones that Daren Mace had been pissing off almost all his life.

The tail feathers surrounding the engine exhaust nozzles hit first, crunching the metal against the destroyed engine and instantly igniting some fuel or hydraulic fluid and starting a black, smoky fire in the aft engine section. The main trucks hit hard, blowing the right tire and starting a small fire in the aft wheel well. The nose hit third, the partially extended nose gear collapsed instantly, and Mace was thrown so hard against his shoulder straps that he lost his breath. The fiberglass radome snapped, broke free, and crashed into the windscreen, destroying what was left of it before flying off.

Still traveling well over 150 miles an hour, the F-111G left the highway and careened out into the desert, threatening to tumble like a mobile home caught in a tornado. The bomber began to spin on its blown right wheel, then on its nose digging into the sand, and finally came to rest nearly a mile past its touchdown spot, buried up to the cockpit in sand.

It took several long moments for Mace to get his wind back—the sudden smell of burning fuel and rubber immediately invaded his half-conscious senses and quickened his recovery. The bomber, with two AGM-131X nuclear-tipped missiles and about fifteen hundred gallons of jet fuel on board, was on fire.

Mace's first impulse was to run, to get away from the burning plane before something blew—but his pilot, Robert Parsons, was also on that plane. He might be dead, especially after the crash, but he couldn't just leave him in the plane to fry. Instead, he hobbled around the decimated nose to Robert Parsons. His restraints had failed on impact and he was slumped over his lap, blood covering his legs and chest, but with the bomber tipped over onto its left side it was easy to pull him free of the plane. With strength he didn't know he possessed, Mace dragged the pilot out across the desert nearly a hundred yards before his strength drained away and he collapsed on the sand.

Laying Parsons down, he carefully removed his battered helmet. Parsons' face was deeply scarred and covered with blood, and all of Mace's bandages had torn off in the windblast. His left shoulder appeared dislocated and shattered. The bandages on his chest were intact but soaked through with blood. The wound across the left side of his chest looked the worst, and Mace had nothing to cover the gaping, bloody wound with except his hands. He applied pressure on the exposed tissue—and to his surprise a low moan escaped from Parsons' lips. Was it just air from his dead lungs being expelled through his—

No! Parsons was still alive! "Oh, Jesus," Mace murmured as he saw Parsons move his head and lips. "Bob, can you hear me? We're okay. We made it. Help will be here in a minute." Parsons' lips moved, and his Adam's apple bobbed as he struggled to speak.

"Don't try to talk, man. You're okay. Don't try."

But Parsons gasped again, leaning forward to get closer to Mace. Over the sounds of the approaching rescue crews and the fire extinguishers being activated against the fires creeping toward the bomb bay, Mace leaned closer to Parsons. "What is it, Bob?" he asked his pilot.

"Nuke . . . you didn't . . . launch . . . nuke."

Then he heard one word from his pilot, but it was a word that was going to change his life:

"Traitor," Parsons coughed. "You're . . . a fucking traitor."

PART TWO

There's nothing I'm afraid of
like scared people.
—Robert Frost

9

The White House Oval Office, January 1995

IT WAS VERY MUCH LIKE A STATE VISIT—THE HONOR GUARD AT the airport, the greeting by Secretary of State Harlan Grimm, the motorcade through the streets of Washington, and the greeting at the White House by the President, the First Lady, and members of the Cabinet and Congressional leadership. The greeting for Valentin Ivanovich Sen'kov, former prime minister of Russia, senior member of the Congress of People's Deputies, and the moderate opposition leader to hard-line Russian president Vitaly Velichko, was almost as grandiose as those accorded a popular state leader.

Sen'kov was in his late forties to early fifties, tall, slender, handsome, and unmarried. He was a former colonel in the SPETSNAZ, the Red Army's Special Forces, a veteran of Afghanistan. Sen'kov was a strong ally of Boris Yeltsin, the now deposed and exiled former Russian President. When Yeltsin was still in office, Sen'kov was named Deputy Chairman of the Congress of People's Deputies, the third-highest position in the new Russian Federation. But with the ascension of Vitaly Velichko, Sen'kov was removed from that post and stripped of most of his official powers. Ideologically, the young Sen'kov was a reformer who wanted closer ties to the

West, and he went out of his way to show the world how exciting it could be for a Russian to embrace the West—he had established very close ties to many Western governments and was a star of his own TV talk show in Russia and in an English-language version of the show shown overseas. Politically, however, Sen'kov swung with the winds. He was careful to make powerful friends both in Russia (including the military) and overseas, especially to show his Russian colleagues what real Western wealth was about. Although not tremendously popular with the bureaucrats or the military, his popularity with the Russian people and people from all over the world could not be ignored. He was certainly a very atypical Russian politician.

There were the usual photo opportunities at the White House, but instead of sitting around in the Oval Office, seated on the usual chairs in front of the fireplace surrounded by photographers, the President, who was a bit younger than Sen'kov and every bit as athletic, took the Russian politician out to the covered, winterized White House tennis courts for a game. The President preferred jogging, but he knew the Russian loved tennis. The press went crazy at every hit. The easy "batting the ball around for the press" turned into a serving warm-up, which evolved into a quick game, which turned into a set, which turned into an all-out head-to-head battle. It was a close game, with no real winner apparent until the very last point—Sen'kov, always politically prudent, lost. They returned for iced tea and ice cream in the Oval Office. Ice cream was one of the President's weaknesses, and it added to his girth. The press was allowed to stay for only a few minutes before being escorted out.

"I wish I could claim a true victory, Valentin," the President drawled in his deep southern accent, as they were joined by the First Lady, "but I had to fight for every point, and I think you let me win."

"I wish I could claim that I let you win, Mr. President," Sen'kov said, "but I cannot." Sen'kov, after spending a long time overseas—including getting a master's degree at the President's own alma mater at Oxford—had only a very slight Russian accent when he spoke English, which made both the President and First Lady feel very comfortable around him. "We must make it a point to play more often."

"That's tough to arrange these days, Valentin," the President said.

They sat in silence for a few moments, drinking iced tea and toweling off; then the First Lady said, "Valentin, I know it must be very difficult for you to leave your country at a time like this. Russia is on the front page every day, especially with that recent tragedy of that transport being shot down by the Moldovan Air Force. How awful."

"I understand you knew many of the men on that aircraft," the President added.

Sen'kov seemed to hesitate a bit, but whether that was from a sad memory or because he was thinking of being double-teamed by this formidable political duo, it was difficult to tell. "I thank you both for your thoughts," he said in a low voice, seemingly choked up by their comment—which, he hoped, would make them feel a bit guilty and perhaps back off a bit. "Yes, I did know some of the senior officers on that plane." He paused again, and the couple could see his expression change from one of sadness to one of rising anger. "It was a senseless thing to do."

"You mean the Moldovans shooting down your transport, and the Ukrainians informing the Moldovans of its presence?" asked the President, putting a big spoonful of ice cream in his mouth.

"No, Mr. President, I mean it was a senseless thing to do to send those paratroopers in the first place like that."

"You mean you would have sent them in at night, or in more than one aircraft, or by a different route?"

"You misunderstand," Sen'kov said in earnest. He hesitated, then decided to be as blunt as possible: "I think it was an insane mission to begin with, perpetrated by an insane man." Well, Sen'kov thought, at least they knew now that he had not supported the Russian mission into Moldova. Sen'kov rested his head on his hands and made a pyramid with his index fingers (he had been taught once by the KGB that doing this made one look very pensive, as if deliberating very hard on a subject), then said, "May I tell you the truth?"

"Please do," the President said.

"I could put a bullet in President Velichko's brain myself for what he has done," Sen'kov said, "and not because he botched the job, but because of the way he is conducting this entire line of foreign policy." He modestly nodded to the pretty blonde

First Lady. "I am sorry if I offended you."

"I understand, Valentin," the First Lady said reassuringly. "No offense taken."

"Thank you. You know what he is about, Mr. President, ma'am. He appeals to those in my country who want the old ways, to bring back the strong central government, to weaken the military, to protect Russians living overseas. Instead of embracing the West and the emerging third world, he shuns it. Instead of trying to strengthen the Commonwealth by strengthening the Republics under a free market society, he tries to strengthen Moscow and bully the independent Republics into allowing Russians to keep all the property and privileges they controlled under the old oppressive regime. It cannot be done. It must ultimately fail."

The First Couple nodded in complete understanding. Shortly after the President had taken office, one of the first crises he'd had to face was the continuing loss of influence and power by Boris Yeltsin, a man the President—and most of the Western World—had hoped could keep the newly formed Russian Republic moving toward democratic reforms. During his first state of the union address, the President had called upon more aid for Russia to help Yeltsin implement his social and economic reforms. But the country, facing an enormous deficit, high unemployment, and a sluggish economy, informed *him* through their Congressional representatives and Senators that it was time to care for America's own first. The President, at the urging of the First Lady, the Secretary of State, and others, was undaunted. He continued to make speeches pressing for aid.

Then, in March of 1993, former President Richard Nixon came back from a trip to Russia—he still knew the country better than anyone in or out of office—and met privately with the President, reiterating the dire need for American aid. Nixon even wrote an editorial in *The New York Times* declaring disaster ahead if America didn't get involved. And then, step by step, things began to unravel for Yeltsin. In an extraordinary four-day session, the Congress of People's Deputies stripped Yeltsin of a lot of his powers, putting them back into the hands of his opposition.

The President, sensing the urgency of Yeltsin's decline, called upon the major industrialized nations to pump up emergency aid for Yeltsin. His pleas fell on deaf ears.

The Germans were struggling with the economic effects of reunification, the Japanese were still reeling from their own faltering economy, the French were typically more concerned about their own country than anyone else, and the British simply had no money.

Nixon, the southern Democratic president realized, had been right all along. Before the summer was over, Yeltsin was out, and Vitaly Timofeyevich Velichko was in.

Velichko was not only President of Russia, but President of the Commonwealth of Independent States' (CIS) Council of the Heads of State; Chairman of the Socialist Motherland Party (which was formerly the Congress of the Communist Party of the Soviet Union); Commander in Chief of the Russian Armed Forces; as well as the Commander in Chief of the Joint Commonwealth Forces. He was the most powerful man in Russia, and he shared ultimate control over the nuclear weapons in the CIS states that still had them with his Minister of Defense and his Chief of the General Staff.

Under the Soviet government prior to 1992, Velichko was Deputy Defense Minister and the chairman commander of the Main Military Council, the principal group charged with maintaining wartime readiness in peacetime (the equivalent to the U.S. Strategic Command). In wartime the Main Military Council becomes the *Stavka*, the highest wartime military body, and the President takes direct control.

After the Soviet Union's humiliating withdrawal from Afghanistan, Velichko's primary job was the restoration of the image and fighting timbre of the Russian Army, and he did it with ruthless abandon. He blamed the failure in Afghanistan not on Russian troops, but soldiers from the outlying, more pro-Muslim republics. Velichko ordered imprisonment and executions for desertion, drunkenness, insubordination, and conduct unbecoming a Soviet soldier. In particular, non-Russian soldiers were policed, even persecuted. Soldiers with Muslim families or a Muslim heritage were removed from the Red Army.

Rather than alienate himself from the military, he actually endeared himself to them, especially hard-line Russians. Velichko was instrumental in continuing many strategic military programs despite huge budget deficits and soaring inflation—the SS-25 and SS-18 intercontinental ballistic missiles, the Tupolev-160 strategic supersonic bomber, the Typhoon-class nuclear-powered submarine, and others.

It was Velichko's job to align the Russian military with the pro-Communist plotters during the August 1991 coup attempt, and when the coup failed and Yeltsin came to power, Velichko faded into the background, remaining in his Black Sea dacha on the Crimean Peninsula of the Ukraine. His popularity with the military was so great that, even after the Ukraine's independence in November of 1991, the Crimean Peninsula became a virtual Russian military enclave, with all naval and naval air bases there remaining in Russian hands. No one dared challenge Velichko and Russian ownership of those installations.

But in a stunning peaceful coup precipitated by threats from the military commanders, in the summer of 1993, Yeltsin was forced to give up his presidency in order to avoid a military takeover. The Congress of People's Deputies, the unelected legislative body in Russia, announced Velichko president, pending elections in 1995. Velichko did not call for elections for members of the Congress, and so he solidified his hold on the government.

Quickly, tactics not seen since the days of the old Soviet Union started emerging. The KGB was refortified and renamed, beefed up with budgetary dollars meant for the people, persecution and disappearance of political enemies escalated, freedoms enjoyed since the fall of the USSR began to evaporate: free speech, the right to openly practice religion, and the right to travel between the CIS states were tightened. He also seized many of the industries that had, during Yeltsin's rule, been taken into private ownership. Velichko ruled Russia with an iron fist reminiscent of Khrushchev, but unlike Khrushchev, many (including the U.S. President and the CIA) felt that Velichko was a psychiatrically defined sociopath. In other words, he was nuts, which made him all the more dangerous.

"You know," the President was saying, "you're gonna have to get your Congress together and tell him he's gonna fail. Big-time. He's going to drag your whole country into war with the United States or NATO, sure as hell."

"It is hard to speak of calm and cooperation in the dead of winter," Sen'kov said. "The truth is, many in my country like Velichko's explosive rhetoric. There are many who blame the Ukrainians, the Muslims, the Romanians, the Balts, for Russia's problems. In their minds, an invasion would solve everything."

"So that transport *was* carrying an invasion force," the First Lady said as if she knew it all along.

Sen'kov looked as if perhaps he was going to deny it; then: "I'm afraid so, ma'am. Reinforcements for the rebels in Kishinev, and SPETSNAZ commandos to stage cross-border raids against Romanian and Ukrainian air defense installations."

"Velichko *promised* me that aircraft was full of humanitarian relief supplies," the President said. "He said those men that died were relief workers and aircrewmen."

"Quite the contrary, sir. It was a small but very lethal fighting force. Petition the Romanian government to examine the wreckage."

"We did that," the First Lady interjected. "As expected, the Moldovans said it was carrying troops. We have evidence that they doctored the cargo to make it look like an invasion force."

"It was, madam," Sen'kov said. "Look at the plane's radar installation. You will find it is different than the normal navigation and weather radar—it has been modified for all-weather terrain-avoidance operations. Normally explosives are planted when military equipment such as this is installed in civil aircraft, to destroy these components in a crash, but I know that most aircrews will disable the explosive device on most low-level flights because they fear turbulence will cause the charges to go off."

The President finished his ice cream, poured himself more iced tea, walked around the Oval Office a bit, then said, "You know, I feel powerless, Valentin. I can't get any more aid approved for Russia until Velichko backs off or is ousted. What else is there to do? What's your prediction here? How far is Velichko prepared to go?"

"I know that I may not be considered an impartial reference, Mr. President," Sen'kov said. "I lost my office to his hard-line socialist party; I have made it quite clear that I intend to run against him in the next election; and I certainly do not share his extreme views. But in my opinion, sir, Vitaly Velichko is a madman. He will not stop until the Ukraine, Moldova, the Baltic states, Kazakhstan, and Georgia are all firmly in the Commonwealth, back under Russian domination. The presence of American warships in the Black Sea, and Ukrainian airmen in Turkey training with NATO forces, is proof to him that

Russia is doomed unless he acts, with all the speed and power of the Russian military."

"But what is he going to do?" the First Lady asked. "How far is he going to take this?"

"Madam, a planeload of SPETSNAZ troopers is only the beginning," Sen'kov said. "Velichko feels he was betrayed by the Ukrainians, with American and Turkish assistance. The recent news that the Ukraine has been stockpiling weapons in Turkey is simply more proof. Romania or Lithuania is not a great threat to Russia—but the Ukraine *is*. He will have to deal with the Ukraine."

The President and the First Lady looked at each other and suddenly felt uneasy.

10

Over Northwest Ukrainian Republic January 1995

PAVLO GRIGOR'EVICH TYCHINA WAS MAD ENOUGH TO CHEW nails. If he heard one more wingman grouse about having to pull another night of air patrols, he was going to put a missile up his butt.

For the sixth night in a row, Tychina was leading a gaggle of twelve MiG-23 fighters, NATO code name Flogger, on air patrol of the Volynskoje Uplands of northwestern Ukraine. To Tychina, it was an honor to lead this large formation of planes. It was unusual for such a young aviator to command such a large flight, especially when the patrol was at night—not to mention the very tenuous political and military conditions under which the patrol was now operating. Because the Air Force had been conducting these patrols round-the-clock for over six months now, the thought had crossed his mind that they were running low on fresh, seasoned pilots and were digging deeply into the less-experienced crews to lead night patrols. He, Tychina, was the leader, and had been for nearly a month and twenty sorties now.

"Lead, this is Blue Two." The radio call came a few moments later. It was Aviation Lieutenant First Class Vladimir Nikolaevich Sosiura again. "My fuel gauge is oscillating again.

It's bouncing on empty. Maybe I better take Green Two back to base. Over."

"Vlad, dammit, this is the second 'oscillating fuel gauge' in three nights," Tychina said. Sosiura's roommate and drinking buddy was in Green Two—how obvious could Vlad be? "Maybe you had better talk to your plane captain and get some different malfunctions. In the meantime, hold your position."

"Go to hell, Pavlo," Sosiura in Blue Two replied. "If I flame out, it'll be your fault." Sosiura's "butt-comfort duration" was about forty-five minutes, and most of the time it didn't take longer than thirty minutes before he or someone else in the twelve-ship formation started seeing "malfunctions" crop up in their planes. Tychina thought they gave "soft" new meaning.

The twelve Mikoyan-Gurevich-23 single-engine, single-seat jet fighters were on a night air-combat patrol of the Volynskoje Uplands, nicknamed the "Polish Bunghole" because of its vast stretches of dark wasteland and its close proximity to Poland and Belarus. Air patrols of the Bunghole were necessary because long-range radar coverage in this region was so poor: the L'vov radar adequately covered the Polish border and even into Slovenia, but radar sites in Kiev, the capital of the Ukraine, and Vinnica in central Ukraine were short-range approach radars only, leaving huge gaps in radar coverage in the northwest. They had installed outdated, unreliable Yugoslavian portable radar units in the area, but they rarely worked, and the more reliable Soviet- and Ukrainian-made mobile radar units had limited range. With tensions this high, the Ukraine needed reliable long-range eyes in the sky.

By forming six gigantic racetracks in the skies over the Bunghole, Tychina was able to fill that five-hundred-kilometer-wide gap. The six ovals were aligned north to south. Each was about one hundred kilometers long, and separated by about seventy-five kilometers, spread from west to east from the Ukraine-Poland border to Zitomir, about one hundred fifty kilometers west of Kiev, from where surveillance and ground-controlled intercept radars would pick up the air defense task. Each oval had two fighters in it, orbiting apart from one another so that when one plane was turning southbound, the other was turning northbound. This way a solid wall of radar energy was always being transmitted northward to cover the Belarus-Ukrainian border west of Kiev. Similar radar pickets had been established in the skies between Kiev eastward to Char'kov, covering the Russia-Ukrainian frontier, and more conventional air patrols were in the skies near the Crimean Peninsula and over the Black Sea.

Almost a hundred MiG-23, MiG-27, and Sukhoi-17 fighters were involved in this night operation, rotating in two-hour shifts from air bases at L'vov in western Ukraine, Kiev and Vinnica in central Ukraine, Char'kov and Doneck in eastern Ukraine, and Odessa on the Black Sea. Three more groups of a hundred planes each patrolled the rest of the day—the patrol operation involved two-thirds of the Ukraine's fleet of combat aircraft. In addition, four-fifths of the Ukraine's eight hundred military and government helicopters—not just combat or patrol helicopters, but transport, communications, liaison, and command helicopters as well—patrolled the Russian, Belarussian, and Moldovan frontiers day and night. It was easily the largest air armada ever launched by a former Soviet republic.

Tychina was proud to be part of this vital mission and happy to be commanding this large air patrol, but a little worried as to exactly why they were up here. He knew that relations were strained to the point of war between Russia and two of its Commonwealth of Independent States' allies—Moldova and the Ukraine—over a tiny enclave of Russians living in the Dniester region of Moldova (what used to be the Moldavian Soviet Socialist Republic). And just last month, Moldova had blasted that Ilyushin-76 Russian transport right out of the sky. Still, that little skirmish was between Moldova and Russia. Or was it?

Tychina finished his northward leg with nothing showing on radar. "Task Force Imperial lead turning," he reported. The rest of the formation was supposed to time their turns with him, but it was easy to get out of sync. One by one the pilots reported their turns to their orbit-mates. The formation was staggered a bit, no more than a minute or two off—the Belarussian border was still being covered. Tychina turned his radar to STANDBY on the southbound leg, started a stopwatch to time his next turn, did a cockpit check, made a few fuel calculations—about twenty minutes left before they headed for home—and settled in his narrow, uncomfortable ejection seat to wait. The next shift of fighters should be calling airborne from L'vov in about ten minutes, and in thirty minutes he'd be back on the ground. They'd be down long enough for a refueling, a bathroom break, a quick snack, and another plastic bottle of apple juice before launching for the second shift.

The young pilot went back to thinking about the mess that seemed to be drawing former allies into battle. One thing he knew for sure: it was important for the Ukrainian people to secure their own borders and get out from under the shadow of their former master. This air patrol, although probably insignificant, was still important. No one, especially Russia, should be allowed to push anyone around, especially an ally.

These round-the-clock patrols were staged more for Moldova's and Romania's satisfaction—and for the Ukrainian people—rather than for any tactical military considerations. Romania and Moldova were charging the Ukraine with siding with Russia in the Dniester dispute, and this was a way of showing them it wasn't true. More importantly, the newly elected liberal government in Ukraine needed support for its policy of international cooperation and openness. So this was a way of showing the world how much they desired peace—and a way of showing the Ukrainian voters how tough they could be.

Yeah, right, he mused. As if throwing a few old fighters up against the cream of Russia's crop showed anything but how desperate you were. Well, if nothing else, this was flying time, and logable formation-lead time, as well as task force leader time. More points toward promotion to Major of Aviation, which young Pavlo Grigor'evich Tychina could expect in—

"Inbound, inbound," a voice suddenly came over the radio—in English, of all languages! "This is Lubin air traffic control center on GUARD, aircraft at zero-seven-three degrees from Lubin at one-three-eight kilometers at one-two thousand meters, descend and maintain one-zero thousand meters, contact me on frequency one-two-seven-point-one, and squawk four-two-two-five normal. Acknowledge all transmissions. Welcome to Poland. Over."

Tychina shook his head, totally confused. Lubin was a Polish air traffic control sector, about a hundred kilometers west of the Ukrainian border—but the location of the unidentified aircraft they were talking to was in the Ukraine. The Polish air traffic controller was obviously giving the Ukrainian jets a friendly "heads-up" about the intruders, disguising it as a standard initial call-up to an inbound flight. But night flights by commercial aircraft were prohibited at night over most of Eastern Europe. Who was out there?

Tychina hit the radio button on his throttle: "Amber Two, this is Blue One, you have contact on that unknown?"

"Say again, Blue One?" the pilot of Amber Two, Aviation Lieutenant Maksim Fadeevich Ryl'skii, replied. Ryl'skii's voice plainly sounded drowsy. Good thing all the aircraft were separated by at least fifty kilometers or else they'd be running into each other for sure.

"Christ, Mak, aren't you monitoring GUARD?" Tychina yelled. "All Imperial aircraft, check your switches and monitor GUARD channel. Lubin air traffic control called unidentified traffic over our airspace, and he *wasn't* talking about us. Northbound Imperial flights, configure for aircraft above one-zero-thousand meters and sing out if you see anything."

Seconds later, Tychina heard, "Imperial, this is Amber Two, I have radar contact at zero-two-zero degrees and thirty kilometers from Reference One, altitude one-two thousand meters." Reference One was the city of Kovel, about seventy kilometers south of the Belarus-Ukraine border . . . the unknown aircraft was definitely in Ukrainian airspace.

Thank God for the Polish air traffic controllers, Tychina thought—the Ukrainians liked to make fun of the Poles, but they may have just saved their asses.

"How many you got, what direction, and what speed, Amber One?" Tychina demanded. *Come on, damn you,* Tychina cursed silently. *Don't go to pieces on me* now—*give me a proper radar report.* Some fighter jocks always sounded so macho, so competent, until a *real* emergency happened, then they turned to putty.

"I got multiple inbounds, headed south, at seven hundred kilometers per hour," Ryl'skii replied several moments later, his voice shaky. He had never seen so many unidentified aircraft on his radar screen before. The Sapfir-23D J-band attack radar in the MiG-23s had been recently upgraded to allow more autonomous air intercepts—the older system was made for ground-controlled intercepts, but that was useless if you no longer had many ground-controlled radar systems. "Andrei, get your ass up here and help me . . . my God, there must be a dozen inbounds up here!"

"Relax, Amber Two," Tychina radioed. "Amber One, you start your turn yet?"

"Affirmative," Aviation Captain First Class Andrei Vasil'evich Golovko in Amber One replied. Golovko was an experienced pilot and a former flight commander, sent back to pushing a jet because of one drunken episode several months ago. Tychina thought the demotion was unwarranted but was glad to have Golovko in his unit. "I have got you and the bogeys on radar; Amber One, you can turn off your exterior lights. Pavlo, we have got multiple inbounds heading south. Jesus, at least fourteen . . . what the hell is going on? . . . Pavlo, I'd call 'em hostile. There could be jokers in the deck. What do you want to do?"

For the first time since leading these patrols, Tychina had to make a real command decision. Their orders were to intercept and, *if necessary,* destroy any unidentified foreign aircraft crossing the border. The caveat "if necessary" disturbed Tychina—it was anyone's interpretation what *that* might mean. It would also be virtually impossible to get a visual identification. Some of the MiG-23s, including Tychina's plane, were equipped with the TP-23 infrared search and track system, and they could use it for a visual identification if they could safely close within about ten kilometers. But closing in that much meant possibly tangling with the "jokers" Golovko was warning him about—enemy fighters. If this was a flight of Russian bombers, it was very possible that they'd bring along fighter escorts.

Pavlo Tychina paused, then ordered, "Amber One, keep the aircraft and Amber Two in sight. Take a high patrol perch if you can. Break. Blue Two and Green Flight, rendezvous with me over Reference Two; I will be at base altitude plus four, so join in the block." Tychina knew that, other than landing in poor weather, most aircraft accidents occurred during night-formation rejoins. He would try to bring his wingman and the two planes in the adjacent orbit areas over to a reference point, stacked one hundred meters below his "base altitude" plus four thousand meters, then hope they could all use radar and visual to join on him.

They practiced a lot of night rejoins, but Tychina could start to feel his own pulse quicken and sweat start to pop out on his own forehead—the rejoin would be difficult and very dangerous under normal training circumstances, and all the harder with hostile aircraft nearby. "All other flights in task force Imperial, I want you to stagger your patrol orbits westward fifty kilometers and shorten your orbits to increase surveillance time along the border. Purple One Flight, contact L'vov and tell them to get task force Royal airborne as soon as possible. Out."

With a steady stream of prompting (as in swearing, yelling, vectoring, and cajoling) from Golovko, the two Amber Flight aircraft joined, climbed to fourteen thousand meters, and approached the unidentified aircraft. They were operating at the very upper end of their altitude capability—a MiG-23 could not fly much above fifteen thousand meters' altitude, and even at fourteen thousand the possibility of flameout or compressor stall was very good—and so far the intruders weren't descending.

Tychina wasn't having the same luck rejoining Blue and Green flights. Suddenly everyone's Doppler navigation systems were running away or frozen, their radio navigation beacon receivers weren't operating correctly, their intercept radars were blanking out, or their identification beacons weren't painting on radar.

Technically it was illegal to join aircraft that had inoperable radars or beacons—but Tychina wasn't going to put up with any shit from his timid wingmen. He performed several 360-degree turns with all of his position and anticollision lights on full bright, shouting on the radio, "Green flight, dammit, I got a visual on you—you should be able to see my lights . . . Blue Two, I've got you on radar, I'm at your four o'clock, six klicks—open your eyes, dammit . . . Blue One rolling out heading three-zero-zero, Blue Two, I'm right ahead of you and above you, c'mon, let's go."

It was a mess and getting worse—no one could do anything right.

"Imperial, this is Amber One, I've got the easternmost bandits in sight," Golovko radioed. Tychina smiled in spite of himself—Golovko, who had visited quite a few Western air bases and even attended a NATO fighter weapons training class in Germany, liked to use American fighter slang like "bogey" and "bandit" a lot. "I have got a Tupolev-95 bomber, repeat, a Tupolev-95 Bear bomber." The nickname Bear was a NATO reporting name, but of course Golovko would prefer to use it. "I see weapons mounted externally. Moving in for a closer look. Stand by."

"Don't move in until you locate and identify any defensive weapons," Tychina called over. "Have your wingman hang back on the opposite side."

"Copy," Golovko replied. "Amber Two, you are cleared to the high perch. Keep me in sight."

"Amber Two copies."

Blue Two had finally joined on Tychina's right wing and was hanging close—he had no IRSTS (Infrared Search and Track System) pod, so he had to rely on Golovko's position lights to stay in formation. Green Flight was taking its time joining on Tychina. "Green Flight, do you have radar contact on me yet?" A few long, irritating moments later, he replied that he had radar contact and that Green Two had him in sight and was closing in. "Blue Flight is climbing to base plus seven and increasing speed."

"Imperial, this is Amber One, I can see a ventral gun turret, repeat, I see a belly turret with twin guns. No tail guns in sight. I call it a G-model Bear. The weapons mounted externally appear to be cruise missiles, I repeat, cruise missiles, probably AS-4, one on each wing. How copy, Imperial? I need instructions immediately. Over."

Tychina swallowed hard. The AS-4 missile was an older-design cruise missile, first developed over thirty years ago, but it was capable of flying over four times the speed of sound—even faster than the R-23 and R-60 air-to-air missiles the MiG-23s were carrying—and from its current launch altitude the AS-4 could fly over five hundred kilometers. It carried 900-kilogram high-explosive warheads, devastating enough to destroy a large office building—or it could carry a 350-kiloton nuclear warhead.

"Amber Flight, this is Imperial, confirm the weapons loadout . . . Andrei, are you sure they're AS-4 missiles?"

"No doubt about it, Pavlo," Golovko said. "I am pulling back to trailing position. What do you want to do?"

Tychina found his throat as dry as an old boot and his breathing was rapid.

Russian bombers.

They were carrying cruise missiles, powerful weapons that could devastate L'vov, or Kiev, or Odessa. He had never thought about the possibility of attacking a Russian aircraft . . .

. . . But what were they doing here?

What was going on . . . ?

"Pavlo, get with it," Golovko radioed. "What are your—"

"Fighters!" Ryl'skii in Amber Two shouted. "Fighters launching missiles, Andrei! Break right! Get out of there!"

Tychina cobbed the throttle to max afterburner and swept his wings full aft to help gain speed. The Russians had just made his decision for him: they indeed had fighter escorts, and they waited at very high altitude until Golovko started moving into attack position. Tychina shouted on the radio: "Imperial Flight, this is Imperial lead, attack inbound Tupolev bombers and unidentified fighters. Check your beacons and lights. Purple Flight, radio to base in the clear, Imperial Flight is under attack by large formation of Russian bombers and unknown numbers and types of fighters. Tell them to declare an air defense emergency! Break. Andrei! Amber Two, what is your condition?"

"I'm in deep shit, that's what, Pavlo," Golovko radioed back. His voice was as icy-calm as if he were sitting in church—the only giveaway that he was locked in aerial combat was the occasional heavy grunting sounds he would make as he strained his stomach muscles against the G-forces to try to keep blood in the upper part of his torso and keep himself from blacking out. "Maksum got hit right away. No radar warning indications—they're firing heat-seekers, slashing down from high altitude, then popping up for the tail shot. I think they're MiG-29s. Go after the bombers, Imperial Flight. Don't try to mix it up with the fighters—they'll eat your lunch for you. Go in fast, take a shot at the bombers, and break up their formation. One bomber turned back already when he saw us coming in—I think they're primed to go home. Come in fast, shoot, and extend. Don't—"

There was a loud *bang!*, a screech of static—or was it Golovko screaming?—and then the transmission abruptly ended.

Two Ukrainian fighters gone in the space of about fifteen seconds.

By then Tychina had passed Mach-one and had moved to within radar range of the Tu-95 bomber formation. His radar picked out two of them. They were still at high altitude, cruising at relatively high speed on the same track as was first reported by the Polish air traffic controller. Straight-and-level attack run—the Russians must've thought they weren't going to encounter any resistance.

At forty kilometers, he armed his first R-23 and locked on to the bomber. The MiG-23's normal armament was a 23-millimeter cannon, two medium-range R-23R radar-guided missiles, and four R-60 heat-seeking missiles. But because there were so many planes involved in this patrol, the IRSTS-capable fighters had been given only two R-60s per plane tonight; the planes without IRSTS had only radar-guided missiles and no heat-seekers, because they would not have enough intercept guidance to maneuver into IR missile position. Tychina hated not having a full-up load of missiles. He knew things were bad in his country, but there was usually no shortage of defensive weapons like guided missiles. He had heard rumors about the black market stealing weapons and equipment.

Pay attention to what's going on, Pavlo, he reminded himself, trying to stay calm. He had passed Mach-1.5, and the R-23 radar-guided missile had a speed limit of Mach-1.2. But Tychina didn't care: speed was life, and he wasn't going to slow down. He did pop the afterburner off to conserve fuel and keep the Russian fighters from picking up his afterburner plume, but he aimed his nose directly at the lead bomber. As he picked up more targets, he adjusted his radar lock-on, always aiming for the leader. If the wingmen saw their leader go down, they might be more inclined to break off their attack.

At exactly twenty-four kilometers he got a steady *ping—ping—ping* indication in his helmet headset, indicating that the R-23 missile was in range and ready for launch. Tychina pressed and held a safety switch on the side of the control stick, which resulted in a rapid *pingpingping* warning tone. The missile's fins were uncaged, the missile was ready to fly.

The entire world seemed to erupt into fire at that very moment. An R-73A heat-seeking missile fired from another attacking Russian MiG-29 fighter missed Tychina's right engine by less than a meter, flew over the fuselage until it was several meters away, then detonated its fourteen-kilogram warhead. The top and top front portion of Tychina's canopy shattered, sending hundreds of razor-sharp shards of glass into the young pilot's head and upper torso. Tychina's helmet was nearly sliced away from his head by the force of the explosion, by the sudden cockpit decompression, and then by the supersonic windblast. Incredibly, the majority of the cockpit canopy stayed intact.

To his own amazement, he was alive and still conscious. The windblast pounded away at his body, but he could no longer hear the thunderous roar. He was protected from the direct supersonic windblast by what remained of his canopy. The subzero air was somewhat soothing, freezing the blood vessels in his nose and face shut and preventing any serious blood loss.

And, more importantly, his jet was still flying, the controls still responded, the engines were still turning—and when he pressed the launch button on the control stick, an R-23 radar-guided missile leaped from its rail on the left underwing pylon. It wobbled frantically as it tried to stabilize itself—now Tychina understood why there was a speed limit on the missile—but just as he thought it was going to spin off out of control, it steadied out and tracked the radar beam. He had to keep his nose aimed at the Tu-95 Bear bomber so the missile could track, but he was rewarded several seconds later with a large flash of light, then darkness, then a stream of fire off in the distance.

His gloved fingers were moving as soon as he saw the hit. He was at eighteen kilometers when he fired his last R-23 missile at another bomber, then immediately switched to the heat-seeking R-60 missiles and started searching for a new target. A second bomber exploded, scratching a blazing meteor in the night sky right down to the frozen earth. All of the Tu-95 bombers started ejecting chaff and flares, but mysteriously stayed on course, and the streams of flares were like large lighted arrows pointing right at them.

Tychina had forgotten all about his wingmen and about everyone and everything else except what Golovko had said before he died: go in fast, shoot at the leaders, and get out.

The infrared search and track system was effective at about ten kilometers, and the bombers appeared as tiny dots on a semicircular indicator in his cockpit. Tychina shut off the attack radar at that point—no use in broadcasting his position any longer than necessary—lined up the seeker boresight reticle on one of the dots, and activated his first of two R-60 missiles. He could no longer hear the telltale growling sound as the missile's seeker detected the hot glow of the Tu-95's huge Kuznetsov turboprops, but he gauged the distance from the readout on his IRSTS indicator and fired the first missile at five kilometers, the missile's maximum range.

Too early. It had not locked on to an engine, but a decoy flare. At Mach-1.22, he was traveling almost a half a kilometer per second, and he barely had enough time to select and fire another missile. The impact of the missile on a third bomber was almost instantaneous, and he could feel chunks of metal from the explosion pepper his plane. Tychina ignored the impacts.

He tried to select another missile, but he carried only two. Damn, what a time to run out of missiles! Tychina switched to his 23-millimeter GSh-23L belly gun pack and fired off a full one-second burst, passing close enough to a fourth Tupolev-95's counterrotating propellers to feel the incredible rhythmic beating of the huge props against his fighter's fuselage. The stream of cannon rounds sliced across the bomber's fuselage, right engine nacelles, and right wing. Tychina cleared for a right turn, saw a Tupolev-95 banking hard right above him with the ventral gun turret aimed at him, and instead threw his MiG-23 into a hard left bank.

When he cleared left after a full 180-degree turn, he nearly yelled in surprise: not one, but *two* Tupolev-95s were going down. The bomber he hit with cannon fire must've turned right into the path of another bomber, because there were two blobs of fire spiraling to earth. He couldn't see the rest of the bomber formation, but another radar sweep told the story—the bombers were heading north again. He had done it! The attack was over! He had—

Tychina saw the missile in its last one-fifth-of-a-second of flight, with a large plume of yellow fire encircling a small black dot, just before the small R-73A missile fired from the pursuing Russian MiG-29 fighter plowed into his MiG-23 and tore off his entire right wing. His head hit the right rear side of the cockpit, finally rendering him unconscious, as the fighter swung wildly to the left and started a lazy spin to the earth.

But luck, even a last bit of good luck, was on his side. The loss of the canopy after the first missile's near-hit had fired all but the last few ejection-seat squib charges and armed the seat. When the fuselage fuel tanks ruptured and exploded from the hit, the shock and vibration caused the ejection seat to fire Tychina's unconscious body clear of the stricken fighter. The seat was automatic and worked properly. Tychina continued in free-fall until about four thousand meters' altitude, when the automatic baro timers fired, releasing his seat harness and tightening a strap along the inside of the seat that snap-launched him from his seat. That action automatically pulled the parachute ripcord, and Tychina was under a full parachute canopy by the time he reached two thousand meters.

Unable to steer himself clear, Tychina landed in a stand of poplar trees that mercilessly raked his face and chest like a wild animal. Townspeople and firemen from the village of Myzovo cut him down several minutes later and found him still alive, nearly conscious, and amazingly unhurt, except for his face and torso, which were horribly disfigured by the trees and by his last seconds in the cockpit of his plane.

But he would live to fly and fight another day.

His victory over the Russian invaders that night would turn out to be the rallying cry for a nation.

11

The White House Cabinet Room, That Evening, Eastern Time

"VALENTIN SEN'KIV HIT THE NAIL RIGHT ON THE HEAD," THE President said. He was meeting with his National Security Council staff in the Cabinet Room of the White House, next door to the Oval Office. Unlike the rest of them, the President was dressed casually in slacks and a sweatshirt—even the First Lady, who was sitting on the President's right beside the Vice President, was dressed in business attire. "He predicted that Velichko would go after the Ukraine, and he did it."

That got a very demonstrative reaction from General Philip Freeman, chairman of the Joint Chiefs of Staff: "Excuse me, sir, but Secretary Scheer and I briefed you on the need to provide support for our NATO allies against an obviously bold and provocative Russia. Now, I never would have expected Velichko to go so far as to invade a fellow Commonwealth country, especially the Ukraine, but the handwriting's been on the wall."

"I hardly think dismissing Mr. Sen'kov's observations in favor of your own is constructive here, General," the First Lady admonished, glaring at him. "I think what's needed here are a few ideas on how to deal with this event."

What Freeman wanted to say was, *Why don't you ask your pal Valentin Sen'kov?* What he did say was, "Very well, ma'am, I and Mr. Scheer do have some recommendations."

"We feel it's essential to pledge full support to our NATO allies, Mr. President," Scheer said. "We need to show them in no uncertain terms that we will not allow Russia to intimidate them. President Dalon of Turkey has requested some assistance, mostly in defensive armament and aircraft, and I recommend we authorize that aid."

"More aid to Turkey?" Secretary of State Harlan Grimm retorted. "Sir, Greece is crying bloody murder about our support for Turkey after the Islamic Wars—they think we're arming Turkey so they can retake Cyprus. Besides, we banned high-tech-weapon exports to Turkey for a reason—if they don't get what they want, they try to steal it. We caught them red-handed with truckloads of Patriot missile technology they tried to steal from Israel."

"Sir, we need to stand by our allies," Freeman repeated earnestly. "If we don't, not only the allies, but Russia as well, will think we don't care what happens in that part of the world. And that invites disaster."

"If I can't get a consensus in my own Cabinet," the President interrupted, "it must mean we haven't got a solution yet. I need more information—on Turkey, on the state of the alliance, on what Velichko has in mind. I think a NATO ministers' meeting in Brussels is in order."

"Let's bring them over here and down to Miami Beach, where it's warm," the First Lady chimed in. She got an appreciative chuckle from that remark.

"Good idea, honey," the President said. "And I need a face-to-face with Velichko, in Europe. Can you make it happen, Harlan?"

"Unlikely, Mr. President," Grimm replied, "but I'll work on it."

"All right. Anything else I need to consider?"

"Excuse me, Mr. President, but there's a whole list of things we need to consider," General Freeman said. "I'm really disturbed about the latest Russian air attack in Europe. The Russians appear to be using their heavy bombers for much more than antishipping and maritime reconnaissance—they had ground attack weapons on board. This is a whole new threat being posed by the Russians, and I think we ought to respond to it."

"How?" asked the President, interested.

"I, and several members of the Joint Chiefs, feel the Russians' actions in Europe warrant Strategic Command gaining the bomber alert force and . . . going back into the nuclear strategic deterrent mode again."

Freeman could have taken off all his clothes and mooned the entire National Security Council and gotten a more muted reaction than he received just then—and the most vocal voice was that of the Steel Magnolia. "Have you lost it, General?" she sneered. "You want to go back to round-the-clock alert with nuclear bombers and missiles? You want to start orbiting the Arctic Circle with B-52 bombers again? I thought the Strategic Air Command was dead."

"Ma'am, let me explain."

But the room was in complete dismay. Donald Scheer leaned over to Freeman and whispered, "Nice try, Phil."

"I think everyone's voiced their opinion on that idea," the President said with a smile. "Now, is there anything—"

"Mr. President, I do think this is important," Freeman pressed on, surprised by the completely negative reaction. "Sir, I'm not talking about going to war, and no, ma'am, I'm not talking about airborne alert—we did away with that in the sixties. I'm talking about sending a credible, rapid, and powerful message to President Velichko—back off or we'll be back in the Cold War business again. I'm talking about taking one-third of our long- and medium-range bombers, about one hundred aircraft, plus three hundred single-warhead Minuteman III land-based missiles, and putting them on alert. We practice it, it's very safe, and my staff has been gathering data on how rapidly we can accomplish this."

The members of the National Security Council quieted down a bit after hearing some of the actual numbers. Not long ago, there used to be over three hundred bombers and over a thousand land-based missiles on alert—Freeman was suggesting a much smaller number, about one-third of what used to be a common thing. "How exactly would we accomplish this?" Michael Lifter, the President's National Security Advisor, asked.

"We're already putting out feelers to the units that will be affected," Freeman replied, "getting hard numbers about what they have available and how fast they can get it all together.

Right now the book says four days from whenever the President says 'go.'

"An order comes down from here to Strategic Command in Omaha—the Strategic Air Command *has* gone away," he said pointedly to the First Lady, "but it's been replaced with Strategic Command, which is the Joint Strategic Target Planning Staff in peacetime and in effect transforms into the Strategic Air Command in wartime. They execute the war plan that we approve. Strategic Command gains aircraft and crews from the Air Force Air Combat Command and other major military commands and assumes operational control of all the nuclear weapons in our arsenals. The commander in chief of Strategic Command, General Chris Laird, reports directly to the President. General Laird becomes responsible for the survival of his forces and for carrying out the emergency war plan, called the Single Integrated Operational Plan, or SIOP."

"World War Three," the First Lady declared.

"We hope not, ma'am," Freeman said. "The primary purpose of the alert force is deterrence. We're hoping that having nuclear-loaded bombers on round-the-clock alert will keep President Velichko from trying anything against NATO."

"So it's MAD all over again," the First Lady interjected again. "Mutually Assured Destruction. The balance of terror."

"It's also a way to assure our allies that we're ready to act in case an attack occurs," Freeman said, looking right at the Steel Magnolia, not the President. "And it is a response to the Russians' newest threat of putting land-attack long-range cruise missiles on their reconnaissance and maritime aircraft. As you know, there are Backfire bombers stationed again in Cuba—the Russians claim these are only long-range patrol planes, but we know now that they could have a land-attack capability and could very easily strike half of the continental United States."

"All right, General," the President said. "I think I've heard enough. I think it'd be a very wise precaution to *investigate* putting bombers on alert again. At the very least, it's a bone we can toss to Dalon and the other allies."

"Sir, with Russia knocking at Turkey's front door, do you think it's wise to just be tossing bones?" Scheer asked. "Perhaps a more positive move is warranted."

"You-all put together what you think that move should be, and I'll look at it," the President said. "Like I said, I need information. The General has given me plenty to think about, but I need more input from the other members before I can decide."

"At the very least, Mr. President," Freeman said quickly, guessing that the President was on the verge of ending this meeting, "allow my staff to brief you on the emergency-action procedures, including responding to the airborne command post and establishing remote and mobile communications with the National Military Command Center."

"Sure, Philip," the President replied, winking away a very concerned glare from his wife. "I think we can squeeze it in tomorrow morning. How about a power breakfast meeting, say, after the First Lady's Health and Human Services breakfast meeting?"

"I'm sorry, sir, but the First Lady doesn't have Top Secret-SIOP-ESI clearance," Freeman said firmly. "She can't attend these briefings."

"She can't?" the President asked incredulously. "How do you figure, General? She can sit in on NSC meetings, she can come and go in the Oval Office at any time—but she can't sit in on a briefing on how to use the doohickey in the briefcase that Navy officer follows me around with all the time?"

"Under current law—"

"Let me have Carl Abell look into it," the President said in a slightly perturbed tone, referring to the White House counsel. "He'll get together with you and whoever else we need and get her a clearance."

Freeman said, "Very good, sir," and he smiled and pretended not to take offense at the smug, satisfied expression the Steel Magnolia gave him right then.

12

Grand Isle, Vermont
January 1995

THE ALARM RANG AT FIVE A.M. REBECCA C. FURNESS WAS already awake, so she quickly slapped the alarm clock silent, then dove back under the covers. The bedroom was cold, so she exposed only her head and her flannel-nightshirt-covered shoulders above the thick down comforter. The chill air was sharp, and as she breathed it in it seemed to fill her body with energy. There was no place like Vermont in wintertime, she thought, even at a frosty five A.M.

The man beside her in the bed rumbled his displeasure when the alarm went off, but he went back to his gentle snoring a few moments later. Furness playfully decided that he shouldn't be allowed to go back to sleep if she had to get up, so she put her hands under the thick comforter and ran them along his shoulders and neck. She was surprised at how cold his skin felt. It was only about 45 degrees in the bedroom—few real second-story country-home bedrooms were heated—but Ed Caldwell insisted on sleeping in the nude regardless of how cold it was. After all, Ed would say, only little boys sleep in bedclothes—even if he died of hypothermia, he would never wear anything to bed.

Her hands moved down to his back, then to his buttocks and

the back of his thighs. Despite only being in his late thirties, a few years younger than herself, Ed already had a small set of "love handles" developing on his waist, but their skiing weekends and his job kept him in pretty good shape otherwise. Rebecca hoped the little bit of cold air drifting across Ed's back and shoulders or her warm touch would wake him up. It would be at least a week before they would see each other again. She wanted to snuggle, talk a bit.

Caldwell pulled the comforter tightly over his shoulders, piled them up around his neck to seal out the cold, and sleepily snorted his disapproval at being disturbed. Five A.M. was definitely too early for Ed. Disgruntled, Becky rolled out of bed, slipped on a robe and a pair of moccasins, and made her way downstairs to make coffee.

Sunrise was still an hour or so away, but the brightening skies to the east rising over the Green Mountains was still spectacular. Furness' house was on the eastern shore of Grand Isle, a large island in Lake Champlain between northern New York State and northern Vermont, and a large picture window in her living room opening up on the lake afforded a spectacular view year-round. She could see as far south as the Highway 2 bridge running from Mallets Bay to South Hero. On clear nights she could see the glow of the city of Burlington on the horizon about thirty miles to the south. The lake was not frozen yet, but the white carpet of ice was running farther offshore every morning and would soon form a near-solid five-mile-wide bridge to the Georgia Plains of northwestern Vermont.

Rebecca Furness lived on a small, secluded plot of land she rented from her uncle, a United States senator from Vermont, nestled between Knight Point State Park, the Hyde Log Cabin Preserve, and Grand Isle State Park. Grand Isle was mostly state parks nowadays, with only three small settlements remaining on the entire forty-mile-long island. Furness' uncle used his influence and was able to get his small plot of land on the shore designated as a wildlife habitat, which kept the developers, the hunters, the skiers, and the state parks commissions from taking his land. The island was like a large, annual version of mythical Brigadoon—it came alive only during the fall for tourist "colors" season, and slept in blissful, isolated peace for the rest of the year, with only a handful of persons a day taking the short ferry ride from Grand Isle to Plattsburgh, New York, or the longer drive on Highway 2 through Grand Isle north almost to the Canadian border.

The house was actually an old barn that had been remodeled into a residence, after the original farmhouse burned down some years ago. Rough-hewn logs and boards made up the ceiling, and huge round rocks plowed up from the surrounding fields made up the big double-sized fireplace. The kitchen was the main room of the house, with a small dining area near the back porch and a huge black cast-iron stove and oven. The large old-style wood- and gas-fired stove provided most of the heat for the house, and even though she would be leaving soon, Rebecca automatically slid another round dry log onto the red-hot coals in the firebox. Normally she would boil water for coffee in the big copper kettle, but she was in a hurry this morning, so she settled for the Mr. Coffee. The thing looked so out-of-place in the house.

When the coffee was finished brewing, she took a cup back out to the living room so she could work on the computer and watch the sunrise through the front picture window. The living room served double duty as a parlor and office, with a large light oak desk and two oak lateral files along one wall. A computer keyboard slid out from the center drawer, and by sliding a few papers out of the way she could see the monitor through a glass panel in the desktop. Rebecca did all her books, scheduling, her record-keeping on that computer—it contained virtually her entire life.

With a few keystrokes, Rebecca was connected to her computer at Liberty Air Service, a small air charter and fixed-base operator at Clinton County Airport, across the lake near Plattsburgh, New York. She owned the company, trained commercial pilots, and did a few cargo or passenger runs to fill in for sick or vacationing pilots—but not this week. Calling up this week's schedule on the computer showed nothing but canceled appointments, all with the annotation HELL WEEK.

Well, Liberty Air could spare the boss for a few days, thanks to the Air Force Reserve.

The electronic mailbox link with her office in Plattsburgh had a few messages, which she briefly answered, mostly with "I'll take care of it when I get back." She noticed that the two late-night runs, one to Bradley International in Connecticut and the other to Pittsburgh, had made it off despite low ceilings and the threat of freezing drizzle. Furness' small eight-plane charter fleet was still composed of all piston-powered planes—all instrument equipped and certified for flight in known icing conditions, but hardly what anyone would call an all-weather fleet. In a matter of weeks she would be looking to buy her first turboprop cargo plane, a single-engine Cessna 208B Caravan with a cargo bay, which would give Liberty Air a true medium-size all-weather cargo capability. Unfortunately, she needed it last week, or even last month. Soon her fleet would be all but weathered in.

Calling up the next thirty days' calendar found it full of FAA inspections, check rides, meetings, deadlines, and of course the beginnings of tax season—all the things that most people put off during the holiday season were now coming due. Things were busy enough with her working six, sometimes seven days a week, but by the time she returned from Hell Week, she would have enough work to last her until spring.

Hell Week was a part of the new American military and a part of Rebecca Furness' new life. She had left the active-duty military in early 1992, during a six-month voluntary RIF (Reduction In Forces) period, in which active-duty Air Force officers were asked to voluntarily resign their regular commissions and accept Reserve commissions before their normal enlistments were completed. The Air Force RIFed ten thousand officers in eight months in an election-year firing frenzy that created so much controversy, so much anguish, that it helped, along with an awful economy, bring down a seemingly unbeatable Republican president.

In one of his very few politically savvy moves concerning the military, the new President eventually invited those officers RIFed in 1992 to join a new program, called the Enhanced Reserve Program, which was meant to increase the capability and viability of the Reserves and National Guard while continuing steep cuts in the peacetime active-duty forces. After all, even with an eye on a huge deficit, the President knew he had to look like a true commander in chief, especially since he had evaded the draft during his own call to duty years ago.

Half of the Reserves and two-thirds of the National Guard were placed under the Standard Reserve Program, or SRP—their basic commitment was one weekend per month and two weeks per year, plus occasional meetings, training schools, and other functions. Those in high-tech specialties such as aviation were placed under the new Enhanced Reserve Program, or ERP, a sort of part-time military where members served at least fourteen days per month, including one continuous week of intensive refresher training. Members in the ERP received approximately half of their active-duty pay, but no other free benefits such as medical care, educational programs, base exchange, or commissary—it was still a cost-cutting system, so all possible benefits and incentives had been eliminated or were offered at reduced cost to members. Reserve and Air National Guard bases were either colocated with municipal airports or were drastically downsized—the base personnel, most of them Reservists, had to rely on the local economy for goods, services, and housing.

Many military experts, including the very vocal members of the Joint Chiefs, feared that the United States was shooting itself in the foot by decreasing the size of the full-time military forces so much—by the end of 1994, the Reserves and Guard composed nearly 50 percent of the total U.S. military force, as opposed to only 30 percent two years earlier. The military budget as a whole was reduced—amid bloodbaths in Congress—by a full 40 percent. The cost savings were staggering. Although the direct effect on the budget after the first year was negligible, the second year the Air Force alone had realized a full 10-percent savings—over 8 billion dollars in just one year. The savings in the future were expected to go even higher, while the national debt was continuing to fall.

As long as no serious world conflicts broke out, the target was a Reserve force of 600,000 men and women, or 60 percent of the total one-million-person American military, by the end of 1996. Of a total 380,000-person Air Force in 1996, over 260,000 were expected to be Reservists or Air National Guard troops.

For the next seven days, Rebecca Furness would leave her business, leave Ed, leave her life on the "outside," and become a soldier.

Furness logged off the computer terminal, finished the last of the coffee, and made her way upstairs to get ready to report to the base. The Enhanced Reserve Program created hardships for a lot of its members because of the amount of time it required, but Rebecca loved it—and needed it. Having Liberty Air Service was challenging, fulfilling, and gave her the time to keep flying for the U.S. Air Force, building up points for retirement—but it paid very, very poorly. Expenses and insurance costs were high, and surviving the lean winter months was always difficult, so her salary was always the first to get cut. She had made the decision to trade in a big portion of her piston fleet for a few turboprop planes to give her more of a year-round cargo and passenger capability, and that had decreased her margin even more. She needed this ERP position to keep herself afloat.

Rebecca showered, staying under the hot water a long time to shave her legs and let the sharp stream of water massage her tense shoulders—hot showers were the only luxury she could still afford. No flying was scheduled today, but just going out to Plattsburgh Air Force Base, the oldest military installation in the United States, and its very busy flight line, always made her a bit tense. After staying in the shower a few minutes longer than she really had time for, she slipped into a big fluffy bathrobe to stay warm and continued to get ready.

For the flyers like Furness, Hell Week was designed as a sort of mini-deployment, so they had to pack their standard deployment items in a big B-4 duffel bag: two flight suits, six pairs of heavyweight socks, thermal underwear, toiletries, T-shirts, and underwear. Since an arctic deployment was possible (and some U.S. non-Arctic bases, such as Plattsburgh, were sometimes cold enough to resemble Arctic bases anyway), they also brought along thick knee-high mukluks, large woolly mittens, fur caps, wool facemasks, and jacket liners. Rebecca had packed most of this stuff the night before, but she did a double-check since there would be an inspection first thing after reporting in.

After rechecking everything in the bag against a predeployment checklist, she zipped the bag up and began to get dressed. Every Hell Week started with a personal inspection, all by regulation—AFR 35-10 (uniform, personal grooming, standards of appearance), AFR 35-11 (weight standards), AFR 36-20 (drug and alcohol screening), AFR 40-41 (civil violations and records check), AFR 50-111 (emergency procedures and aircraft technical order knowledge), and ACC 20-89 (deployment and emergency aircraft dispersal). Anyone not complying with any part of those regulations would be written up in their permanent records and sent home to fix the problem, with a loss of one day's Reserve pay and an "incomplete" for their ERP commitment. Three "incompletes" would mean expulsion from the program.

Flight suits were the uniform of the day, and she had hers cleaned, pressed, and ready to go. Because flight suits chafed so much in the crotch (they were still not allowed to alter their flight suits), she first put on a pair of men's long boxer shorts. They looked silly as hell, but it sure made wearing a rough baggy flight suit all day at least bearable.

"I really hate it when you wear those things," a voice behind her said. Ed Caldwell had finally come to life. He gave her a pat on the bottom as he stalked toward the bathroom.

"When have I heard that before?" she asked. Ed didn't reply, so she continued dressing: heavy wool socks, athletic brassiere, thermal underwear top, dog tags, then the flight suit. It was just starting to feel comfortably warm.

She had just zipped the flight suit up when Ed, still naked despite the near-freezing temperatures, emerged from the bathroom. This time he stood behind her and wrapped his arms around her, burying his stubbly cheeks into the back of her neck to give her a nuzzly kiss. "Mmmm, you feel so good, even in that flight suit."

Rebecca smiled, arched her neck back a bit, and gave him a light kiss on his stubbly cheek. She had been seeing Ed Caldwell for a little over two years, and exclusively for the last year.

Like other lovers and boyfriends before him, Ed had nothing to do with the military or the Reserves. After Rebecca had joined the Reserves, she decided to maintain her no-date policy regarding her fellow officers. Yes, a whisper still passed her ear now and then, questioning her preferences, but far less than when she'd been on active duty. People in the "real world," it seemed to her, were far more tolerant, far less judgmental, than some of the active-duty boys. After all, Reservists had other lives, had to work daily with people of every variation and lifestyle, religion and color . . . a far broader range than what you'd find in active duty. When she thought about it, the Reservists had to be a bit more . . . politically correct. Pull some of the stuff in civilian life that the fly-boys tried in the armed forces, and a corporation would kick them out so fast their heads would spin. "Tailhook," she was convinced, would never have happened at a private-industry convention.

Ed's large hands roamed up and down her flight suit while she was trying to finish zipping it up. "I'm freezing, Becky, you gotta warm me up."

"You are?" she teased. "You're walking around butt-naked and it's only forty or fifty degrees up here. Why not go down and stand by the stove while I finish dressing?"

He slipped the flight suit off her shoulders and let it drop to the floor. He tried to take off the thermal underwear top and undo the clasps of her athletic brassiere, then decided not to wait. He dropped her thermal underwear bottoms, then grasped her by her still-covered breasts, smothering her with kisses, licking the side of her neck slowly, nibbling on her ear . . .

"Ed, c'mon, it's getting late." This was an almost monthly ritual between the two of them. Ed usually waited until she was almost completely dressed in her flight uniform, then he'd playfully try to seduce her. Sometimes it worked.

"Oh, God," she murmured. "Ed, please . . . I've only got twenty minutes to catch the ferry. If . . . I'm . . . late."

Ed, big and strong and completely awake, was working his magical touch all over her, making it increasingly harder for her to resist. The only thing she could say about him, she aggravatingly mused, was that he knew how to make her most hardened resolve and resistance crumble.

"Ed . . ."

He wasn't listening.

"Oh, what the hell . . ." she moaned. "But *hurry!*"

When they were finished, she had to really hustle.

"I'll call you tonight, Ed," she said as she rushed out the door. No reply—he was already sound asleep again. She grabbed her winter-weight flying jacket, watch cap, and wool-lined leather gloves, poured one more cup of coffee, and headed out the door as fast as she could to make the six-twenty ferry.

Thankfully the engine-block heater and trickle battery charger had done their jobs. Her eight-year-old Chevy Blazer four-by-four started right up, and she put it into four-wheel-drive immediately after leaving the garage. The snowplows had not yet been down her lakeside street, so a four-wheel-drive was a necessity. A half mile of four-wheeling on Hyde Log Cabin Road got her to Highway 2 south, where she could feel the crunch of the road salt under her all-terrain tires and put the truck back into two-wheel drive. Four miles south on Highway 2, right on Highway 314, and five miles to the ferry landing. Furness knew the sights of a snowy morning on Grand Isle were beautiful, but she had no time to notice them—the ferry was due to leave at any moment, and she could not be late.

She wasn't. The deck crews were just beginning to hop on board and raise the ramp when she showed her commuter pass, and they stopped when they saw her familiar truck speeding down the road. A few minutes later they were pulling away from shore and crunching through the thin layer of ice on Lake Champlain for the twelve-minute trek on their way to the Cumberland Head landing on the New York State side.

The snack bar on board the Plattsburgh Ferry, which normally served an excellent egg sandwich in the morning, was closed because of the cold, so Rebecca had to stay in the truck, drink cold coffee, and gnaw on a piece of beef jerky she had left in the glove compartment for snowbound emergencies. Enjoying the ferry ride from the inside of her truck, looking out into the black, sooty interior of the ferry, at least gave her a few quiet minutes to think.

She was still feeling that warm postsex satisfaction that went through her after being with Ed, but as fond as she was of him, as wonderful as their sex life could be, she really wished her relationship had remained on a professional level with him. Caldwell was a Burlington banker whom she had met while investigating financing sources for her proposed fleet of turbine-powered planes. Their meetings at the bank had changed to meetings over lunch, then dinner, then Lake Placid . . . finally, to her place. He was, by most women's standards, a real catch. Good-looking, professionally turned-out without coming across as stiff, athletic, and occasionally, when the time really called for it, sensitive.

A bit, anyway.

Ed still had a long way to go in really understanding women. Sometimes she felt he simply indulged her in her passion of flying. He did get her a bank loan of one million dollars for her first fully equipped Cessna Caravan turboprop, after she had to sell three piston Cessnas and collateralize Liberty Air Service to the hilt. But he *did* come through. But sometimes she couldn't help but feel Ed thought of her company as an expensive diversion from doing things like staying in the kitchen and making babies. She sighed. Even in the 1990s, some men—Ed included—would prefer women to stay out of the workplace, stay out of business in what they felt was a man's world. God knows they would never, ever admit it. But they felt it. She knew they did.

As she gazed out of her truck as it made the crossing by

ferry, Rebecca visually drank in the beautiful early-morning surroundings and realized that as content as she should be, something was missing in her life.

What it was, she did not know.

As the ferry moved across the water, she thought back to what had happened to her during the past few years . . . little did she know during those opening days of Desert Storm that her time on that KC-10 Extender, the Air Force's supertanker, were numbered. Thinking about it now, she still resented the chain of events that led her back to Plattsburgh and this new military-civilian career. Although the recent months had been some of the most fulfilling in her Air Force career, Desert Storm—specifically that incident with the FB-111 bomber—had badly tarnished her reputation. She never knew exactly what was going on that day with that navigator named Daren, but whatever it was had been big: the FB-111 incident had been classified to the highest levels in the Pentagon, and the rumors about her only intensified: Furness was a maverick, a lone wolf. A woman who didn't follow Standard Operating Procedures. A woman who put her crew and plane in danger unnecessarily. Yes, Sam Marlowe, the prick, had filed the report he'd threatened to do that day. After that, no one wanted to hire someone like that. In the ensuing RIFs, she lost her assignment at March Air Force Base, then lost her regular active-duty commission, then was turned away from all the major airlines.

So she did two things: one, she decided to start the company, Liberty Air Service, and two, something she had never done before—she called on her uncle, Senator Stuart A. Furness.

It was in his Washington, D.C., office, and for the first time in her life she asked him for a favor.

"I have the skills, I have the training, I have the credential, I have the experience," she remembered telling her uncle. "But I'm getting doors slammed in my face everywhere. I either accept the lowest level of step-pay or go somewhere else. Is there anything you can do?"

The senator from Vermont was tall and wiry, with a lean angular face and short, bushy white hair. Cataract surgery forced him to wear thick glasses, which he removed in anyone's presence, even his niece's. He was always impeccably dressed and carried himself with grace and authority at all times. The photos on his wall told of a man with powerful international connections, both in business and politics. It was sometimes hard for Rebecca to believe this man was a close relative.

But despite his obvious power and command, Stuart Furness was uncomfortable discussing the subject of sex discrimination with his young niece. He didn't seem like the kind of man to fidget, but he was doing a bit of it as he addressed his niece: "Flying is a man's game, Rebecca," he had said. "Why not let them handle it? You're young, and pretty, smart, well-spoken, and a war veteran."

"All of which has added up to zero, Uncle Stuart," Rebecca interjected.

"It may seem that way, Rebecca, but remember the Northeast still is in the grips of a recession—whether it is real or contrived, it is perceived as real and it is affecting businesses everywhere. Perhaps a change of perspective would do some good."

"But I'm not looking for a regular job, Uncle Stu," Rebecca replied with determination. "I'm a pilot. I've been a pilot for over ten years."

"And you were one of the best," the Senator concluded. "But times are tough now. Competition for women in male-dominated jobs everywhere was always tough, and I don't foresee it ever getting any easier."

"I'll put my record against anyone else's," Rebecca fired back. "But I'm getting aced out by low-time rookies. I'm losing jobs to guys that have no jet time, even zero turbine time. I'm losing out to guys with fresh commercial tickets! Look, I'm a flyer. I enjoy military flying. I know the President is trying to increase the size of the Reserve forces and draw down the active-duty forces, but I just can't seem to find a unit to take me."

"Where have you looked?"

"I've applied to every Guard and Reserve unit in the country, Uncle Stu," she said. "I'm on waiting lists in eight units. But I put myself on a mobilization augmentee list in New York so I can get a little better position on the waiting list for an assignment in Plattsburgh, Rome, or Niagara Falls, but that freezes me off the lists in other states." She looked at her uncle carefully, then lowered her voice respectfully and said, "Uncle Stuart, you're on the Senate Armed Services Committee, and you're on the select panel dealing with this new administration's push for an expanded Reserve force. Can't you help me break through some of this red tape?"

He ignored her question at first, staying deep in thought about something else. Rebecca was afraid she had overstepped her family bounds by asking for a favor, but what the hell, what were relatives for?

"Why New York? If you want my help, why aren't you signing up for augmentee slots in Vermont? I'm a senator in *Vermont,* Rebecca."

"I love Vermont—you know that," Rebecca said, "but they have only one military unit, the fighter group in Burlington, and I've read that it may be disbanded or moved. New York has more units. I even heard they want to start a Reserve RF-111G bomber unit in Plattsburgh too."

Stuart Furness looked surprised. "You heard that, did you?"

"It was just a rumor," Rebecca admitted. "The Air Force was considering a Reserve composite wing, similar to the active-duty wings, where each base has its own mini–air force—fighters, bombers, tankers, transports, all that stuff."

"You seem to be very well informed."

"Unemployed people have a lot of time to read the papers, Uncle Stu." She paused, scanning her uncle's distant, thoughtful expression for a moment, then: "What is it, Uncle Stu? You heard something about the new wing in Plattsburgh? They're really going to do it? An all-Reserve composite air battle wing?"

"Yes," he finally said, speaking to her but still lost in thought. "New York State has approved the expansion of the base for up to eight thousand military and civilian personnel, and expanded flight operations. They want to move a squadron of F-16 fighters, KC-135 tankers, and your RF-111 reconnaissance planes there."

"They are? That's great!" Rebecca crowed. "Can you get me an appointment to meet the new commander? Uncle Stu, I would be forever grateful. I'd really make you proud of me." She paused as she noticed that lost, faraway stare again. "You can't recommend me for a slot? Because I'm not a Vermont resident?" No reaction. "Because I'm a *woman?* Is that it?"

"No, that's not it . . . well, in a way, it is," Senator Furness stumbled. "There are a few provisions of the bill that I don't like. First, they want to take the 158th Interceptor Group out of Burlington and move them to Plattsburgh to form the new air battle wing."

"I'm sure you can work out something."

"I don't want to just give it away, Rebecca," Stuart Furness said. "Having a military base in your home state that another state wants has real value."

"Can't they just take it? Can't the Pentagon just order it moved?"

"They can, and they have tried," Senator Furness said. "But although we have a Democrat in the White House and a Democratically controlled Congress, we Republicans in the Senate can still shake things up a bit. They want the 158th—and they want a lot more, too. So they're going to have to pay for it."

"What other things do they want?"

"The big one, Rebecca. The Great Experiment. Women in combat. They want to start putting women in some combat positions this year."

"You're kidding! They're really going to do it?"

"The President made a promise during his State of the Union address, and it looks like he's going to keep it." Senator Furness sighed. "A draft resolution has been in the works for years, but it's never made it out of committee. The Senate sent it to committee last week. My committee." He stood, walked to the front of his desk, and sat on a corner to be closer to his niece. "I'm opposed to the measure."

"You are?"

"I think women have no business in the military, period, to be perfectly honest," her uncle said. "But women in combat, I feel, would be a great mistake. But be that as it may, the House and the President have decided that women should be allowed into certain combat specialties. Top of the list will be Air Force female combat pilots." He paused, studying his niece. She wore an excited expression with a hint of a smile. "Your thoughts, Rebecca?"

"I think it's about time," Rebecca replied quickly. "I think it's a good idea."

"Even with certain . . . extraordinary conditions?"

"What sort of conditions?"

The Senator ticked off the ideas one by one on his fingers, watching his niece carefully for her reactions. "One, they must be experienced—no UPT graduates or FAIPs—First-Assignment Instructor Pilots. Captain or higher, aircraft commander, with at least two thousand hours' total time as pilot in command."

"Nothing extraordinary about that," Rebecca said.

"I'm not finished, my dear. Two—and it's the big one—mandatory, flight-surgeon-supervised, long-term contraception or voluntary sterilization."

"*What?*" Rebecca retorted. "Sterilization? Why?"

"Two reasons. One, pregnant women who strap on a G-suit, climb around fuel and hydraulic fluid, and start pulling lots of Gs can harm a fetus, and I would hate to see that. Children, even unborn children, mean everything to me, and I will not pass a law that could knowingly harm an innocent child.

"Secondly, a woman captured during wartime *will* get raped by her captors," the Senator continued. "No nation locked in war, even those who hold human rights dear, as we do, can guarantee that women captured in combat will not be raped. Obviously the woman can't be concerned with oral contraceptives, because she won't have them after captivity, so the contraceptive method would have to be long-term and unobtrusive, like Norplants or sterilization."

"Norplants?"

"Subcutaneous implants that meter hormones into the body. It lasts for two to three years. You've heard about 'em."

"I should think women would consider that a violation of their rights or something."

"Many will. But women need to make a choice—combat or children. If you want the gift of being able to carry a child, you can't go off to fight. If you want the right to bear arms to defend your country, you should be willing to accept the responsibility of not exposing an unborn human being to such danger."

Rebecca Furness was watching her uncle in stunned silence—she found herself nodding in agreement. "Actually, it . . . you know, Uncle Stuart, it makes sense to me as well. But are you proposing that women who fly in combat can't have children at all?"

"The mandatory contraception or sterilization would take care of that question. Women must make a choice—flying in combat or children. Children may come before or after your flying assignment, but not during. Could a combat pilot afford to miss twelve to twenty-four months of training because of pregnancy and family leave?"

"No way," Rebecca replied. "The unit would need to find a replacement, then find another slot for her when she returns.

It would mean one extra crewmember for every woman in your unit."

"Which would not be acceptable in this day and age of cost-cutting," the Senator said.

"This is getting pretty complicated."

"I'm glad you think so," Senator Furness said. "The public thinks it is an easy call—simply let women do everything men can do."

"It seems to me that if a woman can pass the same qualification standards that exist right now in those other specialties, she should be allowed to serve," Rebecca said. "But don't exclude women just because they're women—exclude them because they're not right for the job."

Senator Furness looked off for a moment, lost in thought once again; then: "Now I have a serious topic for discussion, Rebecca, and it has to do with you. Tell me about the morning of January 17, 1991, Rebecca."

Rebecca opened her mouth to say something, then closed it in surprise. "I know it's classified, Rebecca," the Senator added. He opened a drawer, showed her a red-covered folder with Top Secret/NOFORN marked on it, flipped it open to a page marked by a paper clip, and put his finger on a specific paragraph. It was a short profile on one Captain Rebecca Cynthia Furness, U.S. Air Force, situated within the text of a detailed report on the incident with the FB-111 bomber over Iraq during Desert Storm. "I know their side of the story. Tell me yours."

She did, in short descriptive sentences and making no apologies. After another short pause she asked, "Is that the reason why I can't get a job? Why no Reserve or Guard unit will hire me?"

"Partly so," Senator Furness said. "But it is also one of the most stirring stories I've heard about the Gulf War. It is the story of a true combat hero. Had you not done what you did that morning, the entire complexion of the war could have changed in a matter of hours. The Coalition could have lost the war, and Saudi Arabia and Israel could be in the hands of the Iraqis right now."

"I don't understand. Why? What was that FB-111 doing?" And then she stopped. She suddenly understood.

"I can't get into it with you, Rebecca," Senator Furness said uneasily. "Most commanders below four-star rank don't know the particulars either, so they just assume you screwed up very badly and they don't want to have you in their organization, period. I saw this happening, but I could do nothing to help you—until now.

"I'm going to see how badly they want women in combat, Rebecca. I'm going to use you as a guinea pig. If you want the challenge, if you think you can stand the heat, I'm going to do it."

"Do what?"

"Rebecca, I'm going to make you the first woman combat pilot in the United States Air Force," Senator Furness said proudly. "Not only that, but I'm going to put you in command of a hot new weapon system, the RF-111 strike/reconnaissance plane, at Plattsburgh Air Force Base. It'll be a Reserve assignment, and it won't be a brand-new F-15E or F-22 fighter, but you will be the first American woman to fly in combat. How does that sound?"

Well, it had sounded great, of course. The Women in Combat law was passed, allowing women to apply and compete for all combat specialties, in all branches of service. Women could even compete for elite combat units, such as the Navy SEALS or Army Special Forces, although it was acknowledged by all that few if any women could hope to pass the rigorous physical requirements of those jobs.

Like the Mercury astronauts in the sixties, the first women combat soldiers in each branch of service were chosen, and they were put on display for the whole world to see, one from each of the Air Force, Army, Navy, and Marine Corps. Not all were pilots, and not all services were anxious to have women combat crewmembers, which reflected in their initial assignments. Rebecca Furness got the best of the lot as aircraft commander of a new Reserve RF-111; the Marine Corps woman pilot got a CH-53 Super Sea Stallion transport helicopter, operating in a combat training battalion at Twentynine Palms Marine Corps Depot in California; the Navy copilot received a Navy Reserve P-3 Orion submarine chaser based in Brunswick, Maine; and the woman Army warrant officer, the first noncommissioned female crewmember in the United States, became a crew chief/gunner in a Washington Air National Guard AH-1T Super Cobra gunship. Their training progress was given extensive media coverage—even down to photographers and news crews waiting outside the clinic to interview Rebecca after her Norplant contraceptives had been inserted.

Despite life in a media fishbowl, Furness scored near the top of her RF-111 Fighter Lead-In class in almost every aspect—bombing, gunnery, precision course control, and emergency procedures—and scored impressively well in physical training tests. Her arrival at Plattsburgh Air Force Base coincided with the standup ceremonies for the new 394th Air Battle Wing (AF Res), the first Reserve composite combat air wing, and the dedication of the new RF-111, nicknamed the Vampire.

Nearly a thousand women were now flying combat aircraft in the Air Force, and almost every month brought news stories of yet another traditional male-dominated job being taken by a woman. Although it was very routine work for her now, Rebecca Furness still enjoyed a bit of celebrity status because of her rapid rise in authority within the unit. She became a flight commander just a few months ago, and because of her rank and skill, she was in line to become "A" Flight commander and operations officer in another year and then compete for an Air Command and Staff College slot. Her goal: to be squadron commander within five years, go to Air War College, and to become bomber/recce group commander within ten years.

And she was determined to do it.

13

394th Air Battle Wing (Reserve) Headquarters Command Center Plattsburgh Air Force Base, New York That Same Time

"In summary, the situation in Europe has gotten much worse," Major Thomas Pierce, the 394th Air Battle Wing chief of intelligence said to the dozen persons seated before him in the tiny wing command post at Plattsburgh Air Force Base. "As I stated in my intelligence summary sheet, the Pentagon feels a state of war definitely exists between Russia, the Ukraine, Moldova, and Romania over the Dniester Republic, especially given the unpredictability—and presumed unstable mental state—of Russian President Velichko. Another air invasion can be expected at any time. What effect this will have on continental U.S. units, particularly ours, is hard to guess, knowing the current administration's unwillingness to commit to combat. However, we should expect some action fairly soon. Any more questions?" There were none, so Pierce, a somewhat nerdy but studious forty-year-old, took his seat.

Brigadier General Martin Cole, the old war-horse commander of the 394th Air Battle Wing, was silent for a long moment after Pierce sat down. The atmosphere in the tiny room next to the Wing communications center was quiet and reserved, yet charged with dreaded electricity. Cole was a twenty-six-year veteran of the United States Air Force and the Air Force

Reserve, after serving in a wide variety of positions from duty officer of a radar post in the Aleutians to assistant to the Chief of Staff of the Air Force, and this was his first Reserve combat command. After a year on the job, he was faced with one of the biggest challenges of his long career. He was going on fifty years, and his black hair was thinning, so he kept it cut in a flattop.

"Thank you, Major." Cole sighed, rubbing the bridge of his nose to relieve a bit of the tension he was feeling. "I think that clearly explains the gravity of the warning order issued by Strategic Command at Offutt this morning." It was only about six A.M., but they had all been up for the past two hours when a warning order message from United States Strategic Command, Offutt Air Force Base, Omaha, Nebraska, came in. Strategic Command, formerly the Strategic Air Command, was a joint services command that managed America's nuclear arsenal. Unlike the early days, when SAC controlled all the land-based intercontinental nuclear-armed bombers and missiles, Strategic Command, or STRATCOM, had no aircraft or weapons, only plans and target lists—until war was imminent. Then Strategic Command could "gain," or take control of, any weapon system it required to carry out the plans and missions as directed by the President of the United States.

That time was coming.

"Strategic Command headquarters has advised me that the possibility exists that within the next seventy-two hours all aircraft of the Fifth Air Battle Force, including our units, may be placed on DEFCON Level Four, or higher, for the first time since 1991," Cole said solemnly. "Within three days, we could be back to pulling nuclear alert once again." DEFCONs were Defense Configurations, with DEFCON Five being peacetime and DEFCON One being all-out nuclear war.

There was a murmur of voices through the room, and eyes all around the semicircular table showed both surprise and grave concern. All throughout the Cold War, in order to prove to America's enemies that the country could not be defeated in a surprise attack, American strategic nuclear forces stood on round-the-clock alert. The level of those alert duties changed with world tensions, from peacetime to all-out war.

In 1991, when President George Bush removed all but some nuclear-powered sea-launched ballistic-missile submarines from strategic nuclear alert, the forces stood at DEFCON Five for the first time in over thirty years. They remained that way ever since—until now.

"The warning order," Cole continued, "directs no specific DEFCON or posture for any of the forces, according to STRATCOM regulations. However, it does direct the commanders to evaluate the readiness of his forces and to report his overall readiness state to the Commander in Chief when so directed. Air Combat Command regulations spell out the nature of that readiness review, and that is the regulation we'll follow. I need every group commander to go over those ACC regulations. You'll find they direct a preliminary readiness review report within twelve hours, and a full report with all squadron commanders within twenty-four hours. I make my report to Air Battle Force headquarters six hours later, and the full report goes to Strategic Command, the Pentagon, and the White House within forty-eight hours."

Colonel Greg McGwire, the Operations Group commander, in charge of all the aircraft and aircrews at Plattsburgh, shook his head and leaned back in his seat. "General, with all due respect, how in the hell am I supposed to do that?" he asked in total exasperation. "I'm just starting Hell Week. Everyone is scheduled to fly, including you and me and most of the staff. I've already asked my squadron commanders and some of the flight commanders to work six extra unpaid days a month just to keep up with the paperwork—they don't have the time to do anything else but train during Hell Week."

"Greg, the request from STRATCOM was not optional or negotiable," Cole said.

"STRATCOM puts us through this just to know if we're ready to fight?" McGwire asked irritably. "General, we demonstrate our mobility capability, our operational flexibility, and our warfighting skills *every* day. Send the bean-counters out here and we'll show them!"

"Enough, Colonel," Cole interrupted, lighting up an expensive cigar. "You'll have your opportunity to show General Layton how good your folks are. After all, he's arriving to inspect the Bravo exercise in about an hour." McGwire rolled his eyes wearily, wearing a pained expression as if his back had just broken under the last straw. Cole continued. "I want to see those preliminary reports on my desk by eighteen hundred hours—that'll give us time to clean them up before we transmit them. Get your staffs and your squadron commanders together and get those reports in.

"And just to make matters worse," Cole concluded, taking a big puff of the cigar, "the Reserve training week will continue as planned, and the warning order is not to be discussed outside this office. If necessary, you can tell your staffs that the preliminary readiness report was ordered by Fifth Air Battle Force, period—further explanation is not necessary and not permitted. Questions?"

No response—everyone was eager to get out of there so they could open the regs and start cranking out the paperwork.

"That is all."

The group commanders bolted for the door. Only two men remained: Colonel James Lafferty, the vice commander of the Air Battle Wing, and the Wing's newest group commander, Daren Mace. "Have a seat, Colonel Mace—it'll probably be the last bit of rest you get in quite a while," Lafferty said. Lieutenant Colonel Daren Mace took his seat at the battle staff conference table. Lafferty went over to ask the clerk for coffee, and General Cole used that distraction to get a first look at his newest Wing staff officer. He studied him, in between drags on his cigar.

Frankly, Cole thought, he certainly looked like he could cut the mustard. Well-built, obviously in shape, perfect grooming, alert green eyes. Somewhere in the back of Cole's mind, the image of Daren Mace seemed familiar . . . like one of those faces on television, or that blond guy in the movies his wife always swooned over. The Condor guy. Redfern, or something like that. Cole nodded to himself, savoring the cigar. Yeah, that was it. He looked like that guy in the movies.

He also, Cole thought, looked a helluva lot more like some hot-shit pilot than an Aircraft Maintenance Group commander. Sure, Maintenance was the toughest job on the base, bar none—in charge of three friggin' squadrons and over two thousand men and women, working round-the-clock every day of the year. Tough as hell. No wonder they had the largest percentage of disciplinary actions, AWOLS, personnel turnover, and job dissatisfaction of any group on base. But as Cole himself knew, it was also the most vital position on base, save for that of the wing commander himself, though it was usually occupied by a full colonel. Mace would have to really hump to stay on top of this job.

"Welcome to the 394th Air Battle Wing, Colonel Mace,"

Cole finally said as Lafferty closed the door to the battle staff conference room. "We seem to have brought you on board right in the middle of a hornet's nest, I'm afraid."

Mace shrugged casually and said, "Bravo exercises are important, sir. It'll give me a good opportunity to see the unit at work. And I'm accustomed to working in the midst of an alert as well. Old home week for me."

Mace's last assignment before this one had been as the senior weapons and tactics training officer of the Thirty-seventh Tactical Group at Incirlik Air Base in Turkey, training NATO crewdogs how to fight together as teams. That was back in '93 and '94. The group commander, Colonel Wes Hardin, had said Mace had done a helluva job, running circles around others Hardin had had in that position. The fact that he probably knew more than anyone else in the country of the F-111 weapon system didn't hurt either.

"I'm uh, sorry that Colonel Lambford couldn't be here to help you with the transition, but he, uh . . . well . . ." Cole was nervously rolling his cigar, clearly uncomfortable talking about it. Lafferty and McGwire were doing all they could to suppress smiles, knowing the reason for Cole's discomfort: everyone, including Mace, was aware that Lambford, the old MG (Maintenance Group Commander), had been kicked out of the unit and discharged for calling his squadron commanders' wives while their husbands were on duty, trying to engage them in phone sex. When the commanders found out, they kicked him out so fast he landed right in a psychiatric hospital somewhere. Lafferty and McGwire joked that he was probably playing with himself in some rubber room, trying to figure out what went wrong.

". . . well," Cole continued, "I just want to assure you that you'll get all the help you need from Colonel Lafferty here, Colonel McGwire, and, of course, myself."

Mace said, "Thank you, sir. Colonel Lafferty, in fact, has already been very helpful in working on my relocation, so I don't think the transition will be too bad." Mace watched calmly as Lafferty's eyes clouded in confusion, not sure whether Mace was setting him up or not. As they both knew, Lafferty, instead of really being helpful, had tried to pass off the new arrival's sponsorship duties to his staff, and the staff dropped the ball. Nobody in the room, or Lafferty's staff, knew where Mace was living; if he had a family or what any of his needs were. Nothing. Which was fine with Mace.

"Where are you coming from, Daren?" Cole asked.

"Air Command and Staff College, in residence, just after getting RIFed and getting my Reserve commission," Mace replied. "Before that, I was the deputy commander of maintenance for the 7440th Provisional Wing at Incirlik, primarily in charge of the bomber maintenance departments."

"You were assigned to Incirlik after Desert Storm ended? For Operation Provide Comfort?" Cole asked, raising an eyebrow.

"Yes, sir. I was there for the Islamic War, too."

Operation Provide Comfort, the American air blockade of northern Iraq, was at first passed off as nothing more than a public relations effort by the Bush administration—no one knew that the 7440th Provisional Wing had single-handedly kept the Persian Gulf War from reigniting several times. Jordan, Syria, and Iraq had tried to break the blockade, singly and collectively, and were pushed back by the 7440th's F-15E and F-111 fighter-bombers, and by Turkish F-16s. Overseeing the maintenance for that unit must have been a true nightmare.

Cole noticed Mace's unpolished silver command navigator's wings on his uniform and asked, "Did you fly in Desert Storm?"

Mace hesitated for a moment, then smiled before replying, "Yes, sir."

"I know you were assigned to the 337th Test Squadron at McClellan just before Desert Storm, and an FB-111 squadron before that," Cole said. "Were you involved with the testing for the five-thousand-pound GBU-28 'bunker buster' bomb? That was an incredible development project."

"I can't really discuss my role in Desert Storm, sir," Mace interjected. That denial confirmed Cole's suspicions. "Besides, it was a time I'd just as soon forget."

"It was a great victory, Colonel," Lafferty said, pleased that Mace hadn't hung him out to dry in front of Cole, now kissing his ass. "We should all be proud of it."

"I think the victory we won was not the victory we wanted, sir," Mace said.

"You mean we should have gotten that bastard Saddam Hussein once and for all," Lafferty said. "I agree." Mace was about to open his mouth—to agree, to disagree, to argue, to curse, Cole couldn't tell—but he merely nodded and said nothing.

"Well, we're damned glad to have you aboard, Colonel," Cole said with satisfaction. "It's good to see you came early to in-process, because we need you out on the line today to kick off the Bravo exercise. And you'll need to give a briefing for General Layton later on today." Mace smiled a bit when he heard the name. "You know the General?" asked Cole.

"We've spoken," Mace replied, that same small smile on his face, being careful not to mention that Layton and that ass Army boss Eyers had once ordered him to launch a nuclear missile during Desert Storm that would have killed thousands of people and wiped out half of ancient Babylon in the process—and whacked him for not doing it, *then* praised him for not doing it. "We've not kept in touch, though. I didn't know he was Fifth Air Battle Force commander until he recommended me for the MG position here."

"You might have a chance to get reacquainted," Cole said. "I hate to have you give a dog and pony show on your first day in the harness, Colonel, but we'll give you all the help you need—just let us know. I understand you'll be flying with the squadrons once or twice a month—excellent. I think all the MGs should get some flying time—Lambford never cared to fly. You can't command a maintenance group from your office."

"I agree one hundred percent, sir," Mace replied.

"Excellent." Cole opened a drawer and handed Daren Mace a small foldup cellular phone, spare batteries, a laminated card with phone numbers of the other wing staff officers on it, and car keys with a white plastic Ident-O-Plate vehicle service card attached to the key ring. "Tools of the trade for the MG, Colonel. Your car is outside, gassed up and ready to go. I hope you have utility uniforms handy, then, Daren, because your first task is to grease up eight Vampires for deployment in about twelve hours."

"I'll be changed before I leave headquarters, sir. I want to meet with my staff as soon as possible."

"It's only six A.M., Colonel."

"They've been waiting since five-thirty, sir," Mace replied. "I called them in when I got the call from you."

Cole blinked his surprise, then looked at Lafferty. "Good. Very good. I'll let you get to it, then." They shook hands all around, and Mace saluted and departed the battle staff room.

"What do you think, Jim?" Cole asked, stubbing out the last of his cigar after the newcomer had left.

"Not bad. Maybe a bit too officious," Lafferty said. "But as long as he's got what it takes."

"General Layton installed him in the slot himself. Vouched for him personally," Cole said, rising out of his chair. "Air Combat Command didn't bat an eye. He must be hot stuff."

"Right. But how come we can't find out what he did in Turkey or in Desert Storm?" Lafferty asked. "Pretty strange, if you ask me."

"Doesn't matter," Cole decided. "He may be Layton's fair-haired boy then, but he's in Plattsburgh now. This job has a way of bringing out the worst in a man, and his honeymoon ended about five minutes ago. Let's just hope he doesn't end up in a rubber room like Lambford. Jesus."

The standard Air Force dark-blue station wagon was hubcap deep in snow, and Mace had to brush four inches of snow off the windows and put tire chains on it himself—as if by magic, no one came out of the front door of the headquarters building for the entire time he was working on the car to help him out. Thankfully, the car started on the second try, and he headed for the flight line.

If the sorry status of his vehicle was any indication of the status of the entire Maintenance Group, Mace grimly thought, he was in for a very long tour of duty. If the group couldn't take care of one lousy car, how could they take care of a billion dollars' worth of war machines?

For a few stirring moments he forgot about the bone-chilling cold and looked over the aircraft parked on the ramp—*his* aircraft, until the aircrews signed for them, he reminded himself—especially the sleek, deadly RF-111G Vampire reconnaissance/strike aircraft. Man, what a beauty.

They had once been FB-111A strategic nuclear bombers, back when Daren Mace flew them not too long ago. Everyone said now that the Cold War was dead the world no longer needed nuclear bombers. Sure. That little presumption could end any day now, thanks to the conflict raging in Europe. The military had taken the supersonic FB-111 and given it a photo, radar, and electronic reconnaissance capability. Their top speed was Mach-two, over twice the speed of sound, and with terrain-following radar and advanced avionics, the RF-111G Vampire was one of the world's greatest combat aircraft, even after almost thirty years of service. Of course, this version still retained its strike capability, including laser-guided bombs, antiship missiles, TV-guided bombs and missiles, antiradar missiles, and thermonuclear bombs and missiles. . . .

. . . Like the AGM-131X missile he had almost launched during the opening hours of Desert Storm. . . .

He shuddered even thinking about that day. Besides its being the most harrowing day of his life—flying that Aardvark through Indian country with nothing more than glue holding it together—it also ended on the worst possible note. After almost killing himself to save the camp and his pilot, to then be called a . . . traitor. . . .

All for not launching a nuke that he wasn't supposed to launch anyway.

Both he and Parsons survived the crash fairly well, and the two nuclear-tipped missiles were recovered intact, but while Parsons was recovering from his wounds in a hospital, Mace was confined to an empty barracks at Batman Air Base in Turkey, where he was interrogated for three weeks straight. The interrogation took an inordinate amount of time while Washington and the brass played political football, scratching their heads trying to figure out what to do, while covering their fat asses at the same time. As Mace was entering his fourth week in isolation, somebody with balls at the Pentagon and in the Air Force finally decided what had happened wasn't that bad. That perhaps Mace had done the world a favor by not cooking off the nuke, that the war was going to be won anyway . . . so without another word he was released and returned to his unit.

But word got around. How could it not, being stuck in isolation for almost four weeks? Speculation and whispering was passed from one serviceman to another . . . something had happened out over the desert. Something Mace had done that resulted in the injuries sustained by his squadron commander, the destruction of an expensive aircraft, and the failure of a mission . . . all because of him.

"A flake . . ."

"Coward . . ."

"Screwball . . ."

He had heard them all whispered at some point or another, but the most damaging, the most gut-wrenching of all, was the word Parsons himself had muttered: "Traitor."

As the buzz and speculation continued on base regarding Mace's conduct on that mission, he found himself effectively ostracized from the Air Force flying community. He was taken off flying status for several months until being reassigned into a maintenance officer's role in Incirlik, Turkey, and, to his surprise, he found he enjoyed the challenges of keeping dozens of high-tech war machines in the air seven days a week as much as he had being a radar navigator.

Even after he was removed from the Air Force during the Reduction in Forces cutbacks and then given a Reserve commission, Mace knew he wanted back into maintenance. He was still entitled to fly, and he did so to retain his flight pay, but he no longer wanted to kill for his country . . . at least not directly. Instead, he wanted to care for the machine that saved his life that morning.

That was the mark Operation Desert Fire had left on Daren Mace, and though he loved the maintenance work, caring for those planes, his personal life never seemed as orderly as his military one. While he was based in Turkey, he found the more he came into contact with people, the less he wanted to be around them, as if somehow they too knew what had happened in his other life and would question him, hold it against him. Wait and watch for him to screw up again. He knew it was ridiculous, even a bit paranoid, but at least Mace had the strength of introspection to recognize these feelings for what they were—emotional baggage. And yet he decided to live with it until it subsided. During that time, even contact with his family was limited. His romantic life in Turkey was nonexistent. Daren would see someone for a few dates, and then when they learned what kind of job he had, the women would wax about the romanticism of it all, the power of being in a big cockpit, of having that stick right there, controlling everything . . . and then they'd try to get him to tell war stories, make the fantasy even more romantic.

And Daren Mace would cool down. Withdraw, close up. It usually ended up being the last date with the woman in question once she started getting all hot and bothered by his uniform. He frankly didn't see the point. It was his uniform that had put him in the situation he was in there in Incirlik.

Being hammered for something he correctly judged *not* to do.

The price for Desert Fire had been high for him, but over time, he began to feel he had paid down his debt. He had given the Air Force what they wanted—exile in a shithole base. And he had given himself time to do what he needed—recover. But, stuck there, he'd done the best damned job of his life. Not for them, but for himself. And so, when his group commander, Colonel Wes Hardin, had told him in Incirlik that the Air Reserve Personnel Center in Robins, Georgia, had called and said to him that now–Lieutenant General Layton wanted him to become the maintenance group commander for an RF-111G wing, his old FB-111 Aardvark, he jumped at the chance. He had a love for that plane like no other. It meant going back to the beautiful Northeast, back to changing seasons, back to peace and quiet. As an Enhanced Reserve Program member, he would have steady work and good pay and still lots of time to be by himself. He went to Plattsburgh several weeks early, found a part-time job cleaning and servicing beer and drink taps for local area bars and restaurants—Plattsburgh has more bars per square city block than any city in America. He moved into an efficiency apartment downtown, and found himself ready, even excited, to get started as the new MG when he heard the early-morning roar of F-111s taking off. After a lot of downtime, he was glad to be back in the traces.

Now, sitting in his staff car surveying his flight line, he knew he had a daunting task ahead of him—made worse by the warning message from Strategic Command about some possible action very soon. He was going to have to give this unit a real kick in the ass, shake things up. When—not *if* but *when*—the shit hit the fan and they were tasked to go fight overseas, he wanted these warplanes to be ready.

The flight line was virtually deserted. In the growing dawn, Mace could see snow heaped on airframes, fire bottles buried in snow, and taxiways surrounded by ridges of plowed snow and ice so high that visibility was impeded—one mountain of snow near the flight line, piled high by snowplows and truck-powered snowblowers, was over thirty feet high! Mace remembered back to his days at Pease Air Force Base in New Hampshire when they would put a bomb wing flag atop a snowpile like that and take bets on when the flag would reach the ground—mid-May was the best bet—but now, as the MG and not a give-a-shit crewdog, that pile of snow wasn't funny anymore.

A few crew chiefs were out working on planes with no shelters, no warm-up facilities, no support vehicles, not even a power cart to stand beside for warmth. Security police trucks were cruising up and down the taxiways between planes, the drivers slouched down in their seats, coming dangerously close to aircraft wingtips and pitot booms. Only a few of the tall "ballpark" light towers were on, and each tower was missing a good number of lamps. The aircraft were parked next to one another haphazardly, mainly because the crew chiefs or marshalers couldn't see the taxi lines through the snow. The place was a mess. It was time to kick some butt.

Mace's first stop was the nearly empty base operations building, located just below the control tower, where he changed into green camouflage fatigues over thermal underwear, thick wool socks under cold weather mukluks, a grey parka with a fake fur hood, and a gray fur "mailman's" hat (real fur this time) with black subdued lieutenant colonel's rank pinned on the front crown. He grabbed a cup of coffee and a microwaved egg sandwich while receiving a report from the weather shop.

Mace then drove over to Maintenance Group headquarters, located in a large aircraft hangar adjacent to the flight line. He was met inside the front door by Senior Master Sergeant Michael Zaparski, the Group NCOIC (Non-Commissioned Officer In Charge), a short, thick-waisted, barrel-chested, gray-haired man wearing a long-sleeved shirt and tie. "Colonel Mace?" he greeted his new superior officer, opening the door and shaking hands with him. "Glad to see you, sir. Afraid you might have gotten lost."

"Nice to meet you, Sergeant Zaparski," Mace said. "No, not lost, but I wanted to get a weather report first before briefing the staff." He removed his hat, jacket, and gloves, stamped snow off his boots, straightened his fatigues, then turned on his heels and marched into his office, where the three squadron commanders and three division commanders snapped to attention.

The Maintenance Group consisted of three squadrons, whose commanders reported directly to Mace, and three division staffs of deputy commander status. The largest squadron in the group, and the largest single unit in the entire wing, was the 394th Aircraft Generation Squadron (AGS), with over a thousand men and women, who were responsible for day-to-day maintenance, launch, and recovery of the forty-four planes at Plattsburgh. The AGS was divided into two aircraft-maintenance units, or AMUs, one for the RF-111G Vampire reconnaissance/bombers and one for the KC-135E Stratotanker aerial-refueling tankers. Each AMU was composed of the aircraft crew chiefs and assistant crew chiefs who were colocated with their respective flying squadrons and worked side by side with the aircrew members, plus maintenance specialists that assisted and supported the crew chiefs. The 394th Component Repair Squadron repaired avionics, engines, aircraft systems, fabricated aircraft parts, and maintained the sophisticated electronic sensors used in the aircraft; and the 394th Equipment Maintenance Squadron repaired aircraft ground-support vehicles, performed phase and periodic aircraft inspections, maintained and stored the weapons, and maintained the aircraft weapons release and carriage systems. The group's three division staffs—Operations, Quality Assurance, and Personnel—assisted the group commander in carrying out day-to-day operations.

"It's very nice to meet you all, and thank you for coming in so early," Daren Mace said tightly to his assembled staff. "I wish I could sit down, tell you about myself, and give you my philosophy of life, but this is the first day of Hell Week and the flight line looks like shit, so the honeymoon will never even start." The polite smiles on the faces of the squadron and division commanders abruptly disappeared.

Mace's assistant group commander, Major Anthony Razzano, was impatiently standing beside Mace's desk, obviously perturbed at being awakened two hours early. He was wearing a long-sleeve Air Force blue shirt, a clip-on tie, and dark-blue trousers with Corfam shoes—how the hell he made it into the building without getting a shoeful of snow, Mace couldn't figure. Beside the door Mace noticed a young black female lieutenant, Alena Porter, who was the maintenance group's chief of administration—she was in utility uniform, camo fatigues and boots. Every one of the division staff officers except Porter was in blues.

"First off, nobody shows up in this office during Hell Week in anything but utility uniform," Mace said, affixing his gaze briefly on Razzano to hammer down the point. "This is a combat unit getting ready to deploy, and you will wear utility uniforms. Next, I want—"

"Excuse me, sir," Razzano interrupted, obviously interested in testing the boundaries of the new "old man's" style right away, "but it's too uncomfortable to work in this office with fatigues."

"Major Razzano, I was not considering your comfort when I issued my instructions—I was thinking of the combat effectiveness of this unit," Mace said. "However, speaking of comfort . . ." He turned to Major William LeFebre, commander of the Component Repair Squadron. "Major, perhaps you could explain to me why three CRS troops are on the ramp working on aircraft without a shelter."

LeFebre shrugged his shoulders, looking for help from anyone else in the room, not finding any, then stammering, "I . . . I didn't know about that, sir . . ."

"And why, Major Razzano, was Civil Engineering not advised to clear my ramp and taxiways so my maintenance troops can get out to their planes?" To the Aircraft Generation Squadron commander, Major Charles Philo, he said, "And why do my planes have six inches of snow on them? And why don't I have six airplanes in the shelters ready to generate this morning? You know there's going to be a Bravo exercise, Major."

"Sir, we don't usually start generating aircraft until we're given the word from headquarters," Philo said. "We're supposed to act as if we've been given a mobility order . . . you know, go from a standing start . . . ?"

"Don't give me that *crap*, Major," Mace retorted. "That sounds like a line of bullshit from some of the old, lazy MGs that used to be around, the MGs and their staffs who allow snow to pile up on combat aircraft and who allow their troops to stand in knee-deep snow in freezing weather. This is a *combat* unit, people. We don't do exercises—exercises are for units that have a mission only if combat starts. We *train* for war. Does everybody understand this concept? We don't need exercises, we need to be ready to go to war at any time. Is that clear to everyone?"

"But sir, we're not at war," the Equipment Maintenance Squadron commander, Major Emily Harden, interjected.

"You listen to the news this morning, Major?" Mace interrupted. "You know about Russia invading the Ukraine?" Judging by the expressions on some of the faces around him, it was obvious that many in the room, including Razzano, did *not* know about the events happening half a world away.

"Of course, sir," Harden replied uneasily. "But I'm referring to this Reserve training week. Bravo exercises are not preparations for war—they're just, well, *exercises.*"

"Sergeant Zaparski, give me a copy of the tasking order for this week's 'exercise' and give it to the Major," Mace said. Zaparski did as he was told. "Read it, Major, and tell me if you find the words 'exercise,' 'simulated,' or any such term in there."

Harden read the message quickly, her eyes widening in surprise. After a few seconds, she said, "Well . . . no, but we're deploying to Plattsburgh, for one thing. We're loading training weapons . . ."

"Major, I can assure you, a real deployment order looks exactly the same as that order does," Mace said. "The location may be different, and the weapons loadout would be different, but the order looks just like that one. Now, if you knew that a war was coming, would you wait for that piece of paper to arrive before you began to prepare?"

"But this *is* an exercise, sir," Harden said resolutely. "It's training, pure and simple. We have certain rules, certain 'academic situation' changes that differentiate this from an actual deployment. To give you an example, it says prepackaged mobility stockpiles in certain categories will not be available. Now I *know* they're available, because I check them myself, so it means they're simulated for this exercise."

"Those items are gone, Major," Mace said. "I got the word this morning. They were loaded on a LogAir flight and departed about four hours ago—coincidentally, this was a few hours after the Russian air attack in the Ukraine. Everyone get the *picture?*" Mace could see his new staff member's eyes widening in surprise—they were indeed getting the picture. "Nine pallets, eleven-point-seven-two tons, intermediate destination Langley Air Force Base, final destination is classified."

"That's crazy," Harden said incredulously. "They can't take prepack mobility items without coordinating with me!"

"They can and they did—I confirmed it with Resource Plans Division," Mace said. "They were going to let us know just before the battle staff meeting. You people just lost half your prepackaged spares and tools, and you didn't even know it. We're behind the eight ball, people. You think you know it all, you think you got it wired, you think it'll all go smoothly—and you're all *wrong.*

"Now I know, and *you* know, that the commander is going to order us to generate eighteen bombers and twenty-two tankers in a few hours. Why are we sitting on our asses? Why aren't my ramps plowed? Why aren't we prepared to go to war around here? And how in the hell can you people think that everything is normal when the fucking Russians sent a full squadron of Bear bombers on an obvious cruise-missile launch run over the Ukraine just a few hours ago?

"For us, war begins right *now*, and I don't just mean the Bravo exercise. I want six . . . no, I want eight planes in the shelters immediately, fueled and ready to upload, and from now on I want eight aircraft in those shelters at all times in four-hour generation status. Is that clear?"

"Eight planes on round-the-clock four-hour status?" Razzano asked wide-eyed, already calculating his work load with dread. Four-hour status meant that all of the weapons preload functions had been accomplished, the aircraft had been fueled and preflighted by AGS, and it was ready to upload weapons—no more than four hours from start to fully combat-ready. "Sir, it takes more manpower to get a plane up to weapon preload status than normal training status—keeping eight planes in weapons preload status will be a nightmare. We need to coordinate with security, get permission from Logistics and Mobility to service the shelters—"

"Gentlemen and ladies, whatever it takes, I want it *done*. Weapon preload status will be our *normal* aircraft status from now on," Mace said, impatiently holding up a hand to silence Razzano. "I will not tolerate this arbitrary 'training' status on my airframes. The normal day-to-day status of *all* airframes in a combat unit such as ours is supposed to be category two, which is at least 50 percent of all aircraft in combat preload status. I see nothing in the regs or the wing ops plan that directs the MG of this wing to keep his planes in anything other than combat preload status, so that is what we will do.

"We have eight alert shelters on our flight line, and from now on I want all eight of them filled with bombers ready to upload weapons or photo pods. The same goes with our tankers—I want twelve planes, not just four, on strip alert status, fueled, preflighted—deiced and ready to fly in thirty minutes. Is that clear?"

Heads with surprised faces nodded all around the room.

"Next item," Mace continued. "Squadron commanders, your

place is on the flight line with your troops, not in the office with your feet up. I know you all have paperwork and administrative chores to do, but when you're not working on squadron business I want you on the flight line or in the shops with your troops. They need to see the officer cadre, and you need to know what they need and where the bottlenecks are. You all have cellular phones, so start learning to work on the move with them. Is that clear?" He received murmured "Yes, sirs" from the squadron commanders.

"In order to make the previous directive work, I want division staffs to start taking over the routine daily functions of the squadrons," Mace continued. "Security, compliance, safety, manuals, training, inprocessing—I want all that stuff handled by the division staff instead of each squadron having its own safety officer, newcomers officer, training officer, and so on. These units are spending too much valuable time on shuffling papers and not enough time fixing airplanes, and that will stop right now." Now it was the squadron commanders' turn to smile, and the division staff officers' turn to look grumpy and displeased. Routine staff functions and additional duties not involving aircraft maintenance did eat up a lot of every airman's time, and finally the squadrons were going to get some relief.

"That's all I have right now, ladies and gents—we have airframes to generate. I'll see you all in the field. Major Razzano, a word before you leave."

When the door to Mace's office was closed behind the departing squadron and division staff officers, Razzano crossed his arms on his chest and said, "Well, I think you got everybody's attention now. What do you do for an encore?"

"We make it work, Tony," Mace said, running a hand through his blond hair. "It'll be a ball-buster, but it's gotta be done. We're going to do it until someone orders me to stop." Mace paused for a moment, waiting for another challenge from Razzano; then, when all he got was a disapproving, skeptical glare, Mace asked, "Why didn't they make you group commander, Tony?"

"Why ask me, sir?"

"I checked your records: you have more specialty experience than I do, and although you're not a flyer, that's never been a requirement for MG. Why aren't you in command? I don't see anything in your records that would have disqualified you."

Razzano was obviously stung by the pointed question, and

Mace could see the ire rising in his face: "Why aren't you a wizzo anymore, sir?" Razzano asked, clearly agitated. "I heard you screwed the pooch back in the Sandbox. Is that why they stuck you in maintenance, sir?"

The question stung Mace a little, but it didn't slow his response down. "You're not privileged to hear that information, Major, but I can tell you this: yes, I had my eyes open and my brain in gear and I didn't let anybody else tell me what was bullshit or the truth. Yeah, I got hammered for it, and yeah, I got stuck in maintenance over in Turkey. But when I got in maintenance, I kicked ass. Now I'm the MG for the only Vampire wing in the goddamned world, I still got my promotion, and I still got my wings.

"I know you, Tony. I got the same give-a-shit attitude as you," Mace lectured. "The difference between you and me is that you go around saying, 'I don't give a shit,' and it doesn't get done, while I say, 'I don't give a shit,' and I press on and do it anyway. Most people don't care what you do, Major—they just want you to take charge, take responsibility, do *something*. That's what I want to do.

"I know guys like you, too. You play golf with the brass, go boating together, go to each other's picnics. You can stop me from doing the things I want to do. The question is, are you going to play ball with me or are we going to tangle?"

"You're the MG, sir," Razzano said, "but I've been running this shop now for four years. You want my help, we gotta work together."

"You know how to put together an ACC readiness report?"

The question took Razzano by surprise. He hesitated, searched his memory, then replied, "No, sir, but I—"

"Lieutenant Porter!" Mace shouted through the door. A few seconds later, Porter opened the door and stood in the doorway. "Lieutenant, you know how to put together an ACC readiness report?"

"All I need is the message time, sir," Porter replied.

"Good. Lieutenant Porter, you are the new chief of staff." Her mouth dropped open in surprise. "And since the MG is not authorized by regulation to have a vice commander, Major Razzano, and since you're not qualified to be either chief of staff or MG, you are out of a job. Report to General Cole's office for reassignment."

"*What?*" Razzano retorted. "Hey, you can't do that!"

"I can and I did," Mace said. "I just got here, Major, but I know the regs better than you do. You were made vice MG because the last two MGs were weak-dicks, but they didn't make you the MG, so that makes you a weak-dick too. This group was in your hands for four years, and you let it go to hell, and you've obviously demonstrated your unwillingness to work with me, so you're out of here.

"Oh, and one last piece of advice, for whoever the next unlucky sonofabitch is you happen to work for: impress the new boss, even if you think *he's* a dickhead or you think *you* should have gotten his job. Shovel his staff car out of the snow, drive him to his headquarters, shovel the sidewalks leading to his headquarters, spiff the place up, and make him coffee when he arrives in his office for the first time. You can't even suck up properly. You're out That is all."

Razzano was so embarrassed, so deflated, that he stormed out of the office too shocked to say another word.

"Lieutenant, you're a captain, effective today," Mace said. "Field promotions are authorized in case of unusual staff requirements, are they not?"

"Yes, sir," she replied sheepishly, "with command approval within. . . ."

"I'll either get the approval immediately or get myself shit-canned. In any case, you're authorized to wear the new rank until the orders come down. I suggest you have the clerk send your utility uniforms out to the parachute shop to get the rank changed right away—don't ask me why. The ACC action message came down two hours ago. When can you have the report ready for me?"

"Preliminary report immediately, sir," Porter said. "The divisions update the group status daily on the computer. Full report in about two hours."

"Good answer, Lieutenant," Mace said with a hint of a smile—this one knew what she was doing! "Call me on the phone as soon as the full report is ready. You're in charge of the office and the staff, and your signature is as good as mine as of right now."

He headed for the outer office and started putting on his jacket and gloves. "I'm heading out to the flight line," he told Porter, "but I don't want to see that station wagon ever again after today. Tell Transportation I want the largest vehicle they have with four-wheel drive, preferably a step-up maxi-van. I want all the FM and UHF radios and telephones on board, I want exterior floodlights front and rear, a crew bench in back with heaters, and I want it equipped just like the maintenance supervisor's truck. No use in anyone driving out on the flight line unless they're carrying spare parts and tools. I want to pick the truck up before lunch. Anything for me, Lieutenant?"

"Yes, sir," Porter said. "I'll need you to block out some time for inprocessing, and I'll need your home address and phone."

"My home address and phone are—" Mace looked at the phone number on his staff officer's cellular phone and gave it to her. "That is where you can reach me, now and forever. Mail my paychecks right here to the office. I'll do all the other inprocessing when the 'war' is over. Have a nice day, Lieutenant." He grabbed his coat, hat, and gloves, and hurried out the door.

Alena Porter returned to her desk in a total state of shock. She picked up the phone to call Transportation—the thought of the MG driving a big, lumbering StepVan supply truck, known as a "bread truck," around the base was a funny thought, but that's what the man wanted—but instead went out to the hallway, put a quarter in the pay phone, and took a few moments to call her mother at home.

"Mom? It's me. The new boss arrived today . . . what's he like? He made me a captain . . . yes, just like that, a captain. He's a wild man, Mom. A wild man."

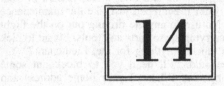

THE FERRY REBECCA FURNESS WAS ON UNCEREMONIOUSLY bumped and slid into the docking slip at Cumberland Head. Furness started the truck's engine and waited her turn to pull out. The roads were much better on the New York side, so she made good time driving into Plattsburgh, arriving at the base a little before seven A.M.

The base was divided into the "old" and "new" sections, with the flight line, flying squadrons, and newer family housing areas in the "new" section (built in the 1930s) to the west, and the command, administrative, and senior housing areas in the "old" section (the original base, established in 1814 and still in use ever since) to the east, bordering Lake Champlain. Instead of heading for the base gym on the east side of the base, Furness took a right turn at the small air museum at the entrance to the "new" base, checked in with the security guard, and headed for the flight line. She had a little time to kill, and Plattsburgh's almost round-the-clock flight line operations were exciting to watch.

The KC-135 Stratotanker aerial-refueling tankers, the largest and loneliest planes on the parking ramp right now, sat silent vigil in the cold morning air. They were going on forty years old, but they would still be in service well after the year 2000, Furness knew. A few of the planes out here, known as R-model tankers, had been re-engined with more modern turbofan airliner engines, which significantly improved their range and load-carrying capability, and a few had been equipped with integral cranes and load-handling devices to give the KC-135 some true bare-base cargo capability. But most of the tankers here at Plattsburgh were A- or E-models, old and slow and underpowered. They were nothing like the new KC-10 tankers, though, Furness thought. The KC-10 could run rings around these beasts. She sometimes missed the old days in the KC-10 Extender, the Air Force's "supertanker"—no alert, few dispersals, comfortable seats, few cold-weather assignments, no cold-weather bases.

But she certainly wasn't complaining.

Rebecca wanted to drive down the flight line road far enough to see "her" plane, number 70-2390, nicknamed "Miss Liberty," but she had run out of time and she had to report in for duty. She made her way to the old side of the base, through another guard gate, drove a few blocks to the base gymnasium, parked in the closest space, grabbed her deployment bag, and headed for the entrance. She saw she was the last to sign in, even though they had fifteen minutes to their scheduled seven A.M. muster time. Anyone reporting in after the scheduled muster time would be given an "incomplete" for the day, and with greater competition for ERP slots, all performance standards, even for Reservists, were stricter than ever before. Being five seconds late for Hell Week could quite possibly get one kicked out of the program for good. The squadron was beginning to line up for inspection, so Furness went over to her place on the gym floor without stopping to exchange pleasantries with anyone.

Plattsburgh had twenty-two RF-111G bombers, matched up with twenty ready crews (eighteen in the squadron plus the squadron and wing commander's planes, leaving one spare plane and one "hangar queen" used for spare parts or ground training). Each plane was assigned a flight crew and a ground crew, both of whom stayed with that plane as long as possible. The Reservists, even in the new ERP that received many former active-duty members, tended to be older, smarter, and, because it was "their" plane and "their" base in "their" hometown, they took a lot of pride in their Reserve duties.

As commander of Bravo Flight, Furness was first in line in the second row. She set her bag down at her feet and lined up directly behind the flight commander of Alpha Flight, Major Ben Jamieson, allowing enough room between her bag and Jamieson's row for the inspector to walk. The rest of her flight lined up on her, and Charlie Flight lined up behind her. After allowing a few moments for everyone to get situated, she stepped out of place and walked down her row to count noses and take a look at her flight before the inspection.

Even though it was considered a "super Reserve" duty, the Enhanced Reserve Program attracted a great variety of characters, and they were all represented right here in Bravo Flight. It was impossible to pinpoint exactly what each crewmember had in common—they all came from diverse backgrounds and had widely varying skill and experience levels:

First Lieutenant Mark "Fogman" Fogelman was Rebecca Furness' weapon system officer, or "wizzo." He graduated with a commission from Air Force ROTC and a degree in business from Cornell University, and was one of the lucky few to draw the new RF-111 fresh out of undergraduate navigator training. The rumor had it that Fogelman's parents, who owned a ski resort and lots of property near Lake Placid, used considerable political pull to get their son a choice assignment, but Furness was not going to bad-mouth that plan of action because she had relied on personal influence as well.

The 715th Tactical Squadron and its sleek, deadly Vampire bomber had attracted a lot of "political" appointees, persons with important families with powerful political ties. Promotion and more desirable positions were almost guaranteed if one was lucky enough to score an RF-111G assignment. It was considered a "front-line" combat assignment—everyone had to be nuclear certified under the Personnel Reliability Program and given a top secret security clearance—but because the unit's primary mission was tactical reconnaissance, it was considered a relatively benign assignment.

Just out of Fighter Lead-In Training at Cannon Air Force Base in New Mexico, "Fogman," only twenty-five years old, was the youngest crewmember in the unit. Because she was so "by the book" and demanding, Rebecca Furness often drew the squadron's new weapon systems officers—it was found that Furness would either straighten the new guys out or drive them so completely nuts that they would quit. She had no doubt that a lot of veteran weapons systems officers preferred not to have a woman aircraft commander, so Rebecca ended up with the new guys who had little say in who they were teamed up with.

The kid never had his uniform completely up to standards, but Rebecca hated helping Fogelman fix his uniform because she always felt like a fussy mother doting over her child. But she had no choice. She ripped the squadron patch off his right sleeve, the F-111 "Go-Fast" patch off his left arm, and swapped the two. "Jesus, Fogman, aren't you ever going to get these straight?"

"I was in a hurry this morning, Becky," he replied, not offering any apologies. He gave *her* flight suit a quick appraisal, found something amiss, and gave her a smug grin. She remembered that she had been rushed, too, and the reason why, and wished she had checked herself in a mirror before reporting in. Oh well, too late now. Besides, she looked ten times better than Fogelman on her worst day. When Fogelman noticed Furness looking at his deployment bag, which looked significantly more empty than everyone else's, he said quickly, "It's all there, Major. I checked."

"I hope so."

"You can check mine if I can check yours," he said smugly.

Furness stepped right up close to Fogman, sticking her face right into his. He did not retreat and had no room to get out of her way—he was trapped. "Was that a joke, Fogelman? Were you trying to make a funny? Or was that a sexual innuendo, like perhaps you were offering to show me your wee-wee? If so, get me a magnifying glass."

Fogelman could feel several pairs of eyes on him now. "Yes . . . I mean, no, I wasn't . . ."

"Or do you want to sniff my underwear? You'd like that, wouldn't you, Fogman? Does women's underwear turn you on? Maybe I'll find some women's underwear in *your* bag if I looked." She backed off right away, giving him a chance to retaliate, but everyone was looking now so he didn't try it. Furness gave him a half-amused, half-exasperated glare and continued on.

She did not presume to try to criticize most of the other members of her flight—they were all fairly experienced flyers. Her wingmen in her flight were Captain Frank Kelly and

Lieutenant Colonel Larry Tobias. Kelly was a five-year veteran of F-111s, and Tobias, the oldest flying crewmember in the unit at age forty-eight, was his weapon system officer. Tobias had seniority over everyone in the squadron except for the squadron commander, Lieutenant Colonel Richard Hembree, but Tobias, a twenty-one-year Air Force veteran, had no command experience, nor had he attended Air Command and Staff College, and so was not eligible for command. He was a flyer, and preferred to stay that way. Furness simply greeted the two crewmembers, asked if they needed anything, and moved on.

Three of her other six crewmembers were new and relatively inexperienced. First Lieutenant Lynn Ogden, married with one child, was a WSO who spent three years as an RC-135 navigator before cross-training to the RF-111. It turned out that Ogden had volunteered for several dangerous reconnaissance missions during Desert Storm, and her reward was a coveted RF-111 assignment. First Lieutenant Paula Norton, unmarried, a former T-38 instructor pilot and C-21 military jetliner pilot, had been a mission specialist candidate for NASA's space shuttle program, and had been given the RF-111 as a sort of consolation prize; she had made it known to everyone, not in words but in her attitude, that being in the 715th Tactical Squadron was a brief "pit stop" on her way to a high-visibility job flying generals and Cabinet officials around in VIP special transport duties like Air Force One. Major Ted Little, married with three children, another WSO and an ex–B-1B bomber navigator, had been out of active duty for nearly two years before joining the Reserves and landing an RF-111. In those two years, he had starred in several major motion pictures, three of which had become major box-office smashes, and had amassed a small fortune. The reasons why he moved from Hollywood to upstate New York, joined the Reserves, and flew the RF-111 were unclear, but he did qualify. Everyone joked he was simply doing research work for another movie. The other five crewmembers—Majors Clark Vest and Harold Rota, and Captains Bruce Fay, Joseph Johnson, and Robert Dutton—were veteran F-111 flyers who had been suddenly and unceremoniously dumped from active duty but had immediately found Reserve billets.

Everyone looked pretty good. Fogelman's hair length was pushing the edge of the envelope, as usual, but that was the worst offense she could see in Bravo Flight. Only Lieutenant Colonel Hembree had access to military personnel and civil records, so there could still be some surprises—having unit members getting busted for DUIs, traffic violations, child support arrears, that sort of thing, was fortunately getting less common, but it still happened once in a while. Furness took her place at the left side of the row and stood at ease until the squadron was called to attention by First Lieutenant Cristina Arenas, the squadron executive officer; then squadron commander Lieutenant Colonel Hembree, operations officer Lieutenant Colonel Alan Katz, and squadron NCOIC Master Sergeant William Tate walked out onto the gym floor precisely at seven-fifteen A.M.

The squadron was ordered to parade rest, and the inspection began.

Rebecca could see this was going to be a tough morning. Colonel Hembree was not picking bags and people at random—he was inspecting everyone. The Alpha Flight commander, Major Ben Jamieson, and his WSO passed, but the first pilot in the flight was pulled out of the ranks and his bag tossed aside by Hembree himself. "Captain, maybe you better just go home and start all over again," Hembree shouted, loud enough for everyone on the floor and almost everyone else in the gym to hear. "Your uniform looks like shit, you got a mustache and sideburns that look like something out of the damned sixties, and it looks like you're ready to deploy to some beach in Florida instead of to a cold-weather base. You just lost one day's training. If you're not back here in one hour with a clean uniform, proper gear and proper grooming, you'll lose the entire week. Get out of my sight."

Hembree broke off his inspection and began circling the squadron like a shark closing in on a wounded whale. Hembree was a big, square-jawed, powerful black man in his late forties, with close-cropped salt-and-pepper hair and dark, electric eyes. His voice all but rattled windows, especially when he was angry—which was right now: "*I will not* have any of you slacking off here. You will report to training week ready to deploy, ready to fly, and ready to fight, or I don't want you here at all. We are not Reservists, dammit—we *are* the United States Air Force. Got that? We are the main combat force. Because we train only two weeks per month, we have to do it better than the active duty units. We have to look sharper, fly better, and move faster. I will not tolerate anyone in this unit who thinks he or she can get away with something here. I am going to pound this fact into you people and make you believe it."

He completed his circle, letting everyone get a taste of the medicine, before resuming his inspection. Fortunately for Ben Jamieson, everyone else in A Flight passed inspection. Hembree assigned Jamieson two nights' worth of duty officer shifts for allowing one of his pilots to report in without his required gear, then moved on to Furness' flight.

She called the flight to attention, saluted, and said, "Bravo Flight, ready for inspection, *sir.*"

Hembree returned Furness' salute, looked up and down the row, then said, "You think you're ready, huh? Well, we'll have to do some pictures first. Perhaps you can tell me about tech order warnings and cautions for the UPD-8 recon pod, Major Furness?"

"Yes, sir," Furness replied immediately. Questions and answers during inspection was something new for Hembree, and this was no idle exercise. Hembree had something on his mind . . . but she had no more time to think about it. She knew the capabilities and functions of all of the eleven different reconnaissance pods that could be fitted to the RF-111 aircraft, and she could recite warnings and cautions in her sleep:

"There are two warnings, two cautions, and seven notes in the tech order about the UPD-8 radar reconnaissance pod," she began. "The most important are: stay clear of the sensor domes until aircraft power and battery power is removed; and ensure all ground crewmen are clear of the aircraft for a distance of at least one hundred feet while running the ground BIT test because of stray emissions—"

Hembree suddenly stepped closer to Furness and interrupted her with, "Did you sleep in that flight suit, Major? It looks like hell." Hembree had caught its postsex rumpled look. Furness fumed inside—not at Hembree, but at Ed Caldwell. Christ, how did she let that happen?

"I know these are only utility uniforms, Major," Hembree snapped, "but if you don't take care of them in peacetime, what assurances do we have that you'll take care of them if we go to war? You have duty officer for two nights after Major Jamieson. Reach into your deployment bag and show me six pairs of wool socks." She quickly did as she was told, then put them back, but Hembree was already moving down the line, so she had to hurry to catch up.

First Lieutenant Mark Fogelman seemed amused by the egg on her face, and Furness wished she could kick him in the balls for wearing that damned grin during open-ranks inspection. Hembree cast an angry look at Fogelman's deployment bag and gave him and Furness a stern, warning look, then moved along. It was obvious that he knew Fogelman didn't have all his gear, and he was silently telling both of them that he knew, but he chose not to put them in a brace about it. That would come later.

"Major Furness, at eleven-thirty A.M. you will brief me on the contents of Air Force reg 35-10 regarding personal grooming standards," Hembree snarled after he finished inspecting Bravo Flight. "Most of your people don't seem to know what those standards are, and since there seem to be so many violations of those standards in your flight, I assume it's because *you* aren't familiar with them. You will also personally ensure that your troops have complied with those regulations. If they have not complied by tomorrow's inspection, you will lose a half day's training for each violation. Is that clear?"

It was clear—and extremely severe. But Furness answered, "Yes, sir."

He finished the inspections for Bravo and Charlie flights quickly, finding one WSO's deployment bag missing a pair of long underwear and nearly throwing the bag out into the hallway in disgust. He went through the crew chief's ranks with the same zeal, this time venting his displeasure at Master Sergeant Tate, his NCOIC, when he found a discrepancy.

"I want another inspection before this week is over, and this time if I find one discrepancy in a deployment bag, I'm sending the offender out in the *street,*" Hembree warned. "This unit *will* be fully combat ready by the end of this week or I'll recommend that Fifth Air Battle Force stand this entire squadron down. Our job is *deployment,* people, and if you're not ready to deploy when you have five days to get ready for it, how the fuck are you going to do it when the call comes in the middle of the goddamned night? Jesus Christ, I will not stand for it! I want performance, I want perfection, or I'll shit-can everybody. Is that *clear?*" Wisely, no one replied. Hembree scowled silently at the entire squadron for a few more seconds, then snapped, "Major Jamieson, take over—if you can." Major

Jamieson called the squadron to attention, but Hembree was already out the door.

They spent a few minutes going over the results of the open-ranks inspection. Mark Fogelman and Paula Norton had been written up for 35-10 violations, and Norton had also been written up for not wearing cold-weather gear for the inspection—she wore a regular cotton T-shirt instead of turtleneck thermal underwear. Furness had Fogelman empty his deployment bag, then turned to Paula Norton. Long hair had to be off the collar while in uniform; she had left two thick strands hang down on each side of her head: "Paula, what gives? You forget how to pin your hair up?"

"Hey, what's with the old man these days?" Norton asked by way of a reply. "He's really got a bug up his ass."

"Forget about the Colonel and fix your hair," Furness said angrily, "unless you want to get kicked out of the program just because some hair is out of place. You know the regs. Why push it? And where's your cold-weather gear?"

"Hell, the Colonel never checked us that close before," Norton sneered. "Usually he checks out my chest and moves on. Did the guy swear off women or what?" Paula Norton was young, blonde, and beautiful, with bright blue eyes and a full, rounded figure. Men of all ages and ranks felt so self-conscious staring at her, especially during an open-ranks inspection while standing at attention, she usually received only cursory glances up close. Hembree was obviously not so distracted this time. "Besides, we just change out of thermals right after the inspection for PT."

"So you thought you'd get ahead of the program by showing up for a winter inspection in a T-shirt?" Furness asked. "Real smart. You have thermals with you, don't you?" Norton nodded. "Have them on for the next inspection. And when it's time to get serious and play war, Paula, even boobs won't distract a guy all the time."

"Tell me about it," Norton lamented as she started to rearrange her hair.

Furness then turned her attention to Fogelman. The little prick had his bag open, but had not begun spreading the contents out as she had asked. "Let's go, Mark, hop to it."

"The Colonel didn't write me up, Major," Fogelman hissed. "Not on my gear."

"Who said anything about your gear, Mark?" Furness asked. The little creep, why in hell would he show up for a required formation knowing he wouldn't pass inspection? "The Colonel gave you a break, then, because your hair is too long and he knows and I know that you don't have all your stuff."

"How do you know that?"

"Fogelman, are you really that dumb or just pretending to be?" Furness said with total exasperation. "Your bag is half the size of everyone else's. Now open it up."

"I wish you'd stop picking on me, Major," Fogelman whined, raising his voice a bit so others in the squadron could hear his complaints. "If you want me out of the flight, just say so."

"What I want is for you to open your damn bag, Lieutenant," Furness said, eyes dead-on him.

He finally did as he was told. "Missing two flight suits . . . no mukluks . . . no mittens . . . no long underwear . . . no socks," Furness summarized as she rifled through the musty, wadded-up clothes and gear inside. She found condoms, money, odd pairs of ski gloves, receipts with women's names and numbers written on them, and parking tickets. Lots of parking tickets, some months old. They hadn't yet shown up on his civil records check. "You left all your winter stuff up in Lake Placid again, didn't you?" Fogelman didn't answer. He liked to use his military cold-weather gear when he went up to his family's resort in Lake Placid—he thought wearing military gear on the slopes made him look cool, like he was some Special Forces arctic commando or something—and he often left the stuff up there. "I hope it's not too cold or too snowy, because you got a long drive ahead of you."

"You want me to drive all the way to Lake Placid? In this weather? After the first day of Hell Week? How about lending me some stuff out of your spare bag?" Fogelman asked in a loud voice. All of the flight commanders had a spare deployment bag filled with odds and ends; Furness had two full.

Furness shook her head. "Because this isn't the first time I've bailed your ass out with my spare bag," she replied, trying to lower her voice to avoid attracting any more attention to her secret stash of gear, "and because you still haven't returned the stuff you borrowed last time—you probably gave my last set of thermals to one of your ski bunny friends. Forget it. Figure out what you're missing and go to Supply during lunchtime. Tell them you lost your stuff, and they'll issue you new stuff."

"And make me pay an arm and a leg for it!"

"It's your fault, Mark. And get a damned haircut."

Physical training (PT) was held every morning of Hell Week and was mandatory for everyone who was not flying. Furness had a good opportunity to observe Hembree during the PT test, and what she saw made her a bit nervous. Instead of allowing each squadron member to count his own reps and laps and report the score to the executive officer, Hembree and Lieutenant Colonel Katz supervised each event themselves, even to the point of coaching squadron members who appeared to be relaxing or quitting. Their voices, especially Hembree's, could be heard echoing throughout the gym, and they weren't words of encouragement—they were words of provocation, even admonishment. Since everyone in the unit could run pretty well, the two commanders carefully supervised the strength exercises, even getting down and yelling at members to grind out one last pull-up or do two more sit-ups "for the Seven-Fifteenth!" It was, she realized, an extremely intense display of . . . what? Determination? Although Hell Weeks in the past had been tough, the commanders usually tried to keep things relaxed and businesslike, not harsh or intense. The more she thought about it, the more Rebecca began to realize that this display by the commanders was more than determination. It wasn't out of pride or creating an esprit de corps.

No, it was a display of concern.

And urgency.

Perhaps even fear.

Something was going on.

EVERYONE PASSED THE PT TEST, ALTHOUGH MANY HAD SCORES that Hembree found unacceptably low, so another test was going to be run at the end of Hell Week. The squadron members had ninety minutes to shower, change back into flight suits, grab a breakfast-to-go from the Burger King right outside the front gate, and report to the squadron for academics, testing, and situation briefings.

The RF-111 Vampire reconnaissance/strike aircraft had twelve "bold print" items—124 words, 27 lines—of such critical importance that they had to be committed to memory and written out or recited word for word. The rest of the morning was taken up with aircraft systems-and-procedures lectures, followed by a multiple-choice test. Fortunately, no one scored below 80, but Furness got another warning stare from Hembree when it was discovered that Fogelman got the lowest score in the squadron.

Then came the blood tests at the base hospital. Along with a severe downsizing in the American armed forces and the growth of the Reserve forces after the 1992 elections was a general distrust of the military, especially the citizen-soldiers who now flew such advanced warplanes. Every military person on active duty, and those Reservists federalized for active duty, was routinely screened for substance abuse. They also tested for sexually transmitted diseases, such as AIDS, and weight and blood pressure, which were considered telltale signs of stress, poor health, and subsequently poor performance.

Rebecca passed all of her physical training, academic, and medical tests, but by the time she had finished all these Gestapo-like "preventive" and "zero tolerance" screenings, gulped down a rabbit-food lunch at the Officers' Club, and reported to the wing headquarters building at one P.M., she felt as worn out as if she had ran a marathon—and the afternoon sessions were just as demanding.

The first order of business was a worldwide intelligence briefing. The officer giving the Hell Week intelligence briefing was one of the sharpest and—in Rebecca Furness' opinion at least—one of the most interesting and best-looking guys in the entire wing.

"This briefing is classified secret, not releasable to foreign nationals, sensitive sources and methods involved," Major Tom Pierce began, "which means you probably saw it first last week in *Aviation Week* or will see it tomorrow night on the six o'clock news. Anyway, make sure the door back there is locked and let's get started." Major Thomas Pierce, the wing intelligence officer, was tall, trim, and good-looking, with close-cropped brown hair, an infectious smile, and round glasses which made his boyish face look even more innocent and inviting to Rebecca. Unfortunately, he was also very married, and apart from her self-imposed ban on dating members of her own wing, married men were definitely off-limits as well. Pierce was an ex-flyer who was bounced out of active-duty flying during the RIFs when the Air Force refused to grant any more medical waivers for his color blindness, so he joined the Reserves as a senior staff officer. He was a major filling a lieutenant colonel's billet, which made him a real fast-burner in the Air Force, and it showed every time he gave one of these briefings.

As it had been for the past year, problems in Europe took center stage. "The conflict between the Ukraine, Russia, and Moldova over the disputed Dniester Republic seems to have gotten worse over the past few weeks," Pierce began. He had an Operational Navigational Chart of the area in question, with the disputed region outlined in black—roughly five hundred square miles in southwestern Ukraine and central Moldova. "Now we know how bad it really is, because Russia tried to launch an air attack last night."

The room erupted with surprise and chaos. Pierce let it burn on for a few moments until they were ready to hear more, then continued. "Well, I see you fly-boys and fly-girls are keeping up with world events. Yes, as you children were sleeping, thinking you were safe and sound, it appears that Russia tried to launch a number of conventionally armed cruise missiles from Bear bombers. Likely targets were air bases in the Ukraine and possibly in Romania."

"Who stopped them?" someone asked. "What happened?"

"The Ukrainian Air Force, such as it is, jumped them in MiG-23s, shot down five, and got the other estimated twenty Bears to turn tail," Pierce replied. "The whole thing lasted about three minutes. No cruise missiles were launched. A few more seconds, and at least one Ukrainian air base would've been history. Four Ukrainian fighters were shot down by Russian fighter escorts.

"As you all remember from my briefings in the past, the Russians living in the Dniester region of central Moldova, including the cities of Bendery and Tiraspol, and assisted by units of the former Red Army's Fourteenth Motorized Rifle Division in Kishinev and the Twenty-eighth Motorized Rifle Division headquarters in Malayeshty, declared themselves independent when the Moldavian Soviet Socialist Republic split from the USSR and declared its independence back in 1991. Although the Russians are a minority in Moldova, they comprise most of the inhabitants of this particular region, which is the industrial heart of Moldova and a major manufacturing and shipping center. Mother Russia has no direct access to the disputed Dniester region, except in accordance with the outlines of the Commonwealth of Independent States treaty between the former Soviet republics. The CIS treaty allows member nations to cross one another's borders in times of emergency. Russia has been stretching this definition to the very limit, thanks to their wonderful President, Vitaly Velichko."

Pierce pointed to the ONC chart and went on. "As you can see, Moldova is surrounded on three sides by the Ukraine and on one side by Romania. Moldova was once a province of Romania.

"This situation obviously stresses out the Russians still living in Moldova because they believe they would become a persecuted people, so in August of 1991, just before Moldova itself declared its independence from the Soviet Union, the Russians in Dniester declared themselves independent from the Moldavian Soviet Republic and formed the Dniester Republic. They formed a militia soon afterward, comprised mostly of men and equipment from the Red Army Fourteenth and Twenty-eighth divisions. The Russians claimed that these two divisions had disbanded and had returned to Russia, but in fact they went underground in the Dniester Republic.

"Like most of the Republics, Moldova tried to annex all Soviet military bases within its borders except for strategic installations like bomber and intercontinental missile bases. They were not successful in Dniester. When the newly formed Moldovan Army tried to enforce the new law, Russian soldiers from Malayeshty resisted. When fighting broke out, the Russian military, contrary to orders from then-President Yeltsin, sent troops to the region to reinforce the militia in the two cities and beef up the Russian garrison."

There was no reaction to any of this, so Pierce raised his voice and stepped closer to the crewmembers to get their attention. "But *how*, you may ask," he shouted, causing one sleepy WSO to jump in his chair, "did they get troops into the Dniester area to help out their fellow Russians?"

"They bullied their way in," someone responded.

"Exactly," Pierce acknowledged. "In fact, Russian supply ships had sailed from the Black Sea Fleet ports near Sevastopol, into the Dnestr estuary, and up the Dnestr River to Bendery, and Russian naval aircraft also landed in Tiraspol's airport—all this without consulting the Ukraine or requesting permission for access or overflight. This obviously ticked off the Moldovans, who accused the Ukrainians of duplicity, so Moldova sent troops to the Ukrainian border, which pissed off the Ukrainians. But the Russians also pissed off the Ukrainians because it was a violation of their sovereignty and a violation of Commonwealth of Independent States joint military agreements."

"And the Ukraine was already pissed off at Russia about the Black Sea Fleet," Furness chimed in, getting into the lively exchange. Pierce had a habit of turning these otherwise dull intel briefings into rather entertaining history–current affairs discussions. "Boy, it sounds like everyone's pissed at everybody else."

"Exactly, O curvaceous one," Pierce said. The room erupted with a few chuckles. Pierce continued. "The disposition of the Black Sea Fleet, about 120 warships and about 300 combat aircraft, including 28 submarines, one aircraft carrier, and one vertical takeoff and landing cruiser, has been a major problem between the Ukraine and Russia since 1991. The original plan was to let Russia keep all the nuclear-capable aircraft and ships, then split the remaining ships equally between the two. But Russia claimed that all but 34 vessels, mostly mine warfare ships and small patrol corvettes, were nuclear-capable—Russia was going to cede only 17 patrol ships to the Ukraine and keep the other 86 ships for itself, as well as the bases on the Crimean Peninsula, which are some of the best pieces of real estate in all of Europe.

"Since 1991, the Ukraine and Russia have been tap-dancing around the issue. There were a few incidents—a Ukrainian crew mutinied and hijacked a frigate to Odessa, a few collisions and near-collisions between ships in the Black Sea, things like that—but negotiations were going along smoothly until the Dniester Republic conflict blew up. So, enough history. Let's bring you up-to-date on what the hell's going on over there."

Pierce pointed to several large circles near Odessa and other towns near the Ukrainian-Moldavan border. "The Ukrainian president, Yuri Khotin, has been trying to gently defuse this entire situation and keep on a defensive stance only, but they're getting pressure from the Ukrainian parliament to act. So recently the Ukraine set up an air defense battalion at the small airfield near Limanskoye, which is right on the border of the disputed region, armed with mostly older 100-millimeter antiaircraft artillery pieces and SA-3 surface-to-air missile units, in response to their warning to Russia to stop overflying their territory. The Russians simply circumnavigate the area. The weapons would not have been capable against the AS-4 cruise missiles, had those Bear bombers managed to launch them last night.

"Anyway, this low-key show of force hasn't satisfied the Moldovans, who have been staging raids into the Ukraine, trying to blow up bridges, canal locks, port facilities, and communications towers to try to slow down the Russian resupply convoys to the Dniester Republic. Romania is actively resupplying the Moldovans with weapons, in preparation for an all-out war, and has mobilized its reserve forces and sent five divisions of troops to the Moldovan border. It is felt that Romania can seize the Dniester Republic in less than a week, but Russia has warned that a state of war will exist if Romania crosses an inch over the Moldovan border.

"Romania mobilized their active-duty units to level-one readiness, and the ready reserves have been mobilized to level-two readiness as well—they could have a half a million men under arms by now, with another half million within six months. They ignored Russia's warnings and sent about half of the Romanian armed forces—two tank divisions, four motorized rifle divisions, a few antitank and artillery brigades—from their bases in southern and eastern Romania, principally in the army bases in Iasi, Bacau, and Braila, into staging bases in western Moldova. Air patrols from Constanta air base in southeastern Romania, mostly MiG-29s, are patrolling the border round-the-clock, and Romanian MiG-27 bombers have been seen over the Black Sea with antiship weapons. All this obviously prompted the Russian air attack last night.

"If hostilities were to break out, Romanian airborne and ground forces would move in from Iasi, led by fighter and bomber units from Constanta. Air operations against the rebels in Bendery and Tiraspol could begin immediately. Four tank and motorized rifle divisions could be in Kishinev to relieve the Moldovan capital in a few days or less, and they could be engaging the rebel divisions soon after that. The Russian and Romanian ground units are fairly equal, considering their sophistication versus numbers. The Romanians can put a lot of air power up front fast, but if the Russian Air Force fully engages in Moldova, it'll be over real quick.

"The Ukraine's trying to stay cool, but their cool *is* slipping," Pierce went on. "In response to the border incursions by Russia, Moldova, and Romania, the Ukraine deployed what they call a Special Action Detachment of approximately thirty thousand light infantry troops along the border, and light patrol boats now patrol the Dnestr River. They are looking for guerrilla forces and illegal cargoes, so they have stopped several Russian, Romanian, and Moldovan vessels, including Russian and Romanian warships. Romania has retaliated by seizing Ukrainian warships on the Black Sea, but that can't last long because Romania's navy is laughable, at best."

Another map of Europe was put up on the overhead projector, this time one of Germany and Central Europe. "One other nonmilitary event is creating a lot of strain on military forces in the region, and that's the refugee problem," Pierce said. "Finland, Poland, Hungary, Slovenia and Ceska—what used to be Czechoslovakia—Romania, and the three Baltic states have taken in an estimated one million Russian refugees in the past five months. Many of these refugees are making their way into Germany and Austria, where antiforeigner sentiment is already at the flash point. Slovenia has closed its borders to Russian refugees, and Romania has imprisoned many of the male refugees over the age of fourteen as possible combatants or spies. Budapest and Warsaw are practically being overrun by starving refugees—their own economic situation wasn't that good to begin with, without another extra quarter of a million hungry mouths added to it. And *now* the Russian government is threatening to punish any country that does not treat the Russian refugees with compassion."

Fogelman commented, "Their economic policies and threat of war forces the Russian people to flee the cities, and then they warn other countries to be nice to them or else? What total buttholes."

"The warning was primarily aimed at Romania, which has been virtually holding the refugees hostage as the Dniester crisis escalates," Pierce pointed out. "But here's something I *know* you haven't seen in *'Aviation Leak'* magazine yet." Pierce put up a slide with some satellite photos of a large military air base, with very large aircraft lined up in exhaust-blacked parking spots. "Here's what else the Russians are doing—this time in our own backyard. This is San Juan de los Baños military air base, south of Havana, the largest Soviet-built airfield in Cuba. Apparently in response to the so-called goodwill visit by the U.S. Navy into the Black Sea, Russia has sent Backfire bombers into Cuba again and based them here, as they did up until 1992.

"The Russians call them 'maritime reconnaissance' planes, and in fact no offensive weapons have yet to be detected, but of course the Russians would be able to move a large number of land attack and antiship cruise missiles into Cuba very easily. So far we count six Tupolev-22M Backfire-C bombers, plus two Il-78 Midas tanker aircraft. The Backfire-Cs have a reconnaissance capability, but they are primarily dash-and-flash bombers. They can carry every weapon in the Russian arsenal, including nuclear and conventional cruise missiles."

"Not much of an offensive force," one of the flight pilots said with a bit of bravado. "The Black Knights can probably take out San Juan de los Baños and all the planes with a sneeze. What about fighters?"

"Well, San Juan de los Baños is also the headquarters of the twenty Mikoyan-Gurevich-29 fighters remaining in the Cuban arsenal—they lose about five planes per year during training missions," Pierce said with a faint smile. "The -29s are the top-of-the-line counter–air fighters, and they have a full ground attack capability and aerial-refueling capability as well. The Cubans also have about three hundred various other fighters deployed around the island, but they put their money in the MiG-29s for sure. Half the Cuban arsenal of surface-to-air missile units is in the Havana area as well.

"That's for air-base defense. The Russians have stationed three MiG-29 or MiG-31 fighters in Cuba for every bomber as possible bomber escorts. You'll notice during Hell Week that the 134th Green Mountain Boys from Burlington won't be playing with you—they're all committed to air defense duties. Some Backfires have been flying as far north as Newfoundland on their coastal patrols. What do you think of your chances now?" The pilot who made the smug remark was silent. The MiG-29 and -31 were the Russians' top-of-the-line jet fighters, almost as good as the American F-15 Eagle and nearly a generation better than the F-111. Not even the Vampire's low-level supersonic capabilities would be a match for a MiG-29 if they got caught over open ocean.

"Christ, I feel like I'm watching TV from the sixties," Larry Tobias said. "Most of you punks probably don't remember the Cuban Missile Crisis, but I do—and this is just like it."

"The Russians have been quiet since the coup in 1991, and they're coming out again in a big way," Pierce concluded. "Bottom line: things are getting pretty bleak over in Europe, and if the two most powerful republics of the former Soviet Union start slugging it out for real, it's anybody's guess what will happen. Russia has committed itself to asserting its position with military force, including in the Western Hemisphere."

"Now, wait a minute, Major Pierce," Major Jamieson said between gulps of coffee. "You're the intel officer here—you're supposed to guess about what's going to happen, or at least pass on what the powers-that-be think is going to happen. Don't cop out on us—tell us."

"Our job is not to give you opinions, Ben," Pierce replied. "We only give you the latest facts."

"Yeah, right. Okay, tell us *your* opinion. Are we going to get involved in a fight in Europe?"

The question obviously made Tom Pierce uncomfortable. Even nervous. Furness could see the anxiety in his face. "All right, I'll tell you my opinion for what it's worth: the Ukraine is the darling of the West right now, especially the United States. Russia has been dragging its heels with economic reforms, while the Ukraine is opening consulates and trade offices all over the place in an attempt to attract foreign investors. While Russia still hasn't cut back its conventional military forces according to the Conventional-Forces-in-Europe-Treaty, Ukraine has fully complied—they have scrapped over ten thousand tanks and other armored military vehicles in just the past two years, plus they halted the sale of that half-completed aircraft carrier to mainland China. And while Russia still maintains a substantial nuclear force, including battlefield nuclear weapons, the Ukraine got the United Nations to certify it as a nuclear-free nation late last year. Besides applying for membership in the NATO alliance, there's talk of the Ukraine joining the European Economic Community—the Ukraine wants to do this because they've been under Russia's thumb for hundreds of years, and a new alignment with the West would help them prosper."

"So we like the Ukraine better than Russia—nothing earth-shattering about that idea," Jamieson said. "But what's going to come of it? What's the chance of a war between Russia and the Ukraine—and U.S. military intervention?"

Pierce nodded thoughtfully, then shrugged his shoulders and replied, "Russia has made it clear that they consider ethnic unrest and foreign military influence in the former Soviet republics a major threat to their sovereignty. They have pledged to use every means at their disposal, including nuclear battlefield weapons, to protect Russians living in the former republics and to secure their borders. Now, they haven't made any threats or done anything to suggest they're ready to start a full-scale war, but Velichko has made his intentions plain. There's obviously a power struggle going on between the civilian and military leaders in Russia, and it has yet to run its course.

"So," he continued, "what if war does break out? The Ukraine has a pretty potent military force, even with all the downsizing and civilian conversion they've been doing, but of course they couldn't stand up for long against Russia, and everyone knows it. Despite their differences, the Ukraine and Russia are still tied pretty closely together economically, socially, diplomatically, politically, every which way—and no one thinks that the Ukraine wants a war.

"But now we got three U.S. warships making a port call in Odessa this week—they call it a goodwill visit, although the timing of this whole visit creates anything but goodwill in the area—and the balance-of-power shift those ships create could push someone over the edge. Russia has repeatedly warned the U.S. about getting involved in the crisis."

"The President's an asshole," Mark Fogelman interjected. For once, Rebecca had to agree with him. "Didn't he realize how dangerous and how provocative that can be?"

"Like Russia sending Bear and Backfire bombers into Cuba again?" Tobias interjected. "It looks like a lot of government leaders around the world are being pretty stupid. But the President had to do something."

"Yeah. Twist the tiger's tail," Fogelman said in disgust. "Piss off the Russkies so they have to respond."

With all the concern and agitation Colonel Hembree seemed to be expressing that morning, Rebecca wanted to know if the crisis in Europe had anything to do with Hembree's near-manic emphasis on readiness, but she put that question on her mind's back burner as Pierce began describing yet another potential world crisis.

"The point of all this malarkey," Major Pierce said in conclusion, "is that there are lots of other forces alive and strong in the world right now, not just the United States, and they have their own plans for the New World Order. We are most certainly the strongest superpower in the world, but that is mostly in terms of military size and industrial potential, and even that is shrinking. If we go at it, we might very well go at it alone."

A fairly ominous picture, Furness thought, from a man usually upbeat. She made a point of intercepting him as he was heading out the door after completing his briefing: "Hey, Tom, you giving up on the human race, or what?"

"Uh, no, Becky. No, nothing like that," Pierce said. "The Wing King is really concerned about events between Ukraine and Russia. He wants situation briefings every morning and every couple hours, which means I'm in here by five A.M. every day. He wants the worst case, too, and I've been inundated by some pretty serious stuff lately."

"Are you concerned about us deploying or something, Tom? I've had this feeling lately. Everyone's uptight, but no one's coming clean. Has the General been getting any messages, any directives?"

"Whoa, whoa, Becky, you're asking the wrong dude. *I know nothing, nnnothssing,*" Pierce replied, imitating Sergeant Shultz of *Hogan's Heroes* fame to emphasize the last part of his too-emphatic denial. "I just report the news, not make it. Talk to the Wing King yourself—he might just tell you. Gotta go. See ya." He gave her a mind-blowing smile and quickly departed.

Well, the *last* thing she needed to do, Furness thought, was to meet with the wing commander and talk about world problems, especially after the day she was having. Better to wait until nearer the end of Hell Week, after a few good flights and a no-writeup inspection before trying to get any information from the brass.

But . . . the feeling of uneasiness persisted. It was a feeling, Rebecca Furness realized, that both excited and frightened her. She tried to shake it out of her head and walked on.

16

AFTER THE LATEST INTELLIGENCE BRIEFINGS HAD CONCLUDED, the squadron members reported back to the squadron, where the next day's ATO, or Air Tasking Order, was just being posted. The Air Tasking Order was the unit's game plan, detailing the location and mission of every aircraft involved in an operation. The usual plan was for Alpha Flight aircrews to launch as soon as possible, with the first six aircraft that were ready to go. Bravo Flight would follow in the next six aircraft, but they would accomplish a strike or reconnaissance mission first, then recover at the "deployment" base. Charlie Flight in the last six planes could do either role, but, because they had the least-experienced crews, was usually tasked to bring more weapons and spare parts for the other planes.

The other units within the Fifth Air Battle Force, the composite-force unit headquartered at Plattsburgh, would contribute to the week-long exercise as well, although, except for the 336th Air Refueling Squadron's KC-135 tankers, none of the other squadrons were based at Plattsburgh. The F-16 C- and D-model multirole fighters from the 134th Fighter Squadron at Burlington Airport, which had long-range interceptor, tactical air superiority, precision bombing, and close-air support versions of the single-engine fighter, would play a dual role in this operation: some would act as escorts for the bombers, while others would play enemy fighters and try to hunt down the bombers while they made their bomb runs. The Wing also used C-130E Hercules transports of the 328th Airlift Squadron based at Niagara Falls International Airport, C-141 Starlifter transports from the 756th Airlift Squadron in Maryland, and C-5A Galaxy transports from the 337th Airlift Squadron in Massachusetts, to practice loading deployment equipment. Sometimes they also practiced joint deployments with A-10 Thunderbolt attack squadrons and even Navy and Marine Corps Reserve units, practicing the important task of joint air operations.

All this was known as the "surge," the most important aspect of the unit's mission—the ability to get a combat tasking order, deploy in the fastest way possible, set up shop at another location, strike targets in just a few short hours after notification, then conduct continuous strike and tactical reconnaissance operations with only the bare essentials until the rest of the Wing arrived. With the drastic downsizing of the U.S. military and the reliance on Reserve forces for national defense, rapidly mobilizing, deploying, and operating inactive combat units was more important than ever.

Lieutenant Colonel Hembree, Lieutenant Colonel Katz, and the Wing Operations staff had already broken down the Air Tasking Order when they arrived back at the squadron building. In the staff meeting that began a few minutes later, Hembree laid out the plan. "Ben Jamieson's flight is already headed out to the aircraft," he began. "So far the first six airframes look pretty good—they should be 'deploying' by sundown. The new MG jumped the gun and started generating bombers and tankers early, but the General obviously likes his ideas, so we're ahead of the game this morning.

"Bravo Flight's attack stream will be launching at about seven A.M. We're looking at two radar bombing platforms, one GBU-15 bomber, two PAVE TACK bombers, and one recon bird in Bravo Flight. The GBU and PAVE TACK planes will have live weapons on board, one GBU-15 and two GBU-24s—Headquarters finally came through and got us a few real bombs to play with, so I want to be able to tell the boss that they weren't wasted. Charlie Flight will be all strike—two laser, four radar, with one GBU-12 and one Mk-84 shape per laser plane. They say more live bombs may be authorized this week." Employing all these precision-guided weapons during a Hell Week was very rare. "The recon bird from Bravo Flight will quick-turn and fly photo recon for both strike packages. Rebecca, that'll be you." Hembree put up a slide on an overhead projector, which showed the schedule of activity for each flight.

Furness was disappointed. In a real-world attack, the first planes over the target were the most important—the first hits had to be deadly to minimize the threat for the rest of the squadron following behind—so you sent your best troops first. Flight commanders usually led the strike packages using the PAVE TACK pod, a combination infrared seeker and laser designator designed to deliver laser-guided bombs with pinpoint precision. The flight commanders were supposed to lead, not come in after the "bad guys" had already been blown away. Flying photo reconnaissance was an important function of every combat operation, but that task was usually left to someone else in the flight.

Not only that, but they had real bombs to use in this surge.

She copied the critical times off the ATO for her flight, double-checking the numbers and weapon loads. "I'll expect package briefings from the flight commanders at sixteen hundred hours," Hembree continued. "I present the packages to the General at five, and then I'll come back with any changes. Questions?" There were none. "Okay, let's do it."

Furness stepped up to Hembree just before he left the briefing room. "Hey, Dick, what about—"

"About you and Fogelman flying the photo bird? General's orders."

"He give any reason?"

"Nope," Hembree replied. "I issued a report to him on the squadron inspection this morning before lunch, including Mark's apparent disregard for 35-10 and for preparing for deployment—but I don't think that had anything to do with the decision. He wants you to fly the photo bird, period. He also specified Ogden on the TV bomber and Little on one of the laser birds. If he has a reason for specifying the lineup like this, he didn't tell me."

"But Lynn just qualified on the GBU-15," Furness said, shaking her head. Every crewmember entered the 715th Tactical Squadron from F-111G fighter lead-in qualified to do level radar, level visual, dive, and computer-toss bomb deliveries only—the unit then qualified them to fly visual toss, photo reconnaissance, PAVE TACK laser-guided bomb deliveries, then finally GBU-15 TV-guided bomb runs. The GBU-15 was by far the most difficult weapon to use because it required a great deal of crew coordination and it was very labor-intensive—the weapon system officer had to use the TV camera in the bomb to guide the plane to the target, then guide the weapon to the target after release, while the pilot initiated evasive maneuvers. Because of the skills involved and because the weapons were so expensive to use just for training, it sometimes took years for a crew to qualify. "She needed five bombs to qualify, almost twice the normal number. Larry Tobias needed only two to qualify, and he hasn't had any since then."

"Rebecca, I hear you," Hembree said, "but the General laid down the law—he didn't make 'suggestions,' he didn't leave it up to me, and he didn't staff it. Ogden gets the Dash-Fifteen, Little on a laser bird. And he wants to see Ogden and Vest do toss releases, and he wants to see a buddy lase." A toss release was a bomb-release procedure in which the bomb is released "whip-crack" style while in a steep climbing turn to avoid overflying a target. A buddy lase was an attack in which another aircraft in an attack formation laser-designated a target for another aircraft carrying the weapons, which allowed more precision-guided bombs to be used with fewer PAVE TACK laser designators.

Both these techniques required an extraordinary degree of crew coordination and planning to accomplish properly. Rebecca didn't doubt that her crews could do these procedures, but it was a lot of work for the first flight of a Hell Week.

As if to emphasize this point, Hembree continued, "It sounds to me like he wants to challenge this unit, to see what the newbies can do."

"I'm just saying that maybe we should be easing into this a bit slower, Dick."

"Becky, give me a break," Hembree said. "The Wing King's also trying to determine the proficiency and combat readiness of our outfit. Look at all the shit going on in Europe, in Korea, in Asia—we could find ourselves up to our asses in alligators in any one of these places at any time. A crew proficient with Dash-15s is an asset; a crew that's not is a liability. We need to change them into assets as fast as possible. I don't want this squadron broken up into crews that can do TV bombs and those who can't—everyone will be proficient in all of our assigned weapons and tactics. I want our crews to be happy, and I want to reward the top performers, but I want combat-ready crews more than anything. Ogden and Vest do the toss Dash-Fifteen, and I expect to see a shack—you, me, the crew, and the General will watch the videotape together. Anything else?"

"You wanna talk about the inspection this morning?" Furness asked. "I'm prepared to give you an Air Force Regulation 35-10 briefing."

"No. Just make sure Fogman has his shit in the bag and Paula does her hair."

"She says she pushed her boobs out for you so you'd be too nervous to stare at her, but it didn't faze you."

Hembree chuckled, and for the first time that day Furness watched some of the tension melt out of his face. "I was distracted, but not *that* distracted. I noticed her damn hair and her uniform. Tell her to stop playing games and get her shit together."

"I did. Fogman too."

"Good," Hembree said. "When the exercise is over, I'll have you give a standup during Commander's Call about 35-10. But General Cole has to hear it through the grapevine that I cracked the whip during morning inspection or I'll be back pushing a crew. 'Nuff said?" Furness nodded, happy that Hembree was at least a little bit back to his old self. "Let's brief here at sixteen hundred with your strike package, and tomorrow morning at oh-five-hundred for the mass briefing. I gotta go check on Ben and Alpha Flight. See ya later." Furness headed back to the mission planning room where the rest of her flight was waiting.

"Well, I guess age doesn't have its privileges anymore," she said as she distributed the takeoff and target times and other information from the ATO. "Lynn and Clark, you guys got a GBU-15 toss tomorrow morning out on the Fort Drum range. Don't screw it up."

"You're kidding!" Clark Vest exclaimed happily. "Man, that's great!"

"Such unexpected largesse for a regular Hell Week," Tobias observed, obviously disappointed that he didn't get the TV-guided mission. "Something's heating up. I know it."

"I think you're right," Furness said, "but I don't know what—Hawkeye's not talking. Anyway, we got some live stuff, so let's make the most of it. Paula, Ted, you got a live one too, a PAVE TACK shape; Bob and Bruce, you guys got the other one, and the Wing King wants a toss. Make sure you got your PAVE TACK preflight procedures down cold—you'll be launching early in the morning with a cold pod. Ted, I expect to see some mind-blowing videotape of an in-your-face shack."

"You got it, Becky," Ted Little replied.

"The flight order is going to get shaken up a bit," Furness continued. "I'll lead cell number one, with Johnson and Norton on my wing. Johnson and Rota will be going in first, dropping 'beer cans,' and then will be buddy-lasing for Norton and Little. Frank, Larry, you will lead cell number two. You'll be a radar bomber with BDUs, and you'll drop beer cans third and buddy-lase for Bob and Bruce." Beer can bombs, or BDU (Bomb, Dummy Unit)-48, were small ten-pound cylindrical smoke bombs that resembled large juice or beer cans with fins—although they were small and did not resemble a bomb at all, their ballistics closely resembled those of a B61 or B83 parachute-equipped nuclear bomb. An F-111 normally carried two SUU-20 racks, one on each wing, with two BDU-48 bombs in each rack. "Paula and Ted, you'll be fifth with the TV bomb. Everyone else, don't feel bad, because it looks like everyone's getting at least one live round this week."

"Buddy-lase, toss bombs, TV bombs, all on the first flying day of Hell Week?" Tobias muttered, just loud enough for everyone to hear. "Man, have the Iraqis invaded again?"

"We've got wall-to-wall brass watching us today, so everyone needs to be sharp," Furness reminded them. "Me and Fogman will be at the top of the block when Johnson goes in, we'll stay at the top of the block while everyone else enters the route, and we'll be tail-end charlie and photograph the entire thing."

"What?" Fogelman retorted, as if the realization of what was going on finally sank in. "How come we're in the recon bird? I got more time on PAVE TACK than Ogden."

"But you don't have as much time on the recon pod," Furness replied. She didn't know that for sure, but there was no doubt that Fogelman's expertise with the reconnaissance suite on the RF-111G was poor. "We also quick-turn and shoot pictures for

Alpha Flight, too, so you'll get lots of practice. I said everyone should get a live round this week, so don't sweat it." Fogelman scowled his displeasure. "Okay, let's get to work."

But while they were assembling the paperwork, they also used the time to catch up on each other's civilian activities. Most of the men in the flight were airline captains with liberal schedules that allowed them to take extended days off for Reserve duties—exactly the same kind of job Furness had been searching for for years.

The technician from Major Pierce's intelligence office came by to hand out the latest "intelligence" of the target area, so each crewmember had photos and computer-generated radar and visual predictions of the targets. Their usual live bomb targets were mock airfields, small buildings made of stacked 55-gallon steel drums, and plywood vehicle-shaped targets. The most important part of the briefing was the position of Multiple Threat Emitter System, or MUTES, transmitters on the range: "They appear to be out gunning for you on this pass," the technician said. He passed out coordinates of four MUTES trailers that would be on the range. The MUTES devices were truck-towed, self-powered radio transmitters that simulated enemy surface-to-air missile and antiaircraft-artillery tracking radars; Air Force technicians would accompany the MUTES trailers on the range and evaluate each crew's evasion techniques as the MUTES sites "attacked" the strike aircraft during their runs. "Latest info says they're on the move as well."

The R-5201 bombing range in northern New York State was only three hundred square miles—four MUTES sites in that small area would place the strikers under almost constant "attack."

"What are we looking at?" asked Furness.

"Brigade or battalion stuff, but they've got the biggest and best waiting for you," the technician said. "Mostly you'll be looking at SA-8 B-model, max range nine miles; the SA-11, max range seventeen miles; and the SA-15, with a max slant range of eight miles. But you can also expect a surprise in the possible presence of an SA-12 that could 'attack' the RF-111 bombers well before they enter the target area.

"The greatest threat you'll face, however, is from fighters," the intelligence technician continued. "If they can spare any—they're busy shadowing those Backfire bombers flying out of Cuba, but we might get a few to play with. Players will have Russian radar emitters installed, so your detection gear will respond just like real." That was a bit unusual. The emitters were simply tiny radio transmitters that mimicked enemy fire-control radars. That wasn't routine for Hell Week.

Mission planning was mostly done by computer after that. In sixty minutes, the planning was done for the entire six-aircraft strike package.

No sooner had the charts and flight plans been spit out of the printer and the mission been briefed than Furness saw Fogelman slipping his flight jacket on. "Going someplace?" she asked.

"I'm going to get my gear and a haircut, like you said," Fogelman grumbled. "Supply was closed during lunch."

"We have to proof these charts and flight plans," she said. "I've got a briefing for the battle staff in one hour."

Fogelman looked at his watch, groaned, and said, "Supply closes at three—I've got ten minutes to get over there. I've got to leave now. Have Tobias proof the stuff for you. Better yet, just take it as is. The computer stuff is always perfect anyway."

Furness was about to rag on him some more, but there wasn't time. Besides, she preferred Larry Tobias' company anyway—in fact, she preferred *anyone's* company over Fogelman's. "All right, all right. But the show time is five-thirty, and you better have a haircut and a complete mobility bag."

"Haircut and three bags full. You got it." He hurried away, leaving Furness to check all the charts and flight plans on her own.

With Tobias' and some of the other crew's help, chart and flight plan validations were over in just a few minutes. Hembree came into the mission planning room a few minutes after they finished, and they briefed him on the morning's sorties. He accepted the briefing without comment, but seemed preoccupied. It wasn't unlike him to say nothing during a mission briefing, especially just before going into the General's office at headquarters to give the same briefing. But Furness didn't knock it.

Like most of the Reservists reporting in for Hell Week, Furness stayed on base in the old alert shelter near the flight line. The dark, windowless alert shelter was a throwback to Plattsburgh's days as a B-47, B-52, KC-135, and FB-111 bomber base, when as many as half the bombers, tankers, and aircrews on base were assigned strategic nuclear alert duties. Rebecca had done that very same thing as a young KC-135 Stratotanker copilot nearly ten years ago, and she remembered it well. A crewdog could expect at least one alert exercise during a seven-day alert tour, and they alternated day or night exercises to keep all the crews proficient in both.

When Furness cross-trained from the KC-135 to the KC-10 tanker in 1988, she no longer pulled alert. *Thank God,* she thought as she unpacked her bags, changed into jogging shorts and a sweatshirt, and put in a two-mile run on a treadmill in the Pad gymnasium. After a shower, she changed into jeans, a heavy wool sweater, a down jacket, and hiking boots, and checked out with the Charge of Quarters.

Until the Bravo exercise was in full swing, the alert facility dining hall was open only for breakfast. So the flyers and their crew chiefs' new social club was Afterburners, a small tavern and restaurant on the lower floor of a hundred-year-old hotel in the center of old downtown Plattsburgh, and that's where Furness met up with most of the members of her squadron.

The flyers and crew chiefs were in the TV lounge portion of the bar, watching the big-screen TV for the latest news about the skirmishing between Russia and the Ukraine over the Russian minorities in Moldova and the sovereignty of the former Soviet republics versus the unity of the Commonwealth of Independent States. "See that?" Captain Frank Kelly, her wingman, said to Rebecca, pointing at the TV screen. A group of protesters were throwing Molotov cocktails at a tank. "Another riot in that Moldavan city. The media are pointing to the Moldovan soldiers and saying they're inciting the riots, but no one seems to be blaming the Russians."

"That's because the Moldavian Army is kicking the hell out of the Russians," someone else said. "If they'd just leave the Russians alone, there wouldn't be any fighting."

"That's 'Moldovan' Army, not 'Moldavian' Army," Larry Tobias interjected. "Get it straight, son."

"Gee, Dad," the other crewmember quipped. "I didn't know class was in session."

"Hey, Larry, my WSO has *forgotten* more than you'll ever know," Kelly said in defense of his weapon system officer. "But as long as you're the expert here, Larry, tell us: What is all this shit about? The rumor is NATO might get involved, which means us. Is that right?"

"Because it is the beginning of the Russians' land grab," Larry Tobias replied. "There are less than one hundred thousand Russians in Moldova, but ten Russians or a million—Russia would still be involved. Russia wants Moldova back. They care about only one thing—secure borders, a secure homeland," Tobias said. "You people may not remember this, but over the past forty years, all of the Russian leaders have fought for the same thing. It is not enough to have massive standing armed forces—they want to put a buffer zone between Mother Russia and all foreign territory, especially those countries with foreign troops stationed on them. A lot of Russian leaders fought in World War Two, and every family in Russia lost relatives in the war. The Russians discovered in World War Two that alliances don't always mean security—occupying and holding land is the key to security for them."

"But why do we give a damn if Russia invades the Ukraine or Moldova?" one of the crew chiefs asked. "Who cares? Hell, most people don't know where Moldova, or Romania, or the Ukraine are on the map. I remember the press had to tell thirty percent of all Americans where Kuwait was before we went to war there."

"We care because Russia is involved," Tobias replied, taking a deep swig of his beer. "Ever since the first Slavic Neanderthal ventured out of his cave, he not only cared about what his neighbor was doing—he wanted to *control* what he was doing. Russia doesn't want the Ukraine to go Ukrainian, or Moldova to go Romanian, or Georgia to go Turkish. They sure don't want any of them to go Islamic, and they sure as *hell* don't want any of them to go democratic. That's probably the worst. Russia will fight to make sure the peripheral republics go *nowhere*. It's as simple as that."

"It doesn't make any sense."

"It makes perfect sense—just not to you and me." Tobias burped happily, glancing at a large wall clock on one wall. A sign on the clock had a 715th Tactical Squadron patch, the words *Drop Dead*, and an arrow pointing at the 7 on the clock, indicating the twelve-hour alcohol limit for those flying the next morning. "We still got fifteen minutes," Tobias said. He turned to Furness. "Buy you a beer, boss? No, wait, you're into red wine, right?"

"Sure, Larry," Furness replied. "Barkeep, last round for the Black Knights over here." They searched for a waitress, but none were in sight. "Yo, anybody awake over there?" She spotted a blond guy, good-looking, carrying two large soda and carbonated gas tanks from behind the bar to the back room. "Hey, guy, how about taking our order?"

"I'm not a waiter."

"You can remember a few drinks, can't you? C'mon, take a chance." The man put the tanks down next to the bar, wiped his hands on his apron, then hesitantly walked over. He was tall and a little weathered, but in good shape, with piercing green eyes. Furness noticed his GI haircut right away—obviously military, a Reservist most likely, a crew chief or clerk, having to pull down a night job to help make ends meet. She knew the tune to that song, all right. "Thatta boy, that wasn't so bad, was it?"

"I'll get your waitress," he said.

"Forget the waitress, guy, you got the job," Furness said. "Got a pencil?"

The man rolled his eyes, losing patience, but he shrugged his shoulders, sighed, and replied, "I can remember."

"You can, huh? Very impressive." Furness gave a sly smile to the rest of the crewdogs seated at the table—they had a little game they liked to play on the new waitpersons at Afterburners. After a little nod to make sure everyone was ready, she said, "Okayyy . . . make mine a 1989 Eagle Falls cabby estate."

Just then, Furness and the other five people at the table got up and, in a mad scramble, changed seats with someone else. The barman couldn't believe what he was watching—it was a mini–Chinese fire drill at the table.

When they were finally seated again, someone else blurted out, "Stoli up with a twist," and they changed seats again.

"Glenfiddish neat with a Fosters chaser . . ." Another seat change.

"Crazy Billy, no lime, tall . . ." They weren't sitting down this time, only changing seats every time another drink order was fired off.

"Bowmore and water, Islay pre-1980 . . ."

"Dos Equis with a lime . . ."

The melee had attracted a lot of attention by this time. The barman waited patiently until they were seated again. Furness asked with a smile, "Okay, sport, you got all that? Or do you want to go get that pencil now?"

Without batting an eye, the barman pointed to her and recited, "Eagle Falls cabernet sauvignon, 1989 estate." To the next person, he said, "Crazy Billy, no lime, in a tall glass. You want salt?"

"N–no . . ."

"Fine. Bowmore scotch and water . . ." He recited them all, perfectly, without a hitch. "Separate checks or all together? You want popcorn, too, lady?" Furness and the others were too shocked to respond, so the man just gave them a smug grin and stepped away. The onlookers applauded, and even a few of the stunned crewdogs at the table had to clap for him.

"He's pretty amazing," someone offered.

"He looks GI," Furness decided. "Anybody know him?" No one did. "Whoever he is, I'd love to have him on my crew."

"Or would you just love to have him, Becky?" someone teased.

Furness gave a sly grin, which made the others at the table give her a knowing "Ahhhh . . ." But she added, "Nah, I don't know where's he's been. He could have the whole viral history of Plattsburgh State College's coeds implanted on his snake for all I know. Anyway, he's got more brains than Fogman could ever hope for."

Just then, the man returned . . . with a tray of six tall beers. "Six Buds, six bucks," he said.

Tobias started chuckling, but Kelly blurted, "What is *this?* This isn't what we ordered."

Furness was surprised at first, then pissed. "Take this back and bring us what we ordered."

"You'll pay me six bucks and drink your beers or you can all get on your fucking knees and *kiss my ass,*" the man snapped, glaring at each and every one of them, including Furness. "I told you I wasn't your waiter, but I played your shitty little game, and now you got your drinks. You can pay up, shut up, drink up, and get back to the base, or we can take it outside to the alley and I'll make you wish you never came here tonight. What's it going to be, children?"

The group was too stunned to reply. Furness considered going to the manager, but Tobias wisely reached into his pocket, pulled out a ten, and gave it to him. The man withdrew his wallet to make change, but Tobias waved it off.

"Have a nice evening," Lieutenant Colonel Daren Mace said, then walked away, picked up his tanks, and carried them into the back room. They didn't notice the cellular telephone stuck in his back pocket, the one that all military personnel knew as belonging to a Wing staff officer.

"Whew," Furness said finally, after a long, stunned pause. "I . . . I think I'd like to get to know that guy better." Everyone at the table knew they had just been told off by one of the best.

"I'm married with two kids," Frank Kelly said, "and *I'd* like to get to know him better."

Everyone laughed.

PART THREE

The grim fact is that we prepare for war like precocious giants, and for peace like retarded pygmies.
—Lester Bowles Pearson

17

394th Air Battle Wing Aircrew Alert Facility, Plattsburgh AFB, NY The Next Morning

AS USUAL WHEN FURNESS WOKE UP AFTER HER FIRST NIGHT in the alert facility, she didn't know where she was. The windowless rooms were completely dark, illuminated only by the red 3:45 A.M. LED numerals on the alarm clock—again, she had awakened several minutes before the alarm. The feeling of vertigo was so bad that she had to feel for the edge of the bed and the cold whitewashed concrete wall before attempting to move out of bed. It reminded her of the reason why she had no curtains over the triple-paned windows on her Vermont farmhouse, and she suddenly longed for its quiet privacy, its isolation, its serene beauty.

Showering in the open-stalled bathroom in the alert facility brought her back to reality very quickly, and Rebecca got out of there as fast as possible. In twenty minutes she was dressed. She was ready to head upstairs to get breakfast when the phone startled her.

"Becky? Ben here." It was Ben Jamieson, the Alpha Flight commander, who was acting as duty officer in the facility for the evening. "You better get up here. Fogelman just made an ass out of himself—and you."

In the CQ office, her heart sank—Colonel Hembree was waiting for her along with . . . Mark Fogelman. At least it *looked* like Fogelman, except this character had a shaved head! "Fogman?" she gasped, forgetting for a moment that Hembree was standing there. "Is that *you . . . ?*"

"Yes, ma'am," Fogelman replied matter-of-factly, his voice uncharacteristically official and disciplined. Not one hint of his usual smug grin.

"Major Furness," Hembree began irritably, "maybe you can explain what's going on here. Lieutenant Fogelman claims that you ordered him to cut his hair like this. Is this true?"

"Wha— *No,* it's not true!"

"With all due respect, ma'am, you're not telling the truth," Fogelman said. The word "ma'am" coming from Fogelman's lips sent a chill down her spine, like fingernails down a chalkboard. "I distinctly remember you giving me an order to cut my hair, and then you ordered me to cut it all off."

"I did no such thing!"

"I will be happy to get witnesses for you, sir," Fogelman told Hembree. "It was right after the open-ranks inspection. She was upset at me after the inspection, and she warned me that I had better not show up today without a haircut, and then she ordered me to cut it all off, to make sure I passed inspection, I suppose. Why would I do this unless she gave me a direct order?"

"Because you're a little *prick,* that's why, Fogelman."

"That's enough, Major," Hembree said. "Addressing a fellow officer like that is out of line, and I won't stand for it, hear me? As far as your haircut, Lieutenant—well, it's within the regs, and you did it to yourself, so you have to deal with it. You are dismissed." Fogelman snapped to attention, turned, gave Furness a satisfied grin, then departed. "Major, I want a word with you." Hembree walked into the adjacent facility manager's office and closed the door after Furness followed him inside.

"Rebecca, what the hell is going on here?" Hembree asked angrily. "I've got the wing commander and the commander of Fifth Air Battle Force coming out here in twenty minutes to view this exercise, and what's he going to see? Two of my crewmembers arguing and sniping at each other like children. What is with you two?"

"I told him to get a haircut and to get his mobility gear together, that's *all,*" she replied. "He made a joke about cutting off all his hair—hell, I didn't think he'd really *do* it. I'm not trying to bust his nuts, Dick, but he shows up for work clearly out of uniform and without his required equipment, and he fights me at every turn—"

"Becky, I could see you two weren't getting along, but I was hoping that would change," Hembree said wearily. "I thought he'd get over this attitude problem he has, especially toward you, and I was hoping you'd straighten him out. I was wrong on both counts, but I'm especially disappointed in you. Fogelman has a suck attitude—I think bringing him out of C Flight so early was a mistake—but you have got a chip on your shoulder the size of a concrete block. Bravo Flight doesn't need someone to constantly challenge them like you do.

"As soon as this exercise is over, I'm splitting you two up and putting you in C Flight," the Colonel said. "Martin Gruber will take B Flight, and you'll take C Flight. I'll put Fogelman with Gruber or Alomar."

"Dick, I don't deserve this," Furness said. "I spent almost twelve months in C Flight, longer than any other instructor. When Fogelman came out of C Flight four months early and before qualifying on PAVE TACK, I recommended against it. Give me Gaston from C Flight and—"

"It's already been decided, Rebecca," Hembree said. "Listen, your experience and knowledge will be good for C Flight, your effectiveness reports will still go to the one-star for his signature, and you and Fogelman won't be in each other's hair."

"If you send me down to C Flight you'll be giving Fogelman what he wants—the satisfaction of busting me."

"This is not a demotion, Rebecca, it's a change that reflects your management style, your expertise in the weapon system, and the need for your knowledge with the newcomers," Hembree said. "The newcomers in Charlie Flight need a strong hand, and your style would fit in better there. Maybe next time you'll think more carefully about what you tell your troops. You like playing games with people's heads, and this time it cost you. And lay off the name-calling in front of the staff—if this shit gets outside the squadron, you may both find yourselves out on the street. Now let's go to work. Your flight will be the first ones through the range today, and half the Air Combat Command will be watching. I want your people firing on all cylinders this morning. Anything else?"

Furness didn't want to argue the haircut incident anymore—it made her look bad. "Are you going to fly with us?"

"General Cole and Vice Commander Lachemann of Fifth Air Battle Force want to observe our deployment procedures, so I'll be on the ground with them while your flight does their bomb runs," Hembree replied. "Alpha Flight has landed from its 'deployment' but hasn't configured for strike yet, so I'm sure the brass will want to watch that, and C Flight is getting ready to 'deploy.' I'll probably fly in C Flight's first strike mission after the brass leaves."

"One more thing, Dick—nothing to do with Fogelman. I've noticed that things seem really . . . well, tense around here. Is anything imminent? Are we going to be mobilized?"

"Who the hell knows, Rebecca?" Hembree replied irritably. "Nothing specific has come down. Everyone's looking for another Desert Storm, but I don't think it's going to happen. No, no one's going anywhere. You just worry about your flight for now. Both Cole and Lachemann want to see the bomb-run video when your planes land, and they want to see shacks. Let's make sure it happens." Hembree stormed out of the office.

Well, that was a great way to start the morning. Chewed out by the squadron commander. And now she had to go fly with Fogelman, the little sonofabitch.

About an hour later, after a quiet breakfast during which Furness and Fogelman silently glared at one another and other crewdogs avoided the lightning bolts shooting between them, the flight held a mass briefing at the squadron. As promised, Brigadier General Cole and Major General Lachemann, a tall, hefty man with dark hair, dark complexion, and an even darker mood, sat in on the briefing. It was times like this, Rebecca thought as she stood to begin the briefing, that she wished she wasn't a flight commander.

After a few minutes, Furness was about to run through the sortie when a beeper on the two-star general's belt went off, and he and Cole quietly excused themselves, ordered that the briefing continue without calling the room to attention, and trotted out. For the first time that morning, Furness felt able to relax and continued her briefing. She spoke about the mission objectives, training rules, the tactical situation, current intelligence, the overall route, formation procedures, force timing, and join-up and recovery procedures.

When she was finished, Larry Tobias then briefed the low-level flying route. Furness asked for questions, then concluded the briefing and turned it over to Colonel Hembree.

"As you can see," Hembree began, "we've got some high-powered visibility today. Everyone wants to know how the Reserve fast-burners will perform. What the generals want is shack scores. What I want is safe, heads-up flying. I want it done right. I want a successful completion of our training objectives, but if the shit starts piling up and you are getting overloaded, fly your airplane right-side up and away from the ground, stop whatever you're doing, and think. Fly aggressively, but fly safe and fly smart. Now get out there and let's show these off-base generals what the Eagles can do."

The crews headed out to collect their gear, and loaded up into crew buses and headed to the flight line. One by one, the bus driver deposited the crews in front of their planes. The crew chiefs for each plane, who had already been out on the flight line for the past five hours, thankfully jumped on board the crew bus to get warm as it stopped, and the crews went over the maintenance logs and preflight inspection checklists in the warmth of the bus before venturing out into the cold. After reviewing the maintenance log, they collected their gear and headed toward the plane.

Working the RF-111G Vampire bomber could best be described as a series of checklists—virtually nothing was done in or around the plane, on the ground or in the air, without referring to a checklist. Before even setting a bag inside the cockpit, the first few items of the Before Preflight Inspection checklist were run right from the ladder, looking into the cockpit with a flashlight without touching anything: external power disconnected, ejection handles and capsule life support systems levers pinned, and battery and external power switches off. It was dangerous just getting near the sleek, deadly aircraft without double-checking to make sure it was safe to start working around it.

After stowing all the personal gear in the plane, the Power-Off Exterior Inspection, or "walkaround," was next. Usually this inspection was accomplished by both crewmembers, especially with weapons aboard, but Furness and Fogelman only had the reconnaissance pods uploaded, so Fogelman went right to work preflighting the camera pods.

The RF-111G reconnaissance plane carried two electronic reconnaissance pods, mounted like external fuel tanks on the number three and six wing weapon pylons. The UPD-8 pod, mounted on the right-wing pylon, was a synthetic aperture radar that took high-resolution radar images of terrain or seas around the plane for a range of up to fifty miles. The radar images could pick out small vehicles hidden under foliage or in bad weather, and had enough resolution to pick out tank tracks in sand or dirt. The AN/ATR-18 Tactical Air Reconnaissance System pod on the left wing was similar to standard optical camera pods, with telescopic, wide field-of-view, panoramic, and infrared cameras for use at night, but the photographs were digitized, stored on computer chips, and data-linked to ground stations up to two hundred miles away. In this way, the results of their photo runs could be transmitted and distributed to friendly forces hours before the plane landed and hours before standard film images were available.

Fogelman simply assumed everything was okay, swept his flashlight around the pods, then scrambled back up into the cockpit to get out of the cold. He stowed his flying jacket behind his seat, closed both canopies, and slapped his left fist against his open right hand, a signal to the crew chief to get warm air flowing inside the cockpit.

The crew chief, Staff Sergeant Ken Brodie, trotted around to Rebecca Furness. He knew that the reconnaissance pods needed power soon to keep from "cold-soaking" the electronics, and he knew that it was damn cold in the cockpit—but he also knew that the external power cart would create a lot of noise, especially for someone up inside the wheel-well areas as Furness was, so he thought it would be better to ask first: "The wizzo wants power," he hollered in her ear over the sound of power carts starting up nearby.

That was the first time Rebecca noticed that Fogelman wasn't going to do the walkaround with her, and it made her angry. "Wait until I'm clear of the main wheel well," Furness told Brodie. "Let *him* cold-soak for a while."

A few minutes after that, Rebecca finished her exterior inspection, climbed into the cockpit, and began her interior power-off, before engine-start, and engine-start checklists. At the briefed time, Furness called for the crew chief to get into position and began the engine-start procedures. Two minutes later, the engines were started and the power-on preflights were begun.

Most of the upgrades on the RF-111G Vampire bomber had been done on the weapon systems officer's side. The navigation, bombing, and reconnaissance avionics were all high-speed digital systems, so getting the ship ready to navigate was virtually automatic and very easy: turn ten switches from OFF to ON or STBY.

All that was left was to preflight the rest of the avionics, check the mission computer for the proper preset data points, and check the reconnaissance pods. All the checks were automatic and mostly done by computer. Preflighting the reconnaissance pods was simply a matter of making sure they had power, checking the data-link system was active, and making sure the radar could transmit—Fogelman did all his checks without referring to his checklist. In less than fifteen minutes, he was ready to go.

Rebecca's checks took substantially longer. After twenty-five minutes, her checks were complete. At the preplanned check-in time, she switched to the squadron common frequency. "Thunder Flight, Thunder One, check in and advise ready to taxi."

"Two."

"Three. Getting a new videotape. Ready in two."

"Four."

"Five."

"Six. I need a few more minutes." Everyone was on frequency. As usual, Paula Norton needed more time to complete the exhaustive after engine-start and before-taxi checklists.

Four minutes later, Norton called in ready. Furness took the flight to ground control to copy their route clearance and get permission to taxi. Furness swept the wings of her RF-111C to 54 degrees, clicked on nose-wheel steering, and turned on the taxi light. "Ready to taxi?" she asked Fogelman.

"Ready. Clear right." Fogelman had properly set the taxi lights and had the NAV mode primary pages up on the two Multi-Function Displays on the forward instrument panel—NAV DATA page on the left and NAV PRESENT POSITION page on the right. He was looking out the right cockpit canopy as if he were scanning for wingtip clearance, but he was pretty quiet and unanimated—he seemed a bit lethargic, as if he had got up too early. Hopefully he'd snap out of this soon.

"Here we go." Furness released the brakes and pushed the throttles up, then pulled them back and tapped the brakes when they started moving. The ramp seemed slightly slippery, but not dangerous. Ken Brodie guided her out of the parking area and watched carefully as she made the right turn toward the parallel taxiway. In order, the rest of the flight followed along, keeping a 150-foot spacing and staggered slightly on the taxiway to keep away from the preceding jet's exhaust. She noticed a blue station wagon following the aircraft, and tried to ignore it—undoubtedly the generals and the squadron commander were watching from there.

There was a short taxi checklist to run, which consisted mainly of checking switches and indicators while turning to make sure everything was tracking. When Rebecca checked the left MFD, however, she noticed that the TIME TO DEST, GND SPEED, GND TRK, and FIXMAG readouts were blank. She checked the right MFD, and the PRESENT POSITION readout was blank. "Something's wrong with your INS," she told Fogelman.

"No, it's—" Fogelman stopped his protest, then issued an exasperated "Shit," loud enough for Furness to hear without the interphone. He hit a switch on his right instrument panel. The readouts on both Multi-Function Displays came back, but they were reading gross values—the GND SPEED readout, the inertial navigation system's computed speed over the ground, was reading 87, about seventy miles an hour faster than their actual speed. "Dammit," Fogelman said, "I forgot to go to NAV." Fogelman had neglected to command the Inertial Navigational System (INS) to stop ground alignment and begin navigating before moving the aircraft. The INS would factor in all aircraft movement less than twenty-five nautical miles per hour and net zero earth-rate movement, and all the velocities in the system would be in error. Fixes, even superaccurate satellite fixes, probably wouldn't torque the errors out—he would have to start over.

Forgetting to go to NAV on the INS before taxiing was a common new-guy error, but Fogelman had nearly six months in the RF-111G—he should have known better. He was behind the aircraft already, and they hadn't even left the ground yet. "Realign in the hammerhead," Furness suggested. "You should have time for a partial alignment at least." Fogelman swore again in reply. *This flight,* she thought wryly, *is kicking off to a great start.*

The quick-check area was three aircraft-parking areas surrounded by thick steel walls where aircraft were inspected, deiced, and, if they were carrying weapons, the armorers pulled the safety wires—in case of an inadvertent bomb release or fire, the revetment walls would protect the other aircraft being armed up. Rebecca pulled into the first parking slot in the quick-check area, set the parking brake, checked that the attack radar and terrain-following radars were off, shut off the taxi light, then called on the radio, "Quick, Thunder Zero-One, radar's down, brakes set, cleared in."

Two maintenance technicians stepped out of a large blue truck. One plugged his interphone cord into the bomber's ground-crew jack, while the other stood by and waited. "Good morning, Zero-One. Quick's going in . . . when you're ready."

Furness placed her hands on the canopy bow. "Feet and hands clear," Furness replied.

"When you're ready, ma'am."

Furness looked over at Fogelman, who was working on restarting the INS. "Fogman, let 'em see your hands." The quick-check crews would not approach the aircraft unless they were sure that a crewmember in the cockpit wasn't going to move a flight control.

"One second."

"Don't bother restarting your alignment, Mark," Rebecca said. "They're going to move us in thirty seconds." But he did not acknowledge her, just continued working for a few seconds, then placed his hands on his side of the canopy bow. "Okay, feet and hands clear."

"Thank you, ma'am," the crew chief acknowledged. His assistant rushed in to check for loose access panels, leaks, Remove Before Flight streamers that might have been missed, and tire cuts. The assistant reappeared a minute later, and the crew chief began to motion for Furness to roll forward. She released brakes and applied power . . .

"Hey!" Fogelman shouted. Furness slammed on the brakes. "Dammit, you just spoiled the new alignment. I'll have to restart it."

"I tried to tell you that, Fogman," Furness snapped. "Let's finish the quick check, *then* start the alignment at the hammerhead." She taxied forward and reset the brakes.

The crew chiefs finished their tire inspection, then had Rebecca run the right engine up to 85-percent power and got into the main gear wheel well area to check for bleed air leaks. When that was done, the crew chiefs unchocked the plane, moved away from the bomber, and waved at the cockpit. "Have a nice flight, Zero-One."

"Thanks, Quick." The crew chiefs unplugged and trotted over to the next bomber waiting in the adjacent revetment. Rebecca taxied forward out of the quick-check area and over to the aircraft hammerhead, the parking area at the very end of the runway. Again, she set the brakes, then called for the Before Takeoff checklist. The wings were swept forward to takeoff position, the flaps and slats were set, and Rebecca checked the flight controls for full and complete movement. "Now you can start your alignment," she told Fogelman. He said nothing.

Another blue sedan, this one bristling with radio antennas on its roof, approached the parked bomber. "Foxtrot moving in," they heard on the radio.

"Foxtrot's cleared in to Zero-One, radar down, brakes set," Furness replied. As the bombers lined up in the hammerhead waiting for takeoff, the blue sedan carrying the Supervisor of Flying, an experienced flyer trained to be the commander's eyes and ears on the flight line during flight operations, began circling them, conducting one last visual inspection.

"No leaks, no streamers, and you appear to be in takeoff configuration," the SOF reported. "Have a good flight, Zero-One."

"Zero-One, thanks."

It was obvious Fogelman was still having problems—the PRI ATT and PRI HDG caution lights were still lighted on Furness' caution panel, indicating that the inertial navigation system was still not ready to go, and it was only a few more minutes to takeoff time. Fogelman was frantically searching through one of the supplemental squadron booklets for something. "How's it going, Mark?" she asked.

"The GPS didn't feed present position for coarse alignment," he replied. "I gotta set in the parking spot coordinates by hand." The INS needed an accurate latitude, longitude, and elevation to start an alignment. The squadron booklet, or "plastic brains," had coordinates for almost every possible parking spot on base, so getting the INS running without GPS shouldn't be a problem, but if you weren't expecting trouble, you usually weren't prepared for it—and that described Fogelman pretty well.

Meanwhile, the last bomber was coming out of the quick-check area.

"Thunder Zero-Six, no pins, no leaks, and you appear to be in takeoff configuration," the Supervisor of Flying radioed. "Have a good flight."

"Zero-Six, thanks," Paula Norton replied. "Lead, six is ready."

"Zero-One copies. Thunder Flight, push button four." The other five bombers acknowledged. Furness was going to tell Fogelman to change frequencies for her. Normally, the weapon systems officer changed radio frequencies via the Computer Display Unit on the right-side instrument panel, but he looked pretty busy, so she decided to do it herself. On the left Multi-Function Display, Rebecca punched the NAV option-select switch in the upper-left corner, which switched the MFD to the master menu page, then pushed the switch marked IFF/COMM, punched the switch marked CHAN, entered 04, then ENT, then RTN to get back to the radio page.

"Thunder Flight, check in button four." All five other planes acknowledged with short "Two . . . Three . . . Four . . . Five . . . Six."

Rebecca noticed that the PRI ATT and PRI HDG caution lights were out on her instrument panel, meaning that the inertial navigation system had finished coarse alignment and was somewhere in fine alignment. That was good enough for now—they had only two minutes to get the flight off the ground. "Plattsburgh Tower, Thunder Zero-One flight of six, ready for takeoff."

"Thunder Zero-One flight, winds two-eight-zero at eight gusting to fifteen, RCR 12, patchy ice, braking action fair, runway three-zero, switch to departure control, cleared for takeoff." The RCR, or Runway Condition Reading, was a measure of the slipperiness of the runway—a low number was good, a high number was bad. Twelve was borderline. The sweepers, with their big revolving bristle drums, had been out here a few minutes earlier, but sometimes the brushes merely polished the stubborn ice, making it even slicker. But Rebecca could see a lot of clear patches in the grooved runway, and the hammerhead and runup areas were clear.

"Zero-One, cleared for takeoff. Thunder Flight, push button five." All five planes acknowledged. On interphone, Furness said, "Stick it in nav and let's go, Mark."

"It's not done yet," he protested, but he punched the NAV line select key next to the steady NAV READY indication on his control and display unit—the INS was now navigating on its own, although with only a partial fine alignment its accuracy was in doubt. He then switched to the UHF RADIO page, tuned the primary radio to Burlington Departure air traffic control, set the backup radio to Plattsburgh Tower, then switched the identification beacon transmitters to ON. "Radios are set."

Furness released brakes and taxied out of the hammerhead. She made one last cockpit check, then "stirred the pot"—moved the control stick in all directions to check for free movement—then, as she turned and lined up with the runway centerline, began pushing in the power. Both throttles went to the first detent, and she scanned the RPM, turbine inlet temperature, exhaust pressure ratio, and nozzle position gauges. When the needles were stable, she started a stopwatch, then moved the throttles one at a time into afterburner zone one and watched the RPMs peg at 110 percent and the nozzle gauge read full open. She then quickly clicked the throttles all the way to afterburner zone five, letting the gradual but powerful kick of the engines shove her back into her seat.

The Vampire bomber sped through sixty nautical miles per hour in a few seconds. No call from Fogelman—the sixty-knot call was mandatory. "Sixty knots, nose wheel steering off."

"Hundred-knot check, instruments good," Fogelman said a few seconds later. *At least he made the call,* Furness thought, although she doubted he really checked the gauges or even really knew what to check for. Her engine instruments were good, the afterburners were still lit, and no warning lights on. He missed the fifteen-second acceleration call as well, but by that time they were almost at rotate speed. Furness applied back pressure, drawing the control stick to her belly, then waited a few more seconds. At the takeoff speed, the Vampire's nose wheel lifted off, followed by the main gear. Because the wheels were so big and the suspension system so rugged, takeoffs in the RF-111G were very smooth and it was hard to tell exactly when they lifted off. She simply waited until the vertical-speed indicator and altimeter were both moving upward a substantial amount, then raised the gear handle and retracted the flaps.

Ten seconds later, Johnson's Vampire crossed the runway hold line and leaped into the sky, Norton followed ten seconds later, and Kelly, leading the second three-ship cell, followed. But Clark Vest in the number-five bomber was a few seconds late getting his plane across the hold line, and tried to compensate by shoving the throttles too quickly into afterburner. The left-engine afterburners lit, but it blew out seconds after the right afterburner was cut in. Vest cycled both throttles into military power, let them stabilize, then tried to relight the 'burners, but the left afterburner blew out again.

"Thunder Five, fifty knots abort, fifty knots abort, fifty knots abort," he called on the Departure Control radio frequency. "Switching to tower." He turned his radio wafer switch to the backup radio. Meanwhile, Bruce Fay in Thunder Zero-Six had started his takeoff roll, but had aborted as soon as they saw Vest's left afterburner wink out. "Plattsburgh Tower, Thunder Zero-Five, aborting takeoff at fifty knots, turning off at midfield. No relight on number one. TITs are steady." Abnormally high TIT, or Turbine Inlet Temperature, would mean that a fire was building within an engine, which was common during afterburner blowouts or power drops. Fay switched to the Tower frequency as well—he wasn't going anywhere now.

"Thunder Flight, Plattsburgh Tower on GUARD, cancel takeoff clearance," the tower controller said. Zero-Five and Zero-Six held their position and acknowledged the order.

Furness and her wingmen heard the abort call on the departure control frequency as they continued their takeoff climbout. "Dammit, what a way to start the week," she muttered. "Now we'll have a royal clusterfuck to get this flight back together."

The big bomber climbed rapidly in the cold, dense air. A few seconds after takeoff, Furness had the gear, flaps, and slats fully retracted and the wings swept back to 26 degrees. At 350 knots indicated she pulled the engines out of afterburner and continued her climb to cruise altitude. "Mark, get on button one and find out about the other three planes."

Fogelman was looking at something in the radar—not a good idea when they were less than ten thousand feet altitude, in scattered clouds, with two wingmen trying to rejoin. With an exasperated shake of his head, he clicked his microphone. "Thunder Flight, go to button one on backup, now."

"Two."

"Three."

"Four."

"Mark, what do you have in the system?" Furness asked on interphone. She was following the standard instrument departure from Plattsburgh and was ready to transition to the mission flight plan, but the autopilot steering bug, or "captain's bars," were pointing behind the plane.

"I'm busy, pilot," Fogelman said. "I don't know where they're at. Switch it yourself." He then checked in the other two planes on the backup radio. Again, Furness couldn't argue, so she swapped nav pages with the right Multi-Function Display, checked her flight plan copy on her kneeboard for the correct computer sequence number, and entered it in the MFD. The captain's bars swung around to the proper heading, and she engaged the autopilot and turned to the first waypoint. Again, Fogelman was either being a jerk or was already too task-saturated to do more than one thing at a time—like set up the mission computers properly.

"Vest aborted because of an AB blowout," Fogelman told Furness. "Fay is going to hold with him."

"Terrific," Furness said. Their morning spectacular was busted almost before it began. Frank Kelly and Larry Tobias in Thunder Zero-Four were dropping "beer cans" and buddy-lasing for Bruce Fay in Zero-Six—he should launch single-ship and let Vest in Zero-Five, who was dropping a TV-guided bomb solo, go when he was ready. "Tell Command Post that Zero-Six needs to launch ASAP. Zero-Five can delay, but we need Zero-Six up here."

"I'm trying to recover my system and get an eyeball on our wingmen," Fogelman snapped. "How about calling them yourself?"

"*Fine.* Sing out when you see Johnson." Furness switched over to the backup radio: "Control, Zero-One, can you get Zero-Six airborne? We've got their bombing buddy airborne with us. Over."

In the background, Furness could hear Burlington Departure Control calling her. Fogelman was checking something in his radar and alternatively searching out the cockpit for the other three planes. Johnson was about two miles behind them, while Norton and Kelly were completely out of sight. Furness wafered over to Burlington Departure. "Departure, Thunder Zero-One, did you call?"

"Affirmative, Zero-One. Have your wingmen squawk standby when they approach within two miles. Say intentions of Thunder Zero-Four."

"Departure, Zero-Four will be joining on Zero-One to make a flight of four," Furness replied. "We're trying to get the status of the other two planes now."

"Roger, copy, Thunder Zero-One. Have them squawk standby when they are joined up with you."

"Zero-One, roger. Thunder Flight, you copy?"

"Two."

"Three."

"Four."

Furness switched over to the backup radio again. The channel was silent—they had been talking, but she couldn't pay attention. "Control, Zero-One, you were cut out, say again."

"I said, Zero-One," the command post controller said irritably, "that Alpha has directed Zero-Five and Zero-Six go as a flight of two. We're trying to get new target times on the range for Zero-Four, Zero-Five, Zero-Six, and you."

"Control, just launch *Zero-Six*—he and Zero-Four can still meet their time over target," Furness radioed back. Each bomber entered the route exactly four minutes apart, and while they were in the low-level route the airspace and the range had to be reserved for them—that meant coordinating new target times through Boston Air Route Traffic Control Center, the Air Force, and the Army. If a plane was going to be late, even by just a few seconds, new reservation times had to be obtained or the flight couldn't go. "You just need a new time for Zero-Five and a new time for me if you want me to go in after Zero-Five. Over."

"Zero-One, Alpha wants a two-ship launch," the command post controller replied. Obviously he was in no mood to argue—undoubtedly the command post folks were feeling a little heat from the brass, too. It was not a regulation, but aircraft with weapons aboard rarely were allowed to fly by themselves unless the weather was crystal clear—if there was an emergency, it was important to have a wingman to help lead the emergency aircraft back to base safely. The fact that they were Reservists and not full-time crews obviously had a lot to do with that unwritten rule—the thought of weekend warriors flying around by themselves with bombs on board unsettled a lot of people. "Request you contact us after your refueling so we can pass new times to you."

"Zero-One, roger," Furness replied. Well, so much for their plan. This was going to be a long fucking day. She had heard no reports on where her wingmen were—it was time to catch up on the joinup. She asked, "Okay, Mark, where's—"

Suddenly she heard Joe Johnson over the primary radio say, "Lead, Zero-Two, I'm overshooting, move out a little bit," in a rather urgent tone of voice. Furness looked out the right cockpit canopy and gasped in panic. Joe Johnson in Thunder Zero-Two was not just overshooting a bit—he was ready to collide. His overtake had been much too fast; his power was high during the climb, and the level-off surprised him.

"Jesus . . . dammit, what in hell are you doing!" She was about to yank the control stick over to bank away, but her right wingtip would collide with Zero-Two if she did that. Instead, she eased the stick down to lose some altitude. Slowly, the two planes slid away. "Shit, Mark, you're supposed to be watching the rejoin!"

"I *was* watching it," Fogelman seethed.

"You watch the rejoin until they're stabilized in fingertip, and you *do nothing else,*" she fired back. "When you got aircraft closing into fingertip, forget the radar, forget the INS, and concentrate on the rejoin. Christ, that was close!"

Johnson knew he had come close too: he said on the backup radio, "Sorry about that, lead. Just wanted you to get a good look at our underside."

"Thunder Flight, this is not a damned race," Furness shouted on the backup radio. She didn't care if the command post or the generals at Plattsburgh could still hear her—the near-collision was way, *way* too close for comfort: "Smooth and gentle on the rejoins. Zero-Three, say range."

"Two miles from Zero-Two," Paula Norton replied. Her voice sounded a little shaky—she had undoubtedly seen that near-collision as well. "We've got you both in sight. I've got Zero-Four on my wing already. He's checked me out already, too." Frank Kelly, an experienced F-111 pilot, had "cut off the corner," joined on Paula Norton's right wing, and had even accomplished a visual inspection. He would simply follow Norton in as she rejoined with Furness and Johnson.

"I want nice smooth turns and no abrupt power changes," Furness said. "Weather looks good in the orbit area. Lead's at 82 percent."

One by one, as they headed southwest toward the first checkpoint, the four bombers joined together. The first sequence of events was an aerial refueling over northern New Hampshire.

The rendezvous with the New Hampshire Air National Guard KC-135E tanker from Portsmouth Air Force Base was uneventful and smooth.

One by one, the formation split up while in the refueling anchor. Two minutes before Zero-Two's end air refueling time, Johnson accomplished a rendezvous to precontact position and then performed a practice emergency "breakaway"—the receiver would chop power and descend rapidly, the tanker would shove the power in and climb, and the other planes would stay on the tanker's wing. Rebecca remembered lots of practice breakaway maneuvers, both in the KC-135 and KC-10 tankers . . . and she was glad to be on the receiver side. She remembered back to those long hours flying over the desert during Desert Shield and Desert Storm as a KC-10 tanker pilot, refueling just about every kind of aircraft in the world—and she remembered how vulnerable the tanker was to any nearby danger. Especially the time during the emergency refueling with the stricken F-111G in the opening day of the war.

God, that seems like ages ago. She tossed it out of her mind and focused completely on getting into that comfortable state of mind where you feel that you're ahead of the aircraft, anticipating the sequence of events—finally in control of the situation. It was a little rocky starting out, she thought, but it was all coming back to them now. . . .

Miracles never ceased.

18

L'vov Air Base, the Ukraine, That Same Time

MIKOLA KORNEICHUK PUSHED HER WAY THROUGH A RATHER large crowd of hospital workers, patients, and bystanders on her way to the hospital front desk. The well-wishers shouted congratulations to the dark-haired, dark-skinned beauty, but she hardly heard one word—her eyes, her heart, her soul were focused only on one extraordinary man.

"Pavlo!" she shouted as the last few onlookers stepped aside to let her pass. The tall flying officer at the outprocessing desk finished the paperwork he had been working on, signing his name with a flourish on the last release form.

Aviation Captain First Class Pavlo Grigor'evich Tychina smiled from behind an antiseptic cotton mask covering part of his face, at hearing his girlfriend's voice. The mask was trimmed at the top, which allowed his curly brown hair to show and partially conceal the mask. Bandages and pads covered his nose and ears, but it was obvious that they were damaged—his left ear and his nose looked as if they were missing completely. Although Tychina wore a flight suit and heavyweight flying jacket—a new one, not the one in which he had bailed out—it could be seen that the upper part of his torso was covered with bandages, and his neck was thickly wrapped. "Mikki!"

he shouted in return. He turned to greet her, but held back.

She paused, taking his hands warmly, her eyes narrowing with concern as she sensed something in his mannerisms. "Pavlo? What is it?"

"I . . . I'm happy to see you, Mikki . . ." But he was pushing her away. Fearing that she might be repulsed by the sight of him, he was trying to keep his distance, not forcing her to get too close because of the onlookers surrounding them.

"Pavlo . . . Pavlo, damn you . . ." Mikola rushed into his arms and kissed him. The hospital staff surrounding them gave them an appreciative "Ahhh . . ." But as the kiss became more prolonged, they broke out into enthusiastic cheers and whistles. She finally released him, hugged him, then took his hand and led him to the hospital doors amidst wild cheering.

The sunshine was dazzling outside the hospital. Pavlo breathed in the crisp, cold air, thanking God and the stars above for letting him live. "All I want to do," Pavlo said, letting great gusts of steamy breath escape from the cotton mask's mouth slit, "is to stand out here and drink it in."

"We'll freeze to death, Pavlo," Mikola said, shivering. "So. Your place or mine?"

"Headquarters first," Tychina said. "I'm going to report back to duty right away."

"Report back to— Pavlo, you shouldn't even be out of the hospital yet!" Korneichuk protested. "You should be in bed and off that left leg! You just survived a high-speed, high-altitude ejection. What on earth makes you think you can go back on duty?"

"Because my injuries aren't serious, and we're at war," Tychina replied as if she should even have to ask. "I didn't say I'd be flying, although I think I'm well enough to fly. They're going to need every soul available to mobilize the armed forces if Russia wants to fight."

"If Russia wants to fight, the best the Ukraine can do is negotiate and beg for help from the West," Korneichuk said grimly. "They can slaughter us like sheep if they decide to invade."

"They can *try* to slaughter us," Tychina said, shaking his head as they walked away from the hospital. "And there may be little hope for us. The Ukrainian armed forces were designed to resist an outside invader until help arrived *from* Russia—not fight *against* Russia. But it's important to fight, Mikki. Whoever the invader is, it is important to fight."

A convoy of trucks carrying base security soldiers rolled by just then, and the truck's driver started to beep his horn when he recognized the young fighter pilot who, almost single-handedly, fought off the Russian air invasion. Soon every soldier in the back of the truck was cheering, and then the entire convoy of ten trucks joined in. Like the scene at the hospital, it was a stirring moment for the young pilot—and for her. Mikola Koneichuk began to realize what her lover was saying: one man's actions could make a difference. Seeing the enthusiastic faces of the men driving by in the trucks, in the faces of those she saw at the hospital, she could no longer say with certainty if her country would be defeated so easily by any foe—even Russia.

It was less than a kilometer to air army headquarters, but it took the couple over an hour to make the short walk because of the numbers of well-wishers who stopped to congratulate Pavlo on the way. Many of them offered the couple a ride, but Pavlo would simply put his arms around Mikola and say, "Would I deprive you unfortunate cretins a chance to glimpse this beautiful woman as you drive by?"

Korneichuk felt enormous pride and love for this man. His life, in many ways, had been so typical of young men in the then-USSR. Born in 1967 in Brovary, near Kiev, Pavlo was the son of Russian parents who made them very proud when he became a member of the Komsomol (Young Communists) and graduated with honors from the Gritevets Higher Military Aviation Academy in Char'kov, Ukraine SSR in 1987. After that, Pavlo was assigned to the Twenty-fourth Air Army in Tallinn, Estonia SSR, flying combat, strike, and maritime patrols in the Black Sea region in MiG-23s and MiG-27s. When the Ukraine declared independence from the collapsing Soviet Union in 1991, Pavlo gave up all privileges in the Russian/Soviet Air Force and accepted a commission in the fledgling Ukrainian Air Force. He did the same duties he'd always done for the Russians, except now it was for his true homeland. As his career moved quickly forward in the new Air Force, he became a flight instructor and flight commander just a year ago. Neither one of them could have guessed what had just happened, barely one year later.

She knew that he had almost been cut out of her life once, and that she should not allow it to happen again. She had always had doubts about being the wife of a military officer, especially a military pilot's wife, and she was never sure if that was the kind of life she wanted. But she now realized that, as difficult as life was in the Ukrainian Air Force, a life without Pavlo Tychina would be even worse. "Pavlo?"

"Yes?"

"I . . . I want to ask you something." She stopped, and Tychina turned to face her. "I've thought a lot about us, and . . . and . . ."

He reached up with leather-gloved hands and encircled her face. "I know what you're going to say, my love," Tychina said. "Believe me, I love you with all my heart and soul, and I want nothing more than to be with you forever. But I . . . I'm not . . . I just think you should wait. I don't want to pressure you into something you might regret."

"Regret? What could I possibly regret?"

Sadly, slowly, Tychina removed his fur hat, then pulled off the cotton antiseptic face mask. Pavlo's face was a maze of scars and lacerations, some requiring extensive stitches to close; others were so deep that they had to be kept open to allow pus to properly drain. His nose was heavily taped, but it was obvious, *too* obvious, that he no longer had a nose. A deep scar missed his left eye by millimeters, making his left eyelid look as if it were twice as large as normal, and it slanted upward, giving him a sinister Oriental appearance. His eyebrows and eyelashes were burned or shaved off. The scars continued down his throat—Mikola saw where a trachea tube had been inserted in his throat sometime during his surgery—and Pavlo revealed enough of his chest for her to see that the injuries continued far down his torso. It was a wonder to her that he could stand the pain without screaming.

"Do you understand now, Mikki?" Tychina asked quietly. "I look at myself in the mirror, and *I* am sickened! I begged my best friend to bring a gun and kill me, but it would be a waste of a bullet that could be used to kill invading Russians. The only thing that keeps me from ending my pain is my desire to keep the Russians off my homeland. I will not compel you to be with a man like me."

"With a man like—" Mikola stepped closer to him, reaching up to his face. He recoiled from her, but she took his horribly disfigured face in her hands and held it. "You are the bravest, kindest, most loving man I have ever known, Pavlo

Grigor'evich," she said. She kissed his scarred lips, holding the embrace until he finally relaxed and returned her kiss. She released him, then, still holding his face in her hands, said, "And if you don't marry me right away, Pavlo, you and I will *both* regret it."

"Are you sure, Mikki?" Another kiss gave him her answer. "Then yes, I would regret it for the rest of my life if I lost you. If you'll have me, Mikola, will you be my wife?"

Her tears of joy and her kiss was all the answer he required.

As they got closer to headquarters, which was only a few blocks from the flight line, they could hear the roar of dozens of jet engines. Pavlo could see more planes than normal parked on the ramp. Instead of just MiG-23 fighters and older Sukhoi-17 attack aircraft parked out there, there were a lot of Mikoyan-Gurevich-27 and Sukhoi-24 bombers. Although the MiG-23 had an integral bombing capability and the Su-17 was a capable, proven bomber, the MiG-27 and Su-24 were true high-tech supersonic bombers. The Su-24 was newer, faster, and deadlier than the Su-17 or MiG-27, and could carry up to eight thousand kilograms of ordnance, far more than any aircraft in the Ukrainian inventory, and it was also capable for use as a tanker to aerial-refuel other Sukhoi-24s for long-range bombing missions. Most Su-24s in the Ukraine were based in Odessa and Vinnica, so obviously substantial strike forces were being moved farther north to counter an expected Russian ground advance into the Ukraine. The smell of war was as powerful as the smell of burning jet fuel—and, truthfully, it both sickened and electrified Pavlo Tychina.

The entrance to the air army headquarters building was heavily guarded now. The guards allowed both Tychina and his new fiancée to enter the foyer, but because the base was on a war footing they could not allow Mikola to proceed past the security desk. Before proceeding, Pavlo made a few phone calls from the security desk, then turned to Mikola: "I've made an appointment with the wing chaplain," he said. "He has agreed to marry us later this evening."

She threw her arms around him, ignoring the guards and staff officers filing around them. "When, Pavlo? When can we go?"

"I've got to check in with the command center and speak with the commanding general," Tychina said. "He's old-fashioned, and he'd probably expect me to ask permission to marry. The chaplain will marry us in the base chapel in three hours, so you have that long to call your friends and ask them to meet us. I'll see you at the chapel then." She kissed him once again and, with her eyes glistening from tears, hurried off to make the wedding arrangements. Tychina checked in with the security guards, then proceeded toward the underground command center—undoubtedly, the air army commander would be down in the deep underground war room rather than up in his fourth-floor office.

A stairway took Tychina three floors down, where his identification was checked once again. Security was extensive, but Tychina was greeted warmly by security and wing staff members alike as he made his way to the command center. A curved, truck-sized ramp led one more floor down, past intelligence, combat planning, and meteorological offices, through another set of steel blast doors, and then into the command center itself. A few of the guards in the security cubicles let themselves out to shake Tychina's hand, and a few curious ex-flyers wanted him to lift his antiseptic mask up so they could see his scars and lacerations. Tychina was happy to see that no one that he could detect was repulsed by his appearance, and he knew he was fortunate. The Ukrainian Air Force was small, very close-knit, and supportive—unfortunately, he thought as he entered the main command center, it usually took a great disaster such as this to remind himself of how lucky he was to serve with such fine soldiers.

After checking in with the final security unit, Tychina met up with Colonel of Aviation Petr Iosifovich Panchenko, the deputy commander of operations of L'vov Air Base. Panchenko, nearly fifty years old, with a bald head and stone-gray eyes, was one of the few senior officers on base that Tychina really enjoyed working with—probably because Panchenko had risen through the ranks in his thirty years of service from a pneumatics technician, to weapons officer on attack helicopters, to rotary and then fixed-wing pilot, to the third-highest-ranking officer on base. He was a former Communist and very influential in the old Soviet Air Force, and could have been Chief of Staff of the Ukrainian Air Force or even Marshal of Military Forces, the highest-ranking military man in the Ukraine, or even Minister of Defense, had it not been for his past Communist Party affiliation and his formerly close ties to Moscow. Best of all was Panchenko's pro-flyers attitude—he still wore a flight suit as his standard utility uniform, even in headquarters.

"Captain Tychina?" Panchenko asked with surprise. *"Dobri dyen,* man, you're out of the damned hospital? How do you feel? Jesus, come on in here." Panchenko led Tychina through the communications center, past the battle staff conference room, and into a suite of concrete-walled offices reserved for the wing staff when they were in combat conditions. "I was going to visit you tomorrow, and I expected to see you either in traction or surrounded by beautiful nurses." He examined the sterile mask, then silently motioned for Pavlo to remove it. Penchenko's eyes narrowed slightly when he saw the horrible lacerations, but soon he stepped over to Tychina, put his hands on his shoulders, and said in a low, sincere voice, "You look like hell, Pavlo. You really do. But I'm damned glad to see you up and around."

"I'm reporting for duty, sir."

"You're . . . *what?* You want to start flying again?" he asked incredulously.

"I'm ready, sir."

"Did you get your medical degree on your last leave, Pavlo? Are you an expert now? Why don't you just take it easy for a few days and—"

"The Russians cut me up, sir," Tychina said in a low voice, "but they didn't hurt me. I can see, I can walk, I can fly, I can fight. I counted at least thirty new airframes on the ramp—do you have enough pilots to go with them? I should remind you that I'm checked out in every swing-wing fighter in the inventory."

"I know you are, Pavlo, and yes, for now, I have enough pilots," Panchenko replied rather uneasily. Obviously unspoken was the fact that if they had to begin a major deployment or, God forbid, an offensive against the Russians, he would run out of fresh pilots in less than twenty-four hours. "Look, Captain, I admire your dedication. I'll tell the General you were by—oh, hell, he'll probably be over at the hospital visiting you tonight."

"I'll wait here for him," Tychina said. "I'd like to ask his permission to get married."

"Married . . . ? Jesus, Pavlo, you're the most active war casualty I've ever seen," Panchenko said. He smiled, then took Tychina's hand and shook it. "Congratulations, son. Miss Korneichuk . . . Mikola, if I'm not mistaken?" Tychina nodded.

"Good man. You were wise to seek the old man's permission, too. He's from the old school, when officers couldn't get a hard-on without the commanding general's permission. But if I know you fast-burning MiG-23 pilots, you already got the chaplain lined up, am I right?"

"He'll do the ceremony in about two and a half hours, sir."

"Ha, I knew it," Panchenko said with a broad smile. "After what you've been through, I wouldn't blame you for not waiting." He picked up the outer office telephone and told Tychina, "I'll get the old man to come back to the command center to tell him you're here. You can ask him for his blessing, then I'll have a car take you to the chapel. You'll make it, don't worry." He made the phone call to his clerk, then added, "As far as permission to go back on duty, it's denied—until after the honeymoon. Four days . . . no, make it a week. May I suggest you spend your honeymoon abroad, as far as your savings can take you—Greece, Italy, even Turkey."

"You're suggesting I leave the country, sir?" Tychina asked with total amazement. "I couldn't do that!"

"Son, I'll give you permission to cross the border," Panchenko said, his face suddenly hard and serious, "and I strongly suggest you do it. First of all, you're a damned hero, a true hero. You put your life on the line to defend your country against astounding odds, and you were victorious. The whole world knows about you, and they would think poorly of the Ukrainian Air Force if we put you back on duty so fast. You should be going to the United Nations or to NATO, testifying on the Russian aggression—in fact, I will request that the commanding general send you to Kiev to debrief the general staff, then send you to Geneva to argue our case.

"Second, you're injured. You may think you're ready to fly, but you're not." He held up a hand to silence Tychina's protest, then added, "Third, you should take your bride out of the country, spend a few days making a future Ukrainian pilot, then leave her out of the country where it's safe."

"Sir, what in hell are you saying?"

"I'm saying that there's going to be a war, son, and Ukrayina is going to be the battleground," Panchenko said, using the less formal and more popular name, "Ukrayina," for their country. "New Russia wants to lead an empire again—Moldova, the Ukraine, Kazakhstan, maybe the Baltic states: the sons of bitches will try to take them all back. We're going to stop them from taking Ukrayina, with God's help and maybe some help from the West. But in the meantime, this will be no place for young Ukrainian wives and mothers."

"Do you really expect a war with Russia, sir?" Tychina asked gravely.

"Unfortunately, I do," Panchenko admitted. "So does the general staff. Ever wonder why you led a major patrol formation the other night with only a partial warload?"

Tychina's eyes lit up from behind his mask: "Yes, dammit, I only had half the close-range missiles I needed."

"There's a reason for that," Panchenko said, "and it's not because of some black market thefts, as the rumor mill is saying these days. You should—"

A klaxon alert suddenly blared just outside the office. Tychina jumped at the sound, but to his surprise, Panchenko did not—in fact, he appeared to have expected it. The door to his office burst open, but Panchenko did not look at the communications officer who had entered—he looked directly at Tychina's masked face with a sad, exasperated expression. "Sir!" the communications officer shouted. "'Majestic' fighter patrol reports large formations of bombers inbound. Supersonic bombers, Tupolev-160 and Tupolev-22M bombers, coming in at very low altitude. They got past the patrols."

"Cruise missile attack . . . and this time it won't be a straight-and-level attack," Panchenko said slowly, as if a great weariness had just come over him. "Lieutenant, launch Crown patrol and any other ready air patrols and aircraft. Sound the air raid sirens. Where's the General and the Vice Commander?"

"The General is in quarters, sir. The Vice is at a city council meeting downtown."

Panchenko knew it would take the commanding general at least ten to fifteen minutes to get back to headquarters, even if he raced back at high speed. He shook his head—he knew he had no choice. "Very well," he said. "Under my authority, seal up the command center and disengage external antennas. Switch to the ground-wave communications network and report to me when full ground-wave connectivity is established."

Pavlo Tychina's masked head quickly went from the excited communications officer back to Panchenko. "What's going on, sir? You're sealing up the command center?"

"We were lucky the other night, thanks to you," Panchenko said wearily. "You turned back what would have been the Russian's warning shot at Ukrayina. If they meant peace, we would have been safe. If they meant war, I knew they would return, only this time with weapons of mass destruction. That attack has begun."

"What? The *attack?* What are you . . . *Mikki!* God, *no . . . !*" Tychina's masked eyes finally realized what the senior officer was saying. He shot to his feet, pushed the communications officer out of his way, and raced for the door. He managed to make it out of the battle staff area and main communications center, but by the time he reached the large blast door outside the command center, he found it closed and bolted. He went back and confronted the security guards outside the communications center, but all he found were men with tight lips and eyes filled with terror who would not comply with his order to open the blast door.

"Even the commanding general must stay out until the all-clear is sounded, Pavlo," Colonel Panchenko said behind Tychina. "He knows that. Our ability to survive and fight would be destroyed if we opened that door. Even love must take a backseat when a nation and the lives of millions are at stake."

The lights suddenly went out, and after several long moments of darkness the emergency lights went on. "We're on generator power," he said matter-of-factly. "We operate on hydroelectric generators that run on an underground river, did you know that? Unlimited water and power. We can even produce oxygen. We have diesel generators and batteries as a backup—we have enough batteries to cover a soccer field down here. I estimate there are a hundred people in the command center, and the supplies were stocked for twice that number. We can survive down here for three months, if need be."

"What's the point?" Tychina asked angrily. His sterile mask produced a hideous effect, ghostly and evil-looking, like some medieval executioner on a rampage. "Is there going to be anything up there to protect?"

"Cicero said, 'While there is life there is hope,'" Panchenko said. He turned, sniffed at the air. "The ventilators have kicked on. We draw fresh air from miles away from the base until radiation levels exceed a certain point, then shut down and go on carbon dioxide scrubbers and electrochemical air-restoration systems, like a big submarine. Come on, Pavlo, let's get back and find out what's going on outside."

Tychina touched the big steel door. He thought he could hear voices and maybe fists pounding on the door from the other side, but the door was sixty centimeters thick, so that was unlikely. "She's gone, isn't she, sir?" he said from behind his mask.

"Pavlo, we don't know," Panchenko said over the loud hum of the ventilators. "All we know is, we've got a job to do. Our country needs us. You may have become the senior pilot of this wing, Pavlo, maybe even of the entire Ukrayina Air Force. I need you to help organize whatever forces we have. Now you can destroy yourself with pity, and I'll understand, because you've been through hell already. Or you can come with me and help me organize the battle against the Russians. Which is it going to be?"

Tychina nodded, took a deep breath, and followed Panchenko back to the battle staff briefing room. Perhaps he was being overly dramatic, he thought. Maybe it wasn't a full-scale attack, or maybe the air patrols would turn the Russian bombers back—the patrols had been strengthened since his incident the other night. He could hear the usual cacophony of chatter coming from the communications room, the clatter of teletypes and fax machines, the hum of computers. Nothing was going to happen, he thought. Dammit, he had let Petr Panchenko, a man he truly admired and wanted to emulate, see his scared, apprehensive side. He had to really take charge now, Tychina thought. He had to—

—suddenly all the lights went dead, a sound louder than thirty years' worth of thunderstorms rolled through the underground structure, and everything in Pavlo Tychina's consciousness went black.

19

Over the Adriatic Sea, 900 Miles West of L'vov Air Base That Same Time

THEY HAD LEFT LOSSIEMOUTH ROYAL AIR FORCE BASE IN Scotland, heading southeast, under the cover of a drenching rain and low overcast skies. The first sonic boom was sixty seconds after takeoff, where only a few fishermen and whales in the North Sea heard it. They stayed at high altitude and at Mach-two, flying in the same jet airways as the Concorde and other military flights, until over the Atlantic far off the coast of Spain, where the flight rendezvoused with a special U.S. Air Force KC-10 Extender aerial tanker. After fifteen minutes, fully fueled, the aircraft turned eastbound again, and let the throttles loose. Passing Mach-two, the normal turboramjet engines were shut down, and the ramjet engines were engaged. Now, twenty minutes and fifteen hundred miles later, they were screaming over the Adriatic at an altitude of one hundred thousand feet.

Every mission in the United States Air Force's newest reconnaissance aircraft, the SR-91A Aurora, was not only an aviation record-setter—it was a totally new experience for mankind. The Aurora was a large, triangular-shaped aircraft made entirely of heat-resistant composite materials—the fuselage was both a lifting body, like a giant one-piece wing, and was also a critical component of the aircraft's combined-cycle ramjet engines. Most of the 135-foot-long, 75-foot wide, three-hundred-thousand-pound gross weight aircraft was fuel—but not JP-4 jet fuel or even JP-7 high-flashpoint fuel as used in the Aurora's predecessor, the SR-71 Blackbird, but super-cooled liquid methane. It was the fastest air-breathing machine ever built.

For takeoff from Lossiemouth, the SR-91A burned gaseous methane mixed with liquid oxygen through the four large engine ducts on the bottom of the aircraft, much like the liquid-fueled engines on the Space Shuttle. At Mach-2.5, or two and a half times the speed of sound, the liquid oxygen would gradually be shut off, the rocket nozzles retracted, and the engines would switch to pure ramjet operation. A ramjet was a virtual hollow tube with a bulged interior that would compress incoming air like a giant jet turbine compressor; then methane fuel would be added and the mixture burned. The resulting thrust was four times more powerful than any other existing aircraft—Aurora was more like a spacecraft at that point. One more refueling over the Arabian Sea, and on to the destination in Okinawa, Japan. Upon approach to landing, the ramjet engines would be shut down, the turboramjet engines restarted, and a "normal" approach and landing—if a five-hundred-mile-long, two-hundred-mile-per-hour straight-in approach to landing could be considered normal—and the mission would be over.

In that mission, the three-person crew would have encircled one-third of the Earth in about three hours, and photographed over seven million square miles of the Earth's surface, transmitting the imagery via satellite to the Defense Intelligence Agency in Virginia. The pictures—synthetic aperture radar, long-range oblique optical, digital charged-coupled device optical, and infrared linescan—along with data from dozens of electronic sensors, would be developed and analyzed long before the Aurora was parked in a special hangar at Okinawa, allowed to cool off—its skin temperature would easily exceed a thousand degrees Fahrenheit, and it would take about twenty minutes before anyone could even approach the plane—and the space-suited crew finally taken off the plane. The next day, another series of recon missions, more records set, and a final landing at their home base at Beale AFB, California.

It was often said by proponents of the SR-91A Aurora that crewmen were an unnecessary redundancy—everything done on Aurora, from takeoff to landing to all reconnaissance and navigation work, was fully computerized. So when the electromagnetic and particle sensors aboard Aurora went crazy as it passed over the Adriatic Sea, the reconnaissance computer merely recorded the data, reset itself, did a complete self-test of its millions of computer chips and circuits, and began recording more information, automatically repeating the process six times a second. There was no report to the human occupants, no warning, no flight plan alterations.

It was as if it were perfectly normal, an everyday routine occurrence, for a half-dozen solar flares to erupt simultaneously—on the surface of the Earth, over Eastern Europe.

"Whoa, baby!" Air Force Major Marty Pugh, the engineer and RSO (Reconnaissance Systems Operator), called out over interphone. Although the plane's cockpit was fully pressurized, all of Aurora's crewmembers wore pressure suits, like the astronauts they were, and they were strapped so securely in place that movement was all but impossible. Very little talking was ever done during the high-altitude, high-speed portion of the flight, so when something happened, an excited voice got instant attention from everyone. "Hey, I got some particle energy readings that just jumped off the scale."

"Copy," Colonel Randall Shaw, the mission commander, replied. "I'm running a flight control check, Snap. Stand by." He got two clicks on the microphone from the aircraft commander, Graham "Snap" Mondy, who merely positioned his hands a bit closer to the side-mounted control stick and throttles. In a conventional aircraft, a flight control check would entail moving the stick, jockeying the throttles, perhaps turning off the autopilot and making a few gentle turns. Not in Aurora—a gentle turn might take them off course by two hundred miles, and flying without an autopilot at Mach-six could turn them into a blazing meteor in seconds. The flight control check was a simple voice command and a two-second self-check in which the flight control computer checked all of its circuits. "Check complete," Shaw reported. "In the green." Two more clicks meant that Mondy confirmed the report.

"Some shit is really going down there off to the north," Pugh said. In the fifteen seconds between his first and second sentence, Aurora had traveled twenty miles, and the sensors had turned their attention to Croatia, Bosnia, Serbia, and was getting ready to take pictures of Greece, Turkey, and the eastern Mediterranean. "You guys see anything out there at your ten o'clock?"

Looking out the window in Aurora was usually an exercise in frustration. The hull glowed so brightly from the heat that it washed out much of the view, and ground features zipped by so fast that even prominent landmarks like a city at night or the Himalayas went by before you had a chance to say, "Look at the Himalayas." But Colonel Mondy swiveled his head around in the Teflon helmet bearings and looked to his left . . .

. . . just in time to see a tremendously bright burst of light, like a laser beam had just flashed directly in his eyes. He blinked his eyes and turned away, but the spot was still there, etched right into the center of his field of view. "Dammit," Mondy said, "I just got flashed by something—an explosion, or a laser beam, something. Damn, I got a spot in my eyes."

"Massive electrical discharge," Pugh reported, "like a . . . a nuclear explosion or something . . . no thermal energy, but particle energy discharges nearly off the scale. Portside CCD optical cameras are out—whatever hit you, Colonel, got our digital cameras too. I've picked up five or six of them."

"Not now, Marty," Mondy interrupted irritably. He lifted his visor and tried to rub his eyes with his right index finger, but the bulky inflated gloves of the pressure suit didn't do much good. "Dammit, Randy, I really got hurt here."

"What is it, Colonel?"

"That flash . . . I got a dark brown spot in front of my eyes, and it's not going away," Mondy said. "I think I got a retinal burn or something. You have the aircraft."

"I have the aircraft," Shaw acknowledged. "You need help? Want to come out of hypersonic range so we can radio headquarters?"

"No . . . dammit, maybe. Let me think," Mondy said. Because Aurora developed a very powerful thermal and static electric field around it during its hypersonic flight, it was usually necessary to slow down to Mach-three, the lowest speed possible with the ramjet, to talk to anyone on the radios. Standard procedure was to remain radio-silent during all ramjet operations. In an emergency you stayed hypersonic until you computed an alternate landing site at least five hundred miles away, because it would take that long to slow down, restart the turboramjet engines, and make an approach—and there were only ten approved landing sites in the entire civilized world for Aurora.

"No, stay with the flight plan—but you'll have to take the plane for the landing, Randy," Mondy said. "Man, I'm really hurt. That dark spot is getting bigger and darker, and I'm getting a really bad headache. Check all systems again, crew—I'm concerned about that blast affecting our systems."

"Hell, we're sixteen miles above and at least six hundred miles away from the location of that disturbance," Pugh said. "Imagine what it was like for someone on the ground."

They did not even want to think about *that.*

20

The White House, Washington, D.C.
That Same Time

FIVE MINUTES AFTER THE TINY BUTTON IN THE OFFICE OF THE chief of the Presidential Protection Detail, U.S. Secret Service, was pressed, a large green and white helicopter was dropping out of the gray, ice-filled clouds over Washington, D.C., and lowering onto the front lawn of the White House. The helicopter was of course Marine One, a VH-3D Sea King helicopter flown by HMX-1, the Marines Corps Executive Flight Detachment from Quantico, Virginia. The engines were never brought to idle upon landing—the Marine Corps pilots held the helicopter on the ground by brute strength with the throttles just below takeoff power until their very special passengers and their Secret Service escorts were on board. Then the pilots shoved the power back in and lifted off, swooping low over the Ellipse before rapidly climbing. Seconds after clearing the area, it was joined by two other identical VH-3D VIP helicopters, and the three craft shuffled inflight position in a prebriefed sequence until it could no longer be apparent to anyone on the ground which helicopter was really carrying the President of the United States, his wife, and members of his Cabinet and staff.

It was a short helicopter ride to Andrews Air Force Base in Maryland, and a high-speed tactical landing just a few feet from the left wingtip of a Boeing E-4B NEACAP, or National Emergency Airborne Command Post aircraft. The huge modified Boeing 747B, white with a dark blue stripe across the sides with the words **UNITED STATES OF AMERICA** in bold letters across the upper half, also had a distinctive bulge on the top of the plane that distinguished this plane from the standard VC-25A Air Force One; the bulge contained a satellite and SHF (Super High Frequency) communications antenna that, along with a two-thousand-foot trailing wire antenna and forty-six other antennas arrayed around the plane, allowed the plane's occupants to literally talk to anyone in the known world with a radio receiver—even if that radio receiver was aboard a nuclear-powered submarine sitting two hundred feet below the surface of the ocean or in orbit two hundred miles above the Earth. Exactly ninety seconds after Marine One touched down, RAFT-104 (as the NEACAP aircraft was known on an open radio channel) was leaving the ground.

The President, his wife, and their daughter had been securely strapped into plush, high-backed seats in the forward flight crew section of the 4,600-square-foot main deck of the aircraft. The President was a big, handsome young man from what many derisively called a "Deliverance" state—lots of farmers and country folk with the joke being that, as in the movie, the men found the pigs more attractive than the women. He had been one of that state's youngest and most popular politicians and one of the youngest chief executives of the United States. Despite his frequent campaign and news shots of him jogging around the running track on the South Lawn, he was plainly out of breath after running up the thirty-four steps of the airstair to enter NEACAP. But if it was from physical exertion or from fear of being roused out of the White House by the Secret Service, it was hard to tell. His wife, in stark contrast, was not out of breath one bit. Much shorter than her husband, slim and trim, with professionally lightened, shoulder-length hair and blue eyes, the First Lady was highly intelligent and very much like her husband. It was often said that the combination of this almost inseparable pair was far greater than the sum of their parts. Many couples in the White House had been described as running a copresidency for a variety of reasons, but although she held no official posts or headed any commissions other than ceremonial ones, in this White House there was no doubt that the President and his wife made a very powerful force to reckon with.

Just a few moments after takeoff, the First Lady turned to their lone colleague, Michael J. Lifter, the President's National Security Advisor, and asked, "What was this about an attack in Europe, Michael? Something happen with Russia and Moldova?" The President's eyes briefly registered his wife's question, and there might have been a hint of irritation at her speaking out before he, but he turned toward Lifter and silently awaited his response.

Lifter, just a bit taller than the First Lady, dark and angular, glanced at the communications panel on the table in front of them. "As soon as the air-to-ground channels are open, I'll get us an update," he replied, addressing them both. "The word I got was that the Ukraine came under attack by Russian cruise missiles, and that nuclear weapons might be involved."

"My God," the First Lady replied. "That's horrible . . . it should be confirmed at once. I hope Velichko hasn't finally gone over the edge."

"It'll take a few minutes for the communications group to get connected into the system and a situation report prepared," Lifter said. He was a former naval officer and a long-time military attaché to the White House, and was very familiar with the interface between the military and civilian halves of the chain of command. Information flowed relatively freely and quickly between military users, especially intraservice, but it flowed less effectively interservice and, in most cases, very poorly between the military and civilian sectors. The First Couple, for example, would never request or accept a standard NMCC SITREP, or National Military Command Center Situation Report—it was so full of abbreviations and acronyms that it would throw both of these Ivy League grads into a royal tizzy. It had to be condensed into a readable, reportable format, and that took time. "Once we're above ten thousand feet," Lifter said, adding a definite number that he knew the couple could comprehend, "the crew can unstrap and all stations can hook in. It'll only take a few minutes."

While they waited, a crew physician came forward to check the President and the First Lady—he had a history of occasional airsickness—and another crewmember distributed a card with a list of crewmembers on board and facilities ready at the President's disposal. There was a flight crew of eight—four pilots, two navigators, and two flight engineers in two shifts—a cabin crew of ten, a security crew of ten—all Secret Service, no Marines—a military crew of forty, a secretarial staff of six, a White House advisory staff of eight, a computer operations crew of two, and a medical staff of four. Only the President, the First Lady, and the National Security Advisor had made it to NEACAP when the alarm had sounded. "Aren't there supposed to be more Cabinet officers on board? What about the Secretary of Defense? Where's Don Scheer?"

"Sir, during a full-alert scramble, it's always unlikely that anyone but those in immediate arm's-length availability with the President will ever make the run," Michael Lifter explained. "The crew of the airborne command post is chosen carefully for its ability to command the military in time of emergency. It is not really intended to be a flying White House."

"It's like a flying Hitler's bunker," the First Lady said half-aloud, almost in disgust. She moved closer to her husband and whispered, "We need to get in touch with Don Scheer and Harlan Grimm right away. We can't be holed up too long with the damned military." Grimm was the Secretary of State and a close friend to the First Couple.

"I know, honey, I know," the President said. "Let's let the boys do their job, though." The First Lady sat back in her seat and affixed Lifter with an impatient glare.

Of course the officers and technicians in the C^3-I (Command, Control, Communications, and Intelligence) area of NEACAP didn't need a "few minutes" or to unstrap to do their jobs—information could flow from all points of the globe no matter how high or low NEACAP was flying—and in far less time than Lifter predicted, a report was delivered to him by an Air Force brigadier general, the chief of NEACAP's communications section, and he reported that the battle staff was ready to speak with the President in the battle staff conference area. The President and Lifter rose and headed back to the conference room; the First Lady deftly moved herself in back of her husband and in front of Lifter as they were led by a steward to the meeting.

The senior military officer on board NEACAP was Air Force Lieutenant General Alfred Tarentum, the fifty-seven-year-old commander of Eighth Air Force, the major command division of the U.S. Air Combat Command, from Barksdale Air Force Base, Louisiana. The chief of the NEACAP battle staff was chosen by the Joint Chiefs of Staff and the Secretary of Defense based on the nature of the current world emergency, as well as by a rotation list of senior military officers; Tarentum, as commander of the Air Force's numbered air force in charge of all bombers and attack aircraft, was the highest-ranking air power expert available for detached duty.

Because NEACAP aircraft had not been deployed on alert duty to Washington for several years (NEACAP followed the President while traveling overseas, but otherwise was rarely used since the end of the Cold War), and because Tarentum was based in Louisiana and not in Washington, the President and very few others in the White House actually knew him—this didn't help to put anybody at ease as he began his briefing: "Mr. President, ma'am, Admiral Lifter, I'm Lieutenant General Al Tarentum, battle staff senior officer, and I have your situation report." He did not wait or expect any other comments, but went right into his briefing:

"About twelve minutes ago, at approximately five o'clock in the afternoon Moscow time, approximately one hundred Russian bombers launched long- and short-range cruise missile and gravity bomb attacks against targets in the Ukraine, Moldova, and Romania. Some of these attacks included cruise missiles armed with low-yield nuclear warheads, what are commonly known as enhanced radiation devices or neutron bombs—"

"Excuse me, General," the First Lady interjected, "but why did we have to evacuate Washington? Was the United States under attack as well?"

"No, ma'am," Tarentum replied. "However, we detected and have been monitoring the deployment of Russian bombers back to bases in Cuba. These bombers are similar to the ones that attacked in Europe. Since we can't be sure of the precise location and number of bombers along the eastern seaboard at any time, when we received notification of the nuclear release in Europe we had no choice but to evacuate the NCA."

"The NCA," Lifter said, "is the National Command Authority, generally meaning the President and the Secretary of Defense or their designees."

"I know who the NCA is," the President said, finding a glass of ice water and taking a sip. He didn't sound nearly as irritated as his wife did—undoubtedly his stomach was causing him more consternation than events were right now. The windows on board NEACAP had been sealed shut with silver-coated shutters to block out any possible nuclear flashes.

"Then how come Mr. Grimm isn't on board, General?" the First Lady asked pointedly.

"Ma'am, our first priority is the safety of the President," Tarentum replied. "The chains of command are intact as long as the President is safe. If any other Cabinet members were present, they would of course be taken along."

"We were fifteen minutes from a morning staff meeting," she said, challenging him. "Surely the others were present or very close by."

"Honey, let's postpone this discussion for some other time," the President said. "Go on, General. What else?"

"We have a call into President Velichko of Russia and President Khotin of the Ukraine," Tarentum said. "However, both men issued statements soon after the attack." A folder was placed before the President with a full text of the two government heads' addresses. "President Velichko said that the attack was a response to the aggression by the Ukraine two nights ago when their fighters attacked several reconnaissance planes legally overflying the Ukraine."

"That's bullshit," the President said, shaking his head. "Everyone knows those planes were Bear bombers." He turned to Lifter, his eyes searching for confirmation.

"Absolutely, Mr. President," Lifter acknowledged. "Armed with cruise missiles. Sources confirmed it."

"President Khotin of the Ukraine in response declared war on Russia," Tarentum went on, "and said he and the Ukrainian people will fight to the last man, woman, and child to keep their country free from Russian domination. There has been no further official communication from Kiev. Sources say that the central government may be evacuating the capital."

"Where could they go?"

"The Pentagon believes they could very well go to Turkey, sir," Tarentum replied. "As we've seen for several years now, relations between Turkey and the Ukraine have grown very close, possibly to the point of mutual cooperation and defense. The Pentagon has speculated that Turkey may have been accepting large quantities of Ukrainian weapons over the past several weeks to be stockpiled there in case of an invasion."

"Excuse me, but I want to know what all this has to do with *us,*" the First Lady interjected. "You spirit us away in this thing like it's the end of the world, and now we're talking about Turkey and the Ukraine—two countries on the *other* side of the world, for God's sake." She turned to her husband and said, "I think we should put this thing on the ground at Andrews and get back to the White House immediately. We look like a bunch of chickens running around with our heads cut off."

"As soon as we determine exactly the status of the Russian bombers in Cuba and other Russian and CIS forces in Europe and the Atlantic," Tarentum said, not believing the balls of the Steel Magnolia. "We'll make a determination—"

"General, my *husband* will make a determination, not you or anybody else," the First Lady said.

That silenced everyone in the conference cabin. The President put a hand on his wife's without looking at her, a silent order to calm down and take it easy, then said to Tarentum, "General, you go ahead and do your evaluation. However, I am concerned about getting back to Washington as soon as possible. Frankly, I'm concerned, like my wife is, about what it looks like if the President abandons the capital like this. The American people will start to think I'm scared, and I *don't* want that. I may be able to direct military forces from up here, but I can't be a leader flying safe and sound thirty thousand feet over everyone's head."

"We need to issue a press release calling this a false jump by the military," his wife said. "Off the record, I'll say we were nearly shanghaied into getting on board this thing—we can authorize *that* to get leaked to the press."

"Let's get the military business over with, shall we?" the President asked. "What do we need to do, General?"

"Your first decision is how to respond to the attack," Tarentum replied, "specifically to the use of nuclear weapons by Russia. From a military standpoint we have no strategic nuclear forces available right now except for a few submarines, which I very much doubt if the Russians think we would consider using in a European conflict. This means we hold no Russian targets at risk whatsoever. If Russia decided to commence a nuclear attack in Europe or North America, our only response right now would be with six Ohio-class submarines, each carrying sixteen or twenty-four missiles, each with one warhead—a maximum of 144 warheads."

"That's a pretty sizable force, I'd say."

"Yes, sir, but the question would be, does Russia think we'd employ those missiles, and would the damage they'd inflict be greater than what the Russians could do on their first attack?"

"What do the Russians have deployed right now that could reach the United States?" the President asked.

"We don't know precisely, sir," Tarentum replied, "but our latest estimates are based on credible forces the Russians had deployed at the time they voluntarily stood down a large percentage of their nuclear forces." He placed another folder before the President; no one touched it. "The primary threat is from approximately two hundred road-mobile SS-25 missiles and about ninety rail-mobile SS-24 missiles. That's almost three hundred missiles, assuming the Russians haven't put multiple warheads on the SS-24—it can take as many as ten warheads each.

"We estimate at least 25 percent of their sea-launched ballistic missile force has been mobilized since recent hostilities started—that's another 250 missiles, not including the additional deployment of sub-launched SS-N-21 Sampson cruise missiles. We've seen as many as one hundred bombers launched in support of the attacks against targets in the Ukraine, and they've been carrying cruise missiles and short-range attack missiles—the Blackjack bomber can carry twelve cruise missiles each—"

"Okay, okay, I get the picture," the President said. "Jesus, I thought the Russians were doing away with all these heavy nuclear forces. Why in the hell are we giving them billions of dollars to dismantle their nuclear forces when they still have all these forces operational?"

"Sir, as you know, final ratification of the START treaty was held up primarily because of the conflict between Russia and the Ukraine," National Security Advisor Lifter said. "The Ukraine refused to eliminate its nuclear weapons until a defense agreement was signed with NATO—that wasn't done until late last year."

"I know, but we've been telling the American people that we've been doing away with Russian weapons of mass destruction, that we've got nothing to worry about from Russia as far as long-range nuclear weapons are concerned," the President said. "Next thing you know, we're up in the Doomsday Plane. How are we going to explain this?"

"Sir, let me get back to the situation at hand," General Tarentum interjected. "I have a specific suggestion to make:

implement the Joint Chiefs of Staff's alert plan right away." The First Lady was no longer paying attention; the President motioned for him to continue: "We can have our land-based bombers placed back on alert within twenty-four hours." He set another folder before the President. "That comprises a force of fifty B-52G and -H bombers, approximately eighty B-1B bombers, and twenty B-2A stealth bombers. We can augment this force with F-111 or F-15E bombers if necessary. The Pentagon suggests that we not mobilize any more sea-launched or land-based missiles at this time. The bombers would represent a low-scale response to a very grave threat."

"I'll have to take this up with the Secretary of Defense and the Chairman of the Joint Chiefs," the President said. "When can I talk to them?"

"We should be connected any minute now, sir," Lifter replied.

The President was silent for a moment; then: "What about mobilizing the Reserve forces? What kind of force mix do we get from that?"

Tarentum had anticipated such a question, and flipped a page in the previously ignored folder to show the President. It was a well-known fact that the Commander in Chief was a firm believer in the cost-cutting advantages of the Reserves, and a primary focus of his administration had been to enhance the viability of the Reserve forces. "There is one B-1B squadron in South Dakota, four B-52 squadrons in New York and Washington state, one F-15E squadron in North Carolina, and four F-111 squadrons in New Mexico and New York, all in the Enhanced Reverse Program," Tarentum replied. "These units are primarily conventional squadrons—the one RF-111 unit up in upstate New York is a reconnaissance and Wild Weasel–type unit—but they are all fully certified for nuclear duties." He paused, watching the First Lady out of the corner of an eye, and added, "They also have the largest percentages of women serving in the tactical air squadrons—*thirty percent* of the crewmembers in these combat units are *women.*"

That got the Steel Magnolia's attention like nothing else. As outspoken as the President was on the value of the Reserves and National Guard, she was equally vocal about putting women in combat. Her reaction was understated, but Tarentum could see her eyes flicker in sheer delight. This was precisely what she wanted, and she made her wishes known by simply placing her hand atop her husband's, a secret, quiet sign—known to everyone in the White House—that she wanted the order given.

"I think this would be a good opportunity to see our women combat soldiers in action," the President declared. "Besides, I don't want to stir things up too much—it's possible that the Russian attack was all a big mistake, and I don't want anyone to get the impression that I think the Cold War is heating up all over again. Ten bomber squadrons is plenty—no subs or MX missiles for now. Get General Freeman on the phone and let's get to it. And I want a report on when we can set this thing down—the sooner the better." He had lapsed into calling NEACAP, the most sophisticated aircraft on earth, "this thing," just like his wife referred to it and all the apparatus of the office of the President of the United States with which she was decidedly uncomfortable.

"Maybe we should go somewhere as if this was a scheduled visit," the First Lady suggested. "Perhaps down to talk to President Carter in Georgia, or Walter Mondale in Minnesota? Perhaps we can pick up Air Force One in Georgia and fly back to Washington in it, so the press and the public will see us flying in it rather than the . . . the Doomsday Plane."

"Good idea, honey," the President said. "Can you see if we can arrange that, General? Let's go see Jimmy. Mike, how about getting the office on the phone and twisting some arms here? And some coffee and juice would be nice. What's the kitchen like on this thing, anyway?"

The meeting over, stewards and secretaries swarming into the conference room, General Tarentum carefully collected up all the classified briefing folders on the conference table and dismissed his staff. Just as he feared, the threat wasn't being taken seriously. What could possibly become World War III was happening right now in Europe, and the President of the United States' response was to mobilize only one-fifth of America's strategic fighting forces, then he was off to see Jimmy Carter, of all people, as if he didn't have a care in the world.

Times had certainly changed, all right.

21

394th Air Battle Wing Headquarters, Plattsburgh AFB, NY That Same Time

"VERY IMPRESSIVE," GENERAL COLE SAID HALF-ALOUD AS Colonel Lafferty, the wing vice commander, entered the office. Cole ran one hand across his black-haired flattop and handed the report he was reading over to Lafferty with the other. "It's the preliminary Air Combat Command readiness report from Maintenance Group."

"What? So soon?" But Lafferty's skeptical expression turned into one of surprise, then grudging admiration as he scanned the report. Lafferty was not the easiest man in the world to impress. A Naval Academy graduate who transferred to the Air Force after Navy flight assignment drawdowns went into effect following Vietnam, Lafferty looked like a typical fighter jock, with a large expensive Rolex, rolled-up sleeves on his flight suit, visible dog tags, and non-military-issue aviator sunglasses on top of his head. He loved fighters and flyers, but wasn't overwhelmed by either until both proved themselves to him. "Well, all *right*—the new guy aces out the other groups his first day on the job. Mace must've really lit a fire under Razzano's behind."

"He *fired* Razzano," Cole said. "Sent him to me for reassignment. Made Lieutenant Porter his exec instead—even promoted her to captain."

"Shaking things up in the old office? Housecleaning?" Lafferty shrugged his shoulders and said, "Well, it's his prerogative. Razzano was on autopilot anyway, waiting for a reassignment, and Mace is a crewdog—he'll cut the ground-pounders out and put in junior officers or other crewdogs every time. But I was afraid he'd do his ex-Marine head-busting routine." He scanned the report, then: "Boy doesn't pull any punches, either—he's saying we're only slightly better than minimally mission-capable. You going to upchannel this?"

"With the boss coming, I have no choice." Cole sighed. "If my MG says it may take over seventy-two hours to generate the force for SIOP or for a max-rate deployment, I have to go along with it. But he's got a plan to compensate. He's moving eight Vampires into the shelters—says he's going to put them into preload status right away."

"We're going to preload *eight* bombers?" Lafferty asked, astonished. "Jesus, spare us from the old retread SAC guys. That means we're going to start flying with external tanks again?"

"Afraid so. With eight planes in preload status, that means he'll need to keep at least ten, maybe twelve planes with tanks on the line."

"God—wintertime with external tanks." Lafferty moaned. "Remember all the problems we had? Frozen feed lines, crew chiefs pounding on tank pylons with wheel chocks to unstick frozen valves, incompatible mountings, upload tractor breakdowns . . ."

"Yeah, and remember the last Bravo exercise we had, where we had to cut the deployment exercise short by two days because three of our tankers went off-station and we couldn't get enough external tanks on our planes?" Cole asked. "We've been kidding ourselves, Jim—we call ourselves mission-capable a lot of times when in reality we couldn't get half this wing overseas in the required amount of time. If Colonel Mace wants to take on the challenge of maintaining one-third to one-half of our bomber fleet in preload status, let him. We'll give him until the end of the second quarter to see if he can do it without breaking the bank or causing his entire Group to resign."

"Well, I'm going to miss flying with slick wings," Lafferty said. "Flying with externals is a real disappointment. What do you want to do with Razzano?"

"I have no earthly idea," Cole said. "I've got a call in to check on his assignment to Seymour-Johnson, but no word yet. You got any special projects you need handled?"

"Right off, he can collect and process all these readiness reports," Lafferty said. "We should—"

There was a knock on Cole's door, and before Cole could respond, Major Thomas Pierce burst into the office. "Excuse me, sir . . ."

"Something wrong, Tom?"

"Something's happening in the Ukraine again, sir," Pierce said, going over to Cole's television and turning the channel to CNN. "About five minutes ago, all the network stations just interrupted their normal broadcasts. About thirty seconds ago, we got an all-stations standby poll from NEACAP. STRATCOM is advising—"

"*What?* NEACAP? The President is *airborne . . . ?*"

Pierce nodded, his face taut and grim. NEACAP, or National Emergency Airborne Command Post, was the high-tech Boeing 747 reserved for the President and others in the military chain of command in case of war. Except for annual exercises, it had not been used in many years. Normally all four of the nation's E-4B NEACAP planes were stationed at Offutt Air Force Base in Nebraska, but one had been moved to Andrews Air Force Base and placed on alert weeks ago when the conflict in Europe started to heat up. "Jesus . . . this is some serious shit."

Just then, Cole's executive officer stuck his head in the door as well; after checking that no uncleared persons were in the office, he said, "Sir, Command Post called. An A-Hour has just been declared."

"A *what?*" Cole demanded, shooting to his feet. "What in the hell is going on? You two, follow me." He rushed out the door, shouting to his executive officer, "Captain, call in the entire staff to the battle staff conference room on the double," as he headed out of the office and downstairs to the underground command post. What the fuck had happened over there? Had Velichko finally gone off the deep end? The declaration of an A-Hour, or Alert Hour, confirmed their worst fears after learning that the President had abandoned the capital: the A-Hour was an order relayed from the President of the United States through his specified commanders to prepare for a nuclear war.

The command post at Plattsburgh had remained virtually the same as it was when it was all but abandoned in 1990, after the FB-111A bombers were removed from the base; except in recent weeks when events had started really heating up, it was used only occasionally for alert exercises. The wing commander and his staff members used a CypherLock keypad to gain entry through the outer door, which was locked behind them. They were now inside a small enclosed hallway, called an entrapment area, where the officer in charge of the command post could see them as their identification was checked one by one by an armed security guard. Inside, they went through a small office area and then into the communications center, where two command post technicians and one officer manned a complex of several radios, covering many bands of the electromagnetic spectrum, allowing them to communicate by voice or data to anywhere in the world. One wall was covered with an aircraft-status board, showing the location, crew complement, and status of every wing aircraft, both at Plattsburgh and at Burlington International Airport.

Cole was about to hurry into the battle staff area, from where he could receive reports and watch the news on banks of television monitors, but at that moment a warbling *deedledeedledeedle* alerting sound came over the loudspeaker, and a shadowy voice, probably a controller from the Pentagon speaking on the microwave link judging by the clarity of the voice, announced, "I say again, I say again, SKYBIRD, SKYBIRD, message follows: two, Bravo, Tango, India, seven, one, seven, Lima . . ." The cryptic message, read out as numbers or as phonetic characters, continued on for a total of exactly thirty-seven alphanumerics, then repeated once again. On one of the readbacks, the controller's nervous voice cracked with the tension, and he had to issue a "Correction, character twenty, Whiskey, reading on beginning with character twenty-one, Uniform, five, five . . ." until the message was reread successfully.

"What have you got, Harlan?" Cole asked Major Harlan Laughlin, the command post senior controller.

"Message from the Pentagon, National Military Command Center," Laughlin replied. "We're officially in DEFCON Four. Strategic Command is generating the bombers for SIOP operations."

Cole sucked in his breath as the tension crept across his neck and forehead like hot air from a bonfire. Defense Configuration Four officially placed selected portions of the Air Force's B-52 Stratofortress, B-1B Lancer, B-2 Black Knight stealth bombers, and other tactical aircraft, including the RF-111G Vampire, into Strategic Command—they were back into the strategic nuclear warfighting business, known as the SIOP, or the Single Integrated Operations Plan, the computerized "playbook" for World War III.

As an experienced Air Force commander and former Pentagon officer, Cole was very familiar with DEFCON Four—that was a low-threat war footing, the readiness level at which they had operated from the end of the Cuban Missile Crisis to the end of 1991. During the Cold War, DEFCON Four was considered "normal," with hundreds of bombers and thousands of nuclear-armed missiles poised to strike at the first sign of a large-scale attack. Now, after years at DEFCON Five, which was total peacetime readiness, DEFCON Four suddenly felt like the beginning of the end of the world.

"STRATCOM and Air Combat Command issued verified repeat messages," Laughlin continued. "STRATCOM issued a Posture Two message just now. LOOKING GLASS is airborne." To further define the actions each unit was to take, STRATCOM messages would direct various "postures," or levels of readiness. Postures were numbered opposite of DEFCONs—while DEFCON One was all-out war, Posture One was the lowest readiness level; and since Strategic Command, with its huge and powerful deterrent arsenal of long-range nuclear weapons, wanted its forces ready for anything, they usually set a posture level one step higher than the military as a whole.

"Have we established connectivity with LOOKING GLASS?" Cole asked. Strategic Command had its own airborne command post, an EC-135 communications aircraft known as LOOKING GLASS because its sophisticated communications abilities allowed it to "mirror" the actions of the STRATCOM underground command center in Omaha and control all of its nuclear forces—it could even launch land-based nuclear missiles by remote control, once given the proper coded orders from the President of the United States. LOOKING GLASS, which carried a general officer, a battle staff of eight, and a very sophisticated communications suite, would take command of the strategic forces as soon as it entered its orbit area over the central United States, within secure radio range of the ICBM missile silos in Montana, Wyoming, Missouri, and North and South Dakota.

"Not yet, sir. May not be up for another thirty minutes. We still have full connectivity with all headquarters, and LOOKING GLASS is not expected to take command of the force." This did not make Cole any happier about these circumstances. The commander of Strategic Command could take control of all of America's nuclear forces at any time from LOOKING GLASS, but the communications networks were not as secure or as reliable. STRATCOM Headquarters in Omaha would retain control until an attack was actually underway.

"Let's get moving with the checklists," Cole said grimly as he headed for the battle staff conference room. Major Harlan Laughlin opened up a thick three-ring binder, then followed General Cole into the battle staff conference room. Cole waited until Laughlin had filled out the blank spaces on a series of overhead projection slides and put them up on a screen in the center of the main wall.

"The Posture Two message," Laughlin began, "establishes an A-Hour, or alert reference hour, and sets the timeline for all other actions. According to the operations plan, the message directs the wing to generate the Alpha-alert combat-capable aircraft for nuclear strike missions."

"My God," Cole muttered. He knew, with all the conflicts and turmoil in Europe, that something like this was possible with Velichko in power, but he never truly believed it would really happen.

The alert was even more surprising because everyone, including Cole, assumed that the nation's fleet of F-111G bombers had been out of the nuclear warfighting business—in fact, he had assumed that the *world* was out of the nuclear warfighting business. Although most F-111s are capable of delivering nuclear gravity bombs (only the EF-111A "Raven" electronic warfare aircraft is unarmed), and the F-111G could launch long-range air-to-ground nuclear missiles such as the AGM-131 Short Range Attack Missile and the AGM-86 and AGM-129 long-range cruise missiles, the Air Force Reserves' RF-111G Vampire had been thought to have only a non-nuclear combat role—the B-1, B-2, and B-52 bombers were thought to have taken over the long-range nuclear bombing mission. Now, with this fresh crisis, one of the first planes to be called upon to prepare for nuclear war was none other than a Reserve RF-111G!

General Cole was fully prepared to generate his machines for nuclear warfighting, but the prospect made him uneasy. The prospect of handling nuclear weapons, the required top secret documents and devices, and responding to nuclear strike orders issued from Strategic Command and the Pentagon instead of a theater commander, was not considered a Reservist's duty—and yet they had been ordered to do it.

"Preplanned bomber sorties one through six and tanker sorties one-oh-one through one-oh-four will be gained immediately by STRATCOM upon generation," Laughlin continued, "and will respond to Joint Chiefs of Staff or STRATCOM emergency action messages. The ops plan directs all other bomber and tanker sorties configured in preload status and available for accelerated generation. These follow-on sorties will not respond to STRATCOM or JCS emergency action messages, but unit commanders may be required to ensure the survival of nongenerated aircraft. This would be done by positioning these aircraft in OCCULT EAGLE or FIERY WILDERNESS airborne alert orbits. These will be accomplished by clear-text messages or by hand-delivered messages authenticated by date-time group."

Laughlin put up slides depicting several large rectangular boxes off the east coast of the United States. OCCULT EAGLE and FIERY WILDERNESS were preplanned airborne alert missions in which nuclear-loaded aircraft were sent to safe orbit areas, far from potential targets, until sent on their grim missions or recalled after the emergency was over.

"Christ almighty," Cole muttered, scratching his flattop. "This is turning out to be one really lousy day." On a small bookstand on his desk in the battle staff room, Cole picked a binder labeled "Defcon" and opened it to "Defcon Four." The binder had checklists that directed all of the battle staff's initial actions to take when notified of a serious emergency—no major actions, especially something as serious as this, was ever left to memory. Cole turned to Lafferty and said, "Jim, start an Alpha recall immediately. Start running your checklists." The recall would direct all available wing personnel to report to their duty stations, ready for deployment or for combat—as Reservists, the Alpha recall meant that they were all federalized as soon as they entered the base. "Thank God we got all of the bomber crews and most of the tanker crews on base already." Cole continued to read and initiate items in his checklist as his staff filed in;

then, one by one, he assigned tasks to his staff officers according to the checklists. Soon every telephone in the room was in use by the General's staff.

One by one the group commanders and key members of the Wing staff hurried into the battle staff room. When Daren Mace entered the room, his first look was at the main projection screen, which had the words DEFCON FOUR TIMELINES at the top and a series of times penciled in. "DEFCON schedules? We changing the Bravo exercise?"

"No exercise, Daren," Cole said to his new MG. "This is the real thing. A shooting war has broken out in Europe, and LOOKING GLASS and the NEACAP are airborne."

"They're— Ho-ly *shit.*" He hurried into his seat at the conference table and opened up his own binder of checklists. The first thing he did was call Alena Porter. "Captain, I need you over here in the command post on the double. The exercise is over, and we have an A-Hour." Mace heard a slight intake of breath on the other end. Porter was sharp: she would know what an A-Hour was and she would hustle. "Make sure the sergeant stays put and near the phone—we're starting a recall. Hurry." It took about ten minutes for Porter to dash over to the command post with a briefcase full of slides and transparencies, fill in the spaces from the main DEFCON time schedule slide, and get an update on the status of the Wing aircraft from Maintenance Control to complete the slides.

"Okay, Daren, you're in the hot seat now," General Cole said. "We need to put the brakes on the Bravo exercise, generate six bomber airframes and four tankers for SIOP missions, and begin predeployment ops." SIOP, or Single Integrated Operations Plan, was the nuclear warfighting "master plan" that would be executed by the White House and Pentagon in case of war, coordinating attacks against thousands of targets by hundreds of weapon systems—bombers, land-based missiles, and sea-launched missiles—over several weeks. "What have we got?"

Mace stood up, took the slides prepared for him by Captain Porter, and put them on the overhead projector. "I feel pretty certain we can meet the twelve-hour time limit for sorties one through four," Mace said confidently. "Alpha Flight's planes, which were in tactical deployment configuration, can be reconfigured for SIOP rather quickly—they have fuel, tanks, racks, expendables, all that stuff ready to go. Fortunately, Charlie

Flight's bombers were not uploaded with training ordnance when the message came down, so those bombers should take less time to generate."

"We'll need to get Bravo Flight back on the ground as fast as we can," Cole said. "Will it be a problem downloading their training stores while you're uploading the . . . special weapons on Alpha Flight?" Another euphemism—the military, even the men and women trained to handle nuclear weapons, hardly ever called them "nuclear weapons"—they were usually called "special" or "unconventional" weapons.

"If the weather holds up, it shouldn't be a problem," Mace said. "If we get that snowstorm later today or tonight, our weapons handlers will be under the gun. We may have to do all loading and preflight actions in hangars and then tow them to their parking spots."

Major Laughlin stepped right in front of General Cole: "Sir, message from NEACAP—we're going to DEFCON Three."

"Jesus," Cole exclaimed as Laughlin put up the DEFCON Three slides and updated all of the Wing's schedule times—the group commanders could see Laughlin's fingers trembling as he put the slides on the projector. DEFCON Three was a medium-threat war-readiness level, not far from all-out nuclear war. "What the hell is going on?"

"Sir, Russia is bombing the Ukraine and Romania," Laughlin said. "I heard it on the news. Massive waves of bombers are attacking several military bases in the Ukraine, Romania, and Moldova. Initial reports suggest that the Russians used low-yield nuclear devices against some Ukrainian air bases." Voices fell silent, and every head turned toward Laughlin and Cole. "Sir, STRATCOM is directing all units near the coastline to disperse their fleets as much as possible, to protect them in case of a preemptive attack."

"I know, I know," Cole said, flipping his binder to the DEFCON Three checklists. DEFCON Three was usually issued when a major conflict began overseas in which the United States or its allies could possibly be affected or involved—or in case nuclear weapons were employed against any nation. The speed at which the U.S. military had moved from total peacetime to DEFCON Three indicated the seriousness of the emergency—it was not unreasonable to assume the worst, that all of Eastern Europe could be at war in the next few hours. Whereas DEFCON Four directed only the Alpha-alert bombers—the first six planes—to be loaded and placed on round-the-clock alert, the DEFCON Three message would direct Cole's entire fleet of Vampire bombers and Stratotanker tankers be made ready for war. Security, crew integrity, safety, nuclear surety, federalization of the Reserve force—it was going to be a nightmare.

Martin Cole had something else to worry about. As commander of the 134th Fighter Squadron at Burlington International Airport, Cole's F-16 fighters were already shadowing Russian Tupolev-22M Backfire bombers out of Cuba that were flying up and down the Atlantic coast. He hadn't thought too much about those sleek, deadly behemoths—until now. Although Plattsburgh was about two hundred miles from the coast and almost three hundred miles from where those Backfire bombers were traveling, it was possible for those surveillance planes to pinpoint each and every one of Cole's planes—and if they were carrying nuclear cruise missiles, they could destroy all of Plattsburgh's planes in one shot.

"All right." Cole sighed. "This may screw up your day, Daren, but those Bravo Flight planes won't be coming back for a while. Jim," he said, turning to Operations Group commander McGuire, "those crews don't have the OCCULT EAGLE orbit-area charts with them, but I want the Bravo Flight crews that are airborne into those orbit areas, at the right altitudes."

"Excuse me, sir, but I need those bombers on the ground," Mace said. He pointed to the updated slide put up on the screen. Instead of only 4 planes in twelve hours and 6 planes within twenty-four hours, now the first 6 bombers had to be ready within eighteen hours, the first 12 bombers ready within thirty-six hours, and the entire fleet at Plattsburgh ready to go to war within three days. Everything was speeded up by 50 percent, and they hadn't even started to move one weapon yet. "Look at those timelines for DEFCON Three. I needed those planes on the ground three hours ago."

"Daren, it can't happen," Cole insisted irritably.

"Dammit, General, this DEFCON Three status won't last long," Mace said. "It's a political thing—they're trying to scare Russia into stopping the fighting. We should at least stay with the DEFCON Four timelines and—"

"Colonel, listen to me, we are at *war!*" Cole snapped angrily, pounding the table with his fist. The battle staff, the entire command center, fell silent. Cole's angry gaze bored into every man's face in the room before affixing on Mace. "The Russians actually nuked the fucking Ukraine, dammit—they dropped a goddamned nuclear bomb. We could be next, Colonel Mace. This is not some Tom Clancy fantasy. We can't second-guess them."

"Then you have no choice but to inform Fifth Air Battle Force that we can't make the timelines," Mace interjected.

Cole's face reddened and his mouth dropped open in surprise. "What did you say . . . ?"

"Sir, we'd have a tough time generating all our aircraft to full SIOP readiness in three days in *peacetime,* with all our planes on the ground ready to go," Mace explained. "We cannot do it in time with planes and weapons scattered all over the ramp."

"Colonel, I am the one who will determine whether we can or cannot make our deadlines, not *you,*" Cole retorted. "I'll inform General Layton of any delays. But DEFCON Three says preserve any combat-ready assets to the maximum extent possible, and I'm thinking of those damned Backfire bombers out there—if they're carrying cruise missiles, bringing those bombers back to Plattsburgh would be a tactical mistake. I've got to think about the survival of my forces. Request to land the four Thunder bombers denied. Every two aircraft generated under DEFCON Three will be launched under positive control into the airborne alert orbit areas as soon as possible."

"We can't call Boston Center to change their flight plans," Lafferty said, "unless they declare an air defense emergency. We'll have to send them VFR, without a flight plan."

"Then do it," Cole said. "Give them the computer sequence point, and have them keep in touch by HF radio or SATCOM. We're going to need a weather briefing for the OCCULT EAGLE orbit area. If the weather goes to shit, we'll have to lie to the FAA that World War Three has just started. Until then, get those four Thunder planes into the orbit area any way you can."

22

Over Central Vermont
That Same Time

SOON IT WAS JUST FURNESS AND KELLY IN THE AIR REFUELING track. Zero-Five and Zero-Six were going to be delayed several more minutes, so Furness and Kelly hit the tanker one more time before the tanker had to depart, and they exited the air refueling track and headed over to the Montpelier radio navigation station, requested and received a safe altitude block, and set up an orbit pattern to wait.

Furness checked to see what Fogelman was up to, now that things had calmed down enough for them to take a breather and get caught up. He had the nav data page on the left MFD and the nav present position page on the right MFD. He stayed in the radarscope a long time, nudging the radar tracking handle onto a radar return and softly muttering to himself. When she checked the FIXMAG readout on the left Multi-Function Display, it read 12600 FT—over a two-nautical-mile difference between where the system thought it was and where Fogelman was trying to *tell* it where it was. "How's your system looking, Mark?" Rebecca asked.

"Shitty," he replied.

"You got a big buffer load in there," she offered, referring to the large FIXMAG reading. "What are you trying a fix on—the

Brookfield overpass?" The radar fixpoints near the Montpelier radio navigation station were well known to all Plattsburgh crewmembers, and the overpass was a good one to use—very easy to identify and aim on. But there were two overpasses that crossed the highway twenty miles south of the capital city of Vermont—and they were exactly two miles apart. If he was on the wrong one, and the system was good, that would be a reason why FIXMAG read twelve thousand feet. If he was on the right one, that meant that the inertial navigation system was off by two miles—bad enough so that it might be better to just start over and reinitialize. "Make sure you got the right overpass."

"I got the right one, pilot," Fogelman snapped. "Stop harping on me." He moved the PRES POS CORR switch to IN, jiggled the tracking handle a few more times to refine his crosshair placement—Rebecca noted that he didn't try to select another offset aimpoint to check his crosshair placement, which would have told him if he was on the right aimpoint or not—then hit the ENT FIX option-select switch on the left MFD.

On Rebecca's right MFD, a message flashed on the screen about twenty seconds later that read PP REAS FAIL. The INS had rejected the fix because of the disparity between where it thought it was and where Fogelman decided it was. The INS itself thought it was navigating accurately. In three years of flying the RF-111G with its two INS systems, and especially after the GPS satellite navigation system was installed, Furness had never seen a fix rejected by the system that wasn't due to operator error. "I think you picked the wrong—"

"The thing has gone to shit," Fogelman complained. "I'll jam this fix in, and if it spits it out I'll reinitialize."

"But don't you think—"

But Fogelman wasn't going to wait. He selected RDR PP on his right MFD to change the fix method, then entered OVR WHL—he was going to "jam" the fix, or tell the INS to accept his crosshair placement as perfect no matter what. He refined his crosshairs once again and took the fix.

Kiss that INS good-bye, Furness thought. An OVR WHL fix, or Override Wholevalue, updated the system present position but did not update the system velocities. Now the INS present position was off by at least two miles, and the INS velocities, which were obviously bad before the fix, were just as bad now and probably getting worse. She had never seen anyone take an override fix except in the simulator, mainly because the INS was always very good. *Expect that puppy to roll over any minute now,* she thought grimly. On the left Multi-Function Display, she saw that Fogelman had just about every possible sensor selected—both INS units, Doppler, TAS (True Air Speed computer), and GPS satellite navigation. The velocities from these sensors would all feed into INS number one through the computers, and eventually INS one would discover that it was out to lunch—then it would "kill" itself, or take itself off-line. That would happen in about . . .

"Thunder Zero-One, this is control, how do you hear?"

Furness keyed her mike. "Loud and clear. Go ahead."

"Thunder Zero-One . . ." There were a few seconds of hesitation; then: "Thunder Zero-One and Zero-Four, we need you to fly to and hold at destination number two-eight-nine, repeat, two-eight-nine. You will cancel IFR, squawk standby, and proceed to that destination. You will be given additional instructions later via AFSATCOM. Attempt to contact Thunder Zero-Two and Zero-Three on the command post or RBS frequencies and direct them to join you at destination two-eight-nine." AFSATCOM, or Air Force Satellite Communications System, was a secure global communications network that transmitted coded messages via satellite from the Pentagon, Air Combat Command headquarters in Virginia, Strategic Command Headquarters in Nebraska, or any combat-unit command post, directly to tactical aircraft. In the 1980s when the FB-111A was pulling nuclear alert, AFSATCOM was the primary method that aircrews received their dreaded "go-to-war" messages. When the Strategic Air Command was stood down and the FB-111 became the F-111G in the new Air Combat Command, AFSATCOM was no longer used. The system still worked and crews still trained with it, but lately it was used to pass routine bombing-range scores and maintenance messages from the planes to the local command posts.

Without waiting on Fogelman, Furness called up the destination number on the left Multi-Function Display and checked its coordinates on her chart. The RF-111G Digital Computer Complex held 350 sets of coordinates, called data points or destinations, which could be a turnpoint, target, or radar offset aimpoint. Most local training missions used only the first two hundred data points; the other data points were never used except for unusual training missions, such as long cross-country flights, RED FLAG exercises in Nevada, or special test flights.

To her surprise, the coordinates weren't on her map, and she had to pull out a standard civil aeronautical chart to find the spot—it was several hundred miles east, about a hundred miles out over the Atlantic Ocean, at an ADIZ entry point called FREEZ. Many times the RF-111G aircraft ran maritime strike and reconnaissance missions out over the ocean or Lake Ontario to practice overwater photo procedures or AGM-84 Harpoon antiship-missile strike procedures. The checkpoint they mentioned was in the middle of a large overwater warning area between Kennebunkport and Brunswick, Maine. When reentering U.S. airspace, aircraft had to enter at a specific spot at the proper time for positive identification purposes or else fighter-interceptors could be scrambled to visually identify the "intruder."

This had to be part of the exercise—they flew many air defense exercises through the years, going supersonic down over the ocean and letting F-16 fighters from Burlington or Massachusetts try to find them. But why were they supposed to go out there, especially with live (albeit only ten-pound BDU-48 "beer can") weapons aboard Zero-Four? Were they supposed to dump the weapons into the sea? If so, why didn't they just tell them to do so?

"Control, Zero-One, stand by for authentication." To Fogelman, Furness said, "Mark, get out the decoding documents and check this message."

"What?" he asked, perplexed.

"The command post wants us to fly out over ocean," she told him, explaining it all to him as if he hadn't heard any of it. "I want to authenticate their instructions."

"Jesus Christ . . ." Fogelman muttered as he removed his lap and shoulder belt so he could twist all the way around in his seat. The classified decoding documents were in a small canvas carrying bag that he had stuffed in the retractable lunch-box bucket behind the seat. You had to be a contortionist to reach it. The bag had enough decoding documents to last them for the rest of the month, including unlocking documents for nuclear weapons.

When he had finally retrieved the bag, he tossed it onto Furness' lap while he strapped back in. She opened the encode/decode book to the proper day's page, selected two characters, and found the proper response character. "Control, Thunder Zero-One, authenticate bravo-juliett."

"Thunder control authenticates yankee." It was the proper response.

"Holy shit," Furness muttered on the interphone. "If this is some kind of a test, I don't get it. They just ordered us to go VFR to an orbit point out over the Atlantic Ocean. We're supposed to try to raise Zero-Two and Zero-Three while they're in the low-level route and have them join on us."

"I guess our low-level has been canceled," Fogelman said. "Maybe they're going to pass us some recon information for a maritime target. That'll be cool—get target information from headquarters via AFSATCOM while the 'war' is going on. Near real-time stuff."

That explanation was as good as any, and Rebecca accepted it. "Boston Center, Thunder Zero-One flight of two would like to cancel IFR at this time."

The controller's mike opened, there was a short hesitant silence; then: "Ah, roger, Zero-One flight. Can you accept MARSA at this time?" MARSA stood for Military Accepts Responsibility for Separation of Aircraft, and it legally allowed military flights to fly in close proximity to one another.

"Thunder Zero-One accepts MARSA with Zero-Two."

"Roger," the controller said, a puzzled tone still in his voice. "I don't know what it is, but you military types are dropping off the screens all over the place. Squawk 1200, maintain VFR hemispheric altitudes, monitor GUARD, frequency changed approved, good day."

"Zero-One copies all, good day." Fogelman set 1200 in the IFF Mode 3 window, which allowed the air traffic controllers to track the bombers and to maintain separation from other planes, but they were not under radar control. It was "see and avoid" for the rest of the day. Rebecca descended to 17,500 feet, the proper altitude for visual-flight-rules aircraft going eastbound. "Okay, they want us to use SATCOM for any more messages," she told Fogelman, "so you can set the backup radio to SATCOM and I'll keep the primary radio in the command post freq. I'll—" Just then she noticed that the present-position readouts and all flight-data readouts had zeroed again. "Looks like your INS just rolled over."

"Fuck," Fogelman muttered. "Just my luck. I draw a piece-of-shit INS my first day of Hell Week." Furness didn't have the heart to tell him it was probably his system management that screwed the INS up. Both INS units seemed to have taken themselves off-line, so he shut down both of them, selected the satellite navigation system for the autopilot and system position and velocity reference, switched INS2 to ATTITUDE mode, then turned INS1 on and began an inflight alignment. The INS would use global positioning system present position, speed, and altitude to begin coarse alignment. It would take twice the effort to maintain the navigation system, and it might never tighten down completely. Fogelman still had a lot to learn about the navigation system—it worked better if just a few quality radar fixes and GPS comparisons were put in, rather than a lot of poor or mediocre radar fixes.

The common post frequency was buzzing a few minutes later as the two bombers overflew the base—Rebecca tried to check in with them, but received only a hurried "Thunder control, unable at this time, out," when she requested an update on their landing time or to check if they had contacted Zero-Two and Zero-Three in the low-level route. "That's weird . . . I guess the exercise must be heating up," she said on interphone. "Some sort of big-time readiness test or something, I bet. Getting a late takeoff and two aborts to start the ball rolling didn't help."

"These exercises are a waste anyway." Fogelman sighed. He had been working hard on the navigation system, punching fixes in every ten minutes or so—far too many, in her opinion. "We practice too much and don't spend as much time flying and dropping real bombs. If they had only two mobilization exercises a year and spent the money they'd save on live bombs and flying time, we'd get more out of these reserve weeks. At least that's how it seems to me."

"You're probably right," Furness agreed, "but mobility is what we do. That's our mission."

"Come on, Furness," Fogelman said. "Everyone *talks* mobility, but do you think they'd ever deploy RF-111s? They'd need half the airlift in the inventory to take our support gear—and that's not including the photointel trailers. Sure, we might deploy to England, to the old F-111 bases in Lakenheath or Upper Heyford, or deploy to Guam, but nowhere else. We're playing the numbers game, that's all. We're keeping F-111s in the inventory just to show that we're not getting complacent about national or global defense. The F-15Es, the B-1s, the

B-2 bombers, the B-52 or ship-launched cruise missiles—those guys get all the glory. We just get to *play* mobility."

"Well, well, Fogman really does have an opinion about national defense issues," Furness chided him, "even if it is motivated by laziness and a total give-a-shit attitude. You really have given this some thought, haven't you?"

"All I care about," Fogelman said, unaffected by either Furness' compliment or her backhanded barb, "is doing my job and getting my ass on the ground. You know what *your* problem is?"

"I can't wait to hear."

"You got this romantic notion about flying and this job," Fogelman said. "You'd sacrifice your business, your personal life, all the real stuff in your life, for the Reserves. Do you think they care about your sacrifice? The Reserves will keep on taking until you got nothing left—no career, no job, no future. Then, just when you've hit bottom, they'll RIF you, just like they did back in '92. You think they're going to let any female Reserve flyer under the rank of colonel make it to retirement? They'll kick your butt out or make life so miserable for you that you'll quit before you collect all your retirement points. Meanwhile you've lost your charter business and your commercial license, you're older, and you're out of work. Thank you very much, Air Force Reserves. I'm not being cynical, just realistic."

Furness admitted he had a point—the tough-ass dude in the bar the other night, obviously in the military and working nights as a maintenance man to make ends meet, came to mind—but she didn't tell Fogelman that. "The solution to that, Mark," she decided, "is to work harder at both jobs. I can make Liberty Air work, and I can make it to O-6 in the Reserves."

"If you say so." Fogelman clucked. "Just remember who told you first. You got maybe five more years in the flying game before they put you out to pasture—and that's if they will still allow women in combat past the five-year evaluation period that ends in '98. You might make it to light colonel and might even make ops officer, but get in your Air War College and squadron commander in five years? I don't think so. All the good slots go to active-duty ass-kissers. And you need to get a command position in a tactical unit before they'll make you a full bird. I hate to say it, but you got screwed when you accepted a Reserve commission. You'd be better off if you just concentrated on getting Liberty Air to go regional, rather than blowing half your time flying these fucking planes. Doesn't that make sense?"

Before she could answer, activity on the primary radio halted their conversation, and he had his head back in the radarscope again. But she had to give Fogelman a bit of credit—he was smarter than he ever let on. If she was given the choice of building her military career or building Liberty Air into a regional carrier, which should she choose?

Liberty Air, of course. There was no other choice, really. She was already stretching herself to the limit by pulling fourteen days of Reserve duty a month—what would she do when it was time to make the big push for squadron commander? Spend an extra week, without pay, working on base? Go full-time to Air War College in residence—for six months? That would kill Liberty Air Service for sure. Even Ed Caldwell, who was the closest thing to a steady guy she'd had in years, wanted her to make a choice and settle down with him.

Sure, there was something to be said for being one of the few top women combat soldiers in the country, even a dash of celebrity. And nothing beat flying the RF-111G Vampire bomber. It was an aviator's wet-dream. But as irritating and aggravating as Fogelman could be, his points were ones she had tried to push out of her mind in the past. But she knew he was calling a spade a spade. She *had* put in time with the military, a lot of time, and Liberty Air offered her the chance to finally build a life for herself. Some security. Some recognition and respect outside of the military. But it couldn't be done if she was going to try and climb the military Reserves ladder as well. She tried to toss the thought out of her head . . . for now. But soon, very soon, Rebecca knew she was going to have to seriously weigh the direction she wanted her life to take . . . and her commitment to the Reserves.

It took about an hour to reach the specified coordinates, and another hour to reach Johnson and Norton and have them join up on them in the overwater restricted area. On the way to the destination, they got the latest weather advisories from Boston Air Route Traffic Control Center. Their nearest alternate airfield, Brunswick Naval Air Station in Maine, was getting light snow showers, and Plattsburgh itself might be snowed in too in about four hours. Their last suitable alternate base, Pease

Air Force Base in New Hampshire, would probably go down in about six hours.

By the time they reached point FREEZ, they were out of radio range of both military and civilian stations. Just to make matters worse, everyone's AFSATCOM satellite communications units in the four-ship cell did not seem to be working—the units were functioning and messages seemed to be going out to the satellite, but no messages were coming in. That meant no coordination for a landing site and aerial refueling. When they tried the high-frequency (HF) radio, they heard absolutely nothing but static. "Anything in the weather briefings about sunspot activity?" Furness asked Fogelman.

"Huh?"

"Sunspots," Rebecca said. "They wipe out HF messages by electrifying the ionosphere so radio waves can't bounce off."

"I didn't hear anything briefed to us about sunspots," Fogelman said. She wondered if he ever listened to weather briefings. Furness sent the rest of the flight out to loose-route formation, set best-endurance airspeed to conserve fuel, and set up a monitoring system on the UHF, AFSATCOM, and HF radios for any instructions from anybody.

Right away, she was feeling more and more uncomfortable with this setup. Problem number one was the weather. After just a few minutes, Furness found she had to bring the other flight members closer and closer in, nearly right back into fingertip formation, so they could stay in visual contact with one another. This immediately began taxing Paula Norton's flying skills—she was a pretty good stick, but long minutes in fingertip formation tended to make her a bit erratic. Rebecca had kept her in her original position in the number-three position, but as the wingmen drew in closer and the weather got worse, the planes at the farther ends tended to shift more, amplifying the other planes' movements, so she put Norton in the number-two position, right on Furness' wing. If they had to go "lost wingman" in the clouds, Rebecca wanted Paula to stay with her as long as possible.

Rebecca made the decision to start heading back toward Plattsburgh after nearly an hour orbiting in the warning area. Johnson and Norton had already been down on the low-level navigation route—Johnson had dropped his "beer can" bombs, while Norton still had her GBU-24 laser-guided bomb—and they were getting close to their fuel reserves. It would take nearly thirty minutes for a tanker from Pease or Plattsburgh to get out to them in the warning area for a refueling, and that was too close a call—if a plane couldn't take on gas, they'd have an immediate fuel emergency. She was going to get an IFR (Instrument Flight Rules) clearance from Boston Center and head back to Plattsburgh before the weather totally crumpled. Exercise or not, things were getting a little too disorganized and dangerous, and it was time to get on the ground and regroup.

Just as they headed inbound from point FREEZ and were about to contact Boston Center for their clearance, they heard: "Unknown rider, unknown rider, off the Kennebunk VOR zero-five-zero-degree radial, niner-five nautical miles, this is WINDJAMMER on GUARD, authenticate kilo-bravo and stand by." The message was repeated several times. They knew exactly who WINDJAMMER was: that was the collective call-sign for the northeast sector of the Air Force Air Defense Zone. The radar controllers that continually scanned the skies for intruding aircraft had locked on to them.

Furness quickly used her left MFD and set the backup radio to GUARD, the international emergency frequency, and said, "Mark, look up that authentication."

"I'm going, I'm going," Fogelman said, quickly flipping back to the proper date-time-group page. Air Defense required unknown aircraft to respond immediately or they would scramble fighters—some of those fighters coming from their own sister squadron, the 134th Fighter Interceptor Squadron at Burlington. Once they discovered you were a friendly, the shit would hit the fan from headquarters on down. No one wanted to be caught busting the Air Defense Identification Zone. "Reply Zulu," Fogelman finally said.

"WINDJAMMER, this is Thunder Zero-One flight of four, authenticates Zulu," Furness radioed on the backup radio. On the primary radio, she said, "Thunder Flight, fingertip formation, monitor GUARD on backup. Zero-Two, try to contact Boston Center on the primary radio and get us a clearance back to Plattsburgh."

"Two, wilco."

"Three."

"Four."

"Thunder Zero-One, this is WINDJAMMER," the air defense controller came back. "Check your IFF for all proper codes, recycle your beacons, and stand by for authentication. Acknowledge."

Furness and Fogelman looked at each other, puzzled. Fogelman hit the CFI, or Channel Frequency Indicator, button on his control and display unit, which gave him a readout of all the beacons and transceivers on the plane. "I got mode one on and set, although I don't know what for," he said, reading off the currently activated radios and their frequencies. "Mode three is squawking 1200, and altitude readout Mode C is on. Mode two and four are standby." Mode two and mode four were special identification codes required for tactical aircraft in a battlefield situation. They were *never* used in peacetime and could be set only on the ground, usually by the crew chiefs before every flight if required. Mode one was a military-unit-identification beacon interrogated only by allied nations and naval vessels; modes three and C were standard civil-air-traffic-control beacons used to transmit flight data and altitude.

"Better turn mode four on," Furness said, "and hope Sergeant Brodie set it right." Fogelman used the CDU and made sure the correct codes were on. It was unlikely that mode two was set properly, but if WINDJAMMER wanted it on, they would turn it on.

But it didn't seem to work. "Thunder Zero-One, this is WINDJAMMER on GUARD, codes not received, turn right heading zero-four-zero, clear of United States warning and prohibited airspace. Acknowledge."

"WINDJAMMER, Zero-One, we cannot turn," Furness replied. "Altering course may cause a fuel emergency. We are talking with Boston Center at this time, requesting an IFR clearance, type aircraft Romeo-Foxtrot-One-Eleven-Golf, slant-Romeo, flight of four, direct Plattsburgh at sixteen thousand feet, cargo code yellow-four. We are VFR at this time. How copy?" Usually flight plans were filed only with an air-traffic-control facility, not with a military surveillance site, but this guy didn't seem to realize who they were, so it would be best to let him copy their information down and get it into the system however possible. The "yellow-four" code, indicating they were carrying explosive ordnance on board, usually got a lot of attention from anyone who recognized the nomenclature, so a flight plan should be ready ver—

"Thunder Flight, this is WINDJAMMER on GUARD, your request cannot be accepted at this time," the air defense controller said. Furness' mouth dropped open. Was this guy *serious . . . ?* "You must alter course and turn away from the coastline until proper identification procedures and clearances are obtained. Turn right immediately to heading zero-four-zero, maintain VFR at seventeen thousand five hundred feet or above, with all lights on and landing gear extended. Acknowledge."

What kind of idiot was in the control tower? she wondered. Rebecca mashed the mike button on the throttle quadrant in total anger: "WINDJAMMER, I am not going to lower my landing gear. We were sent to warning area W-102 VFR as part of a Bravo exercise conducted by Thunder control. We were told to expect refueling support and further instructions at a later time, but some aircraft formations are low on fuel and we need to proceed back to base. If this is part of the exercise, then terminate immediately or we'll declare an inflight emergency and file a written report with the FAA. Over."

The "unknown rider" warning was then repeated several times, with hardly an opportunity in the broadcasts to interject a response. "Christ," Furness mused on interphone, "it's like they don't know who the hell we are. I hate to risk busting the air-defense identification zone, but I think we're lost in the system, and with the HF and AFSATCOM out, we've got no way to communicate with the command post as long as we're out over water." On interplane frequency, she radioed to Johnson: "Two, any luck with Boston Center?"

"Negative," Johnson replied. "They can hear us, I think, and I can hear them talking, but it sounds weird, like there's been an accident and they're clearing out the airspace or something. It's pretty confused, but I don't think they want to talk to us. What are we going to do, Lead?"

"What's your fuel look like?"

"About an hour left, with minimum reserves," Johnson replied. "We'll have about five thousand over the fix, probably less." Five thousand pounds of fuel "over the fix," or at the initial approach fix for an instrument approach and landing, was the absolute minimum for any chosen destination—that would allow enough fuel for perhaps two or three bad-weather landing attempts. "Maybe we should think about Pease instead, or go to Navy Brunswick." Even though they had the National Guard tankers there, Pease, a former Strategic Air Command bomber base and home for the FB-111, was now a civilian airport, and they might not take kindly to RF-111 bombers with bombs and lasers aboard landing beside the tourists and vacationers.

"Brunswick it is," Furness said. On interphone, she told Fogelman, "Mark, call up Navy Brunswick on the computer and give me a heading, then squawk 'Emergency' and keep trying to raise someone on GUARD frequency on the backup radio. This bullshit's gone on long—"

Just then, on the radar threat-warning receiver, a bat-wing symbol appeared at the top of the scope, with a fast, insistent *deedledeedledeedle* audio warning over the interphone. Fogelman was working on calling up Navy Brunswick's destination number and didn't call it out—the warning receiver gave spurious signals occasionally, and this one certainly seemed like a phantom signal. A bat-wing symbol was an enemy-airborne-radar warning, showing the presence of a radar that matched the pulse-repetition frequency and wavelength of a Russian- or Chinese-made fighter. The symbol drifted around at the top of the scope for a few seconds, moving slowly eastbound—the AN/APS-109B Radar Homing and Warning System could not determine the range to the threat, only approximate "lethal range"—then disappeared. "That's weird," Furness said. "Friendly radars don't make that warning."

"Probably a glitch," Fogelman said dismissively. "'Captain's bars' are on Brunswick." Rebecca gently steered the bomber until the nav computer director's bars were centered, then reengaged the autopilot to head for Navy Brunswick. Meanwhile, Fogelman began rooting through the charts and approach plates in the rack beside Furness' headrest, searching for the approach plates and airport diagrams for the base. He set in the VOR radio navigation aid frequency in the primary nav radio as a backup to his admittedly poor INS system. The VOR needle on Furness' Horizontal Situation Indicator continued to rotate aimlessly, and a red OFF flag in the HSI case told them no nav signal was being received. "Brunswick VOR must be off the air," he said. He set in the UHF frequencies for Brunswick ATIS (Automatic Terminal Information Service) to hear a recording of the Brunswick weather and field conditions—no response. Fogelman set in the approach, tower, and ground control frequency into presets. "I'll wait till we get a bit closer to the base, then—"

"Hey," Rebecca interrupted, motioning out the right windscreen with her head into the darkening gray clouds, "there's traffic at—*holy shit, look out!*"

Fogelman looked up just in time to see two F-16 Fighting Falcon fighter-jets in steep 90-degree-plus bank turns, not more than a few yards away from Thunder Zero-Four—and the first fighter appeared to be firing its 20-millimeter cannon at them.

Rebecca could actually see several winks of light and a stream of gas from the cannon muzzle of the lead F-16. The second F-16 fighter appeared to be flying in close trail, directly behind and slightly above his leader, and so he passed right over Rebecca's head, so close that she could see the second pilot's checklist strapped to his right thigh through his large clear bubble canopy. There was no time to react, speak, not even scream—Furness couldn't do anything but let the thunderous roar and the shock wave of the two jets pass over her and pray that death would come swiftly or not at all.

The cannon shells hit with the force of Thor's hammer along the bottom of the fuselage and left wing of Furness' bomber, shaking the plane so badly that Furness thought she'd go into a stall or spin. The MASTER CAUTION light snapped on, several yellow caution lights illuminated on the forward instrument panel, and the navigation computers and most other control and display screens and systems went dark.

The F-16 passed less than half a wingspan away—no more than thirty or forty feet. Their supersonic shock wave smashed into the formation of Vampire bombers, threatening to twist them inside out and upside down. Rebecca saw Paula Norton's plane cartwheel over into a complete roll, caught in the hurricane-like twisting forces of the F-16's vortices—and it was plummeting right into Furness' plane. Furness grabbed her control stick with both hands and pulled sharply to the left to get away from the second RF-111. The cockpit filled with debris from the negative G-forces as the bomber sliced over and down. There wasn't any way Rebecca could control the roll—her controls froze. The roll continued, one after another, and Rebecca couldn't stop it.

Fogelman kept screaming, *"You have it? Shit, lady, do you have it?"* He was frantically looking four directions at once—at the engine instruments, which were probably close to Greek to him; out the window; at his radarscope for some inexplicable reason; and at the ejection handles on the center console next to his left knee.

"I got it, Fogelman, I got it!" she shouted back, first on interphone and then cross-cockpit. He was so excited, with his oxygen mask, arms, and head flailing around so much, that

Rebecca found herself watching the ejection handles, ready to block any attempt Fogelman might make to pull one and punch them out.

"I feel a vibration," Fogelman shouted. "Right under my feet. Did Norton hit us? Jesus, we almost got plastered by those F-16s! All my stuff is out . . ."

"Fuck that!" Furness shouted. "I got the airplane—I got it . . ." *But maybe I don't,* she thought in horror. The nose stayed high and wouldn't come down, the aft end stayed low, and the left roll continued despite her efforts. She mashed the autopilot disconnect lever and brought the throttles to IDLE. No change.

"Eject! Eject!" Fogelman suddenly screamed. Furness saw him make a grab for the right ejection lever and she pushed his hand away.

"No!" Furness shouted. "What the fuck are you doing? We've still got ten thousand feet to work this." She stomped on the left rudder petal with all her might. Suddenly the roll stopped—or did it? The turn-coordinator ball was still hard left and the turn needle was oscillating, although it appeared that the horizon had stopped rolling. She kept the left rudder pushed in, despite her desire to straighten out. Sure enough, the turn needle straightened and the rolling stopped, although the nose was still high over the horizon and the ball was still hard left. The altimeter was still unwinding—they were passing through ten thousand feet above sea level, the recommended safe ejection altitude. Furness pushed the control stick full forward.

"What are you doing?" Fogelman demanded. He tried to haul back on the control stick, but Furness managed to overpower him, and he eventually gave up. "Don't dive! We're already past ten thousand!"

"We're in a flat spin," Furness said calmly as she shoved the wing-sweep handle full forward. The airspeed-indicator tape was reading zero, a strange sensation since they were still thousands of feet in the air. "We've got no airspeed. Hold on—and keep your hands away from the fucking controls!" She shoved the nose seemingly straight down at the ocean. They plunged through a cloud deck, and Rebecca had to fight off a tremendous wave of nausea and vertigo. Her head was spinning wildly, to the right this time, and only by gluing her eyes to the instruments was she able to hang on. A few seconds later they popped through the cloud deck, and all they could see was blue ocean and wind-tossed whitecaps below. Slowly the airspeed began to rise, and when it climbed over one-fifty, she pulled back on the control stick slowly, not letting the airspeed bleed below one-fifty, and fed in power—thankfully, both engines had not stalled and responded immediately. The nose finally rested above the horizon, and she leveled off at about six thousand feet—they had lost over eleven thousand feet of altitude in about thirty seconds.

Carefully Rebecca tried some gentle pitch movements—no problem. But when she tried a gentle left turn, she noticed that the left spoiler, a fencelike drag device atop each wing used to help make crisper turns, would not deploy. "Looks like we got a damaged spoiler actuator on the left wing," she said. "We'll have to lock out the spoilers for the rest of the flight. I think the recon pod got creamed by that bomb, but it's not serious." On the primary radio tuned to the GUARD emergency frequency, she called, "Mayday, Mayday, Mayday, Thunder Zero-One on GUARD, midair collision with two Foxtrot-One-Six fighter planes, approximate position seven-zero-miles east-north-east of Brunswick, Maine, altitude zero-six thousand feet." She wasn't about to say that a friendly F-16 fighter had nearly succeeded in shooting her out of the sky. "My flight is split up and I am in marginal VMC. Thunder Flight, check in on GUARD frequency with status and altitude, over."

"Thunder Zero-Two on GUARD, loud and clear, code one, one-seven-thousand feet, holding hands with Zero-Four," Joe Johnson replied, signifying that they were undamaged and that Kelly in Thunder Zero-Four was with him.

"Thunder Zero-Four on GUARD," Frank Kelly replied shakily, "loud and clear, scared shitless but code one." No reply from Thunder Zero-Three.

"Thunder Zero-Three, this is Thunder Zero-One on GUARD," Furness radioed, "report up on GUARD frequency. Over." No response. "Zero-Three, come up on GUARD frequency immediately, over." Still no response. "Paula, Ted, dammit, come up on any radio if you can! Key your mike three times if you can hear me. Zero-Three, come in!" Rebecca couldn't believe it—they had lost Paula Norton and Ted Little. She obviously couldn't recover from the—

"Becky!" Norton shouted over the GUARD frequency. "Thunder Zero-Three's up on GUARD. Anybody hear me?"

"Paula, this is Rebecca. Are you all right? Where are you? What's your altitude?"

"We're okay," Norton replied, her voice shaking with excitement, fear, and exhilaration all at once. "Ted hit his head—he's a little loopy but he's okay. I'm at one-two thousand feet. I stalled my left engine and it took a few tries to get it restarted, but I'm in the green. I have no damned idea where I am—Brunswick VOR's not on the air, and the nav stuff is out."

"Are you VFR, Zero-Three?"

"Negative. Visibility is poor with snow. Not picking up any ice yet, though."

"All right, Zero-Three, you can start a climb to one-six thousand," Furness said. "We'll try to get a contact to you."

"Roger," Norton replied. "Leaving twelve for sixteen—thank God."

"Zero-Three, Zero-Two's got a lock on you," Johnson radioed, indicating that his attack radar was locked on to Norton's plane. "We're at your four o'clock position high at five miles. You're clear to climb to sixteen thousand five hundred."

"Roger. Zero-Three's leaving fourteen for sixteen-five," Norton announced.

"Zero-One copies, I'm leaving eight for fifteen-five." Rebecca had to give Norton a lot of credit for bringing it back under control.

By the time Rebecca climbed up to altitude, Thunder Zero-Two and Zero-Four, now with Zero-Three within visual range of them, had moved to within a mile. Because Fogelman's nav gear wasn't running, Rebecca put Johnson in the lead and got on his right wing, with Kelly flying beside Furness so he could look her plane over carefully. After coordinating what they would do, Furness moved to twice routeformation distance, about a half-mile from Johnson, and Kelly crossed under and to her left wing, looking at the damage:

"Well, you can kiss that recon pod good-bye," Kelly radioed. "It's departed the aircraft completely. Both bomb bay doors caved in, your nose gear door looks damaged, looks like a few actuators hanging in the breeze. Looks like hydraulic fluid or coolant streaks underneath—better double-check that the pod is powered down and isolated."

"Checked, power off, bomb door switch off, circuit breakers pulled," Fogelman told Furness.

"We got it, Zero-Four," Furness radioed Kelly.

"It looks like the nose gear door might have gotten hit," Kelly continued, "so we'll have to keep an eye on it when you bring the gear down. Moving to the left wing." Kelly eased his bomber over the left wing: "Looks like a possible rupture or break in the skin, Zero-One—I suggest you start transferring fuel out of the right wing, if you got any left, or you'll end up with a heavy wing."

"We're burning off body fuel only."

"Copy. Your left weapon pylon is gone, and you've got a lot of damage on the pylon root. About four feet of the trailing edge of the center flap assembly is ripped off. Some pieces are landing in the slipstream, but not much. Anything else you want us to check?"

"Couldn't stand any more happy news, Zero-Four."

"Roger that. Moving back to fingertip."

Just as Rebecca watched Kelly slide under and out of sight, she looked up and saw four F-16 Fighting Falcon fighters, behind and to Johnson's left about a quarter of a mile. "Company, eight o'clock, Thunder Flight," she called on interplane. "Green Mountain boys returning to the scene of the crime."

"The four buttheads who buzzed us, no doubt," Ted Little chimed in. "You guys are from Burlington? Why the hell did you make a pass at us like that?"

"Hey, Thunder, we didn't know it was you," one of the 134th Fighter Interceptor Squadron Patriot's F-16 pilots radioed back. "We were scrambled against a Backfire bomber from Cuba that NORAD had been tracking all morning." NORAD, or North American Air Defense Command, call-in sign WINDJAMMER, was the joint U.S. and Canadian military agency responsible for the air defense of the entire North American continent, from the North Pole to Panama. "WINDJAMMER must've thought you guys were the bogey and vectored us right on top of you."

No wonder Boston Center and the military command posts were so weird on the radios, Furness thought—they had Russian bombers off the coast to deal with! Well, this wasn't a topic for discussion on an open radio. "Patriots, how about leading us back to Plattsburgh? We've got two birds close to emergency fuel, and now we've got structural damage. Tell Boston Center we'll need weapons-on-board clearance and that we'll be declaring an emergency. Or are you still out chasing Bears?"

"We're heading back to the barn too," the lead F-16 pilot

replied. "We've been rotating these intercepts for days now. And after our little close encounter back there, I'm going to need a fresh flight suit—right before I go downtown and get plastered."

23

"TWO GREEN—CORRECTION, NOSE GEAR GREEN LIGHT OUT, RED light in the gear handle still on," Fogelman called out. Normally he read the checklists very mundanely, with little interest, and recited the usual "two green no red" verbatim without hardly looking—but not this morning. He paid attention to every checklist step and double-checked each light and indicator as if his life depended on it—which, of course, it did.

Rebecca's damaged RF-111G Vampire bomber was handling pretty well as they descended through the clouds and prepared for landing at Plattsburgh, and up until now things had been fairly routine. There were a few snow showers in the Plattsburgh area, and it was overcast and cold, but the runway was open and the ice and snow had been scraped off. The Air Battle Wing had a strip alert tanker ready to launch and refuel the incoming bombers, but the other three bombers had enough fuel to land without an emergency aerial refueling, so the tanker stayed on the ground. Thunder Zero-Two and Zero-Four landed first and Zero-Three last, with Paula Norton taking the approach end arresting cable just in case her aircraft had experienced any serious structural or landing gear problems.

Because Rebecca would be landing without flaps, slats, or spoilers, she needed to burn down fuel before landing in order to get the lowest aircraft gross weight and the shortest landing roll possible. Her plan, as long as the weather cooperated, was to enter the visual pattern into Plattsburgh, being careful to keep the base and the runway in sight at all times, and do a series of low approaches until they were down to five thousand pounds of fuel remaining. Meanwhile, the approach and departure end arresting cables were being reconfigured for her.

Again, it was wall-to-wall checklists—no flap–no slat landing checklist, asymmetrical spoiler checklist, brake energy limit check, approach or departure-end-cable arrestment checklist in case the runway was too icy to stop, plus the normal approach and landing checklists. Now they had an unsafe-gear indication—either the speed brake (the forward main gear door) was not in its proper in-trail position or the nose gear was not fully down and locked. With the damage to the nose-gear-door area, Furness had to assume the worst—the nose gear was not fully locked.

"Delta, this is Zero-One, nose gear indicating unsafe condition, and I'm picking up increased vibration in the nose," Furness radioed on the command post frequency. Delta was the call sign for the Maintenance Group commander, who would coordinate all the recovery efforts for the damaged bomber.

"Copy that, Zero-One," the group commander responded. Furness didn't know the new maintenance group commander—he had just recently arrived—and she was a little skittish about turning over this recovery to a new guy, but the operations group commander, Colonel Greg McGwire, call sign Charlie, and the wing commander had both deferred to the new guy's experience and had turned this recovery over to him. "What are your light indications?"

"Delta, the nose gear light is out, repeat out, the main-gear green light is on, and the red light in the gear handle is on, repeat, on, Thunder Zero-One."

"Okay, Zero-One, leave the gear handle where it is, check your circuit breakers, clean up your checklists . . . and clear me in to your left wing."

"Zero-One cop— Say again, Delta? Clear you in . . . ?" Furness searched out her left side and to her amazement saw an F-16B Fighting Falcon fighter, the two-seat trainer version of the supersonic interceptor from the 134th Fighter Interceptor Squadron in Burlington, climbing and turning to join on them. "Delta, are you in the F-16 closing on me?"

"Affirmative, Zero-One," Lieutenant Colonel Daren Mace said. While the other three RF-111Gs were landing, Mace had requested a two-seat F-16 from Burlington to take him up to inspect the damage personally. "Give us a right turn toward the base. We'll be underneath you looking at your damage."

"Copy, Delta," Furness replied. Somewhere in the back of her mind she thought that voice sounded familiar.

The F-16 reappeared on her left wing a few minutes after she rolled out of her turn. "Okay, Zero-One, your nose gear is not down and locked, and it looks like the wheels are castering in the slipstream. Looks like you're going to take an approach-end cable. Hang in there about fifteen more minutes to get down and get ready. See you on the ground."

It took more like thirty minutes before Delta called up and cleared her for the cable pass. Furness had only fifteen minutes of fuel remaining—she had this try and one more, and then they'd have to take it out over the Atlantic and eject. She was determined not to miss.

"Okay, Mark," she said to Fogelman, "all the checklists are done, right?"

Fogelman had been very quiet for the past thirty minutes. She could see his fists clenching and unclenching on his lap, his nervous, staring eyes, how he jumped at every new shudder and creak the bomber made. He was double- and triple-checking his landing data numbers, reading the checklists over after running them to make sure he had done all the items, and glancing around the cockpit, repeatedly securing loose items, checking switches and circuit breakers. *Nothing like a good old-fashioned inflight emergency,* she thought, *to bring out the best in a crewdog.* "Yes," Fogelman muttered, "checklists are complete."

"Go ahead and lock yourself in," she said, "then pull those straps tight."

"You don't need anything else?" he asked nervously.

"I'm all set. Lock your harness."

Fogelman tightened his straps one more time, lowered both helmet visors, tightened his oxygen mask connectors, then flipped a lever that would lock the inertial crash reel in place. He would not be able to reach any switches or move his body after that reel was locked. He pulled on the straps so hard that his thighs looked as if they'd been severed. "Locked," he said. Then: "You ever take a cable before, Rebecca?"

Hearing her first name spoken by Mark Fogelman was a surprise—this was the first time he had ever said it. She replied, "No. I took a departure end cable once, but it was just a safety precaution. We took the cable going about forty knots—we hardly felt it. I guarantee we'll feel this one. One-sixty to zero like *that.*" She couldn't see his face, but saw him hesitate for a long moment; then, as she turned final and began to line up on the runway, he began straightening his neck, pressing the back of his head securely against the contoured headrest.

The snow had started to fall harder now, and the visibility was down to perhaps three to five miles. There was only going to be one shot at this. "Thunder Zero-One turning final."

"Got you in sight, Zero-One," Delta replied. "Bring her on in. Equipment's ready." No one liked to say "fire trucks" or "crash trucks" on the radio—everyone used the euphemism "equipment" instead.

The touchdown zone had been heavily worked while Furness was in the pattern to make this landing as soft and smooth as possible. Airports did not foam runways anymore—foam was expensive, dangerous to work with, and not always effective—so Mace had used the next-best thing. The runway was scraped clean of ice and snow from its approach end to the arresting cable, but on the other side of the cable Mace had used snowplows, dump trucks, and huge snowblowers, and piled tons of snow on the runway to a depth of several feet. Then he had arranged the dump trucks and snowplows on either side of the runway to act as a barrier in case Furness missed or broke the cable and slid off the runway. Finally, the last half of the runway was again cleared and scraped so she could try for the departure-end arresting cable as a last resort. If she missed that, only the outer fence and some trees would stop her.

Rebecca pulled the yellow, hook-shaped handle, and the HOOK DOWN warning light illuminated. "I see your hook, Zero-One," Delta reported. "Lock your harness and get ready." Furness didn't reply, but lowered both visors, locked her inertial reel, and prepared to land.

Furness' no-flap, no-slat, no-spoiler approach was fast and low. The cold air buoyed her wings, threatening to sail her over the cable, but she was determined not to let that happen. Her wheels touched down just a few yards from the overrun. She held the nose off, using her flight controls to steer the bomber, not trusting the broken nose gear to steer straight on the runway.

As soon as the arresting cable disappeared under the nose, Furness began to lower the nose back onto the runway . . .

Then the hook caught the cable, and the huge arresting-gear brakes kicked in. Rebecca heard a doglike *woof* from Fogelman, and she heard herself cry out as Fogelman's head and torso snapped forward and his head hit the thin metal glareshield—he had either failed to lock his harness or the reel itself had failed. The bomber's nose came down as if the nose-gear strut were compressing as usual, but there was no typical oleo shock absorber bounce—the nose just kept right on coming down until the fuselage hit the snow. Furness held it off as long as she could, pulling the control stick back to her belly, but eventually the cable brakes held and the nose crashed to the ground. The cable continued to reel out for another two hundred feet, sending waves of snow over the canopy.

Rebecca's body strained against the shoulder straps as the bomber began to slow, digging the thick web straps into her shoulders and thighs. The nose was pitched over so far that it appeared that they were rocketing into the ground, and the sound of the fuselage scraping against the porous-friction runway surface was what a building being dynamited must sound like. But Furness somehow had the presence of mind to act. When the bomber settled to a stop, she unlocked her shoulder-harness inertial reel to free her seat straps, yanked the throttles to idle, then to CUTOFF, pushed both fire pushbuttons to isolate fuel from the engines, and lifted the silver agent-discharge switch to activate the engine-compartment fire extinguishers.

Furness ripped her oxygen mask off and raised her visors, then reached over to Fogelman. He was slumped forward in his seat, the top part of his helmet was cracked, and there was no movement. "Mark, you all right?" she shouted. "Mark, answer me . . ."

The bomber was being pulled back slightly by the stretching action of the arresting cable, but Furness could hear voices and footsteps outside. At least a foot of snow was brushed off the cockpit canopies, and a silver-hooded fireman appeared over Furness' head. "Other side!" she screamed through the canopy. "The wizzo's hurt!"

The fireman motioned to someone on the other side of the cockpit, and was then pushed aside by a man in a winter-weight flying jacket and watch cap. "Check your throttles and fire buttons!" he shouted.

"Cutoff and depressed!" Furness shouted back. The fuel valves should have closed and the fire extinguishers should have activated by now, she thought, so she shut off the battery switch as well. "Battery switch off!"

"Good," the man said. Rebecca thought the man looked remarkably calm despite the fact that he was standing atop the broken hulk of a fifty-million-dollar aircraft. "Guard the ejection levers." He motioned someone else clear, then depressed the canopy-release button and swung the left-side canopy open. The first thing he did was put a spare set of safety pins in the two ejection levers and the capsule-recovery handles on the center cockpit beam. That done, he could relax a bit. "Capsule's pinned," he said to the firemen surrounding the bomber. "Clear to go in. Wizzo looks like he might be hurt. Be careful." Puffing from the running and climbing he did, he turned to Furness, smiled, and said, "Nice to have you back in one piece, Major Furness."

Despite the forced landing, despite the damage, despite her hurt crewmember and her own pain, Rebecca could think of only one thing—the man's voice: "You're . . . you're Delta? The new MG?" The man nodded. And then she recognized that incredible face. "You're also the guy from the bar last night!"

"Naw, that was my evil twin brother," Daren Mace said with a smile. When her shocked expression remained, he nodded and said, "Yeah, yeah, it's me. Are you hurt, Rebecca? Can you move?"

Furness found that she was staring open-mouthed at the MG. He looked—well, like a movie star. He had a ruddy, energetic glow in his face, great blond hair peeking out from under his hat, and those green eyes looked so vital, confident, even happy.

"Rebecca?" His face searched hers, looking anxious and concerned but, after realizing she wasn't hurt, he relaxed. He held her left shoulder with his right hand, reached down, and turned the four-point harness connector, releasing all her harness straps at once. "Move slowly, and let me know if there's any pain."

She leaned forward, and he put his left hand on her right shoulder to help ease her away from the seat. "No . . . no, I feel okay. Everything's okay." A fireman was sitting atop the capsule, and with his help Mace eased Furness out of the cockpit. She steadied herself on the canopy sill after her legs were swung out.

Her feet were resting on a mound of snow that had piled itself up all around the Vampire bomber. The nose was almost completely buried in snow, and the wall of snow also nearly covered the wings' leading edges and engine intakes. If she hadn't shut down the engines first, they would have flamed out from having the intakes clogged with snow like that. Overall, the plane looked in pretty good shape considering the nose section was lying on the ground.

Mace covered her shoulders with a rough wool blanket as he helped her off with her flight helmet. "You certainly know how to make an entrance, Major," Mace said. "Let's get you down from there." A fireman put a cervical collar around her neck, and several firemen and medics helped her down off the bomber and into a waiting ambulance. With Fogelman on a gurney with her, Furness was laid on another gurney in the ambulance, covered with blankets, and strapped in securely. The MG rode with her the entire way in the back of the ambulance.

"How bad does my plane look, sir?" Furness asked him.

"Don't worry about that," Mace replied.

"Okay." She sighed. He seemed completely nonplussed about the disaster on his runway, which was pretty amazing for an MG. "How's Mark?" she asked with worry.

He checked on Fogelman, who was being cared for by two medics and a flight surgeon. "Mark cracked his head pretty good. He's unconscious." He saw Furness turn away from him and tears start to flow down her cheeks. Her lower lip trembled, as if from the cold. "Hey, everything's going to be fine. Mark's going to be okay."

"It's not that . . . I just never crashed a plane before," she muttered through cold, chattering teeth. "I never even came close . . ."

"You didn't crash, Rebecca, you brought yourself and your crew back safely and saved the plane from extensive damage or even total loss," the MG said. "You should be proud of yourself. Take a deep breath and try to relax."

"I tried to get away from Paula's plane . . . I pulled as hard as I could . . ." she insisted.

"I said, try to relax, Major," the MG said—she had forgotten his name already, and was already thinking of him as just the MG. "You did good. You were in a no-win situation. I used to be an Aardvark crewdog, too, and I know about crash landings, believe me."

"You do?"

"Yeah, unfortunately." He nodded. "Both me and the pilot got out okay, but I got the grilling of a lifetime—everything but the bamboo shoots up the fingernails and the rubber hoses—and it was all for nothing. That won't happen this time. I'm in charge of the accident investigation board, and I've got procedures to follow, but I will tell you that as long as I'm in charge of the investigation, we'll dispense with the shit they put me through. I promise you."

"What is going to happen, sir?" she asked, biting a nail nervously.

"Can the 'sir' stuff unless it's around the brass," Mace said. "The name is Daren. Daren Mace."

Rebecca's lip stopped chattering when she heard that name . . . and the voice. She had a weird sense of déjà vu, but didn't know why . . . somewhere she'd heard that name before.

"You gotta realize that under the regs we gotta do certain things right away," Mace was explaining. "An aircraft investigation board's been convened. They're going to take blood, and they're going to give you EEGs and X rays and all that shit, and they'll test your urine once you have to use the bathroom. You realize they're looking for . . . foreign substances. They have to do all this right away. A flight surgeon will be with you the whole time, and you can have someone else stay with you if you want—your husband, your parents, anybody. Want me to call someone?"

The ambulance hit a slight bump, which jolted them a bit. She thought about calling her uncle, but he would already be in Washington for the new Congressional session. Ed Caldwell? He'd be useless. Her parents were in Florida, and the nearest sibling was in Dallas, Texas. She had friends at Liberty Air, but no one she wanted to drag out here and stay with her. "There's . . . no one," Furness replied. "Dollie Jacobs will be all right." She had known Dr. Jacobs, the squadron flight surgeon, ever since she arrived at Plattsburgh.

"Fine," Mace said. "She'll meet us at the hospital—she's checking out the others right now. You realize that the accident investigation board's already been sworn in, and we're interviewing the others in your flight, as well as the F-16 crews. We're also retrieving the Boston Center and Air Defense Command recordings." He told her who else was on the accident investigation board—they were all Wing officers, all people she knew and trusted—except the new MG, of course. "The most important thing to remember is that nothing you say to me or the board can be used against you, ever, so I encourage you to talk to me and the other board members, and don't talk to anyone else. The Chief Circuit Defense Counsel has been called in from Langley, so if you feel you want to talk with counsel, we'll do that right away." The Area Defense Counsel was a team of military lawyers who were used as military defense attorneys—they reported only to the Air Force Judge Advocate General and the Secretary of the Air Force in Washington, not to any local commander, and so could not be swayed or influenced by rank or position.

"I'll cooperate in any way I can. I . . . I feel just fine talking with you," Rebecca heard herself say. She hadn't intended on that sounding so personal, but . . . it just came out that way. . . .

"Hey," Mace said, smiling, as the ambulance slowed to a stop at the emergency entrance to the base hospital. "Better stop that—you're starting to turn me on, BC."

Furness' eyes widened and her mouth went dry. She had heard those very same words before . . . but where? "Daren. I know that name. I remember . . . you . . . *you* were in Saudi . . . I mean, Iraq. . . ."

Mace smiled at her, showing her those pearly whites. He squeezed her hand reassuringly. "We'll talk later . . . Shamu," he said. As soon as the ambulance doors opened, he stepped out, and Dr. Dollie Jacobs took his place and began to examine her.

Jacobs had Rebecca transferred to an examining room, where she and two nurses gave her a thorough examination. The entire medical staff was wearing fatigues instead of hospital whites—that was a very unusual uniform-of-the-day combination for the hospital. "We getting an IG inspection or something, Dollie?" Furness asked.

Jacobs was examining Rebecca's ear canals for any signs of bleeding or eardrum rupture: "There's . . . uh . . . you don't know?"

"Know what?"

"We got a message about two hours ago," Jacobs explained. "We're doing a full aircraft-generation—and it's not an exercise, it's the real thing."

"A *generation?*" Furness asked, thinking she hadn't heard right. "Are you sure? Not a deployment?" The 394th Air Battle Wing's primary mission was "deployment," or preparing to move to another location and begin offensive bombing missions. The wing rarely practiced or performed a "generation"—that was when all of the bombers on base were loaded with thermonuclear weapons, and the tankers configured for long-range refueling missions, and both were placed on round-the-clock strategic alert, ready to go to war.

"I'm afraid not," Jacobs said. "Russia has attacked the Ukraine with at least one nuke. The shit, as they say, is really hitting the fan."

24

394th Air Battle Wing Headquarters

"WHERE THE HELL HAVE YOU BEEN, COLONEL?" COLONEL Lafferty, the wing vice commander, asked a few minutes later as Daren Mace entered the battle staff conference room. "The battle staff meeting ended ten minutes ago."

"At the bomber recovery," Mace replied. His fatigues were soaking wet from crawling on the snow-covered plane, and his hair was tousled and sweaty. "I accompanied Furness and Fogelman to the hospital."

"Daren, I need your ass right here at headquarters," General Cole interjected. "I understand that it's important to talk with the crews and see the damage yourself, but we've got a generation to run here."

"Sir, did you receive a report on Furness and Fogelman yet?" Mace interjected. He turned to Greg McGwire, the Operations Group commander, and asked, "Do you know what the status of your crewmembers is, Colonel McGwire?"

"No, but what does *that* have to do with—"

"Well, I know, because I bothered to goddamn *ask,*" Mace said, obviously angry at being rebuffed simply because he was more concerned about the crews than the machines. "If we're generating SIOP sorties, I think it's important to know the condition of those you're handing the codes to, don't you think, sir?

"Major Furness appears unhurt. Mark Fogelman is still unconscious with head injuries. Our movie star, Ted Little, is being examined for a mild concussion. The flight surgeon says that all of them might need a staff PRP evaluation before being allowed back on flying status. That means two crews and two planes down for now." He paused for a moment, then averted his eyes, just enough to show Cole or McGwire that he wasn't trying to challenge anyone, then added, "With all due respect, sir, you can't always run a generation from the command post."

General Cole appeared angry and ready to blast back at Mace, but instead he took a deep breath, simmering, then said, "Thank you for the report, Colonel. Just answer the phone when I call, Daren, is that clear?" Mace nodded, then accepted a cup of coffee and a computer printout on the progress of the aircraft generation from Captain Porter. To the Operations Group commander, Cole asked, "John, let's plan on decertifying Norton and Furness for at least one day, pending a staff review. What will this do to our alert lines?"

"Shouldn't affect the generation at all, General," McGwire replied. "All the alert lines are manned. We can put Furness and Norton together on the Charlie alert lines—as an instructor, Furness is fully qualified as a weapons system officer—which won't come up for at least twenty-four to forty-eight hours. That means we'll be only one crew down."

"That means," Colonel Lafferty interjected, "that we're only one crew or two planes short of going combat-ineffective—and that's if Fifth Air Battle Force doesn't take us all down under PRP anyway."

Mace shook his head at that acronym—he thought he had heard the last of PRP. The Personnel Reliability Program was established in the early years of the Strategic Air Command to certify crewmembers who handled nuclear weapons in any manner. Each person cleared for nuclear duties had to pass a stringent set of physical and psychological standards in order to be cleared for "special"—i.e., nuclear weapon—duties. Certain serious personal occurrences—illness, taking medication, hospitalization, accidents, a personal or family crisis, anything that might cause a person to "not be himself" in any way—would prompt a commander to "decertify" a crewmember, or remove him or her from nuclear duties. Fogelman was definitely off PRP. Under normal circumstances, Colonel Hembree, the bomber squadron commander, would have certainly taken Paula Norton, Ted Little, Rebecca Furness, and maybe even the other two crews in Furness' formation immediately off PRP as well, even though none was injured; a close call like theirs might make them a bit reluctant to fly or might distract them from the dangerous job of handling a nuclear-loaded bomber.

There was seldom any hesitation in temporarily pulling a crewmember's PRP certification—temporary decertification did not affect a crewmember's career or official records. The safe play was to yank PRP—except when it appeared that the whole world was getting ready to go to war. Unless the crewmember showed clear signs of stress, injury, or emotional trauma, they would be kept on the line getting their bombers ready to fight.

"Okay," Cole said, "let's go over the generation so far. I'd like to start with an intelligence briefing. Major Pierce?"

"Yes, sir." Pierce got to his feet and walked over to a map of Eastern Europe, showing western Russia and the Black Sea region. "As you all know by now, the Russians launched a large-scale air attack against the Ukraine, using low-yield tactical nuclear devices, and they used non-nuclear bombs and cruise missiles against military targets in Romania and Moldova. The goal of the attack was obviously to destroy the Ukraine's main offensive and defensive air bases, and to cripple Romania's and Moldova's military units and stop them from mounting any sort of offensive against the Russians living in the Dniester region of eastern Moldova.

"The reports call it a Desert Storm–type air assault, with AS-4 cruise missiles launched from Backfire bombers and AS-15 cruise missiles carried by Blackjack supersonic bombers, followed up by gravity bomb and short-range missile attacks by Bear and Badger long- and medium-range jet bombers," Pierce added, putting up a slide of the suspected Russian staging bases, the types and numbers of bombers, and their suspected routes of flight. "Ukrainian air defense stations reportedly engaged the heavy bombers, but they had no chance to stop them. Reportedly a few of the AS-4 and -15 nuclear cruise missiles were shot down by Ukrainian air defenses, but a total of four nuclear detonations were recorded.

"If there's a bright spot to this horrible attack," Pierce continued, "it's the fact that the Russians didn't use the normal 350- or 200-kiloton nuclear warheads in the AS-4 and AS-15 missiles. They apparently used those rinky-dink RKY-2 devices, which are very small enhanced radiation devices normally used on battlefield nuclear artillery shells. The difference with these devices is that they have no outer shell of uranium to collect and capture neutrons—the neutrons from the first fission explosion are released. Therefore, there are no typical nuclear bomb effects: no gigantic shock wave, no thermal blast effects, no craters, no fallout, no lingering radiation. Their yield is equivalent to about a two-kiloton nuclear device—"

"Neutron bombs," General Cole muttered. "People-killers."

"Exactly, sir," Pierce said. "The neutron stream from the explosion can penetrate unshielded structures with ease. Personnel in shielded vehicles, properly constructed underground shelters, or wearing nuclear-chemical-biological exposure suits are safe, and protected individuals can enter the attack area almost immediately after the detonation."

"And anyone not in shelters or wearing suits?" Colonel McGwire asked.

Major Pierce shuffled uneasily, checked his notes, cleared his throat, then said, "Within a half-mile from ground zero, death from radiation poisoning will occur within twelve hours. Inside two miles from ground zero, death will occur within three to five days, even with medical treatment, depending on distance and level of exposure. Injuries from burns, shock, overpressure, and flashblindness are common within two miles as well." The battle staff was too stunned to react. Of all the ways to die, death from massive radiation poisoning had to be the worst conceivable way—slow, painful, and horrible.

"What Ukrainian bases were hit by these . . . things?" Colonel Lafferty asked.

"Three isolated bases in western and central Ukraine were hit by neutron bombs," Pierce said, putting up a slide of the Black Sea region and the Ukraine. "L'vov in western Ukraine was hit by a neutron missile. Fortunately the base is several miles outside the city of L'vov, which has a population of almost a million. However, L'vov Air Base is . . . rather, *was* . . . the largest Ukrainian air base except for Kiev, and it had been recently reinforced with more aircraft from Odessa. There could have been five squadrons destroyed in the attack."

Unsaid was the fact that Pierce was talking about five squadrons' worth of *people,* about five to six thousand military personnel, since the neutron bomb would have left most of the aircraft intact except those closest to the explosion.

"The central Ukrainian base of Vinnica was hit by one missile, and since the base is very close to the city, here is where we can expect the largest death tolls—possibly close to seven thousand dead or injured, military and civilian," Pierce continued. "Two, perhaps three fighter and bomber squadrons may have been destroyed.

"Krivoj Rog in east-central Ukraine was hit with one missile as well," Pierce continued. "KR was a transport base, with two squadrons destroyed and minimal civilian casualties. Also heavily attacked, but not with nuclear devices, was the port town of Belgorod-Dnestrovski, which is the headquarters of the Ukrainian Coast Guard river patrols. The Russians were obviously going after the Ukrainian river patrols that have been intercepting Russian barges and vessels trying to resupply the Russian rebels in Moldova." Pierce didn't know if anyone was really listening to him anymore, but he decided to press on and get through this godawful briefing as fast as he could.

"In Moldova, the air attacks were centered on the town of Bel'cy, in northwestern Moldova, which had one Moldovan Army division and was a marshaling area for perhaps four or five Romanian army divisions. Kishinev, the capital, was untouched except for antiradar-missile attacks against Romanian long-range radar systems installed during the buildup.

"Three cities in eastern Romania were hit. Iasi, headquarters of the eastern military district and the headquarters for Romanian military operations in Moldova, was hit very heavily with non-nuclear weapons," Pierce went on. "Galati, the main air base in eastern Romania, with six fighter and bomber squadrons based there, was the only base outside the Ukraine hit by neutron bombs—the estimated loss of life is near four thousand. Braila, just a few miles south of Galati, had one army division and was a major Romania Coast Guard base patrolling the Danube; it was hit with non-nuclear weapons."

The immensity of that number simply could not be digested, and nearly everyone at the battle staff conference table shook their heads. Some eighteen thousand people dead, and even more injured—in *one* attack? How could any nation hope to care for that many injured or bury that many dead? It was too enormous to even think about. And what if it happened in the United States? Against Burlington or Plattsburgh, or New York City or Boston? How could anyone deal with it?

"What is equally interesting about these attacks is what was *not* attacked," Pierce concluded. "Kiev, with five fighter and bomber squadrons and four army divisions, was overflown but not attacked, although it fired a great many air defense missiles and shot down several Russian aircraft and cruise missiles. Odessa, with two fighter squadrons, two army divisions, and the thirty-ship Ukrainian Navy; and Doneck, in the eastern coal mining and heavy manufacturing region known as the Don, with six army divisions, were both untouched. In Romania, the large Black Sea military complex at Constanta, with four fighter squadrons, two bomber squadrons, four army divisions, and Romania's only blue-water naval base, was untouched.

"All in all, it appears that the Russians went after air forces and specifically stayed away from attacking large troop concentrations and population centers. They obviously understand that air power is very important, that control of the skies is their first priority, and limiting casualties is important for public relations—"

"Public relations?" Cole asked in amazement. "My God, they nuked the Ukraine! I'd say their public relations efforts have gone down the toilet."

"The best explanation for the use of neutron warheads is that the Ukraine is a powerful opponent and the Russians needed the biggest bang possible out of their big, long-range bombers," Pierce said. "Put a small-yield nuke warhead on some of the missiles, and your mission effectiveness jumps tremendously. It's pretty cold-blooded, but it's an effective way of prosecuting a war. The death toll is going to be very large, but it could have been much worse."

"Jesus. It'll be a pretty sad day when nations determine that they can use nuclear weapons to fight a war. Soon every nation on earth will be using them. This was all supposed to have ended with the Cold War. What a joke."

Daren Mace hoped that no one saw him squirm uncomfortably. *Believe me, General,* Mace remarked to himself, *the Russians definitely weren't the only ones to think of that idea.* What would the U.S. reaction be? If the U.S. government considered the use of low-yield nuclear weapons against a relatively weak foe like Iraq, as they had that opening day of Desert Storm, would the U.S. resort to nuclear weapons if drawn into a battle against a formidable foe like Russia?

"Conclusions, then, Major," Cole asked. "How much of the Ukraine's military was destroyed, and what is their current military status?"

"About half of their military force was decimated," Pierce replied, "mostly their air assets. Although Ukrainian ground forces are fairly intact, with their Air Force so heavily destroyed, I'd say the Ukraine is vulnerable to attack and will not be able to put up much resistance throughout most of the country, with the exception of Kiev, the south, and the Don region—western Ukraine is wide open. Same goes for Romania, although they suffered heavier land forces losses. Conclusion: Moldova can belong to Russia again as soon as Russia is ready to reclaim it, without any interference from the Ukraine or Romania."

"How about closer to home?" Cole asked. "What have the Russians been doing in North America?"

"Their entire force of Backfire bombers based in Cuba was airborne throughout the attack period," Pierce replied. "They were not seen with any weapons when they were intercepted over international waters. However, it is now estimated that the Backfires are each armed with six AS-16 'Kickback' short-range attack missiles in an internal rotary launcher. It is now believed that the Backfires were poised for a strike against the United States if one was deemed necessary. The AS-16 missile is an equivalent to our AGM-69 Short-Range Attack Missile, with inertial guidance, a range of about a hundred miles, a top speed of Mach-three, and a circular error probability of about a hundred feet; it probably would've been delivered during a supersonic low-level dash inland, with a pretty good chance of success. I think we can assume that the Russians have put RKY-2 warheads on the AS-16 missiles as well. It hasn't been officially announced yet, but I think we can expect a directive to come down to shoot down any Backfires encountered from now on."

"I think we'd all agree with that," Cole said grimly. Now at least they had something to focus their anger on, something to take their minds away from dying men, women, and children in Europe, and back to the task of defending their nation. The Backfires were too close to home, and that fact helped them to concentrate. "Okay, gentlemen, let's get down to our job. We've got a helluva lot of work to do. God help us."

PART FOUR

It is the habit of every aggressor nation to claim that it is acting on the defensive.
—Jawaharlal Nehru

25

L'vov, the Ukraine
The Next Day

"WE HAVE BEGUN RECEIVING RADIO BROADCASTS FROM THE outside," Colonel of Aviation Petr Panchenko said. "It is my great pleasure to inform you that although Ukrayina is gravely hurt, the Republic is intact."

The cheer that rose in that conference room was hearty but a bit strained. Panchenko was presiding over a meeting of the surviving officers and senior enlisted staff of L'vov Air Base in western Ukraine, deep within the base's underground command center. The twenty men and women attending the briefing were exhausted and stressed to the point of breaking, both mentally and physically, but an observer who knew nothing of the grave situation outside their earth, steel, and concrete walls would never guess the circumstances the soldiers were under. Panchenko, as senior officer, had prescribed normal dress and deportment, even after all outside life-support systems had been cut off shortly after the attack. Clean, shaven faces, clean uniforms, and spit-shined boots were mandatory, supervised by regular inspections, and twice-daily exercise periods were required for all personnel. Panchenko was determined that military discipline be strictly maintained despite the horrible tragedy that faced them.

"As we surmised, the Russian invaders conducted no attacks in the Ukraine south of the forty-eighth parallel, with the exception of Krivoj Rog army transport base," Panchenko continued. "The reason is simple: more Russians live in the Crimea and Azov regions of the Ukraine than any other. The Don region was untouched, primarily because Russia values the coal and ore mining operations there. The capital received only isolated, non-nuclear attacks to outlying military installations. Obviously, the large number of Russians living in Kiev is the reason for this. So far no foreign troops appear to be marching on the capital, although the M21 highway from Vinnica to Minsk and the M10 highway between Kiev and Moscow across Belarus is closed and is clogged with military traffic."

One officer sitting at the head of the table beside Panchenko was only half listening to the briefing. Captain of Aviation Pavlo Tychina, looking like a sinister Phantom of the Opera with his sterile gauze mask, sat still, eyes straight ahead, arms at his sides. He did not react at all to Panchenko's words of encouragement, but remained motionless, lost in his own tortured thoughts. The Colonel had told him that such self-imposed misery was selfish and useless and nonproductive—everyone in that bunker had lost someone close to them—but his words made no difference. Tychina allowed himself to mourn deeply—and propped up those thoughts with ones of revenge. Nothing would keep either of those thoughts out of his head. He had the skill and the desire to inflict great pain on the Russians who staged the preemptive attack on his homeland, and nothing would stop him from—

"Captain?" Panchenko was asking, trying to get his attention. His commander's voice had a sharp edge. "Your briefing, *please.*"

Tychina didn't apologize for his inattention, but stiffly rose to his feet. His audience's eyes were riveted on him, not only because of his horrible wounds but because of who he was and what he had lost. As Colonel Panchenko had said, everyone lost someone in the hell's fire above, but somehow Tychina's loss affected them all.

"Comrades, I was asked by Colonel Panchenko to interface with other surviving aviation elements in the country to catalog the national defense strike units, namely, the MiG-23, MiG-27, and Su-17 fighter and fighter-bomber units," Tychina began. "Unfortunately, that has been almost impossible. The nuclear explosions aboveground created an electromagnetic disturbance in the atmosphere that until recently has disrupted all normal military communications. The BBC, Voice of America, and Radio Europe report that Ukrainian military units near the capital have been attacked by Russian air raids over the past few hours and that all air defense units in the north have been destroyed or have been rendered non–mission effective. We don't know the full effect of the nuclear attacks against our base or against Vinnica, but I think we must assume that our forces in the north have been destroyed.

"That leaves the Fifth Air Army in Odessa as the only untouched fighter group. So far I have heard no reports about any air attacks into Odessa, so I assume their units are intact and possibly dispersed," Tychina continued. It was good that Panchenko made him do all this research and act as a sort of intelligence officer—it helped clear his head, got him thinking tactically again, and helped keep his mind off the disaster that awaited him aboveground: "The Fifth possesses one MiG-27 bomber wing, two squadrons of about eighteen aircraft each. We may be lucky enough to have a few elements of Kiev's Eighth Air Army who survived the conventional bombing attacks and escaped to Odessa, and we know that as many as twenty MiG-23 fighters from our unit and a few MiG-27 and Sukhoi-17 bombers from Vinnica were airborne and may have escaped the nuclear air raids. Therefore, I estimate that we have a force of approximately one hundred fifty, possibly as many as two hundred fixed-wing strike and fighter aircraft. It is completely unknown at this time how many attack helicopters survived—Odessa had lost one hundred and forty Mil-24 attack helicopters in the Fourteenth Combined Arms Division and at least two hundred Mil-8 combat transport helicopters."

The group was very silent—they knew the devastation was enormous. The Ukraine had had almost two thousand strike planes and helicopters just twenty-four hours earlier—now they had fewer than five hundred, maybe less. How could they ever hope of mounting any sort of counteroffensive? Except for the use of nuclear weapons, which did not seem to be that extensive, the Russians actually seemed to hold back their concentrated attacks, and three-fourths of the Ukraine's air force had been wiped out. What could they possibly hope to do?

"Thank you, Captain," Panchenko said, sensing Tychina's drifting attention and concluding his briefing for him. Tychina nodded and took his seat. To the staff, Panchenko said, "Ladies and gentlemen, I don't know what we'll find up there. We may in fact be down here for quite some time. The main exit appears to be intact but may have suffered damage, and the escape tunnels may be our best option; I have people checking on them now, and they should be reporting in soon. If we can get out, we may take the risk and evacuate to Odessa soon—assuming they can dig us out of here. In any case, I want you all to remember that we are warriors, combatants, and members of the Ukrayina Air Force. We will use whatever weapons we find up there to take up the fight." He paused, scanning the faces around him, and finally resting on Pavlo Tychina. "Is that clear, Captain?"

"Yes, *sir,*" Tychina responded firmly.

Panchenko turned to his intelligence officer for a briefing, but before he could begin, a telephone rang somewhere outside the conference room—it was the first telephone ring they had heard in many hours. A communications technician leaped to answer it. He listened for a moment, covered the mouthpiece, then cried, "Sir! A rescue crew is at the outer door! The door is intact and they are requesting permission to enter!"

Panchenko had no sooner opened his mouth to speak than Tychina was on his feet and sprinting for the door. Panchenko yelled, "Captain! Take your seat!" but it did no good. To the communication technician, Panchenko said, "Clear the security area and weather station, and all personnel, including Captain Tychina, *will* wear exposure suits and respirators before those doors are opened. Everyone else is to be in the communications center or beyond." He dismissed the staff and hurried off after Tychina.

As he expected, by the time Panchenko reached the security area just inside the blast doors, the doors had been opened, the hallway was filled with anxious people—none of whom were wearing chemical antiexposure suits or respirators—and Tychina was nowhere to be found. "I ordered this area cleared and authorized personnel to wear protective equipment," Panchenko said to a senior master sergeant. He couldn't be too angry because he was anxious to get upstairs as well.

"Sorry, sir, they rushed the door as soon as it was opened," the senior NCO replied. "The Captain—the Phoenix—ordered me aside."

The Phoenix—Panchenko had heard that name being muttered around the base and the command center. Tychina's efforts at turning away the first Russian air raid were beginning to take on almost mystical proportions. The quiet, rather introspective young pilot was turning into something of a legend in L'vov. No doubt it would spread throughout Ukrayina before too long—if Tychina survived his anger and thirst for revenge.

"I gave an *order*, and I expect it to be carried out, Sergeant," Panchenko said irritably, "no matter what Captain Tychina tells you. Now clear this hallway."

As the master sergeant complied with his orders, a man in a silver firefighter's suit—not a proper chemical/nuclear exposure suit, but it would offer limited protection—approached Panchenko. "Are you the commanding officer here, sir?" Panchenko nodded. "Chief Warrant Officer Usenko, Twenty-oh-four Ordnance Battalion, Seventy-second Motorized Rifle Division, from Kiev. I'm very glad to find you, sir."

"Thank you for digging us out of here," Panchenko said with relief. "How bad is it up there?"

Usenko shrugged. "Bad? We didn't have to dig you out, sir. A few structures and aircraft were on fire, and the petrol-tank farm was burning from a bombing attack—that's why I'm outfitted like this—but otherwise the base is intact."

"Intact? How is that possible? We were hit, a direct hit . . . our dosimeters registered very high radiation counts."

"Dissipated," Usenko replied. "The Russians attacked with low-yield nuclear weapons, exploded at high altitude over selected targets. They caused only momentary communications blackouts, a few blast damage effects, and—"

"Casualties, Usenko . . . what about casualties?"

Usenko's eyes averted to the floor for a moment, then raised to Panchenko with a tortured, haunted expression. "Too early to tell, sir," he replied. "Each target complex hit with the subatomic weapons had a few initial casualties, mostly from flashblindness, moderate burns, and shock—less than one-half of one percent casualties and injuries, I'd estimate. The weapons produced virtually no extensive damage—no craters, no fires, no fallout. But as you have determined, transient neutron radiation levels were extremely high, and unprotected individuals may have received a fatal dose. Casualties are expected to be very high in the next forty-eight to seventy-two hours."

"You mean to tell me . . . you mean, there are still people up there, *alive?*"

Usenko looked as if he'd been slapped in the face. He shuffled uneasily, then nodded his head: "Uh . . . sir, most everyone that was indoors during the attack, those not affected by flashblindness or overpressure, survived. Persons outdoors but protected from the flash and overpressure also survived or were only injured. But they all would have received tremendous doses of radiation, far above lethal levels. Personnel here in the command center and in other underground or shielded facilities are probably safe, but the others . . . there may be nothing we can do for them."

"My God . . . is there any danger of fallout or exposure now? Is it safe to let my command post personnel outside?"

"Russian fighter planes have been patrolling the area, reconnaissance planes mostly, so we're safe from any more air attacks for now, and as far as the radiation threat, it's safe, yes, sir," Usenko responded. "There is no danger of radiation poisoning, and no fallout. It is probably best that your people be briefed on what they are to expect up there, though. We will be asking all available personnel to assist with medical and mortuary services." Usenko paused, then motioned toward the corridor leading to the surface and asked, "Sir, was that Captain Tychina—the Phoenix? I was hoping he was still alive. I knew he could not die. I wanted to shake that man's hand."

Panchenko stared into the darkness beyond the blast doors of his command center, silently praying for his young pilot. Tychina, and all of them, were going to need all the strength they could muster to get through this disaster.

Tychina was determined to sprint the entire one and a half kilometers to the chapel, but the horror of what he saw was like a vacuum that sucked all the energy from his body. Several buildings and structures were burned down, mostly older wooden structures and the ugly billboards with "inspirational" messages on them that were so common to ex-Soviet military bases, and it seemed that every window in sight was gone—not just broken or shattered, but completely blown away. What he then noticed was the flatbed trucks—dozens of them, lined up outside the headquarters building, the central base personnel office, and other administrative buildings. His eyes were drawn to the trucks' cargo. At first it seemed as if they were unloading tables or medical supplies to set up a triage detail, but when he looked closer he discovered they were loading bodies onto the truck. The bottom rows of bodies were in dark plastic body bags, but they obviously ran out of body bags very quickly because the middle stacks of corpses were covered in sheets, and the stacks above them were covered in clothing, and a few were not covered at all. Each flatbed truck was stacked four or five rows high with bodies, well over two hundred on each flatbed.

But even worse than that sight were the sounds of hundreds of people in agony. For every corpse in those flatbeds, there appeared to be a dozen men and women who were not dead, but horribly injured or maimed from the attack. The sidewalks, the snowy lawns, the entryways and hallways of every building had been converted into makeshift field hospitals, where the dying were crying out for help. It was difficult to fully comprehend—the damage to the base itself was not that extensive, yet the casualties were probably in the thousands. Did the Russian nuclear attack miss its target? Did they use some sort of chemical or biological weapon? Tychina saw a few chemical exposure suits, but most of the relief workers had no protective gear at all. Weren't chemical weapons more persistent than this?

"Look! It's the Phoenix!" someone shouted. "Phoenix!"

"Where were you when the bombs hit, Captain Phoenix?" someone else shouted. "Why couldn't you stop this?"

"Shut up!" an officer interjected. "He's alive and he's with us! He's our best pilot—he won't let us down!"

Tychina nearly stumbled in his hurry to get away. An argument between some of the men in the mortuary detail broke out, some on the side of Tychina and those who were safe in the command center, others who thought that Tychina was on his way to the flight line and cheered him on. Panic seized the young pilot, and he hobbled down the vehicle-clogged street as fast as he could.

But the horrors never ceased. Many were dead in their cars, still behind the wheel or slumped over onto the seat, with a sheen of frost under their nostrils and around their eyes where their dying breath had frozen—they had obviously been there a long time. Most corpses were lying outside, some carrying food or medical supplies, a few carrying other dead souls, probably for medical treatment when they succumbed to the effects of the nuclear weapon the Russians unleashed on the base. Bodies were lining the sidewalks as teams of investigators identified each corpse, tagged it with a baggage tag, moved it clear of the sidewalks and driveways, covered it the best they could with an article of clothing or a sheet, then moved on to the next. Tychina was so transfixed by one body, the corpse of a member of his own squadron, that he nearly tripped over another corpse sprawled in his path. It was like some horrible science-fiction movie about the end of the world.

The base chapel was being used as a mortuary. He asked the sergeant in charge about Mikola Korneichuk, a civilian, and after finding her name not among those who had been identified, was led over to two long rows of corpses of those who had not been identified lined up outside in the snow. The nuclear device set off by the Russians had obviously injected a lot of radiation into these victims, because most had substantial hair loss, huge blisters and lesions all over their faces, bloated skin, and horribly swollen tongues and eyeballs. But Mikki was not among the dead.

"You are Captain Tychina?" the mortuary officer asked him. "You are the pilot that drove the first Russian attack away?" Tychina tried to leave, but the man persisted. "Promise me you'll destroy the Russians for what they've done here, Captain. Promise you'll avenge the dead." Pavlo got out of there as fast as he could.

It was easy to commandeer a vehicle—keys were left in the ignitions, and the dead owners were not about to complain. Security patrols were everywhere. Regular patrols allowed Tychina to pass freely after recognizing who he was, but some roadblocks to the officers' housing area were set up by the local militia, and although he was recognized and his identification was in order, he was told to return to the main base immediately. Tychina wasn't about to put up with any local weekend warriors with shotguns, so he sped through the roadblock. None of the militiamen bothered to pursue him.

The bachelor officers' quarters were about three kilometers outside the main base area in one of the base's many satellite housing areas, a typical bland Soviet-style settlement with many dormitory-style buildings, a park with a few scraggly trees, an exercise area, a small shopette, and an elementary school for the children of young soldiers. Tychina's dorm was a huge, ugly concrete structure in which each unmarried officer was assigned an efficiency apartment, sharing a kitchen and bathroom with the person next door. The entire building, which housed almost five hundred officers, appeared deserted. He took the stairs two at a time to his fourth-floor room and found the door unlocked.

"Mikki!" He had been braced for the worst, but he never expected this: his fiancée was lying on his opened sleeper sofa, head seductively pillowed by an arm, her hair draped across a pillow as if arranged by a fashion designer. She was wearing a long, heavy flannel nightgown against the chill in the room—power had only recently been restored. She looked beautiful . . . even in . . . Pavlo was so overwhelmed that he burst into tears.

Mikola sleepily opened her eyes and smiled at him, the familiar, warm smile he had longed to see. "Hi, baby," she said sleepily.

She was *alive!* Thank God Almighty!

"I waited up as long as I could. Give me a moment and I'll be ready to go with you to the chapel."

"God, Mikki . . . !" He rushed to her side and hugged her close, unabashed in his joy, his tears. "I'm so glad you're safe . . . dear God, I thought you were in the chapel," he moaned, burying his face in her hair. "Are you all right? Were you hurt in the attack?"

"No, I wasn't hurt—scared, but not hurt. I'm still a little tired." She yawned. "It got so cold in here when the power went off, but the loudspeakers said stay in the room, so I wrapped up in blankets and fell asleep, but I'll be better, just give me a few minutes, just let me get out of bed and I'll freshen up and I'll be ready to go. Oh, I love you so much, Pavlo, I love you so much. . . ."

Her voice was trailing away, down to a barely audible whisper, as if she were walking away from him. Tychina noticed that she did not return his embrace, but her arms hung loosely at her sides . . .

. . . and when he lifted her head off his shoulders to look into her face, her hair dropped off her head like clumps of brittle needles from a long-dead Christmas tree. "Jesus Christ, Mikki . . . !"

"Pavlo?" Her voice was as faint as the buzz of a hummingbird, even though she was only inches away. "Pavlo, please help me to the chapel, I'm so tired . . ."

He got off the couch in a near-panic. He had to get her out of here. Had to get her help. She must have gotten a large dose of radiation, Pavlo thought, while she was waiting for him at the chapel. But she survived and somehow made her way back to the dorm room. Except for her hair, it seemed—he prayed—she didn't receive a fatal dose. Perhaps she could be saved. . . .

But when he lifted her into his arms to take her downstairs for help, the skin from her left thigh sloughed off like wet tissue paper, exposing muscle caked with dried, blackened blood. Tychina swallowed hard to hold back the tears, laid her back on the bed, and covered her with blankets. "I'll get help, Mikki," he whispered. "Hang on, I'll be right back." But when he dared look into her eyes, he found them dry and lifeless, clouding up, her perfect mouth slightly open as she tried to draw in her last breath that never came.

"No . . . *Mikki!*" he sobbed, thinking perhaps she'd just gone back to sleep. Yes, that was it . . . she'd need her rest . . . while he went to get help. He held her close to his chest, his sobs growing harder, the tears falling down on her thin hair. He knew she wasn't asleep, it'd been a desperate hope, a fantasy. He tried to bargain with God: *Just take me, let her live, just take me. She's too beautiful, too sweet and wonderful and innocent to die.* He thought she was dead, had prepared himself for it, tried to muster enough strength to face it when he knew, ultimately, that he would. And yet, finding her alive, seeing her come awake, now . . . now only to die.

This is too cruel for any man! he raged silently at the heavens. *Why?* He sobbed even harder, clutching her to him, feeling as if his whole world were collapsing. Not caring whether he lived or died, but only praying for God—for anyone—to bring her back to life.

Mikola seemed so thin, so tiny, to Pavlo as he stapled her identification card to her nightgown and wrapped the body in a blanket. He was about to pick her up and take her down to the car when he heard, "Don't worry about her, Pavlo. We'll take good care of her."

Tychina turned and saw Colonel Panchenko and several members of the command center staff enter the room. A security officer took the body from Tychina's arms, promising to take personal charge of her until he could make proper arrangements. Tychina was going to follow the security officer out, but Panchenko stopped him with a firm, positive grip on his arm. "Not now, Pavlo. You have work to do."

The young pilot shrugged out of the senior officer's grasp and said, "Excuse me, Colonel, but—"

"It's 'general' now, Pavlo," Panchenko said. "I am the new commander of tactical air warfare for the entire Republic. The national military headquarters was destroyed by Russian air attacks. The chief of staff and the service chiefs escaped, but most of the senior staff was killed. I am transferring command to Turkey."

"What? What did you say?" This was all too much. His eyes were swollen, and he felt as if his head were spinning. Mikki . . . Panchenko . . . what was he saying?

"A Ukrainian government-in-exile has been formed in Istanbul," Panchenko said. "The Turks have accepted our pleas for help, and the West is promising assistance. All Ukrainian aircraft that have survived the Russian air raids are deploying to a Turkish training air base near the city of Kayseri. I am organizing the Free Ukrainian Air Force there, and you are coming with me . . . Colonel."

Tychina looked at Panchenko, and although he could see only the young pilot's eyes, he knew that Tychina wore a completely stunned expression. "It turns out that not only are you the senior surviving MiG-23 pilot, Pavlo, but you are one of the most experienced Ukrainian pilots alive. I need you to command the provisional fighter wing, and I can't very well have a captain do it. The promotion is effective immediately. As soon as possible, we will launch whatever aircraft can make the trip and fly to Turkey. Turkish fighter planes are waiting to escort us."

Pavlo tried to clear his head, concentrate on what Panchenko was saying. He tried to look out the window to see Mikki, but Panchenko's size blocked his view. He had to let her go . . . they would try to give her dignity . . . he refocused, as difficult as it was, as tumultuous as the wave of emotions sweeping over him felt . . . and forced himself to listen to what Panchenko was saying.

But it wasn't easy. *You just have to get through it, Pavlo. Just as if you were in a plane during an emergency situation. Stay calm, stay under control. Do your job.* He returned his attention to Panchenko, who was still talking. . . .

"I never finished telling you, Pavlo," Panchenko said solemnly. "We knew this disaster would happen. We, the general staff and the government, knew that the Russians were going to retake Ukrayina. We planned for it. For the past two months we have been shipping weapons and equipment overseas, to Turkey."

"You have?" Tychina asked, stunned by this revelation. "But why Turkey? And how did you know?"

"We didn't know, of course, and we hoped we were wrong," Panchenko explained. "But a war with Russia was inevitable. Conflict over the Dniester was only the spark. Access to the Black Sea ports, removal of nuclear weapons, land and property disputes, free trade, oil, agriculture—the Russians were losing everything of value. Ukrayina wanted to join the West, become a member of the European Community and NATO. Russia couldn't allow that.

"So the government struck a deal with NATO several months ago to rathole one-third of the weapon stockpiles in Turkey. We've been shipping missiles, bombs, spare parts, vehicles, even tech orders and charts to bases in Turkey, right under the noses of the damned Russian naval patrols in the Black Sea. Thousands of tons of equipment and weapons, at least a trainload every week. To pay for the 'storage,' the government has been paying cash and signing basing agreements with NATO for access to Ukrayinan waters and ports after the conflict is over. Now we need someone to start setting up our operating base in Turkey. I want you to do it."

Panchenko kept him in the room until they heard his staff car start up and drive away. What he saw in the young pilot's eyes encouraged him. When he first entered the room and saw Tychina with the body of his fiancée, his eyes looked like a lost child's eyes, full of fear and helplessness. When they took the body, he saw utter despair. Now he was relieved to see fire—and the thirst for revenge—in those eyes. It would take a strong hand to turn that drive for revenge into a more positive direction, to turn the blood lust into a calculating, meticulous planner and leader, but he was certain it could be done. The Phoenix would fly again, and this time he would lead a nation's entire tiny air armada into battle.

Pavlo let Panchenko's words sink in. So much was happening so fast . . . but that was the way it always happened in war. Decisions had to be quick and good. Otherwise you were dead. Pavlo swallowed hard, trying not to think about Mikki but about the matter at hand. He had to be a soldier first. His mouth felt unusually dry and his stomach queasy. And yet he was alive, and he was whole.

And he was going after the Russian bastards.

It was *they* who killed Mikki. It was *they* who had robbed him of the one love in his life. It was *they* who devastated his homeland. It was *they* who killed God knows how many of his countrymen.

He swallowed hard, and with determination he looked into his superior's eyes: "I will do it. And I will get them."

"I know you will. I'm counting on it."

26

The White House Cabinet Room, Washington, D.C., That Same Time

"I GOT IT STRAIGHT FROM THE HORSE'S MOUTH," THE PRESIDENT said in his deep southern accent as he sat down with his National Security Council staff in the White House Cabinet Room. "President Velichko told me—no, *promised* me, man to man, that the nuclear attack on the Ukraine was a mistake that will not be repeated, and that he intends to back off. So somebody explain to me why everyone in Europe's getting all hot under the damned collar?"

The question was not aimed at anyone in particular—a tactic common to the President, designed to make everyone around him uncomfortable and on the defensive—so the men sitting around the table with the President shifted uncomfortably, silently deferring to Dr. Donald Scheer, the forty-two-year-old former professor of economics from MIT who had been chosen as the President's Secretary of Defense. As unlikely as the choice of Scheer was for Secretary of Defense, this young, highly intelligent Bean-Counter Emeritus, as the press had dubbed him, was the perfect counterpoint to the President's big, southern, ham-handed approach to dealing with the bureaucracy. The President was the ax, Scheer the scalpel, when it came to dealing with waste, with the budget, with the Washington establishment.

"Perhaps you should tell us more about your conversation with the Russian president, Mr. President," Scheer said.

"I told you the long and short of it," the President said irritably. "Velichko told me that they were observing the Ukrainian Air Force preparing for a tactical air strike, following the attack on their reconnaissance planes." The President paused as he noticed one of his advisers shaking his head. "Problem, General?"

"Excuse me, sir, but none of that is correct," Army general Philip Freeman, chairman of the Joint Chiefs of Staff, replied. "Our analysis revealed that the bombers the Russians flew over the Ukraine that first night were strikers, not reconnaissance planes. The Russians have a squadron of MiG-25R Foxbat reconnaissance planes within range, but they weren't used. The Ukrainians did have offensive weapons on board some of their fighters following the Russian assault, but what would you expect after just turning back a Russian cruise missile attack?"

"As far as I'm concerned, I'm getting nothing but noise from everyone involved—the Russians, the Ukrainians, the Romanians, the Germans, the Turks—the list goes on and on," the President said wearily, chomping one of the famous cigars that he liked but didn't inhale—even if he wanted to he wouldn't dare. The First Lady all but shot those who tried to smoke, and she would smell it on him. "All I care about is what I'm seeing in the press and in the intelligence reports. Now, from what you've been telling me," he said to National Security Advisor Michael Lifter, "the Russians aren't moving into the Ukraine and Moldova in massive numbers. Isn't that right?"

"That's right, sir," Lifter acknowledged. "The Russians said that their attack was simply a response to Ukrainian aggression, that they plan no other moves into the region unless other factions threaten ethnic Russians in Moldova or the Ukraine."

"They don't need to move into Moldova in force, sir," General Freeman said, "because they already had ten thousand troops stationed in the Dniester region before the attack occurred. The air attacks simply weakened all air defense units in the Ukraine, which gives the Russians free air access over the Ukraine, and they bombarded all the Romanian and Moldovan army positions that could threaten those Russian troops in Dniester."

"Those weren't *Russian* troops in the Dniester region, General," Secretary of State Harlan Grimm said. "Those troops were former Soviet Red Army personnel who stayed in Moldova after independence and who eventually formed a partisan Russian militia during the uprisings."

"Mr. Grimm, I don't believe that for a minute," General Freeman said. "The Russians living in the Moldavian SSR didn't want to leave the Soviet Union after Moldova declared its independence, so the Red Army simply disbanded one of its military units in-place and had them form the nucleus of a resistance movement."

"I'm not surprised you see it that way, General," Grimm said derisively.

"Sir, the point is, the Russians can pull this trick in every vital former Republic," General Freeman said. "They can do it in the Baltic states, they can do it in Belarus, they can do it in Armenia and Azerbaijan."

"I'm not interested in what the Russians *might* do, General." The President sighed, wishing like hell he could go jogging around the White House track, escape all this shit. "I'm more concerned with the here and now. In fact, the Russians haven't appeared to have any desire to move in force against the Ukraine or Moldova."

"It's a fait accompli, sir—of course the Russians are going to promise to back off. They've killed several thousand people already." General Freeman spread his hands to emphasize his point. "Sir, the question is, what are we going to do about the Russian aggression? We can do nothing and continue to voice our displeasure or we can take some action to *show* how displeased we are."

"I don't see anything we need to do, and nothing we *can* do, General," the President said as if the very idea of aggression was distasteful. "If the Russians don't make any more moves into the Ukraine or Moldova, the matter is over."

"The government of Turkey doesn't think so, sir," Freeman interjected, thinking, *What did I expect from a draft-evader, anyway?* "President Dalon appears to be very concerned about Russian reconnaissance flights over the Black Sea. The Russians have repeatedly crossed the twelve-mile territorial boundary in the Black Sea, trying to photograph naval bases near Istanbul and catalog Turkish ships in the Black Sea and in the Bosporus. They've been paying a lot of attention on the military-industrial complex near Kocaeli, about fifty miles east of Istanbul on the Marmara Sea, as well as general military and supply traffic in the Bosporus Strait and Dardanelles."

"Let's try to stick with one problem at a time here, General."

"It's all one big problem, sir," Freeman argued patiently, feeling he was tutoring some ROTC freshmen. "The nuclear strikes in the Ukraine and Romania occurred less than five hundred miles from Turkey, sir, and now Russian bombers and attack aircraft are swarming over the entire Black Sea region. Turkey is getting upset, and they want a pledge by NATO and assistance in defending its borders."

"We've been sucking up to the Turks for almost twenty years," Scheer sniffed to the President. "Reagan and Bush gave them *everything*, and they turned around and kicked us out of their country, made war on Greece, and started ethnic genocide against the Kurds in the southeast. Every time we extend assistance to them, they use it to lash out at an opposition group or neighboring country. They want weapons from NATO, but never *offensive* forces; then, when they *do* want modern Western fighters, ships, and missiles, they badger us into agreeing to a license-build contract, and our companies lose thousands of jobs. They wanted protection against Iraq and Iran, but when they got ground troops they promptly used their own army to go after Kurdish and Armenian bases."

Lifter turned to Scheer and asked, "I suppose now they want military protection against Russia, a powerful showing, perhaps a naval and air presence—but not an offensive presence, anything that might be provocative or make the Turkish people think any foreigners are waging war at their expense."

"They made their request through NATO channels, not through my office," Scheer replied as if enough said. "General?"

Freeman nodded. "It's a similar request as was made during the Iraqi invasion of Kuwait and the Iraqi-Kurdish conflicts in 1993 and 1994," Freeman said. "Air and naval defense augmentation, fill-ins for the weapon systems they don't own. They're requesting more Patriot missile batteries, air defense artillery, strategic and tactical reconnaissance, and suppression of enemy air defense weapon systems. Defensive systems only."

The President rubbed his eyes wearily, then scratched his head through all that bush of prematurely gray hair, a sign that he didn't like any of the options or suggestions being placed in front of him at the moment. "I think this Turkish thing will have to wait," he said. "We start sending any aircraft to Turkey, and the Russians will think we're trying to surround 'em and make them negotiate from the business end of a Sidewinder missile. As long as Russia doesn't threaten the United States and our allies, I see no need to commit any forces up front."

"Sir, Turkey feels threatened, and they feel isolated," Freeman interjected. "Right now they're getting more assistance from the Ukraine than from NATO."

"You mean because Turkey offered asylum to the Ukrainian government, and the Ukraine is flying planes into Turkey, they're going to just ignore NATO?"

"Sir, the Ukraine is moving an estimated two hundred combat aircraft into Turkey right now," Freeman said, "and they've already got an undetermined amount of Ukrainian weapons and equipment. *Actions* not *words,* sir: the Ukrainians might even assist Turkey if the Russians try anything."

"Now that's bull," the President murmured. "And it's that 'undetermined' shit that's got me hot under the collar, too. Who approved a shipment like that? NATO? It wasn't us, that's for sure. Now Turkey won't tell us how much Ukrainian gear is in their country or where it's stashed. Whose side are they on, anyway?"

"Mr. President, we have to decide what our next course of action should be," Freeman insisted, thinking how much he loathed closet pacifists. "I think sending Secretary of State Grimm to Brussels, Moscow, and Ankara is a good idea; you may consider sending him to Belgrade to confer with the Romanian government, and to Istanbul, where the Ukrainian government-in-exile is located."

"That would make the Russians *real* happy," Secretary of Defense Scheer chimed in.

"The Russians started this thing, and they've offered nothing but flimsy excuses for initiating hostile actions," General Freeman said. "The care and feeding of an alliance is just as important as negotiating with the antagonists, sir. We can't assume our allies will follow our lead or do what we want them to do, especially when the major ally in question is a Muslim nation that shares a border with the major antagonist."

"Whatever Turkey wants, Turkey gets, eh, General?" Dr. Scheer said. "Just like ol' Reagan and his lapdog Bush."

"We're doing it because Turkey is important to the West and important to NATO, and because they're truly being threatened by Russia," the General said. "I think relations with them is worth a few squadrons and a few ships."

The President hesitated for a moment longer, then held up his hands as if in surrender and said, "Well, Don, I think we're going to bust the bank on this one, but I tend to agree with the General, at least on the short term. Okay, General, what do you recommend?"

Freeman couldn't believe it. The draft-dodger was coming around. "In accordance with your standing rules regarding limitations on overseas deployments and the use of take-along equipment versus using or creating repositioned stores," Freeman said, "I recommend deploying the 394th Air Battle Wing from New York, flying RF-111G Vampire reconnaissance fighters, KC-135 tankers, and a few F-16 fighters; also three Perry-class frigates from the Sixth Fleet, the *Curts, McClusky,* and *Davis.* These frigates are mostly antisubmarine-warfare vessels, but they have a powerful antiship and even an antiaircraft weapons fit."

"What about these F-111s? Aren't they offensive aircraft?"

"They have an offensive capability," Freeman admitted, "but their primary role is reconnaissance and SEAD—that's Suppression of Enemy Air Defenses, what they call 'Wild Weasel' or 'Iron Hand.' They go after missile sites, radar sites, that sort of thing. The Turks like the F-111, and we've based F-111s in Turkey for almost ten years. The 394th Air Battle Wing has eighteen RF-111Gs, twelve KC-135 tankers, and twenty F-16 fighters. NATO will send one of their E-3C radar planes, and we can send a Special Task Force from the Army's Seventh Air Defense Artillery Battalion with six Patriot missile batteries—that's twenty-four launchers, four missiles per launcher, no reloads. They'd be operated by U.S. Army personnel only, because the Congressional ban on exporting Patriot missile technology to Turkey is still in effect."

"As well it should be, after we discovered Turkey trying to steal Patriot technology last year," Secretary of Defense Scheer added indignantly.

The President looked surprised. He rolled the cigar between his left index finger and thumb. "That's all the Turks want? From what you said, it sounded like they wanted a couple aircraft carriers, maybe a B-52 wing."

"They'd like an entire surface-action group and all our F-117 stealth fighters, sir," Freeman admitted. "We can't, and shouldn't, give them everything they want. The Turks like haggling over levels of assistance—they'll think they're being set up if we send too much. This deal won't totally please them—especially when they find out about the Seventh Air Defense Battalion detachment and the 394th Wing."

"What about them?" the President asked.

"Both units are about one-quarter women," Freemen replied. "Almost half the aerial refueling tanker crewmembers are women; most of the Patriot missile system instructors are women; even some of the RF-111G pilots are women. The Turks don't approve of women as soldiers."

"Screw 'em," the President said. "They ask for help, they're getting help. It's about time we show the world that women can fight just as well as men."

"There may be cultural problems in sending these forces to Turkey, sir," Secretary of Defense Scheer offered. "Putting women in uniform and sending them to Turkey might be considered an insult to Turkey, as if we don't respect them enough, or the Turks might think the women are criminals or head cases. As absurd as it sounds, that's how they think. They may refuse to work with or even acknowledge our women officers. The women we send to Incirlik Air Base in central Turkey have a lot of difficulties when they go off-base or have to deal with Turkish men."

"We'll deal with that problem when it happens," the President said dismissively. "It's about time we start showing the world what American female soldiers can do. Maybe we'll help Turkey join the twentieth century. Don, who's gonna be in charge of this Turkey operation, and what're we gonna call it?"

"Admiral John Carruth will be the theater commander, sir," SecDef Scheer replied. "I'll get together with him and prepare a briefing for you as soon as possible."

"Good. John's a good man. Annapolis wild boy, but a few tours in Washington softened him up for me," the President said. Freeman would have gone a bit further: Carruth, one of General Norman Schwarzkopf's fleet commanders during the Persian Gulf War, had a reputation as a Washington animal with definite political aspirations, spending more time in Washington—not just at the Pentagon, but on Capitol Hill and the White House—than at his headquarters in Florida or at any of his installations. With the increasing importance of the Navy in U.S. Central Command operations, it was logical that a Navy admiral take command of the previously Army and Marine heavy command, but with Carruth it was a political stepping-stone given to him by his buddy, the southern President. This operation might take on a distinct naval flavor before too long.

"Yes, sir," Lifter agreed. "As for a name, General Freeman has the standard computer-generated package name, but we should pick a better one for the press. I suggested Operation Peaceful Hands. Simple, nonaggressive, interdenominational."

"I like it," the President said, truly pleased for the first time during the entire meeting. Of course Freeman hated it, but he had no plan to try to change it. Fights with the White House had to be avoided at best and chosen very, very carefully at worst.

The President was truly enthused now. "Hey, you know I can even go to the Ebenezer Baptist Church for Martin Luther King Day and talk about Operation Peaceful Hands without offending anyone. Good job, Don. Get me a press package on these military units with the women in them—I'll talk that angle up, too. Okay, I think we got a plan of action for that problem right now. Anybody got anything else for me?"

There was a whole slate of things to discuss. The First Lady came in during the subsequent discussions. She was quickly brought up to speed on all the previous topics, and then she joined in as if she had been present right from the very beginning. When General Freeman was notified that the draft military operations order was ready for his review, he excused himself and departed the Cabinet Room. To his surprise, he was stopped by the First Lady, who accompanied him downstairs to the lower lobby.

"I wanted to discuss the deployment of those combat units to Turkey, General," the First Lady said tightly, her face a smile, but her eyes cold as steel. "I—"

"You're concerned about the women in the units, how they'll be treated by the Turks, by the international press, ma'am?"

The First Lady gave Freeman a commending smile and a nod, as if he'd just put the right peg in the hole on "Romper Room." Freeman was one of the few Chairmen of the Joint Chiefs of Staff to wear a moustache, thin and dark with no hint of gray, which many women, both in and out of government, found attractive and bold. The First Lady came up to Freeman's shoulders, and her upraised eyes made her look disarmingly innocent, but Freeman knew better. He had to remind himself of the Steel Magnolia's background, of her training and education and, most of all, of her aspirations to power—but he had always found her attractive, even desirable. That put him at a distinct disadvantage, and he had to keep himself in check.

"I'm also concerned about how Sam Donaldson and Wolf Blitzer treat them as well, General," the First Lady said innocently, as if she were protecting lambs from the slaughter. She had a few laugh lines in the corners of her green eyes, and she was a "touchy" person, adept at the slight, casual touch of an arm, the warm handshake extended a second or two longer than expected. She used such gestures even now with Freeman to disarm and persuade, calculating every move.

"I think you've proven you can handle them, ma'am," Freeman said. "I'm not sure if you've ever taken on a Turkish mullah before."

"No, and the President of the United States, or his men and women in uniform serving overseas protecting American allies, shouldn't have to either," she said with a sudden edge. "I wanted to know what steps *you* will be taking to assure that *our* combat troops deploying overseas will be properly taken care of and given the support and respect they deserve."

"We've had a military presence in Turkey for over forty years, and women have been sent to Turkey for the past twenty-five years," General Freeman said uneasily. "Relations between the U.S. and the Turks have always been good. The key to that success has been the discipline of our troops and the proper respect paid to the Turkish nation by the American government. As long as we treat the Turks like valued allies and not like Islamic-fundamentalist mountain heathens, we won't have any problems."

"Are we treating the Turks as anything more or less than valued allies, General?" she probed, staring at him dead-on.

Freeman knew that anything he said would go directly to the President's ear, and quite possibly to the press and to Congress as well, so he hesitated before answering, but he finally replied, "I detect an attitude in some circles that might suggest we're doing Turkey a favor by providing them military assistance."

"We do tend to jump when they call, General," she said tightly. "And it does seem as if we give more than they offer in return."

"All we want is a stable, strong ally in the Middle East," Freeman said. "We don't have any allies these days who unconditionally agree to everything we say or want. I think it's in our country's best interests to extend to Turkey every possible benefit."

"An alliance, especially one such as NATO, is a give-and-take affair," she informed him. "But reasonable people can differ about all that, General. My concern remains the same: can we expect to see any problems crop up with having American women soldiers in Turkey during Operation Peaceful Hands, and if so, *what* are you going to do about it?"

"The answer to your first question is yes, I do expect some cultural, societal backlash," Freeman replied. "Asking a Turk to accept a foreign woman to defend his homeland will definitely cause problems—to what extent, I don't know. The answer to the second question is, we will do our assigned mission until ordered by the President to withdraw. Any soldier, man or woman, who can't follow orders or who has a problem with any aspect of the indigenous situation will be relieved, removed, and replaced."

"That doesn't sound very fair to me, General," the First Lady said coldly. "A Turkish man whose mind is trapped in the eighteenth century doesn't like the idea of a well-trained, highly intelligent woman defending him against danger, and the woman has to suffer for it? Don't our women soldiers have *enough* to worry about?"

"All our soldiers had better worry about one thing: the threat—and the threat is not from Turkey, but from Russia," Freeman said, putting on his service cap to signify that he was ready to leave. "They should worry about their level of proficiency; their knowledge about potential adversaries, proper procedures, and their own weapon systems; and about maintaining a winning attitude. Everything else is wrong thinking, inappropriate thinking, and it will only hurt the mission and hurt the force."

"What if the threat our women soldiers face is an ally, or even one of their own?" she asked. "How are they supposed to deal with that?"

"They don't deal with that—*I* deal with that, ma'am," Freeman said. "And when it becomes a problem, I *will* deal with it."

"I know you will, General," she purred, patting his arm as if to reassure him. "And I consider it *my* job to deal with such problems as well. I believe in our women soldiers, General. I know they face many more difficulties, real deeply seated societal difficulties, and they need special help to overcome those problems just so they can be given the right opportunity to do their job. I consider it my duty to make sure they are given the proper atmosphere to succeed." She visually sized up the tall general with a glance, as if to say, *your kind doesn't scare me,* then she smiled. "Thank you for listening to me, General—good day."

When General Philip Freeman stepped into his staff car to return to the Pentagon, he found his jaw muscles tightly clenched, and he had to consciously work to relax them. Christ, why couldn't that bitch stick to ribbon-cuttings? He was getting it from all sides of this Administration—including one side he never expected. He knew he served at the pleasure of the President, but sometimes he wanted to know exactly what that meant—was it the man himself, or was it everyone around the man, and did that mean *everyone?*

In certain jobs, certain fields, the women chosen to serve in those positions did outstanding work. Whether or not the environment was influenced or guarded by the First Lady, most of the women serving in the U.S. military were first-rate, and this was recognized by most of their male counterparts. Then why the low-key dressing-down by the Steel Magnolia? Why the veiled threats? Was it just the unknown mystery of Turkey or was something going on he didn't understand?

That question was going to have to be back-burnered for the time being—deploying an air battle wing, an Army battalion, and three combat vessels and their support units halfway around the world in the shortest time possible would require all his attention, not to mention dealing with the Congressional leadership and the press once the operation was made public knowledge. Philip Freeman reached for the secure telephone in the back of the staff car and got to work.

27

Plattsburgh Air Force Base, New York That Afternoon

AFTER BEING RELEASED FROM THE HOSPITAL AND SPENDING nearly an entire day answering questions for the accident investigation board, Rebecca looked forward to her one-day pass. It would be a good opportunity to check in at Liberty Air, have a quiet dinner someplace, sleep in her own bed, and perhaps see Ed. Her shoulders and legs still hurt a bit from the crash landing, but she wanted nothing more than to get that episode out of her life and get back to normal—if generating her flight to fight a possible nuclear war could be considered normal.

But just getting off-base that day proved to be nearly impossible. As she drove off-base and headed toward home, it felt to Rebecca as if she was abandoning the Air Force in the midst of a crisis, abandoning her unit, even her country. A series of signs along the exit road read, HAVE YOU SIGNED OUT WITH YOUR CQ? BASEWIDE ALERT STILL IN EFFECT—CONTACT YOUR UNIT, and ALERT IN EFFECT—UNAUTHORIZED DEPARTMENT PROHIBITED. The line of cars waiting to get into the base was long because the guards were stopping and searching every car, and there was someone at the guards' gate taking down license numbers of those leaving the base. Rebecca had her twenty-four-hour pass from the flight surgeon taped to the inside of her windshield for the guard to check. The expressions she saw from the guard and from those in the line of cars waiting to enter the base were strange and eerie. She imagined them thinking: *Why on earth is she leaving now, with a Defcon Three status?*

Her first destination was Liberty Air Service at Clinton County Airport. The place—indeed, the whole airport—looked like it was deserted. Rebecca found all of her airplanes on the ramp, with a thick layer of snow on them. Why they were out here in the snow instead of in the hangar, she didn't know. Judging by the amount of snow on them, they hadn't been anywhere in quite some time. That spelled trouble, and Rebecca knew why: with the aircraft accident at Plattsburgh and with the alert aircraft-generation in full swing, the Air Force would have requested the FAA close down Clinton County Airport, only three miles from the base, for security and air traffic control reasons. A sign on the door of Liberty Air confirmed it: her assistant manager, Adam Parker, had left a sign which said, CLOSED DUE TO AIRPORT RESTRICTION, along with his phone number in case of emergency.

She went inside, turned on a few lights, and spent a few minutes reading messages left for her on the computer and checking the schedule. Flights were being canceled by the dozens. She put in a call to Base Operations at Plattsburgh Air Force Base, requesting permission for her planes to be shuttled out of Clinton County Airport as soon as possible. She had friends in Albany, New York, and Portland, Maine, that would let her stage her flying service from there (for a price, of course) while Clinton County Airport was closed, but she would need permission from the FAA and from the Air Force before she could launch her planes. After leaving a computer message with Parker to organize the transfer of operations, she went out to look over the maintenance shop.

There was a surprise for her in one hangar, and now she knew why her planes weren't in the hangar: the first of her new million-dollar-plus Cessna Caravan cargo planes had arrived, spiffed up with a great big red ribbon and bow. Obviously it was meant as a surprise for her when she finished Hell Week. It even had LIBERTY AIR SERVICE and her company logo painted on the fuselage, and her name painted in elegant calligraphy below the pilot's-side window. It had been washed, waxed, and polished to a high luster, and the wheels had even been spray-painted with gloss black paint to make them look showroom new.

This was Ed's surprise, she thought happily. The bank loan wasn't supposed to have come in for another three or four days, and delivery of the plane itself wasn't supposed to be for a week after that. Ed Caldwell must've hurried things along for her. Yep, the guy could be a sweetheart sometimes. It was the best thing that could have taken her mind off the incident this morning—and she had Ed Caldwell to thank—*personally* thank if she could catch him. She returned to her office and put in a call to Ed.

The phone was answered on the other end, but whoever had picked it up was obviously distracted with something—or someone—else. Rebecca heard a few giggles, a lot of heavy breathing and groaning, and an unmistakable rhythmic rustling of sheets and bedsprings. Then, a woman's voice, flushed and husky, finally answered with, "Satan's garden of delight, Eve speaking. Satan is having his horn polished, but if you'll leave your name, your number . . ."

The phone was snatched away from her mouth, and Rebecca could hear Ed's voice. "I said, let the machine answer it, baby."

Rebecca slammed the phone back down in its cradle. Well, so much for thanking the sonofabitch. Somebody else was doing it for her. Rebecca didn't know whether to cry or throw the phone through her office window. She sat there, simmering, furious that she'd let herself be lulled into thinking she was the only one in Ed's life. That voice on the other end . . . she knew it from somewhere. Some stupid bleached blonde who worked at the bank, always purring and meowing whenever Ed was around. At least he could have screwed someone with a brain, or a career, or something. But that bimbo . . . it was just too insulting to think *that* was her replacement. That Barbie Doll probably didn't know the difference between the prime rate and prime rib. Rebecca stared at the phone, finally starting to cool down. Well, it really shouldn't surprise her. They certainly had no agreement on their living arrangements. Although the way Rebecca was raised, growing up in Vermont, where you gave a commitment to someone that counted for *something*. At least that's how she'd always felt. Ed obviously had different ideas. Fine. Screw him. He was no different than some of those active-duty assholes she'd had to put up with over the years. Didn't men *ever* change?

The pain in her shoulders from the seat harness was coming back, and the room felt decidedly colder. This had been one hell of a fucked-up couple of days, like a roller coaster out of control. Going home was out of the question now. Ed was smart: he would guess that it was she who called, verify it by calling the squadron, finish snaking Marilyn (he was smart, but he wouldn't pass up a fast screw, either), then head over to her house to explain himself. They would argue, fight, scream and holler; he would be tender, understanding, apologetic, denying everything while reassuring her that she was the only one for him. She would eventually tell him about the crash and the war, and he would tell her about the loan and the plane, and she would collapse in his arms, from exhaustion or surrender or loneliness or fear. He would offer her a massage, dinner, a drink, and they would be back to being an item once more.

Like hell that was going to happen. Maybe in the past, but not now. Who needed that on top of everything else she'd been through? Christ, she wasn't a masochist. Besides, there was nothing at home she needed, so she decided to head back to the base and crash at the alert facility. Her clothes were there, her flying gear was there, and she was going to get called in by midmorning anyway to start generating her sortie for alert. She closed up Liberty Air without stepping into the new Caravan's cockpit—no use in getting too attached to it, since she might have to give it back to the bank if she couldn't start flying again—then headed back to the base.

Her first stop was the base hospital, where she went to the intensive care ward. Mark Fogelman was awake and alert—yesterday she'd been told he was in a mild coma—but he looked as if he should be unconscious just to spare himself a little discomfort. His face, which had hit the instrument panel glare shield so hard it had broken his visor and helmet, was swollen and purple, like a boxer who had taken a pummeling in the ring. There was a thick bandage over his forehead, and his eyes were black and nearly swollen shut. He wore a neck brace, which only served to make his face look even puffier. His shaved head make him look worse.

"Hey, Yot," Furness greeted him, using the pilots' favorite nickname for their F-111 weapons officers, "Yot," which stood for You Over There, on her weapons officer. "You gotta tell the kitchen not to use so much MSG." She sat down beside him on the bed, opened up her flight jacket, and handed him a brown paper bag with a copy of *Penthouse* inside. "I smuggled it in past the nurses. It's my boyfriend's. I knew it would drive you crazy—that's why I brought it."

"Thanks, Becky," Fogelman mumbled. A wad of cotton had been stuffed inside his upper lip where he had bitten through it. He accepted the magazine, lifted it out of the bag to check out the cover, then smiled a very painful-looking smile. "Contributing to the delinquency of a minor. I love it. You're my very first visitor."

"I'm honored, then. How do you feel—as if I couldn't guess."

"Shitty," Fogelman replied. "I see stars everywhere, and I've had a splitting headache. Just breathing is painful, so you can imagine what going to the bathroom does for me. Otherwise, I'm okay. How about you?"

"I'm fine. They had me in here for about a day. I'm heading back to the squadron—my predeployment line should be coming up soon."

"What predeployment line?"

"You mean you don't know what's going on?"

"I've either been drugged to hell or this ringing in my ears and this pain blocks out everything. What's going on?"

"We're generating SIOP alert sorties, Mark," Furness said solemnly. "Russia invaded the Ukraine and hit 'em with low-yield nuclear weapons. Alpha Flight is uploading nukes, and the rest of the fleet is getting ready to deploy." If Fogelman's mouth could have dropped open in surprise, it would have—his eyes widened to nearly normal proportions at her words. "You mean you didn't know? Nobody told you?"

"I don't believe it . . . this really sucks," Fogelman mumbled, coughing. His head dropped back on his pillow in complete exasperation. "Nobody"—he groaned, staring at the ceiling, trying to control his breathing to combat the pain—"has told me shit. Hembree, Cole, no one has been by since I've been awake. I guess I know why now. Shit, a nuclear attack in the Ukraine. It's not as if we haven't been expecting something like this—ever since Velichko ousted Yeltsin. Jesus. Who would've thought it? And we're uploading nukes? I haven't looked over my nuke stuff in a long time. I think I'll stay here until this is over."

"Smart move." She smiled. After a long pause she asked, "They may not have let your folks on base to see you because of the recall and alert," she offered. It was the only reasonable, less painful explanation as to why he had no visitors yet—unfortunately, she expected the painful reason was the *true* reason: no one much liked Mark Fogelman, so why should they care if he was in the hospital? "My planes have been grounded out at Clinton County for the same reason. You want me to give your folks a call? When you get a regular room they'll get you a phone, but until—"

"The doctor called them—left a message." Fogelman sighed. "They're off to the Keys for the rest of the winter, I think. It's no big deal."

Furness never thought it possible, but she actually felt sorry for the guy. The guy crash-lands an armed bomber and goes into a coma for over twenty-four hours from a severe head injury, and when he wakes up he learns that no one had ever come to see him. Not even his parents or fellow pilots. Even if he was an ass, it still wasn't right to just ignore the guy. "I'll call one of your friends. Who was the last one I met? Josette? Judy?"

"It was Josette, but she's . . . not available," Fogelman said, still staring up at the ceiling. Rebecca heard the faint catch in his voice and noticed the glistening of tears. "Just forget it. I'll be okay."

"Are you sure?" she asked with genuine concern.

"Yes." He coughed.

They sat in silence for several long, awkward moments. Then Rebecca sighed. "Hey, the plane made it down in pretty good shape. I met the new MG—in fact, he pulled us out of the cockpit. Turns out I know the guy, from the Persian Gulf War. How about that?" No response. "There's a story behind how I know the guy, and when you're out of here I'll tell it to you over a beer at Afterburners. You won't believe it." Fogelman nodded noncommitally and continued to stare at nothing in particular. "Anything else I can get for you? You want some clothes, toothbrush, anything?"

"No." He sighed.

Furness rolled her eyes in complete exasperation and got to her feet. "Jesus, Fogman, if it's a pity party you want, this is the right time and place for it. A nuclear incident has happened in Europe, you barely survived a plane crash, and we're getting ready to go to war with . . . well, I don't know *who,* but we're mobilizing for a war. But the worst thing of all is that no one has come to see Mark Fogelman in the damned hospital."

"It's because no one gives a shit about me."

"No one came, Mark, because everyone's busy generating planes and moving nukes around the ramp." She wasn't about to say that the real reason was that he was a shit. "You're warm and safe and dry here, and they're freezing their butts off trying to get some thirty-year-old bombers up on the line."

"Well . . . *you* came to visit." He smiled.

"Yeah, and look at me: I crash a plane, my business has been closed down because of the generation, my planes are snowed in, and I've got a new plane in my hangar that's costing me ten thousand dollars a month taking up space that no one can fly and that'll put me in the poorhouse in two months. On top of all that, I catch my jerk boyfriend sleeping around on me. Your situation looks a hell of a lot better to me right now. In fact, move your skinny ass over—I'm staying here. You go generate my sortie."

Furness was surprised to see a painful grin spread across Fogelman's face. "You're making all this up just to make me feel better, aren't you?"

"Yeah, right," Furness said wryly, with a hint of a smile. "Listen, Mark, I'm going to the pad for some rest. I think my line comes up late tomorrow morning, so I'll come by to visit you in the morning. Are you sure you don't need anything?"

He paused for a moment, shrugged his shoulders, then replied, "I might as well start looking over my Dash-One to get up to speed on the nuclear stuff. If you brought my flight bag from wherever they've stashed it, I'd appreciate it."

Rebecca looked at him as if she hadn't heard right. "You . . . what? You want to read your Dash-One?" This was a new side of Fogelman, Furness thought. Hell, he didn't usually get into the books unless it was time for his check ride—now he wanted to read it to pass the time! "You got it, Mark." She got up to leave.

"Rebecca?" She turned toward him. He hesitated, an embarrassed smile on his face, then said, "Thank you for bringing me back okay."

"*We* did it, Mark, not just me."

"No . . . no," Fogelman said emphatically. "I've had a lot of time to think about it, Becky. That was the first time I've ever flown the G-model with serious malfunctions in it. The thing always worked before, so I never much worried about the systems. When everything crapped out, I was nothing more than a damned passenger. I didn't realize until then how much I don't know. If I had a pilot that had the same attitude I had about flying the Vampire, I'd be dead now. *Dead.*" He paused again, staring at some spot far away, then added, "With a nuke going off in Europe there's probably thousands of dead, but that doesn't affect me a fraction of what my own death does. I was ready to punch out. I was ready to drop into the cold Atlantic Ocean hundreds of miles from here rather than trust you with the knowledge and skill I knew you had. I'm a *total* jerk."

"Mark, I don't fly with passengers, I fly with crewdogs," Furness said, patting his arm. "I won't step into the cockpit with someone who doesn't know their shit. You have a relaxed attitude about flying, I'll admit that, but you're not unsafe—just casual. We fly simulator missions and take tests all the time, so I know you know your shit. Just don't give up on yourself. I'll get your books, and I'll even get a weapons officer to come out here and give you a briefing. I know the accident investigation board will be out to debrief you as soon as they find out you're awake. You'll get lots of visitors now."

"Thanks, Becky," Fogelman said. "Back to the real world, huh?"

"If you can call it that, Mark," Furness said. She gave him a thumbs-up and a friendly smile, a sincere one for the first time in many months, and departed.

"Rebecca!" Lieutenant Colonel Larry Tobias greeted her as she entered the squadron building. He gave her a big fatherly bear hug. A bunch of her Charlie Flight crews were in the mission planning room with their helmet bags and flight gear, getting ready to head out to generate their bombers. "It's great to see you, Becky. I see you're on the schedule. How's Fogman? Have you seen him?"

"He's pretty beat up, but he's awake and doing okay," she replied. "I tried to find Ted, but they say he was released."

"They let him go home for a couple of days. I guess he got creamed harder than they thought. Some mucky-muck movie guy from New York City came and picked him up in a limo."

"Stand by for a real shocker," Furness said. "Fogman wants his pubs. Anyone know where they stashed his books?"

"Fogman wants his tech orders?" Frank Kelly asked in astonishment. "For what—to prop up a nurse's ass before he screws her?"

"He says he wants to study," Furness replied, giving Kelly a disapproving glare, "and he even asked for a briefer to get him up to speed."

"That knock on the head must've shaken some cobwebs loose." Kelly chuckled.

"Hey, the guy's on the case. Give him a break," Tobias interjected. Rebecca realized a fellow navigator was actually *defending* Mark Fogelman. The war, the DEFCON change, and the nuclear-alert generation was pulling this unit together very quickly.

Properly admonished by his WSO, Kelly showed Furness where Fogelman's pubs bag was. It was in the squadron commander's office, marked with pieces of yellow tape to signify that they had been inspected by the accident investigation board and were cleared to be returned. A check to be sure that each crewmember's required on-board publications were up to date was routine in investigations such as this—although they did pubs checks often, Furness would be surprised if Fogelman's regs were completely up to date. After retrieving the bag, Furness went out to check her scheduled show time to start generating her alert line.

Rebecca had been assigned one of the last alert lines in the follow-on Charlie force, sortie 39. Because Ted Little was on convalescent leave from his minor injuries during the near-collision with the F-16 fighters, Furness was scheduled as the weapons officer, not as a pilot, and paired up with Paula Norton. The sortie was scheduled to come up at ten A.M. the next morning, but a note pinned to the bulletin board advised all crews to be ready to report in two hours early and to show one hour earlier than posted because Maintenance was getting the bombers ready faster as the generation progressed.

Staying at the alert facility was going to be impossible. Every crewmember assigned to Plattsburgh Air Force Base was there, either generating a sortie or already on alert, and they were already three to a room and breaking out the cots to put crews in the hallways. They had packed up her bags and moved her out of her room in the facility anyway—Rebecca noticed the yellow inspection stickers on all her bags, which meant that members of the accident investigation board had checked all her belongings, looking for any evidence of misconduct or inappropriate behavior that might have a bearing on the accident—prescription or controlled drugs, alcohol, a "Dear John" letter, anything.

There was a small bed-and-breakfast hotel downtown near the lake where Rebecca liked to put guests when they came to town to visit, so she checked in herself for the night, then walked the ten blocks or so over to Afterburners, the Plattsburgh aircrews' customary hangout downtown, for a sandwich.

The place was absolutely deserted.

"Hey, Brandon," Rebecca greeted the bar's owner, a huge, bearlike ex-biker type with a full beard and who wore sunglasses twenty-four hours a day. "Can you find me a good table?"

"Hey, pilot, about time someone showed," Brandon replied, escorting her to the bar and placing a menu in her hand. Rebecca waved off the glass of wine, and the barkeep put a Perrier on ice in front of her instead. Brandon only referred to his patrons as "pilots," "navs," "chiefs" for the maintenance guys, "brass" for the commanders, or "legs" for the nonflyers: "You're the first crewdog I've had in here all night. Had to put up with a bunch of legs whining about the Russians and all the noise you're making out on the airpatch."

Rebecca looked around the empty bar and asked, "Well, they're not here anymore, so what'd you tell them?"

"I asked them which sound would they rather hear," Brandon replied, "the sound of freedom or the sound of Russian bombers screamin' overhead? I think they got the message—go complain someplace else."

"Thanks for sticking up for us," Furness said. She handed the menu back to him. "Burger and fries tonight."

"Uh oh, sounds like the old man got on your nerves."

"How in hell do you know that?"

"You only order the gut-bomb and skids when you're upset at the pencil-pusher," Brandon replied. "Why don't you let me take care of the geek for you, honey? The boys need some excitement." He was referring to his Hell's Angels buddies that Brandon occasionally rode with—they rarely came to the bar, but when they did they seemed to empty a room real fast. Fortunately they got along well with the military, especially the flyers.

"I can handle him, Brandon," Rebecca replied, "but thanks. I don't have many friends who offer to commit mayhem for me."

"Anytime, pilot." The big barkeep shuffled off to fire up the grill and deep fryer, leaving Rebecca alone with the big-screen TV in the corner.

The news was switching back and forth from international to national news, and all of it centered on the outbreak of war in Europe. Moldova, Romania, and the Ukraine had been pounded by waves of Russian bombers. Russian President Velichko was shown in the Politburo pounding his fist on the podium, but she couldn't hear what the voice-over was saying he was ranting about. Thankfully, the use of low-yield nuclear-tipped missiles was not repeated, although the follow-on conventional bombing raids were fierce and probably claimed more lives than the nuclear attacks. For now the attacks were over, but the casualty estimates were astounding—nearly ten thousand dead after the first series of attacks alone. The Ukrainian capital of Kiev had been bombarded and the government had fled, their destination unknown. The Romanian government was dispersed into air raid shelters, even though the capital, Bucharest, was not under attack. Moldova was in the hands of the Russian rebels after the capital of Kishinev was bombarded and the Moldovan and Romanian troops in the western part of the country were pounded by waves of tactical and heavy bombers. Russian military aircraft were patrolling the skies all over the region, enjoying absolute control of the skies.

Now, Russian air bases near the Black Sea, such as Rostov-na-Donu and Krasnodar, were seeing large numbers of smaller jet bombers such as the Sukhoi-24 and -25 and Mikoyan-Gurevich-27 arriving there from interior bases, well within unrefueled striking range of the Ukraine, Moldova, and Romania. The Russian Air Force was encountering little or no resistance. They were taking a breather from the blitzkrieg attack and were now accomplishing a steady generation of tactical forces, preparing for an invasion. Once fully mobilized, she thought, Russia could probably squash Moldova, the Ukraine, and Romania like insects.

Jesus, she thought, if it weren't right there on the television, she would have sworn the whole thing was like something out of a Dale Brown novel. Maybe—she sighed—that's where Russia got the idea.

The network news cut away to the local stations. The Burlington TV station aired a teaser about "confusion over the war in Europe" causing an F-111G bomber crash at Plattsburgh Air Force Base. Rebecca noted that there was no mention of the plane being a reconnaissance jet, choosing instead to highlight its bomber role in light of the war in Europe, and she felt sick at the thought of the accident being broadcast to thousands of homes all over the area. Her neighbors, her family, her uncle in Washington would all hear about it soon. Bad enough going through the ordeal without having the whole world know about it.

She was halfway into her burger and fries and beginning to regret ever ordering them when she saw Brandon shaking hands with one of his employees. When the man turned around, she recognized Lieutenant Colonel Daren Mace, the Maintenance Group commander for the 394th Air Battle Wing. "Colonel?"

Mace turned around. He appeared to be annoyed that someone called him by his rank in this place—or perhaps annoyed that he was recognized—then pleased that it was her. Brandon handed what appeared to be a big fold of cash to him, which Mace refused. Brandon stuck the cash in Mace's shirt pocket and slapped Mace's chest, a friendly but definitive—and no doubt painful—warning that Brandon was not in the mood to argue. Mace then shook hands with the barkeep, moved to the other side of the bar, and sat next to Furness.

"What was that all about, Colonel?" Furness asked, popping a french fry in her mouth.

"'Daren' in here, okay, Rebecca? We had a deal: maintenance work on his taps and condenser units, and a little electrical work, in exchange for room and board. Now he—"

"You were staying *here?* At the bar?"

"He's got a nice couple of rooms on the second floor," Mace said. "He lives on the fourth floor. He's got rooms on the third floor, but I didn't ask what goes on there."

She laughed. "Knowing this place, I can guess."

"Yeah," Mace agreed. "Anyway, Brandon insisted on paying me for my work anyway. He may be a gangster, but he's a decent gangster."

"Well, at least his reputation—and the Harleys outside—keep the college kids and tourists out," Furness said, "which means more room for crewdogs. How long have you been staying here?"

"A few weeks, right after Air War College, when I found out I was coming to Plattsburgh," Mace replied, reaching across the bar and pouring himself a glass of Pepsi from the bar gun. "I came in here for a beer and for a phone book and ended up getting a job and a place to stay."

"What are you doing here now? Aren't you supposed to be at the base?"

"I've been at the base for the past two days straight," Mace replied wearily. "I told them I need a break. Besides, I had to get this one last job done for Brandon. I've got a feeling there won't be many breaks after tonight."

"On your night off from fixing airplanes you fix beer taps? Incredible."

"I guess I'm just an incredible guy," he deadpanned. "But I just quit. I'm going to miss this place. This was a kind of Bohemian place to work, sort of Greenwich Village. Everything was pretty nice"—he waited until she was going to take another bite of the burger, then added—"except for the food."

She stopped in midbite and asked, "What's wrong with the food?"

"Brandon cooks it."

That instantly destroyed Rebecca's appetite for good. She dropped the food back on its plate. Mace slipped a five-dollar bill under the plate and said, "Sorry about that, Rebecca. Let's get out of here and we'll find you some decent dinner."

"I'm through with dinner," Furness said, suddenly feeling queasy, "but I know a good place for coffee. Follow me." They left the bar, got in Mace's pickup truck, and drove down City Hall Place toward McDonough Monument and to Rebecca's bed and breakfast.

The little hotel was right at the end of the Heritage Trail River Walk. From the main enclosed patio, they had a view of the Revolutionary War monument, the canal, and across the marina to frozen Lake Champlain. The bed and breakfast's hosts served hot fudge sundaes and coffee on the patio in the evenings; both officers promised not to tell on each other as they accepted a small splash of Grand Marnier orange liqueur on top of the chocolate syrup.

"Nice place," Mace said after trying his sundae.

"I stay here every chance I get," she replied, licking chocolate and whipped cream off her spoon. "So you work for a biker-bar owner and stay in a biker flophouse. You never looked for an apartment? What were you going to do, stay at Afterburners for your entire tour?"

"Frankly, I never thought about it much," Mace said dryly. He looked around to be sure no one else was within earshot, then said, "After our . . . activities . . . in the Persian Gulf, I've always considered my job in the Air Force Reserve as day-to-day."

"Oh?" she asked, surprised.

Their eyes looked right into each other, as if both knew a secret on the other.

"The Air Force made it clear to me that they weren't going to stand by me," Mace said. "I made a tactical decision during the war and I got hammered for it. I consider myself extremely fortunate to still be in uniform, let alone be in command of a maintenance group. I guess I ultimately made the right decision during the war, and that at least one high-powered angel somewhere agreed and is rewarding me by letting me continue in service. I don't expect that patronage to last forever, though, believe me. I'm not a man of delusions."

Somehow she knew he wasn't. They fell silent as the host poured more coffee for his guests. When he left, Furness asked, "Can you tell me about what you were doing out there during the war, Daren? I remember you weren't on the air tasking order."

"A lot of sorties weren't on the ATO," he said uneasily.

"You had no wingmen, no scheduled tanker, and a bomb load you couldn't jettison."

"We can't talk about this, Rebecca."

"Why not?"

"You know better than to ask, Major," Mace said evenly, using her military rank to firmly punctuate his warning. He quickly added, "Besides, it's the first clear night we've had in days, and the coffee is good and strong. Let's enjoy it." He pointed out the window toward the south. "I can even see the stars out there. That's Sirius, the brightest star in the sky. Amazing what you remember all the way back to nav school."

"They have a telescope set up on the upstairs deck," Furness said. She led him upstairs, then down a side hallway and out a set of French doors to a long redwood patio that had been swept clean of snow. An eight-inch reflector telescope on a motorized equatorial mount had been set up there for the guests. An instruction card on the wall told how to use the telescope and the star drive, but Mace scanned the skies briefly, released the worm-gear drive, repositioned the telescope as if he'd been using it all his life, lined it up on a bright star farther to the east across the lake, using the telescope's small finder scope, and reengaged the drive.

"Aren't we going to look at . . . what's it called, Sirius?"

"Stars don't look any different through a telescope—they're too far away to see the disk," Mace said. "But you'll like this."

When Furness peered through the eyepiece, she inhaled in absolute surprise. "It's Saturn! I can see the rings . . . I can even see the shadow on the rings from the planet itself, and a few of Saturn's moons! How did you know that was Saturn?"

"The weather shop still prepares briefings on which planets and bright stars are up," Mace replied, "and I still get a weather briefing and forecast four times a day. We still calibrate the sextants on the tankers for celestial navigation, even though the tanker crews rarely use them with their GPS and inertial navigation systems—I even did a few precomps and shot the sun the other day. Once a nav, always a nav." He pointed to the sky to the south: "There's Orion with his belt and sword, and Drago the dragon, and Taurus the bull, and the star cluster called the Pleiades, the Seven Sisters."

As they scanned the night sky, Furness shivered, wrapped her arms around herself, and stepped closer to Mace. He responded by putting an arm around her. "See any more constellations?" she asked.

"Yeah. Darenoid, the frozen naviguesser. Let's go inside."

They went inside and headed for the stairs, but Rebecca took Mace's hand and pulled him toward the hallway to the right. He hesitated, searching her eyes, silently asking if she was sure, relaxing his grip, offering her a chance to gracefully back away. She did not release him, and he followed her three doors down and into her room.

There was no talking, no polite conversation, no more requests or replies. As Daren locked the door, Rebecca walked over beside the bed, kicked off her boots, and, standing before him, began to unbutton his shirt. He held her cold face in his hands as she worked, rolling his eyes in mock agony as her cold fingers touched, then explored, his bare chest. His body was lean, rock-hard, and athletic, his chest was square and muscular, even his back was angular and sinewy. Guys never tailored their flight suits or fatigues, so most men's bodies looked the same when in a military outfit—and, in fact, most Air Force men *were* very much alike, trim and fit, maybe toned-up if they were serious about exercise. Daren was not just fit or toned, he was *built,* Furness thought. Taking off his shirt, revealing his incredible body, wrapping her arms around his rounded shoulders and roaming across his fantastic chest and arms was like unwrapping a late but much-anticipated Christmas present.

Her hands wrapped around to his back, and they kissed. The kiss quickly intensified as both tasted, explored, and sought even more. Her hips briefly moved against him, an unbidden but insistent invitation, touching groin to groin for the briefest of moments. That caused a sudden shiver to shoot through him, not from the cold this time but from the pleasure, and his hands began to work the buttons of her cotton blouse. When that was removed, she waited for him to reach around to undo the fasteners of her brassiere, but instead he stepped back and allowed her to remove her brassiere herself. She used the opportunity to full advantage, doing it as slowly as her pounding heart and quickening breathing would allow, then stood before him, topless, watching his eyes roam across her body and his smile beginning to grow.

She expected the rest of it to be quick and catlike, like Ed—and she had to admit that sometimes she liked that. But Daren wasn't going to allow it. He went slow, like a long, sybaritic poem, alternatively smothering her with kisses and grasps, then letting her relax with gentle touches and caresses. He was offering her the spectrum of lovemaking, the hard and the soft, observing which she preferred and delighting in every new discovery. She liked her kisses wet and deep, her breasts handled gently but her nipples teased and moistened into full attention, her buttocks and thighs taken in both hands and firmly massaged. As he laid her back on the thick, soft bed and got on his knees before her, he discovered she liked her womanhood treated slowly, carefully, almost reverently, like kissing a baby's lips, until her breathing became deeper and more audible and her hands moved from the bed, to her own breasts, and then to the back of his head, urging him closer, deeper . . .

He finally stood before her, his well-developed chest moving up and down breathlessly as if he had run up and down stairs, and he started to undo his belt. She quickly sat up, slid off the edge of the bed to her knees, unfastened his belt for him, and slid his jeans and underwear to the hardwood floor. She wrapped her hand around him, feeling its heat and its incredible hardness, then tasted him, once, twice, three times, as deeply as she could. When she released him, she knew neither of them was going to wait any longer. As Daren picked Rebecca off the floor, laid her on her back on the bed, knelt between her legs, and guided himself into her, she discovered him with absolute delight.

It was the beginning of some of the most passionate lovemaking she could remember. His strength was enormous, and he delighted in making her climax time after time until he finally succumbed himself. They made love long and slow. She had thrown out every rule she'd ever made about sleeping with her fellow military personnel, but she didn't give a damn . . . until . . .

They heard the ring of a cellular telephone. She hadn't even noticed it clipped to the inside of his jacket, but of course being the Maintenance Group commander, especially during an alert, it would be a required and constant companion. He withdrew from her, kissing her lips and her breasts and murmuring something softly to her, an apology or a wish, something she couldn't quite hear. But when she looked at him again, his face had completely changed. He had completely changed. He was no longer her tender, passionate lover—he was now her superior officer, the MG of the 394th Air Battle Wing.

He wasn't on the phone long, and he was reaching for his pants and shirt. "What is it?" Furness asked him.

"They figured out what they're going to do with us," Mace said, hurriedly dressing. "We're deploying. To Turkey. Recon and Wild Weasel operations. There's a staff meeting in ten minutes. I've got my utility uniform in the truck; I'll have to change out there," he told her. He put his jacket and boots on, paused, then came back to Furness and hugged her, closely and deeply. They parted, kissed just as deeply, and embraced again.

"I'll see you . . . on the flight line," Mace said hesitantly as he pulled himself away. She could read his thoughts: he wanted to say thank you, to say all sorts of things that lovers say to each other after parting. But his expression, his anxious smile, told her all she needed to know.

"My gear is packed," she said. She was dressed and ready in no time. "I'll drive in with you. They're going to need crews to fly those things out of here."

His smile returned, and he nodded. She was, he realized with a great deal of pride, a flyer first and foremost.

28

Kayseri Air Base, Turkey, Several Hours Later

THE ENTIRE UKRANIAN AIR FORCE WAS PARKED ON THE WEST ramp of Kayseri Air Base in central Turkey. Colonel Pavlo Tychina shook his head in absolute disbelief. Kayseri was a rather large base, one of the largest Western military bases between Germany and Hawaii, so it would make sense for even a large number of planes to be lost there, but the entire Ukrainian Air Force fit in just eight aircraft parking rows. At L'vov Air Base in Ukrayina, just the MiG-23s at that one base filled twelve rows. This wasn't an Air Force, he told himself, this was a recreational-aircraft fly-in. But, thank God, Panchenko had spirited spare parts, missiles, tech orders, and charts to Turkey over the past few months.

Now, this was all they had.

Tychina was at the controls of the last MiG-23 fighter plane out of the Ukraine. General Panchenko had led the formation of survivors to Turkey, and Tychina, flying one of the few Ukrayinan planes that carried any weaponry, was bringing up the rear to cover their retreat. He had been allowed to arm his MiG with the standard GSh-23 gun on the centerline gun station, with only one hundred rounds of ammunition—any plane with a cannon was allowed to carry one hundred rounds of ammunition for self-defense—and he was allowed to carry two R-60 short-range heat-seeking air-to-air missiles on the outer pylons. It was not very much protection for anyone, but at the very least it would allow him to engage any enemy planes and hold them off long enough for the others to plug in the afterburners and get away. He also carried one eight-hundred-liter fuel tank on the center pylon.

He was on a high, wide downwind pattern, parallel to the long northernmost active runway of the large Turkish military complex. He was carefully aligning himself with a Turkish F-16 fighter flying about a kilometer ahead of him, matching every altitude and speed change. Tychina knew that if he strayed too far from his escort his brethren—one F-16 directly astern, another high and out of sight somewhere behind him—would attack. His Sirena-3 radar warning receiver was lit up with threats, and had been well before he crossed the Black Sea into Turkish airspace. Fighter tracking radar, surveillance radar, a NATO Patriot surface-to-air missile system tracking radar—they were all locked on. The Ukrayinans might have been cordially invited into Turkey by the host country and by the NATO alliance, but no one was taking any chances here . . .

. . . including Tychina, who was constantly rehearsing the sequence of events he'd need to accomplish to turn this approach into an attack. Hit the F-16 in front of him with guns, drop chaff and flares, hit the guy to the right with missiles or guns, then drop to the deck and run like hell until he flamed out over Iraq or Syria—go east and south instead of north and west. He wondered if the Americans or NATO would pull some kind of dirty trick, create a trap. He shook his head: in war anything was possible.

"Ukrainian MiG, Kayseri tower," the heavily accented voice said on the radio in English, interrupting Tychina's grim thoughts. "Winds zero-eight-five at ten knots, runway zero-niner, check wheels down, cleared to land."

"Yes, Ukrayinan MiG, landing now, thank you," Tychina replied in broken English on the international emergency frequency. Well, if this was a trap, he was too late—NATO had all the surviving attack planes on their base, including the last one. He was committed. If NATO screwed them now, the world could kiss off Ukrayina for good. He flipped the gear-extension lever down, relieving pressure on the hydraulic gear-retraction system which allowed the gear to free-fall, then reached down to the emergency pneumatic gear downlock pressurization handle on the bulkhead near his right leg and began pumping it, which provided backup pressurization for the gear safety downlocks. He continued to pump until all four green gear-down lights came on—the fourth green light signaled that the large ventral fin near the tail feathers had folded up into its landing position—then extended trailing- and leading-edge flaps and set up for the landing.

Turning final, he could see the pristine deserts and low hills of eastern Turkey spread out before him in an incredible panorama, unspoiled even by the extensive oil fields and refineries south and east of the base near the city. Dominating the landscape was Erciyes Dagi, a large volcanic mountain just ten miles south of the city, its sheer walls rising three thousand meters in just a few kilometers, forming almost a spire reaching over four thousand meters above sea level. Kayseri was an industrial megalopolis in the middle of the high desert, but unlike Russian or Ukrainian industrial centers, Kayseri was shiny, freshly painted, almost beautiful. Not a speck of smoke, only a few puffs of white steam or thin smoke. Where was the smog? he wondered. The area north of the volcano was surrounded by farms tended by circular irrigation systems hundreds of meters in diameter, which in the spring would allow crops to flourish in this very inhospitable region. Everything seemed so clean, so impossibly beautiful, that it put L'vov, Odessa, and even the polluted but beautiful Crimea to shame.

As soon as the dual nose gear wheels touched the grooved runway and Tychina extended the four petal speedbrakes and upper wing spoilers, several armored personnel carriers roared onto the runway. As Tychina coasted toward the end, he looked up in his rearview periscope and saw two huge fire trucks and several more APCs converging on him. "Ukrainian MiG, make the first right turn you can and remain on this frequency. Acknowledge."

"I acknowledge, to turn right, yes I will," Tychina repeated in his best English. The armored personnel carriers ahead of him had formed a corral that clearly outlined the proper taxiway. As soon as he was clear of the main runway, the armored vehicles closed in and he was ordered to stop and shut down engines.

A Turkish army officer stepped up beside his cockpit, signaling him to open the canopy. As he did so, several armed soldiers took up positions around his plane, but he was happy to see that all of them held their rifles at port arms with the actions open—nonthreatening. After Tychina swung open the heavy canopy, the officer made a hand signal to tell him to keep his hands on the canopy bow, in plain sight. Tychina stood on his ejection seat and did as he was told. Technicians put safety pins in his R-60 missiles, and he could hear them installing some sort of shield around the gun ports and a jack under the fuel tank, presumably as safety measures. Finally, a ladder was placed alongside his plane and he was asked to step down.

Tychina was met at the base of the boarding ladder by a tall, slender Turkish security officer, wearing high calf-length riding boots, his uniform blouse festooned with ribbons and badges, armed with a pearl-handled American .45-caliber automatic pistol in a black leather holster, and smoking a thin cigar—very dangerous around a MiG-23 with weapons aboard. He was flanked by two security guards, both carrying M-16 rifles with M-203 grenade launchers attached. It was very ostentatious firepower for one plane and one pilot, Tychina thought, and he wondered if General Panchenko and the rest of his surviving air force got the same display.

"The next time you disobey my orders and do not follow my escort planes as directed," the officer said in pidgin Russian, without identifying himself or offering any sort of greeting, "I will shoot you and your Russian piece-of-shit aircraft from the sky. Is that clear?"

Tychina did not reply right away. He stood at attention just a half meter before the Turkish officer, who was several centimeters taller than the Ukrainian pilot, then removed his flying helmet and tucked it into the crook of his left arm. Tychina was wearing a white flameproof hood with cutouts for his eyes and mouth, which got him a few surprised glances at the unusual headgear. Then, with a flourish, Tychina stripped off the mask, transferred the mask to his left hand, and saluted the Turkish officer with his right hand. "Colonel of Aviation Pavlo Tychina, Fifth Air Army, Air Force of the Republic of Ukrayina, reporting as ordered, *sir.*"

Tychina remained completely impassive, eyes caged, but he could clearly see the Turkish officer's face blanch, then turn green, and his Adam's apple bobble as if he were fighting the urge to vomit. One of the guards dropped his M-16 clattering to the ground—Tychina prayed its safety was still on—and promptly vomited on the tarmac despite a hand held up to his mouth; the other stayed at port arms, but he began carefully examining something on the ground and never did raise his eyes again. Tychina held his salute until the Turkish officer could regain his composure and return a shaky hand salute. Tychina pulled a sterile plastic bag from a flight suit pocket, withdrew a fresh gauze mask, and slipped it on.

"I am sorry I do not speak the Turkish language," Tychina said in English. "I am very happy to be here. Your people very kind. Please, we go to your commanding officer, no?"

"Yes," the officer said a bit shakily, looking immensely relieved that Tychina had put the face mask on and covered his horrible wounds. "I . . . I, uh, will take you to meet the commander . . . Thank you."

"No, it is I who thank you," Tychina said. The Turkish officer tried a weak smile, failed at it, then motioned to his vehicle and led the way.

They headed directly for a driveway between the tower and the fire department, but Tychina noticed the rows of Ukrainian planes parked not far to their right. "Please, may we drive by the planes of Ukrayina, sir?" The Turkish officer gave an order to his driver, who made a radio call and turned toward the parking ramp. An armored vehicle parked every thirty meters or so marked the boundaries of the security area—one M113 light tank had to be rolled out of the way so their sedan could pass.

The Ukrainian planes were in remarkably good condition. As expected, most were MiG-23 fighters. As if on cue, the Turkish officer gave Tychina a copy of his list of foreign planes parked there: one hundred and thirteen Ukrainian Mikoyan-Gurevich-23 fighters, thirty-one MiG-27 bombers, and twenty-seven Sukhoi-17 bombers. The Turkish officer's inventory did not specify which models were present. There were a few two-seat trainer versions—three MiG-23 UB-models and two Su-17 UM-models—both with combat capability. Consistent with the threat of Russian air raids, all of the Sukhoi-17 single-seaters were H- or K-model reconnaissance planes—they would have survived because they were probably all in the air during the Russian bomb runs. They still had the special pylons fitted for long-range fuel tanks, electronic countermeasures pods, and the Ogarkov-213 sensor pod on the centerline station, but all of the external stores had been removed. "Excuse me please," Tychina asked the Turkish officer, "but did these aircraft arrive with tanks? Pods? Photographic devices?"

"They were removed and have been confiscated, for now," the officer replied, his voice a bit tense as he wondered—worried—if the Ukrainian would pull off that mask. "Orders. You understand."

"Yes, thank you," Tychina acknowledged. As long as he got them back in working order, Tychina thought, he didn't care if the Turks took a few apart to study or analyze them. He would gladly trade them for missiles and bombs to arm his planes anyway.

The Sukhoi-17 reconnaissance planes were about twenty years old, and although Tychina knew maintenance on these old birds was usually meticulous, the lack of money for spare parts had taken their toll on them, and they looked their age. The Su-17 was an older model Sukhoi-7 single-engine fighter with the outer one-half of its wings cut off and a swinging variable-geometry section added. The round, open "carp nose" design was primitive and cumbersome, providing very little room for a decent attack radar, but the increased performance of the swing-wing addition was a quantum leap over fixed-geometry designs of the time, and eventually the Su-17 comprised over one-third of the tactical air inventory of the old Soviet Union and was widely exported.

Although the Sukhoi-17 strike planes were valuable, the thirty-one MiG-27s were the prize of Tychina's little attack fleet. They were basically the same as the MiG-23 fighters, but with a greatly strengthened fuselage, lots of armor plating around the pilot, and a big 30-millimeter multibarrel strafing and tank-killing gun replacing the GSh-23 air-to-air gun on the fighter. Most of the MiG-27s here were M-models, about ten years old, with laser rangefinders for precision-guided bombs that could illuminate targets behind and far off to the side of the plane. The -27 could carry just about every weapon in the Ukrainian arsenal—TV-guided bombs, laser-guided bombs, antiradiation missiles, and antiship missiles, as well as air-to-air defensive missiles . . .

. . . that is, if Ukrayina *had* an arsenal anymore. Thank God General Panchenko had had the foresight to worry about a major Russian invasion and sent those weapons shipments here. Panchenko was the hero, not he, Pavlo Tychina. The first order of business would be to organize his aircrews and maintenance technicians to inspect these weapons . . .

. . . that is, if he *had* any maintenance troops here. Tychina had brought pilots, not maintenance troops or technicians. There were no transport planes available to take supplies or survivors out of L'vov—and Tychina assumed it was the same at the other bases—so hopefully General Panchenko arranged for civil transports, overland convoys, or very dangerous sea transportation for the badly needed maintenance guys. These planes weren't going anywhere without proper support.

"I thank you for taking such good care of Ukrayina's fighter jets," Tychina told his host with genuine appreciation.

"You're welcome," the Turkish officer replied halfheartedly. He wasn't sure if Tychina really meant the compliment, since most of the Ukrainian planes looked like shit. They were noisy, smelly, smoky, their radios were bad, and they dropped rivets, inspection plates, large pieces of rubber, and insulation constantly, creating a hazard for the Turkish planes at Kayseri.

They exited the flight line and drove through the base toward the Turkish headquarters. Kayseri Air Base was the most modern, most impressive military installation Tychina had ever seen. The aboveground hangars were huge, thick concrete structures, not weak tin or aluminum over a steel frame like most ex-Soviet facilities in Ukrayina, and Pavlo noticed many gated and guarded ramps leading to underground hangars. Aircraft taxiways were very wide, with enough room for a single Bear-class bomber or several fighter-size aircraft to taxi side by side—many of the taxiways had runway-type markings on them, indicating that they could be used for takeoff and landing if the main runway was in use or damaged.

Although the base was primarily a fighter training base, it was clearly ready for war. Antiaircraft gun and missile emplacements were everywhere, including several Patriot missile batteries and several short-range mobile antiaircraft batteries, including the West's newest weapon system, a combination 30-millimeter Gatling gun with dual feed (antiarmor and antiaircraft explosive rounds) and eight-round Stinger missile battery all on one fast all-terrain truck, using both radar and electro-optical guidance systems. All air defense units were manned at full strength, despite the freezing temperatures. Tychina noted the detailed attention paid to camouflaging every air defense site with realistic-looking white nets and setting up inflatable decoys and radar reflectors around the base. The headquarters building itself was modern and fairly new, but the camouflage makers on base had actually taken great pains to make it more nondescript, to blend in with the snow. The flagpoles and other monuments around the building had been removed, and nearby buildings had similar defensive positions set up around them to make it harder for enemy invaders to immediately determine which building was the headquarters.

Tychina was surprised to see two of his senior pilots, both from L'vov, seated outside the commander's office. They were slouched in their seats, totally bored, with their legs extended straight and their boots tipped up on their heels, tapping them together to show how tired and irritated they were. Pavlo turned to see a Turkish security officer seated across from them, glaring at the two pilots in utter disgust, as if he was ready to pull out his pistol and shoot them both—and Tychina knew why.

The two pilots snapped to attention when they saw him approach. Tychina was overjoyed to see two familiar, friendly faces, but he felt some sort of strain in the room and held his exuberance carefully in check until he found out exactly what was going on. "Captain Mikitenko, Captain Skliarenko," he greeted them in Ukrainian, returning their salutes but then folding his hands behind his back so as to not invite them to shake hands or clasp shoulders, as was customary. Tychina acknowledged the security officer seated across from the two pilots—obviously a guard assigned to the two pilots—who continued to stare disrespectfully at the two young Ukrainians after a polite bow to Tychina.

"Colonel, it is great to see you," Mikitenko said in Ukrainian. "We've been stuck here for the past six hours."

"They haven't even let us go to the bathroom," Skliarenko complained. "I'm about ready to pop. Can you get these guys to let us go to the head, Pavlo?"

On that last sentence, Tychina caught it—the smell of alcohol, strong, fortified Moldovan cherry wine. He leaned closer to Mikitenko and smelled apricot brandy on his breath. "You assholes, you've been *drinking?*" Tychina thundered.

"Hey, c'mon, Pavlo, old buddy," Skliarenko drawled lazily, putting a hand on his shoulder. "We've just been through hell and back. Everyone carries a little nip in the plane—so do you. We just had a little celebration after we landed."

Tychina whipped his right arm up, throwing off the drunk pilot's hand on his shoulder. *"Attention!"* Tychina snapped. Mikitenko snapped to attention once again; Skliarenko was a little slower, his eyes not focusing too well, but he finally moved to attention, weaving unsteadily.

"You bastards could have destroyed any chance we had to regenerate the air force and begin air operations against the Russians," Tychina raged. Mikitenko noticed a line of blood soaking through Tychina's sterile mask—he was so agitated that he had burst a stitch or reopened a wound—and the sight made his throat turn dry, his hands shake with dread. "Don't you two know *anything?* Turkey is a *Muslim* nation. Sunni Muslims. You insulted them to the core by bringing booze into their country and drinking it in front of them. You might as well have pissed on their foreheads. And that's not to mention the fact that it's against regulations to drink on the flight line or during combat conditions. And you were sitting slouched in those chairs with your feet up like lazy pigs."

"Excuse me, sir," Mikitenko interjected, "but we've been here for over six hours."

"Idiots! Sitting slouched in a chair is a sign of disrespect, and pointing the soles of your boots at a Turk is the worst insult you can make," Tychina roared. "Didn't you two notice how pissed off that guard is? You were practically goading him into a fight. Now shut your stupid mouths. I want you to speak only when spoken to. You will remain at parade rest as long as you are here, and you will come to attention if you are addressed by anyone. Is that *clear?"* Both pilots said yes. "Jesus, no wonder this entire country seemed mad at us. I hope we haven't lost the fight before we had a chance to fight it."

Eventually Tychina was shown into the office of the base commander. Brigadier General Erdal Sivarek was a short, round man with dark features and hair that seemed to grow out of impossible places all over his body. The two men were introduced by an interpreter (speaking Russian, not Ukrainian), shook hands, and then Tychina was introduced to an older man in white arctic combat fatigues: "May I present Major General Bruce Eyers, from the United States, chief of operations for NATO Forces Southeast."

Pavlo didn't understand much of the interpreter's thickly accented Russian, but he knew what the two stars on the American's epaulets meant. He quickly checked the American general out. About five foot ten, probably about 225 pounds, a mean-looking sort of man—or maybe just tough—with very short, cropped dark hair, dark eyes, and built like a small building. The American officer squeezed Tychina's hand hard, then asked in a loud voice, "What happened to your face there, young man?" Pavlo was about to reply, but Eyers turned to the Turkish general and laughed, "Looks like the en-tire Ukrainian Air Force is filled with either drunks or walking wounded, eh, General?"

"I apologize for my pilots, sir," Tychina said in English, thinking that the American was admonishing him for the conduct of his two pilots. "They are young and have survived much, sir. Their conduct will *not* be repeated. We will conduct ourselves with very much respect."

"Hell, don't sweat it, chief," the American said easily. "If I just had my hometown blasted to hell by the Russkies, I'd want to toss down a few stiff ones, too. Jeez." He laughed again, but turned much more serious when he found that neither officer was joining in the humor. "I'd advise you to keep a tight grip on your boys, and steer clear of the vodka. The Turks don't go for drinking on this base. It's a pisser, but hell, that's the way it's going to be."

"Our social customs, General, are not 'pissers' to anyone except foreigners, usually slovenly Westerners," General Sivarek said irritably. General Eyers said nothing, but nodded that he understood—and then he made an impatient sigh and crossed his arms on his chest, which Tychina knew was yet another rude gesture to a Turk. General Sivarek glared at Eyers, who didn't notice, then said to Tychina, "*Hos geldiniz, efendim.* I welcome you to the Republic of Turkey and to Kayseri Air Base, Colonel. I am sorry for what has happened to your nation and your home. Under the circumstances, I think we may forgive your pilot's indiscretion. I will make a Russian-speaking liaison officer available to you and your crews so that there will be no more such incidents."

"Thank you, sir," Tychina replied gratefully. "I accept your offer. But I think it's best to keep my crews under cover and working until we can begin air operations. I'm sure General Panchenko and the general staff will want us to be combat-ready in the fastest time possible."

"Hold on there, son," the American general interjected, swaggering a bit now like a bad imitation of John Wayne.

"No one here's talking about *any* air operations. You don't have permission to stage any sorties out of Turkey. You can't even start engines on one of those Floggers without NATO and the President of Turkey giving their okay." He nodded as respectfully as he could to General Sivarek.

Tychina didn't understand all that the American was saying—he made no effort to make himself understood to anyone—but he could sense by the tone in his voice, that lazy swagger, that air operations weren't approved yet. "Excuse me," Pavlo said, "but I anticipate the Russians will begin a full-scale ground invasion of Ukrayina at any time. This we must not allow. I was told you had stockpiled Ukrainian weapons at this location."

"We got nothin' but a hodgepodge of half-assed bombs, rockets, and missiles left over from Afghanistan," Eyers said dryly, looking at the Ukrainian out of the corner of his eyes as if he were a beggar asking for coins. "They're outdated first-generation technology that don't amount to spit and would probably create a hazard for NATO forces anyway. Hell, it's dangerous enough just having those things sit in storage—I can't imagine trying' to upload those things on your aircraft in combat conditions . . . Hell, it'd be like playin' with Tonka toys."

"Excuse me, but we cannot sit here in Turkey while Russian troops march into our country," insisted Tychina as if the man were an idiot.

"There ain't much you boys can do about it, is there, Colonel?" Eyers said, cocking an eybrow. "The only force that can stand up to Russian aggression is NATO *and* the United States, of course. So far, NATO hasn't figgered out what to do.

"Now I'll admit, you got some real interestin' hardware out there, but it's all obsolete, my friend. I wish you'd brought us a few of your Su-24s or Su-37s. NATO will determine whether or not you boys can join our coalition forces and try your hand against the Russkies—although frankly I don't give you a chance in hell. You haven't trained with NATO forces, you don't speak the language, you use totally different tactics."

Pavlo Tychina felt the anger rise to the surface of his skin like a bubble in a boiling cauldron of blood. His breathing became more accelerated, his eyes burning. "I speak English good, sir, very good. And I not need permission from *you* or

NATO to tell me when to fight. You understand?" Tychina turned to General Sivarek and bowed his head politely. "I thank you and your country for welcoming us and giving us the safety. You have given us the opportunity to fight. I ask for fuel and weapons for my aircraft. We will leave aircraft to pay for fuel, and my government will pay; the weapons, they belong to Ukrayina. I require nothing more. We leave soon as possible."

The Turkish general favored Tychina with a hint of a smile, but then tipped his head back slightly, eyes closed—which Tychina knew to be a "no"—and said solemnly, "I am sorry, but that is not possible, Colonel. General Eyers is quite correct: my country offered protection for your government and your air force, nothing more. It is not a wise policy for your crews to fly with our pilots. NATO crews train several times a year together; Ukrainian crews have never trained with us. If there would be an air battle between NATO and Russia, your planes are too similar to Russian rear-echelon planes, even with Ukrainian markings—and some of your planes still have *Russian* markings on them. The confusion would be enormous. It would be dangerous and expose both our forces to serious risk."

"Then we will fly alone, sir," Tychina decided. "When your planes are not flying, we will fight."

"That proves how much you know about Western tactics, son." Eyers chuckled condescendingly. "We don't pause, we don't stop, we don't let up once the ball game gets going. It's just too dangerous. Some overanxious fly-boy would likely put a Sidewinder up your butt, and it'd be a waste of a good missile. Forget it, chief."

Tychina took two tightly controlled steps toward Eyers, his fists clenched. "I am not this 'chief,' and I am not 'son,' sir," he seethed. "I am Colonel of Aviation of the Air Force of the Ukrayinan Republic—"

"And you're way out of line, *Colonel,*" Eyers said, pointing a finger at him as if he were pointing a gun. "We saved your butt from a royal shellacking. You're on our side of the fence now, son. You stay grounded until we clear up this awful mess."

Pavlo was incredulous. He didn't understand all the words, but his tone of voice and his hand gestures said everything—the American general didn't want his Ukrayinan bombers to leave

Turkey. *"No!* My orders are to prepare my aircraft for combat operations," Tychina snapped. "We do not stay on ground. We *fight."*

"You'll do as you're ordered or you'll be placed under arrest!" yelled Eyers, eyes on fire.

"I was not sent here to wait. I came here to fight," Tychina explained to both of them, trying to remain calm. "If I am not given permission to prepare to fight, I will recommend to my commander that our forces be withdrawn."

"Withdrawn?" Eyers' eyes turned the size of saucers. "You listen to me, you third-world shithead . . ."

"Enough!" Sivarek ordered, raising both hands in front of the two officers.

"You stay out of this, General," Eyers said dismissively, waving a hand as if to swat a bothersome insect. "I'm gonna set this pup straight."

"*Hayir.* You will not," Sivarek interrupted. Eyers looked angry enough to commit murder at being shown up by the Turk, but Sivarek went on. "You are my superior officer, General Eyers, but this is still my base and my country, and you are both *guests* here. Is that understood, sir?"

Eyers said nothing, but only glared at Tychina.

"I understand, sir," Tychina said. "I am grateful for any help you give."

"*Tamam.* We shall leave it at that," Sivarek said. Eyers stalked away, finding a pitcher of strong, thick Turkish coffee on a credenza nearby and pouring himself a cup. "Colonel, the decision as to what role your fighters and bombers will play in the conflict which is to come must be coordinated with your country and with any other nations that choose to stand against the Russian aggression," the Turkish officer continued. "So far, none have stepped forward, although NATO—and indeed the entire world—is mobilizing its military forces for intercontinental war, fearful that the Russians may try an invasion of Turkey or the Eastern Bloc republics. We simply have to wait and see.

"We do indeed have a quantity of Ukrainian weapons stored here," Sivarek went on. "My orders are to guard them, nothing more. They do indeed belong to you, and they will be returned to you at the proper time. For the moment, we need help in inventorying and inspecting the weapons stockpile. Can your crews assist in this?"

"They can, sir," Tychina said quietly. "I would like to organize training, intelligence, maintenance, target selection, and communications details as well. I am hoping that General Panchenko can send technicians from Ukrayina, but for now I intend on organizing my aircrews to—"

"What you're going to do, Colonel, is sit tight and don't do anything unless *I* tell you to do it," Eyers declared. "We got you out of your country with your skins, so you owe us. That's all you need to know. You are dismissed. Report here at seven A.M. tomorrow morning and you'll be given your duties."

Tychina saluted Eyers and Sivarek, but the Turkish general held up a hand and asked, "How were you injured, *effendi?*"

"I was leader of interceptor flight that stopped first raid of Tupolev-95 bombers into Ukrayina," Tychina explained. "My aircraft was shot out. But I kill many heavy Bear bombers and make others turn away."

"Yeah, right." General Eyers chuckled, pouring himself more coffee. "You get yourself blown away but still managed to save the day, huh? I heard *that* one before."

"No, I have heard of this man," Sivarek said, impressed. "The young captain who shot down five Russian bombers and averted the first Russian attack single-handedly. You are a hero, young sir. I congratulate you."

"Thank you, sir," Tychina said. He noticed Eyers' skeptical expression and added, "You think I not tell the truth, General Eyers?"

"If you say it's true, it's fine by me," Eyers said easily. "I'll bet that yarn impresses the hell out of your girlfriends, that's for damned sure."

"My girlfriend is *dead,* General," Tychina hissed. "She was killed in Russian attack while waiting for me to marry her." He held out his arms, his hands and wrists tense, as if he were carrying his dead fiancée. "She died of the radiation sickness. In my arms."

"That's too bad," Eyers said in a low voice, feigning his condolences. "But maybe your revenge is making you not think so clear, chief. You just can't go charging back into the Ukraine or Russia just like that—they'll blow your toy planes out there away. Think with your head and not your balls, son." Tychina's open hands, still extended as if he were carrying his dead Mikki, curled into tight fists, then dejectedly dropped to his side.

"You ever think about the fact that if you hadn't stopped those Bears from doing their thing, Russia would've never nuked you?" asked Eyers, raising his eyebrows. "Maybe those Bears were just going to hit military targets in Moldova and Romania, not the Ukraine, or maybe they really were just reconnaissance planes like the Russian foreign ministry suggests. If that's true, what you did was an act of war—against your own people, your own allies."

Tychina turned to Eyers, pure hatred in his eyes magnified by his face mask. "You Americans, no one invade your home, you do not know how to suffer," he said. "You talk big about patience and waiting when Russians drop nuclear bombs on Ukrayina. It will be very different if Russians attack America."

"It'll never happen, son," Eyers said confidently. "Ol' Velichko knows better than to even try it. And don't try to tell me I don't know the score, my friend. I was in uniform defending my country long before you had your first wet dream. Back when ol' Khrushchev was still alive and kicking. Maybe you ought to try listening to how the professional soldiers in the West fight for a change, instead of swinging your dick around looking for a fight. Someone's liable to shoot it off."

The young Ukrainian officer decided he was too disgusted by this guy to hang around for another second. "I will go and inspect my crews now, sir," Tychina said to Sivarek, snapping to attention and saluting. Sivarek returned the salute. "Again, sir, I thank you for helping my country. My countrymen will never forget it. And I apologize for the conduct of my officers; they meant no disrespect to you or your country." Tychina turned and rendered a salute to Eyers, who simply nodded in return, then departed.

"He is a very brave and determined young man, no?" Sivarek asked Eyers after the Ukrainian had left.

"I think he's a peasant in a flight suit," Eyers concluded. He opened the door, then chuckled to himself. "Russia invading the United States—that's a laugh," he said. "I don't know what you see in that kid, General." Sivarek joined in Eyers' laughter as he saw the American to the door and closed it behind him—then ceased his laughing and gave Eyers an obscene "fig" finger—clenching his fist, then poking his thumb out between the index and middle fingers—behind his back.

"I see a fighting spirit that you lost long ago, you pompous American ass," Sivarek said half-aloud. When Sivarek's clerk returned after seeing the American off, the General told him in Turkish, "I want a meeting of the wing staff at oh-six-hundred hours, and I want Captain Yilmez to give me a complete report of the status of those Ukrainian weapons. Do it *immediately.*"

29

The White House, Washington, D.C.

"THIS IS A RATHER SERIOUS TURN OF EVENTS, MR. PRESIDENT," Vitaly Velichko, President of Russia and the Commonwealth of Independent States, said. His English was very good—he was educated both in England and the United States—and it felt a bit strange for the American president to hear a British-sounding accent on the other end of the line and then remind himself that he was talking to a Russian.

"Now, you're not getting upset about a few F-111 reconnaissance planes goin' to Turkey, are you, Mr. President?" the Chief Executive drawled, his feet propped up on the desk John F. Kennedy had once used and that he'd brought out of storage after his inauguration. He popped some M&Ms into his mouth from a big crystal jar on his desk. He glanced around the Oval Office, listening to the Russian president, but visually taking in his surroundings, ignoring those advisers present for this phone call. Even now, in the midst of an international crisis, he never ceased to be amazed that he'd made it here in the first place. A governor from what so many laughingly called a hillbilly, inbred state, with more than a few skeletons in his personal closet, the pundits had called him a dark horse from the start. Laughed off. Well, they sure as hell weren't laughing anymore. His eyes focused on a sculpture on a Federal table by the polycarbonate, bullet-resistant-windowed French doors leading to the Rose Garden. The sculpture was a replica of Rodin's "The Thinker."

Just what the President reminded himself he needed to be doing now. "We deploy these planes all the time to Turkey and you never seem to mind—heck, we landed them in Riga that one time last year, and a hundred thousand people came out to see them. And after all, Vitaly, they're *just* Reservists." He crunched a bit more on the M&Ms.

"We have great respect for both your Reserve forces and for your weapon systems, Mr. President," Velichko said firmly. "Our general staff has modeled our new air force after your excellent Enhanced Reserve Program, and, as everyone knows, the F-111 is one of the world's premier medium bombers."

"They're not bombers, Mr. President, they're reconnaissance planes."

"Ah. Forgive me, sir. Perhaps my information is faulty. I assumed there was only one model of the RF-111G Vampire bomber based at Plattsburgh, New York, and that the six planes you have on nuclear alert there are the same as the twelve planes that you call reconnaissance planes that are being deployed to Turkey. I must instruct my staff at once to double-check their information for accuracy."

"They're *not* the same plane, Mr. President. We're sending reconnaissance planes only to Turkey, that's all," he said, sinking back in his seat in frustration. He released the "dead man" button on his telephone and said to the others in the Oval Office, "Christ, *I* didn't even know how many damned F-111s we had at Plattsburgh—how in hell does he know all this stuff?"

"We released all that information to the press, as part of your openness policy and as a provision of the new START treaty, sir," Secretary of Defense Donald Scheer said. "I think it's smart for the American people and the Russians to know exactly how many weapons we have on alert."

"Yeah, but someone forgot to tell *me,*" the President snapped, all but spitting out the remains of an M&M.

"Mr. President, be that as it may, the Congress of the People here still have very grave reservations about this deployment," Velichko continued. "I'm sure you understand our concerns. I have tried to express my total assurance to you that the bombing raids on the military installations in the Ukraine, Moldova, and Romania were an unfortunate and deeply regrettable incident, purely isolated attacks, and will not be repeated. All of our nuclear forces were at full peacetime readiness, which is to say that no strategic forces were operational except for the six hundred launchers and three thousand warheads authorized under the START treaty, and that neither the United States nor NATO was ever in danger.

"That of course has changed since your country and those nuclear powers in NATO have mobilized additional strategic weapons. We fully understand this reaction, we accept it, we have notified you and NATO of our response, and we will not respond in kind but at a greatly lower level than NATO. However, we are very disturbed by this latest move. The deployment of strategic nuclear forces to Turkey is a clear violation of the START treaty and a serious escalation of tensions."

"Mr. President, let me assure *you,* we are not trying to threaten or intimidate anyone," the American president said. "The F-111s are conducting a routine deployment in support of NATO operations. We—"

"Excuse me, Mr. President, but you said they were F-111 aircraft?"

"Yes, that's what I said, they're F-111s." But he paused when he saw one of Scheer's aides shaking his head. The President released the cutoff button. "What? They're not F-111s . . . ?"

"Sir, they're RF-111G aircraft," the aide said. "There is a distinction. The RF-111G is a reconnaissance and defense-suppression aircraft with a strike *capability*—the F-111 is a *strike* aircraft."

"Well, hell, that's just a difference in wording."

"Sir, it's as different as the Tupolev-22M maritime-interdiction aircraft the Russians sent to Cuba, and the Tupolev-26 supersonic bomber," Army general Philip Freeman said. "Technically they're the same plane, but the Tu-22M is considered a maritime reconnaissance and interdiction aircraft only, not a land bomber. Both sides are allowed to send reconnaissance aircraft to forward operating locations, but not strategic offensive aircraft. Calling the RF-111G Vampire aircraft an F-111 bomber is technically an admission that we're violating the treaty."

The President rolled his eyes again in irritation, dipping his hand back into the crystal jar. "What bullshit." He keyed the button on the phone and said, "Excuse me, Mr. President, I meant they're *R*F-111*G* aircraft. They're reconnaissance planes only."

"Yes, of course, Mr. President," Velichko said. "You *meant* to say RF-111G Vampire aircraft."

"No, sir, they *are* RF-111G aircraft," he insisted, his voice rising a bit. A few members of the President's Cabinet shuffled uneasily in their seats—it was not good to hear the President interrupting the Russian president during their conversation. The Chief Executive had a trigger temper, and it was just like him to get wound up during this conversation.

"When may I tell my government that we can expect this deployment to come to an end and these RF-111G aircraft return to the United States, Mr. President?" Velichko asked.

"I suppose that's all up to you, Vitaly," the President said evenly, a bit of sarcasm in his voice. Secretary of State Harlan Grimm's heart skipped a beat. The President was *baiting* the Russian. He was about to speak, but instead held out two hands, urging the President to take it easy and be calm. But the President had crossed the line, and nothing was going to hold him back now. "The Turks think you're trying to scope out their military bases and that you're puttin' the squeeze on 'em to stop supporting the Ukrainian government in exile. You're makin' a lot of people nervous, Mr. President, and we had no choice but to respond. You got nothing to worry about from me if you just tell your fly-boys to back off and let things over there cool down. As for the -111s, we'll keep 'em over there for as long as it's necessary."

"I understand, Mr. President," Vitaly Velichko echoed coldly. "You will keep the F-111s in Turkey for as long as you think is necessary."

Again, Harlan Grimm, now on his feet while listening in on a dead extension, shook his head, warning the President not to let the Russian put words in his mouth; but the President responded, "That's right. Mr. President, I don't want to send those planes to Turkey. They're just Reservists, and we got young women in that unit that have never been overseas and don't know what it's like to be in action. Frankly, I'd rather not send them to a place like Turkey. But your actions in the region are making lots of people very nervous. We can defuse this whole thing by just backing off. It should be put to an end as soon as possible. How about it?"

"I thank you very much for your words, Mr. President," Velichko replied dismissively. "Thank you very much for speaking with me. Good-bye." The American chief executive barely had time to respond before the connection was broken.

"Jeez, what an arrogant bastard," he said as he hung up the phone, popping some more candy in his mouth. "So. Comments?" No one spoke up. "I hate to deal with world leaders over the phone, but talking with Vitaly's pretty easy. I wish the French prime minister spoke English as well as Velichko. Any other comments?"

No one was about to tell the President that he very well might have insulted the Turks, the women in the Air Force, all military Reservists, and in effect told the Russians that the United States would back off and, essentially, to go ahead with their plans to take over the Ukraine. When there was no response, he said, "Okay, that's over with. The First Lady is flying up to Plattsburgh to see those bombers off, and you're going with her, right, Phil?"

"Yes, sir," General Freeman replied halfheartedly, not at all happy about being on a trip with the Steel Magnolia.

"Good. I know the press coverage makes this whole thing look like a circus, Phil, but I think it's important to show the American people what we're doing to respond to the crisis, that we're not going overboard but that we are responding. My wife wants to get involved in military affairs, and I think it's good—few First Ladies have shown much interest in the military in the past. Good luck with that."

Circus was just about the right word for it, Freeman thought. He said, "Thank you, sir," and departed like a bat out of hell.

30

Plattsburgh Air Force Base, New York
The Next Morning

WITH THE MORNING SUN GLISTERING OFF THE BLUE AND WHITE polished exterior of Air Force One as a backdrop, the two lines of aircrews snapped to attention as dark-blue security vehicles, Secret Service Suburbans, rolled to a stop, followed by two blue VIP limos and another Secret Service sedan. The crowd of about a thousand people, mostly hastily invited guests and local political friends of the President of the United States, gathered against the security ropes about fifty feet away grew louder and more restless. A podium had been set up so the First Lady could make some remarks, and the red security rope was lined with reporters and photographers. This was a rare opportunity to be allowed access to a military base during an actual combat deployment, and they were taking advantage of every moment.

"What horseshit," Colonel Daren Mace muttered under his breath. He was watching a group of photographers being chased away from the outer gate of the alert-facility ramp as they tried to photograph the six nuclear-loaded RF-111G Vampire bombers and six KC-135E tankers inside. They were flashing authorization badges, but nothing they had allowed them to photograph the alert birds. "Just shoot 'em, sky cops," Mace said. "Don't send them away or arrest them, shoot 'em."

"Pipe down, Colonel," Colonel McGwire hissed at him. "They're coming."

As the Secret Service detail and Air Force security police surrounded the area, the First Lady stepped out of the first limousine, waving to the crowd. She was wearing a blue flight suit, given to her when she made a flight with the Air Force Thunderbirds the year before, under a winter-weight Arctic flying jacket with a fur hood. In the car with her was Major General Tyler Layton, commander of Fifth Air Battle Force, plus several Secret Service agents. In the second car was General Philip Freeman, Chairman of the Joint Chiefs of Staff, along with Governor Samuel Bellingham of New York. The two senior officers joined in the applause of the crowd of guests observing this gathering as the First Lady and the Governor began to work the crowds.

The First Lady shook hands with a number of the dignitaries and friends arranged in front of the podium, then she stepped up to the podium and had General Freeman stand on one side and Governor Bellingham on the other. "Thank you very much, ladies and gentlemen," the First Lady began. "It's very kind of you to come out on this beautiful but very cold morning to help me, General Freeman, and Governor Bellingham wish Godspeed and good luck to this exceptional group of airmen—and, not to be outdone or forgotten, air*women*—here this morning."

She spoke in a cold, crisp tone for about five minutes, then got to the heart of the matter.

"I wanted to recognize one more extraordinary group here, and that's the women of the 394th Air Battle Wing. It was just twenty years ago that the first woman pilot in the modern U.S. Air Force graduated from flight training, and only fifteen years ago when the first woman joined a Strategic Air Command combat crew, and only three years since all aviation positions were open to women. You are all witnesses to history in the making again, ladies and gentlemen, because this is the first overseas deployment of a combat-capable crew with women aviators in it, including America's first woman combat pilot, Major Rebecca C. Furness, of the 715th Tactical Squadron 'Eagles.'" The First Lady stopped to initiate the applause, then waved over to the RF-111G side. "Becky, where are you?" As scripted, Rebecca stepped forward onto the red carpet and waved to the crowd. The photographers went crazy trying to get a good shot of her.

The First Lady blew her a kiss and gave her a thumbs-up, then turned to the audience. "There are some who say that women aren't good enough, that they can't handle the pressure, that they don't have the right stuff. Well, my friends, take a look at that woman, and her war machine. That's an American pilot, the best of the best. Rebecca, Eagle Squadron, Griffin Squadron—good luck and Godspeed. God bless you all, and God bless the United States of America. Let's all help get these professionals on their way, shall we?"

The First Lady accepted the loud applause with a wave and a mind-blowing smile for the cameras, shook hands with the Governor and with Freeman, then made her way down the line along the red carpet, shaking hands with members of both squadrons. She spent extra time with all the female crewmembers, making sure lots of pictures were taken with them, and also spent a few moments with movie star Ted Little, who was back after his sick leave. She did a fast tour of the left wing and underside of the KC-135 tanker, then went over to Furness' plane.

Rebecca Furness and Lieutenant Colonel Hembree led the First Lady and several Secret Service agents on a walkaround tour of the RF-111G bomber. "These aren't bombs, are they?" the First Lady asked, her eyes wide, pointing to the objects on the wing pylons.

"No, ma'am . . . we've planned this deployment to be ready for action as soon as we reach our theater of action. So my flight, the first six planes, are loaded with a ready tactical load. The outer pods are radar reconnaissance or electronic photography pods. The middle and inner pylons on each side carries an AGM-88C supersonic antiradar missile, which seeks out and destroys enemy radars, and we also carry a self-protection AIM-9 Sidewinder heat-seeking missile on the side of each middle pylon."

Looking very much like a politician on the stump, the First Lady climbed up the ladder of the maintenance platform and peeked into the cockpit. About a half-dozen photographers and Secret Service agents were on that platform with her, another half-dozen were on another platform on the other side, and more were on "cherry picker" cranes overhead. It was quite a media circus.

What a fucking joke, Daren Mace thought as he glanced at his watch and frowned. It was only ten minutes to their planned engine-start time, but it would take at least fifteen minutes just to get the fucking VIPs out of here, the maintenance stands and cranes moved out of the way, and the crews back in their places. He saw a person come up beside him and said, "Lieutenant Barnes, get Lieutenant Benedict from the Security Police squadron and ask her if she can help get the guests moving toward base operations. The faster we get these rubberneckers out of here, the faster we can get this show on the road."

"It usually doesn't work that way, Colonel," Mace heard a voice beside him say. Mace turned and saw none other than General Philip Freeman, chairman of the Joint Chiefs of Staff, an aide, and General Cole standing beside him. He snapped to attention and rendered a salute, which Freeman returned.

"General Freeman," Cole said, "allow me to introduce my new MG and the architect of my wing's readiness plan, Lieutenant Colonel Daren Mace. Daren, General Freeman, chairman of the Joint Chiefs of Staff."

They shook hands and Freeman said, "I've followed your career, Colonel, ever since the Persian Gulf War. I was given your wing-readiness report unaltered from General Layton, and frankly I was very worried when the best you could give your unit was marginal readiness. I was glad to see this wing came through when the President asked for you."

"I take none of the credit for this wing's success, sir," Mace said. "We've got the best in the business hard at work here."

"You were saying about all the rubberneckers?"

Mace looked at Cole for a brief instant, received a slight nod, then replied, "Sir, why are all these people here? We're supposed to be conducting a tactical deployment. Normally these deployments are classified secret up to one hour before departure."

"The simple answer is, Colonel, that the President and the First Lady wanted it," Freeman replied with clear resignation. "The more politic answer is that our president wants to avert a major conflict and doesn't care too much about sneaking up on an adversary—he believes that being upfront about things like troop movements and public policy is a better deterrent to aggression. Your task is to deliver combat-ready aircraft to

Turkey despite any political or publicity drills imposed on you. Got it?"

"Yes, sir."

"Good. Now there's something *else* I want from you. I want to send you to Turkey—but not to Incirlik with the rest of the wing. I'm sending you to Kayseri Air Base. We have a . . . special aircraft-maintenance task for you. You've got a C-17 at your disposal, and I want you to use it." The C-17 Globemaster, popularly called Mighty Mouse or The Mouse because it was smaller than other Air Force heavy transports but had a larger payload, was the Air Force's newest heavy transport—there were only twenty in the entire inventory—and because of its special unimproved-field and heavy load-carrying capabilities, it was in heavy demand. It was certainly a very special mission if he had one of these behemoths at his disposal. "We've made up a list of the people we want you to bring with you, and you'll need to bring along as much equipment as you can stuff into a Mouse. You'll fly back to Cannon Air Force Base to pick up some personnel and equipment there, then head on out to Kayseri ASAP. Any questions?"

Jesus, Mace thought. *Kayseri Air Base* . . . He had been there a lot after the Persian Gulf War and during the Middle East War of 1993, mostly recovering bombers that had diverted there after accomplishing bombing raids in Syria and Jordan. He had been stationed at Incirlik Air Base, about 120 miles to the south, but Kayseri, a Turkish training base, was an old hangout . . .

. . . as was its sister base, Batman Air Base. The place where they flew the abortive Operation Desert Fire. Just four years after that horrible day, he was on his way back again. . . .

"Yes, sir. Just one question," Mace finally replied. "Why me?"

"I'll give you the usual answer, then," Freeman replied with a smile, his first, Mace saw, on the entire junket. "You're the best. I need multitalented troops on this mission, men and women experienced in many types of airframes, troops with both maintenance and aircrew experience, troops who get the job done and who tell the brass to go to hell if it can't be done. You also know Turkey and Kayseri."

"I'd just as soon forget," Mace said with a grimace.

General Freeman nodded, then glanced around them to see where the closest reporter was—obviously too close, because he said in a low voice, "Your *experience* is needed there, Colonel. You've been through a lot—this is your opportunity to kick some ass again. Any more questions?"

"The others can wait, sir," Mace said. "Thanks for the vote of confidence. Excuse me, but I've got aircraft to launch." He crisply saluted Freeman and walked off toward the security police post himself to begin getting the ramp cleared for aircraft to taxi.

As he did, he looked at Rebecca Furness' Vampire bomber. The First Lady had taken off her flying parka, revealing the very tightly tailored blue flight suit that showed off her magazine-model body to full advantage. She was posing with a couple of female crew chiefs and with Rebecca on the maintenance stand beside the RF-111G bomber while an army of photographers snapped away. Mace shook his head in disgust, then was furious to see reporters and photographers drifting around the bombers, opening access panels on the AGM-88C HARM missiles, looking up into wheel wells and engine intakes. Now each and every aircraft was going to have to be inspected before engine start to make sure a dumb-ass photographer didn't leave something in an engine that would get sucked inside and FOD (Foreign Object Damage) the damn engine out.

Mace glanced to one side and saw Mark Fogelman. This kid, who was injured badly in the crash landing with Furness only a couple days ago, was up and around and was pronounced fit to deploy with the rest of his squadron. He still looked like hell, with bad bruises on his face and missing a couple of front teeth, but he was dressed and pumped and ready to go. But he had been pushed into the background by the First Lady and the White House handlers and the photographers, probably because he looked like a casualty instead of a crewman. By contrast, Ted Little, the actor, who hadn't been hurt nearly as badly as Fogelman, wasn't going to Turkey. The bastard got his Hollywood studio to use a little pressure and extend his convalescent leave.

Several minutes later, when the podium and grandstands and photographers were cleared out of the way, the crews climbed into their aircraft, and on a signal from the First Lady herself, the aircraft started engines and began to depart, Stratotankers first, followed by Vampires. The First Lady stood out in front of Rebecca Furness' bomber beside a female crew chief, wearing ear protectors and holding two taxi wands, and, mimicking the crew chief's actions, helped taxi the first RF-111G carrying the first female combat pilot to her first overseas deployment.

Mace was, by this point, ready to barf. God, how he loathed politicians—male or female.

Well, while the First Lady was putting on a show, others in Washington were fighting this war for real. He was glad someone was on the job.

31

The Black Sea, Near Eregli, Turkey, That Evening

IT WAS THE PRIDE AND JOY OF THE TURKISH NAVY. LAID down on New Year's Day, 1986, launched on 30 August 1987, Turkish Victory Day, and placed in service one year later, the guided-missile frigate F-242 *Fatih* was one of the most sophisticated warships in the world. Designed in Germany but license-built at the modern Golcuk naval shipyards southeast of Istanbul, the *Fatih* was three hundred and thirty feet long, weighed over 2,700 tons, and could reach a top speed of 27 nautical miles per hour. It was a very multinational ship as well, carrying only the best naval weapons from the Western World: an American-made AB-212 antisubmarine-warfare helicopter that could launch British-made Sea Skua antiship missiles; American-designed Harpoon antiship cruise missiles also license-built in Turkey; German Sea Zenith antiaircraft guns with optronic and track-while-scan radar fire-control directors; American Sea Sparrow antiship and antiaircraft missiles; and American-made Mark 32 torpedoes and SQS-56 sonar gear. Once deployed, it was designed to take control of the seas and skies around it for a hundred kilometers.

The *Fatih* was cruising the northwestern coast of Turkey in its usual circuit of the Black Sea offshore from the Bosporus

Strait, along with its escorts, the guided-missile patrol boats *Poyraz* and *Firtina* and, not far away, an ex-German Type 209 diesel submarine, the *Yildiray*, built in Turkey with German assistance and used as an antisubmarine escort for *Fatih*. Also sailing along with the powerful patrol convoy was the large underway-replenishment oiler *Akar*, which dwarfed the frigate and its escorts; she was waiting for first dawn to begin transferring fuel and supplies. Normally the *Fatih* stayed on patrol only for ten to fourteen days, depending on the status of its patrol craft, but with tensions so high in the region all Turkish warships were on almost constant alert, and Turkey's ten oilers and tenders were very busy in the Black Sea keeping Turkey's combat fleet in action.

Fatih's patrol area was one of the most important—control the approaches to the Bosporus Strait and the southwest Black Sea, and defend Turkish territorial waters. Refugee sea traffic from the Ukraine, Romania, and Bulgaria was extremely heavy in the past few months, especially after the Russian nuclear attack, and people were taking anything that could float into the dangerous Black Sea and trying to escape to the West and to Israel. The Navy's job was to keep the normal shipping lanes open for international traders that still dared to risk sailing into the Black Sea, and to keep close tabs on the Russian Navy.

A major source of tension between Turkey and Russia lately was the dispersal of Ukrainian Air Force units to Turkey and the news that thousands of tons of weapons and supplies had been secretly shipped from the Ukraine to Turkey over the past few months. Russia had called for a halt to all military assistance from Turkey, and had called any continued shipments or military support "of grave concern" to Russia. They had said it was another example of Western interference in Russia's internal affairs. The threat was clear: stop supporting the Ukraine or you'll be considered an enemy also. But if the Russians knew nothing else about Turkish history since 1928, it was that Turkey did not respond to threats—they fought back.

Control and access to the Mediterranean from the Black Sea was the responsibility of the Republic of Turkey, and it was an awesome task. The Russian naval fleet in the Black Sea Fleet alone consisted of over two hundred vessels, including submarines and aircraft-carrying cruisers—the Russians classified its smaller aircraft carriers as cruisers because Turkey does not allow aircraft carriers of any nation to transit its waters—and if allowed to break into the Mediterranean intact, it would quickly dominate the entire region. No fewer than five major naval bases, one army base, and three air force bases were stationed in a three-hundred-mile stretch of territory from the island of Cyprus, through the Aegean and the Dardanelles, across the Sea of Marmara, past the Bosporus, and into the Black Sea—half of Turkey's 480,000-man active-duty military, the largest in NATO except for the United States and unified Germany, was stationed in this strategic region.

However, the most important military asset to Turkey was in an oval orbit twenty-nine thousand feet over the Paphlagonia Mountains of northern Turkey, about sixty miles north of the capital city of Ankara—a lone E-3A AWACS (Airborne Warning and Command System) radar plane, owned and manned by multinational NATO technicians and flight crews and commanded by a Turkish colonel. The AWACS plane interfaced with every facet of the Turkish and NATO military establishment in the region.

It was almost midnight when the command radio on the bridge of the frigate *Fatih* crackled to life. "Serpent, this is Diamond, be advised, unidentified aircraft detected at zero-one-three degrees at one-two-zero miles bull's-eye, angels five, airspeed five hundred knots, heading south, number of targets four. We have scrambled Firebrand flight of eight to intercept."

"Diamond, Serpent copies." To Captain Turgut Inonu of the Turkish Navy, skipper of the frigate *Fatih*, the bridge operations chief reported, "Sir, message from the AWACS radar plane, four unidentified high-speed aircraft north of our position, heading south. Eight F-16 interceptors from Merzifon have been scrambled to intercept."

"Very well," Inonu replied. He rose stiffly, stretching the kinks out of his sixty-year-old sea-weary joints. "Sound general quarters. I'm going down to Combat." As the battle stations alert and klaxon alarm sounded, he donned a helmet and life jacket as he left the bridge and headed below.

Captain Turgut Inonu and his small Bosporus task force had received four or five such alerts each and every day since the current Russian crisis began. These were Russian patrol planes, cruising along Turkey's twelve-mile territorial limit over the Black Sea. Most times they were MiG-25R Foxbat reconnaissance planes, the fastest fighter planes in the world, which would sometimes scream past the Turkish flotilla at one and a half times the speed of sound and drop bomblike magnesium flares to take pictures at night—the flares were so bright that shore installations sixty miles away sometimes saw the flares and thought the naval task force was under attack.

The Turkish warships were in international waters, so aircraft could legally fly very close as long as they did not pose a threat or do anything unsafe, but the Russian jets never approached closer than one or two miles. The Russians sometimes sent Tupolev-95 Bear reconnaissance planes as well during the day, and they approached within a half-mile or so from the Turkish ships if they were in international waters, but always with a couple of Turkish F-16 or F-4E fighters on their wing and tail.

It was a common cat-and-mouse game in the Black Sea—Turkey sent F-4E and RF-5A reconnaissance aircraft over Russian ships in the Black Sea every day as well, and even Romania and Bulgaria, both of whom had very small air and naval forces, had overwater patrols these days. Nevertheless, Captain Inonu did not want to appear relaxed or overconfident, even for a moment. The Russians had been pledging they would cease all hostile activities and back off, but they still sent patrol aircraft close to Turkish ships, and that bothered Inonu. The Russians were not successfully demonstrating peaceful intent.

The Combat Information Center on the *Fatih* was a large armored room in the center section of the ship, two decks down from the bridge. It contained two radar consoles for the DA-08 air-search radar; two consoles for the navigation and maneuvering radar controllers; two consoles for the STIR (Separate Track and Illumination Radar) and WM-25 fire control directors, which controlled the Sea Sparrow missiles and the 127-millimeter gun; two sonar operators manning the SQS-56 sonar; two operators manning the radar-warning and signal-gathering systems; and two controller consoles for the TV/infrared/laser fire-control tracking systems for the weapons, one for the front half of the ship and one for the aft hemisphere, which could accurately track and compute attack geometry on aircraft and cruise missiles out to a range of five miles without emitting any telltale electronic energy. Two console operators shared a communications technician/assistant. Each system section (weapons, electronic warfare, and radar) had a director, who reported to the combat officer or ship's captain. Two seamen also manned a lighted manual vertical-plotting board, situated in the center of the compartment in front of the combat officer's station, on which all of the information from the various sensor operators was integrated into a readable pictorial display.

Captain Inonu sat in the combat officer's chair, beside the chief of combat operations who would act as his assistant and communications officer. "Report, Lieutenant," Inonu ordered as he put on a set of headphones and made himself comfortable in the combat officer's seat.

"The ship is at general quarters, sir. Battle stations manned and ready, weapons final check in progress."

"Very well. Communications, this is Combat, broadcast on emergency channels for all aircraft to remain outside ten miles of this task force because of night-flying restrictions and close proximity to resupply vessels. I don't feel like messing around with the Russian Air Force tonight. Radio the contact and our close-approach restriction to task force headquarters at Sariyer." Inonu clicked on the intercom. "Radar, have you picked up those Russian aircraft yet?"

"Negative, sir," the chief of the radar plot section replied. "Should be within range in a few minutes if they stay at five thousand feet. Current position from AWACS plane Diamond has them about one hundred ten miles north of our position." Inonu was ready to acknowledge the call and ask the chief to remind him of the plane's status when the chief radioed back immediately. "Sir, message from Diamond, inbound aircraft were declared an air defense item of interest. Targets now closing at over six hundred knots on a missile attack profile."

"Copy," Inonu said. Dammit, he *knew* it, he *knew* this was going to happen. The fucking Russians! "Combat, go passive." On intercom, he ordered, "Helm, Combat, get the feed from the AWACS plane and put us on the attack forty-five, and make sure we screen the *Akar* as much as possible. EW, begin radar countermeasures and decoy dispersal. Signal the task force to disperse and begin countermeasure procedures." On the shipwide intercom, he said, "All hands, this is the captain in Combat. Air defense is tracking inbound Russian aircraft on a possible attack profile. Go to blackout procedures, go passive on all transmitters, initiate radar decoy procedures. Report in by section when passive condition is set."

"Message from fleet, sir."

"Later. Status report first, all sections."

The one hundred and eighty crewmen of the *Fatih*, along with the thirty-eight crewmen on each of the patrol escorts, configured their ships for combat operations within seconds. All electronic transmissions that might be intercepted and used as a homing beacon were extinguished; the *Fatih* could aim its Sea Sparrow missiles and the 127-millimeter dual-purpose gun with steering signals from the NATO radar plane until the targets got within firing range. The helmsman would receive positioning cues from radar plot to position the frigate "on the forty-five"—at a 45-degree angle pointing toward the incoming planes—they could freely swivel the cannon, the Sea Sparrow launcher, and the two Sea Zenith close-in cannon mounts both before and after the planes passed by, and also present as small a radar cross-section as possible to the incoming planes in case they launched an attack.

The helmsman would also try to position the ship as much as possible between the Russian planes and the replenishment oiler *Akar* to protect it from an antiship-missile attack. Although the *Akar* was liberally armed with six antiaircraft-artillery guns and a Mark 34 fire control radar, its huge size and poor performance underway made it an inviting target. All four Turkish ships carried radar decoys, which were small, boatlike radar reflectors with heat and electronic emitters on board that would act as decoys to radar-guided antiship missiles. As a last-ditch measure, all four vessels could fire chaff rockets to try to decoy a missile away from the ship, and *Fatih* had two Sea Zenith close-in weapon system mounts, which used four-barreled radar-guided 25-millimeter cannons to try to destroy an incoming missile seconds before impact.

"Position of the inbounds?" Inonu yelled out. He did not need to address his request to anyone in particular—the radar director should know that information or direct his technicians to respond.

"AWACS has the inbounds one hundred miles north, approaching at six hundred knots, altitude now three thousand feet."

"Very well." On intercom, Inonu radioed, "Communications, this is Combat, go ahead with instructions from fleet headquarters."

"Yes, sir. Fleet requests you protect the oiler to the

maximum extent possible and detach it as soon as possible," the communications officer replied.

"That's it?"

"Message ends, sir."

Great, Inonu thought. *Not even a "good luck" or a "hang tough."* Shit. "Comm, I want instructions from Fleet on how to handle this hostile, not a wish list. Request instructions."

Inonu turned to the ship's combat officer, a young man named Mesut Ecevit, on his first extended patrol in a frigate after commanding a patrol boat for many years. "What am I forgetting, Lieutenant?" Inonu asked. "Decoys, blackout, passive routine—what else should we be doing?"

The young crewman thought briefly, then responded, "We could get the helicopter airborne . . . perhaps give the bomber crews something in their face to worry about."

"Good thought, Lieutenant. I knew there was a reason we got you off the patrol boats." On shipwide intercom, Inonu radioed, "Flight, Combat, launch the patrol helicopter, have him execute full decoy operations—lights, chaff, radio, the works." His acknowledgment was the warning to all crewmembers that the helicopter was being launched. The AB-121 patrol helicopter, an American UH-1N Huey helicopter modified for maritime patrol duties, could bring a large Sea Eagle surface-search radar aloft, and he would drop chaff and turn on searchlights and broadcast warning messages to the inbound aircraft—suitably separated from the frigate, of course.

The helicopter would also be available for rescue operations—but Inonu didn't want to think about that.

General Bruce Eyers was furious to the point of apoplexy. There, to his amazement, stretched out on the tarmac in front of him, were eighty MiG-23 Flogger-G fighters belonging to the Ukrainian Republic. Half were lined up on the main taxiway of Kayseri Air Base right up to the runway hold line; the other half, the fighters not carrying missiles, were lined up on the taxiways parallel to Kayseri's smaller parallel runway. Two MiGs were on each runway's hold line, ready for a formation takeoff, and the rest were lined up staggered behind it with only thirty feet between tailpipe and pitot boom. All but the last twenty aircraft or so had engines running—the rest had small, truck-towed pneumatic start carts parked underneath the fighter's left wing, ready to shoot high-pressure smoke into the fourth-stage compressor section to start the big Tumansky turbine turning in just a few seconds.

Eyers directed his Turkish driver to park his car right in front of the lead fighter's nose, and after some hesitation and a lot of consternation, the driver finally complied. Eyers considered running out and ordering the pilot to shut down, cracked the door open, thought better about approaching the MiG with its engine running, and grabbed the car's UHF radio. "Lead MiG-23 aircraft, both of you, shut down your engines immediately. That's an order!" There was no response. "I said, shut down your engines! *Now!*" Still no response.

Eyers forgot about the incredible engine noise, stepped out of the sedan, swaggered up to the lead pilot's left side about fifty feet in front of the left engine intake, drew his Colt .45 automatic pistol, and fired two shots into the sky. The muzzle flash in the darkness was big and bright, and the message was unmistakable. Eyers then lowered the muzzle and aimed the gun at the MiG-23's engine intake. A single bullet ricocheting around in the intake would certainly destroy the engine in just a few seconds. Turkish Air Force security vehicles screeched out to the runway hold line, and several soldiers aimed their rifles at Eyers. He ignored them. Eyers raised his left hand, showing five fingers, the gun still aimed at the left engine intake. He then lowered one finger, then another, then another. . . .

The lead MiG-23's engine abruptly began to spool down, and the leader's wingman followed suit. All the rest of the MiG-23s waiting for takeoff kept their engines running, but their path was effectively blocked. Eyers signaled to the lead pilot to open his canopy and step down, and after a few moments, he complied. The canopy swung open a small ladder extended on the left side of the plane, and the pilot stepped onto the runway and walked over to Eyers.

The lead pilot, to no one's surprise, was Colonel of Aviation Pavlo Tychina.

"What in hell do you think you're doing, Colonel?" Eyers yelled over the noise of the other fighters lined up ready for takeoff. He made a "kill your engine" signal to the other fighters, but it was doubtful anyone could see him or would obey him if they did. "Who gave you permission to taxi these planes for takeoff?"

"Permission? No permission," Tychina shouted over the noise. "Air attack in progress. Russian bombers attack Turkish ships. We help fight."

"How did you know an attack was in progress?"

"We hear on radio."

"What radio? Who gave you a damned radio?" thundered Eyers, ready to chew nails.

"No one give," Tychina yelled. "Airplanes has radio. We do listening watch—one plane for each frequency. Easy." Eyers understood: Tychina had his pilots set up a radio listening watch using the aircraft radios—one for high-frequency single-sideband, one for UHF, one for VHF. With an AWACS plane orbiting at twenty-nine thousand feet and with air defense broadcasts relayed across the country, it would be easy for the Ukrainians to pick up the action.

"You're saying that *no one* gave you permission to move these planes?" Eyers roared, all but spitting bullets. "I thought I ordered you to *sit tight* until NATO decided what to do with you."

"No. We not wait. Turkey under attack by Russia."

"I don't give a shit!" Eyers shouted. "I will throw your ass in prison, you Ukrainian sonofabitch! You get up in that Tonka toy of yours and order them to shut down *right now!*"

By that time General Sivarek had driven up to the group, and the Turkish security guards moved in. The General surveyed the two lead fighters on the runway hold line and the impressive line of MiG-23 fighters behind them, then looked at Eyers, to the gun still in his hand, and then at Tychina. He returned Tychina's salute, then strode up to Eyers. "What is happening here, General Eyers?" he demanded, eyes ablaze.

"What the hell does it look like, General?" Eyers snorted. "These kids were ready to blast off—at night, without orders from anyone, without permission, without any way of coordinating with Turkish or NATO air defense."

"You are aware of the attack underway on the Black Sea near the Bosporus, are you not, General?" Sivarek asked.

"What does this got to do with it? General, you just can't send a gaggle of Soviet fighters up in the sky, mixing it up with NATO aircraft. Where's the coordination? Where's the plan . . . ?"

"General Eyers . . ." Sivarek began, then paused and turned to Colonel Tychina. "Colonel, order your aircraft back to parking."

"Excuse me, please, General," Tychina said, horrified by the thought, "but we can still act. We must launch now."

"It is too late," Sivarek said. "It would take you at least twenty to thirty minutes to arrive on station, and your fighters have burned too much fuel sitting here on the ground. Order them to return to parking." Tychina had no choice. He saluted Sivarek, ignoring Eyers, turned, and gave the signal to his planes to turn around and head back to parking. A few minutes later, a maintenance truck with a tow bar came along to tow the two lead aircraft.

As they began moving, Eyers turned to Sivarek. "What is going on here, General? You knew about this? You gave permission for these planes to taxi?"

"Standard base-defense response, General Eyers," Sivarek said. "When under air raid alert condition, attempt to launch as many aircraft as possible."

"That's bullshit, General," Eyers spat. Sivarek's eyes narrowed, his anger barely under control. "You launch as many *friendly* aircraft as possible, not *Ukrainian* aircraft!"

"They *are* friendly aircraft, General," Sivarek snapped. "Can you not understand this? They are here to work with NATO, work with Turkey, to fight the Russians."

"That hasn't been determined yet, General," Eyers declared. "NATO hasn't issued any—"

"No, NATO has *not* responded to my country's plea for help," Sivarek interjected. "A squadron of reconnaissance planes that will not arrive until tomorrow morning, two naval vessels that will not arrive for four days, and an air defense battalion that is half the size we need that may not arrive for a *month*. Meanwhile, Turkey suffers an attack by Russia."

"Well, what in hell did you expect these *Ukrainians* to do?"

"They will *fight*, General Eyers!" Sivarek exploded over the roar of Tumansky engines as the MiG-23s began to turn around. "They carry only one hundred rounds of 23-millimeter ammunition and a few missiles, and not all have attack radars. They have almost no fuel for multiple engagements once they reach the Black Sea, and some pilots are suffering the effects of radiation poisoning, but they are willing to fight, and die, for a foreign power. Yes, I gave them permission to taxi, and I was awaiting permission from Ankara to allow them to launch and engage the Russian bombers. You have been quite effective at stopping them."

"Well, you should've let me in on your little scheme here, General," Eyers said. "You gotta get permission from NATO before you—"

"I *do not* need permission to decide what aircraft taxi on this installation, General Eyers."

"This is a NATO base, General," Eyers retorted. "We funded it, we built it, we upgraded it, and we run it."

"This is *Turkey,* General!" Sivarek shot back. "This is *my* country and *my* responsibility. You and NATO are *guests* in this country . . . and not very good ones at that! It is about time you learn this truth. Captain!" Sivarek's aide stepped up to his commander and saluted. "Release the Ukrainian weapons and external stores belonging to the Ukrainian Air Force. Then order all maintenance chiefs to begin assisting the Ukrainians in arming their aircraft. Request that Colonel Tychina meet with me and the general staff as soon as possible so that we may discuss the integration of their forces with the Turkish Air Force."

"You . . . you can't do that!" Eyers exploded, all but throwing his hat on the ground in fury and frustration. "Those planes can't be armed or launched without permission from Brussels! And I don't want those Ukrainian weapons moved until I get a complete inventory!"

"Your orders mean *nothing* anymore, General Eyers," Sivarek said angrily. "Because of you, my country may suffer at the hands of the Russians. I will not allow that to happen again. I will see to it that these Ukrainian aircraft are made ready for air defense and maritime patrol duties immediately, and I will launch them immediately upon receiving permission from *my* government. You may observe and report your observations to Brussels or to whomever you wish, General, but if you attempt to interfere again you will be placed under house arrest. Captain, order the General's driver to take the General to my headquarters or to his quarters or wherever he wishes, but move that vehicle off my runway *immediately.*"

Captain Inonu leaned forward toward the vertical-plot board as the Russian plane icons were erased and moved closer to the center of the board. "Range to inbounds?"

"Ninety miles by AWACS, sir."

Inonu felt as if he were sitting on a triangle-shaped seat. The Russian bomber was well within cruise missile range now, and could be overhead in just nine minutes. It would take the oiler *Akar* nearly twenty minutes just to execute a 180-degree turn and head for shore. *Akar* would have to fight it out just like *Fatih* and the patrol boats. "Air defense weapon stations, check in."

"Sea Sparrow crews, up and ready."

"One-twenty-seven station, up and ready."

"Sea Zenith station forward, up and ready."

"Sea Zenith station aft, up and ready."

"Thank you, weapons." Captain Inonu knew these crews were ready to go—the section chiefs would have reported in if they were not—but Inonu put the report on shipwide intercom and on the task force network so crews on the patrol boats and crews on the oiler *Akar* could hear it. Hopefully it would make each and every crewmember stay on his toes.

"Sir, decoy pattern one laid down," the EW detail reported. A decoy pattern was a thirty-foot-wide by one-hundred-foot group of floating decoys deposited in *Fatih*'s wake that, hopefully, resembled a large vessel on radar or visually.

"Sir, active Golf-band radar, identified as Tu-22M maritime patrol and targeting radar," the EW section reported. "Electronic countermeasures capable and standing by."

No use in staying passive now, Inonu thought—the Russian bomber had a radar fix and a clear shot. Staying radar-silent now would only reduce their own combat effectiveness. "Clear to begin active jamming on downlink and continuous wave signals, EW," Inonu ordered. "Take down the missile targeting radar as soon as possible. Do not jam their nav radar until they close within thirty miles." Most maritime patrol planes had infrared sensors that could see out twenty to thirty miles, so few used radar within that range at night unless they were lining up to attack; but in any case jamming non-weapon-related electronics such as ship-to-ship radio or navigation radar was considered a hostile act. Inonu wanted to avoid any charges that he was pushing for a fight—besides, the fight was coming to him plenty fast.

"Copy, sir. Beginning active radar jamming now."

The "shooting" had started. Even though no actual explosive weapons had been employed by either side, exchanging electronic signals was just as critical and just as important as firing a projectile. Successfully using radar jammers and other electronic tactics could negate billions of lira worth of pyrotechnic weapons. But being in range of jammers meant that they were well within range of other more deadly weapons. Technically, painting a foreign ship with a missile targeting radar was an act of war, but in the Black Sea it was all part of the game. Who would blink first? Who would "escalate" the "conflict" by jamming? Who would shoot first?

"Radar, where are those bombers . . . ?"

"Sir, range sixty miles, altitude two thousand feet, closing speed six hundred ten knots," the radar officer reported, as if he were reading his captain's thoughts. "We are still passive on air-search and targeting radars. Shall we lock on now?"

Sixty miles—very close for a high-speed Russian missile attack. A Russian AS-4 antiship missile had a range of over one hundred miles at the bomber's current altitude. Newer Russian antiradar missiles had a range of only forty to fifty miles, and a gravity bomb attack over a frigate was unlikely, so if the fight wasn't on in the next fifteen to thirty seconds, these Russians were pissing away their opportunity. But with an AWACS radar plane overhead, the frigate had the advantage—no use in wasting it yet. "Negative. Stay passive until ten miles outside Sea Sparrow range. At thirty miles, I want full-spectrum jamming and active missile targeting—I want to leave no doubts in this guy's mind that we mean business. Comm, this is Combat, call fleet headquarters again and request permission to engage hostile targets if they do not alter course. Make the request in the clear on the emergency frequency and in English. Is that understood?"

"Copy, sir, make request for permission to release batteries in the clear." Seconds later, Inonu heard the transmission in his headphones as the broadcast was made on the international maritime emergency channel 16. This would have the ultimate affect of alerting the media and creating a lot of anxiety among all the governments that bordered or accessed the Black Sea, but Inonu wasn't going to back down.

"Sir, Diamond reports the F-16s have intercepted the Russian bombers," Communications reported. "Radar scan only. Count is now six Tupolev-22M bombers. No word yet on weapons or . . . stand by, Combat . . . stand by for priority red alert."

Inonu touched the shipwide intercom button. "All hands, stand by for priority red alert."

"Combat, red priority, red priority, Diamond sends, F-16 interceptor aircraft engaged by Sukhoi-27 fighters. Count unknown."

Kemal help us, Inonu thought, those fighters must've been flying in close formation with the bombers, screening themselves from radar to disguise their numbers. "All hands, this is the captain, Russian bombers had fighter escorts that just engaged our F-16 fighters. Everyone look sharp."

"Sir, copying mayday calls from two F-16 fighters, range forty miles."

"Range to the bombers?"

"Getting telemetry, sir."

Not fast enough, he thought. "Radar, go active, all stations, prepare to engage hostile aircraft."

"Sir, Diamond confirms three F-16 fighters shot down at forty-two-miles range."

"Dammit, I want range to the *bombers,*" Inonu shouted.

"Sir, radar contact aircraft, range twenty-eight miles, speed six-two-five, altitude five hundred feet."

"Copy that. All stations, batteries released, *clear to engage,* repeat, *clear to engage.* Begin active jamming on all frequencies."

But that was exactly what the Russian bombers had been waiting for: seconds after the radars on *Fatih* were reactivated, they heard, "Sir, missiles inbound, many missiles, ballistic flight path."

"All stations, go passive!" Inonu shouted. "Bearing to incoming missiles?"

"Bearing three-five-zero."

"Helm, come to course zero-four-five, best maneuvering speed." That heading would allow all of *Fatih*'s weapons to be brought to bear on the missiles—they had a better chance of destroying the missiles than dodging them. "Chaff rockets, EW, full salvo. Deploy emitter balloons. All stations, check full passive." Another last-ditch decoy device they used, primarily against antiradar missiles, was tiny radar transmitters tied to large helium balloons—they made tempting targets for not-too-smart missiles.

"Balloons away, sir."

"Very well. Bearing to miss—"

But Inonu did not have a chance to finish that last request. He saw the launch indications for the Sea Sparrow missiles, then saw the firing command and heard the steady pounding of the 127-millimeter gun, and then heard the buzzsawlike scream of the Sea Zenith guns, all in rapid succession—and then the sickening crunch of metal and the sudden vertigo as the normally stable deck heeled sharply over to starboard.

"Ah, *poulako,*" Inonu swore. "Damage control, report!" But Inonu didn't need the full report to see that the Sea Sparrow and aft Sea Zenith gun mount were out or faulted—one of the Russian antiradar missiles must've hit aft of the number-two stack.

"Sea Sparrow launcher is out," Inonu's combat officer reported. "Aft Sea Zenith mount faulted . . . air section reports minor damage to helo deck." The report continued with minor fires on the helo deck while the 127-millimeter cannon and the forward Sea Zenith gun battery opened fire again.

"Where are those bombers?"

He was answered by an immense explosion on the portside forecastle, just a few compartments forward from CIC, followed by another smaller explosion abovedecks. Console lights went blank and emergency lights snapped on. "Damage control, report," Inonu yelled into his intercom. No response. He switched to the backup battery-powered intercom—still no response.

The crewmen sitting behind blank consoles were turned toward their captain, waiting for their orders. None had risen out of their seats, although they clearly heard the sounds of rushing water and knew something bad had happened. Inonu had no choice—deaf and blind down here in CIC, it was no place for his crew.

"One-twenty-seven crew and IR, stay at your posts," Inonu shouted. The 127-millimeter cannon and the passive infrared/laser tracking system were still functioning, and they might get a shot at the Russian bombers still. "All other crewmen, damage-control procedures."

Quickly but orderly, all but four technicians and the section directors rushed for the hatch. Each man departing CIC had a damage-control position topside, and they would stay there until relieved or ordered back to CIC. The CIC section chiefs would try to get the gear working again.

As much as he hated to abandon the post, Inonu's responsibility was now with the ship. Lieutenant Ecevit knew that, and he was standing beside the CIC officer's seat, waiting to take over. Inonu reluctantly rose. "Lieutenant, take over here," the captain said. "Thanks for your work, Mesut. You too, chief. If you pick those bastards up on the IR sensor, blast them to hell for me." The captain clasped his young officer's shoulder and headed topside.

When Inonu made it up on the portside catwalk to take the outside run to the bridge, the sight that greeted him made him freeze in absolute shock. *Fatih* had come through the antiradar-missile attack relatively unscathed—the patrol boat *Poyraz* and the oiler *Akar* had both been hit, and hit hard. The patrol boat looked like it had its fires under control, although occasionally a lick of flame would shoot skyward as a weapon magazine was blown open or another high-pressure line ruptured. *Akar*'s aft crew section, where the radars were located, was burning fiercely in two places. The fires had obviously not reached the fuel storage tanks yet, but there was no sign that the fires were under control either. No searchlights or deck lights were illuminated, and none of the lifeboats or motor launches were unstowed or on deck level—that meant that damage-control procedures were being hampered or were nonexistent.

Inonu jumped as the 127-millimeter cannon boomed once, twice, three times—and then Inonu heard them. They sounded like an approaching freight train, like an avalanche, like what it might sound like seconds before being hit by a speeding car. The Russian bombers careened overhead, slicing crudely through the air, rupturing the skies with their huge engines. Inonu knew what would happen next—he had seen American and Italian bombers do attacks on Turkish ships before, but they had only been simulated then—and he covered his ears tightly. . . .

The supersonic *boooms*, three of them, rolled over the *Fatih* seconds later, far louder than his 127-millimeter gun, louder than any gun Inonu had ever heard. The shock wave was so solid against the chill night air that he thought he could feel it, maybe sidestep it or cruise around it. He heard the shock wave retreat across the sea like a giant knife slicing through paper at a thousand miles per hour. Kemal be blessed, he hoped to turn one thousand years of age before he heard *that* sound. . . .

Inonu had reached the final ladder that led to the bridge when he realized that the Russian bombers had deliberately flown overhead, but had not dropped any bombs or launched any more missiles. Was the antiradar-missile attack going to be all . . . ? No, he realized, there had to be more. "Mine countermeasures!" he shouted as he raced up the ladder to the bridge. It was too loud to be heard, but maybe a lookout would hear him. "Release torpedo decoys, damn you! Lookouts to the forward rail! Watch for mines."

But it was too late.

After launching several AS-12 antiradar missiles from long range, the Tupolev-22M bombers had sown strings of shallow E45-75 torpedoes in the path of the frigate and the patrol boats. Activated by the ship's engine sounds or by detecting the ship's magnetic influence, the torpedoes activated their electric motors and acoustic sensors, maneuvered themselves around, then launched themselves at their targets at high speed. Before anyone could react, three torpedoes had hit the frigate *Fatih* and two had hit the stricken patrol boat *Poyraz*. The weapons were small—the torpedoes' size was spent in speed and maneuverability, not explosive power—but their effects were devastating enough. *Fatih* was crippled and listing badly in less than fifteen minutes; the patrol boat *Poyraz* had capsized, with twelve men trapped belowdecks, in less than half that time.

32

Over the Eastern Mediterranean Sea
The Next Morning

GOOD THING THE DIGITAL AVIONICS AND MULTI-FUNCTION Displays on the RF-111G Vampire translated English measurements into metric, Rebecca Furness thought as she keyed the mike button on her throttle quadrant. "Ankara Air Control Center, Thunder One-Zero flight is with you, level at eight thousand meters, over."

The voice that replied had twinges of Turkish and British accents in it, which made Furness smile—she had certainly heard a wide variety of accents on this trip. "Thunder Flight, this is Ankara Air Control Center, I read you, level at eight thousand. Turn left heading zero-seven-zero, descend and maintain five thousand meters."

"Thunder One-Zero flight, roger, left to zero-seven-zero, leaving eight for five thousand meters."

The new heading put the island of Cyprus on their right wing and the Taurus Mountains of southern Turkey on their left. Ahead about eighty miles was the Nur border region between Syria and Turkey, the scene of much combat over the past few years during the Middle East War of 1993 and 1994. In 1993, a combined military effort by Syria, Jordan, Iraq, and Yemen to rearm and strengthen Iraq, weaken Israel, and take over the

Persian Gulf region (the move was advertised as an attempt to form a strong pan-Islamic fundamentalist nation) threw most of this area in chaos. The decisive military power in the region turned out to be Turkey. With its strengthened military forces, its strategic location, its Islamic heritage, and its strong Western ties, it proved to be a vital factor in allowing the West to drive back a broad-front attack by the Islamic Coalition, as well as negotiate a true cease-fire with the Muslim nations.

This was a pretty pitiful show for such an important ally, Furness thought as she checked out her wingmen around her. Furness was leading a gaggle of twelve RF-111G Vampire bombers, representing the White House response to Turkey's call for help. The flight was spread out into three groups of four, stacked down five hundred feet from one another and spread out to about two miles apart. Although they were very heavily armed—with defensive weapons only, but potent nonetheless—Rebecca would have expected a much greater response from so powerful a friend, in such a volatile part of the world, especially after that ally had just been attacked. When Kuwait was attacked, the United States had fifty F-15C Eagle fighters from the First Tactical Fighter Squadron in Saudi Arabia in twelve hours, and within three days another two hundred warplanes, mostly Reservists and National Guardsmen, were in the Kuwaiti Theater of Operations.

Twelve twenty-five-year-old RF-111G Vampires were sure to be welcomed, but it was not that impressive. She was sure part of it had to do with the President's decidedly less-aggressive stances than his war-hero predecessor.

"Got the Seyhan River valley and Adana on radar, seventy miles straight ahead," Mark Fogelman said. He switched to the tactical electronic warfare threat display and peered into the "feed bag," the black plastic hood around the multifunction cathode ray tube before him. "I'm picking up Echo-3-band search radar from Adana, from Latakia, Syria, in front of us, and from Nicosia behind us. Latakia has a Bar Lock search and intercept radar, probably for an SA-5 SAM system—and I'm picking up Hotel-band Square Pair fire control signals from Latakia, but they aren't locked on to us. Echo-band height finders out there, associated with the SA-5. Too early to get an ID on the missile, but the bearing is from Syria, so I'm guessing SA-5 system." He took his eyes out of the CRT hood, called up the missile launch control page for the AGM-88C HARM (High-speed Anti-Radiation Missile) on his right-side Multi-Function Display, and checked the indication on the CRT. "I've got a good HARM acquisition on the Echo- and Hotel-band radars. Thirty more miles east, and we can kill them. Still not picking up the Lima- or Kilo-band Patriot or Hawk radars in Turkey—they must've been nice and shut them down for us." He took his eyes out of the scope and searched the early morning skies until he located each and every one of the Bravo Flight aircraft. "The flight looks good—looks like people are starting to close in a little. They must be getting antsy with all the bad guys painting us out there."

"Copy, Mark. Thanks."

"Copy" was not nearly an appropriate enough response for the stunning transformation that had come over Mark Fogelman. He was a totally different airman. The old Fogelman would have been asleep five minutes into the flight and would have stayed that way until landing—this Fogelman had been awake the entire trip, nearly eighteen hours now. The old Fogelman would have not touched the radar and would *never* have practiced using the electronic warfare suite to locate and identify radar systems around them—this Fogelman had been giving Rebecca a near nonstop recitation on every electromagnetic bleep within range of their sensors. He had even dry-fired his HARM missiles at simulated targets and run down the proper flight procedures for engaging different threats. The old Fogelman never cared about formation procedures and had considered the control stick and throttles on the right side of the cockpit a nuisance. This Fogelman had been right on top of his formation procedures, constantly checking on his wingmen, recommending flight leader changes and position changes in case someone's neck was getting tired from always looking in the same direction. He was on the radios constantly, talking to air traffic control and overwater-flight following, and he was into his second roll of SATCOM printer paper because he was sending and receiving so many satellite "ops normal" and weather reports. The most shocking request came when Mark actually asked to fly the Vampire into air refueling contact position behind a tanker. To Rebecca's surprise, he was actually damn good at it, and had managed to stay in contact position for a good five minutes until a small burst of turbulence knocked him off the boom and he shyly declined to go back in again.

Fogelman finished resetting the altitude bug on the altimeter tape, after converting the desired metric altitude to feet. "Altitude bug set, five thousand to level. Radio two backup set to Incirlik tower frequency."

It was a good thing he was finally acting like a true officer, because the trip across the Atlantic was a real sonofabitch. Rebecca had filled up three plastic piddle packs. But Fogelman didn't make one remark about her fidgeting or her quiet cursing, never tried to sneak a peek or embarrass her. At one time she thought he was adjusting one of his rearview mirrors toward her crotch, but the wingmen were shifting positions and he was moving his mirrors to keep *them* in sight. The lack of confrontation was almost a letdown, but a brush with death would probably change even Satan himself.

After leveling off at five thousand meters, then accepting and complying with another descent to 4,200 meters, or about 14,000 feet, Fogelman tuned the backup radio to the Incirlik Air Base ATIS (Automated Terminal Information System) frequency and was about to direct the rest of the flight to the same frequency when they heard: "Thunder Flight, you have traffic at your eleven o'clock, fifty miles, flight of four F-16 aircraft. MARSA procedures are in effect." Ankara Air Control Center directed the flight of Vampires to go to their frequency and report to them when they were in contact. It was common for fighters of foreign countries, especially in wartime situations, to escort allied planes through their airspace; Furness had been expecting it.

By wagging her wings, Furness directed the flight of Vampires to close up into fingertip formation, then checked in with the Turkish F-16 flight leader and checked in her flight on the new frequency. When the twelve Vampires were back in close formation, the four F-16 fighters bracketed them in, one fighter in the lead and the others above and behind Charlie Flight. The leader then began to descend; Furness had no choice but to follow. The F-16 leader descended below 12,800 feet, the minimum safe altitude for the Incirlik area. The weather was clear and the visibility was good, but it was still very unusual. "Where in hell are we going?" Furness finally asked.

The flight dropped below 12,000 feet, then below 10,000 feet—now the tops of the Taurus Mountains of southern Turkey were well above them. "We're in the Cardasik River valley,"

Fogelman said. He reached behind his seat and extracted the Turkey FLIP (Flight Information Publication), scanned it, and then set several frequencies into the navigation radios and into the nav computers. The VOR and TACAN radios centered on a station straight ahead, and soon the ILS (Instrument Landing System) director bars became active. "It looks like they're taking us to Kayseri," Fogelman said. "It's a Turkish training base, north of a very large industrial city. Very high terrain south, a big-ass mountain over 12,800 feet high. Two parallel runways, two-six left and right." He reached over and set in the runway heading in Rebecca's horizontal situation indicator to make it easier for her to visualize the runway setup—to her knowledge that was the first time he had ever reached across the center of the cockpit to adjust one of the pilot's flight instruments. "Northern runway is the longest, main part of the base north. Inertial winds are from the west, so we'll probably be landing on two-six left. Field elevation 3,506 feet. Normally has only F-5 and a few F-16s stationed there. Defended by Hawk missile batteries—they probably have Patriot by now—but I'm not picking up anything but search radar and navigation beacons."

"Mark, I'm sorry about all the things I've ever said or thought about you," Furness said. "Your crew coordination on this deployment has been great. After wanting to wring your neck for so long, now I couldn't stand the thought of you on anyone else's crew—I mean that. I think you should get smacked in the head more often."

"Thanks." Fogelman chuckled. "You saved my life, what can I say?" He scanned around outside until the other planes were in fingertip formation, then pointed out the window straight ahead: "Field in sight."

The formation of planes flew west of the city, descended to five thousand feet as they swept north of the field, then turned westbound and lined up on the long runway at Kayseri. The F-16s joined up when the Vampires were five miles from the end of the runway, flew to midfield, then executed an overhead break to enter the visual pattern for landing. Furness did a quick wing jab to the left, indicating that each formation line get in fingertip formation on the left side for a right break, then she swept her wings back slowly to 54 degrees and set 350 knots airspeed. This fast tactical approach allowed the crews to survey the landing runway while still protecting themselves from any ground threats that might unexpectedly pop up.

"Formation's in," Fogelman reported. "Everyone looks good. Field elevation set in the altimeter bug, and I've got radar altitude plus field elevation set for the altimeter setting. Ready with the before-landing checklist. I . . ." He hesitated, checked his threat indicators and the RHAWS (Radar Homing And Warning System) scope, and tapped it in confusion. "I just picked up an India-band search radar, low PRF, no bearing or identification. Could be another aircraft just hit us with a ranging radar. See anything out your side?"

Furness scanned the skies all around them, then shook her head. "Nope, it's clear. Nothing locked on to us?"

"It's gone now," Fogelman said. "Too short for a missile track."

"Well, I hope if they got Hawks or Patriots down there, they'll use them if any bad guys show up," Furness said. "Let's go with the checklist."

As the formation of Vampires passed over the airfield, Fogelman took a moment to scan the field. He saw an enormous number of fighters parked on the northeast ramp—well over a hundred, with service vehicles, trucks, and weapons-loading equipment scattered around. "Looks like we're not the only ones here," he said to Rebecca. "Shitload of planes—they look like British Tornados or Jaguars. NATO must be deploying to this base to set up air ops against the Russians. Jeez, I wish they'd tell us what the hell is going on. I see a Hawk missile site, but no Patriots." He returned his scan to the wingmen as Furness passed midfield and began a 60-degree right break to the overhead pattern for landing. As she continued the break and the airspeed bled away, she eased the wings forward to 16 degrees, and when she rolled out parallel to the runway, she lowered the landing gear handle, extended the slats and one notch of flaps, and began a slow 190-knot descent for landing. Her Bravo Flight wingmen accomplished the same overhead break every five seconds, while Charlie Flight did the same ten seconds afterward.

"I got a green light from the tower," Fogelman said. Visibility for the pilot out the right side of the cockpit was poor, so she relied on the navigator to scan the touchdown area for her. "Runway's clear, no arresting cable, no ice or snow that I can see. Couple of planes on the taxiway moving toward the hammerhead . . . Jesus, what kind of planes are *those?*"

"Lead, *bandits!"* someone shouted on the primary radio. "Ten o'clock high!"

Rebecca's head snapped left and her eyes scanned the sky . . . and there, diving down at them from very close in, was a Russian Sukhoi-17 fighter-bomber. Its outline was unmistakable—a long, thin frame, blunt nose, sharply swept wings with the outer section swept forward for better slow-speed performance. It was carrying two small air-to-air missiles that resembled Sidewinders. The jet was low and slow, but it had Rebecca right in its sights. "Lead, break right!" Joe Johnson shouted again in the command radio. "It's rolling into you! We got it locked up!"

"Don't you dare shoot at me," a familiar voice came on the frequency in English. "Hold your fire, number two—don't you dare put a Sidewinder up my tail. We're just overshooting a little. Stand by." To their amazement, when the Sukhoi-17 finally rolled out right beside Furness' plane, they saw none other than Lieutenant Colonel Daren Mace in the rear seat of the tandem two-place Russian bomber. They then noticed there was no red star or flag on the tail—instead, in large black Latin letters on the camouflaged side were the words FREEZ UKRAYINA AIR FORCE. Even more incredible, the Su-17 was carrying a strange pod that they recognized as an AN/AQQ-901 electronics interface and data pod on one side, and on the other side, it carried an AGM-88C HARM antiradar missile.

"Let us go first—we're a little skosh on fuel," Daren Mace radioed, waving happily at Rebecca. With that, the fighter-bomber accelerated ahead of the lead RF-111G, then turned abruptly toward the runway when it was less than one hundred yards in front of Furness' bomber. Rebecca had to extend a bit to let the Ukrainian fighter land, but in just a few seconds she began her turn to final and set up for the landing. After landing and clearing the runway, Rebecca waited on the main taxiway behind a yellow Follow Me truck as the rest of her flight landed and taxied behind her; then, with wings swept back to 54 degrees, they taxied together to the parking ramp.

The Americans could not believe what they saw—rows and rows of Soviet-made fighters, all loaded with weapons, parked beside the taxiway as far as the eye could see. "Man, this is incredible," Fogelman exclaimed. "They're all MiG-23 Floggers except the blunt-nosed one, which is the Su-17 Fitter, right?"

"Not quite," Furness said. "The ones with the bullet-shaped radomes are the MiG-23 fighters. The ones with the noses that slope downward are MiG-27 attack planes. God, I don't believe this . . . five or six squadrons of Soviet fighters at a Turkish air base—and *we* land twelve RF-111G bombers right in the middle of them."

The reception for the Americans upon landing was raucous and dramatic. Ukrainian pilots—it was hard not to think of them as Soviets or Russians—were standing on their plane's wings, madly waving American and Turkish flags as the Vampires taxied past. A few crazy Ukrainian pilots ran out onto the taxiway and patted the sides of the Vampire bombers before being chased away by Turkish security patrols. A reviewing stand with American, Turkish, Ukrainian, and NATO flags had been set up in front of what looked like the base operations building. The Follow Me truck led the RF-111Gs around the reviewing stand into parking places, and one by one they lined up to the left of Furness' plane, precisely aligning themselves on her. Using hand signals, Furness directed the other aircraft to sweep their wings forward, open bomb bay doors, run up engines to scavenge oil, shut down engines, and open their canopies. Maintenance men put boarding ladders on both sides of the plane, and long red carpets were thrown out leading from the ladder to the reviewing stand, where several vehicles had pulled up and officers began stepping onto the reviewing stand.

The impromptu arrival show worked to perfection, and the growing crowd of pilots and maintenance technicians applauded and cheered wildly . . .

. . . until Rebecca Furness removed her helmet and stepped out of the cockpit, her brown hair unfurling.

The Turkish crews were on the right with a small group of Americans, and it was as if a huge switch in heaven had been thrown and all sound was canceled on that side of the reviewing stand. The Turkish aircrews and commanders were stunned. *A woman is climbing down out of the lead aircraft?* Their astonishment visibly grew as Lynn Ogden and Paula Norton appeared as well. But as if to highlight the silenced Turkish reaction, the Ukrainian crews were cheering, whistling, jumping up and down and yelling like crazy, as if the three flyers were wearing nothing but grass skirts. The Americans were politely clapping and waving, happy to see their fellow wing members arrive safe and sound. The throng of Ukrainian pilots couldn't be held back any longer, and a large group of them rushed forward, picked up Rebecca and the other two women, and carried them triumphantly on their shoulders to the foot of the reviewing stand. Soon there was a large crowd of crewmembers surrounding the foot of the podium.

Brigadier General Erdal Sivarek looked as if he was going to explode with indignation as the three women were deposited at his feet. He fidgeted slightly, twitching as if he didn't know what to do with his hands. His hesitation gave the crews enough time to assemble in front of the podium, and Furness called them to attention. She then stepped forward and said in a loud voice, "Sir, the Seven-Fifteenth Tactical Squadron, reporting as ordered."

Sivarek finally exploded, shouting something in Turkish; then: "Is this some kind of joke? Who is this woman? General, you will explain this to me. *What is this woman doing here?*"

Major General Bruce Eyers was hopelessly confused. He looked Furness over—she was still holding her salute, which only appeared to be making Sivarek and his staff officers angrier by the second—and decided she was doing nothing improper. He shot her a quick salute so she would lower her arm, then stepped over to Sivarek and asked, "What's the problem here, General? This is the crew from Plattsburgh—the RF-111G unit you were told about."

"She is a *woman,* General Eyers," Sivarek said angrily. "You Americans sent a . . . a *woman,* in a *flight suit,* to *my* base, at a time like this?"

"It's no big deal, General," Eyers said easily. "I'm sure she's a good stick. I know they're just Reservists, but they got some—"

"Reservists? These are *Reservists?* What is the meaning of this insult, Eyers? Your President sends female Reservists to my country at our hour of need?"

"Get a grip on yourself, General," Eyers said, chuckling and slapping the Turkish general hard on the shoulder, which he shrugged off. He pointed to the RF-111Gs parked in front of them and said, "She brought those things in okay, didn't she?"

"Then she is just a ferry pilot?" Sivarek asked. "She is simply bringing the planes here, and the pilots are arriving in more aircraft?"

"Excuse me, sir," Furness said, "but I'm not a ferry pilot. I'm Bravo Flight commander of the Seven-Fifteenth Tactical Squadron. All we need is fuel and area charts, and we're ready to begin air operations."

Sivarek silenced her with a sharp word in Turkish that was so loud and so harsh that his staff officers nearby jumped in surprise. One officer quickly rushed forward and, jabbering away in Turkish, stepped in between Sivarek and Furness. Furness stumbled backward, surprised more than hurt or insulted.

But what really surprised her was the reaction from Daren Mace, who was standing on the podium beside Lieutenant Colonel Hembree, the 715th Tactical Squadron commander, and Colonel Lafferty, the 394th Air Battle Wing vice commander, who had flown in with Mace and the other maintenance and support personnel the night before; not to mention Mark Fogelman. Mace grabbed the Turkish officer from behind and whipped him around so they were face-to-face. Fogelman rushed forward and, simultaneously with Mace, body-tackled the Turkish officer down onto the tarmac.

Bedlam erupted. Turkish security guards shouldered their rifles and began pulling at the Americans, and that's when all of the Plattsburgh flyers leaped onto the Turks. More Turkish guards rushed to their comrades' assistance—and that's when the Ukrainian flyers rushed the podium. It was unclear exactly what they were doing, but they generally were trying to keep the guards' M-16 rifles from going off in anyone's face and trying to help Rebecca Furness up off the ramp and into their eager arms. The Ukrainians' charge immediately prompted the Turkish flyers, who were clearly outnumbered but as enraged as wild dogs, to enter the melee. Officers were screaming orders. General Sivarek was shouting orders in Turkish, English, Russian, and Arabic, any language he could think of to make himself understood.

But the only thing that stopped the brawl was the sudden blare of a siren just outside the base operations building. It was echoed by several other sirens on the flight line and by others on the base proper. The Turkish, then the Ukrainian pilots quickly untangled themselves and began running for their planes. "Air raid!" Mace shouted, leaping to his feet as soon as the pile of men got off him. "It's an air raid siren!"

"Jesus!" Lafferty exclaimed, shaking his head. "Get a crew to bring start carts over here, and another crew to get that reviewing stand away from the planes. Furness, tell your crews to taxi your planes toward those aircraft shelters over there. *Move!*"

The American flyers sprinted for their planes and got into the cockpit. Americans and Turks who had been wrestling with each other just thirty seconds earlier, were now side by side hauling heavy external power carts from next to the base operations building to the waiting Vampires, while Turkish guards were helping Daren Mace and a few Ukrainian pilots with broken planes drag the portable reviewing stand out of the way.

Fogelman raced around his bomber pulling chocks and checking to see if any maintenance access panels had been opened, then climbed up into the cockpit and kicked the boarding ladder away clear of the wheels. "Ladder's clear!" he shouted to Furness as she climbed inside the cockpit and retrieved her helmet. "Chocks pulled, panels closed, I'm ready to taxi."

"Okay," Furness shouted. But they didn't need to hurry. The power cart was going to another plane first, it was the only one in sight, and there were no tow vehicles or tow bars moving toward them at all. "Nice going, Mark, but we're not going anywhere right now."

A few moments later their crew chief, Staff Sergeant Ken Brodie, came by and put their ladders back up on the bombers. "Just one power cart out here," he explained. "Colonel Lafferty wants us in the air raid shelter until they're ready to start or tow us." It was one of the most painful things they had ever done to leave their Vampire behind, armed and ready to fly, and retreat to the safety of the air raid shelter under base operations. Before they reached the front doors, they heard a tremendous double *booom!* that rattled windows and seemed to shake the ground. Furness jumped. Fogelman, Brodie, and the assistant crew chief, Bordus, ran on ahead.

But Furness saw some movement out of the corner of her eye and saw Daren Mace dragging a long chain from the fire station beside the base operations building out to the bombers, and immediately she ran over to him. "What are you doing, Daren? They said report to the shelters."

"I talked the firemen into towing planes off the ramp with the fire trucks," Mace said. "I want to get these planes at least out of the open. You better get inside."

But she grabbed the chain and began pulling it toward the planes as well. "At least let's do my plane first," she said.

"Deal."

As they dragged the heavy chain out to Furness' plane and began wrapping it around the nosewheel, she said to him, "Did you start that fight over me, Daren?"

"Heck no," he lied with a smile. "I was trying to stop your wizzo from pounding the shit out of that Turkish officer. Man, he was great."

They finished tying the chain around the nosewheel, then extended it out away from the nose and laid it out on the ramp, ready for the fire truck to hook up. Furness said, "You're a lousy liar, Daren. Thank you. It's nice to have you here."

"Right now, I wish we were back at that bed-and-breakfast," Mace said. "The last thing I want is—*holy shit, look out!*"

Furness turned toward the runway to where Daren was pointing. Careening out of the clear morning sky on the end of a small stabilizer parachute was a string of two large silver bombs, aligned perfectly with the runway centerline. Except for videotapes of training exercises or file footage from Vietnam, neither of them had actually ever seen a parachute-retarded bomb hitting a target before. They saw the weapon at about two thousand feet in the air, and it fell very quickly.

Its shape, its silver color, its thin profile, its large stabilizer 'chute—it looked like an American B61 thermonuclear gravity bomb.

For a brief instant, Furness considered running for the air raid shelter, or at least dropping to the ground and covering her eyes. But that was ridiculous and she knew it. A B61 had the explosive power of twenty Hiroshima bombs and would destroy this base, the nearby city of Kayseri, and everything around it for a distance of thirty miles. She didn't know what a Russian neutron bomb looked like, but at this distance even a fractional-yield nuclear device would kill.

"That boom must've been a sonic boom," Mace said in a low voice. He flashed the middle finger of his right hand at where he guessed the retreating aircraft was in the sky. "A supersonic bomber at high altitude. Long time-of-fall—the plane must've been really up there, maybe fifty or sixty thousand feet. He's gonna get a pretty good bomb score. Lucky son of a bitch."

All Rebecca could think about doing was reaching for Daren Mace's hand as she watched the bombs speed toward the center of the runway. She was pleased to find that he was reaching for her hand as well.

PART FIVE

**The essence of war is violence.
Moderation in war is imbecility.
—John A. Fisher**

33

Plattsburgh Air Force Base, New York
That Same Time

"FOR THE ALERT FORCE, FOR THE ALERT FORCE, KLAXON, KLAXON, Klaxon."

Those words blared out of the loudspeakers at the RF-111G Vampire strategic alert facility at Plattsburgh Air Force Base, and at other alert facilities around the country: a B-1B Lancer supersonic heavy bomber wing in Rapid City, South Dakota, carrying cruise missiles and short-range nuclear attack missiles; an F-111F medium bomber wing, also loaded with nuclear SRAMs, in Clovis, New Mexico; a B-52H Stratofortress heavy bomber wing in Spokane, Washington, all carrying cruise missiles; and a B-2 Black Knight stealth bomber wing in Whiteman, Missouri, the aircraft most capable of penetrating stiff Russian air defenses and therefore the only group still carrying nuclear gravity bombs. The TAAN (Tactical Aircrew Alert Network) radios clipped to aircrews' elastic flight suit waistbands crackled to life with those fateful words, heard by anyone for the first time in over four years, and heard for the first time by one-fourth of the nation's crewmembers—the ones who had never pulled strategic alert before.

The phrase "klaxon klaxon klaxon" was not just a term for a loud raucous horn repeated three times—it was an order, with all the force of federal and military law behind it. Upon hearing those words, or a klaxon sound for longer than three seconds, or by seeing a rotating yellow light on street corners on base or flashing lights marked "Alert" in theaters or hospitals, aircrews on strategic nuclear alert were directed to report to the aircraft, start engines, copy and decode the subsequent coded message that would be read on the network, and comply with the message's instructions. The crews could act like cops on a high-speed chase or fire trucks responding to a fire—they could (cautiously) speed through intersections, drive on aircraft taxiways and runways, even commandeer cars. At Plattsburgh all that was unnecessary: because of bad weather and the base's close proximity to Russian ballistic missile submarines in the Atlantic, the crews were restricted to the alert facility.

Air Force Reserve major Laura Alena, a thirty-seven-year-old computer-aided design engineer in civilian life, had just kicked off her boots and was about to unzip her flight suit and get some sleep when the klaxon sounded. After being in the Air Force Reserves only four years, she had never heard a klaxon before, but there was no mistaking what it was. The sound was inescapably loud, tearing at your auditory nerves, and Alena found herself leaping to her feet.

Her roommate, Captain Heather Cromwell, the Sortie Four weapons officer, was sound asleep when the klaxon went off. She kicked off the old rough green military horse blankets which were tangled around her feet and somehow got up without killing herself. "Shit!" Cromwell yelped, almost rolling off the wrong side of the bed and smacking into the whitewashed concrete wall.

Alena reached for the light switch and flipped it on, instantly blinding them both. "Get dressed, Heather!" Alena shouted. "Don't forget your thermals."

Cromwell fumbled for her thermal underwear and flight suit—she had made the mistake of hanging all her clothes up neatly in the wardrobes, and for a brief moment she couldn't find anything. "Do you think this is an exercise, Laura?"

"No. They briefed us there wouldn't be any exercises," Alena replied. She was formerly a KC-135 tanker navigator, so she was familiar with strategic alert. In the old days, alert exercises were common and expected—not anymore. "It's the real thing, Heather. Hurry and get dressed."

"Jeez, I . . . I can't believe it." Cromwell used to be a T-37 "Tweet" FAIP (First Assignment Instructor Pilot) for a year before she was RIFed out of the active-duty Air Force, and like Alena, she couldn't get an assignment as a pilot and was forced to retrain as a navigator and weapons officer. She spent several years as a Reserve KC-135 tanker navigator before cross-training to the RF-111G Vampire, and had no exposure to strategic alert. As a civilian she was the wife of the president of a major New York construction firm and a mother of one child. Cromwell was a skilled crewmember and good military officer, but her exposure to the realities of life as a combat aircrewman was limited.

Of course, the same could be said for most of the members of the 715th Tactical Squadron, even those who had once pulled alert in the active-duty Air Force. Nuclear war was supposed to have ended. The RF-111G Vampires, although still called bombers and still retaining a bombing capability, were now only Reserve reconnaissance and standoff missile launchers—they were not supposed to carry nuclear weapons deep into enemy territory.

For many crewmembers, especially the young, inexperienced ones like Captain Heather Cromwell, the alert was like a nightmare.

"We don't know what the alert means, Heather," Alena said. "It could be to reposition the alert force, or just a report to aircraft, or . . . something else. Just stay calm. Don't run in the hallways, but once you get outside the doors, run like hell." She finished zipping up her boots, threw on her cold-weather jacket and flying gloves, and headed out the door.

The klaxon horn, an ancient-looking cast-iron thing, was mounted right outside her door, and Alena could hardly hear herself think. Crewmembers were dashing through the halls, knocking into her mindlessly. "Don't run inside the facility!" she shouted. "Walk until you get outside!" But it didn't do any good. A moment later Cromwell came out of her room, started running right past Laura Alena, and plowed headlong into a crew chief who was running out of his room. The impact sent Cromwell flying, but no one stopped.

"You all right, Heather?" Alena asked as she helped her to her feet.

"Yeah, I'm okay," Cromwell replied shakily. With dozens of crewmembers dashing past them, they headed for the outer doors at a slow trot.

"You sure you're okay?" Alena asked, releasing Cromwell. She seemed pretty steady on her feet.

"I'm fine."

"Good. I'll see you after we get back," Alena said, and sprinted off for her pickup truck.

Her partner, Major Robert Harcourt, and their two crew chiefs were already in the truck with the engine running. "Where were you?" Harcourt shouted as he put the little pickup in gear and stepped on the accelerator.

"Somebody smashed into Heather," Alena replied.

"You worry about your own butt, Laura," Harcourt said angrily. "Cromwell is a spoiled brat who can't stand to be away from her chalet in the mountains."

"Hey, go to hell, Bob," Alena responded. "If it was one of your 'bros' on the deck, you'd be helping him out." That was all the time they had for that argument, and the topic was forgotten as they pulled the truck up to the parking space between the shelters. A security guard with his M-16 rifle at port arms flashed a finger sign, Harcourt gave the countersign, and they were waved into the aircraft shelter.

Alena took enough time to pull the engine inlet cover off the right engine and fling it off to the side of the shelter before getting on the ladder and yelling "Ready!" When she heard Harcourt yell "Up!" in response, she scampered up the ladder and undogged her cockpit canopy, making sure that he was doing the same. Crews that manned nuclear-loaded bombers had to adhere to the "two-officer policy," which meant that two nuclear-certified and knowledgeable officers had to be present when access to nuclear release or nuclear launch systems was possible. From the largest nuclear submarine to the smallest nuclear artillery shell, compliance with the two-officer policy was mandatory.

The RF-111G Vampire was indeed loaded for nuclear war. The 48,000-pound aircraft weighed over 119,000 pounds gross weight, loaded to the gills with fuel and weapons. Along with a full internal fuel load of 32,000 pounds, the Vampire carried four external fuel tanks with 14,400 total pounds of fuel—the outermost fuel tanks were on nonswiveling pylons, so the wings could not be swept back past 26 degrees unless those outer tanks were jettisoned, which would be only after the last refueling and when those tanks were finally empty, before crossing into enemy territory. On the innermost wing pylon, the Vampire carried an AGM-131 short-range attack missile with a 170-kiloton nuclear warhead, and on the outside of the number 3 and 6 pylons the bomber carried an AIM-9P Sidewinder missile for self-defense. Finally, two more AGM-131 attack missiles were nestled in the internal bomb bay.

Both crewmen jumped into the cockpit, strapped in, and put on helmets. While Alena retrieved her decoding documents and booklets, Harcourt flipped on battery power, flicked both starter switches on the center console to CART, and yelled "Clear cartridge start!" His crew chief, standing with a fire extinguisher by the left engine inlet, gave him a thumbs-up, and Harcourt lifted the throttle grips up over the cutoff detent, brought both throttles briefly to military to get a good shot of fuel into the system, and set the throttles to idle. When he lifted the throttle grips, battery power set off two large high-pressure smoke generators installed in each low-pressure engine turbine section, which started the turbines spinning. In less than sixty seconds, both engines were at idle power, and Harcourt began bringing up all aircraft systems.

After monitoring the engine start, Alena turned her attention to the coded message. The Plattsburgh command post was reading a long string of characters on the radio. When the controller said, "I say again, message follows," Alena knew it was the beginning of the message, and she started copying the letters and numbers with a grease pencil on a nearly-frozen plastic sheet, one character per box. When she had the first ten characters, called the "preamble," she began decoding, using the proper day-date decoding book.

The first character told the crew if this was an exercise or an actual message—and it read "actual." "Bob . . . dammit, cross-check this," Alena said. Harcourt stopped what he was doing, double-checked that she was using the right decoding document. It was correct. "It's a 'taxi-to-the-hold-line' message," Alena said after breaking out the preamble.

"Authenticate it," Harcourt said.

"We don't need to," Alena said. "We only authenticate a launch message."

"Hell, I'll authenticate it myself," Harcourt said. He clicked on the command radio: "I got a 'taxi,'" he said. It was not proper procedures, but they were playing with real marbles here, and he wasn't about to screw anything up.

"Taxi," another voice said. They recognized it as the Sortie One pilot. One by one, all six pilots of Alpha Flight reported the same thing.

"We take our time," Harcourt said. "I want a full stored heading alignment, I want you strapped in, and I want . . . I want everything *perfect,* dammit. We're not moving until everything is perfect."

A full stored heading alignment took only three minutes, and Alena reported that her system was ready to fly. She motioned to the green padded containers mounted under the instrument panel glare shield. "Tac doctrine says we gotta use 'em," Alena said. Harcourt hesitated, then nodded, and both crewmen opened the containers.

The crew chiefs watched their crewmembers get ready. Suddenly one of the RF-111Gs, the Sortie Six airplane, began taxiing out of its shelter. Harcourt stood in front of his shelter, waiting for the taxi light to come on his bomber. A second bomber taxied out of the shelter. Then he saw his crewmembers take off their helmets and slip something over their heads that he couldn't quite make out before replacing their helmets. Then they clipped something onto the outside of their helmets.

They were PLZT goggles—electronic flashblindness goggles. The other thing they put on under their helmets must've been eyepatches for use in case the electronic goggles failed or if it was too dark to use the goggles. The crew chiefs had had briefings on them and had seen them demonstrated once, but they were never to be used . . .

. . . unless it was the real thing.

With the goggles and oxygen masks in place, Harcourt and Alena looked like two Darth Vaders sitting in the Vampire cockpit. Harcourt turned on the taxi light, signaling he was ready to taxi. The crew chief kept his arms crossed above his head until the second RF-111 bomber taxied past, then motioned Harcourt to move forward, and they taxied clear of the shelter and onto the parallel runway.

Standing in the dark, freezing cold night, with the roar of six nuclear-loaded RF-111s bombarding him, the Sortie Two crew chief saluted the pilot. The eerie death mask turned toward him, looked at the lone figure for a moment, then slowly returned the salute—possibly for the last time.

34

The White House, Washington, D.C.
That Same Time

"WHAT THE HELL DO YOU MEAN, IT WAS A *LEAFLET DROP?*" the President thundered. "You mean to tell me the Russians flew a supersonic bomber right over Turkey, in broad daylight, right over the base where the American planes *had just landed*, and dropped *leaflets . . . ?*"

"That's exactly what they did, Mr. President," General Freeman acknowledged. They, along with the First Lady and their young daughter; the National Security Advisor, Michael Lifter; two Secret Service agents; and a Navy captain assigned to carry the "football," the briefcase with the codes necessary to execute the nation's nuclear forces, were standing in the pouring rain on the west lawn of the White House, just a few yards away from the whirling blades of Marine One. The large VH-53 helicopter had flown out to retrieve the President and members of the National Security Council when the latest alert was sounded. Seconds earlier, Freeman had received word that no attack was in progress, and the group, now drenched, was heading back into the White House.

The President did not go to the Situation Room, but made his way back to the Oval Office instead. He threw his wet raincoat into a corner and ordered coffee and sandwiches. The

First Lady entered the Oval Office a few minutes later with her hair dry and wearing a business suit—it had to be the fastest cleanup in history—and stood beside her husband. "I would like to know," she said crisply, her hands balled into tight fists at her side, "what in *hell* is going on here? General Freeman, getting chased out of the White House twice in just a few days on a false alarm is *not* my idea of fun."

"It was no false alarm, ma'am," Freeman said, swallowing hard, shifting from one foot to the other. To the President, he said, "I've got the intelligence branch on their way over for a briefing, sir."

"All right," the President drawled wearily. He stood by his chair, his fingers pressing into the brown leather back, taking a few deep breaths, then swung the chair around and sat down heavily. "Something in North America or Europe, Philip?"

"Europe, sir, over Turkey," Freeman replied. "Attack warning. There was no reason why the leadership-evacuation warning was sounded. I'll check into that personally."

The Navy captain with the nuclear codes followed along and unobtrusively took a seat in the corner of the room, the case open on a table beside his chair, a cord running from the briefcase to a wall outlet. He then stood and approached the President, waiting for an opportunity to speak. "Captain Ahrens would like to activate your code card, sir," Freeman told the President.

"What for?"

"Sir, we should establish full connectivity with the National Military Command Center immediately," Freeman explained. "When the Russian aircraft were detected on what appeared to be a bomb run, we transmitted a taxi-to-the-hold-line message to the bombers and a stand-by-to-launch message to the Peacekeeper missiles and submarines."

The Steel Magnolia's mouth dropped open in shock—it looked like the President's was about to as well.

"Under these circumstances, the next order would most likely be issued from the portable unit. Since there's still a possibility that an attack against the United States is underway, you should activate the portable sender."

"I told you before, General, I don't want those bombers to launch!"

"Sir . . ." Freeman paused, controlling his emotions and his own shaking voice, cursing the day he was appointed Chairman of the Joint Chiefs. At least Colin Powell got out while the getting was good. "Sir, activating your portable sender doesn't *issue* any orders—it only allows you to be able to do so, should we need to make a run for the helicopter again. At this point, Strategic Command will determine whether or not the bombers launch under positive control. They—"

"What . . . did you say, General Freeman?" the First Lady interrupted. "Strategic Command can launch the bombers? What are you talking about? What do you mean they can launch? Is this some kind of coup?" She turned to the President. "I'm telling you, this smells like *Seven Days in May.*"

"Dammit, ma'am," Freeman snapped, "under DEFCON Two, we would launch the bomber force under positive control as soon as we detected an attack in progress against the United States. That's what DEFCON Two means. Because of the nature of the current emergency *and your orders* regarding protection for our NATO allies, we decided we would launch the bomber force if any attack against any NATO ally, especially Turkey, was detected."

"A policy I totally disagree with," the First Lady said disdainfully, rapping on Jack Kennedy's old desk. "We're supposed to make the world and the Russians think we'll start a nuclear war if *Turkey* is attacked?"

"We already discussed this, honey," the President interjected, trying to calm her, wishing he could take a job at McDonald's or somewhere—anywhere but *here*. "We've got American servicemen in Turkey; Turkey is a strong and valuable ally—it's important we show our support—"

"By starting World War Three? It's insane," she lectured, her lip curled.

The President hesitated. They had indeed argued this point for many hours, with the First Lady not wanting to commit to war with Russia over Turkey and its unilateral decision to assist the Ukraine. She had a point, Freeman thought: world wars were indeed started exactly like this. But the NATO alliance was important to America. Every member—especially its most powerful member, the United States of America—had to back up the others. The single RF-111G recon unit and a few frigates was a paltry show of support—launching the nuclear alert bombers was a *major* show of support. It was a safe and fully controllable response as well—unlike a missile, the bombers could be recalled at any time.

"Our bomber force is so small that reaction time is critical, ma'am," Freeman said. "As soon as NORAD and Strategic Command get a positive attack indication, they flush the bombers. It's the only way to ensure survivability."

"What about the subs and the missiles?" the President asked, sheepishly tearing off the end of a cigar to chomp on—but not inhale. The First Lady glared at him but said nothing. "Strategic Command launches them too . . . ?"

"No, sir. Only you can order the missiles to launch and the bombers to prearm their weapons and execute their strike missions," Freeman replied. "However, under DEFCON Two, the nuclear subs carry out certain instructions if they lose connectivity with you. If the loss of communications continues, the subs can launch an attack."

"I thought you said only *I* can launch the missiles," the President said in exasperation, looking confused.

"Sir, that's true—only you can order a launch," he said, thinking, *Thank God he did avoid the draft—he just doesn't get it.* "But nuclear subs are designed to patrol for months at a time completely undetected. They must expose themselves to receive instructions, which they will do every two to eight weeks, depending on the defense readiness condition. If they come up and don't connect, under DEFCON Two they will proceed to their launch points and try one more time to connect. If that fails, they will launch."

"They can launch *without my orders . . . ?*" he asked, his face still clouded.

"Sir, the sea-launched missiles are our most important, our most deadly, our most survivable weapon," Freeman explained, thinking, *He isn't this dumb. He knew this stuff, why is he doing this? Is he panicking? Well, it sure as hell isn't the time to come unglued.* "If the entire command and control system is destroyed by a nuclear attack, we don't want the subs to be out of commission just because they were down hiding from the bad guys. Therefore, under high-threat conditions like this, sub captains have the ability to launch a limited attack if they don't get the order *not* to do so."

"This is ridiculous, General," the First Lady said through gritted teeth. "This is a nightmare. What kind of control system is this? A nuclear war can start and we didn't even order it . . . ?"

"The President ordered it by going to DEFCON Two, ma'am."

"Well, cancel the fucking DEFCON Two, then!" the First Lady hissed. "I want control of those warheads, General . . . I want—" And then she stopped, finally realizing what she was saying. She took a deep breath, patted her hair, recomposed herself, and smiled coldly. "I think any procedure that delegates any measure of authority for the release of nuclear weapons outside this office is wrong, General. I think something should be done about it . . . that's all. You see my point." She was all sugar and spice.

"Let's worry about that later, honey." The President sighed. "We'll keep the planes on the ground and the subs on patrol for now. I think I've proven to Turkey and the rest of NATO that I'll support them, but if we need to launch the bombers to show Turkey or Russia we mean business, so be it. As far as the subs go, I want to stay in contact with the command center"—the President looked at the Navy captain, at the briefcase, at the top of his desk, at nothing, then said—"*by telephone.* I'm staying right here."

"Yes, sir," Freeman said, glad that that was resolved before the Second Coming. He motioned to the naval officer, who packed up his gear and departed to his office on the ground floor. In the meantime, an officer had arrived from the Pentagon with a locked case full of papers. The President spent a moment looking the cover pages over, handed them over to Freeman while the coffee and sandwiches were brought in, then: "So spill it, General."

"It was a single aircraft, Mr. President, a MiG-25R Foxbat reconnaissance aircraft," Freeman explained. "We've been monitoring many reconnaissance flights over the Ukraine, but this one flew in a long oval track, a total of six hundred sixty miles, right through central Turkey. A simply incredible mission. It passed within sensor range of ten major Turkish and NATO military installations on one twenty-minute pass. Broad daylight, clear skies—it probably took home some great snapshots."

"It made it out of there?" the President asked incredulously, his cigar almost falling in his lap. "How? Didn't they have fighter patrols up?"

"There's a NATO AWACS radar plane orbiting north of Ankara," Freeman replied. "By the time the AWACS plane detected the Foxbat, two hundred miles over the Black Sea, and fighters could be scrambled to intercept it, it was over land. By the time the fighters were set up to pursue, it was in the turn and heading out. By the time the first fighter got a shot off at it, it was back out over the Black Sea. And the Foxbat flies almost as fast as a Sparrow missile. No ground air defense units ever got a shot off at it—didn't even see it. It dropped leaflet canisters near Incirlik Air Base in southern Turkey—the canisters missed by several miles—but it made a direct hit on Kayseri Air Base. They're faxing a copy of the leaflets now."

"Why?" the President asked, amazed. "Why did they do this? What in the hell are they trying to do?"

"It's a clear warning, sir," Freeman said. "More psychological than anything else, but we can't dismiss it as trivial. The tactic's psychological effect can be devastating. The crews see a bomb carrying leaflets one moment, but the next time—who knows?"

"Sorry I'm late, Mr. President," the Secretary of Defense, Donald Scheer, said as he entered the Oval Office. "It feels as if I'm always here, but I always miss the helicopter." He went right over to Freeman, who handed him the report sent over by the Pentagon courier. After reading it for a few moments, he commented, "It's a warning not to get involved, Mr. President. We're playing in the Russians' backyard here, after all. They control the skies over the Black Sea, they have a Coalition-sized force already in place in the region, and they're moving that force slowly south into the Ukraine. All the undamaged Ukrainian aircraft and base facilities are in Russian hands now. We're outgunned and outmanned, and the Russians just wanted to remind us of that little fact."

"It's bullshit. It's hubris. It's grandstanding," the President mused, as if talking it over with himself, calculating their strategy as if this were some election to be won. "Did they think this was going to be productive or something? Did they think this was going to make us stop what we're doing?"

Was the President serious? Freeman was more than a bit worried. Here was a man who could do damn near anything he wanted. He had the power of the greatest industrial nation and the world's finest military behind him—and yet he was concerned about a simple psy-op leaflet drop. The most devastating psychological effect of the Russian mission was obviously done right *here* . . . in this office.

"Mr. President, we've got a great many things we need to do," Freeman insisted. "I think our first priority is to get the Cabinet and the National Security Council in here to go over some options I've drawn up. We need to contact President Dalon of Turkey and the other NATO ministers and get approval for forward basing for coalition forces. We should—"

"You want *more* military forces involved in this thing, General?" the President exclaimed. "Put more troops in Turkey, or Greece, or Italy? We put twelve planes into a small base in Turkey, and the Russians blew a supersonic fighter through there. What in the hell will they do if we move a couple thousand planes?"

"Sir, I'm worried about what they'll do if we *don't* respond," Freeman said. "I'm worried about what President Dalon will say if we don't contact him right *now* with a pledge of military support and additional weaponry to prevent any more overflights."

"Philip, I can't do it," the President said wearily. "I don't believe an increased military response is appropriate."

"But we'd be leaving a valuable ally swinging in the wind, Mr. President," insisted Freeman, disgusted by his Commander in Chief's reluctance.

"The Turks did it to us by not informing us of their intention of helping the Ukraine," the President pointed out.

"That was several months ago, sir, right after the Islamic Wars. When we found out what the Turks were doing, we were glad to have them take over. We wanted nothing more than to pull out and disengage from all military activities in the region, and we wanted Turkey to take charge of its own national defense. Well, in my opinion, now they need our help."

"So why doesn't Dalon just ask for it?" the First Lady asked pointedly. "He's asked for defensive weapons, but he doesn't want offensive weapons; he wants strike aircraft, but he doesn't want Eagles or Falcons or the F-111s other than the reconnaissance models. Why not?"

Freeman was surprised at the First Lady's use of military terminology—shit, she'd obviously been boning up—that was even scarier than the crisis. Well, almost. "Ma'am, the Turks are fiercely proud of their military forces—"

"A lot of good *that* does them," she said dismissively, rolling her eyes.

"—and they'll refuse to admit they need help in driving out their enemies. That's seems to be standard cultural bias for any Middle Eastern country, and for Dalon to express any other view would be political and societal suicide. We have to respect that. But Dalon is a realist: he knows he can't take on the Russians alone. He'll gladly, but secretly, accept our help if we offer it—he will never *request* it."

"So *we* get to name our own poison," the President said bitterly. "We have to recommend aircraft that *we* want to send, troops *we* want to put in danger—and then we take the political heat when Dalon comes back and says he doesn't need all this firepower, or his parliament blames us for escalating the conflict or putting Turkey in danger by sending more NATO troops into Turkey. We shouldn't have to put up with this nonsense."

"It's the price we pay for membership in NATO and for wanting an ally like Turkey," Freeman said. "Sir, we have to make a decision as soon as possible."

The President turned away from Freeman and stared out one of the polycarbonate bullet-resistant windows. The First Lady went over to him, and the two spoke in low tones.

This was the most aggravating part of this White House, Freeman thought: he could have a staff of fifty professional analysts and staff assistants working all night on formulating a strong but measured deployment of forces to Turkey and the rest of NATO, but their work could—and had been in the past—be completely overruled by the Steel Magnolia. Sure, she was intelligent, and politically savvy, and in general she was fair and open-minded—but she was also strongly opinionated and tended to swing with the current popular political winds, especially those blowing from the liberal "left coast."

"All right, all right, we'll act on your recommendations," the President said after several long moments. His wife did not look totally pleased—Freeman hated to think it, but in a way the First Lady's displeasure was a major victory for him. "But I want the full NSC and the Congressional leadership in on this. It has not yet been proven to my satisfaction that the events in Turkey warrant a Desert Storm–type response, and I need more information. The current forces we've deployed in Turkey will have to stand for now."

"Sir, I need to present the entire package to you, and I think I should do it before the leadership arrives," Freeman said. "If it's your decision to keep the 394th Air Battle Wing out there in Turkey by themselves, we must decide to what extent they can be involved in combat activities."

"They can fire only when fired upon," the First Lady interjected. "That seems fair."

"Ma'am, the 394th is primarily a *reconnaissance* group," Freeman said. "They take photos and analyze enemy radar systems from long range."

"They have an offensive capability, General," she fired right back.

"Which they should not use at all until a full combat-ready support group is deployed with them," Freeman said. "Ma'am, the 394th is basically a *support* unit, not a combat unit unto itself. It flies in support of other strike units. Right now the only strike units it can attach itself to are three Turkish fighter units and a Ukrainian fighter-bomber group."

"All right, General," the President said after receiving a cautious nod of tentative approval from the First Lady, "I'll *look* at your proposal and decide on which actions to authorize the 394th to do while they're in Turkey. It won't include combat—it'll be purely defensive in nature, intelligence-gathering and reconnaissance, in support of territorial defense for our NATO allies and information-gathering for the Pentagon, but they'll be able to defend themselves if fired upon over Turkish or international airspace or waters. The rest I'll look at only after discussing the situation with the leadership—"

"And it includes the actions of the alert bombers," the First Lady said. "I realize events and procedures are automatic when it comes to the alert force, but I still think this policy should be reevaluated, with all of our advisers present." The President nodded his complete agreement.

One step at a time, Freeman thought—that was the way to deal with this President. He just hoped that things didn't go to hell in Eastern Europe while the President—and his wife—tried to make up their minds.

"The Joint Chiefs, my staff, and myself have a plan to do precisely that—support a joint Turkish-Ukrainian attack mission," Freeman continued. "The Russian Fleet has been moving steadily southward in the Black Sea, supported by an A-50 radar plane. The fleet has created a strong naval and counterair barrier to try to block any air action by the Ukrainian Air Force, and now they're a direct threat to Turkey. Colonel

Tychina of the Ukrainian Air Force has devised a bold plan for dealing with the Russians, but they need our help."

"What kind of help?" the First Lady asked skeptically.

The General hesitated, glancing at Scheer and the President. "Excuse me, sir, but as far as I'm aware, the First Lady is not cleared to hear this information."

The lightning bolts that launched from the Steel Magnolia's eyes—first at Freeman and then at her husband—could have lighted a city. "We don't have time for that now, General," the President said quickly. "Proceed."

"Yes, sir," Freeman said. He wished he had another witness in here to confirm the President's orders, but his career was on thin ice anyway. "Sir, the number-one threat out there to Turkey is the Russian Fleet and the Russian radar plane, which can keep watch over the entire region. Our Vampire bombers can attack the shipborne surveillance and missile guidance radars—"

"It sounds like an offensive plan to me, General," the First Lady interjected. "Who attacks first, us or them?"

Freeman was dumbstruck by the question. "Why . . . I hope we get a chance to get into attack position before the Russian Fleet can engage our bombers."

"So *we* fire the first shots? I think that's wrong, General," she snapped.

"Ma'am, the first shots have *already* been fired," Freeman said. "This is a response to Russian aggression. We wouldn't allow this fleet within three hundred miles of the American coast, yet they're less than *sixty* miles from the Turkish coast."

"General, I think the First Lady is right," the President said. "Is there any way we can work it to make our involvement purely defensive in nature? Let's let the Turks and the Ukrainians call the shots on this one."

Freeman shook his head in obvious frustration. *Christ, how I loathe both of them.* He took a deep breath and replied, "Sir, I understand your concern, but that's not the way we should operate. Our primary concern is the safety of our crews, and sending them against a hostile force with orders to fire only when fired upon is wrong and outdated thinking. If we launch those Vampire bombers, they should go in fighting."

"This is not between America and Russia, General," the First Lady informed him as if he were just too thick to understand *real* policies. "This is between Russia and the Ukraine. Turkey was an innocent bystander—President Velichko said the attack on the Turkish ships was wrong, and I believe him. If we attack Russian ships without provocation, we'll be drawn into this war, and it'll be *your* fault." She crossed her arms and affixed him with a stare, just daring him to challenge her.

Freeman felt like raising his hands in utter surrender—his words were being deflected away from the President like bullets off cold steel. "Sir, I have a plan for your review," he said finally. "It meets your criteria for defensive action and support for our allies." He hesitated, knowing he shouldn't make any concessions to the First Lady when it came to his troops in the field, but said, "We *may* be able to adjust the rules of engagement to allow only nonthreatening surveillance actions by our crews, but I—"

"I think that's a wise idea, General," the First Lady said pointedly.

35

Over the Black Sea North of Turkey, That Night

REBECCA FURNESS AND MARK FOGELMAN WERE FLYING AT TEN thousand feet over the rugged coastal mountains surrounding the Marmara Sea near the city of Yalova. It was after two A.M. in Turkey, and the night was overcast and very cold—Rebecca could see a light dusting of frost on the leading edge of the wings and hoped the icing wouldn't get too bad. They had barely reached the Marmara Sea, the body of water between the Dardanelles and the Bosporus Strait in western Turkey, when the TEREC (Tactical Electronic Reconnaissance) sensor system and radar threat indicator came to life. "Naval search radar, one o'clock," Mark Fogelman reported. "Analyzing . . . I've got an S-band naval search radar, probably a Head Net or Top Steer radar. That must be the cruiser we're picking . . . nope, wait, now I got two S-band radars, one farther north. The closer one must be the destroyer and the farther one must be the cruiser."

"Copy that, Mark," Rebecca Furness acknowledged. "Let me see the satellite photos again."

Fogelman gave Furness a small binder with satellite photos of Russian warships stationed off the coast of Turkey, delivered electronically just a few hours earlier. There were actually two groups of warships directly off Turkey's northern coast in the Black Sea: a guided-missile cruiser task force, led by the cruiser *Marshal Ustinov,* with two guided-missile destroyers and two light frigates escorting it. Farther east, halfway between the Crimean Peninsula and Turkey, was an aviation cruiser task force, spearheaded by the carrier *Novorossiysk,* which carried missile and antisubmarine-warfare helicopters and several Yak-38 Forger vertical takeoff and landing fighters. The *Novorossiysk* battle group was escorted by two guided-missile destroyers and four frigates with powerful air search radars. Antisubmarine sonars patrolled the waters between the two groups, making sure nothing sneaked in between the two powerful Russian battle groups.

"Thunder One-One flight, use caution for Russian patrol vessels at your twelve o'clock, one hundred miles," the air traffic controller at Istanbul Air Control Center told them. "They have requested that aircraft be vectored at least sixty miles around them."

"Roger, copy, Istanbul," Furness acknowledged. On interphone she remarked, "The magic number: sixty miles. Ten miles outside range of our radar reconnaissance pod."

"And just outside maximum range of the cruiser's SA-N-6 missile system," Fogelman added, copying the details of that call down on his kneeboard. "I'm going to transmit and see if I can pick 'em up. Radar's going to transmit." He switched on the attack radar, set the range to one hundred and twenty miles, and turned the tilt down. "Bingo. Radar contact, three vessels, about one hundred miles north of our position and about eighty miles offshore, due north of Istanbul." He hit the manual video button on the attack radar, which recorded the radar's video image on tape for later analysis. "Can't break out individual ships yet—there's supposed to be five ships in that group, but I only see three so far. Not picking up any jamming yet. Going to 'standby.'" He flicked the mode switch to STANDBY, which kept the system warmed up but did not allow any transmissions that the ships could use to home in an antiradar missile.

"Okay, the cruiser is supposed to have an SA-N-6B Grumble missile system, and we'll be within range of that in about two minutes," Fogelman said, reading from the order-of-battle card given to them by NATO intelligence officers back at Kayseri. "The next system is an SA-N-3B Goblet system. The destroyer has an SA-N-7 Gadfly missile system good out about twenty miles, and that'll be our primary threat."

"That and fighters," Furness reminded him. "We'll be under constant radar contact from that cruiser, so fighters will be under full radar control—and as long as they're over water, they'll have the balls to come down and get us. We gotta stay sharp."

"Bingo," Fogelman called out. "TEREC picked up a strong datalink signal, looks like a Pincer Chord microwave steering signal. Nothing on the RHAWS scope yet, but they don't need a fighter radar if they got naval. Now I'm picking up a search radar at one to two o'clock. That must be the AWACS plane." The *Novorossiysk* battle group was stationed directly under the loitering area of an A-50 "Mainstay" airborne early warning and control radar plane which had been detected flying over the central Black Sea. From its position, it could see the entire Black Sea and detect the approach of any aircraft from sea level to forty thousand feet.

"Well, we can assume we're busted," Furness said grimly. "Let's hope we can convince them we're just taking pictures." On the scrambled HAVE QUICK FM interplane frequency, she radioed, "Okay, guys, we're feet-wet and moving in. Stay as tight as you can."

Two clicks of the microphone was the only acknowledgment from Thunder One-Two, Furness' wingman, manned by Paula Norton and her temporary navigator, Curt Aldridge. Of course, the two RF-111Gs were prepared in case the Russians didn't buy that argument. Furness' RF-111G carried four AGM-88C HARM antiradar missiles and two AIM-9P-3 Sidewinder missiles under the wings, along with the TEREC electronic reconnaissance pallet in the bomb bay.

Norton's aircraft was configured completely differently. She carried an AN/ALQ-131 electronic countermeasures jamming pod mounted between the ventral fins in the rear of the jet and a total of twelve ADM-141 TALD (Tactical Air-Launched Decoy) gliders mounted on pylons under each wing. The TALDs were small four-hundred-pound unpowered gliders resembling small cruise missiles, with small wings that pop out after release. The TALDs carried chaff dispensers, radar reflectors, tiny radar transmitters, and heat emitters that would make the eight-foot-long missiles look like slow-moving attack aircraft to a weapons officer or fire control officer. Two more two-ship RF-111G Vampire hunter-killer formations—half the Vampires deployed to Turkey—had been launched that night to probe the boundaries of the Russian Fleet stationed not far from Turkey's shores and to take an indirect part in the first counterattack by the Ukrainian Air Force against their Russian invaders.

"Thunder One-One flight, warning, you are endangering your aircraft by proceeding in that direction," the Turkish radar controller said. *No shit,* Rebecca thought. "What are your intentions?"

"Thunder One-One is due regard," she replied.

"Understand, One-One," the controller said. Furness noticed that the air traffic controllers sounded much more official and their English was very good—the civilian controllers must have been replaced by military controllers in critical centers such as Istanbul. A civilian controller might not know that "due regard" meant that a military flight was going off to parts unknown—this controller knew and understood right away. "Cleared to proceed, contact me on this frequency when able."

For a moment Furness and Fogelman thought he was going to add "Good luck," but he did not.

"Thunder, go active," Furness radioed. That was the signal to Norton and Aldridge to take spacing as briefed in mission planning and to go to their briefed radio frequency. "Shut 'em down and button up, Mark," Furness said on interphone. Fogelman began turning off exterior lights, turning the identification beacons to standby, turning off the Doppler radar, attack radar, and other transmitters, and buckling up their oxygen masks, donning gloves, rolling down sleeves, and lowering the clear visors on their helmets. Fogelman set 243.0, the international UHF emergency frequency, in the primary radio, and the prebriefed AWACS secure voice channel in the secondary radio.

"Thunder, this is Banjo, good evening," the NATO E-3B AWACS controller said a few moments later. "Fence check, stand by. One-One."

At that, Fogelman briefly shut off the Mode Four transponder which provided secure identification for the AWACS controller, then turned it back on. "Fence check complete, One-One," Furness replied. The controller repeated the process for all the Thunder aircraft. They could not hear it, but Turkish and Russian-speaking controllers on the same plane were checking in other aircraft as well.

"One-One flight, push blue," the controller said. Fogelman switched the radio to the second prebriefed frequency, where one controller would control only their two aircraft. On the new frequency, the controller did not check them in again; he assumed both aircraft had made the jump to the new frequency: "Thunder Flight, you have bandits at two o'clock, high, eighty miles, not paired on you."

"The destroyer is lit up like a Christmas tree," Fogelman reported. "S-band search radar, F-band director for the Gadfly missiles, even the X-band for the cannon. They must not be talking to their AWACS or . . . ah, they're going radar-silent now. I still see a side lobe from an H-band close-in weapon system radar—they're ready for cruise missiles."

"Thunder, range to first target, thirty miles."

"We're well inside Grumble missile range, coming up on Goblet range," Fogelman said. They were still flying north toward the guided-missile cruiser *Marshal Ustinov* and its escorts, still at ten thousand feet. "Inside Goblet range, still no sign of the F-band. They're staying cool. Coming up on Gadfly range."

Then, on the emergency frequency, they heard in English, "Unidentified aircraft fifty miles north of Istanbul heading north, this is the Russian missile destroyer *Stoykiy*. You are endangering yourself by approaching our vessels. Suggest you turn away immediately and maintain a fifty-kilometer space from our vessels. Suggest an immediate heading of zero-four-five for at least ten minutes. Thank you. Please respond immediately."

"Gadfly range, now," Fogelman announced.

"Arm 'em up, Mark," Furness said. Fogelman had already displayed the weapon status page on the right Multi-Function Display. On his weapons panel, Fogelman turned the weapon status and control switch to ALL and made sure that all four of the AGM-88 HARM legends were highlighted on the right MFD, indicating they were powered up and ready. When he received good READY lights from all four missiles, he depressed the number-three weapon cassette, rotated the weapon select switch to the number-three position, and selected BOMB on the mode switch. On the right-side MFD, only the missile on the number-three pylon indicated ready.

"All weapons check good, number-three missile selected," Fogelman reported.

Almost at the same time they heard a brief "Pump" on the secure radio. At that, Furness chopped power and began a rapid descent. Thunder One-Two had released two TALD decoys, which would fly straight ahead and begin a slow descent, and they had also begun electronic countermeasures to try to get the Russian radar plane to break lock and lose track of the Vampires. The pod Thunder One-Two carried was designed to jam the Russian AWACS plane, but not the naval search radars—hopefully this would force the ships to turn on their search radars, and hopefully give Furness and Fogelman a chance to kill it. The TALDs were not programmed to fly closer than fifteen miles to any ship and would crash in the ocean someplace far behind the Russian cruiser . . .

. . . if they were allowed to continue flying. At that moment, Fogelman cried out, "SA-N-7 up, eleven o'clock!"

"One-One, working Gadfly," Furness reported on the command radio.

"The Gadfly's still up . . . okay, it's fading, he's locked on to the decoys," Fogelman reported, activating the radar altimeter and setting the warning bug for one thousand feet. "You've got five thousand to level . . . two thousand to level . . . decoy's been out for thirty seconds . . . one thousand . . . five hundred . . . coming level." They were now flying at an angle away from the lead Russian destroyer, maintaining a range of about twenty miles—just outside the deadly SA-N-7 Gadfly missile's range. "My HARM is receiving telemetry, first one will be from the number-three pylon. Go to 'Attack.'"

"Thanks, Mark." Furness set her ISC (Integrated Steering Control) to ATTACK, which would take range information from the TEREC system and give her steering information to the nearest threat.

"Okay, boys, you gonna just watch them go by or—"

Suddenly they saw a bright flash of light off in the distance, and a missile's motor plume briefly illuminated the profile of a large military vessel—they were twenty miles away, but it seemed close enough to touch. The Russian ship decided not to issue any more warnings—at a range of about seventeen miles, the destroyer *Stoykiy* opened fire with an SA-N-7 surface-to-air missile. "One-One, Gadfly liftoff," Furness reported on the AWACS network. Then, on the international emergency frequency, she radioed in the clear, "Mayday, Mayday, Mayday, any radio, Thunder One-Zero is under attack. Repeat, we are under attack." She started a turn to the left to center the steering bars.

"Missile one is locked on," Fogelman reported.

"Roger." On the AWACS net, she radioed, "One-One, magnum," indicating a HARM missile launch to other friendly aircraft, then said on interphone, "Clear to launch. Kill the sucker, Mark."

Fogelman reached down to his weapons panel, moved the launch switch from OFF to MANUAL, and pressed the pickle button. Immediately the left wing swung up, then stabilized, as the leftmost AGM-88 HARM missile dropped off the number-three pylon. The missile fell for a few seconds as it stabilized itself in the slipstream—which allowed enough time for Furness and Fogelman to close their eyes against the bright glare of the missile's motor. The HARM's motor seemed to explode as it started, and an impossibly bright column of fire erupted in the night sky. In seconds the big missile was traveling over Mach-one, in a slight overhead arc directly at where the SA-N-7 missile had lifted off. About eight seconds after launch, as Furness started a gradual turn back to the east, they saw a bright flash of light on the horizon, followed by several smaller flashes and what appeared to be missiles cooking off and spinning into the Black Sea.

"Banjo, One-One, good magnum hit, I see secondaries," Furness radioed.

"Oh, man, oh, man," Fogelman breathed. He dropped his oxygen mask with a flick of his wrist, as if he couldn't draw enough air through it. "Goddamn, we actually *hit* something. We hit a real live fucking ship."

"C'mon, Mark," Furness said. "Stay focused."

"Becky, it's just that I . . . hell, I never thought I'd actually fire one of these for real." He fastened his oxygen mask to his face, took a deep breath, and began checking the TEREC threat indications again. "Okay, it looks like the F-band is off the air . . . okay, the S-band search radar on the cruiser is back up and hitting us right in the face. He could be taking over the air intercept for the Russian AWACS if he's being jammed. That's the one we want."

"One-Two, give us some music," Furness radioed to Norton.

"One-Two, pump," Norton replied as Aldridge ejected two more TALD glider decoys.

Fogelman selected the antiradar missile on the number-six pylon, then continued to check his sensors. "Still got a lock on the S-band air search . . . shit, the SA-N-6 just came up! I'm selecting the missile on four . . . dammit, c'mon, man, take it, take it . . . got it! I got a fix on both the Grumble and the S-band. Command bars are on the target."

"Turning," Furness replied, and began a steep 60-degree turn toward the Russian cruiser. The HARM missile had to be aimed within 5 degrees of its intended target before it could lock on. She keyed the mike: "Banjo, One-One . . ."

"Missile launch!" Fogelman cried out.

At that, they could see first one missile, then another, then four more missiles rise vertically from the horizon, drawing bright lines of fire in the sky. The lines began to curl a bit—the first one or two missiles were obviously going for decoys, but the cruiser had rapid-fired enough missiles for all of them.

"Missiles away!" Fogelman cried out, and hit the launch button. When the HARM missiles were away and well clear of the Vampire, Fogelman depressed the four jammer switchlights on the front instrument panel, and the forward XMIT light came on immediately—the SA-N-6 Grumble was locked on to them solidly. "Grumble at twelve o'clock," he said. "I lost sight of the missiles . . . I can't see them!"

"Set one hundred feet on the LARA bug!" she shouted, and began a rapid descent to one hundred feet above the sea without changing heading. Their smallest radar cross-section was head-on, and if they turned they would be exposing more of themselves to the Russian missile guidance radar. "Gimme chaff." Furness began a short-frequency up-and-down oscillation, no more than a hundred feet, trying to impart a rolling motion to the missiles that might throw them off.

"I see the missiles! Still headed right for us!" Furness called out. She began a slow side-to-side rolling action. The Grumble didn't seem to be going for it. On the command radio, she shouted, "One-Two, give me a couple more."

"Copy," Norton replied. "Decoys away."

The extra decoys worked. Just as the flare of the missile's motor winked out, Furness could see that the SA-N-6 missile was beginning to climb higher and higher until it was far overhead, tracking the decoys that were hundreds of times better targets than the Vampires. A moment later, Fogelman shouted, "Got it! Shit hot, we got both the air search and the

Grumble missile emitter! We nailed 'em!"

It was confirmed by an entire series of explosions just about twelve miles off on the horizon as the hundred-pound warheads from the two HARMs fired thousands of tungsten alloy cubes in a deadly cloud of metal all across the center and aft sections of the Russian guided missile cruiser, setting off several SS-N-12 "Sandbox" antiship missiles sitting in exposed angled launch canisters on deck.

Just when it appeared the secondary explosions had subsided, a tremendous explosion erupted on deck, illuminating the sea around the *Marshal Ustinov* for miles in all directions. They could even see a helicopter afire on the aft landing pad.

"We might have a kill!" Furness said in delight on interphone. "We might've gotten the cruiser!" She keyed the command radio mike button: "One-Two, did you see that? Banjo, this is One-One, I think we got the cruiser."

"One-One, Banjo, give me an ident." Fogelman briefly shut off the Mode 4 transponder, then turned it back on again. "Received, One-One," the controller said in a low, somber voice. "One-Two is faded at this time. Turn right heading one-one-zero and say what state magnum."

It was as if both Furness and Fogelman had been hit in the stomach with baseball bats. The NATO radar plane no longer had contact with Norton and Aldridge. One of the SA-N-6 missiles that they thought was going after a decoy must have hit them instead.

Just like that, in the blink of an eye, two fellow crewmembers were gone.

The radar warning receiver blared to life, and an "N" symbol appeared on the scope. "Mark?" Furness said. No reply—Fogelman was staring at the TEREC sensor, but he was as still as a rock. "Mark, *come on.* That must be the lone destroyer out there. Let's get this puppy and get the hell out of here."

"God . . . it can't be . . ." he said, mulling over the deaths of Norton and Aldridge.

"Mark, dammit, run this shot." On the command net, she radioed, "Banjo, One-One has one HARM left. Stand by. We're pressing on the easterly destroyer."

"Copy, Thunder. You have bandits at eleven o'clock, fifty miles, may be converging on you. The destroyer is at your ten o'clock, sixty miles. You've got chicks engaged at twelve o'clock, one-two-zero miles."

"Roger." She reached over and shook Fogelman's left shoulder. "C'mon, Mark. Maybe they got out. Maybe they're in the water. We can't do anything for them. Let's burn this last guy."

But without the TALD decoys to induce the Russians to turn on their radars, the destroyer *Rezkiy,* which was patrolling alone between the guided missile cruiser and the aviation cruiser, wasn't going to get sucked in quite as easy. Fogelman even tried turning on his attack radar to attract attention from the ship—nothing. But it did attract the attention of the fighters nearby: "One-One, bandits on you, twelve o'clock, forty miles. Range to the destroyer, fifty miles."

"We'll give it a few more seconds," Furness said. "We're still outside his SA-N-3 missile range." Once they got within range of the SA-N-3, Furness tried climbing slightly—the Goblet had a minimum effective altitude of three hundred feet, so she tried climbing to five hundred feet to get the destroyer to commit. Still nothing. This was the one problem with carrying all antiradar weapons and nothing else—if the radars didn't come up, the missiles were nothing but deadweight.

The destroyer's radar didn't come up because, with the AWACS feeding radar information to them, it wasn't needed. The Russian AWACS was proving to be a real problem. They had a plan to deal with it—hopefully that plan was coming together right about now.

36

THE OTHER FOUR RF-111G VAMPIRE BOMBERS HAD HIT THE *Novorossiysk* carrier battle group from two sides, cutting in from the southwest and from the east in a supersonic pincer. Captain Frank Kelly and Lieutenant Colonel Larry Tobias in Thunder One-Three, the most experienced team in the attack, killed the Russian destroyer *Burnyy* with a salvo of three HARM missiles, but their fourth HARM refused to power up or take any commands. The frigate *Revnostnyy* was hit by two HARMs fired by Major Clark Vest and First Lieutenant Lynn Ogden. After that, all the Russian ships refused to turn on any radars even with decoys flying everywhere—Captain Joe Johnson and Major Harold Rota, firing TALDs for Kelly and Tobias, even fired a decoy directly *at* a frigate, coming within a few hundred yards of hitting it, and the vessel refused to even activate a radar for its close-in weapon system.

Once Russian fighters started showing up, the Vampires were effectively out of the fight—but to the Russian "Mainstay" AWACS radar controller's surprise, the four RF-111Gs turned south only twenty miles south of the *Novorossiysk* and began a *climb,* with radars and radios blaring. The American bombers climbed right on up to twelve thousand feet, well within lethal range of the cruiser's SA-N-3B and SA-N-7 missile systems. But with the destruction of the *Burnyy* by the Vampires, the aviation cruiser wasn't going to risk a sneak attack by the other two Vampires that they knew were operating farther west. After all, they had a full complement of twelve Yak-38 fighters, sixteen helicopters, and over 1,600 sailors on board. So they never fired another shot. It was going to be up to the Russian fighters now.

The Vampires were tempting targets for the Russian fighters operating over the Black Sea in support of the naval task force and now howling south to take up the chase. Deployed to bases on the Crimean Peninsula, only 120 miles to the north, were several wings of MiG-29 and Sukhoi-27 fighters, mostly providing air cover for the Russian radar plane. When the Vampires were first detected by the Mainstay radar plane, the fighter wings at Sevastopol and Yevpatoriya were placed on full alert, and when the attack began on the ships south of the Crimea, the airspace over the Black Sea was filled with over sixty fighters, the maximum the controllers aboard the A-50 Mainstay radar plane could safely handle. Spread out on both sides of the *Novorossiysk* carrier battle group so as to not interfere with the ship's self-defense capabilities, the Russian fighters fanned out to hunt down the fast, low-flying American bombers. Twenty fighters deployed west to cover the *Marshal Ustinov* group, ten stayed with the Mainstay radar plane, and thirty fighters pursued the four Vampire bombers retreating toward Turkey. It seemed as if the RF-111G aircraft were unaware that they were being pursued—the Russians knew the Americans had an AWACS radar plane of their own up, but the Vampires were still flying at a high, very vulnerable altitude.

They were too vulnerable, too tempting a target—and it was designed that way. As the Russian fighter sweep moved south, eighty MiG-23 fighters from the Ukrainian Air Force swept up from the south. The Russian pursuers suddenly found themselves the pursued—what was just a few seconds earlier an easy thirty-on-four advantage had turned into an eighty-on-thirty disadvantage. The Vampires were soon forgotten, and all four escaped to the safety of the Turkish coastal highlands.

The single-engine Ukrainian MiG-23 Flogger, however, was no match for a Russian MiG-29 or Su-27 fighter. Even at night, the more advanced fighters were capable of killing many times their numbers of the older, much less sophisticated Ukrainian fighters, especially with an A-50 radar plane directing them. But they never got the chance—as soon as the Russian fighters started pairing up against their former Soviet brothers from Ukrayina, the MiG-23s turned southbound and ran at full military power without firing one missile. It was a planned retreat—they never had any intention of trying to mix it up with the advanced fighters . . .

. . . and the reason soon became apparent. As the bulk of the Russian fighter coverage moved toward Turkey's north coast chasing the Ukrainian fighters, a flight of ten Ukrainian MiG-27 and ten Sukhoi-17 fighter-bombers swept in from the east at supersonic speed. The Mainstay's radar controllers were swamped with so many planes on the scope that they didn't see the low-flying newcomers until they were only sixty miles from the remaining five ships of the *Novorossiysk* carrier battle group. The Russian fighters were far out of position and had to use precious fuel to turn and engage the large number of bombers streaking in from the east. The Ukrainian tactical bombers were lightly loaded with extended-range fuel tanks—they had to fly three hundred miles farther than their MiG-23 brothers in order to outflank the Russians and successfully sneak up on the aircraft cruiser group—and they carried only one weapon, so they were very fast.

That one weapon—the Kh-59 missile—was the most devastating weapon in Ukrayina's air arsenal. Called the AS-13 Kingpost by NATO and nicknamed the SLAMski because of its resemblance to the U.S. Navy's AGM-84E SLAM (Standoff Land Attack Missile), the Kingpost was a TV-guided subsonic 2,000-pound rocket-powered missile with a 300-pound high-explosive warhead. The MiG-27 and Su-17 bombers fired their missiles at a range of about thirty-five miles from the warships, then turned back to the east. The missiles first climbed rapidly to thirty thousand feet, then began a steep descent down toward the Russian warships. The last twenty seconds of their flight would be controlled by the Ukrainian pilots via a television and steering datalink back to their fighters.

Once the Kh-59 missiles made their climb, however, they were sitting ducks for the Russian fighters—the A-50 Mainstay radar plane could easily track each of the twenty missiles fired at the Russian warships. Since most of the fighters were still too far south to chase down the cruise missiles, the Mainstay directed all but two of its own fighter escorts to try to shoot down the missiles. Eight Sukhoi-27 fighters broke out of their combat air patrols and sped eastbound, locking up the big one-ton missiles on radar and maneuvering to intercept. The radio datalink between missile and fighter was used as a beacon to locate each missile, and the sophisticated track-while-scan radar of the eight Su-27s allowed almost the entire complement of Kh-59 missiles to be targeted . . .

. . . which sealed the fate of the Russian Mainstay radar plane, which was the joint U.S./Turkish/Ukrainian task force's main target all along. While the main bulk of the Russian fighters was turning northeast to intercept the Ukrainian strike aircraft, and all but two of the Mainstay's escorts were trying to intercept the Kh-59 cruise missiles, ten MiG-23 fighters blasted in from the southwest at forty thousand feet.

They were led by Colonel Pavlo Tychina himself.

Like the strike birds, they carried fuel tanks and only one weapon each—an R-33 long-range air-to-air missile with the NATO reporting name AA-9 Amos. The R-33 was one of the largest air-to-air missiles in the world, weighing almost 1,000 pounds, but it was one of the most sophisticated. It had a range of ninety miles when launched from high altitude, a top speed of Mach-three, and a 225-pound warhead. It used three types of guidance: semiactive radar homing, where it homed in on reflected radar energy from its launch aircraft; active radar homing, where a small radar unit in its nose cone steered it toward its target; and passive radar homing, where the missile could home in on radar energy transmitted by other aircraft—especially the big rotodome of the A-50 Mainstay radar plane.

The R-33 missile was not a typical weapon of the MiG-23 fighter—the Flogger's radar could provide only basic navigation information and no guidance signals—but the power of the Mainstay's radar sealed its own fate.

Out of ten missiles launched against the Russian Mainstay, two hit home.

The 380,000-pound aircraft lost the rotodome and its vertical stabilizer, but the main crew compartment stayed virtually intact. Its crew of twenty-four officers, who watched the R-33 missiles home in on them on radar, were alive to feel the impact as the huge aircraft crashed into the Black Sea.

They joined the aircraft cruiser *Novorossiysk* on its way to the bottom of the Black Sea, and because it was easily the biggest, most easily identifiable target for the relatively inexperienced Ukrainian pilots, six of the twenty Kh-59 missiles that survived their short flight hit the cruiser. With its landing deck full of Yak-38 Forger aircraft ready to launch in support of fleet defense, the fires and destruction on board the 43,000-ton vessel were devastating and complete—356 officers and seamen would perish in the attack.

37

Same Time

"THUNDER ONE-ONE, MANY BANDITS AT ONE O'CLOCK, TWENTY miles, high. Chicks at two o'clock, seventy miles. Burner disengage east, bugout south. Acknowledge."

"Banjo, One-One copies, we're outta here," Rebecca Furness replied. She swept the wings of her Vampire all the way back to 72.5 degrees, shoved the throttles into full afterburner, and began to accelerate past Mach-one. "Let's get the Sidewinders on-line, Mark," she said.

"They're ready to go," Fogelman replied. "The HARM is ready to jettison too if you want to get rid of it. I've got trackbreakers on and countermeasures set."

The one remaining AGM-88 antiradar missile on the number-five pylon did not limit their top speed at all, but it did increase drag slightly and made the ride a little choppier. "We'll try to hang on to it for now," Furness replied. "We'll need all the HARMs we can—"

Their E-3 AWACS radar plane orbiting over central Turkey suddenly radioed, "'Apex,' Thunder, twelve o'clock, fifteen miles . . . 'Apex,' Thunder, twelve o'clock . . . 'Apex' . . ."

"Missile launch!" Fogelman shouted. "The Russian fighters are launching missiles! But we don't have a missile-launch indication or an uplink signal. I don't know where they are."

"It's an IRSTS attack," Furness said. The Russian IRSTS, or Infrared Search and Track System, allowed fighters to launch air-to-air missiles by combining range information from a ground or airborne radar with a heat-seeking sensor on their planes. The fighter radar needed to be turned on only for the missile's last seconds of flight. "Stand by, the uplink should be coming."

Suddenly a bat-wing symbol appeared directly in front of them on the threat warning scope, well within lethal range, and they got a bright red MISSILE LAUNCH indication and a fast *deedledeedledeedle* warning tone in their helmets.

"Fighter attack off the nose!" Fogelman shouted. He used two fingers to eject chaff bundles out of both left and right internal dispensers. "Chaff's out! Vertical jinks!"

They could not perform a break maneuver or a hard turn to try to throw the missile off, because they would only further highlight themselves—they had to hope their jammers would take care of the missile uplink and the enemy fighter radars would lock on to the decoy chaff instead.

The sky was filled with air-to-air missiles fired at them—the Russian fighters were close enough now so that they could see the missiles in the night sky as tiny winks of light as they launched. A missile exploded about two hundred yards off their left wing, close enough for them to feel the shock wave against their aircraft.

"Thunder, many bandits twelve o'clock high, twelve miles, line abreast, continue burner east, junk 'em, and hunker down." The AWACS controller's brevity messages were ones of desperation—he was telling Furness and Fogelman to fly balls-to-the-wall right through the line of Russian fighters, continue electronic countermeasures, and hope for the best. "First bandits now at ten miles, twelve o'clock. I've got bandits hooking north—they're expecting you to break south after the merge. Recommend you continue to extend eastbound at best speed. Lead bandits five miles."

Just then Furness heard it—the unmistakable growling of an AIM-9 Sidewinder missile locked on to a target. She did not hesitate, but squeezed the safety release button on her control stick and hit the launch button. The small heat-seeker on the left pylon darted out into space and was quickly lost from view.

"Thunder, bandits breaking left and right . . . head's down." The missile missed.

But it still had a good effect—the Russian attack formation had been broken up and was now on the defensive. "Banjo, can you get us the hell out of here?"

"Thunder, bandits at your ten o'clock, twenty miles high," the controller responded. "What state heat, Thunder?"

"Thunder has one."

"Roger, Thunder, snap to zero-three-zero nose high to engage."

"Yeah, baby, I like it," Fogelman exclaimed. "Let's get 'em." The AWACS controller was suggesting that they try to scatter the Russian fighters who were maneuvering to get a tail shot on them by trying a "snap shot" with their last Sidewinder missile—if they could get those fighters to turn away, even for a few moments, they had a chance to get away.

Furness rolled into a hard left turn toward the middle of the Black Sea—it was a totally unexpected move, with the safety of the northern Turkish coast only sixty miles to the south—and as soon as she raised the nose to 20 degrees above the horizon, she immediately got a growling tone and punched off the last remaining Sidewinder missile at the approaching Russian fighters. She then banked hard right, descended to two hundred feet above the sea, and began a full-afterburner power run to Turkey. They were out of weapons—speed and low level was their only hope now. "Gimme the TFRs, Mark," Furness said.

Fogelman already had his hands on the terrain-following radar switches, and he set them up as soon as Furness gave the word. "TFRs engaged, left TF, right SIT, hard ride."

"Thanks, Mark. Good work." Two vertical lines on the E-scope told them the system was in "LARA override," meaning their altitude over the water was controlled by the radar altimeter until they got within a few miles of the shoreline. On the command net, she radioed, "Banjo, Thunder is 'winchester,' request bogey-dope and vector to home plate."

"Thunder, your bandits are at five o'clock, fifteen miles high, converging rapidly, additional bandits at seven o'clock, twelve miles, recommend . . . *'Apex,'* Thunder, Apex, seven o'clock, eleven miles."

Fogelman was practically sitting backwards in his seat searching visually for the missiles. He then set the threat scope to IR, which used a heat-seeking sensor atop the vertical stabilizer to scan for heat sources behind them. "I don't see them, Becky," he said. "Nothing on the—"

Just then they got a MISSILE LAUNCH light on their instrument panel and a warning tone—the threat scope had picked up another Russian fighter launching missiles and automatically ejected both chaff and heat-seeking decoy flares. Furness shoved power to zone 5 afterburner, rolled into a 90-degree left bank, pulled on the control stick until the stall-warning horn blared, and released the back pressure on the stick. As soon as she did so, there was a terrific explosion less than one hundred feet from their right wingtip.

"Chaff and flares!" Furness shouted. Fogelman ejected more chaff and flares, and Furness rolled into a hard right turn. She had to sweep the wings forward to 54 degrees to keep from stalling the Vampire from all the hard turning.

"Thunder, threats at six o'clock, five miles, suggest you extend left, chicks at ten o'clock, thirty miles . . . threats now at seven o'clock, four miles high, feet dry in two minutes, continue to burner extend . . . threat at six o'clock . . . Atoll, Thunder, *Atoll!*" At the same time as the "Atoll" call, which was a warning against a suspected enemy heat-seeking-missile launch, the MISSILE LAUNCH light illuminated once again . . .

. . . but this time the flare ejector on the left side of the Vampire jammed, so flares ejected only out of the right dispenser. While Fogelman ejected chaff, Furness started a hard 5-G right break—right into one of the Russian AA-11 missiles. The AA-11's 33-pound warhead exploded between the right engine nacelle and the right cockpit canopy, nearly ripping the right engine and wing completely off the Vampire.

It was Rebecca Furness who initiated the ejection sequence, squeezing and pulling the yellow-and-black-striped handle by her right knee. The action fired several pyrotechnic initiators that tightened their shoulder harnesses and set off a guillotine-shaped linear charge all around the cockpit, including the wing gloves, from behind their seats to forward of the instrument panel at the forward tip of the long, slanted windscreen. A split-second later a powerful rocket motor blasted the cockpit capsule free of the stricken aircraft fuselage, with a smaller stabilizer rocket ensuring that the capsule did not pitch over backwards in the jet wash. The force of the primary rocket motor was like being hit in the back by a car going twenty miles an hour—not enough to kill, but guaranteed to make you remember it for the rest of your life.

The primary rocket motor burned for less than five seconds, but it was powerful enough to propel the capsule more than two hundred feet higher than the stricken aircraft. After motor burnout, accelerometers computed when the capsule had decelerated out of Mach speed, and a small pilot parachute and two flaps underneath the capsule "wings" were deployed to help the capsule stabilize. Almost at the top of its parabolic arc, the three main thirty-foot-diameter parachutes deployed. Twelve seconds after pulling the ejection handle, the Vampire capsule was under three good parachutes.

"Mark, you all right? Mark . . . ?"

"I'm here," Fogelman replied weakly. "Over here."

"I hope you're just trying to be funny, nav."

But there was no more time to talk. Four large air bladders—a large mattress-shaped impact-attenuation bag under the capsule, two large pillow-shaped flotation bags under the rear "wing" of the capsule, a mushroom-shaped anticapsize bag behind the pilot's canopy, and a large pillow-shaped righting bag that covered the navigator's canopy—automatically deployed a few seconds later, just before the capsule hit the icy waters of the Black Sea. The gusty north winds kept the parachute inflated for a few seconds after hitting the water, and the capsule was dragged along the sea for a few dozen yards before flipping upside down.

The cockpit was completely dark, and the sudden pitchover completely confused Furness. She was upside down in her seat, hanging from her shoulder and crotch straps, with ocean sounds all around her—it felt as if she were sinking to the bottom like a rock. The capsule was supposed to be watertight and could even keep water out if completely submerged, but that was only if the glass or structure hadn't been damaged. What if the thirty-year-old capsule had split apart or the missile had fractured it? What if the pressure of the seawater was finding some tiny weakness in the canopy and was about to break it wide open?

Don't panic. Don't panic. Don't panic, she told herself. She unbuckled her oxygen mask, then detached it completely and stuffed it in the storage space beside her seat. There was no water collecting on the canopy over her head, only checklists, papers, pencils, and fear—fear was collecting in that cockpit faster than anything else.

She heard a moan—was that from herself or from Mark?—and she reached over to him. "Mark, you all right?"

"I think I broke my face again," Fogelman said. He was also hanging in his straps, but his arms were hanging down onto the canopy. She reached for his oxygen mask—it was already broken free of his helmet. She found blood coming from his nostrils, but it was nothing serious. "Are you okay?" he asked.

"I'm okay."

"Are we still upside down? I can't tell right now."

"Just relax," Furness said. "We'll turn upright in a minute or two."

The large pillow-shaped flotation bag on the right side of the capsule was supposed to automatically right the capsule if it was inverted—the sinking parachutes must be holding it under. On the center overhead beam in the cockpit were four yellow handles. The easy way to remember which handle did which was the "cut-cut, float-float" method—starting from the top, the handles cut the capsule free of the aircraft, cut the parachute risers, deployed the parachute, and deployed the flotation bags. Furness pulled the capsule-severance handle, which unguarded the parachute riser-release handle, pulled the second handle, and a few minutes later, aided by the surging action of the icy-cold Black Sea, the capsule rolled to the left and flipped upright.

Both crewmembers sat in the darkness of the Vampire capsule for several minutes, not speaking and not moving. Both knew how lucky they were to be alive.

38

The Oval Office, One Hour Later, Eastern Time

EVEN AFTER TWO YEARS IN OFFICE, THIS WAS THE FIRST TIME the President had picked it up. In this day of high-speed satellite communications, it was an anachronism, sure, almost a joke—but the Hot Line, the direct line between the White House and the Kremlin, was still in use. Upgraded, it was going to be used right now. "This is the President of the United States. To whom am I speaking?"

"This is President Vitaly Velichko," the Russian president responded. "How are you this evening, sir?" The tone of voice was a bit strained—who wasn't these days?—but it sounded friendly enough. Velichko's English was very good—although the Russian president was an avowed Communist, part of the new right-wing politicians that wanted to return Russia to some semblance of its greatness of the Soviet Union, he was also well educated and rather cosmopolitan.

"I'm fine, Mr. President. I called because—"

The Hot Line was a satellite communications system, so there was no landline delay in their voices. "I am glad you are fine, Mr. President," Velichko said, his voice seething. "I hope you are sane and intelligent as well. If you are, you will withdraw your bomber forces from Turkey, return your nuclear bombers and submarine-based missiles to normal alert, and stop interfering in affairs between Commonwealth allies that do not concern you. Otherwise, Mr. President, I may unfortunately see you roast in *hell.*"

And the line went dead.

"Well, so much for that," the President said wearily. "Talking to that asshole is like talking to a brick wall. Christ, why couldn't people have listened when I wanted to prop up Yeltsin? They wouldn't listen to me, they wouldn't listen to former President Nixon when he warned us about this two years ago. Then our NATO allies gave Boris diddly-squat in aid. Now, look at what we've got. Shit—they can't say I didn't tell them so."

His advisers, and the First Lady, were gathered around the old Jack Kennedy desk, nodding in sympathy. They had certainly wanted more funds for aiding Yeltsin, but they'd seen how the country balked, claiming America needed to take care of its own first. And then when the Russian Congress started chopping away at Yeltsin's powers, bit by bit, the President knew it was a lost cause. Yeltsin's days had been numbered. And it could have been prevented.

A sharp pain shot through the southerner's stomach—his newfound ulcer was acting up—and continued straight up to his temples. The entire evening was grinding him down, something that usually happened only when his wife was being difficult. His entire adult life was in politics. Southern politics—down-and-dirty, rough-and-tumble, the worst kind. Southern politicians in an election were about as nice as starving junkyard pit bulls. It was constant work, constant attention to every detail, constant pressure, just to stay in office. He had never been in the military, but twenty years in public service was, he had always thought, *like* being in the military. It was a way of life, not just a job.

But being the President of the United States was like politics and military service combined, only amplified a thousand times.

All day long there had been a constant procession of people telling him he was wrong, and that exacerbated the ulcer even more. First he heard it from the Joint Chiefs of Staff—all of them. They all had plans on what to do, but one thing was for certain: they wanted *more.* No more bit-by-bit military expeditions—the Joint Chiefs wanted a Desert Storm–type mobilization and deployment. Nothing else would be acceptable. Orchestrated by President George Bush, the 1991 war with Iraq was fought with massive overwhelming strength, and it was over in one hundred days—never mind that they had unlimited fuel, six months to prepare, a third-rate opponent, and it had cost U.S. taxpayers sixty billion dollars. Led by the President, the Islamic Wars of 1993 were fought with units and weapons brought into the theater over a period of several months, and it lasted almost a year—same result, same casualty rate, but it cost only twenty billion. The Yugoslavian question had been stalemated for years until Germany led large numbers of NATO forces into that country, and the peace had lasted for almost a year now. That one cost the U.S. virtually nothing—except its leadership role in Europe, ceded over to a strong, reunified Germany.

Next came the senior senators and representatives, the Congressional "leadership." Most advocated caution. But they also liked it when the President and General Freeman from the Pentagon briefed them on the multinational skirmish in the Black Sea that had just taken place, which netted two Russian destroyers, a frigate, a guided-missile cruiser, an aircraft cruiser, and a Russian AWACS radar plane. Although they had lost two American planes—and the Ukrainians and Turks had lost none—the payback for the attack on the Turkish ships and the gratitude of the Turkish government for the RF-111Gs' action was a tremendous boost to everyone's spirits, and they were asking the President for more. Perhaps another aircraft carrier in the eastern Mediterranean, perhaps two more. Two hundred thousand troops to be sent to Europe—but not any closer than Belgium or Norway. F-15E Strike Eagle and F-16C Falcon bombers deployed to England, but none to Germany, and perhaps more F-111s deployed to Turkey. They loved the F-111, the Turks said. America was retiring and boneyarding all the F-111 Aardvarks anyway—why not sell them to Turkey?

Now he was just finishing up with the third group: the political advisers and media consultants from the President's party. "Economic sanctions of course," the party chairman was saying. "Sends a strong message, lots of feedback in the news, fairly safe, lots of play."

"But if the leadership is so rabid over the apparent success of the air attacks against those Russian ships, why not go for it?" a media type said, tipping his mug of coffee to the First Lady, who gave him a disdainful glare in return. "You hit the media with strong leadership, bold decisions, decisive actions, all designed to look good to the voters during the upcoming election year. This proves what you've been saying all along, Mr. President—limited-action military responses *can* be successful."

"We lost two RF-111G aircraft in that attack," General Freeman interjected. "That probably sounds like a trivial number to you—"

"Hey, General, don't go putting words in my mouth," the media hack said. "I'm sorry for what happened. But to me, the loss was pretty small and the results were pretty dramatic."

"The unit we sent over lost two of its twenty-four crewmembers and one-sixth of their aircraft *in one night,* dammit!" Freeman thundered. "The Russians figured out what was going on almost immediately and shut down their radars, which makes antiradar weapons completely ineffective."

"We can replace the aircraft and crewmembers, General," the party chairman said. "Those men knew—"

"And women," Freeman interjected.

Freeman's comment froze the party chairman in mid-sentence—he had completely forgotten women were involved in the conflict. "One of the crewmembers lost was a woman . . . ?"

"I briefed you ten minutes ago, sir, that the pilot on one of the planes shot down was First Lieutenant Paula Norton." He watched the chairman's eyes grow wide—everyone had heard of Paula Norton. "She was practically a one-person recruiting operation for the Air Force Reserves. Your son probably has a poster of her in his room."

"Let's stick with the subject, which is what to do about any further Russian aggression." The President sighed, dipping into a bag of Fritos sitting next to a glass of Coke.

"Excuse me, sir, but the question is not what to do about further Russian aggression," Freeman said. He hesitated for a moment, wondering if he was going to be burning a very big bridge. "We need to discuss, uh, leadership of this crisis. Mr. President, *what* do you want to *do* about this?"

"I think the President's views are clear on this subject, General," the First Lady interjected, glaring at Freeman. "The President wants the Russians to stop making war on former Soviet republics and stop threatening our allies."

"I know that, ma'am. My thought is, we need to formulate a plan. We need to establish thresholds of action. We need to build consensus and a sense of purpose. What we've done so far is symbolic and reactive—we're responding *after* something happens instead of anticipating and planning what *may* happen, and what we'll do about it *if* it happens."

"Well, how in the hell are we supposed to do that, General?" the President mumbled, the frustration obvious in his voice. "Who would've expected the Russians to invade a fellow CIS member—that's like America invading Canada or England, for God's sake! And who would've known they'd use nuclear weapons?" Little bits of Fritos were flying out of his mouth onto the desk.

"We have some of the best minds in the world working for you in the Pentagon, in the State Department, and right here in the White House," Freeman responded. "We can give you our estimate of what we think the Russians will do next. But it's a very broad list, so our planned response will be sweeping."

"Including mobilizing and deploying hundreds of thousands of troops, I suppose," the First Lady interjected, picking lint off her pants suit.

"I submit, ma'am, that the Russians' course of action, especially their use of low-yield nuclear weapons, means we need to prepare for an equal or greater military response and hope that we can solve this with a peaceful response," Freeman answered. "The Russians set the precedent here, and I haven't seen any sign of letting up. We have little choice but to prepare for an escalation of hostilities—and work like hell to avoid them."

The phone on the President's desk rang. "Yes . . . ? Okay, just for a minute." The President's physician entered the Oval Office, shook his head in obvious disapproval, and had the President use a hand-held finger-cuff device to measure his blood pressure and pulse.

"You look like hell, Mr. President." He clucked. "How about calling it a night early—say, before three A.M. this time? And lay off all this junk food."

"Very funny," the President drawled. The doctor had the President work the device three times to make sure the readings were correct. He was about to take a seat to chat with his patient, but the President said, "Just leave me a full bottle of Tagamets. We've got work to do." The doctor thought about checking up on the First Lady, but she warned him off with a cold stare and he quickly departed. She could see how tired and upset her husband was getting, so she ordered all of the politicos to leave as well.

"All right, Philip," the President said to General Freeman, after everyone but the Vice President, Freeman, Scheer, Grimm, and Lifter had departed, "I'm listening. Give me your best guess as to what's going to happen next."

"The Russians *will* retaliate," Freeman said firmly. "A massive but centralized attack, someplace that will punish the Ukrainians for their attacks and possibly the Turks and us for our role in helping them. My staff's guess is Kiev, the capital of the Ukraine. Secondary target would be Kayseri, where the Russians know we've got most of the Ukrainians based—except now we've dispersed both the American and Ukrainian aircraft to other bases in Turkey in anticipation of an attack, and we're getting the Patriot systems set up as fast as we can.

"The most likely alternate targets: Golcuk, the Turkish industrial and naval center; Istanbul, the historical and cultural center of Turkey and strategically vital; or Ankara, the capital itself. My staff feels the Russians will not restrict themselves to military targets but will expand their target list to include command and control, industrial centers, and communications hubs."

"A nuclear attack?"

"My answer to that, sir, is 'why not?'" Freeman replied. "Why wouldn't they use those neutron warheads against Turkey, like they did in the Ukraine?"

"Because we'd blow their shit away and they know it!" Grimm retorted.

"General, be realistic," the First Lady said wearily. "The Russians would not *dare* to use any more nuclear weapons, especially against a NATO ally. That would be suicide."

"Would it, sir? Would it, ma'am?" Freeman asked. "What exactly would you do if the Russians attacked Turkey? Send in the bombers? Sir, we have not demonstrated the *resolve* to do *anything,* let alone stage a thermonuclear attack on a Russian target. The attack on the Russian ships in the Black Sea was a fluke, a lucky shot, and we only had six aircraft involved in the operation—the Ukrainians had over a hundred. The Russians have used nuclear weapons on multiple targets in the Ukraine, along with destroying several Turkish warships, and you have not had one meaningful conversation with President Velichko of Russia or made any sort of equivalent response."

The First Lady rose to her feet and said icily, "I advise you to *watch* your tone of voice, General."

"I know exactly what I'm saying, ma'am, and it's my job to say it," Freeman shot back. "We deployed virtually *no* forces overseas, we did *not* mobilize any additional Reserve forces, and we did *not* federalize any forces except the ones who would go on strategic alert. The entire Western World thinks we've abandoned them, sir."

"That's bullshit, Freeman, and you know it," Grimm retorted with a snort, looking to the First Lady for support.

"Their neutron weapon is a powerful terror tool, sir," National Security Director Lifter said. "They can set off a nuclear device and actually control the casualties they want to inflict—but it's not a weapon of mass destruction, per se. Over a populated area it can kill tremendous numbers—but over a nonpopulated area, it will do little or no damage."

"Mr. President, killing ten thousand persons by neutron bomb or by high-explosive bombs doesn't make any bit of difference to me," Freeman said, "and it obviously doesn't make any difference to the Russian military or government. In fact, it's a cost-effective and very efficient weapon."

"You sound like some kind of Dr. Frankenstein," the First Lady snapped. "The end justifies the means, is that right, General? Do whatever it takes to get the job done?"

"There's no bad way to kill," Freeman said. "Or any good way to die. There's just killing and death."

The First Lady rolled her eyes in disbelief. "I think that's nonsense too," the President said, popping more Fritos into his mouth along with a few Tagamets. "This is almost the twenty-first century, Philip. Modern-day wars must be fought with restraint and carefully controlled escalation, with stops and checks and pauses put in to encourage the conflict to end and diplomacy to begin again. We're not trigger-happy, for God's sake. We have the weapons and the technology to destroy with precision and strength without resorting to nuclear weapons. Besides, Velichko or some other wacko in Moscow probably's got his finger on the button night and day—we let loose with a nuke of our own, and the whole world goes up in smoke."

"That's a myth, Mr. President," Freeman said. "We've learned that a lot of the ideas we had about nuclear warfighting just don't hold true."

"Like what, General?" asked the First Lady skeptically.

"Like the idea that a finger is poised over a button in Russia someplace, and at the first sign of attack, the whole world is a goner," Freeman replied. "In fact, it takes three persons in Russia—the President, the Minister of Defense, and the Chief of the General Staff—to order a nuclear attack, and only one person to stop it; in our country, of course, it only takes one to start it, but many persons can stop it and it can even stop *itself,* with our system of built-in termination and fail-safes. And this assumes that the Russians can in fact detect a launch or even an impact: we've learned that Russian surveillance satellites and other long-range detection systems aren't as good as we once thought, to the point that a nuclear detonation in Kazakhstan, Tajikistan, or Siberia might go completely unnoticed."

"What's your point, General?" the President asked impatiently.

"The point is, sir, is that wars aren't started or stopped quickly, especially nuclear wars. Russia knows we're ready to fight a nuclear war, sir, and even though we don't have very many weapons on-line, the ones we have are devastating. Velichko isn't insane, no matter what Sen'kov or *The New York Times* says. He would do the same as you're doing right now, sir—meet with his advisers, discuss a plan of action, then proceed. He serves a constituency too."

"Yeah—a constituency of other hard-line neo-Communist wackos." But the President was silent for a moment; then: "So let's assume they attack both the Ukraine and Turkey, and even use more nuclear weapons—maybe even full-yield weapons. What then?"

"That's the question I'm posing to you, sir," Freeman said. "What's our priority? What's your goal? What kind of role do you want to play? Do you want to protect a NATO ally, or punish Russia, or both? Do you want to wait and see or do you want to act?"

"Every time you say that, General, I want to bust you in the face," the First Lady suddenly exploded, "and I consider it *my* job to say it. You make it sound like a cautious, wait-and-see attitude is wrong. You make it seem as if action—and I read that as *war,* pure *violence*—is the only response you'll accept."

"Ma'am, I'm paid to give my professional opinion, based on the information I have and my knowledge and experience."

Freeman sighed. "The President can take my advice, adopt it, reject it, fire me, or hire someone else. If he tells me to jump, I'll salute and ask 'How high?' but I'll also give him my thoughts and opinions on the way up and on the way down."

"I think you need to step back and reevaluate your priorities here, General," she replied coldly, glaring at her husband as if to say, *We've got to get rid of him.*

"I didn't start this conflict, ma'am, and I didn't set the limits. But we've got two dead U.S. airmen now, and an important ally that, I feel, is going to get nailed any minute now. We need to formulate a plan." He turned to the President and concluded earnestly, "I'll do whatever you want, sir. I'm on your team. Just tell me what you want to do."

The phone rang again and the President shook his head. The Chief of Staff answered it, then put the caller on hold. "Sir, it's Valentin Sen'kov, calling from Moscow."

"Tell him to call back later."

"He says it's urgent."

The President was going to refuse again, but this time the First Lady reached over and took the phone. *"Dobriy vyechyeer,* Valentin. *Kak dyela?"* She listened for a moment, then turned on the speakerphone and set the receiver back on its cradle. "I've got you on speakerphone with the President and some members of his staff, Valentin. Go ahead and repeat what you just told me."

"Dear," the President said irritably, "what in hell do you think you're doing?" Along with feeling as if he were being pulled apart by the flurry of voices and activity around him, adding the pompous Sen'kov's voice to the soup wasn't going to help. He also didn't like his wife's growing proficiency in Russian, especially when Sen'kov was involved.

"I am very sorry to disturb you, Mr. President," Sen'kov said on the speakerphone, "but I feel this is very urgent. I know you just called President Velichko. I must inform you that Velichko is no longer in Moscow. He is on the underground railway to the alternate military command center at Domodedovo."

"What?"

"Why is he doing that, Valentin?" the First Lady asked. "We're not doing anything here. We don't have any operations planned against Russia."

"Ma'am, *please,*" Freeman admonished her. "That's an open line!" She ignored him.

"I do not have precise information, sir," Sen'kov continued, "but I believe he has evacuated the Kremlin. He is very disturbed about the attacks over the Black Sea, and I fear he might retaliate immediately."

"Retaliate? How? When?"

"I do not know," Sen'kov said. "I cannot talk longer, sir. But I must say this: Velichko is unstable. The military will follow him, but they are ambivalent and are simply looking for leadership. They will follow Velichko into Hell . . . or they will follow me into true reform and progress. Mr. President, I am asking for your assistance. I know precisely where Velichko will be thirty minutes from now. I am sure your CIA has detailed information on Domodedovo. You have bombers in Turkey, cruise missile submarines in the Aegean and Mediterranean, and intercontinental ballistic missiles. Destroy Domodedovo. Kill Velichko before he starts World War Three."

"Sen'kov, are you insane?" the President retorted. "I'm not about to use nuclear weapons to kill the leader of a nation."

"I am sorry, Mr. President, I can speak no more," Sen'kov said. "I will be in contact with you later," and the line went dead.

The President and his advisers looked at the telephone with stunned expressions, as if the device had just come alive and was squirming on the desk. Finally, after a long silence, the President's advisers began to speak. Harlan Grimm said, "He's totally out of line, Mr. President."

"I don't think that's a viable option, sir," Scheer said. "It's totally out of character for an American president to specifically target a national leader."

"I think it's the first good suggestion I've heard in days," Philip Freeman said.

"General Freeman, are you insane or just having some kind of a nervous breakdown?" the First Lady asked. "Are you trying to be funny? The man just suggested that we try to assassinate Velichko with a nuclear bomb."

"I can't think of a better thing to do, a better weapon to use, and a more rotten person to use it on," Freeman said. To the President he said, "Sir, we had a great victory in Desert Storm, but we suffered one major defeat—we missed Saddam Hussein. That decision, although it seemed appropriate and right and moral then, we now regard as a major mistake. Saddam cost this country a lot when he rose up again two years ago.

"Vitaly Velichko will do the same thing. I truly believe that Velichko will not stop until he precipitates a third world war, or until NATO knuckles under and allows him to take the Ukraine, the Baltic States, and Georgia back under Russian rule. He has used nuclear weapons, and I truly believe he will continue to do so. If we target Velichko now in his bunker in Domodedovo, we'll get him and kill perhaps a few thousand more."

"And risk a massive nuclear retaliation by the Russians," the First Lady declared, her eyes burning on Freeman.

"Not in my opinion, ma'am," Freeman said. "If we get Velichko and members of his cabinet and the military command, and get the codes, no attack will take place. If Sen'kov really can take control of the government and the military—and I think he can—he might be able to head off any kind of nuclear retaliation. But if we don't do it, Velichko will continue to escalate the conflict, hoping we'll back down. Ultimately we'll be forced into a corner and have to resort to a massive nuclear attack on Russia to make the conflict stop. Instead of stopping the conflict after killing only a few thousand—far less than the Ukraine has already suffered—hundreds of millions might die in an all-out nuclear exchange."

The President rubbed his eyes wearily as the First Lady and the Chairman of the Joint Chiefs of Staff shot glares at each other. After several long moments, the President opened a red-covered folder on his desk—it was the Pentagon's joint analysis of the progression of the conflict and a list of recommended military options. "Tell us what you're thinking, Mr. President," Secretary of State Harlan Grimm said.

"I want . . ." the President began, swallowed, took a deep breath, and wondered how in the hell history would judge him for what he was about to do. This was the most critical event of his Administration so far. The people of the country had short memories, but history did not. He had gotten into politics and run for office because he'd wanted to put *his* stamp on America. He had run for President and won against all odds because he'd wanted to shake things up after the complacent four years of George Bush and the eight years of Ronald Reagan's Armageddon view of reality concerning what the

American military really needed. But he had never, never been pushed to the wall like this. And history was waiting, calling him to respond as so many presidents had been forced to do before him . . . from Truman to Kennedy to Reagan to Bush.

"I want this fucking war to *stop,* right now," the President continued. "I want Russia to immediately cease all overflights and patrols threatening our allies. I want Russia to immediately begin a pullback of all ground forces out of the Ukraine and Moldova. I want Russia to immediately withdraw their Black Sea warships to Russian ports—"

"And if they don't, Mr. President?"

"If they *don't,* then I'll—" He looked as if he were on the verge of exploding or totally breaking down—Freeman couldn't tell. "If they don't, we will attack and destroy a military target in Russia."

"What?" gasped the First Lady, horrified.

"The General's right," the President told her. "We've acted with restraint, and all we've gotten is more violence. I don't see an end to it unless we act, unless we answer force with force. I'm not playing the peacemaker anymore. I tried it in the Islamic Wars, and it took the Turks to bail me out. I tried it in Yugoslavia, and Germany bailed me out. So far in this fight, Turkey's bailed me out again. I'm not sitting back any longer.

"I will take the fight to Russia—no economic sanctions, no negotiations, no screwing with words while more American airmen get killed, no more Hot Line phone calls where the asshole *hangs up* on me. The Russian people will find out what it's like to get nuked, to see loved ones die of radiation poisoning, to watch the skies and wonder if the next plane will drop a neutron bomb on their house and destroy everything. I will launch a nuclear bomber attack into Russia against a military target and obliterate it. I will send the stealth bombers into Russia and destroy a military base. I am going to end this damned war or I will carry it through to the fucking *end!*"

There was no sound in the Oval Office for several long moments, except for the sound of the President's deep breathing and the sound of the First Lady pacing back and forth after she'd gotten up. "All right, General," the President said resignedly. "I want a plan to destroy this bunker—this Domodedovo airport. How soon can you have something to show me?"

"Preliminary assessment within the hour, Mr. President," Freeman said, still amazed the President capitulated. "A detailed briefing ready to present to the leadership and the Alliance in three . . . no, two hours."

"I want it surgically done, with as little collateral damage as possible," the President ordered. "Do we have any of those low-yield things the Russians use?"

"Even if we did, it wouldn't work against the bunker, sir," Freeman said. "The neutron radiation can't penetrate through more than eighteen inches of concrete—the bunker probably has more than eighteen *feet* of concrete, if it's anything like Strategic Command headquarters or the NMCC. We have to dig it out, and that means at least twenty kilotons and a direct hit, with an airburst fuzing height of no more than five thousand feet."

"I don't believe what I'm hearing," the First Lady gasped. Over the sudden hubbub of voices the phone rang again, and the Chief of Staff picked it up. "I can't believe I'm actually witnessing the planning of a nuclear attack against Russia." The President took the phone from his Chief of Staff when it was held out to him. He listened for a few moments, then handed it back.

"Looks like we're going to need that plan, General Freeman. There's been a Russian cruise missile attack in Turkey. Ataturk International Airport in Istanbul and the Golcuk naval base were hit."

"Any nuclear weapons used, sir?"

There was a long pause. The President lowered his head and took a deep breath. "Both targets," the President said. "Subatomic warheads, exploded at ten thousand feet."

"My God," Scheer said. "I can't believe it . . . the Russians actually dared to launch another nuclear attack."

"The loss of life may be low," Freeman offered quickly, shocked at how depressed and stricken the President appeared right now—he looked as if he might be on the verge of tears or a violent outburst. "The Turks dispersed the fleet based at Golcuk days ago. The facility is large but fairly isolated, in very rugged terrain, so neutron radiation would be isolated to the local area. The nearest city is ten miles away, out of the hazard radius for a neutron device, and it's small. As far as Istanbul-Ataturk International, it was closed to commercial traffic when the Russians attacked the Turkish Navy, so there would be just a skeleton military security team there. The city is close, about three to four miles northeast, but it would probably not be affected—the danger radius of the weapons the Russians exploded in the Ukraine was only one to two miles. The Russians picked their target well, sir—maximum shock value but very low loss of life."

The President clung to that bit of news and actually seemed to appear relieved. He clasped his wife's hand, who had now gone over to his side, and looked at her stunned face with concern. "It'll be all right, honey," he said in a low voice. "Everything will be all right."

"Sir, perhaps you should think about evacuating Washington," Freeman said. "A flight of Russian cruise missiles launched from a submarine can devastate this city."

"No way," the President said resolutely. "I left once before, and it was the worst embarrassment of my life. I *will* consider sending the Vice President and other Cabinet members out of town—but I'm not leaving.

"I want a statement drafted up immediately, *ordering* the Russians to pull out of the Ukraine and cease all hostile activities. And I want that Russian target list made up as soon as possible. If I don't get an answer back from Velichko immediately, I'm ordering the air strike for tomorrow night."

39

Batman Air Base, Eastern Turkey, That Morning

EVER SINCE HE GOT THE ASSIGNMENT TO PLATTSBURGH AND the RF-111G Vampire, Daren Mace knew he'd be back at Batman Air Base in Turkey. He didn't know why he knew. Obviously the trouble in Eastern Europe, the capabilities of the Vampire bomber, and the Turks' love of the beast had a lot to do with it.

He stood alone on Batman's large parking ramp area, in front of the base operations building. Batman was one of the most modern military bases in the world, with large concrete hangars and extensive underground aircraft-maintenance facilities. It was the headquarters of the Turkish government's defense against Kurdish and Shi'ite Muslim rebels and extremists in the east, as well as being in the center of a powerful industrial and petroleum-production region, and was therefore very well defended and purposely isolated. Located near the headwaters of the Euphrates River of eastern Turkey, with tall mountains to the south and east, the base was also very beautiful. During Desert Storm, Batman was the little-known headquarters of the U.S. Special Operations Command, operating secret combat search and rescue and "unconventional warfare" missions throughout Iraq and the entire Middle East region . . .

. . . and it was also the headquarters of Operation Desert Fire, the mission to destroy an Iraqi military bunker with a thermonuclear weapon if Saddam Hussein used chemical or biological weapons during the war. Back then, Daren Mace had come within seconds of launching the nuke. Now it seemed the whole world was insane enough to use nuclear weapons.

Mace heard a helicopter approach a few moments later. It was a Turkish Jandarma (Turkey's interior militia) S-70 utility helicopter, a license-built copy of the UH-60 Black Hawk. The helicopter had a load slung underneath, and Mace motioned four of his maintenance techs to move a large roller cradle over to get ready to load. It was the escape capsule of an RF-111G Vampire bomber—Rebecca's bomber. The capsule was carefully loaded onto the cradle, and then the S-70 landed and dropped off a single passenger.

Before she had taken three steps away from the jetcopter, Mace had rushed over to Rebecca Furness' side, taken her in his arms, and kissed her deeply. Rebecca returned his kiss, then buried her face in his shoulder.

He finally led her away from the roar of the rotors. "Jeez, Rebecca, I thought I lost you," Mace told her.

"You didn't lose me," Furness replied. "You won't lose me unless you're stupid enough to let me go."

He smiled, then held her face in his hands. "No chance of that," he told her, punctuating his promise with another kiss.

They went over to inspect the capsule. "The missiles blew out the right flotation bag," Furness said, "but we stayed afloat pretty well even though we were low in the water. Everything worked—radios, survival kit, flares." She held up a helmet bag and added, "Two bottles of Chivas Regal—that's all I could scrounge off the Turkish Navy. For your survival specialists and airframe maintenance crews."

"I've got them too busy to drink it right now," Mace said, "but they'll appreciate the thought. Never hurts to suck up to the survival-gear gods. Where's Mark? Is he okay?"

"He's fine," Furness replied. "He aggravated his back injury in the ejection, and the medics found blood in his stool, so he's being taken to Incirlik for tests. He did real good out there—he's turned into a real crewdog after all."

"That's good," Mace said. He held her tightly, then said, "I'm damned sorry about Norton and Aldridge."

"They didn't find them?"

Mace shook his head. "The Russians recovered them and what's left of the plane. They said they'll release the bodies after the fighting stops. Sorry, Rebecca. Norton was a real fighter. She could have wimped out like Ted Little, but she didn't." He hesitated again, then said, "You and Mark did good, Rebecca. The whole squadron did good. Two destroyers, a frigate, and a guided missile cruiser—you and Fogelman got two out of the four. The Ukrainians got the Russian AWACS and the *Novorossiysk* aircraft carrier."

"I remember the excited looks of the crews when they got back from a successful mission over Iraq during the war," Rebecca said. "Funny—I don't feel like that at all. I mean, I'm glad we flew the mission, and that we hit back, but I don't feel like anything was accomplished."

"You heard about Golcuk and Istanbul International?" he asked, referring to the low-yield nuclear attack by the Russians.

"Yes," Rebecca replied. "It's incredible. Were there very many casualties?"

"About two thousand so far," Mace said. "The radiation hasn't run its course yet—they may get several thousand more."

"My God. What are we going to do here?"

"I think we're going to find out," Mace said. "Colonel Lafferty wants to see us immediately. Mass briefing in about fifteen minutes."

The squadron meeting was being held in a briefing room in one of the underground hangar complexes. As Mace and Furness headed for the briefing, Mace suddenly stopped, went down another corridor, stopped at a door marked INFIRMARY, and said, "We'd better stop in here first."

"Who got hurt? I thought everyone made it back okay?" In a room by herself, they found First Lieutenant Lynn Ogden, wearing a paper gown, lying on a bed on top of the sheets, curled up into a fetal position and sobbing uncontrollably. "Lynn?"

When Ogden saw Furness, she gave a loud cry, then reached for her with trembling hands. Furness held her tightly. "What's the matter, Lynn? Are you hurt? Where's Clark? Are you guys okay?" Lynn did not reply, only cried harder. After holding each other for a moment, Lynn suddenly seemed to just melt away from Rebecca, and Daren had to help guide her limp body back onto the table. "Lynn, what's the matter with you?

What happened? I thought you made it back okay. Lynn, stop it, you're scaring me."

"She can't hear you, Rebecca," Mace said. "She's been like that ever since the raid. She and Vest hit a frigate with two HARMS and sent the sucker right down to the bottom—no survivors. She was morose after hitting the ship, but when she found out she *sunk* it, she went schizo. They'll take her to Incirlik for evaluation—probably airevac her out to Germany if it's safe to fly. Her family is flying out to Germany."

"She's not sick? No injuries? Did they take skull X-rays or anything?"

"I've seen this before, Rebecca," Mace said as a nurse guided them out of the room—they could still hear her sobbing even after leaving the room. "Call it shell shock, or posttraumatic-shock syndrome, or battle fatigue—she's so traumatized by the mission that she can't control her emotions. She's aware of everything and everyone around her, but they can't make her stop."

"Shouldn't they sedate her or something?"

"They did. That's her after the sedative wore off."

As they exited the infirmary, they ran directly into Colonel Pavlo Tychina, the wing commander of the Ukrainian Air Force contingent. "Ah . . . Major Rebecca Furness. I am very glad to see you." He shook both their hands and gave her a hug, pressing his gauze-covered cheek to hers instead of kissing. He still wore the white sterile-gauze mask everywhere—he refused to be seen without it. "I have heard of your fellow crewmember, Lieutenant Ogden. I am most sorry. I hope she will be fine."

"*Dyakoyo.* Thank you," Rebecca said, using one of the few bits of Ukrainian she had learned after the short time spent with the Ukrainian aircrews. Despite his horrible visage, she had found Tychina to be a very likable man, animated yet very by-the-book with his men, formal with the Turks, and polite, almost effusive, with the Americans. He was always working and always the commander, although he seemed at least ten years too young for the job. Of course, with the mask on, it was hard to tell if Tychina was thirty or sixty. His nickname "Voskresensky," "Phoenix" in English, was well known throughout the joint air forces, and his heroic story was also well known, as was his sad story about his fiancée's death from neutron radiation. "I think she'll be all right."

"Of course," Tychina said solemnly. "Your crew very brave. You are brave . . . and pretty." They walked together until reaching the main briefing room.

As was their custom, the Turkish aircrews were standing in the back of the room and along the walls. They all looked on with undisguised disgust as Furness entered the briefing room. A Turkish F-16 pilot curled his arms up along his chest, put his fist up to his mouth as if he were sucking his thumb, and whimpered like a dog. The Ukrainians reacted just the opposite—they got to their feet, applauding and cheering, and they slapped her on the back and the butt as if she were a man as she made her way to the front of the conference room and greeted Lafferty, Hembree, and the other American crewmembers. "Welcome back, Rebecca," Lafferty said, putting his arm around her. "Sorry you lost your plane, but you did a terrific job."

"Thank you, sir. Lieutenant Fogelman sends his regards."

"He called from Incirlik," Hembree says. "He's ready to come back already. The docs don't know yet."

"He did really well out there last night, sir," Furness told Lafferty. "I'll fly with him anytime. I'm sorry about Paula and Curt, sir. Lynn too."

"Me too. Their loss is hard on everyone here. Losses always hit small units the hardest. We just need to pull together."

"So what's going on?" Mace asked.

"We're getting a briefing by some NATO and Central Command brass," Lafferty said. "They should be here any minute. You know about the Russian attacks in Turkey, right, Rebecca?" She nodded. "I think the White House is *finally* going to get into gear. I don't know what role we can play, but something's happening."

As if on cue, the room was called to attention, and three officers entered, followed by several Turkish staff members. The American officers snapped to attention . . .

. . . and as they reached the stage and stepped up to the podium, Daren Mace could not believe who he saw: along with General Suleyman Isiklar, the base commander of Batman, and General Petr Iosifovich Panchenko, the Ukrainian Air Force chief of staff who had arrived that morning, was Major General Bruce Eyers, U.S. Army, and Major General Tyler Layton, U.S. Air Force—the very same officers in charge of Desert Fire, the abortive nuclear attack against Iraq four years earlier. He suddenly felt a sinking in his stomach.

"Seats," Isiklar's aide ordered. Everyone took seats—everyone except Daren Mace. Eyers and Layton noticed the one man still standing, but refused to acknowledge him other than giving him a stern look and an unspoken order to sit down.

Isiklar made a short bow to the portrait of Mustafa Kemal Ataturk, the founder of the modern Republic of Turkey—the portraits and little shrines to Ataturk were everywhere in Turkey, and they were treated as politely as if the man were in attendance—then said to the audience without preamble, "Death to the enemies of the Turkish Republic and to evil aggressors everywhere. We begin our campaign to drive away the Russians tonight, with the help of God, the blessings of Kemal Ataturk, and spearheaded by the brave Ukrainians and the Americans. May I please introduce Major General Bruce Eyers, the deputy commander of NATO Forces Southeast." Amidst the growls, cheers, and cries from the Ukrainian crewmembers, Isiklar turned the stage over to Bruce Eyers.

Eyers gave Ataturk's portrait a perfunctory nod, stepped up to the podium, and said, "I am here to inform you that, as of oh-one-hundred hours Eastern European time, in accordance with Article 12 of the North Atlantic Treaty and by unanimous vote of all member nations, the Republic of Ukrayina and the Republic of Lithuania have been formally accepted for full membership in the North Atlantic Alliance. Therefore, in accordance with Article 5 of the North Atlantic Treaty and with Article 51 of the United Nations Charter, all member nations of the North Atlantic Treaty Organization alliance have been put on full military alert, including the forces of the United States of America. Although the Congress of the United States has not made a declaration of war, the President of the United States has ordered two hundred thousand troops deployed immediately in support of NATO operations. The government of Turkey has authorized the deployment of one hundred thousand troops on its soil. An attack upon one member nation shall be considered an attack upon us all."

The Ukrainians went crazy with joy at the news, yelling and cheering like madmen. Colonel Tychina let it go for a few moments, then raised a hand for silence.

"I would like to announce that effective immediately General Petr Panchenko, Chief of Staff of the Air Force of the Republic of Ukrayina, is hereby designated commander of joint

NATO air forces, eastern region, and will be the overall air forces commander of NATO units in Turkey, the Ukraine, and Lithuania. He will report directly to myself as NATO task force commander for this emergency. General Panchenko, the command is yours." Again, the room erupted with sheer bedlam as the crazily happy Ukrainian officers welcomed their leader to the podium.

Panchenko was not proficient in English, so he had Pavlo Tychina translate for him: "The General says that his message is simple and direct. Fellow warriors, today we begin the liberation of Ukrayina." He waited until the cheering and applause died down, then: "However, we have no illusions of grandeur here. Our force is small, and we are committed to the defense of our host country and fellow NATO member, Turkey, as well as the defense of our homeland. We cannot hope to win this war ourselves. Rather, we must hold out until our NATO brothers can arrive in force. But we will not be idle. As we discovered last night, although we cannot kill the Russian bear, we can sting the hell out of him.

"The suppression of enemy air defenses will be our primary mission," Tychina continued, translating for Panchenko. "The more effectively and the deeper inside Ukrayina we can destroy Russian air defense weapons and radar sites, on land, sea, and in the air, the more effective NATO air strikes will be. Our mission is to control the skies over the Black Sea and render all Russian-held air and naval bases along the Black Sea combat-ineffective, which should allow NATO forces free access to the Black Sea to open a second front of attack.

"I will conduct a briefing for all flight commanders immediately following this briefing, in which I will outline my objectives and my outline for the first month. The first launch will be at nineteen hundred hours tonight. Our objective will be the Russian naval base at Novorossiysk and the air bases at Rostov-na-Donu and Krasnodar. If we can destroy these two air bases and the naval base, we can relieve Ukrainian Army units in the Don region from Russian air attacks and cut off Russian naval and air units in the Crimea from routine resupply. This concludes my briefing. May God bless and keep us all."

No sooner had the briefing concluded than Eyers motioned for the senior American officers to follow him into an adjacent room. The door was closed and locked—and Eyers greeted

Daren Mace with a large grin. "Why, hello, traitor—I see you remember me."

"Who are you calling a traitor, Eyers?" Mace hissed. "Who let this psycho in here?"

"I hoped you were dead, Mace," Eyers said evenly.

"I hoped you were alive so I could kill you *myself,* you wacko."

"All right, both of you, shut up," General Layton interrupted. "General Eyers, can we get on with this briefing?"

"What in the hell is going on here, sir?" Colonel Lafferty asked. "Daren, you know General Eyers?"

"Only by voice—and by smell."

"You shut your mouth, yellow-belly. Who in hell made you a colonel, anyway? Certainly nobody in *my* country's air force."

"It appears that everyone in this room has had a promotion in the past four years except you, Eyers."

"I said button it, Colonel," Layton interjected. "General, like it or not, we're all going to be working very closely together in the next few hours, so—"

"We ain't gonna be working together—I'll be giving the orders, and this time you better be carrying them out, sonny boy," Eyers interrupted loudly. He stepped closer to Mace, got right in his face, daring him to shrink from him. Mace did not—which only angered Eyers even more. "If I had my way, chicken-shit, I'd put you in leg irons in Leavenworth or at a nice remote radar site in Thule, Greenland."

"He's not leaving, General," Layton said, "and you know it."

"I know, I know," Eyers snapped. "It's a major fuck-up for the Chairman to choose the bastard that chickened out, refused to obey orders, nearly got himself shot down, and nearly killed his pilot during Desert Storm."

All eyes turned in stunned disbelief at Daren Mace. He said, "They don't know it, Eyers, because it's not true. Maybe they don't know that you were the one who ordered me to launch a nuclear missile on Baghdad during the Persian Gulf War."

"I should bust you for mentioning that, Mace," Eyers said. "That's classified information." All eyes swung back in even more stunned disbelief at Eyers—but this time, instead of a horribly angry face, they found a pleased, satisfied smile. Eyers said, "Yeah, Colonel, I did order you to launch an attack. It was a lawful order from the President of the United States. I was right to issue that order and you were wrong to refuse."

"I refused because it was rescinded."

"It wasn't rescinded. You *guessed* it had been, like some goddamned psychic or something. Well, guess what, hotshot? The President has just ordered *you* to do it again. You're going to lead another nuclear missile attack against the Russian western air forces military district headquarters at Domodedovo."

Everyone in the room was thunderstruck. "What did you say, General?" Lafferty asked.

"You heard me," Eyers said, the smile disappearing. "We're going in with the Ukrainians to bomb Novorossiysk, Krasnodar, and Rostov-na-Donu, but after they finish having their little fun pretending that they're actually *contributing* something to this war, we'll take your RF-111s up along the Ukrainian border, up into Russia, launch a SRAM or two on the Russian bastard Velichko's underground bunker at Domodedovo, and split for Lithuania. The Lithuanians are going to cover your retreat. We take out this base and the underground command center, and the air war is over for the damned Russians. The President wants to teach the fucking Russians a lesson, and that's exactly what we're going to do."

"We've been ordered to launch a nuclear strike against Russia?" Furness asked in complete disbelief. "Are you sure? We'll start World War Three."

"I see you've been spreading your pacifist bullshit along with screwing her, eh, Mace?" Eyers said with a laugh. "Yeah, we've known about you two since you arrived at Plattsburgh, Mace, you and your drug-dealing biker buddies. If you survive this mission, Mace, I'll still see your ass hauled into prison for twenty years for associations with known international drug traffickers. I'm sure we can even trace your smuggling activities to right here in Turkey—I knew there had to be a reason why you had so many consecutive assignments here. . . .

"The President's going to push this war to the next logical step, troops, and he wants us to spearhead the attack," Eyers continued. "He gave the big prize to me." He turned to Daren Mace, gave him a disgusted chuckle, and said, "Now we'll see what you're really made out of, boy. And just for laughs, guess who's going to be your aircraft commander? How about Major Furness?"

"You can't do that, General," Layton insisted in protest.

"Excuse me, General," Colonel Lafferty interjected, "but *I'll* decide who crews these sorties. As senior wing officer, I should be the one who pilots that—"

"It's already been decided," Eyers said with a sneer, "and I don't want to hear shit from any of you. Furness is a flight instructor and training flight commander—hell, Lafferty, she gives *you* check rides, for Christ's sake. Furness is the best pilot, Mace is the most senior weapons officer. End of story. Lafferty, you'll command the backup SRAM shooter, and you'll pick the best four RF-111s you got to fly with you as SEAD antiradar escorts. The rest of the wing will be participating in the air strikes with the Ukrainians. I've got all your charts, your flight plans, your communications documents, and your intelligence material, and the RF-111s with your SRAM-B missiles should be arriving within the hour."

Eyers turned to Mace, reached into his blouse pocket, extracted a red plastic sheath, and gave it to him. "Just to make sure, Colonel, I got you a copy of the executive order authorizing this mission. You'll find the precise procedures for terminating your mission—no more second-guessing, no more chickening out because you think somebody screwed up. If you don't launch the missile, it'll be because you screwed up, you chickened out, or you were killed. I suggest you do your duty this time—*if* you have the guts. I'd hate to see the pretty major there splattered across some Russian peat bog because you weren't man enough to get the job done. Now get out of my sight and get to work. You are dis*missed.*"

40

Batman Air Base, Turkey, Several Hours Later

MACE AND FURNESS WERE PREFLIGHTING THEIR RF-111G Vampire in preparation for launching that evening. They were in a large semiunderground concrete shelter, but the large steel and concrete blast doors covering the hangar were partially open. The aircraft had just come from the United States, and it had been completely inspected and checked in a very short period of time. The internal bomb bay held the two AGM-131 SRAMs (Short-Range Attack Missiles), and the two crewmen were inspecting the weapon right now.

"I've seen these things for years now," Furness commented as they crawled in under the bomb doors with a flashlight and inspection mirror, "but it seems—different this time. It's like this thing is alive."

They inspected the general condition of the weapon. The missile was rather small, with a triangular cross section and three stubby moving fins in the rear—the two missiles fit comfortably in the bomb bay with just a few inches on each side and about one inch between them. It had a soft rubbery outer layer that burned off as it flew through the air at over Mach-three to protect it and to absorb radar energy, making it "stealthier" than earlier models. The nosecap of the missile was hard composite material that covered a radar altimeter for arming and detonating the weapon. There was an inspection access door on the bottom of the missile, and they checked the missile settings together.

"Twenty-kiloton yield," Mace recited. The missile was set for its lowest yield—the highest setting was a full 170 kilotons. "Primary fuzing is an air burst at five thousand feet, with a backup ground burst option. Dual motor burn for a high-altitude climb at Mach-three, then an inertially guided ballistic flight path to impact."

"Checks," Furness said. She stuck the inspection mirror up between the missiles and shined the flashlight up on the right side of the missile. "Warhead safing plug's been removed." She checked the second missile, then handed the mirror and flashlight to Mace, who double-checked both weapons. "Man, I can't believe we're doing this," she said; then she turned to Mace, realizing what she just said. "And you almost *did* it. *That's* what you were carrying back over Iraq when you rendezvoused with me—nuclear bombs."

"I was carrying two of these things," Mace said uneasily. "They were X-models, modified for only a five-kiloton ground burst, no backup fusing option. But yes, I was going to launch one on a bunker south of Baghdad."

"Why didn't you?"

"Because the order was rescinded. They just didn't tell us officially, but I knew it had been," Mace replied. He told her about Operation Desert Fire, how the Scud missile attack on Israel was mistaken for a biological-chemical attack, how his mission was executed. "It was obviously a screw-up—Coalition planes everywhere, hundreds of them right over ground zero. I would've fragged all of them. I withheld the launch—kept the doors closed until the missiles timed out. Eyers was in charge. He didn't plan it properly, and sold the Joint Chiefs of Staff and the President a bill of goods. General Layton was the air boss. He knew there was a problem, knew that the execution order had to be terminated. When the coded terminate order didn't come through, he tried to terminate me by broadcasting in the clear. I listened, and I terminated. I got nailed for it."

"But you did as you were ordered to do."

"Not in Eyers' twisted mind," Mace said. "I disobeyed a lawful order. Only General Layton kept me out of prison."

Furness fell silent for a moment, stung by the enormity of what he had experienced—but there was still one last unanswered question. "Would you have done it?" she asked him. "Would you have launched? If there was no terminate call, no friendlies in the area—would you have done it?"

"Rebecca, I think that's a question every crewdog has to answer for themself."

"I need to know, Daren," she said. She reached out to touch the gray missile hanging before her, but pulled her hand away as if she could feel the radioactivity pulsing within its fuselage. "I need to know . . . because I've never had to face it. I wonder if I can."

"Yes, you can," he said firmly.

"How do you know that?"

"Because you're here, and you're wearing the uniform, and you're under this bomber preflighting these weapons," Mace said. "Everyone here on this base can do it. If they can't do it, they end up basket cases like Lynn Ogden or sniveling cowards like Ted Little—or dead like Paula Norton and Curt Aldridge. You're here because you and Mark Fogelman had the skill and the drive to make it. I hate to talk like this about the dead, Rebecca, but you're here and they're not because you're better than they were, pure and simple. If Mark didn't get his wake-up call when you got nailed by those F-16s, if he didn't pick up his books and get his briefings and screw his head on straight while he was in the hospital back in Plattsburgh, you'd be dead or injured or grounded and someone else would be flying this mission. Crewdogs don't make it because they don't have the mental capacity, the skill, or the courage to kill."

She didn't know what to say, but took his hand and squeezed it to show her thanks. "Plus," Mace added, "you can do it because you got *me*."

His joke finally broke the tension, the unmovable fear burning in her head. She rolled her eyes and said, "Oh, *please*—give me a break."

"This is my baby, Rebecca. This beast and I are one. If it can be done, *we* will do it."

When they exited the bomb bay and finished their preflight inspections, they noticed Colonel Pavlo Tychina standing in the partially open doorway; a security guard was blocking his path. Both Furness and Mace stepped out of the hangar to greet him.

"I shake the hands of all brave crews before an attack," Tychina said. He motioned to the Vampire behind Mace and Furness. Unlike the Charlie-Flight aircraft, the four Bravo-Flight bombers carried external fuel tanks on the number-two and seven nonswiveling pylons, as well as AGM-88 HARMs on stations three, four, five, and six, and AIM-9P Sidewinder missiles on stations three and six—and, of course, the first two Vampires carried SRAMs in the bomb bay. "Extra fuel tanks on an eight-hundred-mile round-trip mission, Major Furness? I not know this."

Furness was a bit confused by his question. "We've got the legs to go all the way, sir," she replied, "but a little extra gas never hurt."

"Ah. Yes, of course."

But Pavlo Tychina still seemed confused. "It's more like two thousand miles on the sortie, sir, not eight hundred," Mace added. "We'll need the extra gas in case we need to use 'burners."

"Two thousand miles, Colonel?" Tychina asked. "I not understand."

Furness and Mace finally got the message: "Sir, the mission against the bunker complex? Domodedovo? Near Moscow?"

"I know Domodedovo," Tychina said, his puzzlement slowly turning into anger, "but I not know about mission. You have a mission to attack Domodedovo?"

"Oh my God," Mace muttered, "you don't know about the airstrike, Colonel Tychina? Rebecca, we should fill him in right away."

"No shit." Furness waved to the shelter guard, telling him that Tychina was authorized to accompany her, and after he was searched and left his helmet bag and equipment with the guard, she took Tychina over to the bomb bay. Tychina's eyes grew wide as he peered at the missiles nestled in the bomb bay.

"These are bombs?" he asked. "Very strange bombs. Antirunway weapons, perhaps?"

Furness hesitated for a moment, then led Tychina and Mace back out of the hangar and away from the guard post, out of earshot of everyone. "No, sir, they're nuclear cruise missiles," she told him. "We have a new additional mission, Colonel—after leading your strikers against your three targets, Bravo Flight is going to launch a nuclear attack against Domodedovo Air

Base, near Moscow. Russian president Velichko is supposed to be holed up in the underground bunker there. Those missiles will destroy the bunker and Velichko."

Tychina's eyes grew wide behind his sterile gauze face mask. "No! Is it true what you say?"

"It's true, sir," Furness said. "I . . . I assumed the Ukrainians knew about this. I think General Panchenko should be informed of this right away."

"I don't think anyone else in NATO knows about it except General Eyers," Mace said. "He's the one who planned it."

"Eyers?" Tychina retorted. "Bruce Eyers is big bullshit. I no like him. Why your government not tell Ukrayina about this secret mission?"

"I don't know," Furness replied. "Maybe because Ukrayina doesn't have the capability of delivering this kind of weapon."

"What you mean?" Tychina asked. "My men, we can do anything, fly anywhere. You only fly four Vampire planes into Russia? You have no escorts, fighter escorts? We escort."

"No air patrols," Mace said. "We go in with antiradar weapons and our Sidewinders only. No fighters can keep up with us."

"What you saying? I can keep up with you, Colonel Daren. My MiG-23s, they can escort you into Russia."

"Your fighters don't have the legs—er, they don't have the fuel reserves, sir," Furness said. "We researched it. It's impossible."

"And you can't fly terrain-following altitudes," Mace added. "We'll be down at three hundred feet or below the entire flight."

"Anything you can do, I can do," Tychina said. "You fly low, I fly low. You fly to Moscow, I fly to Moscow. I escort you."

"Sir, there's only six hours to launch," Furness said. "You can't reconfigure your fighters in time."

"You say *nee, nee,* I say *tuk,*" Tychina said. "I do it. You come off-target at Rostov-na-Donu, I find you, I rendezvous."

Furness and Mace looked at each other. Furness said, "If he can do it, Daren . . ."

"I can get him a chart and a threat map during the weather and final mission briefings," Mace said. "If his MiGs have IRSTS, they can track us without us using lights or radios."

"I go now. I report secret mission to General Panchenko, and I fix planes. I see you." The young colonel picked up his flight gear and trotted away, flagging down a maintenance truck and hopping a ride back to headquarters.

"Well, well," Daren Mace said to Furness as they watched Tychina race off. "Maybe the Iron Maiden isn't quite as hard as I thought. In fact, that was a very *unauthorized* thing to do."

"Hey, we've been given a mission to do and I'm going to do it." Furness shrugged. "Now, I don't know why the Ukrainians weren't told about our mission, but if Colonel Tychina can get us some fighter escorts, at least part of the way into Russia, I'll take it. I'm following orders, but I'm also looking out for my butt. And yours."

"In that case let's finish up this preflight and catch up with Pavlo," Mace said. "I have a few ideas that might turn this whole stinking mission around for us."

41

Batman Air Base, Turkey, That Night

THE LAUNCH BEGAN AT NINE P.M.

The Charlie Flight RF-111Gs launched first—they had more than enough gas for this mission—followed by the Bravo Flight Vampires, then the Sukhoi-17s and the Turkish F-16s. The F-16s would provide air coverage over the Black Sea, but would not cross into Russia. Finally launched were Mikoyan-Gurevich-23s, then MiG-27s, and lastly ten very strange-looking MiG-23s and Su-17s. Eight MiGs and two Su-17s were festooned with fuel tanks: one nine-hundred-pound standard centerline tank; one tank on each swiveling wing section, which would prevent the wings from being swept back past takeoff setting until the tanks were jettisoned; and one tank on each fixed-wing section, for an incredible total of five external fuel tanks—the external fuel load was equal to the plane's total *internal* fuel load, effectively doubling the fighter's range. Instead of six air-to-air missiles, the MiGs carried only three: one AA-7 radar-guided missile on the left-engine intake pylon and two AA-8 heat-seeking missiles on a double launcher on the right. The Sukhoi-17s were configured similarly, but with special stores on the two fuselage pylons instead of missiles.

The last surprise was at takeoff: these heavily laden aircraft used military power for takeoff, instead of fuel-gulping afterburner, with the help of four rocket packs attached to the rear fuselage to boost them off the ground. Even with the added boost, the fighters stayed at treetop level long after they left the runway so they could build up enough speed to safely raise the nose and climb without stalling. As soon as they were safely airborne and clear of any populated areas, the spent rocket packs were jettisoned; then, as soon as the strike force reached the Turkish coast of the Black Sea, the empty outboard tanks were jettisoned, and the planes could sweep their wings back to a more fuel-efficient 45 degrees. The tanks that dropped into the sea were recovered by the Turkish Jandarma for reuse.

Another Russian A-50 Airborne Warning and Control radar plane was up that night patrolling the Black Sea region, and again the NATO air forces under General Panchenko were prepared. A small twenty-aircraft Ukrainian strike force was sent straight north at high speed, aiming for the Russian naval base at Sevastopol on the Crimean Peninsula, along with six MiG-23s flying at high altitude on another anti-AWACS missile run from the west.

The Russian radar plane, which was orbiting over Nikolayev in southern Ukraine instead of over the Black Sea, immediately turned and headed farther north, vectoring in fighters from Simferopol and Krasnodar as it retreated. When the high-altitude MiGs fired their AA-9 missiles, the Russian AWACS shut down their radar, accelerated, and dispensed decoy chaff and flares.

At the same time, a Russian Antonov-12C four-engine turboprop plane accompanying the A-50 radar plane, carrying electronic jammers and other decoys and countermeasures, activated its powerful jammers, making it impossible for any radar transmitters, including the radars in the nose of the AA-9 missiles, to lock on . . .

. . . however, it also made it impossible for any other radars to operate normally as well, including the Russian fighter radars and ground-based radars. The An-12C shut down the early warning and intercept radars along the Crimea and at the naval base at Novorossiysk, leaving it wide open for attack. The naval facility was the headquarters for the Russian Fleet oiler and tanker fleets, and had many vital oil terminals and storage facilities as well as a long-range radar site and air defense missile facility. Being nearly surrounded by the Caucasus Mountains, it was naturally defended by steep ridges and high jagged coastal peaks, a cold, snowy Russian version of Rio de Janeiro.

Not one surface-to-air missile was fired as the Ukrainian attack force swept in. Flying up the coast of Turkey, then crossing into the republic of Georgia and following the Caucasus Mountains, they were completely undetected until just a few miles from Novorossiysk. The fixed SA-10 missile sites and long-range radar sites along the Black Sea coast were hit with dozens of cluster bomb packs and antipersonnel mines from the first group of MiG-27s and Sukhoi-17s, and dock and warehouse facilities and a few tankers in the naval shipyard area of the base were hit by TV- and laser-guided bombs. One MiG-23 flying a medium-altitude combat air patrol was hit by an infrared-guided antiaircraft-artillery gun seconds before a direct hit by a TV-guided bomb from a MiG-27 took out the gun site.

But if the attack on Novorossiysk was unexpectedly easy, the attack on Krasnodar was all the more difficult.

Again, it was necessary for the second strike group to stay at low altitude over the Caucasus Mountains to hide in the radar clutter and avoid detection as long as possible, but the attack on Novorossiysk and the feint on the A-50 radar plane alerted all the other Russian bases in the area.

The short twenty-mile run from the Caucasus Mountains to Krasnodar became an almost impenetrable no-man's-land. The Russians had wised up, and did not activate the SA-10 surface-to-air missile radars or their surveillance radars, but simply swept the skies with clouds of 23- and 57-millimeter antiaircraft gunfire, directed by electro-optical low-light cameras, by infrared sensors, or simply by sound. This forced the Ukrainian Su-17 and MiG-27 strike aircraft up above twelve thousand feet, which made their bombing less accurate and made them vulnerable to fighter attacks.

The MiG-23 fighters engaged the oncoming Russian air patrols, but again the Russian fighters had the advantage—the Ukrainian fighters were no match for the advanced Russian warplanes. Directed by the A-50 AWACS radar plane and armed with superior radars and weapons, the Ukrainian fighters were being shot down with fierce regularity—sometimes two MiG-23s would be shot down simultaneously by one Russian Sukhoi-27 fighter. But the Ukrainian fighters could not run as they did before—they had to keep the third strike team (along with the Domodedovo strike team) from being jumped by Russian fighters before they had a chance to attack the large industrial area and military airfield. They were taking a beating.

The MiG-27s and the Sukhoi-17s from the first bombing group broke the battle open, but at a very heavy price. After dropping their bombs on Novorossiysk and retreating back to Turkey, they arced north, climbed, and made a supersonic dash for Krasnodar at treetop level. The antiaircraft artillery was deadly for low-flying planes, but their range was far less than normal—possibly out of the range of standoff weapons. The Russian fighters had no choice but to disengage from the Ukrainian fighters and intercept the low-level attackers. This gave the Ukrainian fighters who had run out of weapons a chance to flee back to Turkey, and for the rest to set up an air patrol for the third strike team.

The tactic worked.

The Rostov-na-Donu and Domodedovo strike teams proceeded north unchallenged, along with twenty MiG-23s that still had weapons and were not shot up enough to abort.

The attackers from Strike Team Two were able to make high-altitude bomb releases on Krasnodar, and although the mines and bomblets scattered much more than desired and the sticks of bombs were not nearly as accurate, the airfield was rendered temporarily unusuable and the air defense radar sites were seriously damaged.

The twenty MiG-27s and Su-17s from Strike Team One aborted their feint out of range of the murderous guns surrounding Krasnodar's military airfield—right into the waiting gunsights and radar locks of the Russian fighters. In less than a minute, twenty Ukrainian fighter-bombers had been shot down.

Rostov-na-Donu—Rostov on the Don—was the capital of the industrial, mining, and agricultural region of southern Russia, located at the mouth of the Don River. After the breakup of the Soviet Union and the military clashes between Russia and Georgia, Armenia, Azerbaijan, and the Ukraine, the military airfield there grew in importance and size, until it had become a major heavy bomber, tactical bomber, and troop transport base.

Knocking out this base and its associated long-range air defense systems would be vital.

The city was out of range of the A-50 radar plane, so all of Rostov's air defense radars were up and operating—the

Charlie Flight Vampires had a field day launching HARM missiles. Using simultaneous launches, as many as eight surveillance, fighter-intercept, and surface-to-air guidance radars were destroyed at once. The smaller mobile SAM systems and antiaircraft-artillery gun sites were forced to switch to electro-optical or infrared guidance, which greatly reduced their effectiveness.

The RF-111Gs had wised up after their first assault on the Russian warships as well—instead of being loaded down only with AGM-88 HARM antiradar missiles, they carried only two HARMs and a variety of other stores, including two GBU-24 2,000-pound laser-guided bombs, with a PAVE TACK laser designator in a rotating cradle in the bomb bay; twelve CBU-52, CBU-58, CBU-71, or CBU-87 incendiary, antipersonnel, or antivehicle cluster bomb units; two GBU-15 TV-guided 2,000-pound bombs; and twelve BLU-107 Durandal antirunway rockets. Each RF-111 launched its HARM missiles at a radar site, climbed to a safe altitude over antiaircraft guns, and then started aiming and destroying targets.

Two Vampires from Charlie Flight were shot down—one by a Russian MiG-29 from a range of nearly fifteen miles, and the other after peppering Rostov-na-Donu's main runway with an entire load of Durandal rockets. The Durandals parachuted down toward the runway until just a few feet above the surface, when a rocket motor would blast a thirty-three-pound warhead through the concrete surface and heave it upward.

Once the enemy air defense threats were dealt with, the Ukrainians' Strike Team Three moved in on the base.

The major weapon for the MiG-27s and Su-17s here was the AS-10 "Karen" missile, a laser-guided missile with a 240-pound high-explosive warhead; or conventional 500-pound "dumb" bombs. A fully loaded fighter-bomber could carry twelve of these AS-10s or twelve 500-pound bombs, plus two external fuel tanks for the added range necessary to reach the target. There was no time for loitering in the target area, no reattacks, no second chances—every target located was hit with at least one Karen or four bombs, and as soon as their ordnance was expended, they ran for the mountainous Georgian border to safety and then back to Turkey for refueling and rearming.

The Ukrainian fighters again were hammered by Russian MiG-29 and Su-27 fighters, and losses were high.

42

Kayseri Air Base, Turkey, One Hour Later

"FINAL STRIKE REPORT, SIR," THE EXECUTION OFFICER SAID AS he handed the teletyped report to General Petr Panchenko at his headquarters at Kayseri Air Base. Panchenko reviewed the Ukrainian-language copy as General Eyers and General Isiklar read off the English-language version.

"Pretty damn good news, I'd say," Eyers said, his hand resting on the military-issue Colt .45 hostered to his belt as if he were Gary Cooper in *High Noon.* "Reconnaissance aircraft report numerous buildings, warehouses, and oil terminals destroyed at Novorossiysk, along with several docks and . . . good God, they got six tankers, plus two destroyed in drydock. No sign of any signals from air defense radars."

His brow furrowed in dismay as he read on: "Krasnodar appears it might still be in commission, General," Eyers said to Panchenko; an interpreter translated for the NATO air boss. "Minor . . . *minor* bomb damage to the runways and taxiways only, and a damned Su-17 reconnaissance aircraft was shot down by an SA-10 missile from there—I guess we know the SAMs are still operational."

Panchenko said something to his executive officer, who saluted and ran off. The interpreter said, "The General says that Krasnodar's fuel depot was hit, so Russian fighters that land there might be trapped or be low on fuel if they launch. He has ordered Major Kocherga to plan another sortie right away to attack Krasnodar."

"Good thinking," Eyers answered, grudgingly admitting to himself that maybe this Panchenko had something on the ball after all. He read on: "Looks like your boys blew the shit out of Rostov-na-Donu, General. Two runways destroyed, taxiways and parking ramps hit by bombs and missiles, extensive damage to airdrome facilities, several recorded hits by antiradar missiles, no air defense radar signals. Good going, General." Eyers gave a thumbs-up to Panchenko, who acknowledged the gesture with a slight bow.

But Eyers' satisfied grin went away as he read on: "Christ . . . Jesus, we got mangled on this one," he grumbled. "Ten Su-17s lost, fourteen Flogger-Js, and . . . fuck, *forty-eight* MiG-23s destroyed, plus another dozen or so shot up. We're down to eighty-seven operational airframes, *including* the ones still airborne—that's seventy-seven planes here still operational." Eyers closed the report and wearily rubbed his eyes. "We're less than 50 percent, General. I think we're out of the ballgame."

The translator was giving Panchenko a steady stream of words, and up until now he had been nodding, reading, and listening—but now Panchenko was on his feet, shooting a stream of angry words at Eyers. "The General says that he will fight to the last man," the translator said. "Once Krasnodar and the naval air base at Simferopol on the Crimean Peninsula are destroyed, the Doneck and Char'kov army divisions in eastern Ukrayina can start to move west safely, and Odessa can be relieved. With access to bases, factories, and depots in Ukrayina again, the Air Force can be regenerated—"

"Meanwhile, Russian bombers blow the shit out of Turkey," Eyers interjected. "No can do, General. If your fighters get wiped out before substantial NATO forces can arrive, NATO's entire eastern flank could collapse. We're going into a defensive mode, General Panchenko. After Krasnodar is taken care of, your boys start doing air patrols with the AWACS plane. We'll let the surviving RF-111s take care of any ships or air defense radars that pop up—"

Panchenko interrupted him with another blistering retort: "The General says that you are talking about abandoning Ukrayina.

He will not allow that to happen."

"You tell him that the Ukraine is already *dead,*" Eyers shot back, his hand firmer now on the Colt .45. "If we lose all our aircraft on more of these useless hit-and-run missions and allow the Russians to conduct massive air attacks in Turkey, we'll lose two, maybe three NATO countries. If we pull back, we can perhaps save Turkey and Greece. Tell Panchenko that he will reconfigure all his aircraft for air defense missions and set up an air defense plan of attack, and do it *immediately.* If one Russian bomber or cruise missile crosses the border, I'm holding him *personally* responsible."

43

Over Northern Ukraine, That Same Time

"SEARCH RADAR, TEN O'CLOCK," MACE REPORTED. "MUST BE Chervonoye airfield." He adjusted a small red reading light onto the chart in his lap. Chervonoye was a small fighter base in the Ukraine that had been occupied by Russia early in the conflict. "Showing MiG-29s and mobile SAMs there. Forty miles west of us."

Daren Mace and Rebecca Furness were the lead ship of a massive thirteen-aircraft armada streaming into southwestern Russia.

They had successfully navigated the killing grounds of the Kuban and Don River valleys, staying in the Caucasus Mountains as the attack formations streamed into Krasnodar, then staying at two hundred feet until crossing Taganrog Bay and back into Ukrayina. The terrain was flat and forested in the Don region north of the Azov Sea, so once they were outside the radar coverage of the Russian A-50 radar plane orbiting about two hundred miles to the west over the Ukraine, it was safe enough to set one thousand feet on the terrain-following radar and relax a bit.

Flying in close formation with them were three Ukrainian MiG-23 Flogger-K fighters, one on either side and one slightly behind and above Furness and Mace. The Ukrainians were taking an incredible risk flying with the Americans. The Vampires had to leave their electroluminescent strip lights on so the MiGs without infrared sensors could follow the American bombers—one cloud, one bout of the "spins," or following the wrong light strip could be deadly. Twice they had to shut the lights off when they detected fighters nearby, but somehow the Ukrainians always made their way back. Three of their eight MiG-23 escorts had already been shot down by fighter attacks—one as they crossed into the Ukraine from Russia over Taganrog Bay, the other two in isolated dogfights along their route of flight. Their prebriefed procedure was for the MiG-23s to break out of formation and chase down any fighter that might be pursuing the attack force, and although the Russian fighters never made it in, they lost an escort fighter every time.

Five miles in trail behind Furness and Mace was Thunder Two, crewed by Lieutenant Colonel Hembree and Lieutenant Colonel Larry Tobias. They were the "backup shooters." They were escorted by two MiG-23s, who seemed perfectly content to fly just a few hundred feet above the ground in marginal weather without being able to see a blasted thing out their cockpits.

About a mile behind them was Tychina and his wingman, flying Sukhoi-17 "Fitter-K" bombers, with two MiG-23s escorting them. Unlike the MiG-23s, the Su-17s would be able to go all the way with the RF-111s—the MiG-23s would be turning around any minute now. Flying a few miles behind Tychina were Johnson and Rota in Thunder Three—they had no MiGs escorting them because they had already been shot down by fighter attacks as they crossed from Russia into the Ukraine. Thunder Three had one HARM missile remaining. Fay and Dutton in Thunder Four had already expended their AGM-88 HARM antiradar missiles at radar sites along the route and were making the treacherous trip south through occupied Ukrayina back to Turkey, with one MiG-23 flying alongside for protection.

"Step it down to three hundred," Furness said. Daren reached down to the center console and clicked the clearance plane knob on the terrain-following radar control from 1000 to 300, and the RF-111G Vampire obeyed, sliding gently down toward the frozen earth below. The RF-111's terrain-following radar system would automatically fly the bomber three hundred feet above the ground, following the contours of all but very steeply rising terrain.

When they leveled off, the "S" symbol on the threat scope no longer appeared. "Search radar down," Mace said. "High terrain, ten miles, painting over it. City off to our right, power line running across the track line. My notes say it might be four hundred ninety feet high."

"Try five hundred feet on the TFRs," Furness said. Mace stepped the TFR up to five hundred feet, and the S symbol and a slow *deedle deedle deedle* warning tone on the interphone returned when they climbed above four hundred feet. "Nope, they can see us at four. Back to three hundred." The signal went away again at the three-hundred-foot clearance plane.

Suddenly, the S symbol changed briefly into a 12 with a diamond around it, then back to an S.

"Oh, shit, they got an SA-12," Mace said. "They know we're out here." The SA-12 was a high-performance mobile antiaircraft-missile system, capable of shooting down low-flying aircraft out to a range of almost fifty miles, part of a new generation of Russian SAM systems that could pop up anywhere along a strike route and kill with speed and precision.

"Give me two hundred," Furness said. Mace stepped the TFR to two hundred feet, the lowest setting. The S symbol had changed back to a 12 symbol on the RHAWS scope—and then a yellow MISSILE WARNING light on Furness' eyebrow instrument panel came on, and a set of crosshairs appeared around the 12 symbol on the threat scope. "Missile warning, nine o'clock . . ." She jammed the throttles forward to military power, swept the wings back to 72 degrees, and the Vampire bomber accelerated from 480 knots to about 600 knots—ten miles a minute.

"Hey, the MiGs are gone," Mace said. He switched off the exterior formation strip lights—there was no one out there to use them anymore. "Maybe that's why we got the SA-12 up—those MiGs must've—"

Suddenly they heard a fast *deedledeedledeedle* warning tone, the 12 symbol on the RHAWS began to blink, and a red MISSILE LAUNCH warning light began to blink.

"Missile launch, nine o'clock!" Mace made sure the trackbreaker switchlights were all on and that the jammers were transmitting.

"I see it!" Rebecca shouted. Far off in the distance she could see a streak of light disappear into the night sky, followed by another immediately after the first. "It's flying behind us."

"C'mon, guys," Mace muttered. "Where are you?" Just then on the scrambled VHF frequency they heard, "Magnum. Bye-bye." Mace quickly deselected the trackbreaker switchlights. "Magnum" meant that Johnson and Rota were launching a HARM missile—the missile's performance could be spoiled by too much friendly jamming, which was why Mace shut his jammers off. "Nail it, baby, nail it . . ." Seconds later the SA-12 symbol in the threat scope disappeared. "Way to go, boys."

"Nice shooting, guys," Furness said to Johnson and Rota as she pulled the power back to 90 percent and swept the wings forward again to 54 degrees to conserve fuel—there was no way she was going to suggest climbing above two hundred feet again, though. It was now just four of them left—two American bombers, two Ukrainian bombers—and twenty minutes left to go to the SRAM launch point.

The warning tone from the RHAWS system came alive again. "I've got triple-A at nine and ten o'clock," Mace said. "That's the main highway between Moscow and Char'kov. Must be troops heading down that road. My trackbreakers are still off. Two hundred hard ride—we're there."

Triple-A, referring to the radar-guided mobile antiaircraft-artillery unit called the ZSU-23/4, or Zeus-4, had a maximum range of about two miles—they were at least twenty miles away from the road—but the same infantry units that had a Zeus-4 usually had mobile SAM systems as well.

"Search radar at eleven and two o'clock," reported Mace. "Man, it's getting hairy around here."

The closer they got to Moscow, the more they would encounter surveillance radars—Moscow was the most heavily defended city in the world.

"Power's still at 90 percent," Furness said. "I'm ready with a prelaunch check if you're—"

Just then a bat-wing symbol—an inverted V—appeared at the bottom of the threat scope—and it stayed there. "Shit, we picked up a fighter," Mace cursed. "Fine time for the MiGs to bug out." Just then two more bat-wings appeared on the RHAWS scope, this time at the top—and then two more appeared, off to the right near the top. "Crap, we got fighters all around us. Jammers coming on. Step on it, Rebecca."

As Mace selected the trackbreaker buttons again, Furness pushed the power back up to military power and swept the wings back to 72.5 degrees. She was sure she would not move the throttles or wings again until they were out of Russia.

A diamond symbol danced around the bat-wing symbols on the RHAWS, denoting the most serious threat—the fighters behind were gaining fast, while the ones ahead were closing slowly, as if circling above them, getting ready to swoop down for the kill. Mace reported: "The guys on our tail are closing . . . coming up on the turnpoint, next heading zero-two-three, safe clearance altitude one thousand feet . . . one minute to turn, I got a watch running . . . I got high towers left of the turnpoint, two hundred twenty and eight hundred and fifty feet tall . . . power line after we roll."

Suddenly they got a red MISSILE LAUNCH and IRT warning lights, and a hard, fast warning tone—the infrared detection system detected the flare of a missile's rocket motor igniting—and they could see the glare of decoy flares dropping behind them as the aircraft defense system automatically ejected chaff and flares. "Missile launch!" Mace shouted. "Break right!"

Rebecca jammed the control stick to her right knee, rolled into a 90-degree bank turn, pulled on the stick until their chins were forced down onto their chests from the G-forces, then relaxed the pressure on the stick and rolled out, ready at any time to do another break if necessary. The terrain-following radar system faulted and tried to fly them up when Furness exceeded 40 degrees of bank, and the TFR warning lights were still on even after she rolled out. "I got a problem with the TFs, climbing to SCA," she said. With the little finger of her left hand, she depressed the paddle switch to keep the terrain-following radar from trying to do an emergency fly-up, started a gentle climb to the safe clearance altitude for the segment of the route, and reached down to the TFR control panel to recycle the TFR mode switches.

Meanwhile Mace was frantically searching the skies behind them for any sign of a missile launch. It would be nearly impossible to see, but . . . "There!" he shouted, pointing above and to the left. "I see two missiles! I—"

Suddenly they saw a ball of fire erupt in the sky ahead, and there was a lot of joyful shouting on both the UHF emergency channel and the scrambled VHF interplane channel.

"What in hell . . . ? Who is that . . . ?" he asked.

"It's the Ukrainian MiGs," Furness said. She was still recycling the TFR switches—both yellow TFR FAIL warning lights were on. "They didn't leave us—damn, they just shot down a Russian fighter. Call up the next point."

Mace sequenced the navigation computer to the next turnpoint and they headed north. "I got search radars at eleven and one o'clock, and bat-wings all over the damned place," Mace said. "I don't know which is which—they're all bad guys now as far as I'm concerned. Twelve minutes to the initial point. I'm doing a prelaunch check." He configured his weapon release switches, placing the bomb door mode switch to AUTO—and left it there this time. He wasn't going to try to withhold anything this time.

Coming up to the next turnpoint, he checked offset aimpoints in his radarscope. "I got a problem—radar pedestal looked like it crashed," he said. "That last break must've jammed something. I'm resetting my radar." He hit the ANTENNA CAGE button, which should have moved the attack radar dish to its straight-ahead position—it stayed rolled over to one side, producing only a streak of light in his radarscope. He turned his system to STANDBY, waited a few seconds, then back to XMIT—no change. He shut the system completely off, waited ten seconds, then turned it back to STANDBY—still nothing. "Shit, the attack radar pedestal is jammed."

"That means the terrain-following radar is out too," Furness said. "Fuck, we're stuck at SCA."

Mace rotated the TFR mode switches to SIT, which would give them a profile-only view of terrain ahead—it was the only radar they had working now. Without the TFRs or the attack radar, they could not safely descend below the safe clearance altitude. "Christ, what a time for the system to crap out."

The S symbol at the ten o'clock position suddenly changed to a 10, and they heard the fast, high-pitched warning tone of an imminent missile threat: "SA-10, ten o'clock—the Kaluga site came up on us," Mace said as he depressed the trackbreaker switchlights to turn the jammers on again. "Come left and let's get that sucker." Mace made sure his AGM-88C HARM antiradar missiles were powered up and ready. The Vampires did not carry a Tactical Electronic Reconnaissance sensor pallet in the bomb bay—they had a very different load in the bomb bay that night—so the HARM missiles had to find, identify, and process their own attack information, which took much longer than normal.

Furness made the turn, aiming the HARM missile at the SAM site . . . and the MISSILE LAUNCH warning lights came on.

"Missile launch!" Mace cried out.

"I see it, I see it!" Furness shouted. "Chaff—*now!*"

Mace pumped out two bundles of chaff and Furness banked hard left. The XMIT lights on the forward trackbreakers were on, trying to jam the uplink signal steering the missile. The SA-10 missile turned right to follow them.

"Chaff!" Furness shouted again, then threw the bomber into a hard right break. Mace pumped out extra chaff, two bundles at a time.

The SA-10 banked left in response—it wasn't being jammed. It was locked on solid and tracking them all the way. Rebecca had to sweep the wings forward to 54 degrees, then 36 degrees to keep from stalling . . . she had no more airspeed to do another break to get away from this missile.

Furness and Mace saw a huge fireball pass overhead and then heard on the interplane frequency, "Magnum, Thunder One, magnum. Hang in there, guys." Hembree and Tobias in Thunder Two had launched a HARM missile at the SA-10 site, right over their heads. They had to keep on jinking for another few seconds.

"Vertical jink, Becky," Mace shouted. "Go *vertical!*"

Furness shoved the control stick forward with all her might, descended three hundred precious feet—leaving them no more than one hundred feet between them and the highest terrain in the area, although they could see nothing ahead of them and could hit the ground at any second—then hauled back on the stick with both hands. Mace kept on pumping out bursts of chaff. When Furness looked up, she saw the SA-10's burning rocket motor, the only light she could see except for the stars caused by her pounding heart and straining muscles.

Simultaneously, the 10 symbol on the RHAWS scope disappeared as the HARM missile hit the SAM site—and the SA-10 missile self-destructed less than one hundred feet behind them.

The shock wave from the SA-10's 280-pound warhead was like a thunderclap right outside the cockpit canopy. The MASTER CAUTION light came on, big and bright, right in front of Rebecca's terrified eyes. "What have I got, Daren?" she shouted as she punched the light off with a quick two-fingered stab.

Mace checked the caution light panel on the lower left instrument panel. "Rudder authority light . . . TFR lights . . . oil-hot light on the left engine," he said. "We might have an oil leak." He shined a small flashlight that he kept clipped to his flight suit pocket on the oil pressure gauges. "A little fluctuation on the left engine, but it's still in the green. I think we can make it." He checked the other gauges. "Aft-body fuel quantity is fluctuating—we may have taken a hit in the aft-body tank. Fuel distribution caution light. I'll switch fuel feed to the forward-body tank or else we'll be nose-heavy when the aft body drains out. Generator panel's okay. Let's get ready for that other SAM site to the right of track. Watch your altitude—one hundred feet low."

Rebecca pulled back on the stick to correct her altitude and found it took more force than normal to move it. "Stick's getting heavy already," she said as she fed in more trim. She rolled out of her turn with the steering bug centered, then reengaged the autopilot—but seconds after clicking it on, it kicked off again, and the bomber nosed lower. "Dammit, autopilot won't hold it." She cursed, grabbing the stick and feeding in more nose-up trim. "This thing better hold together—I don't want to punch out of two Vampires in one deployment. They won't renew my union card then."

The search radar at two o'clock suddenly turned to an "8" indication, but they were lined up and ready for it.

"I'm tracking the 'Land Role' radar," Mace said. "Processing . . . locked on. Ready to launch . . . now." Seconds later they fired their first HARM missile at the missile site . . . and nothing happened. The 8 indication on the RHAWS disappeared, only to reappear a few seconds after the missile should have hit.

"Two, can you get that sucker for us?" Rebecca radioed on the scrambled VHF channel.

"We got it, lead," Hembree replied. "Magnum . . ." But just as he said the word, they got a MISSILE LAUNCH warning, and they could see four missiles ripple-fire into the sky and arc out toward them. "Missile launch!" they heard Hembree shout on the radio. "I'll go right, lead."

Rebecca hit the afterburners and swept the wings back to 54 degrees. "Chaff!" she shouted, and she banked hard left—she tried to break, but she didn't have the strength to pull the control stick over the heavy nose-low loads until Mace got on his control stick with her, pulling with his left hand while ejecting chaff with his right. Their break was only half the authority of a full-power break, but they quickly ran out of airspeed and had to stop. Their airspeed was down to half normal speed, and nothing else except 24-degree wing sweep would keep the angle of attack in the normal range. Furness pulled the throttles back to military power, and with the wings at 24 degrees they could get 350 knots and six alpha—slow and sluggish, but still flying.

"I don't see the missiles anywhere—" Then, far off to the right behind the right wing, he saw a blazing streak of fire fly into the earth and explode, illuminating the snowy ground for miles in all directions. "God, somebody got hit!" Mace screamed. "Thunder Two, do you read me? Thunder Two . . . ?" There was a long, terrifying pause—no reply. "Thunder Two, *respond!*"

"I copy, lead," Hembree replied. "It was one of the Ukrainians. Thunder Ten, do you copy me? Over."

"Yes, I hear you," Pavlo Tychina, flying the lead Su-17, radioed back. "It was my wingman. I did not see the missiles coming until they hit him."

"We're IP inbound," Mace reported solemnly. "Coming up on the missile launch point in four minutes."

"Okay, Two, we've got a forward CG problem, and we're barely maintaining three-fifty. Dick, you wanna do the honors? You got the lead. I got one HARM left. I'll cover your butt."

"I got the lead," Hembree replied. A few moments later, Hembree said on the channel, "Fence check, Thunder Flight. Arm 'em up, lead is hot."

"God, this is it," Furness muttered. She made sure her flight suit sleeves were rolled down, her zippers zipped up, her helmet and oxygen mask on tight, and her shoulder harness as tight as she could make it. Mace did the same, then checked Rebecca. They then pulled their flashblindness curtains and canopy screens closed, turned on all the interior lights full bright, and turned the cockpit pressurization to COMBAT. She lowered her PLZT (Polarized Lead-Zirconium-Titanate) antiflashblindness goggles in place on her helmet and activated them. "I'm ready, Daren," she said. She looked at her partner after he lowered his goggles in place. "My God, you look like the Fly."

"I feel like it's déjà vu all over again," he replied. He checked the RHAWS scope. "Search radars at one o'clock, Rebecca—that's Moscow. Two minutes to launch point."

"I think we've gotta be crazy, Daren," Rebecca said. "I mean, I can hardly think . . . I can hardly breathe. How can anyone do this? How can anyone launch a nuclear weapon?"

"Part of the fucking job. SA-10 coming up," Mace said. "Give me 10 degrees left and we'll launch our last HARM."

Furness made the turn, the missile processed and computed its target, and they let it fly. The launch and destruction of the SA-10 SAM site was anticlimactic, almost boring. "Two weeks ago, the idea of launching so many HARMs would have been overwhelming," she said. "Now it feels as if I just shot a spitball compared to what we're about to do."

"SA-10's down," Mace reported. "One minute to launch point. Missiles powered up and ready."

Rebecca clicked on the interplane channel. "Godspeed, Thunder," she radioed.

"To you too, Thunder," Hembree replied. "Over and out."

"Thirty seconds. Prelaunch checks complete, doors in MANUAL, center up the steering bars, Becky." The Vampire banked slightly to the right, then leveled out. "Twenty seconds . . ."

"Missile away, Thunder One," they heard Hembree say. The first missile was on its way to its target—it would hit about half a minute before their own.

"Can't get a final radar launchpoint fix . . . I hope the system's running tight enough with GPS," Mace said, his voice still carrying a sharp, determined edge. "Search radar, twelve o'clock . . . that's Domodovedo. They're trying to pick up Dick Hembree's missile. They got an SA-17 system but it'll be too late—"

"Daren!"

"It'll be all right, Rebecca. Let's do it and get it over with." He flicked the bomb door switch to OPEN. "Ten seconds . . . doors coming open . . ."

Rebecca gripped the control stick and throttles as tightly as she could, waiting for the wrath of God to hit. *Something is going to happen,* she thought. She was sure of it. No supreme being was going to allow any human to unleash this much destructive force on—

"Missile away, Rebecca," Mace said as he mashed the pickle button and started a stopwatch. She could feel the three-thousand-pound missile leave the bomb bay, and suddenly her stick felt lighter and control returned. "Left turn, heading two-five-nine, let's get the hell out of here." Rebecca swept the wings back to 72.5 degrees as she cranked the Vampire bomber around and accelerated away from Domodedovo. "Missile-one flight time thirty seconds, impact in thirty seconds." Their speed was building slowly, but they would be over forty miles away from the target when the missiles hit.

"Coming up on missile-one impact . . . now." Rebecca could hear a loud roaring in her ears—her heart was pounding blood against her eardrums like a jackhammer. Daren glanced into his radarscope and turned a switch. "I've got video from the AS-13 missile," he said. He grasped the tracking handle and gave it a few nudges to the right. "I think I see Malino Airfield—I'll try to set this thing in there." Malino Airfield was a small fighter base outside Domodedovo. "Hey, these Ukrainian missiles work pretty well."

Rebecca shook her head, wondering how he could be so flip at a time like this. Just before launch, the order for them to fire the nukes was recalled. It seemed the President had had a politically expedient change of heart. Or the Steel Magnolia did. Anyway, the nukes were still going to go off . . . it was just that the President had decided, and the Ukrainians agreed, that the Ukrainians would do the dirty deed. Which was why she and Mace were now carrying Ukrainian weapons, and the Ukrainians were carrying the American nukes. "Daren—how can you joke about something like this when you know what's about to . . . happen?"

Mace ignored her. "Impact," he said. "Direct hit on the terminal building. Should be plenty of fragments to find." He shut off the attack video system, sat upright, and pulled his shoulder harness tight. "Okay, to answer your question: you *have* to joke about something like this. You think too much about it, well, then you really have doubts. But, Rebecca, this whole mission is a joke, anyway. Leave it to the President to wimp out again. Letting the Ukrainians fight our battle for us is going to make us the laughingstock of the world. But it's what our beloved commander in chief wants . . . or his wife does, anyway. Actually, it's a pretty shrewd political move: the President's getting to knock out Velichko and cover his ass at the same time. Nobody can say *we* launched the nukes, which is a lot more palatable to his liberal constituency than actually doing it. Boy, I bet Eyers was ready to spit bullets. They've robbed him of his chance to play John Wayne."

Furness sighed. "Well, as much as I like Pavlo and the Ukrainians, I'm frankly glad they're cooking them off. After all, it's his homeland and his fight. He might as well have the chance to finish it."

The system was running perfectly, Pavlo Tychina thought. The AN/AQQ-901 electronic interface pod, mounted on his left fuselage pylon, had taken several GPS satellite updates in the past few minutes and had made its final position update. The Doppler radar velocities compared favorably—the system was tight.

Tychina did not need to refer to a checklist—the switches had been configured for him, the computers were in command. The unlock and weapon prearm codes had been entered in for him by Colonel Mace before takeoff—even though they were now allies, no American was going to allow foreign officers any access to classified codes and arming procedures. It was just as well. Pilots should be pilots, not locksmiths.

They had fought their way past the best of Russia's defenses and sacrificed many good pilots and aircraft for this moment. The war had come full circle. Like the mythical Phoenix of his nickname, his life had begun in the radiation-fuel fires of L'vov Air Base, and it was about to end in those same nuclear fires again, this time over the capital city of his enemy. His eyes sought out the control indicator—and just as he focused on it, he saw the MISSILE POWER light begin to blink as the AGM-131 Short-Range Attack Missile he carried on his right fuselage pylon received its final navigation-data dump from the AQQ-901 pod, performed a complete self-test, sampled the air outside the Sukhoi-17 bomber, quickly tested its stubby control surfaces, decided it was ready to launch, then dropped clear of the fuselage.

Three seconds later, the missile's first-stage motor ignited, and the missile leaped into the sky on a long tongue of flame.

The sight of that missile rising into the sky toward Domodedovo made him smile. To think that the Americans, not the Ukrainians, had originally planned to do this awful task! Americans simply had no inkling of what it was like to have their homeland invaded, their people killed by the thousands, their entire way of life ripped away from them far beyond their control. America would have been hated if it had accomplished this attack. Ukrayina was acting in self-defense—it had a moral and legal right to mount any sort of attack in order to defend its homeland.

Pavlo knew that his flight plan said to turn west and try to make it as close to the Belarus border as he could before flaming out—he didn't have enough gas to make it out of Russia, let alone back to Ukrayina—but he kept the nose pointed toward the bright city lights of Moscow and even started a slight climb so he could get a better view. He knew he was supposed to put on his antiflashblindness goggles and close off the cockpit too, but that would be depriving him of the best seat in the house.

It was time to record his last will and testament, indulge in a few seconds of rhetoric—he had earned as much by successfully accomplishing this fearsome task. He set his primary radio to 243.0, the international emergency channel, keyed the mike, and said in Russian, "Good morning, Russia. This is Colonel of Air Defense Aviation Pavlo Grigor'evich Tychina of the Air Force of the Republic of Ukrayina. I am of sound mind and body, acting under orders of the President of the Ukrainian Republic and the Parliament.

"I have just launched an RKV-500B missile at Domodedovo airport, where I understand the butcher Vitaly Velichko is hiding. I wish him a swift journey to Hell." He hoped that lying about the missile, calling it a Russian cruise missile rather than an American AGM-131, would leave no doubt in anyone's mind that the attack was launched by Ukrayina, not America—at least he wanted to get full credit for this deed.

"This strike is in retaliation for my beloved fiancée, Mikola Korneichuk, who was killed by a similar weapon fired by a Russian Tupolev-22 bomber several days ago in the attack against Ukrayina, and for the other nuclear bomb attacks against Ukrayina that left thousands dead or maimed. It is done on behalf of myself, my country, and the good people of the Republic of Turkey, who offered their hand in friendship. I hope this action stops the conflict between Russia and the NATO allies. If it does, I wish you all peace. If it does not, I will see you all in Hell very soon. I hope that—"

He could not finish his sentence because a blinding flash of pure white light obliterated every sound, every sense in his body. He felt no pain, heard no engine sounds. He missed the familiar rumble of the old Sukhoi-17 between his legs, but he knew he had done his task well.

Colonel Pavlo Tychina was twenty miles from Domodedovo airport, ground zero for the twenty-kiloton AGM-131 SRAM-B missile, when it descended and exploded at precisely five thousand feet above ground. The fireball was five miles in diameter, completely enveloping the airport and vaporizing everything it touched, including the entire twenty-story command post and senior leadership bunker set under forty feet of concrete under the airport, and throwing millions of tons of debris a hundred thousand feet in the air with the power of ten volcanoes.

Vitaly Velichko was reduced to superheated gas in a millionth of a second as he conferred with his military commanders, sitting around a table on the sixth floor of the bunker, drinking vodka and plotting the invasions of Romania, Turkey, Georgia, Kazakhstan, and Alaska by Russian troops.

Pavlo Tychina was not caught in the fireball, but the overpressure from the explosion swatted his Su-17 out of the sky like a tennis ball hit with an overhead smash. Only God could see the smile on his face as he crashed into the frozen Russian ground.

EPILOGUE

A nation which makes the
final sacrifice for life
and freedom does not get beaten.
—Kemal Ataturk,
founder of the
Republic of Turkey

....

Vilnius, Lithuania
Later That Morning

DAREN MACE LIGHTLY TOUCHED HER ARM: "REBECCA? Wake up."

"Huh? What . . . *Jesus!*" She was sitting in the cockpit of her RF-111G Vampire bomber, her gloves and helmet on and the canopy closed—but somehow she had fallen asleep, and the airspeed had been allowed to drift almost to zero. It was still dark outside, but she could tell that they were right on the deck, lower than treetop level—the altimeter tape was reading only five hundred feet! She grabbed for the throttles, jamming them forward to military power—

"Easy, Rebecca," Mace said, grabbing for her hands. "We're on the ground. In Vilnius, Lithuania—remember? The crew chiefs are here to load us up." Slightly embarrassed, Rebecca and Daren climbed out of the cockpit, where they had been sitting guard all night ready to launch again, and let the maintenance control team from Incirlik in to do their job.

The Vampires had been refueled as soon as they touched down at Vilnius International Airport, and a maintenance control team that had been sent the day of the attack had fixed the radar and patched the fuel leaks in Furness' aircraft. Now, two hours after landing, a C-17 Globemaster III transport delivered external fuel tanks, Sidewinder missiles, starter cartridges, four AGM-88C HARM missiles, and two CBU-89 "Gator" mine dispersal weapons for each Vampire—a typical defense-suppression load—along with security guards, command post personnel, and a new strike routing, this time targeting armor divisions that might roll across the Russian frontier toward Lithuania. The weapons and fuel tanks were quickly uploaded onto both aircraft, and Thunder One and Thunder Two went on cockpit alert.

"So it wasn't a nightmare," Furness said. "It wasn't a dream."

"Nope, we really did it," Mace replied. They were both wrapped in leather and fur coats borrowed from the Lithuanian Self-Defense Forces, wearing helmets so they could monitor the radios. Both crewmen were wearing survival vests under their coats, complete with .45-caliber automatics—they could be going to war at any time, and they had to be thinking tactical warfare now. A warm-air hose from the external power cart hooked up to the Vampire kept them warm inside the cockpit despite below-freezing temperatures outside. "Pavlo did it."

"Where is he?"

"He never came in," Mace said. "I heard him talking on the radio in Russian while we were getting away—I don't speak Russian, but it sounded like an electronic suicide note to me."

"Damn him," Furness muttered. "He didn't have to do that. He was a hero—he had no reason to kill himself."

"Hard to tell what a guy thinks about after launching a nuclear weapon," Mace said. "But he was doing it to defend his home and his people. That changes things a lot. I'm going to miss him."

Their cockpit alert duty did not last long. Eight hours and two power carts later, Lieutenant General Tyler Layton arrived at the aircraft shelters with several Lithuanian officers and senior NATO commanders. Rebecca and Daren got out of the aircraft when Layton waved them down.

"General Palcikas, I'd like to present Major Rebecca Furness and Lieutenant Colonel Daren Mace," Layton said. "Rebecca, Daren, General Dominikas Palcikas, Minister of Defense of the Lithuanian Republic."

"A great pleasure," Palcikas said, nearly crushing even Mace's strong grip with a huge bearlike hand, then tenderly kissing

Rebecca's hand with a slight bow. Everyone had heard of Dominikas Palcikas, even Furness. He was one of the biggest heroes to come out of the post–Soviet Union states. He was a fifty-five-year-old combat veteran who had trained and risen up through the ranks of the old Soviet Army. But upon the independence of Lithuania in mid-1991, Palcikas became General and Commander in Chief of the Lithuanian Forces of Self-Defense. He named his initial cadre of officers and enlisted volunteers the Iron Wolf Brigade, invoking not only the spirit of the Grand Dukes of Lithuania, but the unit of the same name that had been led by his father in World War II, a unit that once saved Lithuania. Then, in 1992, when an ambitious general from neighboring Byelorussia made a play to take over Lithuania, it was Palcikas (with a little help from the U.S. Marines) who crushed the uprising and kept Lithuania independent once again, earning Palcikas not only worldwide fame but a place in history as well.

"We bring good news," announced Palcikas. "The war is over. Russia has laid down its weapons and is withdrawing from Ukrayina even now."

"That's wonderful!" Furness said, giving everyone there, including Palcikas, a big hug. The big Lithuanian minister didn't seem to mind one bit.

"The Congress of People's Deputies of Russia has appointed Valentin Sen'kov as acting president, pending new elections," Layton said. "He ordered the military withdrawal from Ukrayina, and so far it appears that the Russian Army is responding."

"How badly was Moscow hit?" Daren Mace asked.

"Bad," Palcikas responded, "but not as badly as the Russians did to Ukrayina and Turkey. Much damage to southern Moscow and cities of Podolsk, Zhukovsky, and Ramenskoye. Perhaps twenty thousand dead at Domodedovo, another twenty thousand other places. Russia very lucky the Ukrayinans good bombers. Direct hit on Domodedovo Airport, little destruction elsewhere."

"We're tracking the fallout, and we could see another twenty to fifty thousand casualties from that in time—perhaps some in China and even North America," Layton added. "Radiation could get into the food chain in Asia. It's bad, but like General Palcikas said, it could have been worse, especially if the Russians had retaliated with an all-out attack. I think the world just got a wake-up call, my friends. I just hope we hear the alarm and take action, and don't just hit the snooze button.

"Anyway, you two are off alert. You can turn your classified documents over to the communications detail, and you can run your decocking and stand-down checklists. Once maintenance signs for the plane and the weapons, you two are on your own for a few days. General Palcikas has kindly offered the hospitality of the capital city and his staff."

"Lithuania is cold and blustery place in winter," Dominikas Palcikas said, "but we have many fine ways of keeping our guests warm. You are most welcome. But first show me your beautiful aircraft here. I understand Turkey wants to buy Vampire bombers, and perhaps Lithuania will buy some too. Would you like to come to Lithuania to teach my crews how to fly these beautiful planes?"

"It might just happen," General Layton said. "Negotiations are underway, and the Pentagon will most likely deactivate the Vampire wing at Plattsburgh. Vilnius even looks like Plattsburgh, in an Old World way. You two will certainly be at the top of the list for the initial training cadre—an experienced instructor pilot, a maintenance wizard, and an experienced weapons officer. Think about it, you two."

"Lithuania would be honored to have you," Palcikas added. "You come. We have lots of fun." He looked at the two flyers, noticing how they were looking at each other, then winked at Tyler Layton. "I see the thought of you two being together in foreign land is *very* disturbing. I welcome you to Lithuania." Layton took Palcikas over to the RF-111G and began explaining its features.

Mace turned to Rebecca and smiled warmly, saying, "Hey, all I got left at Plattsburgh waiting for me is some busted taps at a biker bar in downtown Plattsburgh. You have a business to run, a bunch of new planes, maybe a future."

Rebecca thought about her options—for about two seconds. "You know, I think I'll tell Ed Caldwell to take his Cessna Caravans and stick them up his oversexed ass. Pardon my language. I want to fly the F-111s, period. If I can't fly them in New York, I'll fly them in Vilnius, or Ankara. As long . . . as long as you're there with me."

"Deal, lady," Daren Mace replied, taking both her hands in his. "It's a deal."

Rebecca gave him a tight hug, pulled back a bit, then met his lips with her own.

The White House, Washington, D.C.
That Same Time

"Zah vashe zdarov'yeh. Congratulations, Valentin . . . er, I should say, Mr. President," the First Lady said on the satellite telephone call to St. Petersburg. An emergency Russian government had been transferred there until a full assessment of the destruction and fallout from Domodedovo could be completed. "We're very happy for you."

"Thank you very much, Mrs. President," Valentin Sen'kov, the acting president of the Russian Federation, replied. "I am not sure if congratulations are in order, considering the circumstances, but I thank you for your kind thoughts."

"All America is very concerned about the devastation at Domodedovo and throughout Russia," the President said. His feet were propped up on the Kennedy desk, the phone resting on one ear, while he chewed on a chicken leg with his free hand. He had ordered out this evening, over the protests of the First Lady who was on a nearby extension, and a bucket of Kentucky Fried Chicken rested on his desk, along with a huge Coke and a basket of biscuits. He loved the Colonel's original recipe. "Our blessings are with you. And on behalf of the NATO alliance, I want to thank you for agreeing to pull your forces out of the Ukraine and your warships in the Black Sea away from Turkey. A major disaster has been averted, thanks to you."

"I hope what has transpired over the past few days only serves to bring our people closer together in this hour of need," Sen'kov said.

"We share your hopes, Valentin," the President said, wiping his mouth. He saw his chief of staff giving him a signal and pointing at his watch, reminding him that the next news conference was about to start. "We have to go, Valentin. If there's anything you require, you know how to reach us."

"Our blessings go with you," the First Lady said. "It's good to have a close friend and a strong, true advocate of democracy in the Kremlin."

"Yes . . . ah, but there is still one small matter," Sen'kov said quickly. "I understand you are giving another news conference in a short time. I think this would be a good opportunity to propose a reparation plan for the relief of the Russian people. I think—"

"What did you say?" the President interrupted, almost choking on one of the Colonel's legs. "Did you say a *reparation plan?*"

"Yes, Mr. President," Sen'kov said evenly. "We have not come up with any firm estimates on the damage caused by the AGM-131 weapon launched on Domodedovo, but I think a fair, conservative estimate might be in the order of one hundred billion dollars."

"What in the hell are you talking about, Sen'kov?" the President retorted, spitting out the chicken. "Why should the United States or *anyone* pay reparations to Russia for the attack? First of all, it was a conflict between the Ukraine and Russia—"

"Come, come . . . we both know that it was *not* a Ukrainian AS-16 missile, as the pilot who launched the missile claimed during his radio message, but an American AGM-131 missile that destroyed Domodedovo," Sen'kov said. "I think the world would be horrified to learn that you—"

"The United States did *not* launch the damn thing, the *Ukrainians* did!" thundered the President, his feet now off the desk. He looked at his wife, horrified, as if to say, *Now see what you've gotten me into!*

"Be that as it may, Mr. President," Sen'kov said smugly, "the American involvement in the attack can be easily verified, and I think this confirmed story may prove, shall we say, damaging to your reelection hopes."

"But it was *you* who suggested that we attack Domodedovo," the First Lady snapped. "You told us he was in the bunker." Her eyes were as big as saucers; her blonde hair was all but standing on end.

"How in the world would *I* have access to information like that, dear lady?" Sen'kov said. "I am just a simple congressman.

I have no apparatus, no contacts, to get that kind of information. That is top secret information, shared by only a few close to the President, and certainly not with a member of the opposition party.

"Now, may I suggest we split the reparation payments into ten parts, ten billion dollars per year for ten years. Of course, during your news conference, you may call it *humanitarian relief* for the poor people of Russia. I have no objection to that. And we must discuss the procedures for plea-bargaining the lawsuits brought against my government by people affected by the fallout . . . that could go on for another five years."

"This is blackmail!" the First Lady shouted, pacing with her extension in front of the French doors leading to the Rose Garden.

"You pull this shit on us, Sen'kov, and we'll claim the same damages to Russia for its attacks on our NATO allies," said the President, suddenly feeling an ulcer attack underway.

"But Mr. President—it is only fair," Sen'kov said. "Of course, Russia did not use full-yield thermonuclear weapons, like the United States provided for the Ukraine, and it was Vitaly Velichko's government, not mine, who ordered those horrible attacks on the Ukraine and Turkey. However, I am fully prepared to compensate the victims. My government would gladly negotiate reparations for the pain and suffering for the victims in the Ukraine and Turkey, and compensation for the property damage—minimal in our case, since the warheads launched against your allies hardly did any damage at all compared to the *one* missile *you* launched against *us*—provided the United States and NATO pay the same for victims in Russia."

"Valentin . . . Mr. President," the First Lady purred, "why are you doing this? Why are you turning on us like this? Your nation started a war against our NATO allies. Velichko would have started World War Three."

"Dear lady, Mr. President, please understand," Sen'kov explained. "Velichko was a mad dog, but he spoke for many in my country—like myself—that are disturbed by the disintegration of the Russian state. The Communists like Velichko bankrupted our country, it's true, but his ideals are held by many here, including many powerful members of the armed forces. Just because the Cold War is over, the Soviet Union is no more, and the world is changing, does not mean that other countries can take what they want from my country, and we should do nothing about it. Russia should be powerful once again.

"I am not turning *against* you, my friends, I am *appealing* to you. *You* destroyed hundreds of square miles of Russian soil, killed hundreds of thousands of citizens, and poisoned perhaps half our nation. I did not *tell* you to do these things. I am asking for a promise to repay Russia for the destruction you caused. If you are unwilling to live with the fact that you made it possible for your ally Ukrayina to attack us with nuclear weapons, you should help rebuild what you destroyed."

The President was on his feet, the phone cord almost pulling the bucket of Colonel Sanders' chicken onto the floor. He'd pushed back his chair and was now pacing behind his desk. His face was red, puffed up, his eyes burning. "No, you listen to me, Sen'kov, my friend. You're no better than the asshole we just got rid of. This is nothing but blackmail by someone who's now in a position to do it. If we hadn't intervened with NATO, and Velichko had stayed in power, I guarantee you that he woulda had you shoveling shit in Siberia. But *you* came to us. *You* sat in this very office and sold him out and now you're proposing something just as duplicitous. Well, you know what?" the President gritted angrily, "you can go to *hell.*"

"The military commanders of my country would be very disappointed to hear you say that, Mr. President," Sen'kov said. "You understand that my hold on the military is tenuous. I must constantly assure them that I will act to keep Russia strong. They will not be pleased to hear the great President of the United States has turned away from them after precipitating such a terrible attack."

The youthful President was thunderstruck. Was Sen'kov actually threatening to reignite the conflict if America didn't pay up? It certainly seemed that way. The burning ulcer in his stomach came back like a shotgun blast, matching the burning anger in his head. His knees felt weak and he dropped back into his chair as if pushed back into it. "You . . . you sonofabitch," he said, drawing in deep breaths as if he were swimming against a riptide he had just encountered in a seemingly calm, tranquil sea, "don't you dare threaten me."

But the First Lady, listening in to the conversation at her extension, raised a hand to her husband, urging him—then, with a stern glare, *ordering* him—to calm himself. "All right,

Valentin," the First Lady said. "You have a deal. I personally guarantee you that I will head a commission to gather one hundred billion dollars for the 'humanitarian relief' of Domodedovo, and we will establish a commission to compensate any victims of the fallout. You have my word."

"You are as caring and as intelligent as you are beautiful, dear lady," Valentin Sen'kov said. "And I will guarantee that details of the *Ukrainian* nuclear missile attack on my country will never become public. You have my word. The best to you and yours. Good-bye."

And the line was broken.

The President held his head in his hands, breathing heavily. "What did you just do?" he demanded, staring across the Oval Office at the First Lady, who was adjusting her skirt before his press conference. "I can't believe you did that. We fight for our lives, lose all those crewmembers and allies, even risk a fucking third world war to get Russia to stop fighting—and now you've just guaranteed that we have to pay *one hundred billion* dollars to keep it all quiet?"

The First Lady rolled her eyes. "Oh, stop whining. Pull yourself together and start getting ready for your news conference. I'm going next door to my office to freshen up."

"Wait a minute," the President said. "You just gave him a hundred *billion* dollars. Where are we going to get that? Congress won't go for it—they wouldn't give Yeltsin shit after I begged them to. The American people won't go for it, they want it for the cities, for health care, AIDS, whatever . . . and our allies sure as hell won't pitch in."

"I said . . . I'll take care of it," the First Lady said firmly. "After all, look what that attack averted—World War Three. Don't you see? It doesn't matter who launched the weapon, it was *our* attack, *our* plan, and it just saved the asses of governments all over the world. We'll get the money from *them*, even if we have to break their fucking arms to do it."

"But, honey, this is *blackmail*. Sen'kov blackmailed us, now we're going to blackmail our allies?"

The First Lady shrugged. "It's a small price to pay to have a Russian president in one's back pocket," she said, patting her hair. "That attack killed a lot of Russian military commanders and right-wing neo-Communists, and we can certainly prove it was Sen'kov who gave us the information. Valentin Sen'kov belongs to me—I mean, *us*—now. Besides, it's only money, dear. Now come with me and I'll spruce you up before the press conference. As to what you should say, I think the best course would be . . ."

As she talked on, the President and First Lady headed toward the door leading to the other West Wing offices. A Secret Service agent, who'd been in their presence the entire time, opened the door for them to exit. The President was about to go out first, then he noticed the look from his wife. He stepped back. "After you," he said tightly.

"Always." She smiled, marching forward.